Deliver Me From My Past

To a great friend
J. Roger Breckenson

Rich Zeien

4.26.11

Dedications

"It is rather for us to be here dedicated to the great task remaining before us--that from these honored dead we take increased devotion to that cause for which they gave the last full measure of devotion--that we here highly resolve that these dead shall not have died in vain--that this nation, under God, shall have a new birth of freedom and that government of the people, by the people, for the people, shall not perish from the earth."

Abraham Lincoln's Gettysburg Address
November 19, 1863

Because the battle is not yet won.

To those who inspired me to write this sequel to
Before You Seek Revenge.

Mrs. Katie Berry
Mrs. Terri El-Haddaoui
Mrs. Kellie Parod
Major John Calvert
Mrs. Davia Mosley
Mr. Bob Corley

Cover Design
Beth Poirier

Deliver Me From My Past

A Novel By
Frederick Zeier

Chapter 1

She stood in judgment of those who would live or die.

It was not her hand that held the knife, but it was her will that sent it into the heart. When she looked down, it was her hand covered in blood.

She felt the jolt of the gun when her finger pulled the trigger. It was not as violent as she expected. Smoke and fire followed the flight of the bullet and illuminated the spin. She could see the grooves the barrel impressed on the soft lead. The smallest embers of powder still burned bright red on the base. The smell of burnt powder filled her senses.

She looked up. The vile sneer of the man to her front turned into one of panic and surprise. She watched the bullet spinning and traveling ever so slowly and wondered if it would simply fall to the ground for lack of energy. But the bullet did not fall. She saw it start to flatten as it worked its way through his shirt and into his chest. She heard the air escape his lungs and saw his hands grab at the hole to stop the flow of blood.

As the newly dead drifted down into the abyss, they screamed at her; their eyes already gray and hollow and their skin ashen. The screams were loud, and real, and they haunted her.

Danni Walton woke from the disturbing dream, damp with sweat and panting from the effort. It was the same dream, or nearly so—there were many variations—that haunted her for years. She knew she would never be able to fall back to sleep so she rose from her bed and slipped into a robe. She drew the robe tight around her body as she made her way through the dark house and out the back door. The stars provided enough light to guide her down the path she knew so well, and the sea air helped clear the stench of gunpowder from her mind.

She knew why the dream invaded her slumber. She had been thinking of her husband. Today was the fifth anniversary of his death, or his murder, and although she always tried to keep those terrible events in the past they could invade her dreams at their own pleasure. Better to wait for the dawn here, overlooking the Atlantic Ocean, waiting for the sun and the dawn of a new day, where she could control her thoughts and avoid suffering the dreams again.

Lighting flashed in a thunderhead far off the coast and Danni Walton counted the seconds for the rumbles to reach the shore.

~~

Miranda Castillo, known to the family as Mamba, woke early to prepare breakfast. She poured a cup of fresh coffee for Danni, and then discovered her room empty. She knew where she could be found.

Mamba expertly balanced two steaming mugs of coffee and made her way down the path she knew as well as Danni. There, silhouetted against the ribbon of light that distinguished the horizon stood Danni.

"Good morning child. I have brought you a cup of coffee."

Danni smiled at the voice that brought nothing but pleasant memories. "Good morning Mamba."

The two stood in silence; conversation would come in due time. Words can only detract from a sunrise and both women knew it.

Danni was the first to speak. "Mamba, do you know what today is?"

"Yes my child, I know." On the anniversary of such tragic events it was wise to let Danni speak at her own pace.

"I had those terrible dreams again. I hoped they were over, but they keep coming back. Will they haunt me for the rest of my life?"

"I don't know my child, but they are only dreams and your future is bright. I have prayed that one day they will simply vanish from your memories, and you can live for your future rather than regret your past."

Danni understood Mamba's meaning.

"We have come a long way in the past five years." Danni reflected on the marriage of her daughter Hanna…she was happy; she thought about her own life…she was much happier a widow than she ever was married; about her father and about Bill Cannon. "I like it better now."

Mamba picked up Danni's brightened tone. It was a sign the night was over. "So do I, let's go have some hot chocolate with breakfast."

The morning sun warmed their backs until blocked by the thunderstorm pushed ashore by a building on-shore breeze; just as Danni's past was again moving to cloud her future.

~~

Ed Helton watched the same sunrise from his corner office at Coastal Bank. The first faint rays made their way through the giant oak and sparkled off the tinted glass. The fact that the rays even reached the window was testament to the poor health of the tree; and if taken as a snapshot without knowledge of the time of day, the sunrise could just as well have been a sunset.

In years past, the leaves would have completely blocked the sunrise. Now only sparse foliage clung to the bony branches. Even in summer the tree now resembled a skeleton rather than a breathing and vigorous living thing.

He wondered why the tree, the same tree he had looked at for thirty years, came so vividly to his attention on this morning. Was there a parallel between the tree and the country? Maybe there was.

Legend had it that the Georgia signers of the Declaration of Independence posted a copy of that famous document to the trunk of this very oak for all to see. From that day forward the oak was dubbed the Liberty Tree. At the turn of the century, the twentieth century to be accurate, the city fathers formalized the title by erecting a small plaque to that effect. The plaque had long disappeared, presumably removed to make way for the modern convenience of parking meters along River Street.

The Liberty Tree survived pestilence, flood and drought, hurricane and fire. It had survived the great Civil War and General Sherman's march to the sea. It had survived the two world wars and the great depression and the upheaval of the sixties and seventies; but it was now dying.

The grand old tree, still stately and magnificent when viewed from afar, was only a shell of what once was. From a simple acorn into a struggling sapling fighting for survival, the tree had shown such promise. But now, like the country it represented, the infestations and cancerous rot had hollowed the trunk and branches and it grew no more.

To those who passed by, the blackened stubs of branches pruned to maintain the appearance of health, the tree represented only a cool place for the bums and drunkards to find respite from the heat of the day and a place to discard their trash.

3

Was this all that could be expected of the oak tree, was this all that could be expected of the country; a scant two-hundred plus years? Were both doomed to die even before a quarter century was complete? Did they die from old age or did they die from neglect? Was it from the indifference of those who took their existence as something that would always be, and therefore paid no attention to the decay; or was the lifespan of Liberty so fragile, that as an idea, it could not survive the greed of those who prospered under the spreading branches for much more than two-hundred years?

Ed Helton was probably one of those people, and it pained him to admit it.

Could the tree be saved? Probably not.

Could the country be saved? Probably not.

Could the fruits of Ed Helton's labor be saved? Maybe, and he would start today preparing for the inevitable.

~~

Twenty pair of eyes watched the big man circle his prey. Muscles rippled under his skin and he carried 280 pounds on a 6' 7" frame with a dancer's grace. He felt no fear. His size had always prevailed. The man to his front was already defeated; he just didn't know it. It was only a matter of time.

Some would consider challenging the instructor as foolish, but caution was for the weak and the man to his front would go down like so many did in his college days at Michigan. He would pour through them on his way to the quarterback; like he would pour over this old man. He would cast him aside and trample his manhood, and then stand victorious over the fallen foe and revel in the cheers of the faithful. "You're going down old man."

Bill Cannon watched the man circle. At 6' 4" and 210 pounds he wasn't terribly overmatched, but those watching knew it was hard to give away 70 pounds and three inches of reach, and they would understand if the size of the big man would be too much for a man almost 30 years senior. Bill knew the man would charge and waited for the attack.

The big man would disregard his training and come at him in a ferocious charge. Bill knew he would do this because he had proven to be a difficult student, and on occasion would brutalize others with excessive physical force that completely missed the essence of the training.

4

From six feet away, Bill saw the man's nostrils flare as he prepared for the charge. As he raised his rifle over his right shoulder he screamed a guttural roar. Using his rifle as a club he charged.

When he raised his rifle he left his mid-section exposed. From the guard position a forward lunge extended Bill's reach by six feet. The bayonet entered just below the solar plexus and traveled upward into the heart. The strike stopped the big man as if shot. The big man was dead, he just didn't know it; it was only a matter of time.

The big man stared at the rubber bayonet bent against his chest. This just wasn't possible. Rage flashed across his face. The thrust was a lucky one. This old man couldn't defeat him—and reason was lost. His roar was primal as he reached out for the old man. He would choke the life from him.

Bill saw the rage and withdrew the bayonet and stepped forward with a vertical butt stoke that caught the big man under the chin. His head snapped back, his arms flapped uncontrollably at his side, and he staggered; he was defenseless. Cannon stepped forward again and with a horizontal stroke drove the butt of his rifle into the nose of the big man. Blood ran down his face and his eyes rolled up into his head as he fell backwards to the ground. Bill brought the bayonet down to the man's throat, but there was no need, the man was done.

Bill waited until the man's eyes fluttered before he knelt and spoke to him. "Can you hear me?"

The big man managed a weak nod, his hand coming up to stop the flow of blood from his nose.

"You have just been killed by the most basic move. You are not here to learn to fight; you are here to learn how to kill. I hope you understand."

Bill then turned to the assembled class sitting in silence. The combat was quick and violent and caught them by surprise.

"Killing thrusts always come from the inside, not outside the frame of the body. This man was dead after the first thrust. Don't make the same mistake or you will end up just like him."

Bill waited for questions from his young students, all from the Ranger Regiment from Hunter Army Airfield on the outskirts of Savannah. There were no questions; the demonstration just witnessed was enough. A soldier called to Bill from the gym office, "Colonel Cannon, you have a phone call from Washington."

Bill waved at the soldier and then turned to the class. "That's enough for today. A couple of you men get this man to the medics."

Bill grabbed a towel from the clean stack and wiped the sweat from his head before he answered the phone. "Bill Cannon."

"Colonel Cannon, I am William Jefferson. I am one of the Assistant Attorney Generals in the U.S. Department of Justice. You're a hard man to track down."

Bill had no idea why the Attorney General's office would be calling him. "I didn't know you guys were looking for me. What can I do for you Mr. Jefferson?"

"Colonel Cannon, nobody up here thought to notify you, but I thought you should know. Today the Attorney General signed the papers directing the release of Nawaf Al-Mihdhar, Khalid Al-Hazmi, and Mohammad Jarrah from Guantanamo. They are being transported back to their home countries."

Mihdhar, Hazmi, and Jarrah had been captured by Bill Cannon in Iraq after the last desert war. None of the three were Iraqi and all were linked to Al Qaeda. They were captured during the assault on the stronghold where Uday and Qusay Hussein were killed. These men were not simply enemy combatants, they were hard core terrorists.

"You can't be serious. Who the hell made that decision?"

Bill sensed that Mr. Jefferson was uncomfortable explaining a decision he didn't totally support.

"The Attorney General determined there was not enough evidence to continue to hold these men."

What a bunch of crap. Bill Cannon had solid intelligence these three men were involved in a least half a dozen terrorist operations against the United States—everywhere from the bombing of the USS Cole to the attack on the World Trade Centers.

"Mr. Jefferson, I know these men are key operatives in Al Qaeda. Why are we releasing them?"

"I know how you must feel, but the Attorney General has determined any information we have on these men was probably coerced out of them. None of it would stand up in court."

Standing up in court, the new buzz-words of lawyers defending terrorists detained at Guantanamo. The decision by the Attorney General to put terrorists on trial in Federal Court was having the expected effect.

6

Only the most publically known were prosecuted. The rest were being slowly released from detention; often without fanfare or media coverage.

"This is a big mistake. We are going to see these men again."

Jefferson took a moment before he answered. "I'm afraid you're right. Let's hope you're wrong."

Bill Cannon spent more time than usual under a hot shower – cooling off. What was the point of it all? How many men had made the ultimate sacrifice to capture those terrorists? Bill knew he must cast out the bitterness building in his stomach or it might affect his mood, and he was seeing Danni Walton this afternoon. He didn't want to spoil the day.

~~

The word in the yard was a new intern was working the medical section. She was probably from the nursing school in Mobile; it was like student teaching for the nurse trainees. The warden got the use of intelligent and motivated young nurses, and in return all he was obliged to do was take the headmaster on a couple of fishing trips every year. The warden loved the program; after the first few days of screening the worst criminals the state had to offer, the students hated it. Jerome Edward Green knew the interns were an easy mark—at least during the first week.

Hands and feet manacled to a locking belt, and plastic facemask in place, Green was escorted to the screening room. Green sat quietly in the chair facing her desk. His black skin had an ashen look, and he was slightly hunched over. He looked at the desk rather than the intern and never made eye contact, as if to do so was forbidden.

The intern reviewed the file as she had been trained; Green, Jerome Edward, a.k.a. Crack or Crack Daddy, murder one, death, infected with the AIDS.

"What's the problem Mr. Green?"

Green rubbed his chest. "I been having chest pains. I need a shot."

"A shot of what?"

"Painkiller, maybe the doc will give me morphine. It hurts real bad."

7

The intern noted the request in the file. "Wait here. I'll ask the doctor."

The intern found the doctor behind a stack of medical records. "Jerome Green says he's having chest pains. He wants morphine."

The doctor reached for the file. "He always wants morphine. Give him a couple of Percocet and send him back to his cell."

"You're not going to examine him?"

"What for? He's on death row and is dying of AIDS. Just give him the pills."

The intern returned to the screening room and presented the pills to Green. "The doctor prescribed Percocet."

Green accepted the pills, but didn't move from the seat.

"Is there anything else I can do for you Mr. Green?"

Green looked up for the first time. He reached into the pocket of his uniform and extended an envelope to the intern.

"Would you mind mailing this letter?"

The intern saw no threat in a simple letter; and the manner in which it was addressed the post office would probably never deliver it. She dropped it in the box near school on her way back to the dormitory.

Little did she know, as every flood starts with only a trickle and every fire with only a small spark, that the letter she mailed would have such a devastating impact on so many.

Chapter 2

Ed Helton had been in the banking business in Savannah for more than 30 years. His Coastal Bank was profitable and well respected in the community and industry. But banks require a thriving economy to prosper, and like most businesses, struggle during the down times.

The Coastal Bank was not immune to the affects of a declining stock market, delinquent loans and foreclosed houses and business, and increasing Federal regulation. Regulations that bureaucrats in Washington promised would spur the economy, but in reality only made business more difficult. If not for bad news there would be no news at all; and the registered letter sitting unopened on his desk could be the worst news of all.

Everyday brought more challenges and today brought Sean McTavish to Ed's desk. Sean McTavish, President and CEO of McTavish Construction, was an old friend. McTavish could trace his roots back to the first settlers in Georgia. His construction company was now facing bankruptcy.

"Sean, what in the hell happened?"

"Ed, the housing market and construction in general has collapsed. Those builders who haven't already gone under are hanging on by the skin of their teeth. I have liens on ten projects, but you can't get blood out of a turnip. Most of those builders are my friends. They would pay me if they had the money. My equipment is rusting in the yard, and I have had to lay off most of my employees."

Ed could feel the frustration of his good friend. "What are you plans?"

"I am trying to sell my equipment, but what buyers there are, offer only pennies on the dollar. I've asked a couple of the manufacturers to take back the leased equipment, but they want me to live up to my contracts. I'm stuck in the middle, can't pay for it, can't sell it, and they won't take it back. I'm afraid I'm in the same situation with the loan from your bank, Ed. I'll do what I can, but I am going to have to cut back on my payments. I'm sorry, but it's all I can do."

~~

After Sean left, Ed was forced to pick from the lesser of two evils. Either address the letter on his desk or see Ronald Bartholomew, a Federal Bank Examiner, who had made himself a nuisance for the better part of a week.

Bartholomew was all spit and polished when he arrived for the annual inspection. Apparently the Savannah River nightlife was more than the man could handle. In a few short days Bartholomew revealed his true character; he was unkempt, slovenly in stature with a bulbous nose that had turned red along with his eyes, and he reeked of cheap liquor served at the port bars.

Ed knew Bartholomew wouldn't find a thing of substance to report. Not necessarily because the personnel at the bank were perfect in their work effort, or commanded exceptional talent, but simply because this examiner, like so many other bureaucrats, couldn't find his ass with both hands.

With the solemn gravity of a deity pronouncing salvation or damnation of lowly subjects, Bartholomew droned on about loan status, deposit accounts, or investments. He produced endless reports and launched into a mind numbing explanation of figures Ed understood far better than he.

Ed tried hard not to fidget. His mind was really focused on the registered letter still glaring at him from his desk…that and the Memorial Day Celebration planned at his residence on Daufuskie Island.

"I have placed your bank in the marginal compliance category for your failure to properly implement the guidelines in the Community Reinvestment Act."

Ed didn't know if he was more shocked, or insulted, by the rating. The Community Reinvestment Act (CRA) was a cleverly disguised entitlement program signed into law in 1977. The CRA was amended many times over the years with each new law reducing the qualification requirements to secure a loan. Fannie Mae and Freddie Mac, the government sponsored financial institutions providing Federal funds to back the CRA loans, were collapsing and surviving only with billions in subsidies.

Ed Helton showed little emotion, but wanted to know the basis for such a rating for his bank. "Mr. Bartholomew, a marginal rating for this bank after our last review was superior? What specific findings support such a rating?"

10

"Mr. Helton, we think your bank could do more to support the CRA. I'm sure you would agree that banks are established to provide resources to the local population; to help them better their lives."

"No, Mr. Bartholomew, the purpose of this bank is to return a profit to the stockholders and depositors; not to write worthless paper to customers with a history of defaulting on the loans. We're losing money every day in the housing markets. Any additional money would be throwing good money after bad."

"Mr. Helton, I can't force your bank to support the CRA, but I can make you wish you had. The administration has set a new goal of one trillion dollars in CRA loans, and we have some new lending programs that may interest you."

Bartholomew let his voice trail off as if dangling a lure in front of a large mouth bass—and he waited to see if Ed Helton would lunge after the bait. Ed hated to give him the satisfaction of a reply.

"Go ahead, I'm listening."

"The lending guidelines have been eased. We have opened the gates to put all Americans into their own home. We are very excited about it. These new guidelines should put some life back in the home construction business. Your participation in this program would go a long way to getting your marginal rating upgraded."

It went against his grain but Ed asked, "Exactly what loan guidelines are they changing?"

"No down payments, guaranteed Federal assistance to buyers, Federal guarantees on adjustable rate mortgages, things like that. You will be paid to originate and service the loan and Freddie and Fannie are going to buy the paper. It's a winning situation for everybody."

None of the changes made any sense to Ed. Lower credit requirements for the lowest income earners—all backed by Federal money when the country was already on the verge of bankruptcy, seemed like a roadmap to disaster. It was a scary thought to a responsible banker.

"None of that sounds exciting to me. It sounds like a prelude to disaster."

Bartholomew knew these new programs never sat well with the old-time bankers, but in his mind they were the wave of the future.

"I don't think you understand Mr. Helton. All you have to do is originate the loan and then the government will fund the loan. Your bank will still get paid to service the account. It's a winning situation all around. The administration will increase home ownership, Congress will back the mortgages through Freddie and Fannie, and your bank will earn the processing fee. How could that be bad?"

"If the government is going to do that it will drive banks like mine out of the home mortgage business. If the government, with tax-payer money, is going to cut their mortgage rates they are competing in the mortgage markets with an unfair advantage. It will take private funds out of the market, and all the people who managed or processed those loans will be out of work."

Mr. Bartholomew had never given that aspect of the new mortgage programs any thought. But Bartholomew wasn't concerned about the economic future of Coastal Bank. His job was to get the CRA program in gear and running full speed.

"I'm sure your bank will find other forms of revenue. If you do a good job selling the CRA loans, then your economic future should be secure with the fees you will receive from the government."

Ed didn't have time to debate the issues of sound banking and free enterprise with Ronald Bartholomew.

"I will give the proposal due consideration. You can tell your director that I will be challenging the rating of this examination. You can expect a letter from me within the week."

Ed Helton couldn't get Bartholomew out of his office quick enough. "If you will now excuse me I have other matters to which I must attend."

After Bartholomew left the office, Ed Helton returned to his desk to reflect on the meeting just concluded. The marginal rating was a problem, but not a fatal one. If forced to increase the CRA loans, his bank would be on the hook only until Freddie or Fannie bought the paper. The fatal flaw in the government's plan was the extension of so much credit.

The government was taking a tremendous risk with taxpayer money. It was easy to conclude the government was trying to socialize the home mortgage industry. It hadn't worked anywhere in the world and Ed didn't see it working here. Coastal had about $60 million in Freddie and Fannie stock, and about that same amount invested in financial institutions that would probably jump at the chance to gamble with government money.

Ed knew there was great risk investing in institutions so grossly overextended and would begin the process of reducing Coastal Bank's exposure to the whims of the Government.

Ed had avoided the registered letter as long as he could. He finally took the registered letter to read. It was exactly what he expected. The largest liability carried by the Coastal Bank, the loan securing the Daufuskie Island Resort and Spa, was going into default. It was an amount the bank could not afford.

All the hard work to protect the bank from the shrinking economy would be for naught if the Daufuskie Island Resort and Spa could not be saved.

Ed had a plan. It was risky at best, but with the proper infusion of capital, it would save the resort and the bank. Before he left the office he took pen to paper and handed the list to his assistant.

"Please give these people a call. Ask them if it would be convenient to meet me this coming Saturday on Daufuskie Island. If they fly into Hilton Head we will have a boat to bring them to the island. Call Danni, ask her to arrange for transportation from Hilton Head to Daufuskie."

Ed's assistant knew her boss was well connected, but had no idea he had the private cell phone numbers of a U.S. Senator, and so many other influential people. She spent the remainder of the afternoon making the phone calls. Not a single guest declined the offer.

Chapter 3

Ken Carson hated his cubicle. He hated his desk was only a faux wood grain veneer, covering an undersized metal shell. He hated the way the overloaded drawers would fall off their tracks. The banging to dislodge the jam and subsequent screeching of metal on metal would announce to the world his position was only that of a loan officer. His desk wasn't as nice as the receptionist's desk and nowhere near as prestigious as the polished oak of the loan department manager's desk.

He hated his chair. It wasn't much nicer than the two chairs placed in front of his desk for use by loan applicants. After a day processing loans, the chair would dig deep into his back and burn like a heated cattle prod. He yearned for the leather chair in the loan manager's office.

The thing Ken hated most was that Ed Helton had not made the decision on who would be promoted to fill the position of Loan Department Manager.

Ken felt he was the most qualified and deserving of the promotion. After all, he was the senior loan officer, and his finance degree met the education requirement. His loan volume consistently set the standard and his loans were infrequently discounted, earning the highest return to the bank. Ken knew Helton was taking his sweet time simply to torture him.

What Ken hated most was that he had to constantly explain to his wife why he hadn't already been promoted. Ken's bitter attitude was interrupted by the buzzing of the intercom.

"Mr. Carson, Mrs. Carson is on line two, and your three o'clock appointment is here."

"Thank you; I will only be a moment." Ken didn't look forward to the phone call and another barrage of his wife's haranguing about the promotion. He would do his best to keep the conversation short.

"Hello Rachael, what's up?"

"Ken, has Helton made his decision yet?" Rachael could be coy and demure in the right circles, but with her husband there was no need

14

to pretend to be anything but the pushy and impatient woman she had proven to be.

"No dear, he hasn't. He's upstairs with a bank examiner. I'll call you as soon as anything happens."

"Ken, you deserve that promotion more than anyone in that bank. Why don't you just tell the old bastard if you don't get the promotion that you'll quit. You could get a job at any bank in Savannah."

Ken had heard this line of reasoning, if one could call it reason, many times in the past two weeks. His wife had been unrelenting in applying pressure to get this promotion.

His wife was afflicted with a need for immediate gratification, something she concealed rather well during the courtship. He now understood; if his wife wanted something—anything—she expected it now—not later. It was a personal trait that kept Ken on the go. For no quicker than one request had been satisfied, another took its' place.

"Rachael, I may be able to get a job, but then I would probably start at the bottom again. Please be a little patient. We can talk about it later. I have customers waiting. I should be home around 6:30."

"You don't need to rush. I'm going shopping with Karen. You can make something for yourself or pick something up on your way home."

Rachael's sister, Karen, left Nashville, Tennessee, just ahead of a nasty confrontation with the outraged wife of a country and western singer. Only yesterday she moved in with Ken and Rachael. Rachael promised Ken it was only temporary...until Karen could get established in Savannah

Maybe Rachael's behavior, since the arrival of her sister, was simply an attempt to make her sister feel welcome. But in one short day Karen had already driven a wedge into their orderly life. Not so much between the relationship of Ken and Rachael, but certainly a wedge between Rachael and fiscal responsibility. This was the second shopping trip in as many days and Ken shuddered at the expense. Yesterday's trip alone would have paid a lesser king's ransom in biblical times.

"Another shopping trip?"

"That's why you need to get the promotion. Karen wants to go shopping and she doesn't know her way around Savannah."

15

Ken didn't have time to conduct this argument over the phone. "Look, I've got some customers waiting. Try to exercise a little restraint."

Rachael didn't even acknowledge Ken's request when she ended the conversation. "Call me when you find out about the promotion."

Ken was powerless when it came to exerting control over his wife. They had long ago lost, or let fade away, the union of love and respect and any goals and dreams they may have once shared.

In confidence, and out of earshot of his wife, Ken would tell you that his wife's idea of marriage was that he was there for one single reason—her pleasure. In so many ways it was apparent that Rachael took advantage of his need to be with her while she only endured his existence. It was a poor excuse for a marriage and a crappy way to muddle through life.

~~

As the last item on the day's agenda, Ed bent to the task of selection of the new Loan Department Manager.

His recommendation had been a well qualified candidate from Atlanta, but the directors felt it would be better to promote from within. Against his better judgment, Ed withheld objection and the board unanimously approved the promotion of Ken Carson to Manager of the Loan Department.

Ed called a company meeting immediately after closing to announce the selection. The employees greeted the selection with polite applause and extended polite congratulations to Ken.

After the round of congratulations from the employees at the bank, Ed beckoned Ken to join him in the office.

"Ken, I'm having a little Memorial Day party at my house on Saturday. Why don't you and the wife join us? I'd love to have you come and it will give you a chance to get to know some of the other board members."

The promotion was already paying off. Ken had never been invited to Ed Helton's house. He could hardly wait to call his wife.

"Hey baby, you are talking to the new Manager of the Loan Department at Coastal Bank!"

Rachael's congratulations felt somewhat patronizing, but he had grown accustomed to her sometimes cutting demeanor. "You were the

16

best man for the position, just like I told you a thousand times. It's about time you got a promotion."

"Rachael, are you still in the mall?"

"We've only begun to look around and I don't want to hear anything about shopping. I've sacrificed enough already."

Ken knew his comment would surprise his wife. "Don't worry about that. In fact, we have been invited to Mr. Helton's house on Daufuskie this Saturday. Pick up something nice to wear; I want you to look good."

Rachael was excited about the invitation. She had always known she deserved to be in a higher rung of the social ladder, and this promotion was only the first step. Rachael hoped to impress more than just the people at the party; she wanted to impress her sister with her newfound status.

"Oh, Ken, I don't think we will be able to go. I would hate to leave Karen alone on her first Saturday in Savannah. That would be very uncaring on our part. We will have to decline. Please let Mr. Helton know."

"What? Are you crazy? We can't refuse the invitation of the bank president, not the first invitation he extends to us! We've got to go!"

Rachael wasn't about to let Ken start telling her what to do, and only she would determine if they needed to go to a party.

"The only way I'm going to that party is if Karen can go with us. It wouldn't be polite to leave her alone. You can fix it. Go tell Helton my sister is in town. He will understand."

"I can't do that. Jesus, Rachael, I just got this promotion. You want me to mess it up on the first day? Get real! Karen can make do on her own for one afternoon."

Rachael knew the inclusion of Karen was a social faux pas, but wanted her included in spite of it. The party wouldn't be any fun if Ken was her only release for conversation.

Ken reluctantly approached Ed Helton with the circumstances surrounding the invitation. As Rachael expected Mr. Helton calmed all concerns Ken may have had, and extended a welcome to Karen.

17

Chapter 4

The single runway at Hilton Head, just across Calibogue Sound from Daufuskie Island, was doing a brisk business. No less than seven fast-movers filed flight plans with the tiny airport as their destination. The airport manager was in a panic to find enough red carpets to welcome the unexpected guests.

A US Senator, with staff and state trooper in tow, was the first to arrive. Coca Cola, Home Depot, BMW and Wachovia arrived shortly thereafter. Unmarked charter jets and turbo twins completed the arrivals. With the exception of the politician, the airport manager couldn't put names to the faces, but each visitor carried a distinguished and powerful air about them.

A fine looking lady, dressed in casual island attire, entered the front of the airport lounge and announced, "Gentlemen, I am Danni Walton, Ed Helton's daughter. He asked me to escort you to Daufuskie Island. If we could board the bus we will get underway."

With that short announcement the group left the terminal. Something big had to be going on. Maybe the airport manager could get some information from the flight crews, but the pilots proved to be unusually tight lipped.

The bus ride was no more than ten minutes and soon the visitors were boarding a chartered ferry. Danni welcomed each guest aboard and introduced the captain of the vessel.

"Gentlemen, Captain Mike DeAngelo is your skipper, and we should have you on Daufuskie in about thirty minutes. There is a small buffet in the cabin if you would like something to eat. Enjoy the cruise. If there is anything you need, please don't hesitate to let me know."

The principals exchanged greetings and gravitated to the enclosed cabin while the supporting staff remained on deck and enjoyed the scenery and salt air. The seas were calm and temperatures comfortable and the crossing was made without incident. As the ferry maneuvered to dock, Senator Steve Reynolds, the senior senator from the state of Georgia, made his way to the deck. Danni saw Senator Reynolds shield his eyes against the sun and take particular notice of one of the men assisting with the docking of the boat.

The senator walked up to Danni and asked, "Is that man on the dock Bill Cannon?"

Danni was surprised the senator would know Bill Cannon by name.

"Yes, yes he is. Do you know him?"

Danni wanted to ask the senator more, but before she could properly design a question the senator wouldn't consider too prying, he ended the conversation with a polite "Thank you."

The Senator was the first guest down the gangplank. He walked directly to Bill Cannon who was busy securing a mooring line form the boat to the pier.

"Colonel Cannon."

Bill looked up from securing the line. He smiled when he recognized the Georgia Senator. He extended his hand in greeting. "Senator Reynolds, good to see you. Still pulling the wool over the eyes of your constituents, I see." It was a friendly barb.

Bill Cannon met Senator Steve Reynolds years ago during testimony on the second Iraq war. Senator Reynolds was one of many who came to Bill's defense, but even with their support Bill's military career was over and he was forced to retire.

"Hello Bill, it's been a long time. Lucas McLaughlin told me you were bumming around down here. I was hoping I would run into you. How do you like retired life?"

Lucas McLaughlin, more properly introduced, would be Major General Lucas McLaughlin. Lucas had served under Bill Cannon for almost twenty years. When Bill retired, Lucas McLaughlin's service to the country was rewarded with promotion. McLaughlin was now serving in the Pentagon.

"It has its ups and downs, but I'll get used to it." Bill added with a grin, "I haven't been shot at for a while; that part is kind of nice. How's life in the Senate with the new administration?"

The smile left the senator's face. "Bill, we're getting killed. The Dems are in the driver's seat and they're making the most of it. It's going to be a bad four years."

"Well, don't give up the fight."

Senator Reynolds sat on the Intelligence Oversight Committee, one of four Republicans on a committee of ten. Recent legislative changes empowered the Committee to where intelligence agencies would not conduct operations without the specific approval by the Committee. Approval of requests had taken a distinct political tone that fit the President's international agenda, but in Senator Reynolds' opinion, neglected the security concerns of the United States. General McLaughlin assured him that Bill Cannon was the man to talk with if he wanted impartial intelligent analysis of the Middle East.

"Bill, a year ago, the CIA was reporting Iran was well on the way to building a nuke. We haven't heard a thing about their programs since then. You've been over there, you've seen the intelligence; what do you think?"

"About their nuclear program? I can almost guarantee they've been developing a nuke, if for no other reason than Saddam Hussein was trying to build one. Iran is becoming the big dog in the Middle East, and with nukes they would instantly become the dominant power in the region."

The Senator frowned. "What kind of threat do they pose to us?"

"They don't have the launch vehicles to directly threaten us, but would definitely use it as leverage against Israel. The fuse is already lit for the next Mid-East war, so to speak. The Iranians have an intermediate range missile capable of reaching Israel. If they can mate a nuke to the missile, then Israel's hand will be forced and they will launch a strike. We almost went to war over the Soviets putting missiles in Cuba, and Iran is a damn sight more crazy that the Russians ever were. Think how the Israelis feel about a crazy nuclear capable Iran. Israel probably assumes we would never launch a nuclear retaliatory strike against Iran, and probably Iran thinks the same. Unless somebody puts a stop to the Iranian program, there will be hell to pay."

Senator Reynolds rubbed the side of his face, as if massaging a nervous twitch. "It doesn't look like we're going to do a damn thing, a lot of talk and a lot of threatened sanctions, but nothing serious. We've been talking for so long, and lose ground every time we sit down to negotiate. I don't think the Iranians believe we are capable of doing a thing."

Senator Reynolds looked up and down the dock watching the other passengers off-load before he asked, "Do you think they would ever supply a nuclear device to a terrorist group? Would they ever threaten us that way?"

"That would be suicide on their part, but the Ayatollahs may be crazy enough to do it. Besides, they don't need nukes to cripple us. They can cut off our oil, like they did back in '73, and we'll be begging for mercy within a month."

The frown on the Senator's face deepened. "Do you think they would ever launch against Israel?"

"Senator, Hitler told the West what he was going to do in *Mein Kampf*, everybody ignored it. The Iranian President has said the destruction of Israel is one of his objectives. Neville Chamberlain got duped by Hitler; I hope we have learned something from history. Crazy people will tell you what they intend to do if we only listen."

Danni Walton was herding her guests to the golf carts that would take them to the meeting with her father. Senator Reynolds noticed the movement. "Bill, I've got to go, but before I do, if I need a friendly ear in the Pentagon, is Lucas McLaughlin a man I can trust?"

Bill looked the Senator directly in the eyes. "Senator, you can trust Lucas McLaughlin with your life."

Senator Reynolds smiled. "If you're ever in Washington please give me a call. I know a lot of people who would like to meet you, and shake your hand. People still talk about your testimony."

Bill grinned and returned to securing the lines. "Senator, I wish I could forget it. Enjoy your stay on the island."

Danni exchanged pleasant small talk with the group during the short ride, but her mind was on the conversation between Bill and Senator Reynolds. Considering the manner in which Reynolds reacted, it wasn't about the weather.

After getting her charges into comfortable seats around the conference table, she made a bee-line back to Bill. She found him still on the dock unloading beer kegs from the ferry. Mike DeAngelo and Bill made the unloading look easy. Mike would swing a keg up from the deck and Bill would lean out over the water, with one hand holding a piling and grabbing the punched handle of the heavy keg with the other.

"Bill, what was that all about?"

Bill answered without stopping his work, "What was what all about?"

"Senator Reynolds doesn't look happy. You never told me you knew him."

21

Bill stopped his work just long enough to answer. "Miss Danni, I can't ever remember you asking." Just enough of a slight grin crossed his face to let Danni know he was having a little fun at her expense.

Bill wanted to get off the subject. Anything more than that simple answer would only lead to more questions. Bill slid his arm around Danni's waist and pulled her closer to him.

"How about we go find a golf cart and get this beer set up before the ice melts."

~~

Back in the conference room the meeting looked like an assembly of mob bosses. The principals were seated around the table with the staff members and security waiting in the anteroom. Ed Helton stood to start the meeting with the intention of discussing investment plans for the revival of the Daufuskie Resort, but was interrupted by Senator Reynolds.

"Ed, I met a guy on your dock named Bill Cannon. Does he work for you?"

The discussion in these meetings often strayed in many directions, but the question about Bill Cannon caught him a little off guard.

"He doesn't work for me; he was invited to the party this afternoon. He and my daughter have been—not exactly dating—but seeing each other for a while. Why do you ask?"

The senator asked, "What do you know about him?"

"I've known him for about five years. He worked with my daughter in Atlanta. Other than that I don't know much more about him. My daughter seems to enjoy his company. Why?"

"Ed, your Bill Cannon was Colonel Bill Cannon, United States Army…a real American hero. He was up for general officer until he ran into some trouble in Washington and forced to retire."

Ed Helton asked, "What happened in Washington?"

Senator Reynolds suppressed a laugh. "He was called to the Senate to testify before one of those committees. One of the senators accused him of bending the truth to suit his own purpose. The entire incident concerned an Iraqi prisoner's charge that Cannon's men killed captured and wounded fighters. An AP reporter never checked out the allegation, he just published it. The report was investigated by the

22

Inspector General and found to be completely false, but the press had a field day with the accusation.

"Colonel Cannon told the senator if he believed terrorists more than the soldiers of his own country, then he was aiding the enemy. I can't remember exactly what he said but it was something in the oath he took when he was commissioned, *against all enemies foreign and domestic*, and now he knew why the founding fathers put the domestic part in the oath."

Ed answered for the group. "Damn, that took some guts, guts or stupidity. Who was the senator?"

Reynolds paused for effect. "The senator is now the President of the United States."

Chapter 5

Ken Carson thought he looked pretty good in his tan silk slacks and baby blue polo. The dark blue cashmere sweater draped over his shoulders—for later—to ward off the chill of the evening—matched the blue band of his new straw hat. He thought the addition of designer sunglasses made him look like Brad Pitt. He was sure the outfit went way beyond the look of a tourist and simply made him look rich.

As good as he thought he looked, both Rachael and Karen were simply stunning. Their shopping trip was well worth any price because it wasn't often he had two beautiful women, one on each arm, to show off. The sideways glances of the passing tourists fed his ego and he loved the attention. Their trip down River Street to the Daufuskie ferry served as his red carpet. The dresses Rachael and Karen selected were almost translucent. Each time the sun reflected off the window of a passing car Ken could catch the outline of their shapely legs in the windows of the stores facing the river. He knew everyone on River Street enjoyed the same view.

The aromas from the street vendor carts mixed with the perfume of the women and filled the morning with wonder. Every street musician seemed to play in rhythm with their walk and Ken could feel their bodies move with the beat. Ken knew the trio would be the hit of the party and couldn't wait to get there. Every minute of the ferry ride increased his anticipation.

Rachael and Karen giggled their way through the ride with impressions of how a proper southern belle should sound, and how many times they would hear "I declare" during the day. Their arrival into higher society was confirmed when Mr. Helton's guests were transported to the residence by horse drawn carriages and not the gaseous and stuffy buses transporting resort guests to the hotel on the same island.

The horse and carriage made crunching sounds as it made the last turns up the drive to the residence. The house wasn't quite the southern mansion Ken pictured. It was white, but not two story, and lacked the columns he expected; but the grounds were large and maintained perfectly. The driver assisted their exit from the buggy and informed the trio that, "Mr. Helton invites you to join the festivities at the rear of the house. This path will lead you to the party." As Ken's carriage pulled away another was arriving to take its place. This was going to be some party.

Ken and the girls took a moment to take in the experience before proceeding down the shelled path. Even before they could see the festivities they picked up the gentle din of conversation, ice clinking in glasses and the sound of children playing. As they rounded the corner of the house Ken noticed the receiving line. He wasn't totally shocked, but was certainly surprised; the last three people in the receiving line were obviously not related to the President of Coastal Bank.

The line progressed slowly and Ken had a chance to recover his composure before greeting Ed Helton. Mr. Helton greeted Ken's little group as if they were old friends.

"Ken thank you for coming. This must be your wife Rachael, and you must be Karen." Ed engulfed them with genuine hospitality. "I hope you enjoy the party. The band starts in a few hours and we have all you can eat already on the grill. Let me introduce you to my daughter, Ms. Danni Walton." Ed turned to his daughter and introduced Ken.

"Danni, this is Ken Carson, the new manager of the loan department, and his wife Rachael, and sister-in-law Karen."

Danni Walton introduced him to her daughter, Hanna, and to her daughter's husband, what was his name...oh yeah, Major James Madison. Hanna and her husband were young and fit and looked happy like all young couples before they actually experience the grind of a marriage. Ken paid attention to what the young couple said, after all, Hanna Madison was the granddaughter of the president of the bank, and her husband, once he got out of the Army, would probably be worked into the bank management.

Ken was even attentive to the two women that followed. A regal looking lady from the islands, named some God-awful name he could never remember, but everyone simply called her Mamba, and a little old black lady called Aunt Grace. The old lady twittered some mindless babble and Ken struggled to resist the temptation to just walk past her. But Aunt Grace introduced Eric Brown, bringing up the last position in the receiving line.

Ken had a feeling he had met this young man before. Immediately after Ken exited the line he remembered; he was Eric Brown, the nightly news anchor on CNN, the international news network in Atlanta. Ken wanted to go back through the line to make a better impression with Mr. Brown, but to do so would appear strange. Damn, first impressions are important and Ken could have done a better job with Eric Brown.

By the time the three finished the receiving line Ken had his fill of being polite. High society would require some effort. He was proud Rachael and Karen breezed through the line like seasoned veterans. They were proving to be the assets Ken expected them to be.

Ken retreated to the nearest bar and watched Rachael and Karen work the field like bird dogs stalking a covey of quail.

Ken was leaning against the corner of one of the bars set beneath an ancient oak. The huge branches spread far overhead and provided a pleasant dappled light on the ground. Rachael and Karen were slowly making their way toward the group of men in conversation near one of the barbeque pits. Karen said she thought one of the men was a U.S. Senator, and Senators were always a worthy target. You never can tell when you might catch one on the rebound.

Ken felt a presence at his elbow. He turned to find Danni Walton. She started the conversation. "Mr. Carson, congratulations on the promotion."

"Thank you Ms. Walton, I feel fortunate to have been selected. I hope I can live up to your father's expectations."

"Ken, please call me Danni. I'm sure you will do fine. Do you need anything?"

"No, nothing, I'm just enjoying the view. You have quite a place here."

Danni looked for Ken's wife and sister. "Where are Rachael and Karen?"

Ken raised his glass in the direction of the barbeque pit. "She and Karen are on a tour of the grounds." Ken gave a little laugh. "Actually, they are trying to make their way to the barbeque pit to see if there are any single men in that group. Is that Senator Reynolds?"

Danni saw the two women. Their casual stroll, taking an erratic path from one flower bed to another and then to a statue, but moving ever closer to the pit was so blatantly false it was comical; but Danni had seen it many times before when the aura of the powerful turns the brains of idol worshipers into jelly. "Yes it is. He came in this morning for a meeting with my father. Would you like to meet him?"

"I would hate to bother him. Karen and Rachael will probably drag him over here in a minute anyway. Isn't one of the men with him the CEO of Wachovia? I think I recognize him from one of the magazines we get at the bank."

"Sure is. My father is a member of a little group that meets and discusses different things. They've been doing it for years." Danni wanted to end the discussion of her father's visitors. "Will you and Rachael stay for the dancing tonight?"

"We certainly intend to stay. This is a wonderful party. I don't think I could have found a better way to spend Memorial Day. Thank you for having us."

"It is our pleasure to have you. Thank you for coming."

"Ms. Walton, er...Danni, how do you know Eric Brown? I've seen him on the news many times."

Danni knew the question was intended as polite conversation, but the circumstances of their association with Eric and his aunt were better left in the past—deep in the past. "Actually, Eric and his aunt live here on my father's estate. They are like family."

Since Ken was only making polite conversation the guarded answer avoided his question without raising any suspicion. "Well, your father certainly has enough room here, and the lady called Mamba, does she also live here?"

"My father was in business with her father back in the fifties before Castro came to power. She has lived with us ever since."

Ken knew he was at his limit of personal questions and Danni had not excused or dismissed him; it was his turn to keep the conversation going. About the length of a football field from the patio a group of thirty children, ages maybe eight to ten, were being organized into three teams by men who were definitely not normal day care workers. "What's going on down there? All those children don't live here, do they?"

Danni turned her attention to the activity near the beach. "No, they are the children of the 3rd Infantry Division at Fort Stewart, and the Ranger Battalion at Hunter Army Airfield. The three men with them are all retired military. They bring the kids here two or three times a year. They play games, teach them camping and take the kids fishing; things like that. I think it is as much fun for them as it is for the kids. Let me introduce you."

From a distance the men looked like any other, but as Ken neared the children and the games they were playing, the more he sensed these men were different from any others he knew. These men played with the children with complete disregard of how silly it might look to a casual observer. Bill Cannon was the tallest, U.S. Army; Mike DeAngelo, USN Seal, the shortest, but built like a bull and probably the strongest; and Doc Broderson, U.S. Army medic. Ken Carson had the feeling that Doc Broderson was probably the only sane one of the three. The other two, although polite in their greeting, possessed a foreboding aura of danger that made Ken uncomfortable. Ken was glad to be away from these men and found comfort in the company of his wife and Karen.

Between bites of barbeque, Rachael brought Ken and Karen up to speed on everything she knew of their hosts. Most of what she relayed was from the gossip columns and local hair salons she frequented. Once Rachael started with her gossip, she only came up for air when other guests came within earshot.

"Danni Walton was married to a famous preacher in Atlanta. He was found in the Chattahoochee River with a prostitute, both deader than Elvis."

Rachael actually remembered reading about the heroic preacher who was killed trying to find the men who had raped his daughter. Rachael was keen to point out her own interpretation of the gang rape of Hanna Walton, "Probably got what she deserved. I've heard people say she was in a crack house smoking dope. She probably wanted to have sex with the men she claims raped her, but only because she had a preacher for a father did the police call it rape.

"Nobody was ever caught, but I heard that somebody was killed in their house back in Atlanta, and even some people got killed right here in this house. Nobody knows the entire story, but this family isn't all the holy-rollers they want you to think they are. And I heard that Eric Brown—his father was killed in prison. His father was in jail for the murder of his wife, her lover who was a deputy sheriff, and a policeman. I don't know how he got such a cushy job at CNN."

Taking care to ensure their conversations didn't reach the ears of others they spent the remainder of the afternoon trying to conceal their jealous envy of the wealth of their hosts, and taking some evil pleasures from the pain the family had endured. Only with the setting sun and the tuning of the band did they break up their clandestine meeting and made their way to the dance floor.

Later that evening Karen danced with all three of the men that Ken wished to avoid; once with Bill, a few times with Doc Broderson, and most of the evening with the burley Navy Seal, Mike DeAngelo.

Karen was always on the chase for a new adventure and these men were the only men at the party who presented a challenge to her.

At the end of the evening the same line of hosts who received the guests, bid the guests a farewell. Ken Carson, with a second chance to make a first impression, commented how professional Eric Brown handled the evening news. Eric made the show and in Ken's opinion, the newscast would be better if they allowed Eric to anchor the broadcast and go solo. Eric's understanding of the salient points of the news topics was much more insightful than any of the other reporters.

When Rachael finally pried her husband away from the receiving line, Eric watched the trio of Ken, Rachael and Karen board the carriage for the ride to the ferry. Eric shook his head to clear the mush and wondered, what in the hell was that all about.

Mamba moved to Eric's side. Eric turned to Mamba and muttered, "Strange man."

Mamba kept her eyes on the retreating trio. "That man has many shadows in his life. Mr. Helton may have made a mistake promoting him. He is a snake that should always be approached with caution."

Chapter 6

May in Washington D.C. was supposed to be warm.

William Jefferson threw back the quilt and swung his feet to the cold floor. The air in the room made him shiver. It was after Memorial Day and the nights were still chilly. He gazed out the second story bedroom window across the Chesapeake Bay and saw the faintest ribbon of light define the line between the horizon and an angry layer of clouds. Another rainy day and it soured his mood.

As Jefferson made his way to the shower he flipped on the television. A short pause in front of the set told him nothing much had changed: unemployment up, stock market down, TARP and the federal stimulus not producing expected results, increased Tea Party revolt, North Korea rattling the nuclear saber, Iran rattling the nuclear saber, Russia, Israel, the Queen all upset with comments made by the President.

The Offices of the Vice President and the Attorney General both explaining comments made to reporters. Representatives and Senators explaining their misspoken remarks made the previous day. More soldiers killed in Iraq and Afghanistan, and John and Kate Plus Eight were having affairs. Jefferson turned to the Weather Channel and was reminded to take his raincoat today.

The warm water of the shower chased the chill from Jefferson's body. A cold bagel served as his breakfast—wolfed down before the first traffic light. The train ride into Washington provided Jefferson an opportunity to scan the newspaper. After the paper he would lean back in his seat, and although his eyes were closed his mind was engaged on the upcoming day.

First on the agenda was that letter from the President. The Attorney General threw it in Jefferson's office last week.

Too many of these Presidential investigations had come rolling down hill, and to William Jefferson they all seemed to miss the mark. The Wall Street scandals, where billions had been lost, were ignored for investigations into the legality of Tea Party demonstrations. Or the Department of Justice dragging their collective feet in the prosecution of terrorists held in the United States or at Guantanamo, or failing to investigate alleged voter intimidation and election fraud, all the while going overboard to prosecute American soldiers or intelligence agents for heretofore approved interrogations. Well...every new President appoints an Attorney General in tune with the President's philosophy, this one was no different, but to William Jefferson it just didn't feel right.

In forty years with the Department of Justice, Jefferson had earned a reputation as a law and order prosecutor and administrator. Only two items adorned the shelves of the law library to the rear of his desk, a statue of Lady Justice and a plaque presented to him by the producers of the television show *America's Most Wanted*.

The plaque was presented in a private ceremony after the successful prosecution of the 25th criminal on the FBI's ten most wanted list. The plaque was engraved with a saying Jefferson held dear to his heart, "Don't Do the Crime - If You Can't Do the Time." To Jefferson, there wasn't a gray area when it came to the law—either obey it or pay for it.

For this latest investigation, William Jefferson hand-picked and had detailed to the Department of Justice (DOJ), a recent graduate of the FBI academy: Angelina Sanchez. She was not only the youngest of the graduating class, but the smartest. If she performed as expected, then she would be put on the fast track for promotion.

Angelina was notified Friday, before the holiday weekend, to report to the DOJ for special assignment. She bounced between excited anticipation and fear of failure. Everyone knew special assignments were your ticket for advanced promotion, and the rumors said this assignment came directly from the President.

Angelina called her parents to inform them of her selection. The news brought her aging mother to tears and she could feel the pride in her father's voice, and that his emotions were also on the edge of release. Angelina had come a long way from the cinder block house where she was born, and where her parents still lived, to the polished halls in the nation's seat of power. Only in America could the daughter of a Mexican immigrant achieve such success in so short a time.

~~

When Jefferson made it to his office, he ignored Sanchez in the waiting room. He scanned his e-mails and inbox. He removed the letter and the directive from the Attorney General from the top drawer and placed them on his desk before he called for the young agent.

When she settled in the chair to the front of his desk, Jefferson got straight to the point. "Sanchez, you have been temporarily assigned to the Department of Justice to investigate a matter directed by the President."

Jefferson slid a hand-printed letter to Angelina. The letter was short and written in block letters that a third grader would have been embarrassed to turn in.

"The President received this letter a couple of weeks ago. He has directed the DOJ to investigate this allegation to determine if there is any truth to the charge."

Angelina quickly scanned the letter, "Dear President, Only you can help me. A while back a girl had said she was raped, but the police couldn't prove a thing. And now the police in Atlanta killed all the brothers and ain't nobody doing nothing about it."

Attached to the letter was the wrinkled envelope, dated in February and simply stated President, Washington, DC. It contained no return address. It was a wonder the letter ever made it to the President, but now, here it was for action and investigation.

"This is it? This is all we have? An unsigned allegation without any names, dates or places? This is the special assignment?" It wasn't quite what Angelina Sanchez was expecting.

"It's enough for you to get started. I expect your first report in ninety days. If you have a question relating to your investigations, let's hear it. If not, then I suggest you get your butt in gear and get to Atlanta. Do you have any questions?"

"No Sir."

"Then get to Atlanta and get to work."

Angelina Sanchez was going to Atlanta. To accomplish what, it already seemed like a wild goose chase, but it was already warm in Atlanta, so it couldn't be all bad.

~~

Angelina Sanchez may have been looking to escape the chill of Washington, D.C., whereas Danni Walton's daughter, Hanna, and her new husband, Major James Madison were looking forward to the chill that lingered in Washington, and escaping the already oppressive heat and humidity of Savannah.

The romance between Major James Madison and Hanna started years ago. General McLaughlin sent her husband to deliver Bill

Cannon's letter to her mother. He was so handsome in his dress uniform. He stood tall and unwavering as her mother read the letter. Hanna remembered how she blushed, and how her hand shook as she served him a simple glass of iced tea. She couldn't take her eyes from him as he politely sipped from the glass. She could have simply stared at him for the remainder of the day if not for the sobbing of her mother.

Her mother cried for days after reading the letter. The emotional events leading up to the letter, the brutal gang rape of Hanna, the mysterious death of her husband, the home invasion in Atlanta, all seemed to come crashing down with the delivery of the letter.

It was many days later before Hanna was able to sneak into her mother's room and read the letter. Her mother said she feared Bill Cannon was dead, but Hanna only read a sincere apology from Bill, and a statement of love for her mother that Hanna secretly wished would come true.

Some six months after the letter was the next time she saw James. He arrived as a hero should, in the nick of time to free her family from men who invaded their home on Daufuskie Island.

Jimmy wouldn't then, and hasn't since, talked about the men who helped him free her family. One of the men shot and killed one of the home invaders. Two others wounded, Jimmy shot one in the leg, but all Jimmy said was he thought they worked for her grandfather. Hanna knew that wasn't the truth, but it was what they agreed to tell the police. Once Hanna remarked how easily the members of her family accepted Jimmy's claim of ignorance, as to the identity of his two accomplices in their rescue, Mamba advised her to just, "Let it go." So she did.

The night of the home invasion was the same night James asked her mother if she could attend the Ranger Ball as his date. It was their first date and the start of a love affair that only grew.

They were married at the post chapel on Fort Stewart, on the outskirts of Savannah. It was a small ceremony, but it was formal in the military sense. All the officers in dress blues with gilded swords and Hanna believed it to be a fairy tale. The quiet ceremony ended as they walked through the door of the chapel to the roar of 300 soldiers from the 75th Ranger Regiment. What started as a reserved and demure event, turned into an unbridled celebration. And even as the new Mrs. James Madison, the wife of a direct descendent of President James Madison, she never could find how her husband earned the nickname of "Mad Man". She began to wonder if it was a military secret.

She had talked with her mother and Mamba about the hazards of his profession. Even though their first posting was to the Pentagon, a non-combat unit, Hanna knew he could be called at any time to serve. Mamba understood her concerns. She lost her husband at the Bay of Pigs during the invasion of Cuba. Mamba told her, "Tomorrow is never guaranteed. Better to love today than live worrying about what may happen tomorrow."

Hanna's mother wasn't so quick to agree. She had lost her husband to violence and he was in the most peaceful of professions, he was a preacher. But in spite of her reservations, her mother blessed the marriage.

The honeymoon was on the outer banks of the barrier islands off North Carolina. She thought they had walked the entire length, hand in hand at the water's edge. At least half the nights they spent in a small tent that Jimmy carried in a backpack. It was wonderful solitude and they touched each other and nature.

They were assigned quarters on Andrews Air Force Base. Their house was the smallest on the street and their neighbors were all Colonels, and General Officers, but everyone made her feel welcome. The block party served as their housewarming; the party was wonderful and enlightening with the men around the grill and the women chatting on the patio.

The wives knew Hanna was new to the military and they welcomed the naiveté of her questions. "What does your husband do?"

The answer was open and honest, "Oh honey," it wasn't condescending to Hanna to be addressed as such, "none of us are supposed to know what it is that our husbands do." There was a low chorus of giggles from the other wives, "You will never get a straight answer from your husband about what it is he actually does. It's always 'classified' you know. But it's not too hard to figure out. Just watch the news and if he disappears for a week or two, you can expect a present from wherever the hot spot is. But he will never tell you he was there. It's a game we all know how to play. Don't ask because you will never get a straight answer. Just be thankful when he comes home."

"Don't you worry about them?" Hanna hoped she didn't sound unreasonable or even cowardly.

"Hanna, of course you worry. We all worry. It is something you will learn to live with." And then to lighten the conversation the woman added, "Besides, some of our best shopping is done when our husbands disappear; isn't that right girls?"

Lucas McLaughlin broke away from the men and approached Hanna. "Hanna, did your mother ever hook up with Bill Cannon?"

Before Hanna could consider the question, much less formulate an answer, the general's wife scolded her husband. "Lucas McLaughlin, what a thing to say. I can't believe you would ask such a question."

"What's wrong with that? Not 'hook up' the way the children use it, I mean, are they seeing each other. I know Bill thinks the world of your mother, I do too for that matter, I was just wondering, that's all."

Now this was something she really wanted to call home about! So Bill Cannon had the "hots" for her mother. It wasn't an unpleasant thought for Hanna, but she needed to know more. "How do you know Bill Cannon likes my mother?"

General McLaughlin wanted to answer that Bill had said as much on his death bed, but then he would have to explain that whole incident. He had probably already said too much, so his answer was a simple, "No real reason, I just thought they made a good looking couple at your wedding and I thought they might be seeing each other."

Hanna secretly agreed with General McLaughlin and couldn't wait to call Mamba and tell her the new scoop.

~~

John Roger "Doc" Broderson backed his ambulance to the loading dock of the headquarters building of the Georgia Bureau of Investigation (GBI). The building served a multipurpose for the State and housed the GBI, the Fulton County Courthouse, the Atlanta Police Department, and the Hall of Legal Records for the State of Georgia.

As Doc Broderson wound his way through the halls he made the usual stops, and made small talk with the friends he had made over the years. Doc was well respected by the veterans of the police force and was the unanimous choice as medical support when the officers expected trouble.

Doc finally arrived at the Records Department and stuck his head through the door. The front office was empty, but he heard the copy machine working overtime. He yelled his arrival into the depths. "Wade…Wade Griffin, you here?"

Doc heard the records custodian answer from the back. "Doc, is that you? I'm back here. Come on back."

Doc found Wade in the middle of a stack of boxed records with the copy machine producing more by the minute. "Damn, Wade, what in the hell are you doing?"

"Just wasting paper. What've you got?" Wade hadn't even looked up from his task at the copier.

"A copy of the charge bill for that hit and run DOA from last week. It needs to be filed in the report." Doc was amused at the amount of paper that surrounded his friend. "You guys don't have enough records? You have to make more? What's up with that?"

"These ain't for us. They're for some special investigator the Feds sent down here. She wants 'em."

"The Feds? You guys being investigated? Taking too much money under the table? Could be curtains for some I know." That was all in jest, and the barb didn't bother Wade in the least.

Doc ran his eyes down the boxes of records and noted the case names marked on the end of each box. "What kind of investigation?"

"Some special investigation assigned by the Attorney General. I'm making copies of everything we have on unsolved rapes for the past ten years. Do you have any idea how many unsolved rape cases we have in Atlanta? Hundreds! She's real pretty, but can be a real pain in the ass." Wade was finished running copies and packed the last box. "I'm almost finished here and we can file that charge sheet."

Doc noted there were ten boxes sealed for delivery. "You need any help getting those boxes delivered? I've got nothing to do. I can run one of those carts."

"Sure. You take those five and I'll get these. Drop your charge sheet on my desk and I'll file it when I get back."

When the boxes were loaded, the top one had to be held in place or it would slide off. Doc ran into the wall once and the corner of Wade's desk once, before he mastered the art of guiding the cart.

As they rode the freight elevator to the third floor the Wade asked, "Hey Doc, when are you going fishing again. I could use some of those grouper filets again."

"As a matter of fact, I'm going on a little fishing trip this weekend. If I'm lucky enough to catch any I'll bring you some. Now where are we taking this stuff?"

Wade led the way to an unmarked office stuck in the back wing of the building. He stuck his head through the door to announce his arrival. "Miss Sanchez, I have those records you requested. Where do you want them?"

Wade was correct. Miss Sanchez was indeed a real beauty. Her dark hair was pulled back into a pony tail secured by a bright yellow ribbon. The starched shirt, unbuttoned one button too many, revealed a cleverly concealed amount of olive skin; skin that was in brilliant contrast to the white of the shirt. She looked as if she just returned from a week at the beach. The shirt was neatly tucked into pressed khaki slacks and a 9mm Glock was clipped to her belt. She was intently studying a case folder on her desk and with a delicate hand simultaneously made notes on a legal pad. She didn't even glance up before she answered. "Stack them up against the wall, please."

Angelina didn't look up until she noticed Wade wasn't alone unloading the requested records. "Who is you helper, Mr. Griffin?"

Wade stopped his unloading to introduce Doc. "Miss Sanchez, this is Doc Broderson. He drives one of the emergency medical team ambulances. Doc, meet Miss Angelina Sanchez, from the Department of Justice in Washington."

Angelina rose and came from behind the desk. Doc closed the distance and met her at the corner. "It's very nice to meet you, Miss Sanchez. I hope you are enjoying our southern hospitality. Is Atlanta PD taking care of you?"

Angelina's hand seemed small and delicate in the hand of Doc Broderson. "So far they have been very nice. I have no complaints."

The boxes delivered, Doc announced, "Well, I've got to get back to work. Welcome to Atlanta, Miss Sanchez."

As Doc found his way back to the loading dock he ran a quick mental evaluation of Miss Sanchez. Initial impression was that, although very young, she gave the impression she was intelligent and intense and that she would be very thorough in her investigation; an opinion that he would discuss with his friends on the upcoming fishing trip. For not only Doc, but Bill Cannon and Mike DeAngelo would be interested in the subject matter of one of the reports Special Agent Sanchez had called for review.

The report that caught the interest of Doc Broderson was the gang rape of Hanna Elizabeth Walton.

Chapter 7

There may be no better place on earth than the end of a dock at sunset. The heat of the day has dissipated, the winds become calm, and the stars begin to shine through the gathering darkness. Even the sounds of the day begin to fade and it's time for good friends to relax. Bill Cannon, Doc Broderson, and Mike DeAngelo did just that. The day's catch was cleaned and stored and the fish they didn't want to keep had been sold to their favorite restaurant. *Old Ironbelly*, Bill's boat, had been cleaned, put to order, and properly moored in the slip at Mike DeAngelo's Salt Water Creek Marina. The beer was icy cold and beckoned to them for the last hour, but true to their training they always clean up before they beer up.

DeAngelo sat down-breeze of the group to keep his cigar smoke—smuggled in from Havana just last week according to him—from interfering with the delicate bouquet of the bottled beer. His was the only padded chair surrounding the huge wooden cable spool that served as their table. It was—after all—his marina. The beer cooler served as Bill's chair, and Doc's was nothing more than a wooden plank balanced on a pier piling. The occasional boat would pass and the skipper would add to the flavor of the evening with good natured barb hurled at the marina's owner. Their conversation was a continuation of the primary subject covered during the day's fishing trip.

DeAngelo just didn't understand Bill's pig-headed attitude towards Danni Walton. "I don't get it Bill. You and Danni are made for each other! All you ever do is mope around when you're not with her. Why don't you get a pair of balls and tell her how you feel about her?"

Bill felt a little uncomfortable discussing the state of his love life with someone who considered a long term relationship anything longer than a one night stand. "What the hell do you know, DeAngelo? Your last ten relationships lasted what—four hours each?"

"Ohhh, a little testy tonight, aren't we. Hell, Bill, I don't want to see you die a grumpy old man; at least not any more grumpy than you are right now. I think you're chicken!"

Doc Broderson added his advice. "I hate to agree with a Navy guy, but I think he's right Bill. Your problem has nothing to do with your feelings about her. Your problem really is—if Danni Walton would want to even be seen with you. She does have a lot of class and you really aren't a box of chocolates, you know. You might as well get it over with and find out if you even have a chance with her. When is the next time you're going to see her?"

Bill blushed slightly when he had to admit, "I'm taking her fishing tomorrow."

The admission started the good natured ribbing with Mike DeAngelo hitting a new low in decorum. "There you go Bill. There's your chance to make your move, you sly old dog. Get her out on the water and she can't say no, eh?"

DeAngelo added a crude wink to his slanderous comment. Bill knew it was all in jest. All three men respected Danni Walton and this crude dockside humor was only meant for their ears and entertainment among friends.

"You guys are sick." As an afterthought, Bill added, "Doc, are you going to take some of these fillets back with you?"

"Damn right I am." Doc remembered Wade Griffin wanted some filets and that reminded him of Angelina Sanchez and the investigation. "Oh, by the way, the Feds have an agent from the Department of Justice investigating Hanna's rape."

Bill raised his eyebrows with interest. "You're kidding. Why would the Feds want to investigate a rape that happened years ago? The police never got enough evidence to present the case; do the Feds think they can find something new?"

"My friend in records said she is going through hundreds of files; it may turn out to be nothing, but I just thought you would want to know."

Bill knew a detailed investigation, funded by the government and without the pressures of preparing a case for prosecution, could prove problematic. "Who's doing the investigation?" Bill had some contacts in Washington, but none in the Department of Justice. Any inquiries would probably only raise suspicions.

"Hot little Mexican girl, Angelina Sanchez. She's young, but seems capable."

Bill thought how ironic it was that he was just beginning to put that particular part of his past into the dark recesses of his memories that were not often visited. This new investigation proved you can never escape your past.

Everyone Bill cared for could be stung by a new investigation. Certainly Doc and Mike DeAngelo were at risk. Even Hanna's husband, Major James Madison and his senior officer, Major General Lucas McLaughlin, could be brought down with such an investigation. Ed Helton was at risk for unknowingly funding the entire operation. His lifelong best friend, Command Sergeant Major Steve Thunder, had already paid the ultimate sacrifice, but could be caught up in the investigation. It brought a sick feeling to Bill's stomach that the reputation of his friend could be tarnished. Even Eric Brown's new career could be in jeopardy if the investigator dug deep enough. And the person he was most concerned with—the person who had as much to lose as he—Danni Walton may come to regret the decisions she made those many years ago.

Bill thought about all these things before he spoke. "Doc, I think you and I have good cover for this thing. Mike, I think it would be a stretch to link you to the operation, but you need to keep your eyes and ears open. But just in case things go to shit, I will call our friend in Panama to start cutting some cash in case we need to go deep."

Going deep was, in reality, disappearing from all contact with their lives as they now were; something that was always a last resort, but if necessary had to be planned and funded. Their friend in Panama was the Vice President of the National Bank of Panama. He knew enough of Bill's past that he would never question Bill's strange request.

Mike DeAngelo had listened in silence, "Bill, you going to tell Danni about the investigation?"

"Not unless I have to. Maybe the investigation won't turn up a thing and all this will turn out to be nothing; but let's be prepared to move. I'll call Lucas and give him a heads up. I want him to be ready to move Madison if the investigator starts getting too close."

Chapter 8

The day with Danni started with an early morning launch from the Daufuskie pier. Bill arrived at 6 a.m. Danni and Mamba loaded *Old Ironbelly* with provisions and they shoved off at 7:00. By 8:00 they were on the Dolly Madison Reef 25 five miles off the mouth of the Savannah River and by 10:00 they had caught their limit.

Bill didn't want the day to end so quickly so he offered, "What do you say about a short trip down the coast? Have you ever been to Blackbeard's Island?"

Danni couldn't think of anything she would like to do more than spend the day with Bill. "Sounds good to me."

Danni had been on Bill's boat only two other times. The first more than ten years ago—it was on the day he bought it. They met during new employee orientation at Home Depot. The first two weeks were spent in class and traveling the southeast in a detailed introduction to the home improvement giant. Danni was focused on absorbing the company message, and Bill was focused on getting his new boat. Bill extended an invitation to Danni to go on the sea trials before the purchase. Bill put the boat through radical moves that were exhilarating to say the least, and it was the most fun Danni had since before her marriage.

Bill moved from the stern, "Let's get this gear stowed and then we'll get underway."

Danni admired the ripple of the muscles in Bill's arms as he hauled in the anchor. He moved on the boat with a graceful skill that belied his fifty years and she wondered how he maintained a body of a man twenty years his junior.

As Bill pulled on the anchor the wind raised his shirt to expose the tanned skin of his back. Danni noticed the scars from battles long ago, scars she had seen before, but the one she wanted to ask him about was a new one about the length of a dollar bill, just above his right kidney. An unspoken agreement about their past, prevented Danni from asking the question about the newest scar. Their past was filled with secrets and terrible events that were better left alone.

With the anchor finally stowed Bill moved back to the cockpit. "You want to drive?"

Danni thought about the offer for a moment. "No, you're the Captain of this vessel—you set the course. I'll be the galley wench. You want something to drink?"

"Yeah, I'll take one of those waters. Let me know when you're ready."

Danni got two chilled waters from below and then slid into the seat next to Bill. "Let her rip." Danni's leg against Bill's raised a flush on her face that she hoped Bill didn't notice. They both felt the wonderful tension but neither could get beyond the invisible wall that separated them, and they kept their feelings locked within.

Danni yearned to learn when it would be proper to give herself to another man, to expose the true feelings she held within. The violent death of her husband and the terrible years of her marriage always filled her with a fear of total commitment. But Bill was different, Bill made her feel safe, Bill had never betrayed her; but still the fog of fear kept her from allowing her emotions to surface.

Until that day, whenever it may come, Danni's leg against Bill's, and the gentle touch of her hand under his shirt running up the muscles of his back was enough. Danni let her hand slowly approach the scar above his right kidney and as her hand moved gently over the scar she felt the involuntary twitch of his muscles; maybe the day she could give herself to him was the day he would tell her of the scar.

The warmth of Danni's leg against his caused a flush in Bill's face and he hoped Danni didn't notice. The light perfume she wore mingled with the salt spray and Bill believed it was the most beautiful scent in the world. For years he longed for her touch and now she was here, bare skin against bare skin, and the sensation made it hard to concentrate on the wave pattern. Why did he always hesitate to tell her about his desire to have her, to make her his wife? Their past was like the wake of the boat, it was behind them. But Bill knew the secrets he kept may poison her love, so he kept silent. It was enough to have her skin touching his and maybe one day, if he gathered the courage, he would tell her what he knew. But the thought of losing her to the truth was too big a chance to take so he maintained his silence.

Blackbeard's Island lay ahead.

~~

42

Bill and Danni laid in satisfied exhaustion. *Old Ironbelly* gently tugged at anchor a few yards off the beach. The kayak excursion to the salt marshes on the leeward side of the island proved uneventful, but the return trip against the incoming tide had been exhilarating.

The sandwiches and wine capped off a wonderful afternoon and only with effort did Bill keep from drifting off to sleep. Danni's deep breathing, with her head laid upon his chest and arm draped across his belly, was his reward for doing the lion's share of paddling fighting the current during the return trip. Bill knew paradise couldn't be much better than this.

"Bill, my father says the Daufuskie Resort is going to default on their loan. He wants me to manage it. He thinks we can save it."

Bill glanced down at Danni and talked to the top of her head, the aroma of her hair distracted him. "There's no one who could do a better job than you."

"The resort owes the bank a lot of money. Dad thinks it could cause the failure of the bank if we can't turn a profit. It's a big responsibility."

Bill gave Danni a little hug. "With great risk comes great reward. Don't make it harder than it is. Concentrate on the basics and you will turn it around. I know you can do it."

It was then that Bill sensed a change. Something had tripped his alarm. Something, maybe the flushing of birds or a scent in the wind, or sounds of the insects, was warning him they were not alone. Panthers were rare but did frequent the island. Maybe a gator had caught their smell and was making his way around one of the surrounding dunes, or maybe somebody was watching them. Whatever it was, Bill had learned to trust his instincts and he didn't wait to see if it was a false alarm.

"Danni, let's get on back. I don't want to be caught in the dark trying to make my way across the river." As Danni helped load the boat, Bill kept a wary eye on the surrounding dunes and along the skyline. Only when the anchor was up and *Old Ironbelly* skimming across the waves did the sense of caution leave Bill.

~~

After dropping Danni on Daufuskie, Bill's mind wandered as he skimmed through the glassy waters of St. Augustine Creek leading from Wassaw Sound to the Wilmington River. It wasn't the most direct route, but at high tide the creek was a serene ribbon of blue water almost floating on a sea of green reeds. There were just enough bends and curves to the creek that, at full throttle, Bill could put *Old Ironbelly* almost to the starboard gunwale for a couple of minutes to navigate around one of the small islands until putting her on her port side to follow the curve of the creek, and then back on her starboard side and repeating the turns for a mile until finally hitting the no wake zones of the Wilmington River.

The Savannah River docks, commercial piers, and cargo vessels were just to the north but completely out of sight behind the marsh reeds and trees bordering the river. It was an exhilarating ride that perfectly matched the wonderful day with Danni. As the sun settled into the far trees only the sweet aroma of Danni still lingered and the day left him with a boyish anticipation of planning their next excursion.

As Bill idled to the dock he pulled to the fuel pumps. With the tanks full, Bill idled to his slip and expertly backed the boat into the mooring. He made quick work securing the lines and commenced with a wash down when the same tingling of apprehension began to fill his senses once again.

Bill didn't walk through life checking for danger behind every tree, but his sense of impending danger had never let him down, and he had grown to trust this sixth sense. He casually scanned the buildings along the shoreline and looked into the deepening shadows between the buildings and under the trees. He couldn't identify any obvious danger. After coiling the water hose, he returned to the cabin and secured all equipment and hatches and finally emerged from below decks with a light jacket thrown over his arm.

The walk up the long dock was exposed on all sides. The only cover available was the superstructure of some of the larger vessels moored in their slips. Bill eyed each vessel before he passed and chose a rather staggered route that used each piling as cover, what little cover the twelve inch concrete pilings could provide. To a casual observer his gait was one of a man with maybe a little too much to drink or unsure of his footing on the floating dock; it wasn't hurried but could be described as sporadic. Bill knew if he could make it to the base of the pier, where the river met the bank, he could find cover. There was no movement on the bank, but Bill knew someone was there. The closer Bill got to the stairway the more the bank would mask his location from the heights above.

The man watching Bill from behind the dense bushes at the crest of the river escarpment had a distinct middle-eastern look polished to fit into America. He would never warrant a second glance. He was dressed in khaki pants and black golf shirt and could have been a tourist, an exchange student, or business man; and he intently watched the entire docking process of Bill and *Old Ironbelly*.

He knew when Bill walked up the floating stairway he would pass within 15 or 20 feet of his position. His nervous fidgeting and occasional glance to his own rear showed he was impatient to complete his mission and be away from here.

The man in the shadows slowly moved closer to the walkway, but his wait seemed much too long for the short walk. The man on the pier must be delayed for some reason. No problem, he could wait. When his wait turned from moments to minutes he knew something was wrong. With a nervous glance to his flanks and rear he moved from the cover of the bushes, and with his back to the boat house, edged his way closer to the end of the pier. From the end of the pier he could tell the dock was abandoned. He bent far over the rail to look under the platform but could see nothing in the shadows. He had failed.

He hurried back to the base of the escarpment and slid back into the darkness of the shadows. He would wait a few moments longer for his target to appear. There must be another path up from the river that he missed during his reconnaissance. No matter—he knew his man had to pass through the narrow walkway to reach his condominium. When the cold steel of Bill Cannon's pistol nudged against the base of his skull the only thought that raced across his mind was, "Allah, have mercy."

The voice from behind him, barely above a whisper asked, "Are you prepared to die?"

The pressure of the gun didn't vary on his neck and the hand holding it was steady. "If it be Allah's will, but only after I deliver a message from my master, Prince Ahmad Jabir Al-Sabah, to Colonel Bill Cannon, if you be that man."

To his surprise the American addressed him in clear and fluent Arabic. "You have a strange way of delivering a message. Get down on your knees, and then flat on the ground. Do it now."

Bill's voice was firm but quiet. Once the man was spread eagle on the ground Bill placed a heavy knee in the small of his back and his free hand roamed to search for weapons, but his gun never left the base of the man's skull.

The man on the ground had been warned about this American— that he was dangerous and deadly. The Prince himself told him to use caution when he approached him. He had scoffed at such warnings

45

believing they were only told to frighten him and add a sense of intrigue and urgency to his task of delivering a simple message. He believed his training in the Kuwaiti Commando School to have been complete and as good as any in the world, but this American moved like a ghost and now had him at his mercy with his face in the dirt.

Bill, still in Arabic, asked, "Who are you?"

"I am Abul Al-Barrif, second cousin of the Great Prince Ahmad Jabir Al-Sabah. The great Prince thanks you for the lives of his children."

This was exactly the way Prince Al-Sabah had instructed him to address the American. Few knew that Bill, during the first desert war, had mounted a raid against the Iraqi Army to rescue Prince Al-Sabah's children from Saddam Husain's torture squads. The greeting was intended as a means to vouch for the identity of the messenger.

Bill answered, "What is the message?"

The man tried to look back at Bill, "I have a package for you. It's under my shirt."

Bill kept the pistol pressed to the man's skull and felt an envelope taped to his back. "What's in here?"

"My Master ordered that I deliver the package, he did not direct me to look inside. What is inside is for your eyes. I would not disgrace my Prince by opening something intended for you."

Bill wanted to know why there was a need to be so secretive. "Explain the need for secrecy for something that could have been mailed to me?"

"Do not underestimate the danger, Colonel Cannon. Many, even in the house of the Prince, would consider this meeting a treasonous act against Islam. Use extreme caution."

Bill released the man from his pinned position on the ground and watched as he made his way from the wooded area to the parking lot of a local grocery store. Bill waited until he was sure no car followed the messenger from the parking lot.

Bill used the darkening shadows to make his way to his condo using the same sporadic gate as on the dock. No reason to allow any shooter a constant pace for a sniper shot. It had been a long time since Bill felt like he was a hunted man, but the meeting just concluded heightened his sense of caution. Was the messenger the same man watching them on the beach, or were there more eyes than one pair to worry about?

Bill wondered what was going on to require this amount of secrecy. He would wait until he was secure in his house before he opened the package.

Bill avoided the windows and put the pistol on the nightstand before he opened the envelope. The note from his friend was short. "Pictures can tell many stories. Ahmad."

On each picture, an electronic date stamp and detailed latitude and longitude, as if taken from a reconnaissance aircraft. Bill moved to his computer and typed in each set: Port Said in Egypt, Ezbet Abu Segal on the Mediterranean Coast, a walled house in southern Lebanon, the port of Tartus – in Syria, and an isolated piece of desert in Syria. Bill was familiar with some of the locations, but understood none of the significance.

Why had his friend gone to such measures to get these pictures to him? What was it in these pictures that his friend wanted made known, and required him to get them to Bill in such a secretive manner? What kept Prince Al-Sabah from using the normal intelligence channels to relay the pictures to the CIA, or Defense Department, or even the State Department? The man on the river said there was considerable danger. He said many, even in the house of the Prince, would consider the release of the pictures to be a treasonous act. Bill knew he could speculate all night, but then it would still only be a guess. Tomorrow he would call Lucas McLaughlin and Steve Reynolds. They could get these pictures into the intelligence system.

Bill slept with the loaded pistol under his pillow. His sleep was shallow, like days past when you slept with your boots on and your weapons loaded and by your side. This morning, if you asked him, he would have told you that this part of his life was over. He would have told you that he was retired from the rigors of war. He would have told you that his main goal in life was to pursue the woman he loved. He would have been wrong.

Chapter 9

Danni sat with her father in the paneled study. The financial records of the Daufuskie Resort spread before them; they were as expected. Dwindling revenues and bank balances and increasing expenses and obligations. Danni visited every travel site on the web and was shocked to read what she found. Only 10 percent of the comments were positive; and those were customers content with the isolation and solitude of the resort. The other 90 percent detailed a non-responsive staff, accommodations that were often far below expectations, and families quickly bored with a lack of activities for children. It was no wonder the majority of vacationers made Orlando their destination rather than Daufuskie Island. It was just after midnight when Danni asked, "Daddy, are you sure I'm the right person for this job?"

Ed looked up from the last quarterly report filed by the resort. "Danni, this project is vital to the survival of the bank. If I didn't think you were the best person for the job, then I wouldn't put you in it."

"Wouldn't it be wiser to hire a management company?"

Ed put the report down. "The resort already has professional management. Any company we bring in would run the hotel in the same manner it is currently being run. No, what we need is a new look, and some new ideas. I'm pretty sure I can get some new capital investors if we can come up with a concept that will attract customers. I think we have between thirty and sixty days to come up with a plan."

"And if we can't? What then?"

Ed slowly shook his head. "I want us to approach this with the intent and attitude that we will make it work. If we don't...well...we may be forced to declare bankruptcy and close the doors to the bank. A lot of investors will be hurt."

~~

Danni altered her morning run to include the beach facing the resort. As she made her way past a few early rising guests she noticed the only staff activity along the entire beach was a single attendant struggling with an armful of beach umbrellas.

48

He appeared no more than eighteen and had the good looks of a lifeguard; hair sandy blond from the summer sun. His load lightened as he made his way down the tables facing Calibogue Sound and the Atlantic Ocean. On his way back to the storage building he diligently picked up stray pieces of trash washed onto the beach or left by late night beach goers. On Danni's return run down the beach the same young man was cleaning the tables and trying to make repairs to a couple of the umbrellas worn past their useful life expectancy.

Danni wove her way through the cottages adjoining the main hotel and noticed things that had always escaped her attention before. Torn screens, peeling paint and full trash cans left a bad initial impression.

She was back at her house by 7:30 a.m. and called Mr. Porter, the general manager, to arrange a private meeting—followed by a meeting with the department heads. The agenda items would be at the discretion of the general manager or the department heads. Mr. Porter selected 10 a.m. for their meeting, and 11 a.m. for the department heads. Danni reserved comment on the late start.

At 8 a.m. Danni started a leisurely stroll through the grounds. She stopped by the golf course and ordered a coffee from the snack bar. She wandered by the tennis courts and the pool. She wandered past the buses loading and unloading guests either heading to—or from—the Hilton Head Ferry. Danni noticed the resort staff standing by with carts to assist, but none offering assistance unless first tipped.

As Danni made her way into the lobby she watched the guests check in or out, and at 9:45 announced to the attendant behind the counter of her 10 a.m. meeting with Mr. Porter. The young lady, already burdened with checking in guests, directed her to the elevator. "Third floor, turn left, his office is at the end of the hall. You can't miss it." She had barely looked up from her duties at the front desk.

Danni made her way to the elevator and then the third floor. She turned left as directed and at the end of the hall saw the office door with General Manager engraved in black on a brass plate. Danni pushed the door open to a front office appointed with a few couches and a vacant receptionist desk. The desk had been recently occupied because Danni could still see steam rising from a coffee cup on the front corner, but other than that, there was no sign of life. Danni announced her presence, "Hello? Mr. Porter, are you here?"

Danni heard a shuffling of a chair and Mr. Porter appeared in the doorway. "You must be Mrs. Walton. I am Randall Porter, the General Manager. Welcome to Daufuskie Island Resort. Come in and sit down."

Mr. Porter wore a white resort golf shirt tucked into a pair of dark brown slacks. He led Danni to a pair of overstuffed leather chairs with a coffee table positioned between them.

"From what I was told, you are our new boss. I look forward to working with you. In this economy, I hope you have brought some good luck with you. Is there anything in particular you want to see?"

This was about the reception Danni expected to receive. "Mr. Porter, I am new to the resort business. I am at your disposal for the next hour." Danni leaned back in her chair and waited for Mr. Porter's response.

Randall Porter wasn't prepared for such a sudden shift of responsibility. Usually visitors to the resort, wishing to establish their position of authority, would lead the conversation with a line of direct questions. To which Porter would answer with irrelevant and wandering comments that seldom answered the question, but always deflected responsibility to someone other than himself. It was a skillful game of cat and mouse that Randall Porter was expert at playing. Ask him why reservations were down and he would complain about the advertising program. If asked what he thought the marketing theme should be, he would complain the agency had not provided recommendations. If asked when the agency intended to provide a new program, he would answer after the employee surveys were completed. He was expert at the game, but now this lady had dumped the responsibility for the fifty-eight minutes directly into his lap—and he didn't like it.

Desperately trying to formulate a reasonable presentation Porter resorted to the only thing he knew always worked. "Mrs. Walton, would you like some coffee before we start?"

At that moment a woman in her mid thirties, with a skirt at mid thigh and a sweater cut almost to her midsection burst through the office door. "Hey, Randy, that lady from the bank is somewhere in the hotel!" She stopped the instant she saw Danni. "Oh, I see she is already here." She paused long enough to get her bearings and composure. "Mr. Porter, would you like me to bring you some coffee?"

Porter looked at Danni for her answer. She answered, "No thank you. I am fine."

Porter began to blunder his way through information he hoped would placate his new boss. Twenty minutes into the meeting Danni put a halt to the mindless wanderings.

"Mr. Porter, I read you personnel file.   You came highly recommended when you were placed in the position of general manager, so I am going to assume you possess the skills to manage this resort. I will also assume since you have not already tendered your resignation that you either want or need this job. But, this resort is failing with you as the general manager, and I will not hesitate to terminate your employment unless this resort turns around. Do you understand?"

With just those few words this woman convinced Randall Porter that unless he performed up to his potential she would end his employment without hesitation or remorse.   "Yes, Mrs. Walton, I understand."

"Mr. Porter, the fate of this resort is not written in stone. We can turn it around. That is what I intend to tell your staff. I will assume this hotel has been operating under the shadow of closure and our customer service has fallen to levels that will ensure our failure. We are going to start acting like our future depends on our efforts. I will not accept anything but your best. We have thirty days to develop a plan to bring this resort back to profitability. If we fail, then we will all be without a job. Now let's go meet the staff."

Chapter 10

The phone rang in Senator Reynolds' Washington office shortly after 10 a.m. The intern answered as she had been instructed.

"Senator Reynolds' office, thank you for calling, how may I help you."

"This is CNN in Atlanta." The woman's voice on the other end of the connection was curt, short and hurried, as if she didn't have the time to be polite. "Find out if the Senator is available for an on-camera interview after the President's address." Not a please or even a thank you, but the intern remembered her instructions and thanked the lady for her call.

"Thank you for your call. Please hold and I will pass your request to the Senator."

The President was scheduled to make his first address to the United Nations. The White House press leaks indicated the speech would establish his framework for the Nation's foreign policy, and it would send a message of understanding and mutual respect to the world. America was no longer going to force its will on a less fortunate world. The White House staff was giddy with excitement.

The intern called through to Senator Reynolds. "Senator, excuse me, but CNN is on the line and has requested you for interviews after the President's address."

Reynolds paused from reading. "CNN...did they say who would be doing the interview?"

"No Senator, they did not."

"Then tell them to go and pound sand," and the Senator turned back to his reading.

In the short time the intern served in Senator Reynolds' office she had learned enough to be more diplomatic than her boss. She took the waiting call off hold. "I'm sorry; the Senator will be unavailable for interviews this afternoon. Can I be of any other assistance to you?"

Rhonda Fleming, Eric Brown's assistant, hung up the phone without-so-much as a goodbye. She knew Senator Reynolds wouldn't do the interview; it had been a waste of time to even try.

Rhonda was perfect for the CNN newsroom. Early thirties, vegetarian skinny, communications degree from Berkley, could be doing more with her life, but so many different causes required her attention; much more so than work ever would. She would never admit it, but protesting against the sins of capitalism was easier than actually making a contribution.

"Eric, Senator Reynolds' office said he wouldn't be available for interviews. I knew he would just blow us off. I don't know why you always want him, he only complains about the programs the President is putting in place. He's just a right-wing nut, if you ask me."

Eric Brown looked up from his desk. "Rhonda, whether you realize it or not, we are supposed to be a news organization and should provide both sides of any argument; that, and he is the sitting Senator from our state. Did you talk with the Senator?"

"No, I just talked with the girl who answered the phone."

Eric extended his hand, "Give me the number, I'll call him."

Rhonda gave Eric the number and then stormed back to her desk to brood.

When the intern answered Eric's call she was surprised when the Senator asked for the call to be transferred. "Steve Reynolds."

"Senator, this is Eric Brown. I hope I'm not interrupting anything. Do you have time for a few questions?"

Senator Reynolds realized the invitation he so rudely rebuffed was probably from Eric. He hoped the intern hadn't relayed his exact sentiments. "Eric, was that your office that called a few minutes ago?"

"Yes it was. I hoped you would do some on-camera stuff with me this afternoon, after the President's speech at the United Nations."

"Are you going to be doing the interview? I'm not on the best of terms with some of the anchors at CNN, and I don't want to get in some ridiculous debate."

Eric laughed, Senator Reynolds didn't pull any punches during his televised interviews, and that he was not on the best of terms with some of the anchors was putting it mildly. Some anchors took more joy in placing him in indefensible positions than they did in reporting the Senator's point of view.

Eric still had the reputation of a fair and unbiased news journalist and that is why his answer to Senator Reynolds' question was important. "Yes sir, I'll be lead on the interview. Has the White House released any of the President's speech?"

"Just the leaks you've probably heard. They're playing it very close to the vest. It should be interesting."

"Yes, Senator, it should be interesting. We'll have our cameras set up in the rotunda. I'll talk to you after the speech."

~~

Mike DeAngelo threw Doc Broderson a beer from the small refrigerator conveniently built into the counter at his *Saltwater Creek Marina*. "Hey, Doc, why don't we cruise on up to Paris Island and roust a couple of Marines. I understand they got new girls at the club at Port Royal."

Doc considered the offer. If the trip was going to be a repeat of their last trip—where he would end up watching his friend get drunk, take on the entire Marine garrison from Paris Island, patch him up, and then be forced to negotiate the tricky sand bars in the middle of the night—he didn't put it on the top of his to-do list.

"I've got a better idea. Why don't we stay right here in Savannah and act like adults?"

"Getting scared in your old age?"

"Shut up DeAngelo, let's watch Eric on the news. I know you can't read, but if you shut up and listen you might learn something."

DeAngelo slid a bowl of peanuts between them and the two veterans settled in for the nightly news.

"This is Eric Brown reporting from CNN Headquarters in Atlanta. Today, in his first address to the United Nations General Assembly, the President announced to world leaders that, 'America does not accept the legitimacy of continued Israeli settlements,' and further called for an end to Israeli 'occupation' of Palestinian lands seized in the 1967 war...."

DeAngelo let out a low whistle, "Damn, talk about throwing Israel under the bus. I guess the President doesn't think we need any allies in the Middle East."

Doc leaned back on his stool. "What in the hell are we doing? By that one statement the President has just reversed fifty years of US foreign policy."

Eric continued, "...political observers suggest this represents a major shift in American policy supporting Israel, our long-time and often only ally in the Middle East. The President met later in the day with the Prime Minister of Israel and the President of the Palestinian Authority to further the peace process..."

DeAngelo, as gruff as he always appeared, understood the tenuous balance of power in the region. "Peace process, my ass. If the President wants peace then the first thing he should do is go and kick Iran's ass and get them to stop funding all the terrorists. Peace process...what a joke!"

"...The Israeli Prime Minister's only comment to the press was that, 'Israel retains the sovereign right to protect our borders and the well being of the citizens of Israel. We will take whatever action is required to protect our nation...'"

Mike had enough of the news and headed for the switch. "Let's turn this crap off. I can't take it anymore."

Doc diverted his attention. "Throw me another beer."

"...the UN's International Atomic Energy Agency (IAEA) announced the operation of a secret Iranian nuclear processing plant..."

Now Doc came with the low whistle, "That's where the real trouble is. If Israel attacks the Iranian nuclear plants then the entire region could go up in smoke; some peace process."

"...Military analysts are not clear if this belligerent warning is a response to the continued acts of terrorism launched from the Gaza Strip or the increasingly apparent nuclear threat from Iran..."

~~

Senator Reynolds immediately understood the possible implications of the speech, and Eric Brown was right on the mark with his questions.

"Senator Reynolds, the President has criticized Israel for developments in the West Bank. Do these decisions reflect a new direction for US foreign policy?"

"Eric, the President's announcements came as a surprise to me. The growing threat from Iran in armaments and the processing of weapons grade uranium is real. Iran has a new intermediate range ballistic missile capability that has been well publicized. Iran can reach into central Europe as well as most of the eastern Mediterranean Sea, to include Israel. I know the President wants to portray America in a new

55

image, but he is playing a dangerous game of international politics that neither he nor anyone in his administration has much experience."

After the interview, the other network commentators scoffed at Reynolds comments. Eric was the only one in the newsroom that feared that Senator Reynolds was right on the mark. After a while it became such a burden that he simply stopped trying to reason with them.

~~

As Eric Brown concluded the evening news, Danni Walton was pacing the floor in her new office. Her message to the employees had been a simple one. "Your future and the future of this resort is your responsibility. For without your best effort we will surely fail. There is no other option except performance at the highest level. Our customers are our most valued assets. We will treat them as if our lives depend on their pleasure—because it does."

Danni hated the phrase "outside the box." It was a cliché that had worn thin with overuse by obtuse people who used it to justify their inability to apply linear logic to problem solving. But that is exactly what Danni was trying to do—think "outside the box." And there in her office, overlooking Calibogue Sound and the Atlantic Ocean, she paced—pausing on occasion to watch the young man on the beach tend to his duties. The same young man she noticed on her first visit to the resort. It was a pleasure to watch him.

Danni knew it was his effort that would save this resort; but his effort alone wouldn't be enough. The best efforts of the entire staff couldn't save the resort. What really troubled Danni was that the staff was better at their jobs than Danni was at her own. Like the boy on the beach—his job was well defined and with proper attention to detail, easily accomplished. The jobs of all the staff were well defined and with proper attention to detail, easily accomplished. And Danni's job was ill-defined and not easily accomplished. Soon the hotel staff, the bank, and her father would want to know what it was that she had accomplished.

Danni looked at the table model of the resort and knew the marina where Mike DeAngelo would launch fishing charters wasn't enough. She looked at the models of the two golf courses and knew the new tournaments wouldn't be enough. She looked at the model of the horse stables and knew the riding lessons wouldn't be enough.

As Danni pondered the fate of the hotel, she noticed the young man on the beach bend over and with the utmost of care and patience he removed something from the sand. She was far too distant to tell what the object was, but whatever it was held the attention of the young man.

Danni saw him walk to the lifeguard tower and gently wrap the object in a towel. He placed it in the box attached to the tower. He couldn't help but go back again and again to look at his treasure. What was the object that held his attention to the degree he couldn't simply leave it in the box until his shift was over?

The allure of the object captured Danni's interest so much that she headed to the elevator that led to the beach. "I need a break," she told herself. She wasn't accomplishing anything confined to the office. This "thinking outside the box" produced about what she had expected—absolutely nothing!

The setting sun was warm on her back as she made her way to the beach. The young man didn't look up from his duties until Danni called to him. "May I ask you a question?"

The young man glanced skyward and then stood straight up when he noticed who it was that had addressed him. "Oh, excuse me. I didn't hear you come up. What can I do for you?"

"I'm Danni Walton." Danni extended her hand to the young man.

The young man stood forward and accepted her greeting. "I know who you are Mrs. Walton. How can I assist you?"

"I know I should know your name, but there have been so many new faces for me to learn."

"How impolite of me," said the young man, "I am Brian Vance, it's very nice to meet you."

"I was watching you from my office. You picked something out of the sand. What was it?"

His face lit up like a Christmas tree. "Mrs. Walton, you should see it! It's the largest one I've ever found. I was just lucky to see it in the sand."

Danni followed the young man to the lifeguard tower and watched as he un-wrapped the towel from around the object. He was so gentle that one could guess it was explosive. The young man could barely contain his excitement. "Take a look at this!"

There on the towel, blackened with age lay the fossilized remains of the biggest tooth she had ever seen.

"Oh my goodness, what in the world is that?"

"This, Mrs. Walton, is the tooth of the largest shark that ever lived. This is the tooth of the megalodon shark."

"Good Lord! That's a tooth from a shark? I don't believe it. The thing is huge!"

The tooth measured at least four inches across and was larger than the palm of Brian's hand.

"Yes ma'am it is. The experts believe the megalodon shark grew to maybe 60' or longer and may have weighed 70 tons.

"And you found that tooth on the beach?"

"Yes ma'am I did. They find a lot of these in mud pumped out of the Savannah River channel."

"When did it go extinct?"

"The first one has been dated back 18 million years, and they went extinct about 1 million years ago during the ice age."

Brian handed the huge tooth to Danni and she marveled at the mass of the thing.

"How do you know so much about this thing?"

"My dad and I dredged one up pulling a shrimp net about 10 years ago. I've been fascinated with 'em ever since. "

If the boy dredged a tooth while shrimping, then his family probably lived nearby. "Do your parents live on the coast?"

"They used to. They died in an auto accident. I was enrolled at the Citadel when it happened. They got caught in a thunderstorm and missed a turn and drove off a bridge."

Danni could have kicked herself for raising such a tragic event. "I'm sorry to hear that. Are you still enrolled?"

"No ma'am, not right now. When my folks passed, I didn't have enough money for school. That's why I'm working here. Another year and I should be able to go back." He grinned before he continued, "That's why we need to make this resort successful again, Mrs. Walton."

As Danni walked back to her office she took note how refreshing the conversation with Brian Vance had been. Thinking outside the box had not produced results, but her little trip outside the office planted the seed, a bold concept, to save Daufuskie Island Resort. She couldn't wait to explain it to her father.

Chapter 11

Special Agent Angelina Sanchez learned an important lesson her first weeks in Atlanta. These special assignments were not all they were made up to be.

She was received professionally enough, and assigned a reasonably sized office, but the initial excitement of the case was soon replaced by the loneliness of not knowing a single person in Atlanta. More than a few police officers introduced themselves, but Angelina had no desire to strike up a relationship. It wasn't that the officers weren't acceptable candidates—some were, but once the investigation was complete she would move back to Washington, and she would never start an affair simply for something to do.

The futility of the assignment was almost overwhelming. The letter specified, "...the police couldn't prove a thing." The dead files were the place to start. It was sobering to review so many rapes. Each was painful. It was difficult to tell if you were moving in the right direction. So many cases and so many dead ends; it was like walking in a forest in the dead of night without a light.

Another thing she learned about rape—nobody escapes unscathed. The scars and wounds run deep and remain painful; they are never erased from memory. Her interviews of the victims and alleged rapists always produced the same results. The victims felt justice had been ill served, and the suspected perpetrators denied involvement or claimed the sex was consensual.

During every interview the smoldering pain and resentment of those terrible events, buried in the deepest recesses of memory, were fanned back to life. Angelina could see fear come back into the eyes of the victims. Some would shake with anger while others would sob with pain or fear—but always, there was a reaction. So much pain for so little gain; Angelina didn't find a trail of killings or murders associated with any of the rapes.

When she reported as much to William Jefferson—along with a request to be transferred back to Washington—she was told in no uncertain terms to, "…do your job the way you have been trained, quit whining and get back to work!"

There was no relief from Washington so Angelina, in spite of her conviction that she was on a wild goose chase, dug back into the stack.

How many had she already reviewed; close to 50? So many that she lost count. The file she opened late on Friday was like all the others. The names didn't mean a thing. It was a gang rape in Atlanta. Walton, Hanna Elizabeth…age 15…daughter of Reverend Peter Walton and Danni Helton Walton.

The executive summary was written in the concise language of the police department. The case was closed with the approval of the District Attorney and the Chief of Police: Insufficient evidence to continue the investigation.

There was a list of suspects, of course, by name. Transcripts of each interview attached. One possible witness and the transcript of her interview attached. The statements from the victim and parents were attached. The investigating officer noted the victim was unable to identify any of the suspects. No DNA samples available, officer's note: destroyed by family doctor prior to investigation. That was unusual. Why would a doctor destroy critical evidence? The question, if it was even considered, wasn't enough to keep the investigation open. The DA's statement was clear, they had insufficient evidence to continue— and the case was closed.

It wasn't the first time a rape was thrown in the dead file because the victim couldn't identify the assailant. Victims either too frightened, or in this case maybe too stoned to remember what happened.

The facts of the case were not uncommon. Young white girl in a bad part of town, trying to fit the gangster lifestyle kids tried to copy, and things went bad…really bad. The toxicology reports had the victim full of THC, the drug found in marijuana, among others. The girl was lucky to survive the mixture of drugs. Looking at the pictures, Angelina hoped the drugs helped spare the girl the pain of the savage beating. The pictures were difficult to look at, but there was no trail of dead bodies. It was simply another dead end.

Angelina leaned back in her chair and stretched. She looked up at the clock. Almost 6 p.m. and her body ached from inactivity. She would have to start working out or she would put on 50 pounds before Jefferson would see the futility of this investigation, and let her get back to some real field work.

She closed the file and tidied up her desk. She didn't look forward to another meal at Burger King and gave a quick thought to changing the monotonous routine and going to the Golden Corral steak house. They had a decent salad bar and she could top off the tough steak with some soft serve ice cream. She would start her workout program on Monday.

She had her hand on the light switch when she paused. There was something in that file that wasn't right. She knew it would eat at her all weekend if she didn't take one more look.

What was it that bothered Angelina? There, on the list of suspects, the name, Thomas, Bomani. It was an unusual name, and she had seen it before. It took a moment to boot up her computer. It was the least she could do, to check out the name; a Google search shouldn't take but a few moments.

The name, Bomani Thomas, listed almost a thousand articles and computer hits in the hundreds of thousands. If she added up all the hits, they would surely near three to four million. What she read amazed her. Bomani Thomas arrested for rape, not Hanna Walton's rape, but another. During the trial he escaped confinement; beat the female escort officer close to death. With the officer's sidearm he murdered, in cold blood, the judge and three others. The articles painted the picture of a city in panic as the police searched for Thomas. Eventually captured, Thomas pled guilty in return for a life sentence without the possibility of parole. Bomani Thomas was later killed in a prison fight; too bad for him. But there was no mention or association in the articles concerning the rape of Hanna Walton.

Thomas may have been a rapist and murderer, but Angelina couldn't link his death to any action by the police. Tough luck for Thomas, killed by another convict; he wasn't such a bad man when he wasn't raping and beating up young girls or shooting unarmed victims. Justice had been served in a perverted sort of way.

She found the Google search on Bomani Thomas interesting; maybe she could find something on the others. She ran the names of the other suspects. Only one generated any articles; a Jerome Edward Green. The article was a short one. Green, high on cocaine, plowed into a group of grade school children, killing six. He was on death row in Alabama awaiting execution.

Angelina Googled the witness; nothing came up…she Googled Hanna Walton…nothing; Googled her mother, Danni Walton…nothing. When she Googled the father, Peter Walton, she let out a muffled whistle. The headline of the first article was a story in itself, The Reverend Peter Walton found dead in the Chattahoochee River. There were articles about his heroic attempt to find the men who raped his daughter, and the injustice of his tragic death. There were articles about his funeral and how he was loved by all in the church, and how God would punish the men who killed him, even if the police couldn't find his killers.

It was enough to get Angelina back into the antiquated police computer. The three suspects that failed to turn up any information on Google, were listed in the police computer data base; all three dead. She typed in the name of the witness…dead. It didn't take a genius to see that all the suspects and the witness, and the Reverend Peter Walton were killed within a week of each other.

Five, no six, if you counted Peter Walton, deaths within a week's span, and no further investigation? The fact that the female witness was found dead in the Chattahoochee River with Reverend Walton began to border on the absurd. The fact that one of the suspects was killed in the house of the Reverend and Mrs. Danni Walton was downright incredible. All this and the police couldn't build a case for prosecution in any of the deaths?

Was this the smoking gun for which Angelina had been sent to Atlanta? Four of the five suspects, all black males, die violent deaths and not a single investigation into the circumstances concerning the same? Were these deaths vigilante justice and completely ignored by the police? Angelina Sanchez grinned when she realized she had free reign to find out. Finally, she had direction. Maybe something would come from this special investigation after all, and she had never been to Alabama. Now was as good a time as any to go.

It was well past midnight when Angelina turned off the light in her office. She would get a burger on her way home. Monday morning couldn't come quickly enough.

~~

Angelina didn't like using the long winded introduction, but would resort to it if she wanted to establish her position of authority.

"Warden Farber, I am Special Agent Angelina Sanchez, detailed to the United States Department of Justice, conducting an investigation ordered by the Attorney General at the direction of the President."

The obvious pause at the other end of the phone made an excellent point establishing Warden Farber's own position of authority.

"Is that right? Good for you. What are you people from Washington investigating, how many illegal aliens we have locked up?" Warden Franklin Farber ran the Holman Correctional Institution in Atmore, Alabama, a town of about 8,000 just north of the Florida panhandle. The Holman facility held more than nine-hundred total inmates and held the two-hundred or so inmates on Alabama's death row.

"Warden Farber, I am on assignment to investigate a complaint the Justice Department received concerning a rape case."

Angelina used the rape case as a way to cover the real purpose of the investigation—to determine if the police in Atlanta were on a vigilante killing spree. Investigating a rape would be more palatable to law enforcement officials than investigating their own. "One of the suspects listed in the case was Jerome Edward Green, also known as 'Crack Daddy,' one of your inmates."

Investigating an old rape didn't make any sense to Warden Farber, but it was just like the Feds to waste money doing just such investigations. "Why waste time? Crack Daddy is on death row. You won't get anything out of him."

"These investigations are directed by the Attorney General. I hope you understand to do a complete investigation, I need to interview your inmate. Crack Daddy was listed as a suspect. I would like your cooperation."

State penitentiaries have always been considered the private fiefdom of the governor, and their hand-picked jailors; and no matter how you sugarcoat the visit of a federal official—you just weren't welcome. So it was with Warden Franklin Farber; he didn't want Angelina Sanchez or any official from the Justice Department snooping around his prison.

Farber could tolerate the FBI agents or the U.S. Marshals because they were law enforcement officers and often turned a blind eye toward the harsh realities of prison life—but officials from the Justice Department—you just never knew what in the hell they were looking for. The story Angelina relayed to the warden, simply didn't ring true; she had to be looking for something else. "I don't suppose you have any warrants, charges, subpoenas—you know—legal stuff that will require counsel to be present, do you? I'm sick and tired of paying for legal counsel for convicts when you Feds come down here on your wild goose chases."

"I can get my boss to send you an official request, if you feel that is necessary. But, as far as I know, we do not intend to file any charges in the State of Alabama. Your prisoner is my only lead and I want to close this assignment."

"Miss Sanchez, I'm sure you know, Crack Daddy's on death row. He was high on drugs and ran into a bunch of kids getting off a school bus; killed six of them, and crippled two more. The governor isn't going to cut any deal for you. Crack is headed for the table, and he knows it. I seriously doubt anybody would waste the time and money to bring an old rape case back to trial. Sounds like a waste of time and money. Besides, Crack Daddy is dying of AIDS and will be dead long before you could file any charges. The doctors give him only a few more weeks to live."

"Even so, I would like to have a chance to talk with him. Like I said, Crack Daddy is the only lead I have." Angelina knew she was getting nowhere with Warden Faber and decided to play her last trump card. "I am required to make written reports to Director Jefferson on these investigations. I know he would really appreciate your cooperation."

Not that the name startled or intimidated Faber, for he had worked with Jefferson on an international child porn ring years ago. Jefferson had proven to be a diligent and persistent investigator, a lawman's lawman, and he had earned Faber's respect. "You work for William Jefferson?"

"Yes sir, I do. I know he would appreciate your help in this matter."

"Jefferson is a cantankerous old son-of-a-bitch, isn't he?"

Angelina agreed with this assessment, but found no reason to criticize her boss in this backhanded manner. "Mr. Jefferson is very professional in every respect. Should I include your personal assessment of the Director in my report?"

Farber gave a hearty laugh at the challenge in Angelina's voice. "No, Miss Sanchez, but you can tell him hello from me. You are a feisty one. Most people wanting my help wouldn't be so quick to threaten me; good for you. Shows you may have more guts than brains. I'll set it up so you can have an hour with Crack Daddy on Wednesday morning—say 10 a.m. Will that work for you?"

"That will be fine Warden Farber. Thank you for your help. I will pass your greeting to the director and note your cooperation in my report."

"I still think you are wasting your time. Be at the visitor's entrance at 9 a.m. It will take about an hour to process you through. No weapons inside the fence for any visitors. If you want a guard to monitor your visit I can arrange that.

"No thank you warden, I may have better luck getting him to talk if there are no guards around."

~~

The warden's instructions to the guards were simple: allow access to the prisoner she requested and nothing else.

"Lady, Crack Daddy is dying, but don't forget he is still a murderer and has nothing to lose. So be on your toes. The panic button is by the door. All you have to do is hit it and we can be inside within 30 seconds, but a lot can happen in that time. Are you sure you want to be in there by yourself?"

Angelina did appreciate the warning. "Thanks for the warning and your concern, but I want to talk with him alone."

"Suit yourself. It's your ass. I will check to make sure he is strapped to the gurney before I leave the room. Remember he has AIDS, so stay far enough away from him where he can't spit on you or anything like that."

Angelina knew those type acts of violence were not uncommon for condemned men. "I will remember."

Before the guard unlocked the cell he donned a plastic face shield and verified through the window imbedded into the door that the patient was in the bed. He opened the cell door just enough to announce, "Crack Daddy, you have a visitor."

After verifying Crack Daddy didn't pose a threat, the guard entered the room. "This lady came all the way from Washington, D.C. to see you. The warden wants you to be nice to her. I'm going to strap you in."

Through the window Angelina couldn't see Crack Daddy's face, but did see the guard give a tug on three straps tying the patient snuggly to the bed. The guard then manacled arm chains to the guard rails of the bed before pulling a chair from the wall and placing it about five feet from the bed. Angelina felt a twinge of guilt that Crack Daddy was so rudely strapped to the bed just for her visit. He was in a terrible emaciated state and looked closer to a skeleton than the body of a human being; he looked incapable of lifting his arms much less inflicting any physical harm to anyone.

Crack Daddy didn't even open his eyes when Angelina entered the room, and surely he heard the cold clash of steel on steel of the cell door closing, and the sound of the key seating the deadbolt lock in the door. Angelina knew that sound—to a man on death row—must sound like the doors of hell closing on a soul lost to eternal damnation.

Angelina thought the manacles securing Crack Daddy to the bed rails were a little excessive. His black skin actually looked a shade of charcoal gray against the clean white sheets. The head of the bed was slightly elevated so he was sitting partially upright. His face was covered with a full clear plastic shield and he fogged the shield with each breath. He was so still Angelina believed he may be asleep, and if his breath wasn't visible on the shield, she could have mistaken him for the cadaver he was soon to be.

Once in the room Angelina felt alone and abandoned; why had she insisted on this interview? Here she was in the same room with a killer, a rapist, a man infected with the HIV virus; maybe refusing the company of a jailer wasn't such a good idea. The bed was in the middle of the room far from any wall or table. It was obviously a medical treatment room but there were no medical supplies, no medical equipment, nothing an inmate could use to attack a guard or medical personnel—only a stainless steel table pushed against the side wall and a small table with a pitcher of water and a glass. Angelina assumed the water was provided for her comfort and not intended to be used for the comfort of Crack Daddy. The entire room was glaring white and the only way out was the door to her rear and the drain in the floor. Then Angelina had a chilling thought. This is the room where they bring the bodies after execution!

Well, all the spooky feelings wouldn't get over any quicker unless she started asking questions. "Mr. Jerome Green, I am an investigator with the United States Department of Justice. Somebody wrote the President a letter that the police in Atlanta were killing suspects in a rape case. Did you write that letter?" It was a simple way to start the interview.

Angelina waited for some response, some acknowledgement from Crack Daddy, but he didn't move a muscle—he didn't even open his eyes. "You were one of five suspects listed in the rape of Hanna

Elizabeth Walton, a fifteen-year-old white girl. Do you remember this case?"

Angelina began to believe the warden was correct in his assumption that this condemned man wouldn't cooperate with any investigation. She debated if she should entice him with an offer of immunity for his involvement in the rape if he would cooperate, but she didn't have that authority, and her integrity wouldn't allow her to lie about such a thing.

"Mr. Green, you are dying of AIDS, on death row in the state of Alabama. Do you think you could get in any more trouble by helping me? I am sure you know all the other suspects listed in this case are dead. Helping me certainly won't hurt them."

Even that logic didn't sway him to respond. Angelina felt more pity than frustration with Crack Daddy. His emaciated body reeked of death and the manacles on his arms looked terribly uncomfortable. Angelina asked, "Do they keep you shackled to the bed like that all the time?"

Crack Daddy slowly turned his head to Angelina and opened his eyes. The chain link of the shackles clicked against the steel of the bed rails as he raised his arms. "No, these are special attire for visitors. I did get a clean set of sheets though."

"I'm sorry. I didn't mean to cause you any more trouble. Maybe this was a bad idea. I would like your help with this case. The only thing I can offer you is a little redemption for your soul. But I can't make you answer questions. I am simply asking you to talk to me about this case."

Crack Daddy turned his head away from Angelina, dropped his arms back to the bed and closed his eyes. The warden had been right. Convicts don't help the law unless they get something in return, and Angelina had nothing to offer. She was almost to the door when Crack Daddy said, "Lady, I could use a drink of water."

When Angelina turned back, Crack Daddy was staring directly at her through the plastic face mask. Angelina remembered the warning of the guard. Angelina didn't hesitate, but filled the glass with water and walked to the side of the bed. She had to lift the face shield to place the glass to his lips. Crack Daddy savored each drop as she poured the water into his mouth. When she withdrew the half empty glass Crack Daddy simply said, "More," and he drained the remaining liquid. When finished with the water Crack Daddy breathed a contented sigh and licked his cracking lips. All he said was "Thank you." Angelina replaced the mask and turned to go, but he stopped her with, "Take this mask off me and I will tell you what you want to know."

Angelina remembered the warning. For some reason, she did not feel threatened and against all advice she removed the mask and returned to the chair. Crack Daddy started his story.

"We did it. Five of us did it. Young white bitch all fucked up on weed. Bomani Thomas slipped her some stuff in a drink and then started ripping her clothes off. We each did her a couple of times, roughed her up pretty good too, and then left her in the house.

"The police investigated about a week later. Picked up a bunch of the boys who worked the streets off Industrial Blvd., but you could tell the police didn't have no idea who did it. They just tried to muscle confessions out of everybody. The police harassed everybody for about six months and then they just quit looking. So nothing ever happened."

"Didn't anybody see the rape? I mean, it happened in the early afternoon. You would think they could have found someone who knew what happened."

"The girl came with some friends who was upstairs fucking. You could hear them through the ceiling. We was gone before they came downstairs. They didn't see nothing. One of the brothers said he had seen a hooker named Jasmine in the back room. She was doing a white man. Bomani scared him off and they didn't see nothing. They might of heard something, but they didn't see nothing. Thomas looked up the hooker and put a knife to her throat and threatened to kill her if she ever said anything."

"Is the brother you are referring to named Bomani Thomas?"

"Yeah, he was the one who did her first."

"Did the police take any fluid samples from you or any of the other people they rounded up?"

"A black man ain't gonna let no cop take stuff like that. Besides, I heard one of the cops say they didn't have no DNA evidence because the doctor who treated the girl destroyed all the stuff. Too bad for them, I guess."

"Did anybody try to find the white man? He was the only other material witness."

"We all knew who the white man was. Bomani said he was a regular with the hookers. I didn't see him, you know, but Bomani said it was the Preacher in the house with Jasmine when we was banging the girl."

"Why didn't somebody report that to the police?"

"Why would anybody do that? The white man ran like a chicken to get away. Why would a brother report that to the police? So they could solve the crime and then we all go to jail?

Angelina realized the stupidity of her question. "Good point. It was a stupid question. You said the white man was named Preacher. How did you know his name?"

"I didn't know that was his name, that's just what the girls called him. We all seen him on the television. He was one of them preachers on TV, but nobody knew his real name."

Angelina mentally reviewed what Crack Daddy told her with what was in the report. Everything matched. The victim was transported to the house by her high school friends. They were smoking pot before the couple went upstairs, leaving Hanna alone downstairs. The hooker Jasmine was also in the report. The police effort to develop a list of suspects was pretty standard. Angelina knew from the reports that the DNA evidence, so heavily relied upon by the police to solve the crimes of rape, had been destroyed by the family doctor. The only new information was the man with the hooker was white, and they called him the Preacher.

"Mr. Green, do you realize all the other suspects listed in this case are dead? All died violent and unexplained deaths?"

"Shit, lady. Why do you think I left Atlanta and came to Alabama? I was in county lock-up for possession when all the killing started, that's probably why they didn't get me. I heard one of the boys was killed right outside the house where we banged the girl when there was people inside, and nobody heard a thing; somebody broke his neck. There was a lot of killing going on. Word got around that they was killing all the brothers. I think it was the police so when I got out of jail I left town as fast as I could. I ain't never been back."

"You know Thomas was killed while in prison by a man named John Brown Jackson? Do you know anything about him?"

"I heard the name after it hit the news. No big deal. Prisoners kill each other all the time. I was more worried about them boys that was killed who wasn't in prison. That's the ones the police probably killed."

"Another was found with a bullet in the head in a car in the Okefenokee Swamp. Know anything about that?"

69

"I don't know exactly who did it if that's what you mean. I think it was the cops, but them boys in the car was working for Tyrell Biggs. He was the biggest drug dealer in Atlanta. Maybe they stiffed him, and Biggs killed them. I don't know for sure; I think the cops did it."

"You said, 'boys,' was there more than one victim in the swamp?"

"There was four people killed in the swamp. They all worked for Biggs. I don't know how many others were killed exactly, but there was more."

"Mr. Green, one of the men in the rape was killed in the girl's house. Do you know anything about that?"

"No, I heard about it, but I don't know anything about that. There is one man who might know. He was Tyrell Biggs driver. His name is "Frenchy" Guidry and he lives somewhere in Louisiana."

Angelina stood to leave. Finding Crack Daddy had been easy. Finding a man named Guidry in Louisiana may prove more difficult, but at least she had a name to follow.

Chapter 12

Ken Carson knew the decline in the loan volume at Coastal Bank was not his fault. The economy was killing everyone and everything. He knew managers at other banks. They were complaining of the same thing. The lack of loan traffic was affecting them directly in their paychecks.

Ken's monetary expectations with his promotion were far greater than what a bad economy provided; and there were no indictors pointing to anything but the same. But Ken Carson was smart enough to work around the inconvenient constraints of a bad economy; and it didn't take him long to find another stream of income.

Ken leaned back in his leather chair and liked what he saw on the spread sheets arrayed on his desk. What he saw was growing balances in various bank accounts and stock portfolios. It had been a long trip, but his diligent efforts were beginning to pay handsomely.

The growing balances were not simply the result of good luck; luck had nothing to do with it. Only the most precise accounting, planning, coordination and discipline made the growing balances possible. It was tedious and detailed work that required a sharp mind and complete focus. There was no room for mistakes—and Ken made no mistakes.

Ken didn't think of it as fraud—he thought of it as effective management—effective leveraging—of money. He had made close to $100,000 for the bank and close to $6,000,000 for himself.

His first fraudulent loan was nothing more than an experiment. He just wanted to find out if he could do it. He had to admit the thrill of it—the excitement of the deed was more electrifying and satisfying than any sex. The rush lasted much longer.

It was a simple thing. Review the county tax records for under-valued homes; usually in the older and more established areas of Savannah. The perfect profile would be elderly citizens with well-established credit. Check the bank records for a name match and get the social security number and then it was a simple matter of filling out the home improvement loan. Deposit the money into a bank in one of the small towns on the outskirts of Savannah. Set up an automatic electronic payment schedule with deposits on the loan. Take 80 percent of the loan and play the market. Don't dally—take your profits and get out. Pay off the loan and no one was the wiser; older folks never check their credit records, and the early payoff would only help their credit score.

Ken started slowly, only the one loan until he was convinced he was well below the suspicion threshold. The first loan was followed by many more, and Ken Carson had accounts in banks from the Florida state line to North Carolina and as far west as Birmingham. His nifty little experiment proved very profitable. Ken convinced himself the bank received their fair interest payments. This was the reward of management. His fraudulent loans had passed various forms of review, both internally and by bank examiners. To top it all off, Ken was commended by the Board of Directors for a loan department that was still profitable in spite of a souring economy.

He was very conservative with his profits. No extravagant spending, no new car for him, his Lincoln Town Car served his purpose and helped maintain a low profile. Not a lot of new clothes and nothing excessive or showing off to his fellow employees.

His only weakness was his wife, Rachael. She accepted the new diamond rings and diamond necklaces and matching stud earrings without question. She didn't question the cash Ken dropped in the casinos in the Bahamas—the first class accommodation seemed suited to her sense of entitlement; first class was where she was born to live. The new Mercedes, a surprise from Ken, fit her new life style. Rachael began to believe her decision to marry Ken was going to finally pay off.

Ken knew when he took Rachael to the new beach house on Tybee Island, he would be amply rewarded. He could barely contain himself. He wanted to call her, but he wouldn't because he wanted it to be a surprise.

He would ask her to take a ride that afternoon—if Karen came along it would even be sweeter. He would casually drive into the gated beach front community overlooking the Atlantic and then in the most nonchalant manner, he would ask her if she liked the house. Then he would watch her reaction. It was hard to contain his anticipation.

Ken's gifts to his wife kept her spirits high and even Karen began to show flashes of jealously—and to Rachael that was an added bonus. Now, when Rachael and Karen went shopping, they traveled in style in the new Mercedes.

But as women can do, Karen always found a way to throw a damper on Rachael's newfound opulence. On their most recent shopping trip, Karen raised the question about the extravagant gifts.

"Ken seems to be doing really well."

"What do you mean?" Rachael feigned innocence, but she knew exactly what her sister meant.

"You know...diamonds everywhere, new car, new clothes; Ken's job must pay a ton. Lucky you."

Karen directed her attention to the fine leather stitching of the console and enjoyed the new car aroma. Her hand traced the stitching to the disappearing radio built into the polished wood grain of the dash before she turned to her sister for the answer. "Well?"

Rachael wanted to tell her sister it was none of her business. For the first time in their adult lives Rachael was reaping rewards far greater than any of Karen's boyfriends could bestow upon her. Rachael knew her sister was consumed with jealously. Why she always felt on the defensive when Karen talked to her in that tone of voice, she didn't understand.

"Ken said he has some investments that have really done well. I don't ask for any details. Making the money is his job, mine is to spend it."

Rachael giggled when she answered, hoping the false levity would direct her sister's attention elsewhere. It didn't.

"Let me ask you a question, dear sister. Why, when you and Ken go to parties, do you always drive his old Lincoln? I've noticed you never wear any of your new jewelry when you do anything with people at the bank. Why is that?"

Rachael had asked Ken the same question. "He says bankers are very conservative and he wants us to fit in. He just doesn't want us to show off."

"Yeah, right, I'd watch my ass if I were you, dear sister."

Karen committed herself to solving the riddle of Ken's new wealth. She was just the girl to do it.

~~

Danni couldn't believe she was actually nervous. On the other side of the double doors sat the Board of Directors of Coastal Bank;

assembled today to hear her plan for the salvation of the Daufuskie Resort.

Sixty days ago it was nothing more than a challenge to find a way to save the grand old lady, but now it had grown into love, almost an obsession with Danni. The money her father raised was only enough to keep the hotel running; she would need more to make the hotel a success. The single major factor in her favor was that the bank would suffer significant loss if the resort failed. The single major factor against her was that putting major money into a failing resort in these tough economic times was akin to pouring money into the Savannah River and watching it float out to the Atlantic.

When Danni entered the board room she could sense an underlying level of tension.

"My purpose here today is twofold. First, I will review the current state of the Daufuskie Island Resort, and will propose a plan to restore the resort to profitability.

"Since the resort went into receivership, held by the Coastal Bank, we have yet to have a profitable month of operation. You have all seen the profit and loss statements. We are still losing money, but at a decreasing rate. Last month we posted a loss of a little over $175,000. Our best projections are that we will break even in the month of December with an increase in holiday vacationers, but will fall back into the red in the months of January through March. We expect a profitable month in April with the golf classic on Hilton Head Island.

"The reality of the situation is that Daufuskie Island Resort, in its current form, can't compete against the family venues in Florida. Unless we change the concept we might as well close the doors today."

Danni's comment raised a buzz around the table, and raised her father's eyebrows more than a little. This wasn't what he expected from his daughter. He couldn't believe that he had misjudged her to this extent.

Danni continued her briefing. "But, this box holds the secret to Daufuskie's revival." Danni slid a white cardboard box down the length of the table to just in front of her father. Ed Helton and the eyes of every member of the board focused on the box. Inside, packed neatly in cotton cloth was the fossilized tooth of the megalodon shark.

Danni's father was the first to respond. "Holy smokes! What the hell is this?" He was joined in his amazement by every other member of the board. They had forgotten the purpose of the briefing and were interested in passing around the huge tooth. After the tooth had made one and a half laps around the board table, Ed Helton redirected everyone's attention back on Danni. "Danni, what is that thing?"

Danni paused to ensure she had everyone's attention. "That is the tooth of the megalodon shark, the largest shark to ever swim the seven seas; an older brother to the great white shark. The megalodon ruled the oceans for almost 20 million years and went extinct just under a million years ago."

Ed turned the huge tooth over in his hand and placed it on the table to his front. "What does that have to do with the Daufuskie Resort?" The eyes in the room went from Ed Helton to Danni.

"That tooth was found in the sand on the Daufuskie Island Resort. They are quite commonly found when dredging the Savannah River."

Ed grinned at his daughter before he asked his next question. "And how does this relate to your plan for the Daufuskie Resort?"

Danni was ready for the question. "Our marketing research shows that about 70 percent of America has been to either Disney Land or Disney World and most say they will visit again. The kids love it. The parents tolerate it.

"What the parents in our demographic profile really want is a more substantial vacation that will enlighten their children with more than Mickey, Minnie and Pluto. I intend to make Daufuskie Island Resort a five-star educational destination for the arts, sciences and sports that will have no rival in the United States. We will effectively balance entertainment, leisure, and education for a vacation experience unmatched anywhere. This unique approach is our only chance for not only survival, but profitability. A detailed plan is contained in the packets to your front. I am prepared to discuss any of your questions in detail."

The board poured over the plans. They were brief and to the point. Danni allowed time between each section for questions. The briefing lasted more than two hours and in the end she was dismissed by her father for the private deliberations of the board. He escorted her to the door and whispered in her ear, "Great job," and then kissed her on the cheek. She was exhausted but received the funding for the resort.

~~

It was past 8 p.m. when Bill arrived at Andrews Air Force Base. The Officer's Club was doing a moderate amount of business and Bill entered without a second glance from anyone. There, in the far corner sat Senator Reynolds and Major General Lucas McLaughlin.

It wasn't unusual for politicians and senior military officers to meet at the bar; it was the unofficial meeting ground of the political and military leadership of the country. Bill wanted to get straight to the pictures. He opened the envelope and spread them on the table in a manner only the men sitting at the table could view the images.

"Prince Al-Sabah sent me these photos the day before yesterday." Bill thumbed through the photos. "This one is of Port Said in Egypt. This one is of a village on the Mediterranean about 50 miles south of the Gaza Strip. This one is of south Lebanon. This one is of Port Tartus in Syria, and this one is of the desert in Syria on a direct line from Tartus to Kuwait City."

Senator Reynolds and Lucas McLaughlin traded the photos. Reynolds asked, "What do you want me to do with these?"

"You're on the Intelligence Oversight Committee. Get them into the system. These photos mean something; we have to find out what it is."

Senator Reynolds turned the photos face down on the table. "I can't do that. The President has issued an executive order that only he can approve intelligence operations against any Arab state. These would fall in that category. If I put these into the system, then they will be killed."

Bill scowled. Who was running the ship?

Lucas joined the conversation. "I may know someone who may be able to help." Lucas collected the photos. "It may take a day or so. You want to hang around?"

"No, I want to get back home. Let me know if you come up with anything."

Chapter 13

Major General Lucas McLaughlin walked into the office of the Deputy Director of Strategic Reconnaissance at the Defense Intelligence Agency for an unofficial office call.

Miss Terri Toth was a square woman, not what you would call a raving beauty, but a wonderful person. She was smart as a whip and always full of laughter and life and Lucas had known her for more than 20 years. They first met when Terri was a CIA field agent and Lucas was only a lieutenant on Bill Cannon's strike team busting drugs in Panama.

Terri always worked diligently collecting electronic evidence on the Noriega drug operations and proved to be reliable with her analysis, and never squeamish to put the finger on those who she considered "dirty." She never married, not that she was against the institution, but her dedication to the job didn't leave much time for romance. She spoke five languages, six if you counted English, and lived more in the office than in her small condo on the outskirts of Washington. Lucas respected and trusted her as much as he trusted any person.

Terri looked over the photos. "What do you want me to do with these?"

"I got them from Bill Cannon. He got them from Prince Al-Sabah of Kuwait. Bill thinks they mean something. Can you run an analysis on them? Senator Reynolds has seen them, although I didn't tell him I was bringing them to you. Reynolds said they would be killed if we put them into regular channels."

Terri Toth put the photos back into the envelope. "I'll see what I can do. I can't promise you anything."

~~

Terri didn't open the envelope until she cleared her inbox. She called her assistant and told her to hold her calls except from Directors and above, and no visitors. After typing up a short memo of her meeting with Lucas, she spread the five photos across her desk and decided to start at the beginning, at Port Said.

The photo contained an automatic time stamp burned in the photo. Five ships in the harbor, "Let's see if we can confirm that." Terri turned to one of the three computers arrayed to the rear of her desk and typed in her access code. After a few moments the screen came to life. In the flashing box she typed in her request: Satellite Image – Port Said, Egypt...and the time stamped on the image. The computer took only a few seconds and the identical image as in Bill's photo appeared on the screen; five freighters, same as in Bill's photo. "Enlarge X-10".

Even with the magnification, Terri couldn't make out the names of the vessels or type cargo, so she turned to the second computer to type her request: Harbor Master Logs, Port Said, Egypt. Again, only a short delay and the detailed list of the five vessels appeared on the screen. All the statistics you could ever want about each vessel was available with the simple click of her mouse. Name of the vessel, skipper, length, beam, tonnage, registry, port departed from, arrival at Port Said, cargo offloaded, cargo loaded, departure, destination, names of the crew, insurance company—everything. Nothing appeared unusual with any of the ships or their cargo.

It was easy enough to verify the route of the vessels. "Satellite image – seaborne vessel, and she typed in the names of the five vessels and backed up two weeks from the date on the photo, and requested four hour intervals.

The request took a little longer, but before long the image of the world with little red dots—four hours apart—marked the vessels route and progress until they arrived at Port Said. The first vessel departed Bayonne New Jersey, with a load of humanitarian wheat, and was bound for Somalia. The second vessel was from Kobe, Japan, and had just completed the northward passage of the Suez. It was bound for England; nothing unusual there. The third vessel was Russian and departed the Black Sea port Tuapse with engine parts for Egyptian tractor manufacturers and would continue to Morocco—nothing unusual there. The fourth vessel left the Iranian port of Bandar Abbas with a load of pipe for the Egyptian natural gas industry, and bound for the Egyptian port of Alexandria—nothing unusual there. Finally the fifth vessel and the smallest of the lot departed the Syrian port of Tartus, dropped a shipment of fertilizer, and should have returned to Tartus—nothing particularly unusual there—except Terri didn't think Syria produced fertilizer. How and why would they be exporting something they didn't produce?

Terri called up a classified report on Syrian manufacturing—no fertilizer production in Syria. Terri drew a little red flag next to the

Syrian vessel. Five vessels and only one with any activity that may warrant further study. Not much for three hours work. She moved on to the small town on the Mediterranean, Ezbet Abu Sagal.

There was absolutely nothing going on in the town of Ezbet Abu Sagal. No unusual port activity. No unusual vehicle traffic. No assembly of vehicles or people, and at first glance it was a quiet seaside town. It would have never caught her eye, except everything else looked so peaceful, and she had not yet tired of the wild goose chase. She decided to track the route of the single small freighter—maybe even a fishing trawler—a few miles off the coast, heading directly for the small port. She typed in: Satellite image – seaborne vessel unknown two miles off Ezbet Abu Sagal, Egypt.

After a delay of five minutes the red dots appeared on the screen. "Well, that's interesting." The vessel was making round trips from the Port of Tartus, Syria to Ezbet Abu Sagal. The vessel had made three such trips during the month preceding the date of the photograph. It was interesting but not damning from an intelligence point. But Terri had learned the art of intelligence is to put the pieces of the puzzle together— and Prince Ahmad had given them a roadmap to the picture. It was her job to find the pieces and put them together.

"All right," she said to herself, "let's take a look at who is visiting Ezbet Abu Sagal." And she typed in nine sets of coordinates covering the only roads leading into and from the port town. The images were four hours apart and it was tedious work trying to put any semblance of order to the vehicle traffic. She had near run out of patience when it hit her. The three truck convoy arriving from the west played in her mind. Three trucks, not 20 yards apart leaving Port Said were still 20 yards apart when they were 100 miles out of the port, and still together 100 miles outside of Ezbet Abu Sagal. Her intuition told her she had seen these trucks somewhere else. Back to Port Said: Enlarge X 100, were the instructions. There on the pier—three trucks— if they weren't the same trucks bound for Ezbet Abu Sagal she would kiss a pig.

She wouldn't bet her life they were the same trucks, but the coincidence was outside the normal probabilities that three trucks from Port Said would be heading to the small town of Ezbet Abu Sagal at the same time, at the same speed. If Terri's math was correct, at a rate of about 60 miles per hour and the distance to cover from the last image was about another 100 miles. That will put the convoy in Ezbet Abu Sagal at about 8 p.m. local time." Terri challenged the computer: Image - Ezbet Abu Sagal at 8 p.m. the date of the photos.

Terri played the one hour loop three times. All three trucks unloaded cargo at the same warehouse in the port area; all three trucks departed south on highway 22. Red flag number 2.

It was now 11 p.m. and she wasn't going to spend another night in the office. With the computers locked down and the photos in her private safe, she headed home.

~~

A good night's sleep provided a refreshing break from the monotonous study of information that may or may not be intelligence.

The study of the truck cargo raised suspicion but not hard facts. The Iranian pipe looked pretty much like pipe, but it was covered the entire time the satellite was overhead. But, Egypt had plenty of pipe used for oil transport, and why would Azbet Abu Sagal need pipe from Iran? Egypt had enough pipe to build a bridge from Cairo to Rome. Terri assigned a small red flag to the Iranian pipe connection.

The Russian engine cases looked like engine cases, although much more sophisticated than a regular engine case. The containers looked like something the U.S. would use for electronics or hazardous or sensitive material. The harbor master log at the Russian port listed the cases as engines, but Terri couldn't track their origination past their arrival at the port. If it doesn't fit perfectly, then it raises concern in the doubting mind of an experienced intelligence officer; another little red flag.

She moved to the picture of the house in South Lebanon. It was larger than most and sat atop a commanding hill with residential districts all around it. To the north of the house was the Latani River. Terri couldn't see anything unusual about the house. Maybe the walls were a little thicker than most, and the courtyard larger, but nothing that would set it apart. She knew she could get a signal signature, via satellite if necessary, but the lack of activity made it hard to justify the reprogramming of the satellite.

The port of Tartus in Syria didn't show much promise either. Terri could track the arrival and departure of the vessel identified yesterday, but could put no rhyme or reason to anything else in the port or in the area depicted in Lebanon. Vehicles changed with each delivery, no special security precautions, nothing to raise any doubt. She couldn't believe she had already hit the wall in her investigation. The only thing left to look at was the spot in the empty Syrian Desert in the last photo. She decided to come in on Saturday to complete the task.

Talk about boring. You can only look at sand and rock for so long before you start seeing mirages. The frustration of wasting a Saturday to look at the same rocks and sand was beginning to fatigue Terri. "Lucas McLaughlin is going to hear about this!" she muttered. Terri decided to run a month long loop of images of five minute intervals with half-second flashes. Maybe something would catch her eye. She programmed the request to start 30 days before the date in Bill Cannon's photos.

The national intelligence computer network struggled to compose the images, and for the hour before the request was complied Terri processed the inbox she had neglected yesterday chasing Bill Cannon's ghosts.

The computer finally signaled it was ready to run the requested images. Terri channeled the images to the large high definition screen mounted on the office wall. After five minutes of watching brown sand turn into black night, Terri returned to her inbox with only a cursory look at the screen.

In the corner of her eye, from the black of the desert night, Terri saw the flash. A few clicks on the keyboard replayed the images. No doubt about it. That was a flash of light. Nothing more than a pin-prick, but it was a flash of light! "Enlarge X 100." Terri gazed intently at the frozen image. That was a match, or maybe a lighter; but it was a man-made light. "Infrared Scan" one hour prior and one hour after showed a hot vehicle engine and personnel apparently loading a truck.

The bevy of nighttime activity completely disappeared during the daylight hours. Terri watched the remaining 30 minutes of the original program with renewed interest. As surprising as the burst of light was the appearance of a black rectangle the morning of the 28th day. Nature doesn't make straight lines—"Enlarge X 100." The low morning sun etched a long black rectangle on the brown desert. It was the dark shadow of a door. A well camouflaged door, but a man-made door in the middle of the Syrian Desert. A door that the U.S. intelligence community never knew existed until this moment. That alone was worth the Saturday.

~~

Danni and Mamba didn't exactly fight over the selection of the gown, but their discussion was heated in a mother-daughter kind of way. Danni felt something conservative, more concealing than revealing, something elegant but business-like would be more appropriate for the ball; Mamba insisted on seductive and alluring.

The Southeast Conservatory annual fundraising ball was an unexpected windfall for Daufuskie Resort. The Conservatory's ball was initially scheduled for Hilton Head, but the hotel with the booking became a casualty of the economy and closed their doors. Danni jumped at the opportunity. It was their first opportunity to influence a lot of important people, people with money, and Mamba wanted Danni to look nice.

"You are not an old maid, Danni girl, don't dress like one."

Danni fought back against the pressure. "Good grief Mamba, what's the big deal? Nobody cares how I look."

Mamba's smile ended the jousting. "You never can tell; maybe somebody will ask you to dance."

Mamba finally pressed upon Danni a stunning shirred chiffon gown with beading that added highlights to the dark blue of the dress. Mamba insisted on the dress because the dark blue would be a beautiful contrast to the diamond wreath necklace and matching earrings of graduated rows of different style cuts. The set was valued at $750,000. The owner of the jewelry boutique forced it upon Danni; there was no better advertising than having his jewels grace the beautiful body of Danni Walton.

With her father in Texas on business, and without an escort, Danni monitored the serving of dinner from behind the mirrored window overlooking the banquet facility. The kitchen and serving team did themselves proud. Each course was served exactly on time and it took no more than five minutes to complete the service. It was a sight to see from above.

Danni elected to eat in the office. The table rounds of eight were perfect for the couples attending the event and Danni had no desire to be seated with odd pairings of the single men and the few single women in attendance. She did not want to be captured and forced to make small talk over dinner; there would be more than ample opportunity for that during the ball that followed.

Danni made her way to the ballroom with the slightest twinge of envy of those couples sharing the events of the evening. At $2,000 a ticket, Danni wanted to greet as many of her patrons as possible.

She was the picture of elegance as she greeted her guests. The blue of the dress seemed to caress her skin. The sparkles of the diamonds never matched the warmth of her smile. The flow of guests into the ballroom finally eased and Danni circulated among them. Most were delightful and complimentary of the services rendered and of Danni's choice of attire, but eventually she was cornered at the open bar nearest the orchestra. The three men meant well but in reality Danni quickly bored of their attempts at humor and desperately wished for the opportunity to escape to less confining encounters.

"Excuse me gentlemen. Miss Danni, may I have this dance?"

She started to smile even before she turned. There was only one man who addressed her as Miss Danni. There were no words of greeting exchanged, only the connection of their eyes. Bill Cannon extended his left hand to her and beckoned with the other that she should join him on the dance floor. The feeling that nagged at her the entire night vanished with the touch of his hand.

Danni fought against the urge to circle Bill's neck and boldly kiss him. It took all she had to turn back to the men at the bar. "Thank you all for coming. Each of you has made this evening very special. Please excuse me." Danni meant every word.

Bill escorted her to the dance floor as the orchestra began a gentle rendition of a tango. Danni was pleasantly surprised when Bill drew her close to him and expertly led her through the dance. The surprise on her face must have been apparent to Bill.

A sheepish grin lit his face. "I took some lessons with the great expectation of one day getting to dance with you again. Unfortunately it is the only one I know, so make the most of it."

Danni giggled and allowed herself to be drawn into the spirit of the dance. It was calming and thrilling at the same time. Bill's hand on the small of her back was warm to the touch through the fabric of her dress and she was lost in his embrace. Each move, each touch made Danni wonder why this man had such an effect on her. Why did Bill always make her feel young and vulnerable and secure at the same time? When the dance ended Danni hoped her guests would not notice the flush on her cheeks.

Bill offered his arm to Danni. "It looks like things here are under control. Would you like to take a walk in the moonlight? I promise to have you back by midnight."

Danni smiled, but before she answered she scanned the room to ensure all was in order. "Mr. Cannon, I would love to take a walk with you."

They took the footpath to Calibogue Sound and followed the beach path north. Danni slid her arm in Bill's. "You look very handsome in your tux. Why didn't you tell me you were coming?"

"I knew you would be busy, and I didn't know if maybe you had a date. I was too chicken to ask."

"And if I did have a date, then what?"

"Then that would have been one expensive dinner."

Danni smiled at the confession. "You still could have let me know. I felt like a chaperone at a high school dance. I would have felt better if I knew you were going to be here." Danni paused and turned to Bill. "How did you get in here anyway? This was supposed to be by invitation only."

Bill looked offended. "I bribed the security guard. I hope you don't mind."

Danni would never put something like that past Bill, but she didn't really think he would go to such measures. "Seriously Bill, how did you get in here?"

Bill grinned. "Danni, I've been a member of the Conservatory for years. When they e-mailed the members that the conference had been changed to your hotel, I sent my money in..." Bill sent his money in with the hope of seeing Danni in a setting different than his normal shorts and sandals attire, but he had to add, "...and saving the whales is important to us all."

"I'm glad you did."

That was just about the most romantic thing Danni Walton had ever said to him.

The quarter moon was late in rising and only now started to climb into the night sky. Bill started the conversation with a safe subject. "Oh, by the way, when I was in Washington, I asked about Hanna and the Mad Man. Lucas McLaughlin said they are doing just fine. Do you talk with Hanna much?"

"We talk about twice a week. Hanna likes Washington but *James*, and I wish you would stop calling him Mad Man, can't wait to get back with the Rangers." Danni barely had time to take another breath when she decided this was as good a time as any to solve the Mad Man puzzle. "Bill, just exactly how did James get the nickname of Mad Man?" It was a topic discussed since the day Hanna and James met, but the story behind the name remained a mystery.

"If he hasn't told Hanna, then I damn sure am not going to tell you. You will just have to ask Major Madison."

Bill finally had Danni exactly where he wanted her—alone on the beach. But now as the lights of the hotel faded into the darkness and only the call of the night owls would interrupt their conversation, Bill hadn't planned his conversation any further than his first comment. It was bad planning on his part. With his hands shoved deep in his pockets and Danni's arm hooked through his he could only muster,

"That was some kind of meal."

What? That's it? Danni was finally alone with Bill Cannon, the man she enjoyed more than any other, and all he can say is that was some kind of meal? She was hoping for something like, your eyes are like emeralds, or your skin is like velvet, or anything, but 'that was some kind of meal!

She wanted to say those things but her reply was simply a proper, "Thank you."

It was a full minute before Bill spoke again. "How do you like working at the hotel?"

Was this going to be the entire conversation? Was this romantic walk alone on the beach going to be nothing but proper platitudes? "It has its ups and downs, but I enjoy the challenge. It sure keeps me busy and, since Hanna moved to Washington, it gives me something to do."

The rising moon reflected off the water and an owl hooted from the trees. It was the calming elixir they both needed. Bill broke the silence. "Danni, you've done a wonderful job with the hotel. Are you going to keep it or sell it?"

Bill hoped for some sign, any sign, that Danni was tired of the task of running the hotel. He didn't get it.

"I'm so glad the bank gave me the opportunity. If the price was right the bank would sell it in a heartbeat, but we still have lots of mountains to climb before we can consider the rebuilding a success."

"Things like what? This place looks great and from what I hear everybody is impressed."

"We still have to operate at a profit. Since we started making money, the state has raised the room tax three times. The taxes have quadrupled since the day the bank took over operation of the resort. It doesn't affect the super-rich, they will always have money to spend, but about 90 percent of our business comes from regular folks who may save for a year to take a nice vacation. The politicians promise no new taxes, but the ferry rides to and from the island have doubled and the state authorized the power company to raise our rates to help subsidize the power for federal housing on the mainland. Even our garbage fees are triple what they used to be. They may kill the goose that lays the golden egg; the government and the unions will drive us out of business."

"I didn't know you were under a union contract."

"We're not, at least not yet, but the government is talking about an amendment to an old law that will allow more control over business they consider vital to the economic well-being of the nation and individual states. It will grant unprecedented powers to unions. The ISU…"

Bill interrupted, "Who the hell is the ISU?"

"The International Service Union had a general meeting of the staff about a week ago. They talk a big game; higher wages, more benefits, more security, more days off. Only one employee, Brian Vance, rose to talk against the union; the rest of them bought-in hook, line and sinker. I don't think we could survive a union contract."

"Who is Brian Vance?" Did Danni catch just a hint of jealously in Bill's question?

"He's an employee here at the resort. He used to work the beach, making sure the umbrellas were out and the grounds clean, but now he is in charge of our sailing school and takes the kids on excursions to find fossils. He was enrolled in the Citadel before his parents died. He's such a hard worker. I'm going to start a scholarship fund to get him back in school. He was the only employee who spoke against the union. It took a lot of guts. I'd like for you to meet him."

"Citadel cadets have always impressed me. You can count on me to help with the fund. If the unions are beginning to give you trouble, why don't you get out now and cut your losses? We can lie on the beach and let the government and the unions try to run things for a while."

Danni did notice the "we" in Bill's last comment. She also had given the "we" much thought over the past few years, but every time she started to think of the future with Bill, the only man she would consider making a future with, the deeds of her past came to haunt her. Danni knew that Bill Cannon could never truly love a woman who had paid for the execution of a man. It was her terrible act of revenge for the rape of her daughter. Maybe justified, but something that could destroy the foundation of love if not revealed, so she carried the burden of revenge within; a lonely life was her penance.

Danni tried to focus on the present. "Bill, I'm not going to quit until I'm beaten. There is still a chance we can beat the economy, the union, and the government. What about you? What exactly do you see in your future?"

Bill only had one plan in his future, but to blurt out that his future plans were only her, would have been impolite. His answer avoided the subject. "I'll continue to run my school, but other than that...I don't know...maybe I'll crew out on one of DeAgnelo's fishing boats."

"Bill, I've seen how you fish." Danni remembered years ago when Bill brought a date to a party on the island. The date jokingly complained that she was famished. Bill had promised to catch their breakfast only to come up empty. "I want my guests to actually catch something."

Bill saw the smile on Danni's face. "We did pretty good the other day. I've learned a few things."

"Yes, you have."

And they walked deeper into the moonlight.

"Bill, do you have any regrets, anything you would change if you had the chance?"

It was a dangerous question to ask. Of course he had regrets. The most overwhelming regret he had was that he didn't meet this woman before she married the deceitful and unworthy Reverend Peter Walton. She probably would have never chosen him to marry, but at least he would have asked. He would never allow her to suffer the way she had. He always wanted to come right out and ask her to marry him—country and hotel be damned—they could move to Costa Rica and live the remainder of their lives in peace.

His second regret, the other thing he wished he could change, prevented him from doing just that. His second regret was that he was responsible for the murder of her husband. Something that once revealed would certainly destroy the woman he loved. So Bill lived with the heavy burden and would continue to work simply to ease the pain of not having the woman he had truly grown to love.

For now it was better to avoid the true answer. "Danni I try to focus on today and tomorrow more than the past, but I do regret one thing in my past. I regret I didn't take more dance lessons when I was a kid."

Danni laughed at the joke.

"How about you? Do you have any regrets?"

"Only one I can discuss. I wish I had more children."

"We can still do something about that you know."

"Bill, you're such a romantic."

The groundwork laid, Bill went out on a limb. "Danni, have you ever thought about getting married again?"

Bill felt Danni tense at the question. Without noticing that she did, Danni removed her arm from around Bill's. The memories of her marriage flooded back. She hadn't given the specific question much thought, but her first marriage wasn't something that she liked to dwell upon. Danni answered slowly, "I really haven't given it much thought. My first marriage wasn't exactly what I thought it could be. I really don't know."

Danni wished she could take it back. She wished she could clarify the statement and the way she answered. But the past was still a raw and painful wound in her life and although she didn't think time would completely erase the terrible emotions of the past she wished she had answered the question in a different way, and she knew it hurt Bill when he abruptly stopped.

He didn't explain his actions, but slowly turned his head to the side. Danni saw that his eyes were closed and he held erect his index finger in front of his mouth signaling for quiet. Danni trusted Bill's instincts. They had saved her from robbery, maybe more, years ago in a parking garage in Atlanta. After a moment he whispered to her.

"There's something in the trees ahead. Stay behind me but stay close."

Bill slowly made his way to the trees ahead. She wondered how he moved through the grasses and twigs without making a sound; he took pause every few steps to listen. "Wait here."

Bill disappeared into the darkness of the trees. Danni suddenly felt very alone.

"Danni, come ahead."

"What is it?"

"It's a boy, badly beaten."

Danni finally recognized Bill's crouching outline in the moon shadows of the trees. Danni was more than eager to make her way to Bill's side. The body at Bill's feet did not move. "Is he alive?" The thought of such violence on Daufuskie Island disturbed Danni.

"Just barely, do you recognize him?"

Danni bent low to study the beaten face. The dappled light from the rising moon was just enough to make out the swollen facial features. She did recognize the young man. He was lying so still and bleeding so profusely on the pine needles.

"Oh my God! It's Brian Vance. What happened to him?'

"I think the union just got serious about silencing the opposition."

As Bill and Danni waited for the ambulance, Bill felt his phone vibrate indicating a text message. The message from Lucas McLaughlin was simple and direct. "Need to talk. Come to Washington ASAP."

Chapter 14

Rhonda stuck her head into Eric's office. She was surprised to see him still at his computer terminal.

"Eric, you're going to be late for the production meeting."

There was concern in her voice. Bernie Stein, evening news managing director, was cantankerous and unreasonable at his best, and could be downright brutal to anyone late for his meetings.

"Rhonda, have you seen these reports coming in from Iraq? Three suicide bombings in Baghdad and two attacks on government offices in Basra, over 300 dead, and a government army unit is surrounded and being cut apart. And look at this report from the Cairo desk."

Rhonda was more concerned with getting her boss to the meeting than reading reports from Egypt. "Eric, you're going to be late. You can tell me about the reports on the way."

Eric collected the reports and talked while he walked. "The Cairo desk reports Egypt has announced joint military exercises with Russia and Iran! Hell, the Egyptians just kicked the Russians out of their country 25 years ago, and what the hell are they doing with the Iranians? All this when the President is pulling our ground troops out of Iraq? It's going to make the Secretary of State's visit look a little premature, like we're pulling out before the country is really secure and allowing Russia and Iran to dominate the area. I think it should be our lead story."

"Stein isn't going to lead with that. He probably won't let you bring it up." The CNN intelligence network in Washington was as good as any, and they had learned the President intended to withdraw all American combat forces from Iraq, Kuwait and Saudi Arabia. The only force he intended to leave in the region was the naval forces of the 6th US Fleet.

"We'll see about that."

~~

The second hand on the wall clock was approaching the 6:00 o'clock position; 30 seconds late.

Bernie Stein impatiently tapped his pen on the metal and glass table; everyone in place except the lead anchor for the evening news. Eric's co-anchor still applying the finishing touches to her makeup; weather, sports, entertainment, politics, business, video, cameras, sound and a few others twitched in their chairs waiting for Eric.

Eric ignored the nervous tension in the office and boldly asked, "Bernie, have you seen these reports from Iraq and Cairo? We've got a small war going on over there." He slid the papers towards Bernie as he took his seat.

Bernie glanced at the reports. "No, Mr. Brown, I have not seen these reports because I was here waiting for you. If you can't get to these production meetings on time, I can always find another anchor."

Eric ignored the empty threat. Eric's ratings were the highest on the network and Stein would have a lot of explaining if he tried to fire Eric. "I think we should lead with Iraq. Do we have any video?"

"We're not leading with Iraq. Nobody gives a rat's ass about what is happening over there. People could care less about the war, and are tired of hearing about it. We're going to lead with the President signing the amendment to the '34 Banes-Adams Act."

The amendment the President signed earlier in the day gave the Government power to designate business in the private sector as vital to the national economy. The amendment allowed unprecedented government oversight and control of those private businesses, and allowed states to do the same with businesses in the individual states.

Stein turned to the video director, "Play that cut of the President."

The video of the President filled the screens in the conference room. The President was eloquent as always.

"In light of the current economic conditions these additional regulations are needed to stabilize employment and wages in the private sector. These oversight measures should prevent those companies, vital to our national economy, from repeating the same mistakes that caused the economic crisis we find ourselves in today. With proper oversight, these measures should hasten our economic recovery. This new amendment also empowers the individual states to pass similar laws at the local level."

The screens turned blue and Stein continued. "We will follow the President's statement with a report from Donna Davis…Eric you will do the lead-in. Run the clip."

More clicks on the computer and the pre-recorded report from Donna Davis started to run. "I'm Donna Davis reporting from a small suburb of Detroit."

Behind Donna, marching in orderly fashion, were union members in protest. "I'm standing at the locked front gate of the American Axle and Spring Company, which until recently produced the axles and suspension springs for the American automotive market. This factory was the latest in a long line of failures of manufacturers associated with the industry. In a press release the owner of this company blamed personnel expenses and the increasing burden of the new value added tax to his cost of materials. In his statement he said the domestic automotive manufacturers could buy his products cheaper overseas than he could produce them here. It left him no choice but to close the door of this factory that had been the mainstay of this small community for 100 years."

Eric watched the tape with the others. "Mr. Stein, do we have anyone lined up to explain what the owner of that factory meant?"

Stein almost scoffed at Eric. "Don't be ridiculous! Nobody wants to hear why the economy is going to the crapper. They just want answers."

Eric was going to respond but Stein held up his hand. "Forget it Brown, it's a dead subject. Sports, what's on your outline?"

And down the table Stein progressed and soon the evening news began to take shape. Before they concluded the meeting Eric asked, "Are we going to give any time to the Secretary of State's visit to the Middle East?"

Stein answered, "Only if we have video to support it."

Eric turned to the video director. "You got anything yet?"

Video called up the menu. "Looks like we just got something, but we'll have to edit it before we run it. We can get that done before deadline."

"Okay, we'll run the State visit in the world wrap up. Brown, since you're so hot on this trip, you can write the script. Alright, everyone have their scripts done in an hour and loaded in the teleprompter. Wet run at 4 p.m., now get to work."

The wet run went with few glitches and was the first time Eric Brown had a chance to view the video of the Secretary of State's visit to Kuwait. He nudged his co-anchor. "I've met the Prince of Kuwait."

She turned to Eric. "You've been to Kuwait?"

"No, I met him at a funeral here in the states. He was a pall bearer at the funeral of a friend of my father."

Eric silently kicked himself. There was absolutely no good reason to brag about meeting the Prince of Kuwait; it was part of his past. A past he had worked so hard to conceal. Eric welcomed the next segment of the rehearsal.

~~

The Secretary of State's meeting with the Prince of Kuwait went exactly as expected. The US was pulling all combat forces from the Middle East and sending the majority of those to hunt terrorists in Afghanistan. The cost of maintaining a standing force was just more than the US economy could bear. Prince Al-Sabah accepted the news without any visible sign of objection.

The Secretary of State quickly moved to the rising price of oil. "Prince Al-Sabah, the President of the United States sends his respect and has directed me to ask your help to bring the price of oil down, and to increase your production and shipments to the United States."

Prince Al-Sabah slowly nodded, "Madam Secretary, the price of oil and production quotas are established by OPEC. What would you have me do? One tree cannot stop the advance of the desert. My brothers in OPEC would consider any deviation from the agreed upon price and quota to be a breach of faith and would subject my country to sanction."

"Prince Al-Sabah, you have the support of the United States. We have spilled American blood to protect your country. The American President and the American people expect your economic support in return."

"Madam Secretary, we do not tell America what to charge for wheat. I am surprised you think to dictate the price of our only commodity. It seems contrary to the free enterprise system you Americans are always bragging about."

"Prince Al-Sabah, we are taking measures to bring America's consumption of oil in line with the rest of the nations in the world. Until that time we need your assistance to get us through these bad economic times."

"Madam Secretary, every nation feels the pain of America, but my Arab brothers would not understand if I broke their trust. My country has been bitten by the snake of invasion before, and now we shake with fear at the sight of a rope. I must do what I think is best for my people. "

"Prince Al-Sabah, America has proven to be a worthy ally of Kuwait. We will stand by our treaty obligations. You can count on us."

"Madam Secretary, if your country must withdraw from my country for economic reasons, then the future costs of your return may be too great a price to pay. Now you abandon us to chase Osama Bin Laden in Afghanistan. Your President has called the American efforts to stabilize the Middle East as an illegal war, and the defense of my country as a cause for terrorist recruiting. Perhaps your President will find oil in Afghanistan."

"Prince Al-Sabah, our efforts in Afghanistan are not the issues I came here to discuss. America is crumbling under the weight of the price of oil."

"An ailment your country has brought upon itself. Madam Secretary, your promise of support is nothing more than a cloud of hope and hope will not protect my country. Kuwait lives in the middle of a den of lions eager to find reason to pick over our bones. We, alone, have supported the United States for years; and now your country is concerned only with the price of a gallon of gasoline, and will come to the aid of my country only if it suits you. Your newspapers and media say the American public is tired of the war and your President will join with the family of nations as an equal. Your citizens think the money you spend here is wasted and could be better spent at home. They have come to expect rewards, but have forgotten the price that must be paid to secure their prosperity."

"Prince Al-Sabah, the United States has the most powerful military on the face of the earth. You can rest assured we will come to your aid if needed."

"Madam Secretary, an army of lions led by a sheep would be defeated by an army of sheep led by a lion. The Russians invade the free nation of Georgia, and America does nothing. Iran and North Korea threaten the world with nuclear weapons, and America does nothing. You have the power yet you lack the leadership and the national will to be considered a trustworthy ally."

Perhaps the Secretary of State concluded she had lost the argument. The Hail Mary to convince Prince Al-Sabah her words were true—fell on deaf ears. "Prince Al-Sabah, I give to you my word that America will always stand with Kuwait."

"Madam Secretary, your words are like the wind in the desert, strong today but gone with the setting sun. The American Army rides a slow camel and I fear only the echoes of your words will reach my country in time of war."

~~

Lucas McLaughlin reserved a meeting room in the Army-Navy Club in Washington for the meeting. It was one of the few places where Bill Cannon's presence would not raise questions.

As a polite gesture Lucas introduced Bill to Terri Toth. "I remember Terri from Panama. It is good to see you again."

Lucas motioned to the table in the corner of the room. "Why don't we get right to it?"

After the group was seated Terri Toth turned to Senator Reynolds. "Senator Reynolds, I know you sit on the intelligence oversight committee. I assume you are aware of the President's order to restrict intelligence operations against any Arab state without his specific approval?"

Senator Reynolds returned Terri's stare. "Yes Miss Toth, I am aware of that restriction. Please rest assured that my office thinks I am here for lunch and nothing more. I have not, and will not make any record of anything discussed in this meeting. What we discuss here is for our ears only; I give you my word on that."

"Good enough."

Terri removed the photos from her briefcase. "Gentleman, I ran these photos through our computers and our intelligence data base. The conclusions are my own and have not been reviewed by any other analyst. This should be taken into consideration before you make any decisions or take any action."

Terri pulled the photo of Port Said in Egypt. "Three of the five vessels in port are what I consider suspicious. The first is the Iranian vessel. This vessel off-loaded a load of pipe for the Egyptian oil industry. The problem is threefold. First, Egypt has enough pipe to lay across the continent of Africa without importing any from Iran. Second, the pipe appears to be a larger diameter than the standard size pipe used in oilfields. And third, the pipe was delivered to a small town in the Sinai, Ezbet Abu Sagal. Ezbet Abu Segal doesn't have an oil production facility within four-hundred miles."

Terri used a pen to point to a second ship in port. "This ship sailed from a Russian port on the Black Sea. The manifest indicated they

95

delivered engine or engine parts in closed containers. The containers are the type we reserve for jet engines, sensitive equipment, or hazardous cargo. The containers alone raise doubts as to the content being simple engine parts. I attempted to backtrack the parts to Russia manufacturing and found no connection. These engine containers were also delivered to Ezbet Abu Sagal. There are no manufacturing plants or any other business in that city that would require in excess of 100 of these engine containers."

Terri pointed to a third ship. "This ship is from Syria. It delivered pelletized fertilizer that was also shipped to Ezbet Abu Sagal. Ezbet Abu Sagal is nothing more than a fishing village with some limited crop production and a tourist stop. It does have a need for fertilizer, but… Syria doesn't produce fertilizer; I would suspect it is something else."

Terri slipped the port photo back into the envelope and removed the photo of Ezbet Abu Sagal.

"This is Ezbet Abu Sagal. A quiet fishing town located 30 miles south of the Gaza Strip. Other than the delivery of the goods I have already mentioned, I didn't see anything unusual there, except this small trawler just north of the port." Terri pointed to the fishing trawler.

"The boat has been making a shuttle run between the Syrian port of Tartus and Ezbet Abu Sagal. No record of its cargo exists, and you would think maybe they were selling their catch in Sagal, but not once did I ever see it deploy its nets. This trawler loaded drums in Tartus and then offloaded the drums every time it docked in the port."

Terri pulled the photos of southern Lebanon from the envelope. "The electronic signature of this house leads me to believe it's a headquarters building. The foot traffic to and from the house was higher than any of the houses in the surrounding area, but more than that I can't even guess."

Terri continued. "The really interesting photo was this photo of the Syrian Desert. As you can see the area is devoid of any buildings, life or vegetation. Only when I ran a month long loop on this area did I find this."

Terri pulled a new photo from the envelope, one that Bill had not provided. "When I ran an IR scan, I found this." Terri slid an infrared photo across the table. The photo clearly showed heat images of trucks that were being loaded. "I also found this." Terri presented a satellite photo of the black rectangle on the desert. "Gentlemen, nature doesn't make anything with that many straight lines. I believe that is a cleverly camouflaged door to an underground storage site that we have not known about until now."

All three men sat in silence digesting what Terri Toth had presented. Senator Reynolds asked, "Miss Toth, what conclusion have you drawn from your research?"

"Senator Reynolds I would hate to say I can draw any specific conclusions, but my hypothesis is that we have discovered the storage site where Saddam Hussein shipped his chemical weapons before our invasion of Iraq, and somebody is sending it to the Sinai Peninsula and building rockets, possibly chemical rockets, to launch into Israel."

Senator Reynold's face looked years older, "Miss Toth, you've been in intelligence for years. What would be your recommended course of action on your findings?"

"Senator Reynolds, I would recommend direct action against these targets."

"By direct action do you mean an attack?"

Terri shook her head. "No, by direct action, I mean putting the CIA on the ground to confirm the content of those deliveries. But with the President's order, only he can order direct intelligence operations. If you want action to take them out, then you would have to talk to guys like Lucas or Bill."

Lucas McLaughlin spoke up. "Senator Reynolds, are you aware of the joint operations between Egypt, Russia, and Iran? If the Russians and Iranians deploy to Egypt, then the combined Egyptian, Iranian, and Russian force would be the largest armed force in Africa since World War II, with only the Suez Canal between them and the Israeli border. The combat multiplier of a chemical strike capability could be devastating. That amount of combat power arrayed against Israel may force Israel to conclude their only option to ensure their survival would be to escalate and retaliate with a nuclear response."

Terri was glad someone other than she brought up the nuclear response scenario.

Apparently the thought was more than Senator Reynolds had considered. "Israel would never do that."

Lucas responded to the Senator's comment. "I wouldn't put it past the Israelis. They were dusting their nukes off in '73 during the Yom Kippur War. I don't think they would hesitate to use a nuclear response if they were facing an overwhelming force following a massive chemical strike."

Reynolds asked, "I wonder if the Israelis know any of this? We need to send someone over there and fill them in."

Bill Cannon had been waiting for just such an opportunity. Although it wasn't a terrible concern, the investigation by the federal agent in Atlanta always played in the back of Bill's mind. If Major Madison and Hanna were out of the country then two critical components would be removed from the investigation. It was a long shot that the investigator would ever follow the trail to Hanna and Madison, but Bill considered it the prudent thing to do. He didn't see any downside to it.

"Lucas, why don't you send Major Madison? You can assign him as a military attaché to the Embassy."

Getting Madison out of the country would solve more than one problem.

Lucas McLaughlin thought for a moment. He saw the utility of sending someone from his own staff and Bill's warning of the Atlanta investigator was not lost on him either. "I can make that happen."

Putting the decision of moving Madison to Israel behind him, McLaughlin refocused on the pictures. To no-one in particular he voiced the thought. "You know what we really need? We need a man in Kuwait. Price Al-Sabah obviously knows something is going down. He wouldn't have given us these photos if he didn't."

Bill Cannon nodded his agreement. "Who do you have in mind?"

Lucas McLaughlin paused a moment before he looked at Bill. "You."

The thought of leaving Danni Walton crossed Bill's mind, it was a thought that didn't sit well. "I'm retired. You need to find someone else."

"Bill, you know Al-Sabah better than anyone; and he trusts you. Think about it. He wouldn't have given you those photos unless he needed our help. The entire Middle East may be going up in flames and you're going to sit down in Georgia and just watch? I don't believe it. Besides, you may get over there and find out it's nothing. You could be home in a week."

Lucas had a point. His friend trusted him to get the photos analyzed, and it wasn't in Bill's character to turn his back on a friend.

"Okay, I'll go, but I have a few things I have to tidy up. It may be a couple of weeks."

Chapter 15

It took Angelina Sanchez two weeks to get a lead on Frenchy Guidry. The time between dead ends Angelina took to study Tyrell Biggs.

The Google search on Biggs painted the picture of a successful black business man heavy into the gangster scene, rap, hip-hop, and all the biggest hip stars. There were hundreds of articles and pictures, and even commercials for corporations trying to break into the hip-hop market. Angelina noted with interest his involvement with numerous charities and social events in and around Atlanta.

The police computer told a different story. It painted a picture of a local drug king pin, maybe the largest in the South, and when he was found dead from a broken neck on a pontoon boat in the Savannah River, the police closed any investigation when the coroner ruled his death a simple boating accident.

Maybe the man in Louisiana could connect Tyrell Biggs to the rape of Hanna Walton and the death of the rape suspects. At least that is what Angelina hoped.

But right now, Angelina questioned the stupidity of her decision to question Frenchy Guidry, and her skin crawled with the kind of apprehension that had the hair bristling on the back of the neck. Every sense in her body was telling her to turn around and get back to Atlanta, and to leave the southern Louisiana swamps to the Cajuns who made these foreboding backwaters their home.

Every ripple in the dark waters surely was either a snake or gator lying in ambush for unwary prey. This world was alien to her; so far from the desert southwest where she was raised. There, in the wide open spaces of the desert she had mastered the art of avoiding the snakes, scorpions, occasional coyote and other hazards to one's health. The desert never closed in on you like the swamp was closing in on her now. The only similarity between the two locations was that you could disappear in the swamp just like you could disappear in the desert—and never be heard from again. That is probably exactly why Mr. Gerald "Frenchy" Guidry had chosen to move here after the death of Tyrell Biggs.

The directions to Guidry's stilted shack were very accurate: Highway 38 north past the second bridge, turn right onto the first dirt road, three miles to the end of the road and then take the footpath atop the small water control dike and use the footbridge to cross the creek. Guidry's house should be around the bend ahead. Angelina received the directions from the local sheriff, a big black man wearing a dirty khaki shirt stuffed into Levis covered with beer stains, blood and fish entrails. A small tarnished badge—the only visible sign of his office—was pinned to a pocket stuffed full with a pouch of chewing tobacco. Getting the directions from the sheriff was akin to getting water from a barrel cactus—a lot of hard work for a little bit of relief.

After a full explanation that the purpose of her visit was to complete an investigation directed by the President, and that she neither had warrants to serve or persons to charge, nor were there any suspects in the local area, did the sheriff provide her directions to the house.

Far be it that he was interested enough in the investigation, or Angelina's safety, that he might feel obliged to actually accompany her into the swamp—that may take valuable time away from cleaning fish. The sheriff did, however, tell Angelina to inform Guidry that he had provided the directions and that he should answer her questions. Angelina assumed this advice served the dual purpose of a warning about Guidry and also granted her safe passage and that, if nothing else, the sheriff knew of Angelina's trip and he would expect her eventual return.

Following the footbridge and the ensuing trail around a stand of palmetto bushes and brush Angelina found herself on the beaten dirt and weeds that constituted Guidry's front yard. The ramshackle house stood on stilts 6'off the ground. What was left of storm shutters hung askew on the windows, the screens covering the open windows were rusty and torn. The cypress siding was weathered but looked in reasonable condition. The skinned carcass of an 8' – 10' gator hung from a hook secured to the cross beam supporting the porch roof. The gator's hide was rolled and tied neatly into a bundle and adorned the top step of the stairs leading up to the porch; as if ready for pickup or shipment. There wasn't a breath of air and the sounds of the buzzing flies and mosquitoes filled the air. If there was a spot close to hell on earth, Angelina had stumbled upon it. There was no movement in the darkened house and try as she could she didn't hear any movement in the house or on the surrounding grounds. Except for the gator carcass still dripping blood onto the porch, you would think the shack had been abandoned for years.

Secure in the belief that her escape path to her rear was clear, and hesitant to approach the house without invitation, Angelina called out loudly to announce her presence. "Mr. Gerald Guidry, I am with the Department of Justice in Washington. I would like to talk with you. The sheriff gave me directions."

Angelina was a little startled that her voice sounded so loud in the quiet of the swamp. She called out again, "Mr. Guidry, I have come a long way to talk with you. I want to talk with you about Tyrell Biggs." The sound of her voice floated through the surrounding cypress trees and over the waters of the swamp, but all she got in return was silence. The silence only built upon the nervous tension she felt. The snap of a twig, directly to her rear, caused her to react.

Angelina reached for the Glock clipped to her belt and stepped forward to create distance between her and the location of the breaking twig. The sound of a pump action weapon cycling a round into the chamber and a deep Cajun voice stopped her. "If I be you then I would not do that."

Angelina should have paid more attention to the bristling hairs on the back of her neck. But now was not the time to lose her nerve. "Are you Gerald Guidry?" As she was asking the question she moved her hand away from the pistol and slowly turned to face the voice behind her. She prayed that she would at least be able to see the face of the man who held her fate beneath his trigger finger.

The man to her front was at 6' 4" and close to 300, maybe more. He was darker than most of the Cajuns she had seen in town, his unruly hair and beard matched the matted hair on his barrel chest and he looked more like the elusive Sasquatch than man. Angelina was looking down the barrel of a well worn but cleaned and oiled twelve gauge pump action shotgun that was unwavering and pointed directly at her chest. At the man's feet was a pit bull squatting of all fours. The dog's eyes never left Angelina.

"Are you Gerald Guidry?"

The barrel of the shotgun didn't move. "Who are you?"

Angelina slowly reached to her pocket to pull her badge. "I am Angelina Sanchez. I work in Washington for the Justice Department. Your friend—"Crack Daddy" Jennings—said you might be able to help me with an investigation. Do you remember "Crack Daddy" Jennings?"

"Maybe I do, maybe I don't. Why would Crack tell you to ask me for help? I've never been to Washington." Guidry had to give this woman some credit. Most men would never venture into the swamp alone, and the woman was either very brave or very ignorant to do so.

Angelina glanced down at the pit bull. Drool slowly oozed from his jaws and the eyes of the dog, like the barrel of the shotgun, were still trained on her—the dog's obsession only added to the surreal atmosphere of the swamp.

"Mr. Guidry, Crack Daddy wrote a letter to the President. He said the police were killing the suspects in a rape case that they never had enough evidence to take to court. It was the rape of a 15-year-old girl. There was never a trial, no one was ever charged; they were never punished by the law, but with the exception of Crack Daddy the rest of the suspects were killed.

"One of the suspects in that rape was found in a burned-out limo in the Okefenokee swamp."

Guidry's eyes narrowed slightly, but the shotgun didn't move.

"There were four men in that limo. The bodies were burned to a crisp, but the cause of death for three of the men was a bullet hole in the head and one through the heart, and the fourth was almost decapitated; probably a knife through the throat and out the back of the neck. Crack Daddy said you were the driver for Tyrell Biggs, and that the limo belonged to Tyrell Biggs. Any of this ring a bell with you?"

Angelina waited for some response from Mr. Guidry. "Mr. Guidry, I did a little checking around. You ran with a pretty bad crowd. Somebody killed your boss too. I've counted up the bodies, what was it, a total of eight men dead? That doesn't raise any questions with you?"

It wasn't an outright accusation, but it must have caused a change in something in the big man and the dog at his feet felt the change and started a low warning growl. The dog proved to be an accurate lie detector system.

Guidry was well aware of the four bodies in the limo. He was the man who drove the limo to the burning Georgia swamp hoping the fires would completely erase any trace of the four dead men. But the swamp fires didn't complete the job and the Georgia swamp didn't swallow up the evidence.

Angelina waited for some type of response from Guidry, and the long silence between the two heightened the noise of the insects. Angelina continued, "That limo was registered to Tyrell Biggs, the big hip-hop record producer in Atlanta. Crack told me you were Mr. Biggs' limo driver. You don't have anything you want to add?"

Angelina noticed the barrel of the shotgun was now slightly raised and was pointing directly at her head. "I don't know anything about that. Why would Crack want to help you?"

"Mr. Jennings," - the name didn't register with Guidry - "Sorry, Crack Daddy, is dying of AIDS in an Alabama prison. Maybe he wanted to confess to gain forgiveness before he dies. In any event he told me the entire story. You have nothing to worry about from me. The only thing I am investigating is the murders of the other suspects. I am just asking for a little cooperation from you, something the Sheriff told me to tell you—that you should answer my questions. You were Mr. Biggs' limo driver, weren't you?"

Guidry knew the local Sheriff had his own reasons to cooperate with the Feds. Get 'em in and get 'em out as quick as possible without raising any more suspicions. The last thing the Sheriff needed was a bunch of Federal agents snooping around the swamp. The 40 acres of Jamaican marijuana growing not two miles from this spot was reason enough to get Guidry to cooperate with this lady. And if Crack Daddy had confessed to the rape, then he probably told this lady from Washington everything she already needed to know. Guidry concluded her trip to the swamp was to confirm her findings. Guidry had nothing to do with the rape or the four dead men in the burned limo.

"So? Bad luck for them. I didn't have anything to do with raping the girl. Why are you telling me these things?" The barrel of the shotgun still held steady on her head.

At last Angelina had a response from Guidry. "So you were Mr. Biggs' limo driver. How did four dead men get in your limo and end up in the Okefenokee Swamp?"

Guidry's answer was completely unrelated to the question. "The company lawyer reported the limo stolen. Why don' you go ask him what happened to the limo. I was just the driver."

Angelina took another path in her questioning. "Mr. Guidry, how long have you lived here in the swamp?"

"I been living here for five years, maybe a little more. This house was my momma's house. After Hurricane Katrina she went to Texas and asked me to watch over it. She died, so the house is now mine."

"When did you leave Atlanta? Was it before Mr. Biggs drowned on the Savannah River, or after?"

Mr. Tyrell Biggs and a companion died rather mysteriously on the Savannah River not more than six months after the four charred corpses were found in the swamp. His neck was broken but the coroner concluded it was a self inflicted injury when he lost his footing, or was caused when a freighter leaving the docks rammed his pontoon boat. In either event, he was cold and dead and not too many officials in law enforcement missed his passing. His companion, a man known as "Brownie" was never found.

"After the Big Man died there wasn't no more paychecks, so I came here."

"Mr. Guidry, I want you to consider this. We have just talked about the deaths of your associates. I can piece together the killing of the men who raped the girl, that makes sense, but I don't understand the killing of the other men."

"Why do you care about those men? All that happened a long time ago. It's over and I don't want to talk about it."

Indeed Gerald Guidry didn't want to talk about that part of his life. He considered himself to be the lucky one to have escaped from the wild men that killed his friends so easily and quickly. He always considered his escape to the swamps as the only thing that had saved his life. His one brush with the men this woman sought was enough to convince him to get out of Atlanta. They were deadly and Guidry didn't want to talk about them.

"I think it is time for you to leave. It will be dark soon and bad things can happen in the swamp at night. You should leave and don't come back here."

"Mr. Guidry, I care about these dead men because this entire mess looks like a war zone. It stinks of vigilante justice or a new organized crime syndicate. Either way, I am committed to getting to the bottom of these killings. And unless you want me to come back with a federal warrant, and take you to a grand jury you better come clean with what you know."

Angelina had no intention of fulfilling this threat, after all, the investigation she was charged with completing was limited to the deaths of the rape suspects, but she had a feeling that Gerald "Frenchy" Guidry didn't want any more dealing with the law than this short meeting with Angelina.

Guidry took a single step forward and the barrel of the shotgun pressed under Angelina's chin. For a brief moment Angelina knew

Frenchy was going to kill her and hide her body in the swamp as food for the gators. She was defenseless. She wondered if someone would find her body and tell her parents, or they would wonder about her fate for years to come. Guidry didn't pull the trigger, but stepped forward and removed the Glock from her belt and tossed it a few feet away. She felt his hand run over her shirt and figured what he was looking for when he asked, "Are you wearing a wire?"

Angelina hoped her sigh of relief was not as loud as she knew it must be, but with his question her senses told her the immediate danger had passed. She pulled her shirt from her slacks exposing her midriff. "No Mr. Guidry, I am not wearing a wire. Anything you tell me will stay between us."

Guidry lowered the shotgun from beneath her chin and stepped back. "I didn't have anything to do about the rape of the girl. I didn't know nothing about that until way later, and then only because the Big Man lost some money on a drug deal, and thought the girl's daddy might know where it was."

A drug deal associated with the rape? That was a new twist. "Tell me about the drugs."

Guidry spoke slowly trying to put his thoughts in reasonable order. "A couple of months after Bomani Thomas got life for killing those people at the courthouse, he sent word to Mr. Biggs that a con on the inside had people on the outside that had heroin to sell. Biggs agreed to the deal. Biggs told me that he figured he could make maybe $20 - $25 million.

"When they made the buy, the police were waiting for them. They lost the drugs and the $3,000,000 they had for the drug buy. It was a setup. Biggs had the people who lost the drugs killed. The Snowman killed two and left them in the lake. The people who sold them the drugs got away with the money. Biggs didn't think the police tried very hard to find the sellers, but as long as the police hadn't found them, then the Big Man still had a chance to get his money back."

Angelina interrupted the story. "Who is the Snowman?"

"He worked for Biggs, just like me."

"Go ahead."

"Biggs told Bomani to get the dealer names from the con on the inside. They both killed each other in a fight. Biggs sent a man to the con's funeral—Jackson was his name I think—and only two people showed up; the preacher and his wife. A couple of the boys recognized the preacher. The Big Man figured he must be connected to the drug deal, and that he knew who had his money."

"Say that again."

"What?"

"The part about the preacher attended the funeral."

"The preacher went to the funeral. Ain't no reason for a big preacher to go to a con's funeral unless he was in on the drug thing."

What was Reverend Walton's connection between Hanna's rape, the drug deal, and the killings in prison? "I don't understand. Why would Biggs think the preacher would have any idea who did the drug deal and where the money was?"

"Everybody else was dead. The Preacher was his only lead."

"Why would a high society preacher go to the funeral of a convict?"

"Maybe it was because the con killed the man who raped his daughter."

Angelina was stunned by Guidry's answer. The Reverend Walton knew it was Bomani Thomas who had raped his daughter?

"When did the preacher know it was Bomani Thomas who raped his daughter, and how did he know? Why didn't he report it to the police when the rape occurred?"

"The preacher knew it the day it happened. The preacher came down to Atlanta all the time to fuck with the hookers. He was in the house, in the back room, when Thomas and his gang was banging the girl. The preacher saw Thomas head-on, but he didn't do anything. He ran away. The preacher left the girl in that house to get raped and didn't do nothing to stop it."

Angelina could hardly believe what she had just heard. Crack Daddy had mentioned someone called the preacher had witnessed the rape. Was it possible the preacher who witnessed the rape was, in fact, the Reverend Peter Walton? It was hard to focus on the details when visions of the brutal rape continued to play in her head.

"Did the preacher know the girl was his daughter?"

"I don't think so. He never saw the girl. He probably just heard her crying. He probably didn't find out it was his little girl until later."

Angelina didn't want to hear the rest of what Frenchy had to say, but knew she must. "Go ahead."

"So Biggs tricked the preacher to come to Atlanta and tried to beat the information out of him, about where the money was. But the preacher didn't know nothing about the money, but the Snowman killed him anyway. Biggs figured the momma of the girl must know about the money, so he sent some of the boys to grab the momma. They went to her house, but got the girl instead."

Angelina noticed the entire story was in the second person. It was always the other guys doing the kidnapping and making the drug buys, never Mr. Guidry. Maybe he was protecting his own skin, but Angelina believed if he was involved with any of what was just said, then he would have pulled the trigger on the shotgun many minutes ago. Maybe this wild tale was the truth.

"The boys brought the girl to Biggs house. Biggs was going to use the girl to get to the mother. But before we...I mean, before they could get to the mother, some men snuck into the house and stole the girl from us. They came from nowhere. They didn't make any noise or nothing, and they broke into the house and killed everyone and took the girl. It took only a minute. I've never seen anything like it. I got off one shot and I think I hit one of them in the back, but nobody ever caught them. I think they were the same people that killed Mr. Biggs and Brownie on the river in Savannah. After Biggs was killed I came here. Those men was like ghosts. Every time the noise in the swamp stops, I expect to see them at my door. That's all I know."

Mr. Guidry lowered the shotgun to his side and started walking up the steps to his cypress prison. He stopped when he reached the top of the porch. Standing next to the skinned gator he addressed Angelina again. "Those men that did all that killing—they haunt my dreams. If I was you I wouldn't try to fuck with 'em. I don't think they would let you walk away like I am. Don't never tell no one that I told you those things, and don't come back here no more."

Guidry looked through the trees blocking the remaining rays of the setting sun. "It's getting dark and bad things happen in the swamp at night. If you value your life, get out before the dark comes."

Mr. Guidry and the dog entered the shack.

Picking up her sidearm, Angelina began the hike to her car and decided to take Mr. Guidry's advice and drive back to Atlanta tonight. The trip to the swamp had been very productive indeed, but raised more questions than it answered.

Chapter 16

The drive from Louisiana to Atlanta exhausted Angelina. The details of what she had learned rattled around in her brain, but the fatigue prevented any logical conclusions. She arrived at the condo at 3:30 AM but didn't really fall asleep until well past 4 a.m.

The work day was ruined. She was late to work, and then kept nodding off. She surrendered to the urge to sleep and finally stretched out on the couch in her office. She didn't stir until well past 6 p.m. When she woke, the hours on the couch caught up with her. She felt 60. She needed a workout. A couple hours at the gym might restart her body clock.

Angelina's gym was a vacated and remodeled grocery store just outside the high-rise area of downtown Atlanta. It certainly wasn't the flashy spas most young women select. Here, the clientele were hardcore exercise enthusiasts and concentrated on the physical tasks at hand rather than performing the peacock parade of beautiful bodies on the troll for a mate; doing just enough exercise to generate the glow of exertion but never enough work to actually break a healthy sweat.

She focused on the weights; forcing her mind on something other than the Hanna Walton case. When she finally found a vacant treadmill, the rhythm of her pace finally helped to focus her thoughts.

The miles ticked off as Angelina reviewed the case. What she knew: Hanna Walton, 15, was gang-raped and nobody charged with the crime. The mother was in New York on business and upon returning to Atlanta found that her husband had moved his daughter to Chattanooga for medical care. It may be worth her while to talk with the doctor—he may have insight into the bizarre behavior of the Reverend who ordered the destruction of evidence.

The one glaring question Angelina had was the connection between the rape and the drug deal talked about by Mr. Guidry. How and why was there any connection between the two? That didn't make sense and continued to bother her; that and the growing number of bodies. Where to go to learn about the drugs? The Atlanta PD would be a starting point, maybe the DEA. She should have access to both with her investigative charter from the Department of Justice.

And why was it so hard for the Atlanta Police department to connect the deaths of suspects with the rape, and the rape with the drugs, and the drugs with the murders? She connected the three events with two interviews. Just bad police work or a cover-up?

Angelina's treadmill, as were the others, was located at the front of the gym—probably by design. Since treadmills, stationary bikes and Stairmasters were the exercise machines most preferred by women, the image presented to those passing the front of the gym was designed to attract new customers. The close proximity of the front row of exercise equipment to the reflective glass, coupled with the bright lights inside the building reflecting back off the darkness of the night, provided an excellent mirror for Angelina to see everything happening to the rear of the gym.

In the back right corner of the gym was an area of linked rubber floor mats reserved for floor exercise. Tonight it was in use by two men locked in the most intensive combat she had ever seen; their struggle so violent that many had stopped their own exercise to watch. This was no show to impress the onlookers; the two combatants focused on the man to his front, watching his every move—fearful to let his opponent gain advantage. Even when the two broke from the fight they didn't sneak a look to see who they had impressed with their skills, but maintained focus. Angelina had received endless weeks of instruction on close combat techniques at the FBI Academy; enough to know these were not techniques to subdue, but to maim and kill. It was a chilling thought.

It was obvious the older of the two men was the instructor. He would stop the action—patiently explain shortcomings to the student—before they would re-engage. And when they re-engaged it was full speed, no pulled punches, no slow motion—full-out until the fatal blow was stopped just short of the target.

The instructor was a big man maybe 45 to 50. He was 210 to maybe 220 pounds and stood 6' 3" maybe 6' 4". From Angelina's vantage point there didn't appear to be any fat on his body—he looked like a Greek statue and almost as hard as the stone from which they were carved. She identified him as the instructor because after explaining a particular series of moves he would allow the student to flail away at him with reckless abandon—but the student could never land the killing blow. After allowing the student the opportunity to attack without regard to counter-attack, he would separate, and indicate the following session was full speed on both sides. Every time the student would be disabled within moments—helpless against the more skilled fighter who would then patiently repeat the lessons.

110

The one who really caught Angelina's eye was the student; a handsome black man about her own age with close cropped hair and an excellent physical specimen. Maybe she felt some compassion for the young man because—try as he did—he could never penetrate the defenses of his instructor. It didn't seem to cause him any embarrassment or concern that everyone in the gym could see he was getting his ass kicked. What was obvious to Angelina was that he soaked up every bit of instruction and was eager to learn more. He had a handsome face and somewhere in Angelina's past she knew she had seen this man before.

And then the session was over. So riveted to the action at the rear of the gym, Angelina had spent a solid hour on the treadmill. In so doing she ignored any more analysis of the Hanna Walton case. She realized she didn't feel the least bit fatigued after the long workout. Angelina thought how funny it was that the body could work so hard if you didn't allow your brain to think about the pain you were enduring; so engrossed she was with the two men at the rear of the gym that she had far exceeded her normal performance. A lesson she hoped she could always remember.

As she toweled the sweat from her face and arms she watched the two men. As the instructor slipped into tennis shoes and collected his things from a small pile of towels, keys, wallets and watches, the younger man bent at the waist with his hand on his knees—recovering from the exertions just endured. They engaged in conversation for a short while and when the instructor started toward the side exit, he put his arm around the shoulders of his student and together they walked to the door. It was a moment of tenderness that was more like a father consoling his son than an instructor and student, and it was a moment far from the violence of the lesson. The instructor turned and waved farewell to the student, and then he was gone.

The student collected his things from the mat and disappeared to the men's locker room. Still in Angelina's mind she knew she had seen the student before and the vaporous thought began to become an obsession; an obsession to figure out where she had seen this man before. But it was late and Angelina would have to figure that puzzle out another time.

Angelina stood outside the front entrance and let her eyes adjust to the dark of the night before venturing into the parking lot. Waiting for her eyes to adjust was the prudent and safe thing to do. Besides, the night air helped to cool her down from the excessive time on the treadmill.

And then the door to the gym opened, hitting her in the back at its full extension, and the young student was standing next to her. Her presence must have been a surprise to him. "Oh, excuse me. I didn't know anyone was here. I hope I didn't hurt you."

Angelina jumped a bit with the force of the door. The man was more attractive than she had first imagined and she found herself somewhat stammering for words. "It was my fault. I shouldn't have been so close to the door. No damage done."

The man looked into the dark depths of the parking lot and understood the concerns a woman would have walking to her car unescorted at this time of the night. "I'm Eric Brown. May I escort you to your car? That parking lot is kind of dark."

Angelina was impressed, not only with the manner in which the man offered his help but in the manner in which he addressed her; with respect and without the normal "Yo, Girl or mamma, or some stupid and hackneyed pick-up line.

Angelina extended her hand. "I'm Angelina Sanchez. Thank you for the offer, but I was only waiting here for my eyes to adjust to the dark. I can make it on my own. But thank you for the offer."

But Eric Brown suspected there was a little bravado in her refusal. "Nonsense, there is no reason for a woman to be alone in this part of town in the middle of the night. Please allow me to see you to your car. You really should park closer to the door. You never can tell who might be out there."

Normally Angelina, as most women, would decline such an offer from a stranger, but for some reason she felt more secure in the presence of Eric Brown than she was worried about a possible lack of character in him. "OK, I'm parked near the front of the lot."

As they walked through the parking lot Angelina brought up the just completed session of martial arts training. "I watched you and your instructor. You guys really go at it pretty hard."

Eric gave a slight chuckle. "You're right. He's a pretty intense guy, but he's not my instructor. He's just a friend."

"Where does he teach?" This conversation was as good as any to have with someone you just met; it really was their only common ground. As Angelina carried on the conversation she couldn't put it out of her mind that she knew this man from somewhere else in her past.

"Are you interested in the martial arts?"

"No, not really, it just seemed to be different than anything I've ever seen. It didn't seem to be a sport, but more intense, more dangerous. That cut on your lip and that bump on your head is evidence of that."

Eric ran his tongue to the corner of his mouth and tasted a trace of blood; his hand over his forehead and felt the growing bump on his head. "Oh, great! That's going to look real good at work tomorrow."

That's when Angelina knew where she'd seen her new acquaintance before. "I thought I recognized you! You're a news anchor on CNN aren't you? I knew I'd seen you before."

"Yep, sure enough, I'm one of the talking heads. Do you watch the show often? I haven't been doing it that long and could use any constructive criticisms."

Up to this point Eric had enjoyed the conversation because it had not been centered on his notoriety as a television celebrity. If this girl was like so many others, the fawning would now start about how good he was, and how he made the entire newscast, and usually would continue ad-nauseam to the point of driving Eric away. But this girl surprised him.

"I've seen you a couple of times. I think you do a good job. Do you enjoy it?"

"I'm getting used to it. It took me a while to read from the teleprompter without following each word with my eyes. I still have a lot to learn."

To Eric's surprise Angelina's questions and comments were just as often critical as complimentary. It was refreshing. Eventually Eric was able to steer the conversation to Angelina.

"How about you, what do you do for a living?"

Oh, great, now comes the part where she scares him off when he finds out she is a Federal Agent. It was only a small white lie, "I am doing case studies on women's health; boring, but it pays the bills."

The walk to the car had been at a pace more suited to discussion than covering the distance. Once at the car Angelina couldn't think of any topic worthy of continuing the conversation. "Well, here we are. Thanks for walking me to the car. I will try and watch you tomorrow. I hope that bump goes down."

Eric waited until Angelina was seated and buckled in before he assisted in closing the door. He bid goodnight with, "Nice talking with you."

Eric enjoyed the time with Angelina and hoped he would have the chance to see her again.

Chapter 17

Ken Carson couldn't explain how the affair started. Was it the flirtatious looks from Karen when Rachael's back was turned that always led to the banter that degenerated into innuendo and coy sexual challenges? Or, was it the way Karen always positioned herself in just the right manner to reveal more than a generous amount of cleavage every time she removed a beer from the cooler? It was so easy to take the next step, and it happened shortly after they moved into the Tybee house. It was the weekend he and Rachael celebrated the opening of their new pool.

Rachael invited Karen and her latest boy-toy. Karen always had an ample supply of boyfriends; Ken knew she rode 'em until she broke 'em. As soon as the gifts of jewelry or clothes started to dry up, Karen could easily trade up to one with even more money. Where Rachael's beauty carried with it a demanding and haughty nature, Karen's beauty was even more stunning and her demeanor exuded not quite a sinister aura of sexuality, but more that of the forbidden fruit constantly dangled before him. Always just out of reach until that day at the pool.

The new house, deck, and pool, all overlooked the Atlantic Ocean on exclusive Tybee Island. It was the first big purchase since his promotion. In Ken's opinion, this home more accurately reflected his status and importance as a senior manager—almost vice-president level you know.

With only a few improvements they would be ready to begin entertaining in the manner expected of such an important and influential man. Ken knew the house was premature for his current income, but Rachael had been adamant and therefore the decision was out of Ken's hands.

And so on that day, with Ken sketching a landscape plan for the pool, and Rachael fluttering around with accent pieces to gain just the right look, and the boyfriend soaking up the tanning rays, Karen presented the forbidden fruit to her brother-in-law.

Only Rachael noticed Karen's departure from the pool. The sisters exchanged ever-so-slight smiles and Rachael allowed her sister to get into the house before she asked, "Ken honey, would you bring that box of colored glass balls from the garage? You know the ones with the rope nets around them? I think they would look great under these tables."

Ken put down his rough drawings and pulled another beer from the cooler. He needed the beer because no telling where that damn box was, and it was hot in the garage. As Ken made his way to the house Rachael's eyes followed his progress until he disappeared through the sliding glass door into the den.

As was his habit, Ken stopped by the refrigerator and rummaged around, clanking glass jars until he found the kosher dill pickles. He pulled the largest one from the container and stuck it in his mouth. With pickle in one hand and bottle of beer in the other he made his way down the hall leading to the garage. And there to his left, the short hall leading into one of the guest bathrooms, door ajar, he had clear sight of Karen in front of the mirror. Her tanned body glistened in the lights of the mirror while she rubbed lotion on her face, breasts, and down to her stomach. Ken stood transfixed. He couldn't take his eyes off her seductive body.

When she slowly turned her eyes to Ken it didn't seem to bother her that she caught him in the act of spying on her. Karen knew every man was a voyeur at his core and in many ways she enjoyed the power she held over them.

"Oh, Ken, I didn't hear you come in. You surprised me." Ken noticed she didn't stop the slow application of lotion to her body. "Would you mind putting some of this lotion on my back? I don't want to burn."

Ken gave a furtive glance back down the hall to the kitchen, wondering if this venture into the bathroom was worth the risk. He could see through the cracks of the window that Rachael was still busy with her decorating, and that Karen's boyfriend seemed fast asleep on the pool deck. He threw caution to the wind. "Sure. No problem, anything you want."

Ken left the door ajar when he entered the bathroom and then placed his beer and pickle on the counter. He took the bottle of lotion from Karen. "How much should I use?"

Karen turned back to Ken, brushing her breast against his extended hand, "That should be enough. You will have a lot of rubbing to do. Make sure you spread it evenly."

Ken rubbed the lotion between his palms. He started at her shoulders and worked down her back and forward to her sides. Her skin was soft and supple and Ken would swear a moan of pleasure escaped from her lips. As he worked his way down her back to the top of her bikini bottom he saw her reflection in the mirror. Her eyes were closed and head tilted back and she looked somewhat flushed, her checks and throat seemed to almost burn red with passion. "Make sure you get under the straps and under the hem."

Ken reached around Karen and added another squirt of lotion to his already saturated hands. As he placed the bottle on the counter he felt Karen tilt her hips back and up and gently push back against his groin. The sensation was one that Ken had yearned for since the first time he laid eyes on his wife's sister. Ken's hands slid easily under the thin straps that were straining to hold Karen's breasts, and when he did so Karen reached to the door and pushed it shut. "Here," she said, "let me help you with that," and Karen reached behind her an unbuckled the strap.

Ken's hands moved forward to the sides of her breasts and then forward to fully grasp them and slowly massaged the tender skin and hardening nipples; and she did nothing to resist and let escape another moan of pleasure. Ken's lotion covered hands moved down the sides of her body easily sliding into and under the elastic of the suit. He hooked his forefinger and thumbs into the suit and easily pulled the garment down over her buttocks. The tan of her skin contrasted the white purity of the skin covered by the suit. As he gazed in wonder at the beauty of her body he felt her hand reach back and fondle his manhood through the cloth of his shorts.

It was over in a moment. All the sexual pleasures that Ken dreamed in his years of coveting the sister of his wife were laid before him for the taking. The low moans from Karen and his panting breath echoed off the tiled walls of the small space; and his legs quivered with the exertion of the act. As he stood pressed up against Karen he glanced into the mirror and saw the beads of sweat dripping onto the back and buttocks of Karen. Karen didn't move away, but held pressure against Ken as if she didn't want the experience to end, and that fed Ken's ego even more. He ran his hands from her hair and down her back and circled her waist pulling her to him again and wondered at the beauty of her skin and how beautiful it looked pressed to his. He exhaled a deep sigh of satisfaction, but was startled back to reality when he heard the hall door to the garage close. He looked through the crack in the window, there by the pool lay Karen's new boyfriend, but no Rachael!

117

Waves of panic engulfed him. How would he explain this to his wife? There could be no reasonable explanation; he had cheated on his wife with her sister. Hoping to escape with some dignity he pulled his shorts up and with nothing more than, "Oh, shit!" and Ken eased out of the bathroom. The hall was empty. Karen must be in the garage looking for the glass balls. Ken quickly retreated upstairs, taking the steps as lightly as possible but two at a time to the guest bath at the top of the stairs. Once there he made great ado with raising and dropping the toilet seat and flushing the toilet. That would explain his delay in returning to the patio.

As he made his way down the stairs he heard Rachael call out to him, "Ken!" And then she called again, "Ken!"

As he turned from the stairs toward the garage he came face to face with his wife. She was standing in the short hall directly in front of the bathroom where he had been just moments before. "Where have you been?" Rachael's voice carried the same demanding tone that it always did when she addressed her husband.

"I had to use the bathroom. Is that O.K.?" Ken's heartbeat started to drop closer to normal. Maybe he hadn't been caught. "I'm getting the balls now. I'll be right out."

"Don't bother. I don't think they will look good anyway. That's what I came in to tell you."

It was then that Karen emerged from the bathroom with some casual remark about the, "sun's going down…can't waste it." When Karen moved out of the doorway, there on the counter of the bathroom lay Ken's beer and half eaten pickle. If Rachael noticed and put two and two together then all would be lost. Karen slid her arm through Rachael's, "Come on big sister, let's go see what you've done with your decorations."

~~

That was their first encounter and every succeeding one was just as seductive and exciting. Karen had a way of making Ken feel like a man. She always responded to his touch and satisfied his every forbidden desire. Karen never mentioned her sister, and Ken was more than willing to leave the taboo subject at rest. It was their secret and Ken believed Karen received as much satisfaction from their times together as did he. Karen was a good listener and simply an uninhibited sex machine in bed.

Ken took little notice when Karen started to guide their conversations to money. "Ken, you seem to be doing really well down at the bank. What's the secret?"

Ken wanted to impress Karen with his modesty. "I guess I've just been lucky with some of my investments."

Karen slid her hand under the sheets and onto Ken's abdomen. "Ken, I hate to bring this up, but I could use some help. I haven't been able to find a job. If I can't find something soon I'll have to move to Atlanta. There are more jobs up there."

Move to Atlanta? That was the last thing Ken wanted to hear. It may take a few more loans, but he would find a way to keep Karen in Savannah.

~~

The excitement in Danni's voice was obvious. "Dad, you've got to get over here and see what McTavish has done. The guy is a genius! Half the cottages are already renovated, he has half the foundations laid for our main street shops, he has three docks in the lagoon completed, and the classroom and theater are almost complete. I can't believe somebody this good couldn't find work."

Ed was proud of what Danni had accomplished at the resort. She had thrown herself into the task with a dedication that did not surprise her father. The main street shops were taking shape, and Danni had commitments from the finest shops and boutiques in Savannah and Charleston as tenants on the new Main Street. Professors at five southern universities agreed support their summer educational programs with lectures, and young Brian Vance passed his Sea Captain Certification test and was setting up the sailing school. There was a lot of work to be done, but the gamble looked like it would pay off. Reservations for the summer months were up 25 percent over projections, and twice as many as the resort did last year. The Daufuskie Resort was the only bright spot of economic activity from the Florida State line to North Carolina, and the word was getting out.

As his daughter continued to bend his ear with details of progress, Ed casually reviewed his lengthy list of emails. Danni was so enthusiastic about the resort that only occasionally would Ed be required to add to the conversation, and then only with a simple, "Uh huh," or "I like it." He enjoyed the musical tone of his daughter's voice and could have passed the afternoon simply listening to her, but an email came up on his screen and soured his disposition.

"Danni, something has just come up. Can I get back to you?"

"Oh, I'm sorry, Daddy. I guess I do go a little overboard. I'll let you go, but only if you promise you will visit soon. There is so much I want to show you."

As the email from Ronald Bartholomew came to life on the computer screen, Ed answered his daughter. "I promise."

A redundant, but accurate, description of Ed's understanding of the message sent by Bartholomew was simply incredulous disbelief. Ed scanned the message twice and the words must have been meant for another bank, not the Coastal Bank. "…in accordance with the Banes-Adams Act it has been determined that the Coastal Bank is vital to the economic stability of the economy of the United States of America…transfer of $500,000,000 to your account…normal fees and repayment apply…repayment after your bank is deemed financially sound…your current salary and bonus schedule and the same for your vice presidents and board of directors…under penalty of law...meeting in Atlanta to discuss new Federal Regulations…"

As Ed printed two copies of the email he reached for the phone. "Mr. Carson, I'm forwarding you an email from Bartholomew. There is a meeting in Atlanta to discuss new Federal Regulations. I want you to represent the bank."

~~

Danni was a little rebuffed by her father's sudden dismissal of her. She didn't have long to dwell on it though when Mamba entered the room. Her message was strange. "Tell Hanna she shouldn't go."

"Go where?"

"I'm not sure, but tell her she shouldn't go."

"Mamba, you're talking nonsense. Hanna hasn't said anything about going anywhere. What are you talking about?"

The phone interrupted Mamba's explanation. Danni picked up the phone. It was Hanna on the other end, and she was bubbling with excitement.

"Momma, Jimmy got a new job. We're going to Israel!"

Chapter 18

Bill wanted to tell Danni about the trip to Kuwait. Not that he needed or wanted her approval, but for the first time in his life he felt it was proper to inform someone of his decision.

Bill was a little shocked when asked by the gentleman attending the information counter if Mrs. Walton was expecting him; in essence, did he have an appointment? Maybe Bill's baseball cap, island shirt, Bermuda shorts and sandaled feet didn't fit into the swank lobby of the resort, but Bill had seen many guests dressed exactly as he was, or maybe this stuffed shirt knew he wasn't a hotel guest. Maybe that was his reason for the cold reception.

"Just tell Mrs. Walton that Bill Cannon would like to see her for a few minutes. It is a personal matter."

It was only a short wait before Bill was escorted into the depths of the hotel to an office overlooking the Atlantic Ocean. "Mrs. Walton is expecting you Mr. Cannon, this way please."

Bill found Danni standing behind a conference table with detailed drawing of the resort grounds spread from edge to edge of the large table. She didn't notice Bill's entrance until the secretary announced him. "Mrs. Walton, Mr. Cannon is here." Bill had suddenly become an appointment. He didn't know if he liked that.

Danni looked up from her work—she didn't come from behind the desk and greet him with a kiss or hug as he would have liked—not that she had ever done that before, but there was always that hope.

"Bill, I'm glad you came. Come here and take a look at this little lagoon. Do you think Mike would be able to run fishing charters from that lagoon without dredging a channel?"

When Bill came around the table and stood beside Danni, he could smell the soft aroma of her perfume. Bill watched her mouth move as she explained her concept of a fishing charter for the hotel guests. Her hair fell in front of her face and only added more mystery to this woman he wanted as his own. But she wasn't interested in romantic overtures that Bill never found the words or time or courage to explain; she was interested in the lagoon. "Bill...Bill, what do you think? Can Mike launch from this lagoon?"

Bill finally looked to the drawings on the table. "It's big enough and well protected from the sea, but will probably require some dredging to accommodate low tide, and the tides can run 15 feet in this area. You get it dredged out and I think he could do it."

Danni went from the lagoon to new proposed riding trails, a concept to build an antebellum street of shops for the guests, a par three golf course to compliment the two championship courses already in operation, expanded riding stables with riding classes for children, and the list went on. Bill enjoyed listening to her talk. The task of turning the resort around had given her new focus on life. Bill secretly hoped one day he might become her new focus. A knock of the office door interrupted Bill's thoughts.

"Mrs. Walton, the chef is here for your 10:00 o'clock appointment."

Bill's hour had been squandered on hotel plans and Danni realized she hadn't given him a chance to state the purpose of his visit. "Have him wait for only a moment. I'm sorry Bill. I seem to have forgotten my manners. I never let you get a word in edgewise."

"I just wanted to tell you I'll be out of the country for a while. I'm going to Kuwait. I don't know how long I will be gone."

The grandeur of Danni's visions for the resort suddenly didn't seem so important. Did she hear Bill correctly? "You're going to Kuwait, why?"

"Lucas McLaughlin asked me to go check out a few things, and it's been a long time since I've seen Prince Al-Sabah." Bill saw no reason to bother Danni with the questionable circumstances surrounding his visit.

"You can't just send a letter or call him?" Danni couldn't explain, but why did she suddenly feel less secure? Would it be fair to ask Bill to stay? No, it wouldn't.

"Danni, he's a good friend. It's been a long time since I've seen him."

She knew Bill was right, but it didn't make her feel any better. "Well...you're right, but I can't say I'm happy about it. Oh, by the way, Hanna called the other day. Jimmy is being assigned to a military attaché post in Israel. Maybe you can look them up when you get over there."

Bill grinned, "Israel and Kuwait aren't exactly neighbors, but I will try."

This could have been one of those awkward moments, you know the kind where you don't know if you should kiss good bye, hug, shake hands, or just leave. But the awkward moment didn't touch Danni in the same manner as it did Bill. Maybe it was simply a defensive mechanism, or maybe she was hurt that Bill would rather visit his friend than stay and help her with the resort, but Danni turned her attention back to the drawings.

As Bill retreated from the office Danni called to him. "Bill." He wondered if this was the goodbye where she would come from behind the table and tell him hurry back, that she would miss him, and ask him not to go. But instead, all he got was, "You won't forget to check in on Hanna and Jimmy?"

"No Danni, I won't forget."

The hall leading from Danni's new office now seemed a cold and confining maze. Maybe he wanted her to say, "Don't go." Maybe he wanted a reason to decline the offer to visit his old friend; but that didn't happen. Danni had politely dismissed him as she would have anyone intruding on her busy schedule. Bill left Danni's office a much more lonely man than when he entered. There was nothing holding him here.

Danni felt "it" when Bill left the office. The "it" was Bill's departure pulled the oxygen and life from the room. The hour they spent together had flashed by and now he was gone. Danni felt a pang of what she could describe as panic, not the panic of fear, but the type you feel when you can't find your credit card. Something always taken for granted until you can't find it. Did you leave it at the store, or at the restaurant, or simply misplace it? Was it in the kitchen or on your dresser or had it fallen to the ground and now in the hands of someone enjoying a shopping spree on your dime?

Danni realized she didn't want Bill to leave. She knew she couldn't stop him—he was his own man—but she always felt secure knowing Bill Cannon wasn't far away. He had in many ways become her security blanket. Danni knew she was always safe when Bill was near—and now he was leaving the country. She really hadn't concentrated on what Bill said. How long would he be gone? Maybe he hadn't said. How could she get in touch with him if she needed him? He hadn't told her—no—more accurately she hadn't given him a chance to tell her these things.

Danni threw her pen and notes on the table and in that hurried gait women use to get passed people they want to ignore, walked through the waiting room. Her assistant and the head chef looked a little stunned when she rushed by them with only a, "I'll be right back."

Danni caught Bill in the hall waiting for the elevator. "Caught" might be a slight misrepresentation—actually she ran into him while he was waiting for the elevator. She turned the corner and "bam!" there he was. Now that she caught him, she couldn't think how to phrase a decent question and an embarrassing blush started to color her cheeks. Danni tried to stammer her way out of this compromising situation. "Uh, Bill, ummm…when are you coming back?"

Bill almost had Danni in his arms and didn't want to totally release her. He let his arm circle her waist for a moment too long before he started to relax his hold. It would not have been proper to kiss her here in the halls of her hotel—he wanted to, but would not be so forward.

"I'm not sure; maybe a couple of weeks to a month, at most. When I get to Kuwait, I'll call DeAngelo with my number. You can always get in touch with me through him."

Danni felt Bill's arm slide from her waist. Why hadn't he just pulled her closer to him and given her a reason to kiss him goodbye? She knew the answer: because he was Bill Cannon and wouldn't do that. Danni kept her hand on Bill's forearm and said, "Thank you for coming to say goodbye." And Danni did it before she really knew why. She stretched up on her toes and kissed Bill on the cheek. Now Bill's face burned red. "Hurry back and be safe."

Danni was smiling as she turned on her heels and straightened her suit as she made her way back to her office. She heard Bill stammer something barely coherent like, "Umm, yeah, you…I will."

Danni felt like she had just found her credit card—right where she remembered she had left it.

Bill decided in that instant there was indeed something holding him here. Danni was the reason to come back.

While Bill Cannon was bidding farewell to Danni, Ken Carson was struggling to pay attention at the conference in Atlanta.

~~

Every word was important. The essence of each new Federal policy, if one understood how to use the system to your own benefit, could make even more money for Ken Carson. Even with the future at stake, Ken Carson found it hard to pay attention to Donald Bartholomew and the other administrators at the conference.

The Government declared The Coastal Bank, and every bank at the conference, vital to the economic stability and recovery of the nation's economy. What that meant was more oversight and regulation.

The government would buy, at current stock price, 50 percent of the bank's preferred stock. Taxpayer money used to gain control over the banking business. The American public generally supported the measure; after all, the government and spin-doctors placed the blame for the economic collapse directly on the banks and Wall Street. The public bought it hook line and sinker. The government believed the cash infusion should make it easier for the banks to loan money again, and that would ignite the economy.

Banks would be allowed to purchase back the stocks when the government determined the economy was sufficiently recovered, and the individual banks were solvent.

Carson knew what Helton would say. He would say the government was buying stock at deflated prices, holding them during the recovery, and then selling them back at inflated prices. It would cost Coastal Bank millions. Ken Carson couldn't care less; he didn't hold any Coastal Bank stock.

There was also the billions of dollars the government would loan the bank. Carson also knew what Helton would say about that. He would say that a reckless loan program was exactly what got the country into this economic mess. Ken knew they would have to make loans with the money. Not even Coastal Bank could afford to pay the interest on the government money without getting the money into the economy, and Ken Carson would earn commission on every penny loaned.

Ken found the information valuable but it was more enjoyable to think about the night ahead with Karen. They would hit all the hottest clubs, and then spend the rest of the evening in their suite high atop the Atlanta Westin Hotel, you know, the one with the revolving restaurant on the top. They would lay naked with the curtains pulled back for the world to see. The conference was perfect for the rendezvous.

But until tonight he had to concentrate. He knew Helton would want a detailed explanation of the new regulations.

The Atlanta night life was everything Ken thought it would be. Ken knew he looked good driving the Mercedes and Karen was absolutely stunning in her dress that must have been painted to her body;

how she could reveal everything while revealing nothing was an amazing thing. At every club, Ken could feel the envy of the other men, and knew the women thought he must be rich to have such a beautiful woman at his side.

Karen played the clubs like Cinderella at the ball. Making small talk—intermingled with delightful little squeals of humor—with the men who eyed her with lustful looks, but she always returned to Ken; something that only fed Ken's ego.

The deeper into the evening the more the liquor flowed and the more Ken was captured by Karen's beauty. Karen always had a way of being seductive; her hand lingering too long on your arm, or getting close enough to just brush her breasts against you, or bending forward while reaching for a drink in such a way you could almost see to her sculptured stomach. She had an alluring way of standing, with her feet positioned at a perfect right angle, arms dangling at her side, and then turning her head and upper body to the side exposing the perfect silhouette. Ken had to admit, his sister-in-law was one luscious package, and she was his for the taking, and he wanted her now.

"Karen, let's get out of here."

Karen leaned against Ken, "Why, aren't you having a good time?"

"Sure, but I want to have a different kind of good time."

Karen giggled. "Silly, we can do that right here."

"We can't do what I have in mind right here."

Karen pressed her firm buttocks against Ken while they waited for the valet to retrieve the Benz. Ken thought he should buy some stock in the company that designed and built the Stairmaster because from his vantage point it was working wonders on Karen. She alternated pressing against Ken and reaching back to feel with her hand to gage the affect she was having. She wasn't disappointed. Ken had a hard time walking to the car in such a manner as to conceal his aroused state.

By the time they reached the penthouse Ken was ready to explode. Karen moved Ken to the side of the bed and exposed his manhood and knelt before him. Ken's moans of pleasure told Karen what she wanted to know—he was hers for the taking. She stood and said, "Let's see what you've got, big boy."

Karen undid the belt and let his trousers fall to the floor. As Ken struggled with the remainder of his clothes she moved to the dresser and removed the blue sapphire pendant from around her neck and the matching bracelet from her wrist. She had purchased them last week specifically for this trip. She purchased them in the same department store where she purchased the miniature digital video camera she concealed in her purse.

As her gown fell to the floor, two thoughts crossed her mind. The first was that technology is amazing. The second was that men are so stupid.

Chapter 19

Angelina's visit to the doctor in Chattanooga, the man who destroyed DNA evidence at the order of Hanna's father, did nothing but confirm he did what Reverend Peter Walton requested. "Better to keep this quiet," was the only reason Peter Walton had given to justify his strange request.

How Tyrell Biggs ever linked Peter Walton to the missing drug money was still a mystery. It was beyond the pale and almost an unbelievable coincidence that both Crack Daddy and Frenchy mentioned a preacher in the house when the girl was raped, and Frenchy as good as identified Reverend Peter Walton as that preacher. Was Peter Walton witness to the rape of his daughter? Was Peter Walton involved in the heroin deal? Both were stupid thoughts and Angelina tried to push them from her mind, but it seemed all too possible that both were true.

You are judged by those with whom you associate, and getting killed with a prostitute in your car, especially one listed as a witness in the case of your daughter's rape, certainly tarnished the sanctity of the Reverend Peter Walton. Angelina wondered if the wife of Reverend Walton, Danni Walton, was aware of these bizarre circumstances.

With Crack Daddy's confession, the facts of the rape case were now firmly established. What remained to be discovered: if the deaths of the rapists were the result of vigilante police justice as Crack Daddy thought, or a rival gang of ruthless killers as Frenchy seemed to indicate. In either case, the truth was always there, hidden somewhere in violence of the rape, the drug bust, or the deaths of so many. The death of the gang leader, Bomani Thomas, at least had a name associated with the event: John B. Jackson. The killers of the others remained free.

Frenchy said Bomani Thomas brokered the drug deal from inside the prison, and served as the conduit for the information. Was Jackson the conduit for the drug information into the prison? If he was, then his past may shed light on the truth.

Angelina knew the deaths of the other three rape suspects were never linked to the rape. In fact, the death of the three probably would have been welcomed by the police; culling the herd, so to speak. The rape case was closed and put deep in the dead file before any of the suspects met with their deaths. She supposed there was no valid reason to open a dead file to post the demise of the suspects, but it did raise questions as to the competency of the Atlanta PD.

Frenchy said the murder of Reverend Walton was associated with Tyrell Biggs trying to recover the money he lost on the drug deal. It didn't take long to find the details of the most famous drug bust in Georgia history. The Internet was full of articles about the joint operation between the Atlanta Police Depart and the Drug Enforcement Agency.

All the killings occurred after the bust and a full two years after the rape. Angelina concluded the drug deal was the catalyst for the killings. One name in particular was mentioned in all the reports: Officer Steve Thunder, Atlanta PD.

Officer Steve Thunder was the leader of the Atlanta PD Anti-Drug Task Force. It was his intelligence that pinpointed the location of the drop. It was Officer Steve Thunder who tracked the buyers through the North Georgia woods and recovered the drugs. It was Officer Steve Thunder who mounted a one-man campaign to prove Tyrell Biggs was behind the drug deal.

Steve Thunder seemed to be the perfect police officer. Dedicated and unwavering in his pursuit of justice, but Angelina had her doubts. Thunder's name also appeared on the investigation into the death of Reverend Peter Walton. Thunder's contribution to the report established the premise that Peter Walton was killed during a personal investigation into the rape, and that he was killed when he was close to identifying the rapists. It read well and the rationale made it easy to close the case; but Angelina knew it was a total fabrication and nowhere near the truth.

She had only one problem. Officer Steve Thunder was killed on a drug raid, but he had to have a file and he had to have friends she could question. Angelina put the review of Officer Thunder's file on the white board secured to the wall in the office.

Was the good reverend involved with drugs? Certainly the articles on the Internet didn't paint that picture. Everything on the net was a glowing report of a leader in the community and a beloved leader of one of the largest churches in Atlanta. The police files didn't have much more. The first entry under Reverend Walton was the reported rape of his daughter. The second entry dealt with his death and the investigation surrounding it. The third entry was an innocuous entry concerning a home invasion of the Walton residence. Angelina was preparing to exit from the report when she noticed the date of the home invasion. It was the same date Reverend Peter Walton was found murdered on the river. That couldn't be a simple coincident.

When she clicked on the report, Angelina was amazed by two items. The first was the brevity of the report, and the second, the content. The executive summary read that a burglar broke into the Walton residence. When discovered, the burglar killed the house-keeper. The perpetrator was shot and killed by a man named Buford Long.

Buford Long, a name from out of the blue—no official title, no department affiliation, nothing but the name on an official report of a death in a private residence. That was unusual.

Angelina Googled the name and the details were impressive. Buford Long was a retired law enforcement official. During his extensive career he served with the FBI, was the head of the Georgia Bureau of Investigation, and finally retired after serving 20 some years as sheriff of Chatham County. Okay, maybe he had the credentials to sign off on a report of the home invasion, but what was he doing in the Walton residence on the day Reverend Walton was murdered?

The FBI's national data base was full of cases involving Buford Long. The data base accurately listed all his cases with the FBI, his cases as head of the GBI, those as the sheriff of Chatham County, and even the home invasion of the Walton residence was listed.

There was only one additional entry. It was strangely similar to the home invasion of the Walton residence. Except in this report, Buford Long was a victim of a home invasion as a guest of Mr. Ed Helton, on Daufuskie Island, South Carolina.

A home invasion where one man was killed, two wounded, and three arrested. The report of the home invasion on Daufuskie Island was as brief as the report of the home invasion in Atlanta. Maybe Buford Long simply attracted trouble, but the interesting thing about this second report was the name of the owner of the residence: Ed Helton. Where did Angelina see the name Helton? Oh, yeah…Helton was Danni Walton's maiden name.

That's it? Two sketchy reports to cover armed home invasions of the Walton residence in Atlanta, and then the Helton residence on Daufuskie Island; reports that mention the death of the intruders only in passing?

Were the police blind or did they intentionally ignore the connection? Home invasions didn't happen every day…and the same family victim of two such events in a relatively short span of time? It was near impossible to believe the police didn't connect the violence at Helton's residence with the same event at the Walton residence. They were in-laws for God's sake. It was an amazing coincidence or blatant cover-up—that no-one made the connection until now. Angelina rose from her computer and put Buford Long's name on the board.

When Angelina reviewed the day's work, the sequence of events and persons of interest that now crowded the board in her office resembled the ramblings of a day-time soap opera. When she tried to put them in a logical sequence, she knew the investigation was ambitious and only beginning. The rape, the drug deal, the death of Bomani Thomas, the death of Peter Walton, the associated killings, the home invasion, the names of people to investigate; it was an overwhelming undertaking, but no better time to start than now.

She called down to records. "Mr. Griffin, would you please pull the personnel file on Officer Steve Thunder and bring it to my office?"

"I'll be right up."

Angelina leaned back in her chair to contemplate the task that lay ahead. She would research Thunder this weekend and get to Buford Long and John B. Jackson next week.

"Here is the file you requested. Why do you need Thunder's file? He was a drug guy and I hate to tell you, but he's dead."

"I am well aware of that Mr. Griffin. He conducted an investigation of a murder that may relate to one of the cases I am studying. I wanted some background information on him, that's all. You wouldn't happen to know if any of the officers he worked with are still with the force?"

"I don't know any of the officers on his strike force, but his best friend was Doc Broderson."

"Who?"

"Doc Broderson, the medic; you met him your first week here. He helped me bring the records up. Thunder and Doc were in the Army together. When they retired, Thunder signed on with the police department and Doc signed on with the county as a meat-wagon driver."

Angelina did recall meeting the medic. She thought nothing of him at the time except he looked harder than most. She would put the medic on her list to see next week.

"Thank you for bringing me the file. I should be finished with it this weekend and will return it on Monday." Angelina dismissed him with, "Have a good weekend."

Angelina dove into the file. The report of his death was tragic in that he wasn't killed by a crazed out of control druggie, but by an 89-year-old woman simply trying to protect her home. He was shot in the back of the head by the home-owner when he tried in vain to stop a no-knock warrant. The intelligence for the raid was provided by a confidential informant named Brownie. Angelina noted the name immediately. Was this Brownie the same Brownie that disappeared on the Savannah River with Tyrell Biggs? Did she read that in a report? Or, was it Frenchy who mentioned the name? It didn't matter; the connection was worth checking out.

She reviewed the entire file and only one other name was listed as a confidential informant. That name: Bomani Thomas. For an officer on the anti-drug task force she would have expected a more extensive list. Was Bomani Thomas the source that pinpointed the drop? Stranger things had happened.

How many were killed after Thunder's death that had the possibility of being linked to what Angelina considered a growing conspiracy? By her count at least three: Tyrell Biggs, Brownie, and one man in the Helton residence. Did Steve Thunder have friends on the police force who were not afraid to exact revenge? Who were the men who avenged the death of Steve Thunder and were they the same men Frenchy referred to as ghosts and still feared to this day?

All this went through her mind in the brief span of 30 minutes. So intriguing the mystery, she probably would have worked into the night; if not for the email tone on her computer.

"Hello, are you working out tonight?"

Angelina looked at the sending address and didn't recognize it, *talkinghead@cnn.com*.

She typed back, "Who is this?"

"Eric Brown. We met the other night at the gym, remember?"

The brief visit with Eric Brown had been the highlight of her social life in Atlanta.

"Of course I remember." She hadn't given any thought to working out this evening but now her plans may have to change. "I had planned to; got to keep the butt small enough to fit into my jeans." She regretted her silly attempt at humor the moment she hit the send button.

"May I treat you to dinner after the gym? I know a quaint little spot. Good down-home cooking."

More work, or dinner, with the first man in Atlanta she found interesting? It wasn't hard for Angelina to make the decision. "Eric, I would love to have dinner with you."

"Great, see you at the gym."

It wasn't necessarily her nature to be suspicious, but she didn't remember giving Eric her email address, or where she worked. She typed, "How did you get my address?"

"I'm a famous reporter. It's my job to find out these things. I've got to get to a meeting. See you at the gym after the news." Eric had simply asked the gym operator for the email address on her club application.

If she hurried, she could get home, change, pack some clothes for dinner, and catch some of the broadcast before going to the gym. She didn't often take the time to watch the broadcast, but tonight she wanted to catch the entire show to have sufficient ammunition for discussions during dinner.

Angelina gambled that black slacks with low heels, a cashmere sweater and single strand of pearls would be sufficient to gain entry into any restaurant. As Eric signed off the news she loosely packed her clothes to avoid wrinkles and made her way to the gym. She hung her clothes in a locker and started her stretching routine. She kept her eye on the front door when she was startled by a greeting from the rear.

It was Eric. "Angelina, what do you have planned tonight?"

Angelina regained her composure and brushed a lock of hair from her face. "Hello Eric, I really hadn't given it much thought; a light round of weights and then maybe the treadmill."

"Great, if you don't mind the company why don't we work out together?"

Angelina planned a light workout, but once she and Eric started lifting, the competitive juices started flowing. Eric pushed her to the limit on every exercise and she enjoyed the challenge. There was no small talk, no chit chat, just an intense workout like the martial arts sparring she had witnessed that first night in the gym. Almost without notice a solid hour passed and she felt the satisfaction of physical exhaustion.

It took her a full 30 minutes to cool down and shower, and another 20 to get her hair in some decent style. Eventually she gave up and pulled it into a ponytail if for no other reason than it wouldn't obey any other commands. It would have to do.

She found Eric waiting patiently sitting on a bench near the front entrance. He was casually dressed in a polo golf shirt, khaki slacks and loafers. He brightened when Angelina approached. "You look great! Are you hungry?"

Angelina smiled, "More exhausted than hungry, but it will come. Where are we headed?"

"Finest dining in Atlanta; do you want two cars…your car…or my car…it's your choice."

For some reason Angelina appreciated the opportunity to choose. "It's your town, you can drive."

Eric led her back through the gym and exited the side door. She showed her surprise when Eric opened the passenger door to a rather plain looking pick-up truck. The truck was cleaned and polished and the interior reflected detailed attention, but the truck surprised her; so unassuming for one so visible. She turned to Eric before she stepped up into the cab.

"I never would have expected you were a pickup man."

"What's the matter? You don't like pickups?"

"Are you kidding? I was practically born in a pickup. Saddle up cowboy and let's get rolling."

The finest dining in Atlanta turned out to be an Atlanta landmark, the OK Café. Angelina felt as if she stepped back in time, or at least had traveled back to her humble roots in New Mexico. The huge sign indicating the wait flashed 45 minutes, but the time passed quickly. There was never an embarrassing lull in the conversation and everything was new and revealing. Eric was attentive and allowed the conversation to drift in the direction Angelina wanted it to go. At least a dozen or so fans found the courage to approach for an autograph and Eric made each feel comfortable. He didn't rush his visitors off but treated each with the respect she found refreshing. Eric made her feel the same way.

When finally seated in the famous café Angelina asked Eric about the huge Confederate Battle Flag carved into the wood above his head. She pointed at the symbol most black men reviled and asked, "That doesn't bother you?"

Eric turned and gazed up at the carving. "Not at all, it's part of the heritage of the South. I understand that flag represents a lot of things to a lot of people. To some it represents slavery; to others it represents individual freedom and state's rights. But look at us, a woman of Mexican descent and a black man, sitting here among people of many colors, backgrounds and beliefs, and we are accepted. Many black men fear the flag, but I do not. I fear more the men who hide behind the belief that their failures are still caused by that flag. It just isn't so." Eric paused before he continued. "Try the collard greens. They cook 'em with honey. You'll love 'em."

It was if their entire dinner was within a cocoon where the hustle and bustle of the restaurant never penetrated. To Angelina the evening passed in slow motion and relaxed grace. Eric's smiles and laughs were meant only for her and it ended too soon. The dinner was followed by a stroll down the famous Peachtree Street and included a childish ride to the top of a hotel where they enjoyed a cocktail while Eric pointed out landmarks as the restaurant slowly revolved.

"Do you have anything planned for tomorrow?"

Angelina didn't even give Steve Thunder's file a moment's thought. "No, nothing at all."

"How would you like to ride the raging rapids of the Chattahoochee River? Every newcomer to Atlanta has to do it at least once. You're going to get wet so dress accordingly."

Chapter 20

Angelina met Eric at the north end of Cumberland Mall parking lot. They enjoyed a quick breakfast at a local McDonalds, and soon were bound for the river. Angelina glanced at the white water cascading over the smooth rocks and assumed the rapids Eric spoke of must be down river for there was nothing to instill fear in her at this point. She had rafted the Colorado River at full flood and was sure she could handle anything a river in Georgia could dish out.

"We're here. Help me launch our trusty vessel."

Their trusty vessel turned out to be nothing more than two inner tubes with a cooler of beer and wine tied between them. Two short paddles were secured to the handles of the cooler. "We're going to run the rapids in that?"

Eric's charade now revealed, he grinned when he said, "Well, we take things at a little slower pace here in the South. Climb aboard."

The water was refreshing and only cool, not cold. The pace of the trip was almost imperceptible but the trees along the bank did show they were making progress. It was to be a day of lazy relaxation with good company.

Angelina had to ask. "Eric, are there any snakes in this river?"

Eric popped a beer before he answered. "You don't have to worry about the snakes. That's why we have paddles. What you have to worry about are the gators."

"There're gators in this river?"

"Don't worry. I'll protect you." Angelina took comfort in those words because she believed he would. "You want a beer or wine?"

As they drifted the lazy river the conversation ranged wide and was relaxed. It seemed the pair fit like hand and glove, but neither completely opened to the other. Angelina relayed her youth, but withheld the fact she was trained at the FBI academy and currently working for the Department of Justice. She had no valid reason to believe Eric would reject her because of her profession, but it had happened enough times in the past to exercise caution. She didn't want anything to complicate the day. There would be opportunity in the future to reveal all; at least she hoped so.

Eric detailed his childhood. He lived in Cairo, Georgia with his Aunt Grace. He talked about his trip to relative fame as the reporter covering the historic campaign of Barrack Obama, and subsequent promotion to anchor at CNN. Angelina wondered why there was no mention of his mother or father, but was polite enough to not pry. Eric was free with details of the present and dreams of the future, but was guarded as to the details of his past.

As the hours drifted by, the needs of mother-nature required attention. "Eric, are there any restroom facilities along the way?"

"No problem. There is a small park with facilities about 20 minutes down river. Can you make it?"

Her legs were stiff with cold when they pulled their raft to the bank. It took a moment to get the circulation moving again and both stiffly climbed the bank. Angelina enjoyed Eric's steadying hand on her arm as he helped her up the bank. They walked to the facilities almost touching elbows—close enough to feel the warmth of the other. Neither gave much notice to the gathering of migrant workers assembled a short distance away, but the beautiful woman of their heritage walking with a black man had certainly been noticed by the group.

Eric heard the mumblings of the group of Mexicans as he waited outside the facility for Angelina. This group of eight was more than migrant workers. The low pants, tattoos and red bandannas trailing from the back pocket of their pants told a sinister story. The biggest one, always the leader, slowly moved his herd closer to their raft. Eric watched as they raided his beer cooler. Their terrible conduct and the vulgar grabbing of their crotches and taunts only increased when Angelina appeared from the rest facility.

Angelina didn't give Eric a chance to offer an alternative to completing the trip down the river via walking trails bordering the river. "I see someone left the chicken coop gate open again, and all the roosters have escaped."

Eric almost laughed at her description of the men at the raft. He wondered why it was that women often ignored obvious danger. Was this a test? If it was, it was an awful dumb one. The two inner tubes and beer cooler could be easily replaced and they were not worth placing the girl at his side at risk. But her arm, now linked through his, was relaxed and unafraid, but still he asked, "Are you sure you want to do this?"

Their walk was not hurried back to the raft. In fact, it was much slower than the walk up the bank, but then a few moments ago the call of nature urged them to a quicker pace. "Eric, I've known men like these all my life. They will crawl back to the chicken coop when challenged."

Eric appreciated the bravado but questioned her sanity. These eight had more the demeanor of a pack of wolves than chickens loose from the coop.

Angelina looked up to him and flashed a disarming smile. "Do you speak any Spanish?"

"Not a lick."

"Good, I don't think you would like what they're saying about you right now."

"Is that right?"

This was silly, challenging these people over a worthless raft and a few beers; but Eric felt the adrenaline begin to pump into his body. He knew if they attacked it would come from one of the two men flanking the leader, and it would come from the side.

The leader was the most vulnerable to attack, but the presence of his gang always put the victim on the defensive; but Eric would take him first. Their initial attack would be slow and sloppy, and usually never intended to kill but to bring down their prey. If you were fast enough and gained the initiative you could escape.

Bill Cannon drilled it into him: attack, evade then attack; defend, disable, and then kill. Don't hold back. Fight with all your might. Fight without fear. Strike to kill for your life depends on it. Eric had no fear.

Angelina launched a verbal attack on those around the raft. The heated conversations were in Spanish and Eric didn't understand a word, but Angelina more than held her ground against the five. Eric heard the air escape from one of the tubes and saw the knife in the hand of one of the five who said in English, "La paraditas (street hooker) likes the black man more than her people. Maybe we make her not so pretty," and, encouraged by his friends, waved the knife near Angelina's face.

Eric had become distracted by the knife and noticed too late the movement to his right. He knew he was late and that he couldn't completely avoid the punch, but the throat of the leader was there, it was vulnerable, and it was his target. The rigid fingers of Eric's right hand sunk deep into the throat of the leader and he felt the cartilage surrounding the wind pipe collapse. The leader fell to the ground gasping in vain for air. The punch aimed for Eric's head glanced off his shoulder and allowed him to turn into his attacker and block his second punch with his arm while he drove the palm of his left hand up and into the nose of his attacker. Blood exploded from his nose and he stood there motionless, stunned from the blow. Eric blinded him with a thumb pushed into his eye socket. He was defenseless and available for the kill at Eric's leisure.

The third man reacted slowly and Eric blocked his attack with his left arm. He slid his hand down his attacker's arm to secure his wrist and held him there while he hammered at the side of his neck with the edge of his right hand. Angelina heard the bones in the man's arm break as Eric turned and pulled the arm down over his shoulder.

"Eric, watch out!"

Angelina's warning came a moment too late. The knife thrust caught him in the back, on the shoulder blade. Eric felt the tip scrape the bone but he felt no pain. He rolled away from his attacker and regained his feet in one smooth movement and his attacker made the mistake of trying to press home his attack. With knife arm raised above his head the man charged Eric. It was over in a moment. Eric caught the downward thrust by forming his arms into an X above his face. Eric stepped under the raised arm and turned into his attacker but he did not release the man's arm. The turn brought his attacker's arm swinging down and Eric only assisted with direction as the knife buried deeply in the attackers abdomen. It was only a heartbeat before the attacker realized the knife protruding from his belly was his own.

Eric prepared for the next attack but none came. When Eric regained his senses, he scanned the other members of the gang. They all stood in stunned disbelief, to include Angelina, as to what they had just seen. As electrically charged as Eric was, he could hear the buzz of the insects and also the moans of those now in pain on the ground. In the background he heard the distance sound of sirens that were growing louder with every breath.

Eric kept a wary eye on the remaining members of the Mexican group when he addressed Angelina. "Get behind me. Are you hurt?"

Angelina made her legs work to move behind Eric. "No, I am not hurt."

Frantic park goers who witnessed the event waved the arriving police cars to the restroom facility. The remaining members of the gang scattered, but could not escape the growing number of police officers. They had nowhere to run and were searched, handcuffed and placed in the back seats of the police cruisers. The police called in the medical response units to treat the wounded.

Angelina ran to the rest facility and returned with a handful of paper towels to stem the flow of blood from the stab wound on Eric's back. Eric winched when she pressed against the cut. "I'm sorry, does it hurt much?"

"I didn't even notice until now. I feel a little shaky. I better sit down." As the adrenaline in his body receded not only did the magnitude of what had just occurred hit Eric, but his own capability for such violence shook him. He had lost control during the fight. If given the chance would have killed them all.

Was this the same manner in which his father responded when he caught his wife—Eric's mother—in bed with another man? Did he kill them in an emotionally charged rage before he knew what he was doing? Eric now understood how it could happen and it concerned him. It concerned him that his father's blood ran through him and that the capability to kill came without warning. Was his genetic makeup such that he was doomed to follow the path of his father? He had learned to love his father in spite of what he had done, but by necessity had separated his life from the shame of the past, and now it may all be revealed. All that he had worked for may be lost for this day.

With one hand on his knee and the other pressing the towels against the wound Angelina sensed something had changed. "Are you feeling OK?"

Eric wasn't worried about the wound but his future. "I could have killed those men."

"But Eric, you didn't do anything wrong. They attacked you. It was self-defense."

"It was almost murder. They can't find out about this at work."

Eric hung his head and wished he had never asked Angelina to the river. He wished he was back on Daufuskie Island with Aunt Grace among the people he loved and where there was no danger. His thoughts were interrupted by a voice calling his name, it wasn't Angelina's voice but it was a voice from his past, it was a voice he instinctively trusted.

"Eric," the sharp smell of ammonia invaded his nose. "Eric, it's me, it's Doc, you with us?"

Eric looked up and the smiling face of one of his "uncles" was there, hovering over him with great concern but with smiling eyes. "Oh, hey Doc, I was just thinking, that's all. I've kind of made a mess of things."

Doc glanced around at the four wounded still laying where they had fallen.

"I'd say you did fine Eric." Doc lifted Angelina's hand and took a quick look at the wound. "It's not too bad; I'll have you patched up in no time."

Doc replaced Angelina's hand with the instruction, "Keep pressure on that until I get back."

As Doc turned to his ambulance additional medics arrived on the scene. "What's the priority here Doc?"

Doc stopped and pointed to the man with the knife still protruding from his belly. "Get that guy immobilized on a stretcher and get a drip going in him. If he's stable he should be the first to go. Leave the knife where it is and notify Grady Hospital you've got an abdominal knife puncture and he'll need surgery right away."

Doc pointed to the man who led the attack on Eric. "Irrigate that socket and push his eyeball back in. Throw a patch on it and tape it closed." Doc pointed to the leader still gasping for air. "Snake a trachea tube down him and throw an air cast on him and transport to Grady."

The medics turned to work and soon Doc returned with a medical case to treat Eric. "I'll take over now miss. You did a great job. Maybe you should be a nurse."

As Doc worked on Eric, Angelina went into the rest facility and washed the blood from her hands. Her emotions caught up with her and her knees almost buckled. It was her foolish bravado that almost got Eric killed. He had warned her, but no, she had to prove how tough she was and her vanity overwhelmed her good sense. It took her a few moments to regain her composure. The least she could do was ensure Eric's name was kept out of the report.

When she left the rest facility she searched out the senior police officer on the scene. Her badge and federal identification was all she needed to get his attention.

Doc cleaned the wound to Eric's back and gave him a running commentary of what he saw. "Not too bad but will require some stitches. No real damage to the bone but it should be x-rayed just to make sure. I'll throw a couple of sutures on it to stop some of the bleeding and then I'll take you to Saint Josephs. They've got an excellent surgeon on duty. He will make it like it never happened. Let's go."

As Doc helped Eric to his feet, Eric asked, "I just can't leave Angelina here. Can she come with us?"

"Sure, get her over here and let's get rolling."

When Eric called, Angelina hurried to his side. Angelina recognized Doc Broderson immediately. "I remember you. You're Doc Broderson, I met you my first week in Atlanta."

"And I remember you Miss Sanchez. Hop in the back and watch over my boy until we get to the hospital." Before Doc shut the doors to the ambulance he had to add, "No playing doctor in the van. Keep your hands to yourselves."

The ride to the hospital was without siren or lights. Doc watched his passengers in the mirror and noted the ease of their conversation. The violence of the fight behind them Doc could tell these two were connected and comfortable in the presence of the other.

Doc Broderson...the man Angelina wanted to talk with for information on Steve Thunder. This was neither the time nor the place. Eric was now the focus, and her investigation could wait. If she questioned Doc now Eric would wonder why, and she still didn't want Eric to know she was a Federal Agent

While Angelina was exercising caution, Doc Broderson was thinking about Angelina Sanchez...the woman turning over so many dead bodies that should remain undisturbed, and a threat to so many friends. Did Eric know of her investigation? He doubted it, or surely he would have mentioned something. He wanted to confront her, but this was neither the time nor the place. Doc wondered if it was time to tell Eric the truth, but that wasn't for him to decide alone. Doc knew there was reason for caution.

~~

Angelina reviewed the police report Monday morning. "Officers responded to a 911 call reporting apparent Mexican-Americans engaged in a fight at the Riverside Park in the Chattahoochee River National Recreation Area. Four injuries, two serious, non-life threatening. Suspects held in the Fulton County Jail and US Immigration notified. Suspects scheduled for deportation. Names and aliases listed on first attachment to this report. End of Summary.

Angelina was struck by the brevity of the report. She was thankful there was no mention of her or Eric Brown. She was also struck

142

by the similarity of this report and the reports filed by Buford Long. She asked her conscience if the omission of fact was the same as a cover-up.

Her conscience knew the answer, but she refused to listen.

Chapter 21

Interesting development, the attraction between Eric Brown and Angelina Sanchez, and Doc Broderson didn't exactly know what to do, or how to handle it. Mike DeAngelo wasn't the man Doc would normally turn to for advice, but with Bill in Kuwait he had no other alternative. He caught DeAngelo at the Marina before his fist charter.

"Remember the little Mexican number I told you about? She and Eric Brown are dating."

Doc new DeAngelo always looked on the dark side of every issue. His pessimistic nature came through the phone. "What a sneaky little bitch! That's got to be more than just coincidence. She must be setting him up for something. I can't believe with all the people in Atlanta these two people met by chance. I think we need to warn Eric."

Doc disagreed. "Warn him of what? That his girlfriend is a federal agent investigating a rape in which he had nothing to do?"

DeAngleo understood the logic, but still had concerns. "What if she finds out about his money? What then?"

"He's never been flashy with his money and I can't see any reason he would start now. She wouldn't dig into his finances unless she's investigating him. Besides, I'm not sure she really knows who Eric is, and for that matter, I don't think Eric knows she is investigating Hanna's rape."

DeAngelo had a way of putting things in terms everyone would understand. "Smells like week-old fish if you ask me. We can always go south if she is getting too close."

"I know. I'll keep an eye on her and try to find out what she's doing."

~~

If Doc was worried about how he would keep tabs on Angelina Sanchez, he needn't be; he had a message on his desk when he reported to work Monday morning. "Doc, a federal agent named Angelina Sanchez wants to talk with you the next time you are downtown. She said you know where she works."

144

No time like the present. Doc took his time making his way to Angelina's office. He stopped at the offices he normally visited. Only this time his good natured discussions always included a question about the hot Federal agent on the fifth floor. She was dating a friend of his you know, and did anybody know anything about her? He didn't learn a thing until he stopped by and visited Wade Griffin, the records custodian.

"Wade, do you know anything about Angelina Sanchez? I think she's dating a friend of mine. What kind of girl is she and what has she been doing since she got to Atlanta?"

"She seems OK to me. Works hard and I've heard nothing bad about her. I know she went to Alabama and Louisiana not too long ago, but other than that she just comes to work every day like everybody else. She did ask for Steve Thunder's file the other day and wanted to know who he had as friends. I told her you were probably his best friend. What's up with that?"

"Damn if I know. I guess I'll find out soon. She wants to talk with me about something; maybe that's it."

Doc walked into Angelina's office, "Miss Sanchez, I got a message you wanted to see me. You didn't get hurt in that fight, did you?"

"No, I'm fine. Thank you for taking such good care of us. It was a scary situation."

"What in the hell happened. How did the whole thing start?"

"It was probably my fault. All my life I've had to deal with the Mexican gang thug mentality. They ruin so many lives and nobody ever challenges them. They were saying such horrible things about me and Eric, I guess I thought if I just stood up to them they would leave us alone. I was wrong."

As casually as he could Doc asked, "How did you ever hook up with a guy like Eric Brown?

For a moment Angelina wanted to answer that it was none of his business, but the question was innocent enough. Eric Brown was a national figure, considered a celebrity by many, and the question was conversational, not prying. "I met him at the gym. I didn't recognize who he was at first. He emailed me last Friday inviting me to dinner and then rafting. I hope he doesn't consider me bad luck or a trouble-maker."

"Have you talked with him since the fight?"

Angelina laughed, "Now that you mention it, I don't even have his phone number."

"Pretty soon we'll be seeing you on TV, on the red carpet. We'll all say, we knew her before she got famous."

Both laughed at the joke. Doc asked, "Does he know you're a cop?" Doc knew cop wasn't the proper description, but it carried the same meaning as federal agent.

"No, I haven't told him. Every time I meet a guy and they find out I work for the FBI, or Justice Department, it just scares them. I suppose if he ever asks me out again I will have to tell him."

Doc took that as his opportunity to exit. There was nothing in her demeanor that gave any indication she was investigating Eric. "Well, I better be getting back to work. Are you sure you are OK?"

"I'm fine, really. Thanks for asking."

As Doc turned to go Angelina remembered the reason she asked him to her office. "Doc, that's not why I wanted to talk to you."

Doc thought he had made good on his escape and grimaced slightly before he turned back to Angelina. "Oh?"

"Doc, I'm doing an investigation, and an old friend of yours keeps popping up, Officer Steve Thunder. I understand you served together in the Army."

Doc knew it best to never try to conceal facts. They have a way of working to the surface. You can conceal thought, intent, emotion, objective, and anything else that can't be proven, but facts are easy to bare. Acknowledge the facts and conceal all other.

"Yes we were."

"You both retired at about the same time; Thunder joined the police force and you joined the county medical unit."

"That's right."

"You were with him the night he was killed. Do you know anything about the case he was working?"

Doc remembered the night vividly. He was having coffee with Steve Thunder in his police car. The dispatcher questioned the validity of the address of the drug raid. Thunder realized the information from Brownie, his confidential informant, as a set-up. A raid on a house owned by an 89-year-old woman who had been burglarized a half dozen times in the previous 12 months would result in the seizure of no drugs

146

or weapons, but only ridicule and scorn by the media and a black eye for the department.

"It was a drug raid. Steve requested me for medical backup. He found the info on the target was bad, so he tried to stop the raid. When he turned his back to the house, the old lady shot him in the back of the head. He was killed instantly. It was tragic, but then so many deaths are."

Angelina reminded herself that, as of this moment, she had no proof of any crime or police cover-up, and that she must exercise caution with her questions, or risk raising the suspicion of the Atlanta Police Department. The last thing she needed was a police department suspicious of her every move. Don't get ahead of yourself, stick to the basics.

"Officer Thunder also worked with the Feds on a big heroine bust. Do you know anything about that operation?"

"If you mean the one in the Georgia Mountains, I know that Thunder busted the buy and recovered the dope. I was on vacation when all that went down, so I don't know much about it."

"Thunder recovered the dope, but does anybody know what happened to the money?" If there was a connection between the drug money and Reverend Peter Walton's death then she had to find it.

"I never heard anything about any money. I think the Feds were so happy to get the drugs that they didn't even try to chase it down. You're going to have to ask somebody in the police department or the Feds about that."

Asking the police department was the last thing Angelina wanted to do. "There were about a dozen deaths that I can connect to this drug bust. None were investigated by the police. Do you find that a bit unusual?"

That may have been the dumbest investigative question she had ever asked. What would a county medic know about police investigations except for second hand hearsay?

"Miss Sanchez, I'm a medic, that's all. I don't know what the hell you're talking about. I think you need to be talking to people in the police department, not me."

"Yeah, I guess you're right, only a couple more questions. Steve Thunder worked on the anti-drug task force, why would he participate in the murder investigation of Reverend Peter Walton, and considering the number of deaths after Thunder was killed, who would want to avenge his death?"

Doc moved closer to Angelina's desk. His face had visibly hardened. "Since this is sounding more like an official investigation let me answer those questions this way. To the first, I didn't know he was part of the investigation of the Walton murder. As to the second, and it's off the record, who would want to avenge his death besides me, probably a dozen other guys who deal with the scum of the earth every day, and don't have the luxury of sitting behind a desk in a clean white shirt and question what they did years ago. You've asked me a lot of questions. I have one for you. Exactly what kind of investigation are you doing?"

"I can't tell you that."

"Then let me tell you this. Steve Thunder was a man of honor and he was my friend. He served his country with valor and courage his entire life. He was always upfront with everybody, he never hid what he did for a living from anybody; unlike some people I know. I have a bit of advice for you. If you need medical help...don't call me."

Angelina knew he was referring to the concealment of her profession from Eric and understood the offense he took with the questions about his friend. It was an expected reaction. She hoped she would eventually be able to patch things up with Doc, but the law came first. When she reviewed the session with Doc, she realized she didn't know a bit more than she knew an hour before.

Doc concluded Angelina suspected a police cover up of the drug bust. They were safe for the moment, but there was reason for caution.

~~

Ken Carson worked deep into Sunday night finishing his report on the banking conference. He emailed it to Ed Helton on Monday morning.

Knowledge is power, and Ken knew he must put his new found knowledge to work on his loans and his stock portfolio. He knew he must reduce his exposure in some areas and accelerate his investments into others. These new banking regulations would make him a rich man.

Ken was engrossed in a detailed analysis of his many and varied investments. It wasn't easy to decide where to sell and where to buy, and some of the loans at the bank should be paid down or off to effectively leverage his new position.

Ken had two computer screens working. The one to the rear of his desk with his accounts listed by broker; the one on his desk was used to send instructions on which stocks to sell. Back and forth he went, from the back screen to determine which to sell, to the front screen sending instructions to his brokers. For two hours he worked uninterrupted. Slowly he built the cash reserves to pay off the loans that he listed on a single sheet of paper on the corner of his desk. When enough cash was assembled he would scratch through the loans. The list was getting shorter.

He was interrupted by the small ding of the front computer telling him he had received a new email.

The icon on the lower right corner of the screen flashed, "You've got mail: From Karen, Here is a memento..."

Ken had been totally focused on the computer screens and felt the tension in his neck. The email brought a smile to his lips. He needed a break and Karen's emails always provided some racy relief from the boring life in the bank. He clicked the icon and the computer automatically opened the email.

"My Darling Kenneth, Here is a little memento from our special night. I love watching it. It's not as good as you next to my side, but fills the emptiness until we can be together again. Enjoy. Love, Karen."

Ken clicked open the attachment and immediately moans of pleasure filled his office. They were unmistakable; the sounds of passion could not be confused with any other sounds. Ken feared the sounds of their lovemaking would spill into the hall and reach unintended ears and he frantically searched for the volume control. Once the sound was turned down to nothing more than a whisper Ken leaned back in his chair to enjoy the show.

It never crossed Ken's mind how Karen made the recording of that night in Atlanta; for now it was enough to enjoy. Karen's body glistened with the exertion of their lovemaking and Ken silently complimented himself on his performance. Viewing the recording was in some respects even better than the actual act. Maybe it is the voyeur in all of us that lets the imagination run wild—what he would do with Karen's body, or what she would do to his—the next time they met.

Ken should have been thinking of the purpose of such a recording, and why would Karen not tell him of her desire to record their lovemaking? Ken's clouded thinking concluded the exhibitionist in Karen was always looking for release—the manner in which she dressed and the seductive way she always moved, the sexual acts she encouraged in public places, always excited him. He wanted to give this line of thinking more thought, but his attention was pulled back to the computer screen.

He enjoyed the video attachment and clicked the replay button. He could have spent the remainder of the morning reliving that night, but he was interrupted by the rude and incessant ringing of his phone. The screen on the phone showed, "Ed Helton."

Ken muted the screen and answered the call. "Yes sir."

"Mr. Carson, I read your report on the conference. You did an excellent job. I have a few questions, I'll be right down."

Ken almost panicked. His first two attempts to shut the video off missed the mark. Ken heard the footsteps of Ed Helton on the carpet runner in the hall. It took him two attempts to close his email. When Ed turned into Ken's office, the incriminating email and video were closed, but staring Ken in the face was the broker account, to his rear was the status screen of his investments, and under his right arm the list of fraudulent loans he planned to repay.

Ed was on top of him, spreading his report on the corner of Ken's desk. Should he close the remaining screens or count on Ed Helton's manners to allow the information on the screens to remain private? One click on the screen to his front closed the broker site, but there was nothing he could do about the screen to his rear, or the list of accounts.

Ed Helton pulled a chair to the corner of Ken's desk. "What in the hell is the Fed doing? Is this correct? Does the government think we are going to sit idly by and let them buy fifty percent of our stock?"

"Mr. Helton, the President and his team of economic advisors put that into the law. If you don't allow the government in, then they will pull the federal charter of the bank. We won't get any money out of the Federal Reserve, nor will we be allowed to do business across state lines. I don't think there is anything we can do about it. The Fed will sell the stock back to the bank when they consider the economic crisis is over."

"That could cost us millions! Didn't anybody object?"

"Oh, yes sir. A lot of the banks objected to that provision—that the banks would be buying their own stock at inflated prices—but the government said it's the only way the American taxpayer can get back their investment in the banks."

Ed Helton shook his head. Government control of the American banking business was something Ed Helton never thought he would see in his lifetime. "Do we have to take the stimulus money?"

"Yes sir, we do."

"Or...?"

"Or they pull our charter."

"What if we take the stimulus money and pay it back right away?"

Ken knew that question was coming, if fact, he asked the same exact question at the conference. "The Fed won't allow us to pay it back until they consider the economy recovered. They want us to loan it out."

Ed made a note on Ken's report. "Well, we can't afford to pay interest on billions of dollars. We're going to have to get it moving. Did they establish any guidelines on the money?"

Ken knew his answer would upset Helton. "Yes sir, the CRA guidelines were mentioned more than once."

Ed was disgusted, "Damn, same old crap that got us into trouble in the first place!" Ed rolled up his copy of the report and used it to punctuate the air in Ken's direction. "This is a bag of shit. We are going to be forced to make interest payments on a half-billion dollars and the economy is so bad that all the businesses are shutting down. The only people trying to borrow money have such bad credit they couldn't finance a Snickers Bar. This is only more of the same. Lend money to people who can't afford to pay it back, or lose your ass making interest payments on money we don't want to borrow. It's insane! Do you have any ideas?"

Ken knew his answer would please Mr. Helton. "Mr. Helton, you could use the Stimulus money to finance the Daufuskie project."

Ed Helton paused. That wasn't a bad idea, but a Federal loan to Danni meant Federal involvement, and she was doing fine without the help of nosy bureaucrats. "No, we're not going to do that; at least not yet."

Before Ed left Ken's office he glanced at the document on the desk. "What are you working on?"

Ken noticed Ed's attention on the list of loans. He picked up the sheet and held it in two hands. "I'm just checking the status of these loans. So far, they are all on schedule."

Ed paused and reflected for a moment before leaving. "Good…" Ed waved the report at his Loan Manager, "…and good job on this report."

Ken breathed a silent sigh of relief. Helton had missed everything, and Ken thought briefly about his boss, "What an idiot."

Ken decided one more look at the video was in order before he erased the email. After all, Karen would have the complete copy if they wanted to watch it together; and it never occurred to Ken to ask the question…why would Karen make a video?

~~

Ed Helton walked slowly back to his office. If you passed him in the hall you could tell he was deep in thought. When he entered his office he stopped by his secretary's desk. His request was simple.

"Get Buford Long on the phone, and hold all my other calls."

Chapter 22

Major James 'Mad Man' Madison wondered what his wife would say if she knew what he was doing. He told her he was on an inspection tour of the northern border. He would be gone only a few days, and there was no danger. He regretted the lie, but she had enough to worry about getting settled from the move. He doubted she would understand the need to go on the raid into the Sinai, but it was his report that put men in danger, and only a coward would send men in harm's way and not be with them.

Madison had learned two things about the Israeli Army. First, what would take weeks or months to evaluate and plan in the Pentagon, took only two days in Tel Aviv. Second, there were no half or measured responses to terrorist threats in Israel.

He briefed Bill's pictures to Israeli intelligence. He noted the ships in Port Said, and their cargo and the shipments into Ezbet Abu Sagal. Coupled with the shipments from the location in Syria, there was a possibility that rockets capable of carrying chemical agents were being shipped into the Gaza Strip.

The Israeli general's questions were direct. "Has this been briefed to the President?"

"No sir, it has not."

"…to the Secretary of State or the Secretary of Defense?"

"No sir, it has not."

"Why not?"

"Sir, only three people in Washington know about these photos. I was directed to brief you as a trusted ally. These photos have not been entered into the intelligence data bases, because quite frankly, my boss didn't want to run the risk of this information getting lost in the political shuffle in Washington. I trust you understand the sensitive nature of this briefing, and we hope these photos will be held in the strictest confidence. Many careers and lives may be at risk."

"We understand your concerns, Major, but we have concerns of our own. The lives of our soldiers are as valuable to us as your skin is to

153

you. We don't like sending our soldiers on…how would you say it…a wild goose chase, without high confidence that what you have presented is true." The general paused, "Where did you get these photos?"

"Sir, I am not at liberty to say. You will have to make your decisions based on what I have told you, and understand that my boss thought this intelligence was important enough to completely circumvent normal channels to get it to you." General McLaughlin's instructions on protecting the source of the photos were crystal clear. If it ever leaked that Prince Al-Sabah was the source of the photos, there would be hell to pay in the Arab world.

One of the officers at the head table leaned to the general and whispered into his ear. The general turned to Madison. "You work for Lucas McLaughlin, don't you?"

"Yes sir, I do."

The general nodded. "You can tell Lucas his secrets are secure with us."

The next day Colonel Abraham Wetzel, his point of contact with the Israeli General Staff, casually asked if Madison would like to accompany the commando unit on the raid. Madison should have thought twice and declined the offer, but now he lay half covered with sand on a dune overlooking the coastal road running from Ezbet Abu Sagal to the Gaza Strip.

"Colonel Wetzel, what will happen if the Egyptians, or for that matter, if the UN finds out the Israeli Army attacked across international borders into Egypt. What happens then?"

Madison found Wetzel's answers, if you could get past the sarcasm and contempt, always accurate and either well thought out or well rehearsed. "If we find the missiles you say are there, then the UN will pass a resolution condemning the stockpiling of chemical weapons, but will do nothing. If there are no missiles, the UN will pass a resolution condemning us, but will again do nothing."

"Have you considered the political fallout in America?"

Colonel Wetzel was somewhat condescending with his reply. "Did you before you gave us this information?"

Madison gazed over the rough desert. "I don't think that even crossed General McLaughlin's mind, but if this goes to shit, the political fallout could be trouble for Israel."

Wetzel's answer was the truth. "That's the trouble with you Americans. Everything with you is now political."

Military protocol aside, Madison took offense at the statement. "Excuse me sir, what the hell is that supposed to mean?"

Colonel Wetzel's face softened somewhat before he answered. "Major Madison, where is your home?"

"I'm a military man; so was my father. So I guess my home is the Army post where I am stationed. My wife is from Daufuskie Island, South Carolina, so I guess I would have to call that home."

"Do you have any children?"

Madison smiled at the thought. "Not yet."

"I have two children; a boy and a girl. If what you say is true, then those missiles will not fall on Daufuskie Island, South Carolina, they will fall in Israel on my wife and my children. This is not a political exercise; it is our fight for survival. We do not have the luxury of two oceans to serve as a buffer between my enemies and my family. If there are chemical weapons in the Gaza then we must find out now. We cannot afford to retreat in the face of our enemies. It is naïve to think our enemies do not intend us harm, as America is beginning to believe. We have nowhere to retreat. Already you American's have forgotten the lessons of 2001. Will it take another attack before your country will understand that your enemies are dedicated to your destruction? They only understand victory or defeat; and consider negotiation only as a path to victory. If you have no stomach for what we must do, then you should have stayed behind."

Madison had the stomach for it, but as he lay prostrate on the sand overlooking the coastal highway he wondered why he didn't have the sense to stay in Tel Aviv.

The political discussions behind them, Colonel Wetzel and Major Madison now had only one objective: conduct the raid, get the evidence they would need to justify their actions to the world, and get back to the relative safety of Israel, without bringing the entire Egyptian army down on their heads.

The plan was straightforward. The Mossad (Israeli Intelligence) would trail the target vehicle and report progress to Wetzel. A second Mossad team would block the bridge over the deep gorge where Wetzel's soldiers waited in concealed positions. Snipers would take out the driver and the trail vehicle would force the truck into the gorge. Wetzel's team would secure at least one missile and using fire and smoke and the gathering darkness to cover their escape, make their way to the sea where they would be picked up by an Israeli patrol boat.

When the trail vehicle reported the target vehicle a few minutes out Colonel Wetzel asked Major Madison, "Somebody told me you are a descendent of your President Madison. Is that true?"

Major Madison was proud of his heralded ancestry, but avoided making it known. President Madison was part of his past, but he was more concerned with making his own contribution to the country. "Yes I am."

Colonel Wetzel turned to his younger companion, "Then why do you serve in the Army? You should be in politics, not rolling around in the sand as a soldier."

"I gave some thought to politics, but I have found serving as a soldier is more honorable. Politicians are too quick to compromise; a quality I have not mastered."

Colonel Wetzel actually laughed. "Good for you. After your service in the Army you can then go into politics and become President."

Madison took Wetzel's comment as a compliment, but wanted to focus on the mission. "What do you think the Egyptians will do when they find out about this little exercise?"

Wetzel's face reflected his own concern. "You Americans think you have bought control of Egypt with your financial support of the military, but there are many in Egypt who wait for the government to fall. If the Egyptian leadership knows about these shipments and have been supporting them, then their reaction will be immediate and severe. They will not want the world to know what has been going on here. If only the radicals in their government know about this, and the government moves to stop these shipments, then the radicals may try and turn the masses against the government for their lack of support for those aligned against Israel. In either case the next war could start here, today.

"If the government is unaware of these missiles, then there will be no immediate response. If they find out we did this thing, even if we prove chemical systems are being assembled in their country, they will probably be forced by the other Arab nations to stand against us."

Madison added, "The Russians and Iranians won't help."

"No, the Russians and Iranians could be a problem." Wetzel directed his attention to the highway. "Here comes the truck."

Madison watched the ambush unfold. On cue, the trail vehicle started to overtake the truck and started to pass the truck some 1,000 yards before the bridge. When the chase vehicle was abreast of the truck, Madison saw the windshield shatter from the sniper bullets ripping into the driver. The Mossad vehicle turned into the truck and forced it off the road before it made the bridge. The only sound was the revving of the engine as the truck sailed into the deep gorge. There was no initial explosion, only a growing fire as fuel hit the hot exhaust. Before the fire spread to the cargo area, Wetzel's soldiers removed one of the rockets and four men lifted it to their shoulders and at a slow running gait started toward the sea. When they were well clear, the rear guard set explosives to the fuel tank and rocket motors and beat a hasty retreat.

Madison heard Wetzel's order, "Let's go," and noticed the Mossad vehicles disappear down the highway.

~~

Bill Cannon's flight from Atlanta to Kuwait was spent contemplating two subjects: The current state of international affairs in the Middle East and his relationship with Danni Walton. He had a good understanding of the first, but made no headway with the second. But the flight had passed quickly because of the complexity of both.

His arrival into Kuwait was with more fanfare than he would have liked. The airlines upgraded him to first class, probably on order of the Prince, and he was first off the plane and escorted to a waiting limousine parked on the tarmac.

When Bill entered the limo, the driver informed him, "Prince Al-Sabah sends his regrets. He must attend to some official functions this evening. He will meet you at your residence for breakfast."

The driver maintained a steady pace and Bill noticed his route had been cleared and Kuwaiti police manned the intersections. Bill tapped the window of the vehicle and felt the solid thud of armored glass and wondered if the security provisions were really necessary. The driver approached a walled compound—not a military compound but more like a little castle—and never stopped but only slowed to weave his way through an armored gate. Bill noticed military guards lurking in the shadows as the vehicle passed.

The car stopped within the confines of the entrance gate completely protected from all sides. When Bill exited the vehicle he was met by an elderly gentleman dressed in traditional Arab garb. "Colonel Cannon, my name is Karim. I am your host during your stay as a guest of Prince Al-Sabah."

Karim briefed Bill on the entire compound. It was often used by the Prince, members of his family, and dignitaries. The walls surrounding the compound were 20' high with walking guards at all times. The walls were 4' thick and built of reinforced concrete with sensors placed on all the walls to detect any intruders. They also controlled four houses outside the walls with guards controlling access to the walls. The roof could be used as a helipad and there was a bomb shelter in the basement. Bill concluded this was more of a fort than a residence. From the balcony of his room you could see the moon reflecting off the Persian Gulf. It looked like paradise but felt like trouble.

It obviously wasn't all paradise or else the loaded .45 semi-auto wouldn't have been neatly tucked under his pillow. Additional magazines were available in the drawer of the nightstand. A quick fieldstrip of the piece to ensure it was properly functioning was the last thing Bill did before slipping it beneath his pillow and drifting to sleep.

~~

Daylight revealed the grandeur of his accommodations; gilded ceilings and marble floors with ribbons of gold running randomly through the stone. Bill began his morning ritual workout; slowly at first and then building in speed and intensity and forty-five minutes later his morning shower prepared him for the day. Maybe Karim had him on video, or more likely timed his call after the shower stopped.

"Colonel Cannon, breakfast has been prepared for you on the veranda. Prince Al-Sabah will join you in a few moments."

The veranda commanded a million dollar view of the Persian Gulf. Bill could clearly see the oil tankers moving north and south in the shipping lanes. The table was set with fine china and crystal glasses. Fresh fruit under glass and dark Arabian coffee were presented amid a delicate setting of green. Bill decided to wait for his friend before eating, but sipped the strong coffee and read the English newspaper folded neatly on the corner of the table. Bill was through the first two sections before the arrival of his friend.

Prince Ahmad Al-Sabah looked as fit as he did when he and Bill traveled deep into Iraq to rescue his children. The Prince was dressed in the traditional dishdashah and gutrah head covering. The heavy mustache was the first thing you would notice, but Bill saw the deep lines of responsibility that now etched his friend's face; those lines of worry had not extinguished the fire in his eyes or removed the smile from his lips

"My good friend, you have blessed this house with your presence."

"Thank you for allowing me to come." Bill gestured at the grandeur of the house. "I don't know if I warrant this kind of attention."

"My tent is your tent as long as you wish to stay. I assume you are pleased with the security?"

Security was a topic Bill wanted to discuss. "The security is fine, but why so much? I thought things were pretty much under control over here. Have I missed something?"

A slight frown crossed Prince Al-Sabah's face. He avoided answering the direct question with, "Bill, the map of the world is changing and I believe we are approaching troubled times. Much of what happens in my country depends on what happens in yours. We will have time to discuss all these things during your visit."

Bill started to ask about the photos, "My friend, I would like to ask you about the pic…"

Prince Al-Sabah held up his hand, and Bill stopped in mid sentence. Prince Al-Sabah placed his hand on Bill's arm. "Trust me. We will have time to discuss all things, but now is not the time."

Bill understood the pictures were not to be discussed until raised by Prince Al-Sabah. Bill allowed his friend to lead the conversations during breakfast.

The conversations were not rushed, and between bites of fruit and coffee the Prince talked of various subjects: Strange bedfellows, the Russians and Iranians in Egypt…the Iranian claim to ancient Mesopotamia…the continuing conflict between the Shia Muslims in Iran and southern Iraq with the Sunni Muslims currently holding power in Iraq…the withdrawal of American ground forces…American politics…the world economy…and he talked of his dream for peace.

Bill listened attentively. Prince Al-Sabah would not be discussing these things if there were not lessons to be learned. When his friend allowed an interruption Bill asked, "The newspapers back home said you were pretty rough on the Secretary of State. You haven't burned any bridges, have you?"

Prince Al-Sabah turned to Bill, "Old friend, the time for subtle moves is over. You know as well as I the dangers my country faces. I need America to be strong. America has always been the beacon of hope for the world, and only America has the power to prevent disaster, but

America has lost her way. Perhaps, with the blessing of Allah, we can save both countries." And Prince Al-Sabah grinned.

"Bill, I have something very special for you today. OPEC has called an emergency meeting in Qatar. I would like you to attend as part of my staff."

"That should be interesting."

"Make sure you bring the .45. Put it on under your coat."

Bill raised his eyebrows; carrying a weapon in the presence of the Prince was unusual.

Prince Al-Sabah noticed the hesitation. "We don't expect trouble, but everyone at this meeting will be armed. It's a cultural thing. Americans carry law books, Arabs carry weapons."

"Now, what is it exactly you want me to do at this meeting?"

"Nothing but to learn my friend; one of my aides will interpret the discussion for you."

"No need to do that Ahmad, I speak and understand Arabic very well. If I have a question, I will not hesitate to ask you about it."

With a little grin Prince Al-Sabah replied. "I know you speak Arabic, but many do not. We will keep this secret to ourselves for the time being. We will allow others the freedom of their tongue without guarding their speech."

"I'll keep my ears open and mouth shut."

Chapter 23

Israel was an enchanting land. As much as she enjoyed learning about Washington, Israel was that many times more interesting. From their small apartment near the American Embassy, Hanna looked forward to a historical excursion almost every weekend.

After his inspection tour of the military installations, James took Hanna to Jerusalem. They walked the Via Dolorosa, the same path Jesus walked and carried His cross to His crucifixion, at what is now the most holy of Christian sites, the Church of the Holy Sepulcher, where the New Testament says Jesus was crucified, buried and resurrected.

Along the way James pointed out the golden dome of one of the most famous Islamic shrines in the world, The Dome of the Rock, where Muslims believe the Prophet Muhammad ascended during his Night Journey to heaven. James then led the way to the most revered Jewish site in the world, the Wailing Wall, said to be the only remaining wall of the first temple built by King Solomon.

Hanna found it difficult to remember all the civilizations James rattled off that ruled over modern day Israel: Egyptians, Assyrians, Babylonians, Persians, Greeks, Romans, Arabs and the Crusaders, the Ottoman Empire and then finally the British before the modern State of Israel was declared in 1948. Hanna was beginning to understand the complexity of the continuing clash of civilizations and religions over Jerusalem.

She thought how shallow most Americans were of the historical footprints of civilizations around the world. American history always began in the year 1492, when Columbus discovered America. So little thought was ever given to the ancient civilizations of Central and South America, much less the American Indians, and to consider the Vikings may have been the first Europeans to discover North America would be considered a ridiculous assertion.

Their weekend trip to the Old City in Jerusalem was amazing. The smells and sounds of the old city overwhelmed her and it felt like she had only touched the surface of the culture that was the West Bank of the most contested piece of ground in modern history.

It was nothing compared to their trip to the Negev Desert. James surprised her when he announced before a three-day weekend, "We're going to the largest Bedouin Market in Israel. We're going to Beersheba. You'll love it."

The famous Bedouin market was everything James said it would be. The mix of races and cultures added to the din of the market and they spent the entire day wandering the streets with merchants hawking their wares. Hanna picked out a beautiful Bedouin scarf for her mother, a dark blue—one of the traditional Bedouin colors—embroidered with gold and jeweled studs. Hanna could think of hundreds of uses for it.

They ended the day at a café surrounding an ancient well that had been restored to working order. The café owner touted the well as the famous well dug by Abraham in ancient times. James said it was more likely a well dug by the Turks at the turn of the twentieth century, when the Ottoman Empire ruled over the lands that were now Israel.

"James, of all the places we've been, this town seems so at peace with itself. There doesn't seem to be the tension here that I felt in Jerusalem. Everybody here seems at peace with each other."

James thought about her comment for a moment. "I agree. Maybe because the Bedouin Market is the main tourist attraction in the Negev part of Israel. But for whatever reason it should give everybody some hope that the Arabs and the Jews can live together in peace."

"What are we going to do tomorrow?"

"We'll spend the night here and take in some of the night life of a Bedouin camp. The people in the Embassy say you will never forget it. Tomorrow we'll head north to Gaza, and then swing over to Tel Aviv and spend the night there. The clubs there are supposed to be world famous. We'll hit a couple of the clubs and get back to the apartment on Sunday. "

~~

As Hanna and James drove west and north to the Gaza strip she reflected on their Bedouin adventure. When they left the hotel it was as if they had stepped through a time warp. Their hosts were gracious and the wine they sipped was chilled as was the cheese. The meat was cooked exactly as she ordered and the four courses rivaled the best restaurants anywhere in the Mediterranean Sea. She was sure most was staged for the tourists, but James was right; she would remember it for the rest of her life. She would remember it not only for the magical ambiance of the desert, but that was the night James and Hanna conceived their child.

But that was last night and the further north they drove the more she came to realize she wasn't in the 19th century, but the 21st, and the signs along the road warning of rocket attacks from Gaza made her want to reverse course and return to the serenity of the Negev Desert.

From their vantage point atop a small hill Hanna could see the wall erected by Israel around the Gaza Strip. James told her the history of the Gaza strip and what precipitated the wall. Since the erection of the wall, terrorist bombings from Gaza had been replaced by random Katyusha rocket and mortar attacks.

"The rockets aren't very accurate and Hamas launches them with no regard as to what they might hit. It is the worst kind of terror. You can be sitting down to dinner and be subject to a rocket attack. Israel tried to clean the terrorists from Gaza, but every time they try they only succeed in turning world opinion against themselves."

As if scripted to James's explanation, three dirty exhaust streaks rose from inside the Gaza wall. The rockets headed northwest and made a graceful arch against the blue sky. Hanna followed their progress until the motors burned out and the rockets went ballistic. Without the exhaust, the rockets were impossible to follow but Hanna kept her attention directed in the general direction of their flight. She never saw or heard the impact. It was as if they disappeared. But she knew they had to come back to earth.

As she followed the path of the rockets she felt suddenly alone and vulnerable and she moved closer to James and grabbed his arm. Not in panic or fear, but just for the company of a civilized man. "I hope those things didn't hit anybody."

"So do I," was all James added. They stood in silence on the small hilltop for a few moments longer before James said, "Let's get to Tel Aviv. This place gives me the creeps."

~~

Their ride to Tel Aviv was mostly in silence. The three random rockets had put a terrible damper on what had been a relaxing respite from the modern troubles of Israel. It was obvious James was thinking the same thing.

"James, if Jews and Arabs can live together peacefully in Beersheba, why is there such animosity in other places of the country?"

163

"I think most Arabs and Jews want to do just that, live together in peace. But too many of the radical Arabs are simply bent on the destruction of Israel as a state. I'm not an expert, but I think Israel has been willing to make concessions to the Palestinians, but there is always something that sets the negotiations back. This country is a real powder keg just waiting to explode. I hope I'm a long way from it when she blows."

When they finally arrived in Tel Aviv their enthusiasm for clubbing was replaced by a quiet dinner overlooking the port and an early night.

In the morning James and Hanna walked along the boardwalk between the beach and busy restaurants and shops facing the sea. It was such a beautiful morning that trouble was the farthest thing from Hanna's mind until two men, over dressed for the mild morning, hurried past Hanna and James. She felt James tense.

James moved a little closer to Hanna. "Hanna, those two people that just passed us, the two men; something's not right about them."

Hanna glanced in the direction James indicated with her eyes. "What do you mean?"

"They're not from here. I think they are from Iran."

"So? What makes that so strange?"

James couldn't place what caused his concern with the two men. There were hundreds of people on the boardwalk. Why did these two men get his attention?

He only caught a snippet of their conversation as they passed. What was it? The taller said something about, "the first bus and you take the second..." and the other replied, "Allah be with you." But that wasn't what gained his attention. It wasn't their words so much as the dialect. It wasn't Arabic they were speaking, but Farsi, the common language of Iran and the language he specialized in when he attended the Defense Language School. James had been lucky to catch enough of the conversation to make the identification.

"I heard the tall one say he would take the first bus, and his friend should take the second. And look at them, I know it's a little cool this morning, but they are the only two people wearing heavy coats and they look like they have vests underneath the coats."

Hanna looked closely at the two strangers. James was right. Something was a little different about the way they walked, as if with heavy loads. They walked like fat men walk with their arms never touching their sides—only these two were not fat.

The pair separated. The taller man heading to a bus parked near an exit to the beach, the other walking toward the bus parked directly behind the first.

"Wait here." James started on a run, not a full run but at the pace most would use to catch a bus before it departed—fast enough to get to the bus, but not so fast as to show the world you were late. James increased his speed slightly to make sure he got to the door of the bus before the tall man and rudely cut in front of the Iranian. When he did, Hanna saw James trail his hand across the mid-section of the man. It was done with the skill of a pick-pocket.

When James cut in front of the Iranian he gave him his ugly American, "Excuse me." He knew instantly his suspicions were confirmed—explosives. James didn't hesitate. He had made his decision while running to catch the bus. He would have to take the target out quickly. His right hand continued up to the man's throat while with his left he grabbed the sleeve of the man's right arm. The only tricky part was hooking right leg behind the Iranian's right leg, but he was so quick the man didn't have time to react. James pushed hard on the throat and jaw with his right hand and held the left arm preventing the Iranian from breaking his fall. With the impact of his head on the pavement the Iranian lay motionless. James ripped open the jacket, and there exposed was the explosive vest of a terrorist bomber.

Hanna saw the next few moments in amazing clarity - as if time stood still. She saw James kneeling over the downed man trying to regain his senses. She saw James turn his head toward the second bus and make eye contact with the second terrorist. She saw the look of disbelief on the man's face that he had been discovered and saw him raise the detonator high in the air. She saw the people begin to scatter and saw the Israeli policeman raise the Uzi and begin to take aim. She saw James turn his head back to her and yell, "Run!"

~~

Hanna felt the heat and blast from the explosion as she dove to the curb. The concussion shattered the glass of the store fronts and deafened her ability to hear. She felt blast particles falling from the facades of the stores and she didn't move for almost a minute. She was dazed and confused.

Her hands and knees were skinned where they had taken the brunt of her dive to the pavement. There was blood on her legs, but to her delight and then to her horror, the blood wasn't her own. The body of a young girl, maybe six years old, lay against the curb. Her little arm was missing the hand and the blood from her arm was that which covered Hanna's leg. Her eyes had the look of death.

It was an epiphany for Hanna; she knew the young girl would die if she didn't take action. She stopped the flow of blood with the girl's belt wrapped tightly around her little arm and the Bedouin shawl, over her bloody body to provide the warmth the girl needed to avoid falling into shock. Hanna stayed until relieved by a shop owner who staggered from his shattered store. As Hanna left the young girl, she was rewarded with a flickering smile from the child.

Hanna walked to where the first terrorist lay. His head had been cracked open by projectiles from the bomb and his gray matter was slowly oozing onto the pavement; his explosive vest still intact around his body. All around Hanna lay the wounded and dying from the attack. After the violence of the explosion, the silence on the boardwalk was eerie—there was no sound of the sea gulls or even the waves lapping on the beach—all had been drowned out by the blast. To try and determine why no sound reached her, Hanna felt of her ears and face—both felt numb to the touch.

Once the sounds of the cries and moans of the young children began to register she wished for the silence of her deafness to return. Most of the children were in shock and only low moans of semi-conscious pain escaped from their small bodies. At least the ones moaning were still alive. Hanna teetered between an emotional breakdown at the horrors that lay strewn on the boardwalk—the tears welling up in her eyes at the discovery of another torn and mutilated body, and the strong urge to empty the contents of her stomach at the sight of so much blood and small body parts askew on the pavement.

"Hanna." Had someone called her name, or did she imagine it? But then she heard it again, "Hanna, help me up."

Oh My God, James! Where was James? James!

"Hanna, I'm over here. Help me up."

Hanna considered it a miracle that James was alive! Bloody from the blast, James had been spared the brunt of the explosion by rolling behind the front tire of the bus. He looked up at Hanna and said, "If you help me up, I think we should get back to the embassy."

Hanna knelt and cradled her husband as if he was a young babe. She kissed his lips and tasted his blood. And the salt from her tears mingled with his blood and she didn't care. He was alive.

"Hanna, help me up. We need to clear this area. There may be more bombs here."

As they staggered from the scene they did what they could for the children near them. Soldiers and medical personnel started arriving, even before the news media, and James and Hanna were able to make it back to their hotel.

~~

Achmad Nardiff had spent the night in prayer with his two martyrs, the two young Iranians that would sacrifice their lives to gain the kingdom of Heaven. Allah be Praised. They visited the holiest of Islamic shrines, the Dome of the Rock, yesterday and dedicated their sacrifice to Mohammad.

Achmad filled the time between prayers with heroic stories of martyrs who walked the path of salvation before them; and how the fruits of Heaven await them, and how their families would be showered with gifts and fame for their sacrifice. Death to All Infidels and Zionist Pigs, It is the Will of Allah, Allah be Praised.

Achmad walked with the two believers to the boardwalk facing the sea. He joined in the prayers spoken just above a whisper to help the young men focus on the valor of their deed and the pleasures that await them in heaven. He stayed with them as long as he dared; for it would be a terrible waste of training, planning and resources if they were to realize there were pleasures here on earth they had yet to enjoy, and they may still abandon their mission so close to the target.

And the target had been carefully selected. Two buses of Israeli school children visiting the shore. Achmad knew it was easier to kill snakes when they are young; before they are capable of defending themselves. The explosive vests hidden beneath their clothes would surly kill all the children on the busses; and with luck would kill some of the infidels standing nearby.

Achmad wondered if the young American couple that they had passed would be caught in the blast. Having spent five years in New York, he always enjoyed the opportunity to speak the English he had learned. He would have enjoyed spending the day with the tourists from his adopted home; if not for the more pressing matters at hand.

Achmad watched from the alley between shops as the American left his woman and made his hurried way to the lead bus. Silly American, he thought, those buses are not for hire. He knew the American was running to his own death. Allah's Will, be done.

To Achmad's horror the American did not attempt to board the bus of children, but instead, knocked one of the martyrs to the ground and exposed the explosives beneath the clothes. Just before the blast, he heard the American give the alarm, "Run!" to his woman.

As he slid away from the carnage of the blast he knew that the stupid American had destroyed months of work. For his meddling, the American's should be his next target, but Achmad had an important meeting in Qatar, and he had little time to spare.

~~

Of the six OPEC members attending the meeting - Iran, Iraq, Kuwait, Qatar, Saudi Arabia, and the United Arab Emirates – the only head of state attending was Prince Al-Sabah. Only the Kuwaiti delegation included an American - Bill Cannon. Only the Iranian delegation included a holy Imam, the Ayatollah Khommani, and a Russian. The six countries represented 58% of all known oil reserves in the world.

The opening remarks clearly established the Iranian agenda was more political than economic.

"Since the days of my grandfather the Arab states have lived under the oppressive policies of the West. Their decadent ways have begun to poison our young and turn them away from the true path to heaven. Even before the imperial powers of the new world divided our lands after the first Great War, our ancestors were murdered, our women were raped, our children killed, and our cities pillaged and burned in the Holy Wars. Allah has blessed us with the strength to survive those injustices. He has granted us the wisdom and the power to establish a new order where the followers of Allah will assume their rightful place as the leaders of the world and champions of the true faith.

"It is written that believers are due the Jizya (non-believer tax) from those who do not follow the word. It is our duty to now collect this through the blessings bestowed upon us by the most merciful and gracious Allah. Our nations must now bond together and double the bounty we charge for the oil that Allah has so graciously allowed us to control. It is the way that will allow us to spread the word of God."

168

It was a righteous call that many at the conference had heard before, but never before had Iran been the dominant power in the region. Only Iran pursued nuclear weapons and either possessed them or nearly did so. Only Iran brought the Russians to the conference. Only Iran was engaged in joint military operations with the Russians on the continent of Africa.

"Already we have driven the Great Satan from the lands of our fathers. The imperialistic states of Europe are weak with internal strife and weak economies. Our OPEC brothers in Africa will rush to join our cause and even Venezuela and Ecuador despise the Americans."

The Iranian slowly looked around the assembled members, as if to let his words gain strength. He then raised his hands as if praying to Allah and then turned briefly to the Russian. "We have extended to our Russian brothers an invitation to join with us in this crusade. We will control eighty percent of the world's oil. The non-believers and Zionist pigs will be brought to their knees before the will of Allah."

The rhetoric was powerful and well received by the states attending. Only Prince Al-Sabah found the courage to stand against the tide.

"What you say is true. Allah has blessed us with oil. Why in His wisdom did he not also bless us with the fertile valleys from which we could feed our brothers? Why has he not blessed us with the ability to heal our sick without the medicines we get from the West? Without the technology we get from the West our cities will rust in the sun like the oil fields in your country now do. Without oil to fuel the world's economy these things will not reach our shores. We must understand the impact our decision will have on our own children."

The Oil Minister spread his hand to the Russian as if the answer was sitting on the stage with him and that it should be clear for all to see. "Our friends from the north can provide for our needs. Our trade with Russia will grow and we can share in their bounty."

Prince Al-Sabah shook his head. "No, the Russians cannot feed their own people. How can we depend on them to supply for the welfare of our citizens? All the trade from the Russians must pass through the mouths of the people of Iran before it can reach us. When many camels drink from one stream there is little water left for those at the end."

The Ayatollah Khommani, sitting next to the Iranian Oil Minister spoke. "If the followers of the true faith must suffer to spread the Word then they will be rewarded in heaven. Why does my Kuwaiti brother speak against spreading the true word of God?"

169

Prince Al-Sabah paused before he answered. "Do my brothers not understand that a hungry lion is more dangerous than one that carries a full belly? If we pluck out the eye of the eagle do my brothers think he cannot still fly and fight with one? We tread on dangerous ground when we think we can do these things without the possibility of the world uniting against us. Have the Russians poisoned your reason? They will use us to weaken their old enemy and then put us under their boot of oppression." Bill Cannon was proud of his friend for having the courage to voice dissent.

The Ayatollah answered slowly. "It is known to be true. The enemy of my enemy is my friend. The friend of my enemy may not be." It would be hard to describe it as anything less than a direct threat from the most powerful religious leader in Iran, and it was directly leveled against Prince Al-Sabah.

Prince Al-Sabah bowed, "I am but a humble servant of God, and I only seek a just peace for my people."

"Then my brother from Kuwait will find it in his heart to help those who fight for a just peace?" It was a new voice from the far side of the room, a voice from the past that Bill Cannon instantly recognized. His hand instinctively moved to the .45 concealed under his coat. Prince Al-Sabah put a restraining hand on Bill's shoulder.

Prince Al-Sabah didn't miss a beat. "Peace be with you, Achmad Nardiff. Would $30,000,000 convince you of my loyalty?"

Achmad Nardiff bowed deep. "My brother is very generous."

~~

Bill sat across from Prince Al-Sabah and General Al-Wadi, his senior military advisor, in the back of the limousine. The trip to the airfield was only a short 20 minute drive.

"Your highness, do you know Achmad Nardiff is responsible for most of the terrorist bombings throughout the world?" Bill noticed General Al-Wadi stiffen at the mention of the name.

"Which man who loves peace does not know of Achmad Nardiff? He spreads terror like most men spread cheese on bread."

"Your generous gift surprised me."

Bill's statement could be considered insulting, questioning the Crown Prince of Kuwait. General Al-Wadi responded as any loyal officer would and leaned forward to challenge Bill. Bill did not fear Al-

170

Wadi and in the close confines of the limousine he was no threat unless he moved to grab his sidearm. "Colonel Cannon, you do not know…"

He was stopped by Prince Al Sabah's hand. "General Al-Wadi, Colonel Cannon deserves to know the truth." When Al-Wadi leaned back in his seat the Prince turned to Bill.

"Achmad Nardiff is the worst kind of terrorist. He will kill Muslims for Jews, Jews for Muslims, Christian, Americans, Arabs, Russians, any race, any nation, any religion; he will kill anybody for money. He is not on jihad; he is an arm of the devil. We pay, as do all countries in the Middle East for his protection. When I say 'his protection,' what I really mean is that we pay him to spare our citizens and property from his acts of terror. Your country and nations around the world have done the same. America, when it was young and weak, paid $2 of $10 in the treasury to the Barbary Pirates. Nations now pay the pirates in Somalia to let their vessels pass the Horn of Africa. It is easier and cheaper to pay Achmad Nardiff for his protection than to turn over every rock to find his tunnel to Hell. It is something I hate to do, but I must consider the safety of my people. It is a small price to pay."

Chapter 24

The meeting with Doc Broderson could have been better. Angelina Sanchez had to admit the only things she accomplished were to piss off Doc Broderson, and probably alert the entire police force of her suspicions of a cover-up. A cover-up of what…she still couldn't quite put her finger on.

Did the police cover-up the killings associated with the Hanna Walton rape? Four of five suspects killed and not one investigation. Or was there a police cover-up of the killings associated with the drug bust, at least a half dozen dead bodies and not a single investigation; she didn't consider the sketchy reports by Buford Long as anything near an official investigation. Or, this was a growing possibility, were the police involved in the drug deal and their lack of adequate investigations was an attempt to hide their involvement?

The sole item in her growing list of suspicions that had a clear beginning and a clear end was the death of Bomani Thomas. "Mr. Griffin, I need all the records you have on a Bomani Thomas. He was sentenced to life…"

Mr. Griffin interrupted her request. "I know who he is. You're all over the parking lot, aren't you; who's next, the chief of police?"

It was obvious by his tone that Doc Broderson must have already spread the word of her suspicions. It wasn't going to help her investigation. She knew her decision to talk with Doc Broderson was a bad idea.

"You can save your sarcastic remarks, Mr. Griffin. Just bring me the records. And also bring me what you have on a John Brown Jackson."

"Who the hell is John Brown Jackson?"

"He's the convict who killed Thomas in prison. Bring me what you have on him."

Angelina felt chilled. Was it the temperature or the sudden realization that her careless questioning of Doc Broderson created a hostile environment in which she must now work? When Wade Griffin

172

finally delivered the requested files on Bomani Thomas it wasn't with the courtesy he had delivered files in the past. There was no greeting or casual talk. He normally stacked the records neatly against the wall in her office, these he simply dumped in the middle of the floor. "I don't have any records on John Brown Jackson."

"He was convicted of murder and was killed in the state pen. How would you not have records on him?"

"His records and his personal belongings are stored at the Bureau of Prisons."

"Well, can you get them for me?"

"Not my department lady. You will have to fill out a request and get it approved by the Chief; in fact, any additional records you require will have to be by written request."

"Mr. Griffin, do you consider that necessary?"

"Full cooperation. That's what we said we would provide to your investigation. That's what you will get. You need something, request it, and you will get it. By the way, you said you were going to return the Thunder file today. Are you finished with it?"

So, that's the way the game was to be played. Angelina handed the Thunder file to Mr. Griffin. Without so much as a thank you, he simply turned and left her office. The chill didn't leave with him.

It was unnecessary and extra work, but Angelina typed a request for John Brown Jackson's file and forwarded the request to the office of the Chief of Police. She wouldn't need the Chief's approval to get the Federal records maintained on Steve Thunder; after all, she was with the United States Department of Justice on special assignment for the United States Attorney General. She had clout and the full weight of the United States Government behind her, and would show these country hicks what a professional investigation should look and feel like.

She sent her request for Thunder's records to the Inter-Agency Liaison Office, Department of Justice, Washington, D.C.; she added the name of John Roger 'Doc' Broderson as an after-thought. Let's see if these people had anything to hide.

Her fingers flew over the letters on her keyboard and didn't slow until the quiet ding of the computer announced she had incoming mail. "How about lunch? I'm buying if you come to the CNN Center." It was from Eric Brown.

The thought of Eric Brown brought a much needed smile to her lips. If she left for home now, she could change and be at the CNN Center by noon. But then she caught herself. Doc's accusation still lingered in her ear. If she was to have a future with Eric Brown then he would have to accept her for what she was, a Federal Law Enforcement Officer. Take it or leave it. Today was as good a day as any to find out what part Eric Brown would hold in her future.

"I'll be right down," was her reply. For the first time since arriving in Atlanta, she thought it best to lock the door of her office as she left for lunch.

~~

All the bravado about telling Eric her profession left her as she drove to the CNN Center. Maybe just a couple or more dates before she told him. There was no reason to rush into a confession before she knew Eric felt the same way about her, as she felt herself growing towards him. She removed the Glock from her belt and placed it in her purse. Eric met her as she was walking from the parking garage.

Eric smiled as he approached Angelina. He circled her shoulders with his left arm and gave her a slight hug. "Thanks for coming. I've got an hour. Let's eat and then I'll take you on a tour of the studio. Does that sound good to you?"

Angelina liked the way Eric's arm felt around her. "Sure. How's the shoulder feel?"

"Not too bad. It's a little stiff, but I don't think I'm going rafting any time soon anyway. How about you, everything OK?"

"I'm fine. Eric, I want to apologize for that thing on the river. If I had not been so foolish, the entire thing could have been avoided."

Eric hugged her closer. "Don't worry, no real damage done. Just next time, if you want to rumble with the boys, let me know before we go. I'll bring some friends along."

Both laughed at the comment, Eric's a hearty laugh, Angelina's more reserved and nervous.

"Oh, and by the way, what did you say to the policemen? Absolutely nothing came across the wire about our little scuffle."

"I told him who you were, and that you were two-timing your girlfriend. If she found out it would cause you a lot of trouble."

"Good thinking." Eric pushed open the door to the atrium of the CNN Center. "For taking such good care of me, I have planned a lunch for you at some of the finest dining establishments in Atlanta."

Eric swept the expanse of the atrium with his good arm. "Take your pick. There's chicken, burgers, Mexican, Chinese; it's your choice."

Angelina almost laughed when she saw the choices Eric offered. The entire expanse was almost wall-to-wall fast food restaurants. She turned to Eric with a smile, "You really know how to impress a woman, don't you."

Eric led the way to Chick-Fil-A. "Spare no expense when you're trying to impress the ladies—that's my motto."

Angelina never would have believed a chicken sandwich could taste so sweet. Their lunch was leisurely and relaxed. The small tables allowed their hands to touch on occasion near the joint pile of waffle fries. Eric was witty and Angelina giggled at his silly jokes. They lingered over their drinks not wanting the lunch to end until Eric looked at his watch. "If I'm going to show you around the studio, we better get going."

Eric gallantly cleared the small table and led Angelina to the double glass doors that led to the CNN studios. With a wave to the guard behind the glass of the security office Eric swiped his security card through the reader and led the way into a long corridor. Angelina heard the beep and knew instantly her charade was up. The frame of the entrance doubled as a cleverly disguised metal detector. Angelina noticed the guard move from the office and another emerged from behind another security station at the end of the hall.

The first guard politely asked, "Mr. Brown, may I talk with you a moment?"

Eric had never been stopped by security before. Maybe he needed to sign Angelina in. He excused himself and walked to the guard. The guard beckoned Eric behind the glass enclosing the security office. Angelina knew they would always try to separate employees from a possible intruder to prevent any hostage situation.

"Mr. Brown, is everything OK?"

"Sure, no problems, do I need to sign her in?"

"You know we take security very serious. We can't make exceptions for anyone."

"I didn't know it was against the rules to give personal tours. What's the problem?"

"I believe the woman with you has a gun in her purse. We are going to have to search her."

"Angelina? Don't be ridiculous."

"I'm sorry Mr. Brown, but there are no exceptions. Please ask her to come here."

Eric turned to call to Angelina and noticed the guard from down the hall was much closer now and although his weapon was still holstered, his hand was on the grip. "Angelina, this officer wants to search your purse. It's just routine security."

Eric was surprised and somewhat taken aback when Angelina's holstered Glock 9mm tumbled from her purse. Angelina saw the guard's hand move under the countertop and heard the unmistakable click of an emergency call button; probably summoning the police.

"Miss, weapons are not allowed in the CNN studios, and carrying a concealed weapon is against the law. Do you have a concealed weapons permit?"

"Yes I do, it's in that folded leather wallet, there."

The guard moved the Glock away from Angelina's reach before he opened the wallet. There in blazing gold was the federal badge of the United States Department of Justice and above the identification card with Angelina's picture embossed in the plastic of the card. The gig was up.

"I'm a Federal Agent with the Department of Justice." She turned to Eric. "I'm sorry Eric, I wanted to tell you, but never got the nerve. I'm sorry."

Eric regained his composure from his obvious surprise. "Don't be sorry. I feel safer already!"

The crisis was averted because there was no crisis. Eric needled her during the entire tour. Maybe later they could play some games with her handcuffs and with a nudge and a wink, "If you know what I mean," and maybe next date they could go and arrest some drunks.

Before Eric returned to work, he escorted her to the same door where they entered. Angelina stood on her tip toes and kissed him on the cheek. "Thank you."

It was a simple good-bye but Eric remembered it through the entire broadcast. His anchor partner asked why he was grinning during the entire broadcast. She found his reply a little puzzling.

"Because the world looks pretty good to me right now."

~~

The hour lunch with Eric had turned into almost three. Angelina's fears of rejection were unfounded and she found a new spring in her step and a great weight off her shoulders. Lunch was so pleasant that she gave thought to taking the afternoon off simply to extend the feeling. Ignoring her emotions, she returned to the dungeon that had become her office. Such was her euphoria that she didn't notice the furtive glances cast her way, but she did hear the incessant ring of her telephone even before she unlocked the door to her office.

"Angelina Sanchez."

"Please hold for Director Jefferson."

While on hold, Angelina clicked her email and had visibility of the files request. The request went through the liaison office to the Military Personnel Center. The Military Personnel Center forwarded it to the Pentagon requesting guidance. The Pentagon sent it to William Jefferson requesting justification. William Jefferson dispensed with the civility of email; Jefferson worked best on the phone.

"Sanchez, what in the hell are you doing requesting military personnel files?"

"Mr. Jefferson, I found the man who wrote the letter to the President. He was a member of a gang that raped a young girl in 2003. Five suspects were listed...none prosecuted...and four of the suspects were killed. One of the suspects was killed in prison. Three other suspects all died violent deaths, and none of the deaths were investigated.

"Somehow, and I haven't figured it all out yet, but the killings may have been linked to a drug deal more than the rape. I checked with DEA about the bust. The intelligence they had was that heroin was imported by US soldiers stationed in Afghanistan. The DEA arrested and prosecuted the soldiers but never recovered the heroin. The heroin recovered in the drug deal here in Atlanta was from Afghanistan. The DEA recovered the dope, but made no attempt to recover the money. There are at least nine deaths associated with the drug deal; none of which were investigated.

"Those facts lead me to believe there is reasonable suspicion to investigate the Atlanta Police Department in the vigilante murders of three members of the gang that raped Hanna Walton. Second, there is reasonable suspicion to investigate the Atlanta Police Department for conspiracy in the murder of nine people associated with the sale of heroin. And third, there is reasonable suspicion to investigate the Atlanta Police Department's involvement in the sale of heroin to persons unknown."

William Jefferson took a moment to digest what he heard. "How do the military records of Thunder and Broderson enter into your investigation?"

"It was Officer Steve Thunder, retired US Army, working on the Atlanta Police Department Anti-Drug strike force, who pinpointed the location of the drug buy. It was Officer Steve Thunder who recovered the drugs for the DEA. It was Officer Steve Thunder who participated in the murder investigation of Reverend Walton. Thunder's name was the only common denominator in all aspects of the crimes involved. That is unusual."

"And Broderson, how does he come into play?"

"Broderson is a medic with emergency services here in Atlanta. He and Thunder served in the Army together."

Apparently Angelina's explanation was satisfactory; for all Director Jefferson said was, "Watch your back. I'll get back to you."

Chapter 25

Was it the human emotion of envy that she felt?

When Ken finished with her, he slipped from beneath the sheets, went to his pants draped carelessly over the chair and removed the box. He made a show of hanging the solitaire pendant around her neck and draped the stone between her breasts, his hands caressing her as he did so. The diamond was nice, but she had received larger and more brilliant stones before; or was it that the diamonds Rachel wore were larger?

Or was it that Ken would leave her and drive to his wife and enjoy the pleasantries of home and her sister, and leave Karen to the loneliness of her apartment and the remainder of the night alone? Or was it the common vice of greed that she wanted more, that helped her make the decision?

Those things may have been part of it, but the real reason was power. The power she craved was the power to control her own life, and power to control Ken, and even power over her sister. The thrill of the chase was long forgotten and there were new adventures to be sought, and new men to be conquered. She could do all those things now.

No longer would she endure the weight of his body on hers, and his meager thrusts and sweating body. She had given him what he demanded, and now it was her time to savor the rewards of her labors. And she would have those things she desired, maybe a house on the ocean, or a new Mercedes, maybe she would be the one to enjoy the warm beaches of the Bahamas and the services of the young men offering her drinks in frosted glasses.

Karen's night was filled with dreams of those things and they would be within her reach. She deserved better, she deserved more, she deserved the best life had to offer; and tomorrow she would get it.

~~

Ken leaned back in the leather chair and smiled. The balances on the screen were impressive and his expectations were high. Life couldn't be much better.

The phone call from Karen was unexpected, but a lunch date could be worked into the schedule. Maybe they could drive to that spot on the river and Karen would reward him for the diamond. Just the thought of Karen's soft lips on him stirred his desires, and he had to shift in his chair and concentrate on the numbers on the computer to regain his composure. Lunch couldn't come soon enough.

Karen's phone call had an ominous urgency to it, and when he reflected on it later, he would describe the sinister edge to her voice as demanding. There was none of the usual coy sexual banter, none of the innuendo that usually laced their conversations. She simply told him to, "Meet me at Pepper's at noon."

The dim lighting in the bar and the crush of the crowd made it difficult to find Karen. She wasn't at the bar where she always made sure she was the center of attention. Ken continued his search in the more private corners of the establishment. He finally found her in a booth on the second floor. She was nursing a tall drink and the condensation that had collected on the napkin told Ken she had been waiting for a while.

"Hello sweet baby." Ken leaned forward and expected a kiss but none was offered. When Karen turned away from his advance he retreated and slipped into the facing seat of the booth.

"Karen, is something wrong?" Karen seemed distant and distracted. Ken had never seen her in such a manner. The pendant he purchased was missing and he wondered why.

"Why aren't you wearing the necklace?"

"Don't worry about the necklace. You've got more important things to worry about."

The comment surprised Ken. It was unlike Karen to be so rude. "Is something wrong?"

"Nothing is wrong. I've given this a lot of thought, and I think it's time you started sharing the wealth a little. I need more help."

This wasn't the reception Ken expected. "Karen, I already pay most of your bills. You know I will always take care of you. How much do you think you need?"

Karen had given the figure she wanted considerable thought. She needed enough to live on and then added enough to make life comfortable. "Forty thousand a month."

"Forty thousand a month? That's outrageous! I could never hide that much money from Rachael. I can't do that."

Karen calmly replied. "You can, and you will, or our little love video will find its way to more than one computer. What would Rachael think? For that matter, what would the bank think? "

"This is blackmail!"

"You can call it whatever you like. I call it payment for services rendered. I expect a check every week. You're smart enough to figure out how to do it."

Ken sat in the booth for almost an hour after Karen left. When he finally left the bar, he paid no attention to the lone man sipping a beer in the booth far across the room. If Ken would have been more alert, maybe he would have noticed the directional microphone and camera concealed beneath the newspaper he read.

~~

The walk back to the bank, normally a relaxing break from the pressures of the bank, only heightened his feeling of hopelessness. Years of extraordinary risk and hard work were lost with the unrealistic demands of Karen. Ken leaned forward and cradled his head in his hands. How had his life come to this?

To compound the already shitty day, the window on his phone flashed Ed Helton. Concentrate! The mental lashing was important. Don't compound an already bad day by making a mistake with the bank president.

"Yes Sir?"

"Ken, are you busy?"

Ken Carson noticed Ed Helton called him by his first name. Ed Helton never did that. It was always Mr. Carson, never Ken. That in-of-itself made the phone call different from all the others. Ken knew better than to let the sudden familiarity cloud his thinking; Ed Helton was still the president of the bank.

"I am reviewing loan applications. How may I help you?"

"When you get a moment would you mind stepping into my office? There is something I would like to discuss with you."

Again the familiarity; never in his tenure with the bank did Mr. Helton seem so inviting. "Certainly sir, I'll be right up."

181

As Ken collected the loan applications, his palms began to sweat and he felt his pulse begin to quicken. Had he been caught? Was the inviting tone of Mr. Helton nothing more than a ruse to get him to go quietly into the waiting arms of a federal marshal? He considered running away, but knew he had nowhere to run. There was no escape. If he had been caught, and would spend the next years in jail, then at least he wouldn't have to pay Karen for silence. There would be some small comfort in that; so there was a bright side to his impending arrest.

As he walked the hall to Helton's office he decided that he would claim his innocence, and indignation, and would threaten a law suit for defamation of character, and would then hope his lawyer could find some loophole in the law to spare him the maximum sentence. There were some low-security white collar crime prisons in Virginia that wouldn't be so bad. All these thoughts raced through Ken's mind the closer he came to the president's office.

Ed Helton met Ken at the door of his office. Ken was shocked when Mr. Helton actually put his arm around his shoulders and welcomed him. Apparently Ed Helton didn't notice Ken's relief that there was no sheriff or marshal with handcuffs waiting in the office.

"Thanks for coming up." Even before they were through the door Ed Helton called to his assistant to bring some coffee.

Ed Helton led Ken away from the formal setting of his desk to the low coffee table and deep leather chairs near the picture window overlooking the Savannah River.

"Ken, you've done a wonderful job as the manager of the loan department. Your office is the most profitable in the bank and I wanted to personally thank you for a job well done. In fact, I wouldn't be surprised if a vice presidency isn't in your future."

Ken was flattered. "Why, thank you Mr. Helton. I appreciate the compliment." Promotion to vice president would fit nicely into Ken's personal recovery plan. In the current economic morass that was America everybody had a recovery plan. The US Government had a recovery plan, and a promotion to vice president would help Ken execute his. Ken's plan involved cleaning up all his financial loose ends, and then taking Rachael and moving far away from Karen.

The conversation slowed to almost nothing as the coffee was placed between them. Ed Helton waited for his secretary to leave the room and close the door before he continued. "You know, Ken, the economy has really hurt a lot of people."

The statement about the economy was obvious. Ken could only agree. "Yes sir, it has."

Ed was bent slightly forward with his attention directed to the coffee on the table. "Probably the hardest hit has been those in real estate and construction."

"Yes sir, those and many others." Ken wondered where this conversation was leading.

"Ken, I have a friend who has really been hit hard by the economy. His name is Hans Dieter. He's the president of a BMW dealership in the upstate. If the owners find out about his finances they will probably fire him. I want to help him clear up some of his problems. I want you to clear your calendar this afternoon and take care of him. Needless to say, this will require a certain amount of discretion. I want you to personally process the paperwork."

Ken noticed Ed Helton remained focused on the coffee. Almost as if he wanted to avoid direct eye contact with Ken.

"Sir, I can do that. That shouldn't be a problem. Will this be a commercial loan or a personal one, and do you have any idea of the size of the loan Mr. Dieter seeks?"

Ed continued to gaze at the coffee table. "He needs $2,000,000. Make it a commercial loan, interest only for the time being."

"If he is using the assets of the dealership as collateral, that amount shouldn't be a problem. I can have it done right away."

Finally Ed looked up from the table and looked directly at Ken. "That's where the discretion is required. He can't use the dealership and his personal finances won't qualify. This will be a non-secured loan. He has some things in the works that should allow him to repay this loan in a very short time."

This was exactly the type deal that got many loan officers in trouble. But these instructions were coming directly from the president of the bank. "Are you sure we want to make an unsecured loan for that amount?"

"He's a good friend and I trust him. It will be OK." Ed Helton paused for a moment. "And Ken, I want this paperwork to disappear when the loan is paid off."

Destroy the paper trail? That was a strange request coming from Ed Helton. Maybe Mr. Ed Helton and his friends aren't so high and mighty after all.

"Do you want to see Mr. Dieter when he comes in?"

Ed Helton redirected his attention back to the coffee table. "No, it will be better if I am not involved in the loan. In fact, I will be out of the office this afternoon. Just take care of him and keep it quiet."

As Ken gathered the few items he brought to the meeting, he knew he was leaving the strangest meeting ever with Mr. Ed Helton.

When Mr. Hans Dieter arrived to process the loan, his actions were as mysterious as Mr. Helton's earlier in the day. Dieter gave the sense that he was being stalked during the time it took to arrange for the check to be processed. His nervous twitches and glances towards the door when footsteps approached even had Ken on edge.

But within two weeks Mr. Hans Dieter paid the loan in full and was all smiles and gracious when he produced the bank draft from the National Bank of Panama that covered the entire amount of his loan.

~~

Ken would have considered this incident a once in a lifetime event, if it were not for the call he received the day after Dieter paid his loan. The phone call was from, "...Jerry Evans. I'm a friend of Hans Dieter, he referred me to you. I was wondering if I could come in and discuss a loan."

Simply the reference to Hans Dieter made Ken nervous. "May I ask what type of loan you are considering?"

Mr. Evans described the loan in the terms Ken clearly understood. "The same kind of loan Hans Dieter got."

Ken didn't like the idea that the Hans Dieter loan had become public knowledge. His good sense told him that he must find a delicate manner in which to tell Ed Helton that his friends couldn't be blabbing the details of the loan to their friends—no matter how well connected they might be.

"Mr. Evans, what is the size of the loan you will be requesting, and when will you need the money?"

"I need a million dollars and I need it today."

Jesus Christ, thought Ken, these guys don't play around.

"Mr. Evans that is a rather large sum of money; what is the purpose of the loan?"

Evans didn't hesitate when he answered. "I'm a little over-leveraged right now and I've got an inside line on some investments. I'm about 20 minutes from the bank."

Before Ken could answer the line went dead. Did this stranger just expect to call the bank and get a million dollar loan? Ken shook his head in disbelief. Mr. Evans acted as if his request would be automatically approved. It made Ken more than a little resentful toward the man he had yet to meet. Ken knew he better get guidance on handling this particular loan request and he reached for the phone.

"Mr. Helton, I just received a strange request from a friend of Hans Dieter—a Mr. Jerry Evans. He has requested a sizable loan similar to the Dieter loan. I thought it best to ask for your guidance."

Ed Helton didn't seem at all surprised. "Jerry called huh? When he gets in your office, have him give me a call."

And that is exactly what Ken did when the demanding Mr. Evans burst into his office. After the rushed introductions, Ken placed Evans in the chair facing his desk. "Mr. Helton has asked to speak with you before we proceed any further."

Jerry Evans showed no concern at the mention of Ed Helton. "Not a problem. I haven't talked with Ed in a while."

Ken dialed the number and waited for Ed Helton to pick up. "Mr. Helton, I have Mr. Jerry Evans for you. Please hold."

Ken handed the phone to Evans and waited for the fireworks he knew were to come. Ken only heard Jerry's side of the conversation but, it was enlightening to say the least.

"Hello Ed, how is the family?"

It was a casual start to what Ken expected to be a one sided conversation, but Jerry didn't seem to be bothered in the least. His answers flowed easily as if he had nothing to hide from the president of the bank.

"I need a million and I need it today....The cartel meets tomorrow in Miami....It's supposed to have something to do with the government in Zimbabwe...no, not long. The turn should be less than a week....fine, I'll do it, thanks."

Mr. Jerry Evans handed the phone back to Ken. "He wants to talk with you."

Ed Helton's instructions were short and to the point. "Ken, make the loan—same deal as last time."

Ten days later Mr. Jerry Evans showed up in Ken's office with a bank transfer of $1,400,500 dollars. Mr. Evans instructions were also clear.

"Take the entire loan from this and then transfer half the remaining money to my business account and half to this account in the Cayman Islands."

As Ken processed the request, the two men had a few moments where the silence between them became a noticeable embarrassment. Ken decided to try and break the ice.

"That was some kind of investment to return over 40 percent in just a little over a week."

"Yeah, we knocked it out of the park with this one."

Jerry Evans actually rubbed his hands together like a greedy man would do before counting the rent money from poor tenants. Ken should have felt revulsion at a man so bent on making money, but what he actually felt was envy. Envy that this man, no smarter than he, could make this kind of return when Ken was struggling to maintain his investments on the American stock exchanges. The payments he had made to Karen made his meager returns a bitter pill to swallow.

Ken ventured a casual question. "Which market are you using: New York, Chicago, Japan?"

Ken tracked all these exchanges on an hourly basis. Nowhere could he identify anything that returned the kind of money Mr. Evans just deposited in the Coastal Bank.

Evans took a quick look over his shoulder before answering. "I'm a member of an investment syndicate. We bid on investment opportunities presented by an international investment cartel." Jerry Evans rubbed his hands together once again; it was a habit that Ken Carson was beginning to find offensive. "We're making a killing!"

This was exactly the kind of returns that Ken needed to dig himself out of his financial troubles. "I've got a little money lying around to invest. How do you sign up for this investment cartel? Is it on the web?"

Maybe Mr. Evans simply wanted to boast about his good fortune—why make money if you couldn't brag about it? "You can't. You have to be invited. It's very exclusive and very private. Besides, it takes a lot of cash to play. The minimum syndicate bid is $10,000,000. I doubt you could afford to play."

Ken took offense at this obnoxious man's evaluation of his financial status; if Mr. Evans was that well-to-do, then he wouldn't be begging for a $1,000,000 loan. Ken kept his composure at the insult—he wanted to challenge his visitor to a comparison of personal balance sheets—but he wanted to learn more about these investment syndicates.

"You're a member of a syndicate? How many members do you have?"

"We have five members. I don't know how many others there are. They come from all over the world."

"It may surprise you Mr. Evans, but I have a considerable portfolio I can invest. Let's just say that I wouldn't need to rush to a bank to get a loan for an investment opportunity tomorrow."

"Is that right? How much do you have you could invest?"

Ken didn't try to play coy with his reply. He was proud to announce that he had, "Millions," to invest. Ken noticed an immediate change in Mr. Evans attitude toward him, and now it was Ken who could play the condescending one.

Mr. Evans took his time before answering. "Well, Mr. Carson, we could always use another investor. I'll mention you to the group."

As Ken thanked his guest and escorted him to the door, he wanted one more bit of information. "Mr. Evans, is Mr. Helton a member of your syndicate?"

Jerry Evans manner turned from boastful and overly entertaining and engaging to stern and distant in a single moment. His tone conveyed the intensity of his comment.

"Mr. Carson, that is a stupid question; don't ever ask it again. This isn't calling your broker and placing a bid on 20 shares of Coca-Cola. You only know who is in your syndicate and no one else. These people shape the economy of the world. Don't make the mistake that they give a rat's ass about you or me. This isn't a country club, it is high stakes investments. These people will do anything...*anything* to protect the security and privacy of the cartel. Forget I even mentioned it."

Ken got the message loud and clear, but forgetting what he had heard was not going to be possible. "Mr. Evans, I apologize if I was out of line, but I would like to hear more about your business."

Chapter 26

Angelina studied the white board in her office. Like Officer Steve Thunder, Bomani Thomas was a common denominator in the rape of Hanna Walton and the drug deal.

For the number of crimes committed by Thomas the files were surprisingly sparse. Thomas wasn't on the legal radar until arrested for the rape of his ex-girlfriend, and his killing spree in the same building in which she now sat; sloppy police work and three dead at the courthouse. It turned Angelina's stomach.

The file made no mention of any connection between Thomas and Hanna's rape, or Thomas and the drug deal. The only thing left to do was watch a video news report of his death. The quality of the video is what you would expect of a security camera, grainy and shot from a great distance. But the events in the prison yard were obvious.

Thomas and two other inmates attacked John Brown Jackson, the inmate fingered by Frenchy as the inside source for the drugs. Jackson was standing alone near the prison yard weight benches when Thomas and two others attacked. Time and time again they lunged at Brown, to no avail as Brown easily eluded them. Not until Brown turned Bomani Thomas's own knife back upon him were the others able to get to Brown. But Brown would not release Thomas and both died in the prison yard. Angelina couldn't put her finger on it, but there was something vaguely familiar about the fight. She knew the video made national news, and maybe she had seen it before she enrolled in the academy.

No matter, in Angelina's mind it was poetic justice; Brown and Thomas died by each other's hand. The murdering rapist was killed by a murdering drug dealer. They deserved each other.

The phone rang as she finished watching the video for the fourth time. The call from Wade Griffin was abrupt and short. "Sanchez, those files on John Brown Jackson you ordered from the Bureau of Prisons is on the loading dock."

"Well, are you going to bring them up?"

188

"I didn't order them, you did. If you want them, you can get them."

Three large boxes stood abandoned on the loading dock. Angelina checked the shipping label on the top box. It said, "Deliver to Agent Angelina Sanchez, US Department of Justice at Georgia Justice Center, Atlanta, Georgia. Personal Effects and Files on John Brown Jackson, Prisoner #C428-M331 LWOP, January 7, 1994, Died August 12, 2003." Angelina guessed the LWOP meant life without parole.

Angelina called Wade Griffin from the loading dock. "Why did the Bureau send me the personal effects of Jackson? I don't need all this stuff."

"You asked for everything they had on Jackson, that's what you got; full cooperation." Wade Griffin hung up without saying so much as a good day.

It would take Angelina the better part of an hour if she had to move the boxes individually back to the office. Finally, she found a hand cart with a wobbly wheel on which to load the boxes. No one offered to help. By the time she made it to her office and stacked the boxes next to the wall she was fed-up to the point that she put the hand cart in the elevator and pushed the button to the basement. Full cooperation meant someone else could find a place to store the cart.

Not wanting to mix any evidence, Angelina boxed up the Bomani Thomas files. As she was doing so she noticed a totally unpleasant odor beginning to fill the office. "What is that smell?"

The odor was coming from one of the three boxes stacked against the wall. Retrieving a letter opener she cut the tape on the top box. Nothing in the first or the second, but when she cut the tape on the third the full impact of decomposing flesh almost overwhelmed her. There in the third box the decomposing carcass of the biggest rat she had ever seen.

Her tirade to the Chief of Police didn't produce the expected results. His only comment was, "There are a lot of rats in prison. I have no idea how one got in the files. It happens." She at least did get a custodian crew to clean her office.

It was obvious the word of the rat spread like wildfire to the officers on duty. She could hear the laughs and childish comments from the officers passing in the hall. "Sure don't smell like tacos in there," or "I smell a rat." Even though the stench of the rat was not completely gone from the office, Angelina closed the door. The stench was easier to stomach than the comments coming from the hall.

The first thing she noticed was the uniform Brown wore on the night of his arrest, the boots and uniform still dusty from some far off battlefield. She wondered if the blood stains, now turned brown with age, were from his victims or the blood of an enemy soldier. On the shoulder of the uniform was sewn the patch of the 75th Ranger Regiment and on the front above the pockets on the chest simply his name and US Army. In the front pocket she found the letter from his son that precipitated the terrible events of his trial. In the unsure hand of a young boy the damning words, "…Mommy is sick all the time, and her boyfriend hits me and locks me in my room."

The pictures in the bottom of the boxes were personal; and all of better times. There were pictures of Brown, his wife and son together. Sharing life as all families would like to do. The terrible outcome of this wasted life affected Angelina in a way she never expected. It was a tragedy and all too common. The Bible was well worn but there were no highlighted lines or passages that would shed light on this man. Inside the back cover of the Bible was a carefully folded newspaper article. The caption to the picture read, "Members of the Cairo Cub Scout Troop enjoy a tour of the Military History Museum at Valdosta Air Force Base." Angelina wondered if the young black boy in the foreground was Jackson's son. As far as Angelina could determine, it was the last piece of civilization Jackson received before his death.

Death…it was exactly what her office smelled like and she couldn't take it anymore. She went to the nearest two restrooms and took every block of industrial deodorant she could find and scattered them around her office.

Maybe by the time she got back from Savannah and her interview with Buford Long, the stench in her office would be gone.

~~

As Angelina walked to her car she wished Eric would call. It's not that she wasn't tough enough to weather the storm at the office, but it would have been nice to simply lean against him and gain strength. She would have hit the gym, but getting out of the clothes inundated with decaying rat carcass seemed a more pressing issue.

She stripped naked in front of the washing machine and added extra soap to the heavy duty cycle. Her shower also heavy duty - extra hot and extra long, only when her skin was almost raw from vigorous scrubbing, and almost burned red from the hot water, did she leave the shower.

With a towel wrapped around her she ran her clothes through another cycle. It was then she noticed the blinking light on her cell phone.

"This is Eric. How's my favorite federal investigator doing? I'm sorry I missed you. I want to let you know I will be out of town for the next few days. My aunt isn't feeling well and I wanted to spend some time with her. I'll give you a call when I get back."

Angelina missed the call by 20 minutes. She called, but could only leave a message. "This is Angelina, and how is my favorite news anchor doing? Sorry to hear about your aunt. Let me know if I can do anything. This is good timing, I'll be out of town the next couple of days also. I miss you. Give me a call when you're back in town."

~~

Buford Long was every Southern sheriff stereotype Angelina ever had—he even had an old bloodhound lounging on the porch next to his rocker. As she opened the gate and walked through the white picket fence, the bloodhound gave her a glance and then laid his head on his paws. Dusty work boots snaked into khaki trousers held up by red suspenders over a white short sleeved shirt and all topped with a straw cowboy hat. Buford Long alternated taking sips of sweet tea and spitting tobacco juice over the rail.

From below the porch she said, "Sheriff Long, I am Angelina Sanchez. Thank you for seeing me."

Angelina withdrew her credentials from her purse and extended them for Long's review. "May I come up?"

Buford Long waved her onto the porch and closely reviewed her identification. He nodded Angelina to a rocking chair next to the small table separating the chairs.

"What can I do for you miss?"

"Sheriff Long, I have reviewed your record. It is quite impressive: FBI, Director of the Georgia Bureau of Investigation, 25 years as Sheriff of Chatham County."

Long let loose with a long stream of tobacco juice over the rail. "You said you had some dead cases you wanted to discuss with me. Get to it."

191

It was an offensive but natural gesture, the spitting of the tobacco juice; but it was the manner in which Buford Long used it to punctuate his impatience with her that bothered Angelina.

"In 2003 you were listed as the investigating officer in a home invasion at the residence of Reverend Peter Walton, in Atlanta, where their housekeeper was killed. The report said you were wounded in an exchange of gunfire and killed the intruder."

Long let go another stream. "I remember the report."

"Six months later you were involved in another home invasion where another intruder was killed. That's a lot of action for a retired police officer."

"Miss Sanchez, if all you are going to do is tell me things that I already know, you are wasting my time."

Sheriff Long had a point.

"Mr. Long, what was your association with the Reverend Peter Walton?"

"None."

"But you were in his house the day he was killed. Why?"

"Reverend Walton was married to the daughter of a good friend. He asked me to poke around and make sure everything was okay."

"Mrs. Walton's maiden name was Helton. Are you are referring to Ed Helton? There was a home invasion at his house, where you filed the report."

"Good for you Miss Sanchez, great police work."

"What is your association with Mr. Helton?"

"I do security work for him."

"Mr. Long, do you think the Reverend Walton was involved in drugs?"

"Miss Sanchez, what exactly are you investigating?"

"Mr. Long, the Department of Justice has been directed to investigate the police in Atlanta; that they may have been involved in the murders of suspects in the Hanna Walton rape. Your name has come up too many times to be a coincidence. I'm just trying to get to the bottom of a lot of suspicious killings."

Buford Long didn't bat an eye. "Miss Sanchez, who is your boss?"

"I was assigned this investigation by Director William Jefferson."

Buford Long pulled his cell phone from his shirt pocket and dialed a number and simply asked for, "Bill Jefferson please, Buford Long calling." Buford let fly another stream of juice as he waited. How often did Buford Long call the Department of Justice if he knew the number by heart?

Long's face brightened when his called was answered. Angelina could only hear one side of the conversation. "Bill, this is Buford Long...Yeah, I'm doing fine...Oh yeah, he's doing fine but he couldn't track a sausage truck now, getting too old I guess." Buford reached down and scratched the bloodhound behind the ears. "Bill, are you doing an investigation on me?"

Buford Long listened and then nodded. "Well, I've got a young lady from your office making a fuss about a couple of my cases from years ago."

Long leaned forward and handed Angelina his phone. "Bill Jefferson would like to talk with you."

Angelina heard Director Jefferson well before the phone was to her ear. It was an onslaught that she had never experienced. It was hard to follow the entire conversation, "...Buford Long...legend...law enforcement...what in the hell are you doing in Savannah...outside your instructions...get your ass back to Atlanta...I'm getting on a airplane...meet...airport...damn good expla..." Angelina handed the phone back to Buford Long even before Director Jefferson was finished with his tirade.

"Apparently I am needed back in Atlanta. I apologize for interrupting your day."

~~

Eric thanked Mike DeAngelo for the ride from Savannah to Daufuskie. Rather than use one of the golf carts available for transport of hotel guests he decided to walk the mile or so to the house. There was a noticeable change of atmosphere surrounding the resort. Maybe it was the news of Aunt Grace's illness that dampened his spirits, but the blowing trash along the road, unheard of at the resort, lent to his mood. It was a simple task to bend over and pick up the wayward paper and he couldn't understand why the employees of the resort seemed to ignore them as they walked by. It was enough to get him to turn and enter the lobby of the hotel

"Hello, I am Eric Brown. I don't have an appointment, but would it be possible to see Danni Walton?"

"She's been in meetings all morning, but I'll check."

Much to the surprise of the girl at the front desk, Mrs. Walton asked the young man to come right up.

Danni ambushed Eric with a big hug as he exited the elevator.

"Eric, it is so good to see you."

Danni looked the same. She had the same fit body and the same elegance she always possessed; only the deepening lines around her eyes gave any indication of her stress. Danni stepped back and surveyed her young friend.

"You're looking well. Atlanta must suit you." It was then Danni noticed the wadded up paper in Eric's hand. "What do you have there?"

"Just some trash I picked up on the grounds. Have the maintenance crews all gone on strike?" Eric said it as a joke, but it was close to the truth.

"No, they're not on strike, just a work slowdown. The union is trying to organize the workers and one of the things they are doing is telling the employees picking up trash isn't in their job description. If we want the trash picked up, we should hire more workers to do it. The vote comes in a week. We'll see what happens."

"I thought South Carolina was a right to work state. When did the unions move in?"

Danni face became stern. "When we were designated vital to the state's economy."

"How do you think the vote will go?"

"It could be the death of the hotel. I'm praying for a miracle."

"I hope you can work it out."

Danni hoped so also. She knew Eric wasn't here to discuss the hotel's business. "Have you been to see Aunt Grace?"

"No, not yet, I'm heading that way now. How is she doing?"

"The diagnosis caught us all by surprise. She is a strong woman and is ready for whatever comes. I know she is looking forward to seeing you. Let me get someone to drive you home."

"No, thank you, I think I would rather walk. It's not that far and I think I need some peace and reflection before I see her."

Danni knew exactly what Eric meant. When they first heard the news, she was almost afraid to confront Aunt Grace. Why would such a terrible disease afflict one so pure and gracious in every way and spare herself, one riddled with guilt of the indiscretions of her past? But Aunt Grace was not afraid or bitter and was prepared for life here or in the hereafter, whichever was God's choice. Danni was sure Aunt Grace would bring the same peace to Eric.

Eric first tried the cottage that had been his and Aunt Grace's home after their hurried departure from the shack of poverty in Cairo. When he found it empty he made his way to the main house on the Helton estate. There he found Aunt Grace sitting peacefully at the table in the kitchen watching as Mamba busied herself with dinner. Aunt Grace looked no worse for the news of her cancer.

Their conversations through the afternoon were not filled with dread. They acknowledged the trials that lay ahead and also acknowledged the obstacles they had overcome. Yes, there was concern, but there was not a great amount of fear. Aunt Grace was prepared for tomorrow whatever it may bring. There would be time for mourning, but now life was still a celebration and Aunt Grace would not allow it to be otherwise.

It was later in the day when Mamba stopped her work with preparing dinner. She turned to Eric.

"Eric, there is something different about you; more mature and wiser, of course, but also more content. Is there something that you want to share with us?"

Eric grinned at the question. He debated during his entire trip to Daufuskie if this time, considering the terrible news of Aunt Grace, would be appropriate to bring up his feelings about Angelina Sanchez. The conversations of the day made it easy to share the news. The trio enjoyed the stories of new and budding love. Eric found it easy to relay his inner most feelings and both women had advice on how to most impress his newfound love.

Chapter 27

Angelina waited for Director Jefferson in the arrival lounge of the Atlanta airport. As hundreds of travelers rushed passed, she tried to finalize her argument for the continued investigation of the Atlanta Police Department. She knew she was far from the objective of the original assignment, and maybe she was due a reprimand. She was prepared to accept that. The thought did cross her mind that Jefferson was known to fire his subordinates in person, never on the phone. Angelina hoped it wasn't that.

Maybe the purpose of his visit was nothing more than to scare her back to the scope of the original investigation. After all, the letter to the President only talked about the killings associated with the rape of Hanna Walton. Maybe Jefferson was taking heat from his superiors for her lack of progress. But, she was convinced crimes had been committed that had gone unpunished.

Now that she faced the prospect of justifying her investigation she admitted few of the crimes she was investigating fell under Federal jurisdiction. The gang rape, despicable as it was, did not involve crossing state lines so it was clearly within the jurisdiction of the State of Georgia. All the killing associated with the rape and the drugs were under state jurisdiction.

She knew her argument was weak unless she could present solid evidence that the Atlanta Police Department was corrupt and subject to the Federal Racketeer Influenced and Corrupt Organizations Act (RICO), or maybe a civil rights violation. Death, if that wasn't a violation of someone's civil rights, what was?

With the limited evidence she had, she knew any prosecution would be a stretch. The more she debated her case the more she came to realize the only solid Federal Jurisdiction involved the drugs, and drug investigations were under purview of the Drug Enforcement Administration. She just made a strong argument for her own firing and started to feel queasy in the stomach.

Finally she saw Director Jefferson crest the escalator bringing the passengers from the tunnels connecting the arrival lounge to the arrival gates.

"Welcome to Atlanta, Mr. Jefferson. How was your flight?"

"The flight was fine."

Mr. Jefferson didn't even slow down as he passed Angelina heading for the rental counter. As Angelina struggled to catch up, Jefferson opened his briefcase and pulled out a large sealed envelope and handed it to her.

"What's this?"

'That's what you wanted. That is a copy of Sergeant Major Steve Thunder's military personnel file."

Angelina was relieved that Jefferson did not intend to fire her on the spot; maybe he would fire her later, but it appeared he was going to let her plead her case in the privacy of the car or her office.

As she trailed her boss to the rental counter she opened the clasp to the envelope and pulled the military personnel jacket from the envelope. There on the front of the jacket in two inch red letters the word SECRET. A black line was drawn through the classification and a large black stamp UNCLASSIFIED and smaller letters For Official Use Only now covered the folder. It had been declassified only yesterday.

"I didn't think military personnel files were classified."

Jefferson didn't slow his advance on the rental counter but did look back at Angelina. "Most aren't. His was."

When Angelina opened the file she immediately noticed many blacked-out portions.

"What are all these blacked-out parts?"

"Those were the classified parts. DOD wouldn't let me have the file until they cleaned it up."

"How am I supposed to do a complete investigation if half the file is blacked out?" Her question didn't sound like whining to her when she asked it, but maybe Mr. Jefferson perceived it as such.

"Jesus Christ, Sanchez! You're a trained investigator. Start acting like one; or are you going to insist I bring Thunder back from the dead? You have raised a lot of eyebrows at the Pentagon asking for that file. Sergeant Major Thunder was a decorated and respected soldier. A lot of people think you are on a witch hunt and are dragging the memory of a true patriot through the mud for nothing."

Angelina did not consider her investigation a witch hunt. The tone of her challenge could have been considered by some as insubordinate. "Just because he was a good soldier doesn't mean he could not have turned bad."

Jefferson stopped in his tracks and turned to Angelina.

"I didn't say that, Sanchez. I got you that file because you may be on to something. What I do know is that you are charging all over the southeast investigating things that are not under our jurisdiction. You have pissed off the entire Atlanta Police Department and a retired law officer well thought of in Washington and here in Georgia, impugned the integrity of a dead soldier who can't defend his honor, and so far you have not produced one single piece of evidence - not one. It's getting close to the time where you will have to put up, or shut up and get back to the job you were sent here to do."

Everything her boss said was true. So rather than try to defend her investigation she used the time in the car studying Thunder's file. Although many parts were blacked out those that she could read were impressive: three purple hearts for wounds received in action, two Legions of Merit, Silver and Bronze Stars for Valor, combat tours in Serbia – Somalia – Kuwait – Iraq, US Army Rangers, Special Forces, Delta Force and others. By the time they reached the Atlanta Justice Center, she understood why so many in the Pentagon would consider her investigation a witch hunt.

Her comment summed up the experience of reviewing Thunder's file. "Wow."

Jefferson put the car in park, but left the engine running. "Makes you wonder, doesn't it? How could a man like that turn bad?"

Her response truly reflected her feelings. "Yes, it does. I hope you're right."

Angelina assumed Mr. Jefferson needed directions to the parking garage. "The parking deck is around back."

"I'm not coming in."

"You're not? You came all this way to bring me this file?"

"That and to patch things up with Buford Long. Look, Sanchez, use your head. Unless you can come up with something concrete pretty soon, all you are doing is pissing in the wind, and I still need your report on the assignment from the Attorney General. The question you really have to ask yourself is, can you build a case?"

Jefferson left her standing on the curb. As he pulled away some of the fear and apprehension she felt toward her boss faded away as unfounded. He was concerned about her investigation and obviously respected her opinion, or he would have shut her down.

Angelina had to admit Jefferson's question crossed her mind, but she had found a connection in Thunder's file that warranted further investigation. If her hunch panned out it would go a long way to doing just that, build a case. Sergeant Major Steve Thunder and John Brown Jackson, the man who killed Bomani Thomas and served as the prison contact for the heroin buy, both served in the 75th Ranger Regiment and fought together in Bosnia and Somalia. The connection was not simply a coincidence, and it was too strong to ignore.

~~

Angelina compared Thunder's service record with Jackson's. It was clear; the two had served in the same units in Central and South America, and in Somalia. The letter she found in Jackson's uniform explained his sudden departure. The rest was history.

She was trying to fill in the blanks in Thunder's file, those blacked out by the Pentagon. What was Thunder doing during those times? The blackened boxes in the file may hold the secrets she sought.

Her cell phone interrupted her thoughts.

"Hello?"

"Angelina, what are you doing this afternoon?" It was Eric, and she smiled.

"Eric, how's your aunt?" She almost could feel the spirit of the phone call die with the question.

Eric paused somewhat before he answered. "She has cancer. I'm so proud of her. She knows it's going to be a long fight, but is in great spirits. I don't know if I could be so brave."

"Is there anything I can do?"

"Angelina, I know it may sound crass, but Aunt Grace is in good hands. There's nothing we can really do, and I would like some time away from it, if you know what I mean. How would you like to go for a little hike this afternoon?"

"You don't have to work?"

Angelina felt a little life come back into Eric. "No, not until tomorrow, I have the rest of the day off. How about you? Can you sneak away?"

Jefferson was on his way to Savannah, and the files on her desk would be there tomorrow, and the lingering stench in her office made the decision an easy one.

"I'd love to go hiking." Spending the day with Eric was well worth the risk of getting caught goofing-off. "Tell me where and when, and I will be ready."

"Great, be at the gym in one hour. I'll pick you up, and what size shoe do you wear?"

"Why do you need that?" She knew her quick response sounded silly. It wasn't like Eric was asking her age or weight, for God's sake. Would he consider her size seven too big or too small?

"You are going to need some special shoes and I will pick them up for you."

"Well, I wear seven and a half in high heels but a seven in flats and sandals, but in loafers I like them to fit a little more snug…"

Eric's laugh interrupted her. Eric knew a woman could go on for an hour on shoe sizes so he narrowed the question. "Angelina, what size do you wear in a tennis shoe?"

"Seven."

"Seven it is. I'll pick you up at the gym at 11."

Eric was standing next to his truck when Angelina pulled into the parking lot. Eric extended his hand to assist her from her car, and then took her other hand; she thought he was going to kiss her. He didn't, and her pulse fell back to normal. He held her at arm length and surveyed her from head to toe.

"Perfect," was all he said, and then led her to the passenger side of the truck, opened the door and helped her climb into the cab.

"Where exactly are we going?"

"The North Georgian Mountains to a small town named Dahlonega."

"What's in Dahlonega?"

"Well, there are woods, rivers and mountains in Dahlonega; a perfect place for a hike."

Eric served as the local guide during the remainder of the drive and Angelina enjoyed every minute of it. They laughed and teased each other, and the cab of the truck was warm and inviting, much more so than the poisoned atmosphere of her office. Here there were no cutting and snide remarks from her fellow law enforcement officers; here there was the freedom to let down your guard, and the hour drive ended much too soon for Angelina.

If Angelina thought a hike with Eric would be a gentle walk in the woods, she was mistaken. The back packs, the coils of rope, the helmets, the climbing boots, the harnesses, the snap-links, the climbing hammers that Eric unloaded from the truck all indicated this wasn't to be a romantic walk along marked trails under the forest canopy. The equipment was more appropriate for an assault on Mount Everest.

Eric pointed to a backpack and unceremoniously said to Angelina, "That one is yours."

Angelina had trooped the woods in a backpack before. It was part of the training program at the Academy, so she didn't hesitate slinging it to her back and adjusting the straps. Eric loaded her down with a couple of coils of rope before collecting his pack and the remaining gear.

Eric did a last check of the gear. "Ready?"

"I'm ready, but where are we going?"

"I'm taking you to a place that's very special to me; I think you will enjoy it."

As they walked down a small trail Angelina noticed the sign, US Government Property – Contact Army Corps of Engineers for Access. It wasn't hard to miss; this wasn't a small sign nailed to a tree, it was large enough to see from 500' away and Eric walked passed it without a second glance. In fact, you had to turn your body to miss it.

"Eric, are we supposed to be in here?"

"Probably not, but you're the Federal Agent. If we get caught, you can say we're tracking a suspect." Eric turned his head and Angelina could see his smile as he talked.

"I swear Eric, if you get us in trouble I will never forgive you. What is this place?"

"This is where the Army Ranger School conducts mountain training. My uncle used to bring me up here every summer. He said he wanted me to learn how to climb, but I really think he came up here just to get away from civilization and relax. It's a special place to me. I hope you enjoy it."

"You have never mentioned you had an uncle nearby. Does he live near here?"

"No he lives down on the coast. He's not really my uncle, but he looked after me when I was younger."

"I've got a bunch of uncles, but I've never met even one. They're all still in Mexico and probably the only Mexicans who don't want to come to the United States. Maybe one day my family will go south of the border and I can meet them. I think I would like that."

"Where do your parents live?"

"They have a small farm in Roswell, New Mexico, you know, the place where the aliens landed. They have lived in the same house for 50 years."

Eric brightened at the mention of Roswell, "Hey, you know what? We have a Roswell, Georgia, in the northern suburbs of Atlanta. I have never seen any aliens up there; at least not the outer space kind."

The path they were walking started to increase in grade. "Eric, you never have talked about your parents, do they live near here?"

Angelina's head was down with the strain of the pace and the increasing grade, so she didn't see Eric stiffen at the question. "Both of my parents are dead."

It's easy to walk into a stupid question and Angelina felt bad about bringing up the issue of Eric's parents. "I'm sorry Eric, I had no idea. How did they die?"

"I don't want to talk about it."

Angelina noticed a definite increase in the pace of their walk. There wasn't any more conversation until Eric announced, "We're here."

Eric's smile and excitement told Angelina the awkward situation created by her question had passed. Where Angelina stood was at the base of a rock cliff that towered hundreds of feet straight up.

"Good Lord, Eric, we're not going to climb that thing, are we?"

Eric laughed, "Not the whole thing, only to that ledge," Eric pointed to a rocky outcropping about fifty feet above them. "There is a natural pool up there that is fed by rainwater and it's a great view. It's a hard climb, but it's safe."

"How can climbing straight up be safe? Are you crazy?"

"Only about you, but look, there are safety anchors already in the rocks all the way to the ledge, and we'll be tied together the entire time. I've seen you on the treadmills at the gym; I know you have the legs for it. What do you say? I brought you some climbing shoes, are you game?"

Against her better judgment Angelina agreed to the climb.

True to his word, Eric stayed with her and talked her through every move. Those few times when Eric offered assistance over the more difficult parts of the climb, she refused his help. This was her mountain and she would conquer it. After two hours of grueling effort they crested the ledge.

As Angelina lay panting on the rock of the ledge she asked, "Now what?"

Eric sat down next to her and loosened the laces on his boots. "I don't know about you, but I'm taking a swim," and he charged off to the face of the cliff. Angelina saw him jump and then disappear from sight immediately followed by the sound of Eric plunging into the pool of water captured by the rock formation. "Come on in, you'll love it."

Angelina walked to the edge of the pool. The water was deep, clear and inviting. Eric was floating on his back, eyes closed, letting the strain of the climb ebb from his muscles. Angelina suddenly knew she had a need for this man. She reached down and removed her boots, and then loosened the belt to her shorts and let them drop to the rock, and pulled her shirt over her head. The sun glistened off the sweat on her body and she stood naked on the rock and unashamed.

Eric watched as she slowly entered the water and made her way to Eric, and they met and folded into each other's arms. Their love was intense yet gentle, unhurried, yet at times frantic and fulfilling. As they lay drying on the warm rock they realized they had crossed a threshold, and now searched for the right words to express fear they felt for the future.

"Angelina, I didn't bring you here to..."

Angelina put her hand on Eric's, "Eric, don't say anything right now. I came to you because I wanted you. This was my decision and I don't regret it. Don't ruin it by trying to think of something clever to say. We can talk about it later."

"OK."

After a few moments, Angelina turned her head to Eric. "This was a pretty good move on your part. How many girls have you brought up here?"

Eric turned to look briefly at Angelina before looking back up the cliff face. "You are the only person I have ever brought up here. I told you, it is a very special place to me. I used to come up here and think about my parents, and the struggles of my life, but now when I come here I will probably think more of you."

Angelina closed her eyes and smiled. She felt Eric move beside her and felt the warmth of his lips on her shoulder. It had been hours since she had given any thought to Steve Thunder, the Atlanta Police Department, Buford Long, or Hanna Walton and she wasn't going to start now; she even ignored Eric's comment about his parents. This was her day and she was going to enjoy it.

Chapter 28

It wasn't exactly a panic attack that consumed Ken. It was more a total feeling of being trapped. He was like the trapped animal struggling against the snare that held a leg and all manner of struggle only tightened the noose. If he could sever the entangled member, like the animal chewing off a leg, he would, but there was nowhere to turn. He knew more loans were too risky, and it would only take one that caught the attention of Helton and the game would be up. There had to be another way out.

His temples throbbing and nerves on edge, he jolted at the sound of his cell phone. Since the vicious double-cross by Karen, the phone had become almost useless to him. There wasn't a number on the phone screen, only the word PRIVATE. He was sure it was nothing more than a misdialed call.

"Hello."

"Is this Ken Carson?"

"Yes, who is this?"

"Ken, this is Jerry Evans." It was Ed Helton's friend, the one who made such a show about his investment group. "If you have some time this afternoon, I would like to discuss some investment opportunities with you." It was an introduction Ken had heard many times before, but this call had his interest.

The mysteries of the investment syndicate shared so brazenly by Jerry Evans had stayed with Ken. He couldn't dismiss the image of Evans bragging about the money he made in such a short time. Ken believed he was simply showing off, with his outrageous claims of an international investment cartel and secret syndicates of investors. It all had to be a fairy tale, but, then again, he did bring in a sizeable check and not only paid the loan, but transferred money to other accounts like it was simply another day at the office.

Another oddity, the only thing Ed Helton ever asked was if Evans paid back the loan. When Ken added that Evans repaid the loan, and transferred an additional $450,000 to his company account and an offshore account Helton only muttered, "That lucky bastard." Ken was starting to wonder what kind of friends Mr. Helton really had.

Ken's answer to Jerry Evans was guarded. "I may be. Tell me how you got this number."

Evans dismissed Ken's question. "Don't worry about that. Ken, this is a limited time opportunity. If you are interested, then we can meet this afternoon, if not, I have other clients I can contact."

Ken saw the faint glimmer of easy money and it would cost him nothing to investigate the outlandish claims of Jerry Evans. "Mr. Evans, I may be interested, but I would like a full briefing on the investment."

"Of course, that's not a problem. Are you familiar with the Salt Water Creek Marina on the Wilmington River in Thunderbolt?"

"Somewhat."

"We'll be expecting you around 5 p.m. We'll be on the yacht *Crescent Moon*. She's tied up at the end of the marina. We'll take a little cruise and answer all your questions."

Ken was impressed when he pulled up to the marina. From the bluff overlooking the river he tried to guess which vessel was the *Crescent Moon*. As he walked the pier, the yacht to his left was resting peacefully at anchor and he guessed it was 75 feet if it was an inch, but it was dwarfed by the yacht tied at the end of the pier. And it was from the largest boat where Jerry Evans hailed Ken.

Jerry Evans met him with a smile, a handshake and a slap on the shoulder. "I'm glad you could make it. Let's get a drink. We'll cast off in a few minutes."

Jerry stopped with only one foot on the gangway. "Oh, before we board, do you have your cell phone with you?"

"Yes, I do."

"Could I have it please? We do not allow cell phones on the boat. It will be returned to you when we dock. Any other electronic devices...pager...iPad...recorder?"

Ken thought it odd, but handed the phone over to Jerry, who in turn handed it to a crewmember manning the gangway. The crewmember placed it in a briefcase and started walking away from the boat.

"Where's he taking my phone?"

"Ken, your cell phone has a tracking chip in it. That man will drive around Savannah until we dock."

It was an aspect of security Ken had never considered. These men, whoever they may be, were serious about their security.

Ken followed Jerry through a passageway and up the ladder to the stateroom overlooking the stern of the boat. Ken felt the engines rumble as the bow cut into the current. Jerry asked, "Martini okay?"

"A martini will be fine."

A burly attendant, not the pretty face in short skirt you would expect on a luxury yacht, manned the bar and prepared the drink. As Ken accepted and sipped on the drink, the burly man stepped from behind the bar and waved an electronic wand over his complete body. "He's clean."

Jerry invited Ken, "Come on, let's go meet the rest of the boys."

The introductions were brief and cordial and only the first names were revealed. Ken remembered Hans Dieter from the bank, and the big man named Henry was obviously from Texas, and Edwardo's Latino accent pegged him from Mexico or further south. The four men cautiously welcomed Ken into the group.

Once outside the river channel and with Savannah fading to a ribbon of green on the shore, the five men settled into deep leather chairs surrounding a low polished table. Hans Dieter started the conversation.

"I understand Jerry told you a little about the cartel and our investment syndicate. We are looking for the best and brightest investors to join our team. You come highly recommended. Do you want to hear more?"

"Of course, but why the spy stuff? Why here? It's a great boat and very impressive, but why not meet in an office like normal people do?"

Hans leaned forward and placed his drink on the table, the condensing water forming a ring at the base of the glass. "Let me be very clear about this, Ken. Members of the cartel and even members of our syndicate are very private individuals. They value their anonymity; and will do what it takes to remain anonymous. You must understand this is a lifetime commitment before we go on."

"If this is so secret, then why did Jerry spill the beans to me?"

"Ken, we know just about everything there is to know about you. We know who your brokers are, we have a good idea about your net

207

worth, and we know you are a genius when it comes to the market. We all consider ourselves to be tuned into the market, but you have a gift, and we would like you to become part of our team. When Jerry was in your office, he was simply testing the water…so to speak."

"Are you telling me that once you join, you can't get out?"

"Ken, I hate to use the cliché, but these people are the movers and shakers of the world's finances. Once you're brought in—you can never leave. You might stop investing, or break off to form your own syndicate, but what you learn here will go with you to the grave. I don't want to sound too ominous, but any violation of our rights to complete privacy will be dealt with harshly and immediately. That means you don't make any notes and leave them in your desk or even your safe at the office or home. You don't talk about it with your wife or your girlfriend. You never discuss it with anyone unless the syndicate approves the move; like we approved the decision to recruit you. Do you understand?"

Ken understood the implications of the veiled threats and understood with great risk often comes great reward. "Yes, I understand."

"And you would like to continue?"

Was this the miracle Ken needed to escape the clutches of Karen? He had nothing to lose. "Yes."

The International Investment Cartel (IIC) was formed after World War II by European industrialists. The initial objective was to fund investments free from interference and control of the governments that had just destroyed the world's economy. Since that time the IIC had grown to encompass almost every facet of the world's economy.

"Now, they have a worldwide network of syndicates just like ours. We bid on and fund those projects that may not stand the light of day; or the close scrutiny of more conventional banking systems. Requests for money flow into Switzerland; they do the analysis and then offer the proposals to the syndicates for bid."

A great sales pitch if Ken had to say so, but it sounded just like so many small business loans he had processed over the years. They all sounded good in the boardroom, but the reality was that most failed.

"If this is such a great deal, then why bring anybody else in? Specifically, why do you need me and my money?"

"One of our biggest players broke off to form a separate syndicate. Second, the more the syndicate can invest, the greater the return. The top bidding syndicate earns a substantial bonus, so we're looking for partners with money to invest."

The entire organization, as described, fell into place in Ken's mind. It all made sense. "You mentioned the risk involved in these investments; talk about that."

Hans Dieter didn't miss a beat. "Switzerland does a great job analyzing every funding request. There are always risks; but the rewards can be sweet." Hans rubbed his hands together and grinned.

"How does Switzerland develop the leads on the projects?"

"They get most of their leads from projects presented to the Federal Reserve, the International Monetary Fund, the World Bank, the United Nations and other organizations who fund projects. The IIC has contacts in just about every major bank in the world and in every world organization that monitors economic activity."

"How does the syndicate put together the bids on projects?"

"We all get the same briefing. If a project interests you, you determine the level you want to invest. We consolidate our bid and offer it to the IIC."

"How about taxes and how do you transfer large amounts of money without alerting the IRS to the process?"

"Most new players start small with transfers of money to off-shore accounts. We use banks that are controlled by the IIC and understand our process; banks that keep our assets secure and private. You only pay taxes on the money you transfer back into the United States. Most of us just keep our money offshore."

Ken moved forward in his chair to the edge of his seat; a sure sign that he was too eager for more details. He forced himself to relax and lean back. He brought the martini to his lips and drained half the drink. There wasn't a single hole in the plan or organization.

In his wildest dreams he often thought how he would set up such an organization, and the financial freedom such an organization would bring. If he used a portion of the profits to pay his fraudulent loans he could keep the majority offshore, free from the prying eyes of the IRS.

"Can you give me an example of the investments?"

Both Hans and Jerry grinned. "In 1994 the cartel invested in the political campaign of one Hugo Rafael Chavez with a ten million dollar investment in his bid for the Presidency of Venezuela. We have made over two billion dollars on a ten million dollar investment, and are still receiving oil royalties from that country. How's that for a return on investment?"

Ken was surprised. "The IIC funded the communist takeover of Venezuela?"

Hans replied, "With us it's business, not politics."

Ken liked what he had heard. "Gentlemen, your syndicate sounds like it is right up my alley. When can we start?"

After a round of handshakes and another round of drinks, Ken asked, "What's my first move?"

Jerry Evans answered the question. "Start liquidating some of your assets. With whatever amount you feel comfortable. All bids are cash, gold, gold bearer bonds, Eurobonds, or Panamanian bearer bonds when they go out, and are the same when you are paid."

Ken noted that every means of payment accepted by the IIC were untraceable; a fact that didn't bother Ken in the least.

Ken felt the rhythm of the boat change and noticed they were off the mouth of the Savannah River channel and it occurred to Ken that he had been on this beautiful boat for more than an hour and didn't even know who owned it. "This is a beautiful boat. Do either of you own it?"

Hans laughed before he answered. "I only wish I could afford this boat. No, the largest investor in our syndicate owns this boat. He allows us to use it from time to time."

Now it was Ken's turn to laugh. "Who is it? Some oil sheik from Arabia?"

Jerry smiled when he answered. "Maybe."

Ken marveled at the international connections that were now available to him with the simple commitment to join this investment group. It was the status that Ken believed he deserved. The long hours perfecting his craft had finally paid a handsome reward. He had arrived.

It had to be described as an epiphany for Ken; a sudden realization that the men sharing the observation deck were already known to him. Ken knew of them even before they made themselves known to him to request their loans; or made polite introductions at the beginning of this little cruise. The island just to the north of the river brought the past into sharp focus. The first party he attended at Ed Helton's house on Daufuskie Island is where he saw these men drinking beer and laughing near the barbecue pit. There was no mistake; these men were the friends of Ed Helton at the meeting on Daufuskie Island during the Memorial Day party.

"Let me ask one more question. The man who left to form his own syndicate, was that man Ed Helton?"

Their collective silence was all the answer Ken Carson needed.

Chapter 29

Angelina slowly woke from a deep and refreshing sleep. While still under the covers she stretched to her full length and the soft moan escaping from her lips sounded like the purring of a content cat. The cotton sheets felt like satin and she gave thought to turning over and trying to fall into another dream about her day with Eric. She would have done so if not for the morning shadows telling her that she had long missed her normal waking time, and that she would surely be late for work. It didn't bother her in the least.

Her morning coffee seemed to be richer and more aromatic than she remembered, and the water temperature for her shower was perfect and required no adjustment. There wasn't a cloud in the sky and she thought she actually heard the pleasant chirping of morning birds. She caught most of the traffic lights on her way to work and those that she didn't were only a short wait, and the busses or garbage trucks normally spewing asphyxiating fumes into the window of her car were nowhere to be found.

She saw no one in the parking lot and therefore didn't have to challenge the eye contact of her fellow officers, nor did she have to avert her eyes to ignore others. It was a beautiful day! There was fresh air in her lungs and she decided to forgo the dank and dingy confines of the elevator and take the stairs instead. She took the stairs two at a time and didn't slow until she crested the final step on the fifth floor.

She bent at the waist to catch her breath and smiled when her pulse started to return to normal in less than a minute. What a way to start the day.

It was then she noticed the door to her office wide open. She was sure she closed and locked it yesterday when she left. Why would anyone break into her office? Unless they were trying to tamper with the reports or the evidence already collected. She slowly approached the door, not hugging the wall, but a step or two clear of it to gain maneuver space.

She cautiously stepped in front of the door and noticed two shoes casually propped on her desk; somebody was in her office. It was

Director William Jefferson casually flipping through Jackson's military personnel file that she left stacked on her desk with the file of Steve Thunder.

Jefferson casually looked at his watch, "I'm sorry to interrupt your lunch schedule."

It was nowhere near lunch time, but Angelina got the message loud and clear. "How did you get in here? I locked the door when I left."

"The custodian let me in. I think you owe him a favor because he told me you are usually the first person in every morning. I must have caught you on a bad day, huh? I tried to call you a half dozen times yesterday afternoon. You don't check your phone or messages?"

Angelina grabbed for her belt where she normally clipped her cell phone. It wasn't there. Come to think of it, she couldn't remember taking the phone from Eric's truck. It was either in the truck, her car, or she left it at home.

"I was doing some field work yesterday and I must have left it in my car. I'm sure it will show up eventually. I thought you were going to fly out of Savannah. How did your meeting go with Buford Long?"

"Obviously. I did intend to fly out of Savannah, but I thought I would give you a chance to explain your conspiracy theory."

Jefferson tossed Jackson's file back onto her desk and wrinkled his nose. "What is that God-awful smell in here," and pointing at the boxes of Jackson's personal effects, "and what is all this stuff?"

"Those are the personal effects of Staff Sergeant John Brown Jackson, and the smell is the dead rat that the prison shipped in one of the boxes. You'll get used to the smell in a while."

"Nice touch. Too much heat for you here?"

"No sir, not at all."

"Alright, let's get to it. Show me what you have."

Angelina moved to the erasable board and wiped it clean.

"You sent me here to investigate the killings associated with suspects in a rape that was never prosecuted. I am convinced the case the letter referred to was the gang rape of Hanna Walton, age 15."

Angelina wrote 'Hanna W.' in the center of the board. Above Hanna's name she wrote 'Peter W., and Danni W.', "these are her parents." Above Danni's name she wrote the name Ed Helton. "Ed Helton is the father of Danni Walton, and the Grandfather of Hanna."

Angelina moved the chalk back to Hanna W. in the middle of the board. "Hanna Walton was raped by five men," under Hanna's name she wrote 'Bomani Thomas,' three small circles, and then the name of Crack Daddy. Beside the name of Crack Daddy she wrote, 'Alabama.' "The police investigated but couldn't put together a case. Some years after the rape the killings started."

"When I ran the names of suspects, four of the five suspects had been killed within a month of each other. Bomani Thomas was killed in prison by Jackson, the man in the file you were reviewing, the other three suspects were killed within two weeks of the Thomas killing; one of these men was killed by your friend Buford Long..." she paused just long enough to add emphasis to her point, "...in the Walton residence the same day they discovered Peter Walton's body. Only Crack Daddy survived. I interviewed him in prison in Alabama. He told me he was the man who wrote the letter to the President, and he admitted to the rape." Angelina put an 'X' over every name or symbol of the deceased.

Angelina wrote the name Jasmine under Peter Walton. She put an 'X' over Peter Walton's name and Jasmine's. "Jasmine was a prostitute and probably was witness to the rape. She was killed with Peter Walton and they were both found in Walton's car in the Chattahoochee River. When I asked Crack Daddy about the murder of Peter Walton, he gave me the name of a man named 'Frenchy' in Louisiana." Angelina wrote 'Frenchy' and Louisiana, on the board.

"I interviewed Frenchy. He said the Walton murder was associated with the DEA drug bust of a heroin shipment, and had nothing to do with the rape.

"Frenchy told me his boss, Tyrell Biggs, received the information on the heroin by Bomani Thomas. Thomas got the lead on the drug deal by another inmate. I assume that inmate was John Brown Jackson." Angelina wrote the name Tyrell Biggs and J.B. Jackson on the board and connected the names with arrows with points on each end.

"Jackson and Thomas killed each other in prison."

"About six months later Tyrell Biggs and another of his associates were killed on the Savannah River. Your friend, Buford Long," again she paused for emphasis, "was involved in another home invasion of the Helton residence on Daufuskie Island where another man was killed. Long didn't do the shooting, but did file the report."

By the time Angelina finished with her diagram the board was full on names, arrows, and 'Xs'. Jefferson took a moment to take it all in before he asked. "Where does Steve Thunder come to play in all this?"

"Thunder was involved in the drug bust, the investigation of the Peter Walton murder, and was hot on the tail of Tyrell Biggs before he was killed."

Jefferson picked up the Jackson file and tossed it in Angelina's direction. "You missed a critical component of Thunder's involvement. It's in there. I'm surprised you missed it."

Angelina was somewhat taken aback by the criticism. She picked up the Jackson file and started to flip through it.

Jefferson said, "Look at Jackson's efficiency reports. Who wrote most of those reports?"

There, on the back of the efficiency reports, clear as day, the name of Steve Thunder.

"You may have a conspiracy, but I don't think it's the Atlanta Police Department." Jefferson pulled a typed sheet from his pocket. "I did a little checking of the other file you wanted, the file of Doc Broderson, it's very interesting. Doc Broderson, Steve Thunder and Jackson all served in the Rangers at the same time and in the same unit. Now that's more than a coincidence."

Angelina was embarrassed that she missed that obvious connection. "Do you think…"

Angelina's question was interrupted by a knock at her office door. "Excuse me, are you Angelina Sanchez?"

Angelina looked up. "Yes, I am."

"I have a delivery for you. You have to sign." The delivery man handed an open box with chiffon paper covering the contents. "Be careful, you might spill it."

Angelina placed the box on her desk and signed for the delivery. She looked to Jefferson to continue her question, but he stopped her. "Well, aren't you going to see what it is?"

Angelina gently removed the object from the box and set it on the desk. When she removed the wrapping paper she almost laughed out loud. There on her desk was a water filled crystal bowl. On the bowl was a red ribbon and affixed to the ribbon was her cell phone. The attached note was from Eric. She removed the note and placed it in her desk. She wanted to read it immediately, but not with Jefferson in the room.

Jefferson leaned over the bowl and asked, "What the hell kind of flower is that?"

Angelina again almost laughed, but with effort she controlled herself. "It's a water lily."

Jefferson noted her cell phone attached to the ribbon. "I see you found your phone; field work, my ass."

Angelina felt her face flush with embarrassment and wondered what to do next. Jefferson helped her out.

"Sanchez, I think you may be on to something here. Keep up the work. I'll tell you what I'll do. I'll see if I can't get the Army to run a computer check on matches of other soldiers who served with Jackson and Thunder. There's got to be somebody else involved."

"What gives you that idea?"

"Who pulled the trigger on all those people after Jackson and Thunder were killed? They didn't kill themselves. You also need to establish a motive that would tie all this together. Right now all you have is a bunch of bad guys getting killed; to establish a conspiracy, something the Department would investigate, you have to tie it all together. If you can't do that, then we don't have a case."

Jefferson left her office with a last glance at the crystal bowl, "A water lily, huh?"

Angelina waited until she was sure Jefferson had left the building before she withdrew Eric's note form the drawer.

The note read, "Angelina, if you have no plans tonight, would you consider accompanying me to a round table discussion group at my old university. I am a member of the discussion panel. It will only take about an hour. We can have dinner afterwards. I have provided you a phone which you may use to inform me of your decision. In either case I would love to hear your voice. Eric."

~~

She was breaking all the rules, accepting a date on such short notice, but she couldn't think of anything more appealing than spending an evening with Eric. The plain, but fitted, black dress and heels with a string of pearls were perfect for the occasion. Angelina waited at the front of her apartment and paid little attention when a black Mercedes pulled up. To her surprise, Eric stepped from the car and walked towards her. He offered her his arm and escorted her to the car.

"What happened to the truck?"

"I like the truck, but on special occasions I pull this thing out of the garage. I know it isn't as stylish as the truck, but I hope you don't mind."

Angelina rubbed the plush leather. "You're right. It's not as nice as the truck, but I guess it will do. Oh, by the way, thank you for the wonderful flower arrangement. My boss really appreciated it."

Eric had a look of concern. "I hope I didn't get you in any trouble."

Angelina turned to Eric and smiled, "Well, he didn't fire me, but I think he suspects that I wasn't really working yesterday."

Eric turned back to Angelina, "It was worth it, wasn't it?"

Angelina smiled. "Yes it was."

Now that they had put yesterday behind them Angelina focused on the evening ahead. "What is the topic of this discussion?"

Eric pulled a paper from his coat pocket, "The role of government in family development, the war on poverty, and their affect on inner-city youth."

"Wow, that's quite a title; I wouldn't think that would be a subject with which you would be familiar. What was your major?"

"I graduated in '07 with a communication degree. Besides, when was the last time you saw one of these discussion groups bring in real experts. They always bring in people that will support their own point of view. I think they asked me to participate simply because I'm on television." Eric turned and looked at Angelina before continuing, "It's always good to have a pretty face on television." Both of them laughed at the joke.

"I wouldn't take you as a government type of guy."

"Oh, I'm not; far from it. I suppose I will be the only free market guy on the panel. It could be bloody."

~~

The round table discussion was held in the executive conference room of the university. A small group of dignitaries were invited to attend and they were seated two rows deep just outside the halo of lights

217

illuminating the discussion group. Video crews hovered near the table to capture the comments of the panelists.

Angelina could have listened to Eric talk on the subject all night, but she quickly tired of the rhetoric of most of the members. She retreated to the rear of the conference facility, took a seat next to the wall and counted the minutes to the scheduled conclusion of the discussion.

On the table next to her chair lay copies of the university yearbooks. She picked up the year 2007 and began to thumb through the pages. She didn't notice Eric's picture in any of the photographs, so turned to the listing of graduates. She ran her finger down the list of Bs and never found Eric's name. The light was rather poor and so she carefully reviewed the names again. Eric's name was missing from the list. So engrossed was she in her search that she didn't hear Eric's approach, until he was standing next to her.

"That wasn't so bad, was it? Are you ready for dinner?"

Angelina looked up and smiled. "Eric, you did great." It was a small lie; she had tuned-out the entire discussion long ago. With the annual in hand she asked, "I thought you said you graduated in 2007? I couldn't find your name in the annual."

"It's in there. Here, let me show you."

Eric took the annual from her and flipped through the pages. When he placed the annual in her lap he pointed to the list of 'J' graduates. "See, there I am; Eric Brown Jackson."

Angelina raised her eyebrows slightly. "Why don't you use your full name now?"

Eric took the annual from her and placed it back on the table. He extended his hand to her to help her from the chair. "A lot of television people don't use their real or full names. It gives you a little more privacy. Where do you want to go for dinner?"

Angelina would let Eric surprise her, she didn't care. She was more engrossed in which name had more of a ring to it, Angelina Brown, Angelina Jackson, Angelina Sanchez Brown, Angelina Sanchez Jackson. It would require much more analysis than a few repetitions during their drive to dinner. She couldn't wait to see which looked better on paper and she knew she would have to consider everything before she could make a choice. Not only was her name important, but which name would look best if they had boys or girls, or both. It was a difficult decision and would require much more thought.

Chapter 30

Danni was exhausted. She unbuttoned the jacket of her suit and unceremoniously slumped into the deep chair across from her father. A strand of rebellious hair worked loose and fell to cover the corner of her face. She closed her eyes and leaned back in the chair and breathed a deep sigh of relief. She simply wanted a break. Ten hours in negotiations with the Service Union and their lawyers over the new hotel contract had almost drained the fight from her.

Ed looked to his daughter. "Tough day?"

"One of the worst. It started with Reverend White. Do you know Reverend White?"

Ed laughed. "Who doesn't? He runs a tax exempt charity in Savannah, and has made a living putting pressure on local businesses to contribute, but I think he is nothing more than a political scam artist. The bank used to make a contribution every year, but I cut him off when he started spending more money on political contributions than food for the poor. What did he want with you?"

"He wants us to let the kids use our recreational facilities. I told him no. I don't think that would go over with the few customers we have left. He said he had influence with the union...said if the hotel would contribute to his organization, he would help with the contract."

"Do you believe him?"

"Dad, I think Reverend White would tell the devil he could get God to forgive him and get him into heaven, if the devil made a contribution to his organization."

"Did you contribute?"

"No, and when I didn't he basically threatened me. He said that his friends in the union would own the hotel before long, and then I would get what's coming to me."

"How goes the new union contract?"

Danni didn't even open her eyes. "They are idiots."

219

Ed hid his grin from Danni. "The union has been in business a long time. They know all the tricks in bleeding a company dry. If you value the hotel, and I know you do, then fight for every penny."

"Dad, I went into this negotiation with the intention of signing a contract that would be beneficial to the union and their workers and the long term success of the hotel. But, I tell you, I believe the union could really care less about our future. My labor costs have doubled and the bureaucracy they are setting up will hamstring my managers. Wages are up and they are demanding redundant employees to provide more flexible schedules and increased sick days and personal days. The health care package alone may kill us. I don't know how they figure we can absorb all these additional costs."

"Danni, believe me, they haven't given any thought on how to fund their demands. They expect you to do that. You are management and they are labor. They expect you to make it work."

"They are making it hard to do. You know what bothers me the most? The new labor laws give the negotiating edge to the union and the power to arbitrate to the government. Every issue we submit to the State Labor Board for arbitration has ruled for the union and against us."

"How are the employees holding up?"

Ed could see the lips of his daughter curl in contempt before she answered. "Dad, we were doing so well before the union showed up. They were happy and motivated and dedicated to serving our customers. Now they seem surly and disgruntled, especially to the customers; almost as if they despise the wealth of the people staying at the hotel. Our customer satisfaction is way down, complaints are way up, and the reservations are starting to slide. I am trying to get the union to agree to a wage package that reflects the customer satisfaction ratings we get; ratings go up they get more bonuses, ratings go down they don't. The union hates the idea and won't budge. I think it's the next thing they are going to send to the Arbitration Board. I have a good idea what the results will be."

Ed Helton weighed what his daughter revealed. It was as he expected. It was enough to help Ed make his decision.

"Danni, how much does the hotel owe the bank, in rough figures?"

Danni knew exactly how much remained on the note to her father's bank. "$30 million."

"What is your best guess on the total worth of the hotel?"

"Right now, I would say, based on our last year's performance, we could get maybe $50 million if we could find a buyer; but, finding a buyer in these times will be nearly impossible."

"Danni, what would you do if the bank called in the loan?"

"What?!" Danni couldn't believe what her father just asked her. "Why would the bank call in the loan? We have a contract. You, yourself approved it! Why would you want to yank the rug out from under us?"

"Danni, can you separate family from business?"

The fatigue of the negotiation earlier in the day left her. "Yes, I believe I can. But what I just told you was not in your board room, it was in our living room."

"What you just told me, the bank has suspected; you have confirmed our suspicions. Think about what you just admitted to me. You are losing control of the hotel to the union and government regulation. The bank loaned you that money based on a viable recovery plan. The assumptions and conditions of your plan have changed. The money we loaned you isn't my money. It is the money of thousands of investors who expect us to be good stewards of their life savings. We don't think you can save the hotel. We may have to pay a fine when we call in the loan, but we won't lose all our money."

"Are you telling me the bank is going to call in the loan?"

"It is being considered, yes."

"We have a contract you can't just cancel it. That would put us out of business!"

"Maybe it would, maybe it wouldn't. We are prepared to file suit and go to court, if need be. Business is business, Danni. I hope you can understand that."

After Danni slammed the door to the library, Ed heard her heavy footsteps recede down the hall. Only when he knew he had complete privacy did he pick up the phone and call his friend Byron Wilson, at the Ford production plant in Detroit.

"Byron, do you have anyone inside the United Auto Workers Union?"

"That's kind of a strange question. Are you getting in the auto business?"

"No, I'm trying to stay in the banking business. I wonder if the UAW would share with their brothers in the Service Union that the Daufuskie Resort is trying to raise capital and may be ripe for a buy-in."

Byron and Ed Helton had been friends for a long time. Byron paused quite a long time before he answered. "I'm pretty sure they would."

Danni understood business as well as anyone at the bank. That didn't change the fact that her father had abandoned her. As she tossed and turned in her bed that night she softened the feelings that overwhelmed her immediately after the discussion with her father. Business was business and he had given her warning. It took her well into the night to understand what her father said was true. She had lost every battle with the union and the government. She had to find a way to preserve the hotel.

~~

The meaning of Mamba's dream was not clear. She saw the joy of Hanna's return, but there was more to the dream than the return of Hanna; there was an ominous ending that Mamba refused to see. It was such that it woke her twice during the night; both times from a deep sleep. Hanna's return was clear; even the baby boy Mamba saw that Hanna would carry was clear, but the meaning of the dream was not clear. There was more to the dream than Mamba wanted to see.

Fearing the revelation of the ending, Mamba dressed and made her way to the kitchen where she put on some coffee. Whatever would come would come, but Hanna's room still needed to be cleaned.

The commotion in Hanna's room woke Danni from a troubled sleep. The sour mood of the discussion with her father still lingered, and on a day that should have been filled with joy. Today was the day Brian Vance, the boy hurt in the fight with the union thugs, was to be released from the hospital.

Danni felt a deep responsibility for the full recovery of the boy. Not only did she respect his valiant stand against the union, but he had no one else to care for him in his time of need. There was more than enough room at the estate and her father agreed to help nurse the boy back to health. Her father even agreed to consider funding Brian's return to the Citadel after his recovery. How could a man that generous turn against his own daughter? The noise coming from Hanna's room did nothing to brighten her mood.

"Mamba, what in the world are you doing at this hour? It's not even 6 a.m."

Mamba didn't look up when she answered for she feared her eyes would relay her concern. "Hanna is coming home. Her room needs to be cleaned."

"What? Why didn't you tell me? When did she call?"

"She did not call. She does not yet know, maybe today she will be told, I am not sure."

The initial excitement in Danni ebbed somewhat with the strange answer. She yawned deeply trying to chase the troubled sleep from her body. "Then how do you know she's coming?"

Mamba stopped her work momentarily. "I know." Even Mamba couldn't help but smile with the remainder of the news. "She will be with child, a boy."

Now the sleep was gone from Danni. "A boy!! That's wonderful! What time is it Israel? Let's call her. I can't believe she never told me!"

Mamba smiled again. "It would not be wise to call now. I saw these things in a dream. They will come to pass in their own time. Be patient."

Although it was only a dream Danni couldn't wait for the visions to come true. "How long will they stay?"

"I did not see Major Madison in the dream."

In the excitement of the moment, it simply didn't register with Danni that James would not be coming with Hanna; it was only a dream so it raised no alarm with Danni. "Let me get dressed and I will help you."

"No. You should go to work. You will drive me crazy with questions all day if you stay here. I can take care of this."

~~

Late in the afternoon, Ed Helton picked up the phone and placed a call to Ken Carson. "Ken," again the familiarity, it was becoming more frequent of late. "Could you come up to my office after we close? I have something of a personal nature to discuss."

"Certainly sir, let me close the loans I am working on and just as soon as I lock up the department, I'll be right up."

223

When Ken walked into Ed Helton's office he noticed him cover handwritten spread sheets with unmarked folders. The spread sheets he could not conceal, he stacked them together and turned them over face down on his desk. With only a quick glance, in the mirrored reflection of a picture on the desk, Ken saw a list of accounts on the computer screen. It was only a glance, but Ken knew what Ed Helton was doing. He was moving money.

Ed directed Ken to a chair facing his desk as he got up and headed for the door to his office. "Take a seat Ken, let me lock this door to give us some privacy."

While Ed's back was turned Ken studied the reflection. He couldn't clearly see the amounts listed on the transfers, but he knew one thing for sure; the logo at the top of the screen was none other than the Barclay International Bank in the Cayman Islands. He knew this for a fact because the Barclay International Bank in the Cayman Islands was one of the cartel's recommended banks. It was the same offshore bank Ken was using to manage his investment money.

Ken was studying the trees out the window when Ed returned to his seat.

"Ken, I'm thinking of calling in the Daufuskie loan. If I did, it would kill the resort and I don't want to do that. What are the chances the resort would qualify for a government loan?"

"I'm not sure the Fed would invest in a hotel, sir. That's a pretty high-risk business."

"It might be high risk, but the government has designated it as vital to the economy. By that designation alone it should be considered important enough to get a Federal loan. You have a pretty good relationship with Bartholomew; he could approve the loan. I want you to process it."

Ken's relationship with Ronald Bartholomew was a hell of a lot better than Ed Helton's. Ken knew Bartholomew held Ed Helton with a certain amount of disdain and contempt. Ken felt a certain sense of importance and power that Ed Helton would have to come through him to get a loan for the resort.

"I'd be happy to talk with Mr. Bartholomew. I don't see any reason why he wouldn't approve the loan. The Fed likes to show support to union shops."

Ed Helton reached into his top drawer and withdrew a plain white envelope. It fell with a thud when Ed tossed it in Ken's direction.

Ken stared at the envelope unsure of his next move. Accepting money for any transaction at this bank was strictly forbidden. Any breach of those ethics was grounds for immediate termination. Fraudulent loans aside, it was a rule that Ken never violated. He had to ask the question.

"What's that?"

Ed Helton didn't bat an eye or squirm in his chair. His answer was so matter-of-fact that it could have been a pack of gum, but it wasn't. "It's $10,000; in case Mr. Bartholomew needs some help deciding what to do on the loan."

Six months ago the package on the corner of Ed Helton's desk would have more likely been moon rocks as an envelope full of money to pay-off a Federal Bank Examiner, but many things had changed at the bank. Ed Helton didn't give Ken time to make a decision.

"There is another thing I would like you to look into for me. You are better in the stock market than I am, and I need a buyer for the stock I have in the hotel. It's currently holding steady at $10 a share and I have about $2,000,000 in it. I don't want to go through my broker; it wouldn't look good if it got out that I was dumping the hotel stock."

"I don't know, Mr. Helton, hotel stock in this economy is a pretty hard sell. How soon do you want to sell it?"

"If I am going to sell it, I've got to sell it within a month. I will hold the price at $10, unless it goes down of course, and will guarantee to buy it back within a month at a 10 percent profit."

"That's a pretty sweet deal, but I don't know anybody with that kind of money to invest."

"I thought maybe you could mention it to Reverend White. I know he wanted to get his kids out to the resort to use the recreational facilities. It would be rather difficult to turn him away if he was an owner in the hotel."

Ken knew the Reverend White didn't give a rat's ass about the kids he always used as leverage to extort money out of local businesses, but now that Ed Helton mentioned him Ken knew it was a perfect match.

"I'll mention it to him. I can't guarantee anything."

Ed stood from behind his desk indicating the meeting was over. He picked up the envelope and handed it to Ken. "Ken, if you can make it happen, there's another one of these with your name on it. Do what you can."

~~

225

Danni suffered through the work day. She jumped at every phone call expecting the call from Hanna, but it didn't come before lunch. She tried to busy herself with the details of the day. At 3 p.m. she began to believe Mamba was wrong. At 5 p.m. she was almost dejected and irritated that Mamba would play such a cruel hoax on her. As she left the office just before 7 p.m. her assistant stopped her in the doorway.

"Mrs. Walton, you have a call on line two."

Danni walked to her desk and punched the flashing light.

"Momma," Danni's heart jumped at the sound of her daughter's voice. "Guess what? I'm coming home!"

The day's wait was worth the joy. Even though she had been told by Mamba, the news was even better from her daughter. "That's great honey. When will you get here and how long will you stay?"

"I'll be there within a week. I don't know how long I will stay. That's not a problem is it? You haven't made my old room into s sewing room or anything like that, have you?"

Danni laughed at the question. "No, it's not a sewing room. You come on down and you can stay as long as you like. Will James be coming with you?"

Danni felt the change in tone, "Not right now. There are some things going on over here, and General McLaughlin said he has to stay."

If there was trouble in Israel, then Danni had completely missed it on the news. The President was making a trip to the Middle East, but she didn't think he was going to Israel. That part of the world was the last thing on her mind. Life at home was trouble enough, worrying about what was happening half a world away simply never hit her radar.

Mamba's dreams were once again on target. If she could predict Hanna's arrival then maybe Hanna was concealing the other news for announcement when she arrived. A little fishing was in order. "Do you have any other news you might want to tell me?"

Danni held her breath and waited for Hanna's reply. "Momma, I'm pregnant! We're going to have a baby! I didn't tell you before because I wanted to be sure. I'm so excited!"

Danni Walton was going to be a grandmother. She liked the idea.

Chapter 31

Hanna didn't understand the change in her husband's attitude. He returned from a meeting at the Ministry of Defense, earlier in the day, he told her she had to go back to the States. He rejected her pleas to stay, and offered only a simple statement that, "It's not safe here anymore. It's not safe for the baby."

Hanna found his change in attitude puzzling—almost insulting—that he would not offer any more of an explanation.

After the terrorist attack in Tel Aviv, there wasn't any discussion about her returning to the States, and there hadn't been another such incident since. For all intents and purposes, Israel was at peace; but for the first time in her marriage her husband would not listen to reason.

"You are going home, and that's final. Take only what you can carry in your luggage. I'll ship the rest to you as soon as I can."

~~

The Israeli commando raid on the Tartus to Ezbet Abu Sagal fishing trawler spurred Major Madison to action. They took the craft 40 miles off the Lebanon coast. There were no survivors. The boat wasn't due in Ezbet Abu Sagal until the following day, and maybe wouldn't be missed for another. The Israeli General Staff had a window of twelve to thirty-six hours in which to make a decision and James would ensure his wife was safe before that deadline.

James was in the command center when the photos of the vessel's cargo were sent via secure satellite link, and watched with interest the reaction of the Israeli Prime Minister. In the heavy accent that the world knew was the Prime Minister, he directed, "Enlarge those photos, please."

The technician entered commands into the computer. He centered the clearest pictures and enlarged it until the writing on the drums was clear—the drums simply read 'Isopropyl Alcohol.'

James leaned to Colonel Wetzel, "That's nothing more than regular rubbing alcohol."

Wetzel only said, "Wait for all the pictures."

The screen flashed more drums. These were not labeled quite so clearly, and the technician enhanced the images. Each image was slightly clearer than the one before. Finally the writing on the drums was legible. James asked Colonel Wetzel, "What in the hell is isopropylamine solution?"

Colonel Wetzel whispered back to James, "Some companies use it in weed killer. Some people mix it with isopropyl alcohol and methylphosphonic difluoride."

"Makes a hell-of-a slow gin fizz, huh?"

James thought the joke was worthy of at least a soft chuckle, but Wetzel wasn't amused. "Mix those three chemicals together and you've got Sarin, NATO designation GB. The same stuff Saddam Hussein used against the Kurds. What you've got there is nerve gas."

~~

James was not included in the discussions that came next except for the terse statement directed to him by the Prime Minister. "Major Madison, you brought this intelligence to us. We are in your debt. Thank you."

After the departure of the Prime Minister and General Staff, Madison turned to Wetzel. "What are they going to do?"

"What did your President Kennedy do when the Russians put nuclear weapons in Cuba?"

"You don't think they will order an attack into the Gaza, do you?"

"I don't know."

~~

James placed a secure call to General McLaughlin. McLaughlin rousted Senator Reynolds from a deep sleep and reported the meeting to him. Senator Reynolds notified the White House Chief of Staff. The National Security Council, with the President on a state visit to Saudi Arabia, the Vice President presiding, assembled in the White House bunker by 4 a.m.

General McLaughlin briefed what he knew. The Vice President, always fixed on the political implications of every event, asked, "Do you think the Israelis will launch an attack while the President is in Saudi Arabia?"

"The Prime Minister left the briefing room without making a decision. I don't know."

The Vice President turned to the Attorney General. "If the Israeli Commandos attacked the boat in international waters would the World Court consider that an act of self-defense?"

The Attorney General looked up from the notes he had taken. "I think the Israelis are on shaky ground. They didn't actually find all the components for nerve agent. If you ask me, the World Court might consider it an act of piracy."

"Shit, that's what I thought. Well, we've got to notify the President." The Vice President turned to the Under Secretary of State. "Send a message to our Israeli Ambassador. Tell him to inform the Israeli government that we urge restraint on their part. Tell them we think this is something that should be brought before the United Nations Security Council. Tell them that we will consider it an act of aggression if they launch an attack on the Gaza Strip without exhausting all diplomatic channels."

~~

When Lucas McLaughlin finally laid his head on his pillow after forty-eight non-stop hours of work, the visions in the night were almost as grim as those during the day.

The wise-man whispered into the King's ear.

"My Liege, you are in grave danger. You must be on guard. We must fill the moat and raise the bridge, and let only those pass we know to be our friends."

The King turned to the wise-man. "Surely you jest, for I am the most beloved in all the lands. Who would intend me harm? Are you my council, or a jester sent here to tell stories?"

The wise-man bowed low. "I am nothing, but to serve the Kingdom, great King. I have many eyes and ears and they bring the message that men from the east will unleash a great plague on the kingdom."

"Your eyes and ears deceive you, old fool. Have I not spread my words of love and peace to the ends of the earth for all to hear?"

The wise-man lay prostrate on the ground. "Your words of love and peace have not reached the hearts of those who hate and still fear the kingdom."

"Have I not made offerings to the men from the east? Have I not withdrawn my armies from their shores and released their brothers from my prisons? Surely in all their days they have never seen one such as I who has made these offerings! They must know my words of love and peace, are true."

The floor began to tilt and the wise-man slowly started to slide away. "Great King, allow my eyes to look, and my ears to listen and let us begin to question all the men from the east to see what is in their heart."

"Old fool, if we question the men from the east they will think I do not love them, and they will spread the word of our deeds to the far corners of the earth that my words of love and peace are hollow."

The King turned to the High and Lofty Sherriff of the Kingdom. "Great Sherriff, do not the new laws say we will question the men from the east no more than we question the men from the north, from the west, or from the south?"

The High and Lofty Sherriff opened his Book of Laws and his crooked finger traced down the page until he found the law of international love and peace. "Great King, the law is as you say. We will question one no more than the other, for peace and love will reign across the land."

The wise-man tried to slow his slide and asked, "Oh, Great and Merciful King, your faithful subjects look to you for their protection. You cannot let this plague come unto our lands."

"Old fool, my subjects are happy with my presence. They have no wish to be bothered by such things. They are happy in these days, and they dance and sing and celebrate my reign."

The wise-man looked to others gathered in the royal court. Some covered their ears so they would not hear the truth, others covered their eyes so they would not see

230

the truth, and others covered their mouth so they would not speak the truth. The floor collapsed from under the wise-man and he fell into a black pit. He could no longer be heard because he was falling faster than his words could escape.

Lucas McLaughlin woke in a cold sweat, with his sheets pulled from under the mattress. He had struggled during the dream and only hoped it was nothing more than a dream.

~~

As Air Force One began its descent into the international airport in Saudi Arabia, an Iranian Airlines flight bound for Mecca and the holiest shrine of Islam, pulled away from the Tehran terminal.

Iran Flight A380-323 Heavy was the newest plane in the Iranian fleet. The Airbus 380 carried 555 passengers on two decks. The flight was expected to cover the thousand plus miles between the cities in well under four hours, terminal-to-terminal.

The Iranian flight was special in that it was the single largest Hajj pilgrimage to Mecca...ever. What in years past may have been a month long arduous and often dangerous journey could now be accomplished in under four hours in the air-conditioned comfort of a modern jetliner. It was historic in a sense and the Iranian television interviewed the passengers and videoed the Mullahs bestowing their blessings.

The flight from Tehran to Mecca was special in another sense. The pilot, co-pilot and select members of the aircrew had been specifically selected for this particular flight. They were assigned this flight the day following the State Department's announcement of the President's scheduled visit to Riyadh. It was the first flight for half the pilgrims on board; it would be the last flight for all.

Once airborne the Iranian flight became an item of interest to the American forces providing security for the President's visit to Saudi Arabia. A satellite link notified the crew on board Eagle Watch, the American E-3 Sentry AWACS loitering over the Persian Gulf, of the departure. The flight was only one of hundreds tracked by the early warning aircraft. Within twenty minutes the revolving radar mounted on the fuselage of E-3 had the Iranian flight on radar at 31,000 feet and on course to pass north of Kuwait City. A380-323 Heavy began to receive more attention when the track of the aircraft deviated south of its projected route.

231

The Airbus Captain announced to his passengers that they were in for a special treat. They would reduce altitude and fly down the Persian Gulf. The passengers buzzed with excitement for even in the clear air above the desert there wasn't much to see from 30,000 feet.

When the Iranian flight was clearly deviating from its authorized route, the watch commander on Eagle Watch notified the flight of four F-18 Hornet fighters assigned combat air patrol during the President's visit.

"Hornet leader this is Eagle Watch. Investigate Iranian commercial flight deviating from assigned route. Bogey descending through angels 25, speed 300 knots, vector is 030 degrees at one hundred thirty miles." Angels 25 was the terminology to designate altitude in thousands of feet.

"Eagle Watch this is Hornet 1, bogey is Iranian commercial at 030 degrees, 130 miles, roger, Hornets 3 and 4 on the chase."

The watch commander noted the radar blips of the F-18s break formation and close the distance to the wayward Iranian flight. "Hornet 3 this in Eagle Watch, your bogey now 60 miles at angels 20 and descending."

"Hornet 3, roger, Angels 20 descending at 60 miles."

The watch commander turned to the operator of the ground radar monitor. "Ground watch, what do we have on the surface in the path of the Iranian airliner?" If the Iranian flight was having mechanical difficulty then search and rescue may be required.

The ground operator answered. "Only American vessel north of Bahrain is the USS Garcia." The *Garcia* was one of the newest and most capable guided missile destroyers in the US Navy.

The watch commander contacted the bridge of the *Garcia*. "Garcia this is Eagle Watch. Be advised you have an Iranian commercial airliner heading in your direction with possible mechanical problems."

The duty officer on the bridge of the *Garcia* called the information to the Captain's quarters. "Skipper, Eagle Watch just notified us that an Iranian commercial flight is heading our way with possible mechanical problems."

The skipper of the *Garcia,* Commander Louis Scott, was a seasoned veteran of combat operations in the Persian Gulf. There wasn't much he could do to help a crippled airliner except fish any survivors out of the Gulf, if the plane went down. "Tell Eagle Watch to keep us advised. Alert damage control of the situation."

"Hornet 3, this is Eagle Watch, your bogey now twenty miles at angels 15."

"Eagle Watch we have bogey on radar, expect visual any moment."

The F-18s reduced speed as they approached the Iranian aircraft. Hornet 3 approached the airliner and Hornet 4 maintained altitude above and to the rear of the airliner. Hornet 3 flew down the port side of the airliner and noticed no visible signs of mechanical problems, and then reversed course and flew the starboard side of the aircraft, and then above and below the airliner. There was no indication of any mechanical problem. The pilot could see the faces of the passengers through the windows of the plane. Nothing seemed out of the ordinary.

"Eagle Watch this is Hornet 3, bogey now in escort. No visible signs of problems, standing by."

"Roger Hornet 3, contact him on the emergency channel and escort him to the west."

The Iranian airliner did not respond to the pilot's radio call or the international signal of waggling his wings directing the escorted aircraft to "follow me".

"Eagle Watch this is Hornet 3, no response from bogey. Bogey is now angels 10 and descending."

Now the USS Garcia clearly saw the picture of the Iranian airliner and US fighter jet on their radar screens. The duty officer called Commander Scott. "Skipper, that airliner is making a beeline right at us. He's at 50 miles at 10,000 feet."

The skipper's orders were clear. "Zero nine zero on the rudder. All ahead flank."

The *Garcia* heeled over and shuddered under the increased speed. Commander Scott left his quarters and entered the Combat Information Center (CIC). The CIC was the nerve center for the combat systems and was buried deep within the vessel for protection. The red combat lights and bright colored blips on the radar screens could have been a science-fiction movie, but everything in CIC was deadly serious. With each mile they sailed the skipper noticed the Iranian airliner made minor adjustments to follow their path.

"Bridge, steer two seven zero on the rudder, maintain maximum revolutions."

It didn't take long for the skipper to notice the airliner adjust their flight path. There was no doubt; they were being stalked by the Iranian airliner.

"Bridge, this is the Captain. Sound battle stations. Warm up the missiles, flex the guns and turn on all video cameras, and radio 5th Fleet that we may be under attack by an Iranian airliner."

The duty officer paused before he hit the battle stations alarm. "You want me to report to Fleet that we're under attack by an airliner?"

"Get to it Mister. I'm on my way to the bridge."

When the Captain arrived on the bridge his first call was to Eagle Watch. "Eagle Watch this is *Garcia*, what are your intentions with the Iranian airliner?"

"What do you want me to do? I can't shoot him down."

"This is Commander Scott, that son-of-a-bitch is tracking my every move. At least order some warning shots across his bow. Let's find out what his intentions are."

Captain Scott turned to the Officer of the Watch. "Steer one eight zero and make smoke. Let's see if we can run from this bastard and blind him at the same time." The Airbus was at forty miles and 8,000 feet and closing.

The young officer of the watch asked, "If we make smoke, won't that make it easier for him to see us?"

"On a clear day like this he can follow our wake just as easy and he has radar in his nose." The skipper turned to the electronic warfare officer (EWO). "Find his radar frequency and on my order I want you to scramble it. We're going to steam south as long as we can and then turn back into our own smoke. If he is after us, he may fly right over us. If he comes back, then we will know for sure he is after us."

The pilots of the Airbus 380 ignored the 20mm tracers that passed dangerously close to the nose of their aircraft. Their attention was riveted on the rising plum of white smoke on the horizon. "The Americans try to run and hide. It will not help them." Only twenty miles and 4,000 feet remained to the target.

Commander Scott called the watch officer on Eagle Watch. "Eagle Watch, this is Garcia. Will you order the Hornets to engage?"

"We cannot engage until a hostile act has been committed."

"Fire one more warning then clear your aircraft. We are going weapons free if that bastard doesn't pull off." The skipper knew the watch officer's hands were tied. The world would never believe a commercial airliner would commit a hostile act against an American warship, even though four such airliners killed more Americans on 9/11 than the US Navy lost in the Japanese attack on Pearl Harbor.

When the Iranian airliner didn't respond to the second burst of cannon fire the pilot radioed to USS Garcia. "Garcia this is Hornet 3. Your bogey is still inbound. I am leaving your airspace. You are cleared for weapons free. Good luck."

The mile long smoke cloud on the water obscured their target, but the radar in the cabin of the Iranian airliner cut through with smoke. "The Americans can't hide. They should prepare for their death." The pilot and co-pilot grinned at each other.

The skipper of the Garcia turned to the EWO. "Fire your chaff curtain."

Four small rockets left four streaks of exhaust as they streaked toward the airliner. The aluminum strips scrambled the airliner's radar with hundreds of false targets.

If executed properly, the 'crashback' maneuver would reverse the course of the ship within three or four lengths of the ship, and they would be well within their own smokescreen before the pilots figured out where they were. The approaching airliner was at ten miles and 2000 feet.

"All Stop!"

Commander Scott felt the ship lose momentum. "Left full rudder!"

As the ship took the first 30 degrees of the turn he ordered, "All back full, right full rudder."

The powerful engines began to pull the stern to starboard. It took only a minute to complete the next 100 degrees of the maneuver, but it was an eternity to the men on the bridge.

Finally Scott ordered, "Left full rudder, all ahead full."

As the USS Garcia entered the security of the smoke screen at thirty knots, Captain Scott ordered. "EWO, full jam."

The nose of the airliner entered the upper levels of the smoke screen when the radar screen went white. There was momentary panic in the cockpit of the airliner. "Where is the American?"

"I can't see him. He is in the smoke. Pull up, we must go around. He cannot escape!"

Crashing into the sea with 555 passengers on Hajj would have probably served the purpose of the pilots, but now they were determined to send the infidels on the American ship to hell. The whine of the four jet engines was deafening to the men on the USS Garcia as the plane passed over the ship less than one-hundred feet above the tallest masts of the superstructure.

The EWO gave the Skipper the bad news. "Skipper, he is coming back."

Commander Scott evaluated the situation. They wouldn't miss this time. "Weapons, report radar lock."

The hand of the young officer manning the launch station shook and sweat covered his brow, but he answered as he had been trained. "Sir, we have radar lock, we are prepared to fire."

This is what it always comes down to, it's either them or us. There was no easy answer. Would the sacrifice of his vessel and crew prevent the political uproar that he knew would follow, or was it his moral responsibility to protect the men under his command?

Commander Scott did not hesitate when he ordered, "Fire."

Chapter 32

Captain Scott watched the missile blow through the launch tube protective cover. The missile responded to the initial guidance command and closed on the Iranian airliner. The entire sequence was over in seconds, but Scott's brain processed it in slow motion.

The missile penetrated the windscreen and decapitated the co-pilot with the swipe of a control fin. The thrust of the missile was such that the captain didn't feel his flesh burning before the missile tore through the security door and detonated mid-cabin, directly above the massive fuel tanks in the wings. The explosion ripped the mid-section of the airliner apart and ignited thousands of gallons of fuel. Only the wingtips and tail section remained intact to fall into the sea.

Shaken by what he had just seen Commander Scott returned to the bridge. The officers and sailors on the bridge stood in stunned silence, color drained from their faces.

"Ahead—dead slow. Put a man on the bow and we will search for survivors."

"MISSILE ALERT! Three bogeys off the port quarters 150 miles and closing supersonic."

Scott silently vowed that this was not going to be another incident like the USS Stark. The Stark was hit by two Exocet missiles launched by an Iraqi fighter in the'80's, thirty-seven sailors lost their lives and the crew fought for two days to keep the cruiser afloat. "Weapons, full automatic. Engage."

Three missiles jumped from the vertical launch container system and streaked to port. "Stand-by with electronic countermeasures and chaff, Phalanx to automatic, helm, full speed ahead."

The weapons officer reported, "Hits on missiles one and two. Missile three is still flying, impact in thirty seconds."

"Launch countermeasures!"

The same chaff containers that confused the radar on the Iranian airliner were again launched; this time with the added assist of the ECM officer jamming any signal the remaining missile may be receiving from the launch station.

"Weapons, status please."

The weapons officer intently studied the track of the inbound missile. "Missile is still flying straight and true—right at us, Skipper."

"Then let's hope the guns work."

The seconds ticked by as the crew waited for the impact of the missile. Their last and only chance was the 6 barreled Phalanx gun. Capable of firing 4,500 rounds per minute, the gun system was the mainstay of the close-in defense system of the ship. The men on the bridge heard the low growl of the gun as it spewed out one-hundred round bursts. Once, twice, and a third time the gun fired, each time tracking both the depleted uranium rounds and the path of the missile and constantly updating the intercept solution. The fourth burst caught the inbound missile square on the nose. The explosion was greeted by a cheer from the sailors on the bridge.

The pilot of Hornet 3 swore softly at the scene below him. Hornets 3 and 4 had the entire engagement on digital camera, everything from the attack of the airliner to the USS Garcia's defense against the incoming missiles. "Eagle Watch this is Hornet 3, I've got that entire attack on camera and a visual on the missile launch site. It has a smoke trail leading directly to it. It looks like they are reloading. Request permission to engage."

"Hornet 3, this is Eagle Watch. Weapons free on the launch site. Keep your cameras rolling."

"This is Hornet 3, understand weapons free on the launch site and keep cameras rolling. Stand-by for battle damage assessment."

The attack on the missile site would have been more difficult against a coordinated defense of air-defense missiles, or anti-aircraft guns, but the Iranians were not prepared to defend the launch site. A single shallow dive and a thirty second burst of the 20 mm Gatlin gun in the nose of the F-18 silenced the site.

"Eagle Watch this is Hornet 3, the launch site is out of action."

Eagle Watch relayed the information to the bridge of the USS Garcia. The immediate danger was over.

Commander Scott ordered, "Radar, keep a close eye on those missile sites. Officer of the watch, take us through the wreckage. Let's see if there are any survivors."

Their search was in vain.

~~

The first sign something extraordinary had occurred was the call from one of the second string correspondents, the first team always traveled with the President, with the rumor that the President had cancelled the remainder of his Middle East tour and was returning to Washington. The White House was tight lipped and refused any and all inquires. That set the news machine in motion. Calls went out to correspondents stationed around the world for news on the President's location.

The news team with the Vice President reported he was pulled from a fund raiser in New York and was put on Air Force Two to return to Washington. No reason was given for the unusual action.

The correspondent reports from the news bureaus in the Middle East began to paint a horrific picture. A US Navy warship shot down an Iranian airliner full of Muslims on Hajj to Mecca. Additional reports described the scenes of floating debris and human remains in the blue waters of the Persian Gulf. The news from Al Jazeera TV reported the attack on the missile launch site as an unprovoked attack by US Navy fighter jets on a peaceful Iranian research project.

By noon the White House acknowledged the cancellation of the remainder of the President's trip, but deferred all questions concerning the rumors of the downed Iranian airliner. The State Department simply said they were studying the situation and will address it after consultations with the President and other concerned parties. The Pentagon refused to answer any questions citing national security issues. The Secretary of Defense would address the press after consultations with the President and the National Security Council. Only the news outlets at the United Nations had anything to report, and they had UN Ambassadors lined up for interviews.

Condemnation after condemnation spewed from the mouths of the Ambassadors. Only Eric Brown dared question the utility of allowing the Ambassador's unsubstantiated charges of war crimes to be broadcast to the American people. "Why are we broadcasting this crap? We don't even know what happened yet."

The producer provided the answer. "We don't have to know what happened. All we do is report the news." The producer was beaming and rubbed his hands together in excitement. "We've got 'em now, that's for sure. They won't be able to cover this up."

239

"We've got who?"

"The Pentagon! They aren't going to get out of this one."

The more Eric watched the video reports coming in from around the world, the more he began to believe the producer was right. The reports showed hundreds of thousands of people marching in the streets of every major city in the Middle East; all chanting "Death to America!" Video reports of burning offices of American businesses, and no effort by local authorities to stop the rampage. The reports of American citizens in a panic to buy tickets on any flight leaving the region reminded Eric of the films of Americans fleeing South Viet Nam. The most disturbing reports were of American exchange students stoned to death at universities across the region. Eric Brown would be the anchor most visible explaining the growing chaos to the American people.

The 6 p.m. news hour stretched into two hours and then three and then four. At 8 p.m. the President arrived in Washington and immediately went into emergency session with advisors and the Joint Chiefs. At 9 p.m. the White House announced the President would address the nation from the Oval Office at 10 p.m.

The hours of stress were evident on the President's face as he approached the microphone. Eric introduced the President to the millions of viewers on the world-wide networks of CNN.

"To the citizens of the United States of America and citizens of the World, I stand before you tonight with a heavy heart. The terrible and needless loss of life in the Persian Gulf is tragic and beyond comprehension. My prayers and the prayers of this nation go out to the families of the victims.

"American involvement in the internal affairs of the countries in the Middle East has for decades been justified by my predecessors as vital to the national interests of the United States. There has been a long debate in this country as to our involvement in that region. The terrible and unnecessary loss of life has made one thing clear to me; this nation's insatiable thirst for oil must be fulfilled in a more civilized and humane way. No longer will this country hold our friends in the Middle East hostage at the point of a bayonet or looking down the barrel of a gun.

"To that end, as Commander in Chief of our Armed Forces, I have ordered the redeployment of the 5th US Navy Fleet from Bahrain to the island of Diego Garcia in the Indian Ocean. I have directed the detention of the Navy personnel involved in this terrible incident until a thorough investigation has been made. I extend an invitation to the nation of Iran to participate in this investigation.

"In the trying times ahead I ask that we all exercise restraint in our actions. To the people of the world, tomorrow is another day, and unlike the days of the past, tomorrow will dawn on a new America. A United States committed to understanding the sovereign rights of all nations to determine their own path. A United States committed to living in harmony with all nations.

"Thank you and good night."

The President ignored the flood of questions, turned and left the podium. Eric started the commentary on his speech.

"That was the President of the United States' address to the nation and the world about the terrible incident in the Persian Gulf, where apparently the US Navy shot down an Iranian commercial airliner. I found it interesting that he never specifically mentioned that fact. He also said he has ordered the detention of the personnel involved and extended an invitation to the Iranians to participate in that investigation. In an effort to reduce the tensions in the area he also ordered the 5th US Fleet to deploy to the island of Diego Garcia. If I remember my geography, Diego Garcia is about 3,000 miles south in the Indian Ocean."

Eric's co-anchor, a woman recently moved from one of the nightly entertainment programs to the national news desk, added, "That's right Eric. The President also extended his condolences to the families of the victims of this terrible event and promised a new foreign policy that will live in harmony with other nations of the world."

As she was speaking the producer was talking into Eric's earpiece. "There's a briefing at the Pentagon. We are going live in 30 seconds. Get her to shut up and get us to the live shot!"

Eric's eye was on the clock and he was prepared to kick his co-anchor under the table, but apparently she ran out of irrelevant things to say. "We have just been notified that we are going live to the Pentagon for a briefing on the day's events. Let's go to our reporter at the Pentagon for the details."

The screens in the control room were filled by the CNN Pentagon reporter. "Eric, the officer you see behind me is introducing General Harold Beechman, United States Air Force. He has served as Chairman of the Joints Chiefs of Staff for two years and is the senior military advisor to the President and the man responsible for all combat operations worldwide. This is a bit unusual, that the Chairman of the Joint Chiefs would conduct a briefing that many here at the Pentagon thought would be given by the newly appointed Secretary of Defense,

241

Mr. Alvin Gray. We have no details on the General's speech and can only assume it deals with the tragic events in the Persian Gulf. Let's listen."

General Beechman walked to the podium and opened a simple manila folder.

"Ladies and Gentlemen, earlier this evening the President made clear our concern over the incident in the Persian Gulf. I will add my condolences to those of the President for the families of the deceased. Many of the dead are innocent victims of the reckless and deliberate actions of a few.

"The reaction of the world has been predictable. That reaction and the increasing violence against Americans will not bring back the dead. I ask the world to exercise restraint and offer protection to our citizens abroad as we would protect your citizens in our country.

"The President has ordered the redeployment of the US 5th Fleet from Bahrain to Diego Garcia. I have already issued orders directing local commanders to execute the President's order with the utmost speed and urgency. This deployment, 3,000 miles south of the 5th Fleets operational area, will reduce, but not eliminate our ability to respond to crises in the area. In joint consultation with our allies we will restructure our shared responsibilities to ensure continued peace and unimpeded access to the Persian Gulf."

General Beechman paused and reflected a moment before closing the folder from which he was reading; as if his address was complete.

He continued in a softer, but a more resolute tone. "That completes my prepared remarks, but I would like to address one additional topic.

"I have proudly served in this Nation's Armed Forces for 34 years. Like many soldiers, sailors, airmen and Marines, I have often struggled with the moral dilemma of war and the violence of it. If the bombs I have dropped killed the enemy deserving death, or did they fall on innocent victims who yearn for nothing but peace. Only my belief in God and the moral fiber of this great country helped me through the horrors of war. There is no one who yearns more for peace than the soldier sent to fight the war.

"Too often we are quick to criticize those who risk their lives doing the bidding of our county. And already there are those who demand we punish our soldiers even before the facts are known. These are not mercenaries who fight for the spoils of war; they are our brothers and sisters, our mothers and fathers, our sons and daughters and they serve with honor and integrity. Thank God so many have heard the calling to serve. Too often their sacrifice is their only reward for their service.

"America is the leader of the free world; some in our nation would prefer we retreat from that position. The fact remains that we are the nation so often challenged, because so many others have retreated in the face of a growing threat of radical sects and nations. We as a nation must accept the responsibility of preserving the hope of free men everywhere. As Chairman of the Joint Chiefs of Staff, I must accept my responsibility to defend the actions of my brothers in arms when all others have retreated in the face of adversity and are so quick to condemn them."

General Beechman picked up a television remote control from the podium. "Ladies and gentlemen this is what really happened in the Persian Gulf. You can decide, and the American people can decide where the blame lies for the death of the passengers on that Iranian airliner. The pictures you are about to see were taken from the reconnaissance cameras on board a US F-18 Hornet flying air-cover over the entire incident. "

General Beechman turned on the monitor and began. "As is standard security procedure, we deployed an E-3 AWAC airborne command post to coordinate security for the President's visit to Saudi Arabia. We also, as standard security procedure, deploy combat aircraft to fly a constant air patrol providing security for the President in flight and while on the ground. In this instance, we had naval vessels not only in the Persian Gulf, but deployed in the northern Indian Ocean along the coasts of Yemen and Oman and in the Red Sea. These are standard security procedures and are defensive in nature.

"If you listen closely, the watch officer aboard the AWAC alerts the Hornet flight that an Iranian airliner has drifted off course. The AWACs directs the F-18s to investigate. The watch officer also notifies the USS Garcia that an Iranian airliner is headed in their direction.

"The airliner did not respond to repeated radio requests, nor did they respond to the international signal for intercept. The F-18s fired two warning salvos to warn the Iranian aircraft, but again they did not respond. The commander of the Garcia started to generate smoke to conceal his exact location. Here you see the Iranian airliner, after missing their target, return for another pass at our vessel. The USS

Garcia did not fire at the Iranian airliner until repeated attempts to avoid conflict and then only when the attacking airliner demonstrated beyond any doubt to the captain of the USS Garcia; that they were the target.

"After the engagement, the USS Garcia slows to begin a search for survivors. The weapons officer on the USS Garcia caught the radar signature of the missiles launched at his ship. The USS Garcia destroyed the three missiles launched to attack the ship.

"The F-18's followed the smoke trails from the missiles to their source and did not engage the launch site until there was evidence the launchers were being prepared for another salvo."

General Beechman turned off the monitor. "The complete text of the radio transmissions between the AWACS, the Hornet aircraft and the USS Garcia are available for your use. These are the facts concerning the downing of Iranian Flight A380. The American people can decide if the action of their military was justified."

General Beechman placed the control on the podium and retrieved his folder before stepping to the front of the stage to answer questions.

"General Beechman, how do you feel about the order to detain the military personnel involved in this incident?"

"Concerning the President's directive to detain all personnel involved in this incident; it is my sworn duty to carry out the orders of the President of the United States, and I have ordered that detention. I would be a coward to leave such an unpleasant task to my successor."

Eric's producer was screaming in his earpiece, "Eric, ask the General what he meant by that. We've got a rumor that the President has relieved him. Don't let him get away!"

Eric relayed the question to the Pentagon reporter. "General Beechman, we have heard a rumor that the President has relived you of you duties. Is that true?"

The question caught everyone by surprise and the buzz in the room stopped; you could hear an ax drop.

General Beechman stood alone to face the question.

"After I issued the orders directed by the President, I offered my resignation through the Secretary of Defense to the President. The President accepted my resignation and effective at midnight tonight I will retire from active service."

Beechman turned and directly faced the nearest television camera, almost as if he was trying to connect with the people across America while ignoring the reporters directly to his front.

"It has been my honor to serve America and to serve with the members of our Armed Forces." It was a simple closing, but one that chilled Eric Brown to the bone. "God save America."

~~

Bill Cannon understood the meaning of General Beechman's farewell, "God save America," not "God bless America." Bill wondered how many more of his old friends would follow Beechman's lead.

Bill Cannon and Prince Al-Sabah watched the entire broadcast. Only the chanting crowds in the city streets disturbed their thoughts.

Prince Al-Sabah turned off the broadcast and broke the silence. "So my friend, America once again retreats and will not face the lies of her accusers."

It was an unusually harsh criticism from his friend. Bill got up from his chair and moved to and opened the window. The sounds of the rampaging mob filled the room.

Bill turned to his friend and said, "You now know the truth. Will you speak the truth to your people? Which man carries more shame, the man who runs from the lie or the man who fails to speak the truth? Both carry the burden of shame."

Prince Al-Sabah realized his thoughtless comment cut his friend to the core. "You are right my good friend. Please accept my apology for my unruly tongue. I fear the future without a strong America to provide the light for those who desire freedom and democracy. I fear the mobs will smother us all."

~~

After Bill left the personal residence, Prince Al-Sabah called General Al-Wadi. "The Americans are leaving. We have no choice but to continue. Call Achmad Nardiff and tell him to proceed."

"Yes, your highness."

Chapter 33

It was Wednesday afternoon—near closing—when Ken got the first call. "Ken, Jerry Evans...do you have time for a drink after work?"

It was the first call Ken received from anyone in the syndicate. After all the secrecy surrounding the cruise, he expected action a little more dramatic, but it had been a month. He'd be lying if the thought that the whole thing was some charade hadn't crossed his mind more than once. But why would these men go to such extremes if their claims didn't carry the weight of truth?

Ken and Jerry met in the Hilton Hotel bar on River Street. It was a common meeting place for businessmen and their meeting wasn't noticed.

"Ken, we've got a line on a deal. We want to put up a million. If you want $100,000, you can have it."

Ken had that much cash available. "What's the deal?"

"A contractor in New Orleans needs a $10,000,000 bond to qualify for a government paving contract. We put up the money; if he gets the contract we double our money within a week. If he doesn't get the contract, we get our money back. It's a pretty clean deal."

Ken liked the deal. "When do you need the money?"

"This Friday."

There was always a certain amount of risk associated with these kinds of monetary exchanges. What would prevent Jerry Evans from simply taking Ken's money and disappearing? "Where is the meeting?"

"In Atlanta, this weekend, do you want some of the action?"

"Maybe. Who's going to be at the meeting?"

"Only me. This is a no-bid deal, so I'm the bag man for this one. This is small potatoes and the amounts are already set. We're getting one-tenth of the deal. We think some of the boys from Chicago are taking half." Jerry hunched his shoulders and added an Italian accent to his last statement.

"Boys from Chicago? Are you trying to tell me that there is still a mob in Chicago?"

Jerry grinned. "We don't know who they are, but Chicago always bids high on construction work. We think it's the mob, or somebody like the mob. It's kind of an inside joke, not a good joke, but that's what we think."

Jerry Evans, alone with one million dollars, this he had to see. "Isn't that kind of dumb? A million in cash…alone?"

"I won't be alone. I will have security with me."

Did Ken really trust his new partners? Their story sounded convincing, but scams bigger than this had been pulled on unsuspecting victims many times. Let's see if Jerry Evans would shy away if he wanted to tag along on this one.

"Jerry, it sounds good to me, but I would like to go with you on this. This will be my first investment, and I would like to see how the whole thing works."

Did Jerry pause before he answered? Ken couldn't really tell. "Not a problem with me. I'll have a motel room on the airport Marriott. Be there by 9 p.m., and don't be late."

~~

Jerry's security surprised Ken. When Ken was through the door and into the room, the 5' 4" blond, that couldn't have weighed more than one-hundred-twenty pounds, pinned him to the wall and buried the barrel of a gun in the base of his skull. With her free hand she expertly searched his body for weapons. "Put your briefcase on the floor and take a seat."

When Ken was seated, Jerry picked up the briefcase. "Hello Ken, let's see what you've got here."

That was the limit of the greeting, and Jerry didn't say anything else until he completed counting Ken's money. "Now we wait. Do you want a drink?"

Ken and Jerry sipped from the small glasses provided in the hotel bar. Ken wondered if the case on the table behind Jerry actually contained $900,000; Jerry didn't see the need to show Ken the money, and Ken wanted to give the impression he had done this sort of thing before.

The security escorting the silver haired gentleman from the IIC looked like security. Big and burly with ominous bulges under their coats where you wouldn't expect bulges to be, they avoided eye contact and positioned themselves where they could watch both the door and the two cases of money.

With only a silent nod to Jerry, the IIC man arranged the two cases and started counting. Ken watched as blocks of ten-thousand dollars were moved into blocks of one-hundred thousand dollars. Ken's money was the last to be counted and he was slightly embarrassed that the small denominations made the counting more difficult, but if the IIC man was in any way aggravated, he didn't show it.

When the counting was done, the IIC man transferred Ken's money into Jerry's larger case. With a nod to Jerry the man closed the case and stood to leave. Ken almost panicked; all that money and no receipt? It took all his self-control to remain silent. One burley guard and the female checked the hall, and the other guard and the IIC man left the room.

Maybe it was the banker in Ken, "Jerry, we don't even get a receipt?"

Jerry was patient with his new partner. "Ken, we told you, this is a cash only business. There are no receipts, no records, nothing."

Ken still felt nervous. "Is the security lady coming back?"

"She wasn't my security. She was IIC security. We don't have the money—why do we need security?"

Ken had to admit, Jerry had a point.

~~

Bill Cannon had to admit, Prince Al-Sabah had a point.

Bill studied the reconnaissance photos. Everything Al-Sabah claimed was substantiated by the photos. Protected storage facilities along the highways leading from Iran to Iraq and Kuwait were circled on the photos. Heavy transport trailers hauling armored vehicles, indiscernible to the naked eye, were circled on the highways. New army barracks, two-hundred miles west of their previous locations were marked. Assembly areas full of artillery pieces were marked. Facilities that appeared to be nothing more than a rest area along the highways when photographed with an infra-red camera clearly showed the underground fuel tanks of fuel depots. The dark shadows in the passes were underground storage sites for armored vehicles and ammunition. Bunkers dug into the cliffs overlooking the Persian Gulf were obviously launchers for the new anti-ships missile system imported from Russia. Two new Iranian corvettes were circled in the port of Bandar-Abbas.

248

Transports from Russia were highlighted on the northern highways into Iran. The convoys were spaced hundreds of miles and days apart, but there was no doubt, it was a concerted effort.

There was no doubt in Bill's mind the Iranian Army was moving slowly, but inexorably, to the west.

Prince Al-Sabah's frustration was evident, "Bill, these things are clear. If we can see these things, then surely the CIA can do the same. Why is the United States ignoring these provocations?"

"My friend, I hope that they are not."

General Al-Wadi asked, "Colonel Cannon, how do you think the American Pentagon views these movements?"

"Well, first the military would analyze these events from the Iranian perspective. The only valid justification for the movement of military forces to the western approaches would be if they felt threatened by a ground invasion from Iraq, or some other nation to her west. Since the departure of the American ground forces, Iraq's military is in complete disarray and does not have the capability. Neither are your forces, nor those of Saudi Arabia, even combined, capable of mounting offensive operations. In my opinion, there is no valid justification for these movements. Therefore, I believe they would conclude these movements are offensive in nature. In fact, the only threat to Iran is from the north; and they are foolish to believe the Russians, whom they now court, will not exact some sort of payment."

"Colonel Cannon, if these movements are prelude to an invasion; how would you plan such an invasion?"

Bill knew that every military, to include the Kuwait general staff, constantly studied scenarios such as this.

"I would expect the main attack will come in southern Iraq, probably through Basrah and Kuwait City with a strategic objective of Riyadh, Saudi Arabia. Supporting attacks will be made north to Baghdad to fix Iraqi forces in the defense of their capital, and another on the left flank of the main attack to secure the Saudi oil facilities along the Persian Gulf. The attack will be preceded by Iranian Special Forces infiltrating the local populations to activate insurgent Shia groups to support the attack. Once across the international borders, I would close the Straits of Hormuz to stop the flow of oil to the world. Once I occupied the oil facilities along the Persian Gulf, I would be in a position of power to negotiate with Europe and the United States to trade oil for their pledge to stay out of the affairs of the regional conflicts. If the buildup continues at the same rate it has been, then they could launch an attack within a year, and control the world's oil within two years."

Prince Al-Sabah and General Al-Wadi listened to Bill's assessment with the stoic demeanor of condemned men. "If the Iranians attack, will America come to our defense?"

"I don't know."

"Will the American people not see that their future will be different than their past? Do they not understand that their sworn enemy will control most of the world's oil? Will they not demand action?"

Bill hung his head for a moment before he answered. "Some will; but there are too many who think we should not be involved here. They only look to the government to make their life easier and do not look beyond their own comforts." It was a sad commentary on his country, but true.

Prince Al-Sabah's voice carried a tone of contempt. "Then the Americans will let us fight this battle alone. We will be washed away in the flood. The Americans have become like a small barking dog that only makes noise, but the barks will not turn our enemies from our borders."

Bill understood the feeling expressed by his friend, but many of his own friends had died in the defense of this piece of sand floating on oceans of oil. "Prince Al-Sabah, I understand your frustration, but the Kuwaiti flag still flies over this house, not the flag of the United States of America. Perhaps it is time you call your citizens to arms to defend your country."

Prince Al-Sabah walked to his friend and put his hand upon his shoulder.

"I apologize for my words of ignorance. I must confess that my people hold little allegiance to Kuwait. If you ask them where their allegiance lies most would answer they are Shia, or Sunni, Arab, or of some ancient tribe; very few would first answer they are Kuwaiti. Too few understand the value of a modern country. It has always been my dream to bring my people into the twenty-first century. Like the American, I think my people have eaten at the table of plenty for so long they have forgotten there is a price to pay for their freedom. Their allegiance blows like grains of sand in the wind. It is a burden I have long carried.

"Since I was a child I have seen America as a great savior, but perhaps I see America as it once was—as I want it to be—as I wish it to be, and I find it difficult to see her for what she has become. Like many great civilizations, she is destroying herself from within, she is collapsing upon herself.

"America has burned bright. Brighter than any other, but now it fades. The Romans, the Greeks, the Persians, the Mongols, in their time - ruled for thousands of years. America has been the guiding light in the world for two-hundred years, but now will sit idly by and watch as evil spreads death and destruction across many lands.

"America is becoming the great negotiator and hopes to contain evil with words rather than deeds. You can criticize my small country for depending on America for security, and I will accept that criticism, but Kuwait is not a superpower, America is."

Bill understood the feelings his friend was expressing, lately, he had many of the same misgivings. "Prince Al-Sabah, why did you allow me to see all these things?"

Prince Al-Sabah spoke in a softer tone. "Because you saved my country once, you saved my children; I hoped you could so the same again."

"It is America that saved your country. What I did for you many others would have done the same."

"That may be true, but your deeds speak louder than your words. Even today you choose to stand with me to defend my country rather than excuse yourself to the comforts and security of your home. You continue to stand with me even though your country has abandoned us both."

The frown on Prince Al-Sabah's face was obvious. "Bill, one last question, if this happens, would the government of Israel take action? Would they feel threatened enough to attack the Iranians?"

Bill didn't answer immediately. "Prince Al-Sabah, with the Egyptians, Iranians and Russians lining up on the western side of the Suez Canal, I think Israel is effectively neutralized. They wouldn't risk an attack from that combined force. Unless the United States, or maybe NATO, would put a heavy force in the Sinai, to guard Israel's western border, they aren't going to do a thing. I think Israel has all it can handle right now in the Gaza Strip."

~~~

Indeed, the Israelis had all they could handle in the Gaza Strip. The resistance was more than expected and the attack had stalled. They called up the armor too late, and then the confining streets limited their effectiveness. The airstrikes killed more civilians than Hamas fighters, and the Israeli Army had not discovered the nerve gas. They uncovered many caches of the new longer range rockets, and the binary warheads, but without the nerve gas the world would ignore Israeli claims as just more propaganda.

And, the American's were helping the Israeli government, and Al Jezeera television had proof.

Major James Madison went in with the command group of the 1st Brigade, and was kneeling behind a low wall when the man next to him was shot through the chest.

James did what he could until the medical evacuation team arrived. He cut away the uniform and tried to seal the entry and exit holes of the wound. And the entire incident was filmed from a window overlooking his position.

Within twenty-four hours his picture and the American flag on his shoulder made headlines around the world. The White House Chief of Staff had also seen the video and he was mad as hell, more than mad, he was livid.

Lucas McLaughlin had 30 minutes to get to the White House. He had the distinct impression of being brought before judges of the Inquisition; and they were obviously looking for a confession. In addition to the Chief of Staff, the Director of National Intelligence, the Deputy Director of Collection, the Director of the Central Intelligence Agency, the Secretary of Defense and the Chairman of the Joint Chiefs of Staff, political appointees all, were in attendance. The Chief of Staff was the only man who spoke.

"What in the hell have you been doing? The President gets ambushed and you stand there looking stupid! I want to know why you shouldn't be fired right now. What do you have to say for yourself?"

Lucas broke the stare of the Chief of Staff. He also had seen the video, but there was no reason to volunteer information. What did the Chief suspect? "Pardon me, sir. What exactly are you talking about?"

"You damn well know what in the hell I'm talking about! The Israeli's launch an attack on the Gaza Strip based on some trumped up bullshit about chemical weapons being smuggled into the strip, given to them by somebody from our intelligence community, and you don't know what I'm talking about? And who the hell is that American officer pasted all over the news? How can the President push his world agenda for peace in the Middle East if it looks like we are supporting Israel when

252

it attacks into the Gaza. If the President can't depend on his own military and intelligence agencies for accurate and timely information how can we forge a lasting peace?"

McLaughlin was cautious with his reply. "Sir, Israel did not inform us of their intent to attack in the Gaza. It came as a complete surprise. I have seen the video, and it clearly shows our man is not armed. He is simply an observer. There are many exchange officers serving with different militaries around the world."

The Chief of Staff exploded. "That will be enough out of you! You people just don't understand the complexity of the situation. From this point forward, nothing goes to the Israelis without coming to this office for approval first, and get that idiot out of Gaza! Is that understood?"

Those instructions, maybe given in haste, would virtually kill the exchange of intelligence between the United States and Israel. Lucas McLaughlin knew it; so did his superiors in the room, but none of the Directors, the Secretary, or the Chairman raised objection. The pause before McLaughlin answered only infuriated the Chief of Staff.

"Do you understand!?"

"Yes sir, I understand."

~~

On the same day James Madison received orders to leave the Gaza, Ken Carson got a phone call from Jerry Evans.

"Ken, the money is in. How do you want it?"

"What are my options?"

"You can get cash, or you can split it into cash and some to an offshore account."

Ken wanted to see if this could possibly be true. Did he really just make $100,000 profit in one week? It was almost too good to be true. If he took it all in cash he could pay off a couple of loans, enjoy the remainder, and put the initial investment back into his accounts.

"I want it all cash."

"Not a problem. Pretty sweet deal, huh?"

Ken was grinning from ear to ear when he answered. "Damn sweet!

Chapter 34

The financial reports were painting a grim picture. Danni swiveled in her chair and let her eyes scan the horizon, and let her mind drift to the last fishing trip will Bill Cannon. They had launched from that same pier on their last fishing trip. She remembered the smell of the ocean and the sting of the salt spray, and closed her eyes when she remembered the warmth of Bill's leg next to hers. How long had he been gone? She missed him. She could have spent the remainder of the day dreaming about that fishing trip, but her phone brought her back to the present with a harsh ring.

"Ms. Walton, you father is calling."

She was still upset with her father, but would never ignore his call. "Put him through."

Ed Helton sounded much less troubled than his daughter. "Danni, how many years has it been since I treated you to dinner?"

Danni found the question a little ludicrous. Her father was the cause of most of her current problems, now trying to make amends It was difficult to let her love shine through at this particular moment.

"I don't know if I would be good company tonight, dad."

"Nonsense, you have a solid partner running the hotel. It's about time you started to loosen up. I'll send DeAngelo to pick you up. Come exactly as you are. Mike will be at the dock in one hour."

Honor thy father and mother. It was the passage that swayed Danni's decision. "Okay. I'll be ready."

An hour later, Danni saw DeAngelo's boat skirt the sandbar formed by the Savannah River. Mike greeted her in his normal off-color way. "Danni, when are you going to quit pretending you're not attracted to me? We'd make a beautiful couple you know."

"Fat chance DeAngelo, I don't date pirates." Mike DeAngelo had a hearty laugh at his own expense. Her sharp wit was one of the reasons he liked and respected Danni Walton. Mike knew Danni was Bill Cannon's true love and his advances were all in jest. Danni was Bill

Cannon's girl even if neither Bill Cannon nor Danni Walton would admit it.

Danni was mildly surprised when DeAngelo didn't turn west up the Savannah River, but kept the bow of his vessel pointed to the open ocean.

"Where are we going for dinner, Bermuda?" It was a joke, but Danni didn't know how close to the truth her guess was.

"Not now, maybe later. Your father has a special treat for you."

It wasn't long before the running lights of a beautiful yacht glimmered through the gathering darkness. Her father met her at the rail. He was all smiles.

"Welcome aboard. I hope you enjoyed the trip."

Danni's attitude, sour before the sight of her father, began to soften. "Daddy, where did you get this?"

"It belongs to a friend of mine. He's letting me borrow it for a while. I thought you might need some cheering up so I arranged a special dinner for you."

As the yacht cruised up the Atlantic coast Danni and her father sat on the fantail. The gentle sway of the boat began to have a calming effect on Danni and before long she actually began to enjoy the rhythm of the boat, the gentle breezes and moonlight glittering in the wake. Except for the steward silently appearing to serve the drinks and appetizers they were alone. They talked about Hanna and the baby, and of her husband in Israel. They reminisced about the times when Danni was young and her mother still alive, and the boat rides they took, and the picnics they enjoyed on the beaches. They talked about Bill Cannon and wondered when he would return. It was wonderful and relaxing until her father asked.

"Danni, I want to ask a favor of you."

The luster of the evening vanished. Was this nothing more than a charade put on by her father to put her in another compromised position? She had seen the tactic employed so many times before. Get the opponent alone, preferably on your own turf, dazzle them with something grand—the yacht—pour a couple of drinks down them to soften them up, and then spring the trap. Danni regretted that her father felt the need for such deceitful practices.

"What now?"

"In about a week, I want you to request a loan from the bank. About $40,000,000 should do."

"Forty-million dollars! Now why would I want to do that?"

"I want you to buy all the outstanding resort stock."

"Dad, you just pulled the rug out from under me when you called in the bank loan. Now you're going to loan me $40,000,000? That doesn't make any sense, besides, why would I want to buy up all the outstanding stock of the hotel?"

"Because, honest people invested in the hotel and I would hate to see those people lose their money."

The comment was almost considered an insult to Danni. "Thanks for the vote of confidence. You didn't answer my question. Why would you loan me $40,000,000?"

"I wouldn't, but the government will. Nothing would please the administration more than funding a union controlled resort. I wouldn't be loaning you the bank's money, the government would be loaning you stimulus money. There's a difference."

"Not much of a difference. Government money is nothing more than money taken from the taxpayers and taxpayers are honest people too, you know."

"That's the way it is supposed to be, but it's not that way today. The government is printing money that is backed only by their creditors; places like China and other countries that buy our country's debt. They went way beyond tax payer money a long time ago."

"Even if I agreed with the idea, I can't request that loan without the approval of my new partners, the union, thanks to you. I don't think they would sign-off on the idea."

"Sure they would. Want to know why? They will sign off on the deal because they are greedy. You start buying your own stock and the price of the stock will go up. They will think you are the smartest person in the world. You will be a hero."

"Dad, in what kind of crazy scheme are you getting me involved?"

Ed Helton had cleared the first and most difficult hurdle; he got his daughter to listen.

"Why don't we discuss it over dinner?'

~~

DeAngelo returned her to the hotel pier. It was the first time Danni could remember where DeAngelo didn't keep up a running dialogue on something…the weather, fishing, politics, the Braves – it never mattered if the subject made any sense at all, but once DeAngelo started he could ramble on for hours. On this night DeAngelo kept his thoughts to himself.

Even after spending an hour with her father, Danni still had trouble putting what he told her into perspective. It was so far from the values that he had preached to her over the years. She had a hard time believing the words came from her father.

The lights of the hotel lit her way through the grounds. She could take a golf cart to her home, but maybe the solitude of the walk would help her understand the events discussed over dinner.

She tried to ignore the weeds in the flower beds. The union contract allowed the gardeners to tend to the gardens only twice a month, and the weeds would be allowed a few more days of growth before they were removed; the same contract applied to the once perfectly manicured polo field.

She tried to ignore the day-sailor that was awash in the marina, left there to rot since the departure of Brian Vance. The piers looked naked since the departure of DeAngelo's fishing fleet. After DeAngleo refused to join the union, the hotel simply stopped booking fishing charters, so he simply moved his charters back to his marina in Savannah.

She tried to ignore the vacant shops on Main Street that closed when the union doubled the rent. The shop owners simply packed up their wares and returned their inventory to their main locations. All these things Danni tried to ignore.

The lights of the hotel faded into the darkness of the night, and the dirt road reflected enough light to guide her way. The sounds of the woods were familiar and comforting. Only the sound of the approaching siren dampened her spirits.

She stopped and glanced down the road to watch the approaching emergency vehicle. The red blinking lights and blaring siren violated the calm of the night. They sped past Danni at close to 60 miles per hour, a speed unheard of on the small roads of the island.

Danni turned and started to run. There was only one house down this road; her house.

Danni could still see the lingering dust cloud where the ambulance turned from the main road to the driveway leading to her father's house; only another quarter mile to go. Don't think, just run. Could it be the baby, or Hanna? Was Hanna losing the baby? Was it Hanna that was in danger? There, through the bushes, the red lights of the ambulance silently flashing. Why did we choose to live on an island? The nearest hospital was in Savannah and even if Mike DeAngleo had a boat in the marina it was a 30 minute trip, probably more if you added the time it would take to get Hanna to the hospital. Unless Mike was docked and his cell phone on, then it would be difficult to even reach him.

Danni felt a quick pang of conscience when she hoped it was Brain Vance, rather than her daughter. Maybe he had a blood clot or something. She was ashamed at the thought and asked for forgiveness.

Mamba was standing on the porch as she made the last 100 yards. Out of breath, sweat staining the silk blouse, hair dangling across her face Danni gasped out, "Where's Hanna?"

Mamba held her hands up as if to stop her charge, "Hanna's inside. Both she and the baby are fine. Aunt Grace collapsed. She had a heart attack. The medics are working on her now. They have called for a helicopter evacuation to Savannah."

"Can I see her? Will she be OK?"

"You would only get in the way. She was unconscious, but the medics shocked her back. She is alive, but delirious. I would think it would be better if you comforted Hanna. She is very upset. She is the one that found her."

Danni was only able to hold Aunt Grace's hand for a moment as the medics rushed her to the waiting helicopter. The hand was cold and had the feel of death and Danni shuddered at the thought that Aunt Grace may not return to the island.

Danni turned to Mamba and asked, "Has anyone called Eric?"

~~

Eric drove from Atlanta and was at her side when she died. The doctors did all they could, but the cancer treatments were just too much for her heart. Just before she passed, she opened her eyes and turned her head to Eric.

"Dearest Eric, I have talked with your father." Her voice was weak and words came slowly, and Eric had to lean close to her lips to hear. "He loves you and is proud of you and he will watch over you."

Eric thought those were her last words, but she continued. "I am proud of you. You have grown into a good man and will find happiness. Have no sorrow for me for I am going to a better place, I have seen the light of salvation."

Tears streamed down Eric's face and he was not ashamed to cry for this lovely woman who cared for him when all others abandoned him. "Please thank our new family for all the love they have shown us. Tell them I am sorry to have been such a bother. I want to be buried next to my husband. Keep your faith."

And then she closed her eyes and passed. The doctors rushed in when the monitor sounded the alarm and the lines went flat, but Eric knew there was nothing they could do. Aunt Grace was gone. He stood against the wall, away from the medical staff, and Eric felt more alone than ever in his life. There was no more family he could turn to; his father and mother, and now Aunt Grace, were all gone. The world was suddenly a lonelier place. He wondered if he had the strength to make it through life without the comfort of knowing he could always find love in their presence.

When Eric walked from the intensive care unit he looked upon his new family and friends. Ed Helton, his daughter Danni, her daughter Hanna, and Mamba, and his other friends—those friends of his father— Mike DeAngelo and Doc Broderson, were waiting in the lounge. These people, he knew, would help him through life. Bill Cannon would always be there too, he had promised as much to his father. And now Angelina was coming into his life, and the passing of Aunt Grace made him realize he was not alone.

"Aunt Grace is in heaven. She thanks you for your love. She wants to be buried next to her husband in Cairo."

Eric's family rose to comfort him, but he stopped them. "I am going to see my father."

Eric left the hospital and drove to the burial grounds outside the state penitentiary. The guard referenced his father's name and showed Eric where the marker could be found.

For the first time since his father's death, Eric Brown Jackson knelt at his father's grave and prayed. He then sat on the ground next to his father and told him of his life and his new family, and of Bill Cannon and his other friends, and of Angelina. When the creeping edge of night covered the burial grounds Eric promised his father he would one day come and remove him from this field, and find a place of honor for him to rest.

The guard noted it was dark when the young visitor finally returned to his car and drove off.

Chapter 35

Angelina struggled to focus on the investigation. Since Eric's call that his Aunt had taken gravely ill she simply lacked the motivation to concentrate. He hadn't called for three days and if he didn't call today, that would make four. She realized she missed him.

She tried to get back into the Hanna Walton case, but it simply took too much effort. She reviewed her notes, nothing new jumped from the pages. She reviewed the file on Bomani Thomas, and reviewed the video of the fight in the prison yard, but there were no new secrets revealed.

She flipped through the military records of Steve Thunder and Jackson, but found nothing new. She scribbled in her notes the association of Doc Broderson with the two other men, but that had already been established, and the fact they served together in the Army was not conclusive proof they were conspirators in the drug case. It would be pure speculation that Steve Thunder and or Doc Broderson ever had any contact with Jackson after his sentencing. The visitor logs to the prison were detailed in every respect. Neither Steve Thunder nor Doc Broderson ever visited or called Jackson during his confinement.

Every letter, every postcard sent or received from the prison was logged. No letters, post cards, phone calls, or visits to help build the circumstantial evidence required to prove a conspiracy. In fact, the only visitor ever logged for John Brown Jackson was a distant aunt that visited him once a quarter during his confinement. So Angelina wasted time tracing silly figures on her notes and hoped Eric would call.

The smell of the dead rat now at a manageable level, Angelina removed the personal effects of Jackson from the boxes received from the prison. The foul odor of the dead rat still lingered on the uniform, but the uniform revealed nothing. The few letters he received were all from his aunt and contained no hint of new information. They simply tried to tell the story of his growing son and life outside the prison walls. The letters were always handwritten and Angelina could tell they were always written in a loving hand.

The pictures of his young son and the last picture in the news article visiting the military museum at Valdosta Air Force Base were the same pictures she had already reviewed. Only in the pictures of the Jackson corpse did she notice something new, a distinctive tattoo, barely legible on his black skin, of a knife through a rope braided into a figure eight. It was unique enough to catch her attention, but nothing more.

She neatly placed the effects back into the boxes. Just as the last box was sealed Eric's voice brightened the room.

"How's my favorite investigator?"

Angelina jumped up from her sitting position on the floor and ran to Eric and gave him a hug and a short kiss appropriate for the office setting; they both wanted more, but their manners and comportment called for restraint.

"Why didn't you call me? I've been worried sick about you. How is your aunt?"

Eric held Angelina's hand in his own, almost as if he was providing strength for her at the news he was to relay. "My aunt passed away. The cancer therapy weakened her heart and she had a heart attack. I was with her when she died."

Angelina wanted to go to him, and hold him, but he seemed so strong. She did not want her affections to be considered patronizing to someone who had already mastered his grief. "I'm so sorry, Eric. I know she meant a lot to you. Is there anything I can do to help?"

"It would mean a lot to me if you would accompany me to the funeral."

~~

The transition from the hustle and bustle of metro Atlanta to the slow and sometimes depressed rural areas of Georgia was quite remarkable. Once outside the metropolitan counties that surround Atlanta, the impacts were obvious and devastating. Too many men lounged along the streets of the small towns, and every third or fourth house along the highway displayed personal belongings behind huge signs that read yard sale, or the more ambitious would read estate sale. It was an increasingly depressing trip.

When they arrived in Cairo, Eric checked them into separate rooms at the Best Western Motel; it was the proper thing to do. Their dinner at the Western Sizzling Steak house, obviously the most refined restaurant in town, reminded Angelina of the steak house outside her home town in New Mexico, where her family ate meals when they could afford the luxury of eating out.

After dinner Eric took her on a tour of his home town. The high school was still in use and, although small, was well maintained. The home he shared with Aunt Grace was maybe 800 square feet, but weeds and vines had taken over the grounds and begged the question: "How long ago did you move from this house?"

"About eight years ago. We moved to South Carolina. Aunt Grace wanted to be buried here, near her husband. There's a small family plot up the road a bit. I'll take you there next."

Eric drove them to a small church set well down a country dirt road. The wood siding of the church had been painted so often that Angelina guessed the paint was now thicker than the wood it covered. The church stood between a stand of huge oak trees draped with Spanish moss, and the small fenced cemetery. Angelina could see the freshly dug pile of dirt next to the resting place for Aunt Grace.

Eric took her through the cemetery and pointed out the headstones of Grace's husband, and of relatives long passed. He could trace his linage back through the days of slavery and told her stories that had been passed down through generations of his family. He could trace his roots to before slavery when his ancestors resided on the upper reaches of the Nile River in Africa. He pointed out the first relative who earned his freedom after the Civil War, and the first man in their family to own his own business. He pointed out the headstone of a distant aunt who bore 22 children, and apologized when he couldn't relay the stories of those children.

"Too many left here to find a life elsewhere and they just drifted out of our history. I wish I had the time to track all of them down."

Angelina noticed that none of the history that Eric relayed included any of his close family. "Eric, is this where your parents are buried? You haven't talked about them at all."

"My mother is buried in Albany."

"Where was your father laid to rest?"

"My father is not buried here."

Angelina thought it strange that Eric didn't elaborate any more than his simple statement. She wanted to know more, but now was not the time to ask.

They returned to the motel after dark and parted ways with a tender kiss before heading to their individual rooms. The service was scheduled to begin at 10 a.m.

Eric wanted to be at the church early to greet friends of Aunt Grace. When they arrived at the church, the casket was already displayed near the podium and Eric discussed the service with the Pastor.

The Pastor reminisced with Eric about how fine a woman Aunt Grace was and how the congregation missed her. Angelina didn't think the Pastor's question about their sudden and completely unannounced departure from the area was inappropriate, but she saw Eric visibly stiffen. Eric's answer, that they thought a location on the coast would be better for her health, seemed rather abrupt. The Pastor didn't press the issue and said he was happy Aunt Grace decided to come home.

Eric asked if it would be proper to allow Angelina to greet the guests with him. The Pastor smiled at Angelina before he said, "If she is part of your life then, by all means, it would be most appropriate."

Angelina wished Eric would have discussed his plan to include her in the ceremony, but quickly decided she would have conceded to his wishes, and obviously he wanted her by his side.

The first guests were Aunt Grace's oldest and dearest friends. Their conversations with Eric were filled with condolences and motherly pats on his hand. Distant relatives, some Eric had never met, arrived and introduced themselves. Before long 20 to 30 of the seats in the small church were filled. The introductions of Angelina were comfortable and the guests seemed to accept her presence.

Near 10 o'clock a late model SUV, one of the larger models—all black and shiny, pulled to the walk leading to church. The SUV was followed closely by another car that stopped directly to the rear. Angelina watched as the driver of the SUV, a distinguished looking man in his early sixties, in a well-tailored suit, circled the vehicle and opened the passenger door. The passenger in the trail vehicle, a large bearded man with a deep chest and arms that strained to break free from the confines of his suit, opened the rear door of the SUV.

The driver helped the front passenger, a pregnant young lady about Angelina's age, steady herself as she slid down from the high seat. The girl laughed when her dress rode up the seat, and the driver held her hand as she straightened her dress. Angelina got the initial impression that the two ladies in the back seat, one black and one white were the royalty of the group. Both stood tall with the simple elegance of confident women. The small group took a moment to get organized and allowed the large bearded man to move the vehicle to the parking area.

Angelina felt a growing excitement in Eric and he beckoned her to meet these people on the front steps of the church rather than inside the vestibule.

Eric turned to Angelina and said, "Angelina, I've been wanting you to meet these people for a long time. They are my new family. I hope you like them."

Angelina had no reason to believe she wouldn't like the people coming up the walk. They carried themselves with dignity and even at such a solemn occasion as a funeral all seemed to have quick and genuine smiles on their faces.

Eric stepped forward to greet the tall lady first. "Mrs. Walton, thank you for coming. It means a lot to me."

The lady bent forward and kissed Eric on the cheek, "Eric, Grace was a wonderful woman and she meant the world to us. It is our honor to help put her to rest."

Before Eric could introduce Angelina, the young pregnant woman threw her arms around Eric's neck and gave him a big hug. "I called Jimmy and told him about Aunt Grace. He sends his love and condolences." The young woman stepped back and said, "You know what? You look better on TV than you do in person."

Eric smiled and Angelina thought for a moment he was too embarrassed to respond to the strange compliment, but he wasn't.

"And you look better pregnant that you ever did as a skinny little girl," and the pair had a playful connection as only old friends could.

The black woman addressed Eric in a strange way. "Master Eric, I hope this day of joy finds you well."

Eric turned to face the black woman. "It does Mamba. Everything is right with the world. Thank you for coming."

Mamba directed her attention towards Angelina. "So this is the girl who has brightened your path. Would you be so kind as to introduce us?"

Eric turned and gently led Angelina into the center of the women. "May I introduce someone who is very special to me; this is Angelina Sanchez. Angelina, this is Mrs. Danni Walton and her daughter, Hanna, and this is Miranda Castillio, but everybody calls her Mamba."

265

Angelina was bombarded with emotions. First, she had to deal with the introduction, someone who is very special to me, what was that supposed to mean?

She was distracted by the names of those just introduced; Mrs. Danni Walton and daughter Hanna. Her mind kept racing from the steps of the church, to the reports in her office, and back. Could these women be the same Danni Walton and daughter Hanna that she had been studying for the last months? She wanted to retreat to solitude to gain her bearings and regain her composure. Mamba, in her wisdom, helped her back to the present.

Mamba held her hand and looked deep into her eyes. Angelina heard her voice, but never did she see her lips move, but the message was clear. "I can see you have questions and are confused. Enjoy this day of joy. Your questions will be answered in due time. Welcome to our family."

Angelina watched the three ladies walk the side aisle to Aunt Grace's casket. They each paused and bowed their head and then moved to and sat on the benches near the pulpit. Angelina almost jumped at the touch on her arm.

"Angelina, I want you to met Mr. Ed Helton."

Angelina had not recovered from the shock of meeting the women, and when Ed Helton introduced himself she was sure he thought her to be slow witted, at best. She found it difficult to answer his simple questions and she did the best she could with a simple yes or no and a charming smile. As she watched Ed Helton move to the pew, she heard a voice that was familiar.

"Eric, Bill Cannon is on the phone, he wants to talk with you." It was the voice of Doc Broderson.

Angelina heard Eric excuse himself, and then felt him move away to take the call. When she turned back to look to the front, she turned directly into the barreled chest of the bearded man. The big man made Doc Broderson, standing to the man's left, almost look small. Doc Broderson introduced his friend to Angelina.

"DeAngleo, this is Special Agent Angelina Sanchez. She is the one I was telling you about."

This was at least something tangible, something Angelina understood. She turned first to Doc Broderson. "Hello Doc, what are you doing here?"

"I'm a friend of the family. The question is, what are you doing here? Is this official business; who are you investigating now?"

Angelina squarely met his stare. "I am here for Eric."

The big man to her direct front stuck his hand out and introduced himself. "I'm Mike DeAngelo. Doc was right; you are a pretty little thing."

Angelina's hand was dwarfed in the paw of the big man. "I am Angelina Sanchez, very nice to meet you Mr. DeAngelo. What else did Doc say about me?"

It was a dumb question and she knew there was no real reason to open the discussion in this setting, but she felt like challenging Doc's innuendo.

DeAngelo still held her hand in his. "Doc and I think you should be careful on whose name you try to smear. Steve Thunder is dead and buried; let him rest in peace."

She didn't feel threatened by the big man. She sensed he was dangerous and maybe even deadly, but she didn't see anything in his eyes that lead her to believe she was in immediate danger. Eric's return ended the standoff.

"Let's go on in. We're holding up the service."

~~

Eric discreetly covered her hand during the service. She stood next to him during the burial and the whole time her mind bounced between the service and her reports back in Atlanta. She tried to tabulate how many questions had been answered with how many new questions she now wanted to investigate. Every time she started to get close to a final count, another would pop into her mind and she had to start counting again.

Eric must have noticed something was amiss because he asked her on the way to the reception, "Are you feeling OK?"

She turned to Eric and smiled. Letting her attention wander had been very impolite. "I feel fine. It was a wonderful ceremony. I'm glad I came."

~~

The Best Western went all-out for the reception. Krispy Kreme provided the donuts and the Western Sizzling steakhouse provided the sandwiches. Doc and DeAngelo spiked the punch and had to warn the

267

older guests away from the refreshments in the corner. The punch bowl at the other end of the table was safe.

Danni, Hanna, and Mamba, as best they could, adorned the room with pictures and mementos of Aunt Grace. Angelina allowed Eric the freedom to entertain other guests, and she, with Hanna as her guide, toured the room. Hanna explained each picture. One picture seemed out of place in the gentle life of Aunt Grace. It was a picture of eight soldiers in full combat gear, taken in a jungle clearing many years ago.

"Tell me about this picture."

Hanna leaned close to the picture. "I think Aunt Grace kept this picture more for Eric than for herself, but she was always proud of her nephew for serving in the Army."

"Why would she keep it for Eric?"

"Because…her nephew is Eric's father. You didn't know that?"

"No, I didn't. Which one is her nephew?"

Hanna pointed to a young black soldier second from the left, "That soldier there, that man is Eric's father. That guy on the end is Doc Broderson."

"Do you mean our Doc Broderson?" Angelina directed her attention to the two men in the corner of the room sipping punch. "Do you mean that Doc Broderson?"

Hanna smiled and giggled, "Yes, that Doc Broderson. He was a lot younger back then. Looks rather fearsome, doesn't he?"

The entire group looked rather fearsome to Angelina.

"Do you know the names of any of the other men?"

"Sure." Hanna pointed out the other men in the photo, "The one in the middle is Bill Cannon, that man there is Lucas McLaughlin, he's a General now and is in the Pentagon; and that man to the right is Sergeant Major Steve Thunder. He's buried in the cemetery in Thunderbolt near Savannah. I don't know who the others are, but Eric does. Do you want me to get him?"

"No, let him stay with his guests." Angelina stood and looked at the picture. Hanna probably wondered why the photo was such an interest to her. Angelina wanted to sit down and sort out what she had been told. There was so much to organize, but she couldn't do it now; that would have to come later. She turned back to Hanna and asked, "Did I hear correctly that your husband is in the military?"

Hanna answered, but Angelina could tell some of the enthusiasm in her voice was lost. "Yes he is. He's on assignment in Israel."

Angelina immediately knew it was an emotional subject with Hanna. "I'm sorry. I shouldn't have asked the question, it was thoughtless of me."

Hanna smiled a weak smile. "Oh, that's OK. I knew he was a soldier before I married him. I just hope he gets home before the baby is born."

Hanna noticed her mother waving to her, "Please excuse me for a moment; I think my mother wants me to meet some of Eric's family. I'll be right back."

Hanna's departure was fine with Angelina because she needed time to collect her thoughts. Maybe it was her wrinkled brow that attracted the attention of Doc Broderson.

Doc handed her a large plastic cup of punch. "You look like you could use a drink."

Angelina looked up and accepted the offering. Her first sip almost came back through her nose. "Good Lord, Doc, what's in this stuff?"

Doc laughed, "I don't know, DeAngelo doctored it up and Navy guys will drink just about anything. Its' got a kick to it, doesn't it."

Angelina struggled to keep down the second sip. Pointing to the picture she asked, "Hanna said that's you in the picture. Tell me about it."

Broderson looked at the picture. "That was a long time ago in Colombia, South America. That was our first mission as a group. We were trying to stop the drug cartels from shipping cocaine into the United States."

Doc paused and took a long swallow from his cup. "We lost Tex on that mission. We were teamed up with the Colombian army to blow up a big shipment of dope. The Commander of the unit was on the take and left us in the jungle. Tex got shot through the throat while we were trying to escape. I couldn't stop the bleeding and he died on the chopper."

Doc took another long drink. Angelina could see the battle fought many years ago still haunted Doc Broderson. "I'm sorry Doc, I didn't know."

"It happens. It's always a deadly game. There are only three of us still alive, me, Bill Cannon," pointing to the large man standing in the center of the picture, "and Lucas McLaughlin." Doc pointed to the men in the picture as he spoke, "We lost Sparks to a RPG hit in Somalia, and Edwards was killed in Iraq trying to rescue a wounded buddy."

Doc drained his cup. He wasn't nearly as animated as he was five minutes ago. The recollections were powerful and the emotions raw. "Thunder and Jackson were killed after they left the Army. You know about Thunder."

These were obviously good friends, more than good friends, comrades in arms, and Angelina saw the tears begin to well up in Doc's eyes. Doc turned away and mumbled, "I'm getting another drink."

Angelina was numbed by the alcohol and by the revelations. She wished the women would have selected a different photograph to display; any photo other than this one would have been better. The drink was strong, but there were only eight names. Cannon, Broderson and McLaughlin were still alive; Tex, Sparks and Edwards killed in action; that only left two men to account. Angelina knew how Thunder died; and the only other name, and Doc didn't hesitate when he said it, was Jackson, the soldier Hanna pointed out as Eric's father—Jackson not Brown. Angelina wanted to believe there was some other way to explain it, but she knew she was only lying to herself.

As the reception ended and Angelina walked with Eric to the car, she was deeply troubled by what she learned. The truth must have been hard to conceal for when Eric took her by the arm he again asked, "Are you sure you're feeling OK? You don't look real good."

Angelina smiled weakly. "It must be the punch. I think Doc and DeAngleo must have put transmission fluid in it."

Eric gave a little laugh and hugged her shoulders. "Those two should never be let out in public; they're a hazard to regular people."

As they stepped onto the parking lot Angelina heard a commotion to her left. An old lady, 60 maybe more, was pointing a gnarled finger in their direction and shouting to a young man with a portable tape recorder hooked to his belt, "There he is. That's him."

The young man ran up to Eric and stuck the microphone in his face.

"Mr. Brown, I'm Dwayne Carlton, I work for the Cairo Courier and I'm doing a story on your family. Do you have anything to say about the passing of your aunt?"

Eric quickened his pace. "She was a fine woman and lived a Christian life and may she rest in peace. That's all I have to say."

"You're a world-famous TV personality now, why don't you use your real name of TV?"

"No comment. Interview over."

"How does it feel to be the son…"

His question was interrupted by the flash of the burley image of Mike DeAngleo crossing in front of Eric and Angelina. The reporter didn't see him coming and Mike walked right into him knocking him to the pavement. Angelina looked back and DeAngleo had one foot on the throat of the reporter and the other on the recorder grinding it into the pavement.

Angelina heard the low rumble of DeAngelo's voice. "You stinking coward, who are you to butt in here today." Angelina saw the reporter struggle under the increasing weight of DeAngelo's foot.

"Mike! Stop!" It was Doc Broderson who shouted the command. "Let him up."

DeAngelo took his time removing his foot. As the reporter struggled with breathing, Eric took Angelina by the elbow and hurried her along. The old woman was fast approaching and started screaming.

"Murderer! Son of a murderer! I hope you die! Murderer! Son of a murder! I hope you die." The screams were almost insane.

Eric didn't stop or turn, but only continued his way to the car. "Get in. Let's go."

It was an hour before Angelina got the courage to ask, "Who was that?"

Eric took one glance in her direction and then concentrated on the road.

"That was my grandmother."

271

Chapter 36

The drive from Cairo to Atlanta was in complete silence. Eric was stoic and concentrated on the road. Angelina had nothing to do but fidget in her seat. She didn't know if it was the smart thing to do, but she finally mustered the courage to ask, "Do you want to talk about it?"

She didn't know what Eric was thinking; his expression never changed, but she hoped he had not completely shut himself off from her. He pulled into a rest area, got out of the car, and started walking the trails. Angelina waited for a moment to see if he would return and when he didn't, she ran after him.

When she caught him she said nothing, but only wrapped her arms around one of his and walked with him. Maybe it was the warmth of her touch that helped him decide, but whatever it was he knew this woman deserved to know the truth.

"I was six years old when it happened. My dad was with the Rangers in Somalia. We had a little house in Cairo, I didn't show it to you because there are only terrible memories there. It was just my mother and me.

"She was young and probably lonely and it must have been a hard life for her; a young mother trying to raise a son alone. She started drinking and then got into drugs. I really can't remember ever having a home-cooked meal, unless Aunt Grace came over to fix one. I would go to school and steal the lunches of the other kids. I can remember the terrible arguments my mother and Aunt Grace would have, and my mother would leave and Aunt Grace would sleep on the couch. Sometimes my mother would come home and sometimes she wouldn't.

"We had enough money, my father sent most of his paycheck home, until my mother got a boyfriend, and then the drugs got real bad and he took our money and gambled it away. I found out later that Aunt Grace called the sheriff and a deputy came out to the house and arrested the man. But, then my mother started sleeping with the deputy.

"The deputy had a mean streak in him. The other guy took our money, but the deputy would beat me and my mother, and lock me in the closet while they had sex. Most nights they never unlocked the door and

I would sleep there. At least he wasn't hitting me, but I hate dark and confined spaces to this day.

"Aunt Grace would come over and do what she could for me, but the sheriff covered for his deputy. Aunt Grace told me they were dirty cops, I didn't know what that meant back then, but she was trying to get the state to come down to investigate. I don't know if they ever did.

"I didn't know what else to do so I wrote my father a letter, telling him as best I could about what was going on in our house. When I think back, it's a miracle my father ever got the letter. I addressed it to Sergeant John Jackson, US Army in Africa. It was a long time from when I wrote the letter to the night my father came home.

"I was locked in the closet and only heard the front door break. I heard some men yelling at each other, a gunshot, and my mother scream, and then I heard another shot. I didn't hear anything for a long time and then I heard the key in the lock start to move. I was scared to death that it was the deputy, but it was my father. He was still in his uniform and I could see splashes of blood on his shirt.

"He picked me up and we sat on the sofa until morning. He hugged me almost all night, and he would cry and then tell me everything was going to be OK. The police surrounded our house in the morning. I think my father was going to give himself up, but a young police officer broke through the door and my father shot him. Maybe the police officer scared him and my father reacted so fast I almost couldn't see him move, but he killed the officer with a single shot.

"The police arrested my father, he went to trial; I wasn't allowed to attend any of the hearings. They sentenced him to life without parole. I never saw him again. The state was going to send me to an orphanage, but Aunt Grace said she would care for me. We had no money and everyone in town never let us put what my father did behind us.

"Aunt Grace would visit my father, but never let me go, not that I cared to go. Life was bad when my mother was on drugs, but at least when she wasn't stoned, she could be a loving mother. In my mind, my father was the cause of all the bad things that happened in my life.

"Aunt Grace and I were on a cruise when my father was killed in prison. We could barely afford to eat, I never figured out how we could afford a cruise. I wasn't even in the country when my father was buried at the state penitentiary. That's why I never mentioned him.

"A week after we got back from the cruise, Mrs. Walton came to our house; I'd never seen her before. She convinced Aunt Grace to move to Daufuskie Island and live on their estate. All Aunt Grace ever told me was that our life would be better, and it was. I would have never returned to Cairo, but Aunt Grace wanted to be buried next to her husband."

Angelina tried to hide the tears that streaked her face. She didn't know what to say, so she said nothing. Eric took a deep breath and looked up into the gathering dusk, "We better get going. Let's go back to the car."

A few miles south of Macon, Angelina said, "Eric, let's stop here for the night."

"Why? Atlanta is only one hundred miles up the road. We will be there in about two hours."

Angelina reached for his hand on the steering wheel. "Let's stop here for the night. I don't want to get back to Atlanta tonight. Tomorrow will be soon enough."

When Eric pulled into the motel, a considerable upgrade from the Best Western in Cairo, Angelina said to him before he left the car, "Eric, only one room tonight, please."

~~

Angelina woke with her back snuggled deep into the body of Eric, his hand gently resting on her bare legs under the covers. Their lovemaking had, at times, been intense and other times gentle and it had lasted well into the night. But, the sun was filtering through the window and she was due back at work, so the trip to Cairo must end. She felt Eric stir at her back and she took his hand and moved it to her breast.

"Hey Tarzan, Jane has to get to work, it's time to go." It was an inside personal joke from their lovemaking last night.

Eric gently nudged her; she could actually hear the smile on his lips, "Are you sure?"

Angelina mentally calculated the remaining time to her office. There wasn't enough time to play and still get to work on time. "I'm sure. You're going to have to get our stuff from the car." They didn't take the time last night to bring in their luggage.

"Damn, you're right. You wait here." Eric gave her breast a gentle squeeze and kissed her on the back of the neck.

Angelina stretched to her full length as Eric visited the bathroom. When he put on his pants and before he threw on his shirt

Angelina noticed the pink scar of the knife wound he received on the river. "Eric, did I ever thank you for what you did for me on the river?"

Eric turned back to her and snaked his hand under the covers and tried to tickle her. "I thought that's what last night was all about."

Angelina dodged the creeping hand and managed to throw a pillow in Eric's direction. "You pig!"

Eric captured control of her hands and leaned forward and only a couple of inches from her lips, "Angelina, you have captured my heart. I have fallen in love with you." He kissed her deeply but tenderly. When he released her hands, she circled his neck and drew him close to her and they embraced. As he slid under the covers he asked, "I thought you had to get back to work?"

Angelina laughed, "I do. Quit tempting me, now go get the luggage."

As Eric made his way to the car Angelina rose and showered. Eric was laying out the luggage on the rumpled covers when Angelina left the bathroom with a towel neatly wrapped around her body. "You make a towel look real good."

As Eric showered, Angelina dressed and sat at the mirror to start her makeup. When Eric left the shower she watched him in the mirror as he dressed. The long muscles leading from his legs to his buttocks reminded her of a cheetah, they moved in a graceful and smooth rippling effect, but she knew the power they possessed.

"Eric, I'm glad you told me about your father and mother."

Eric stopped dressing and turned to her, "I'm glad you know. I felt terrible not telling you from the start, but I was afraid you would leave me." It was exactly why Angelina never mentioned her profession to him. Now was the time for her confession.

As she brushed her hair she talked. "Eric, you know I am an investigator with the Justice Department."

"I sure do and I'm damn proud of it."

"I was sent to Atlanta to investigate old rape cases." It was easier to say than her new objective of investigating the drugs and those killings.

"One of the cases I am investigating is the rape of Hanna Walton."

Eric sat on the bed and pulled on his socks and shoes as he spoke. There was no reason to hide his limited knowledge of the event.

"I don't know much about it. It happened two or three years before I met the Waltons. Nobody ever talked about it, but over the years Aunt Grace and Mamba told me what happened. We all know it happened, but everybody is trying to put that part of their lives in the past. I would see Hanna crying for no reason, and I always figured that was why. I would sit with her and hold her hand until she stopped, but we never talked about it. I don't think they ever caught the guys that did it."

Angelina continued to run the brush through her hair. "Eric, did Aunt Grace explain why you were moving to Daufuskie?"

"Mrs. Walton came to our house and told us we would be safer on Daufuskie. I never asked why. My father made a lot of enemies when he killed those police officers. Cairo is a small town and hatred can run deep. I didn't care why we were leaving, I was just glad to get out of that town. I haven't looked back. I haven't regretted one day since I left. Mr. Helton is like a father to me, and Mrs. Walton, Hanna, and Mamba, they are family to me too."

Angelina turned in her seat and faced Eric. "Eric, if I told you that the man your father killed in prison was one of the men who raped Hanna, what would you think?"

The comment stunned Eric. He sat at the foot of the bed and let his hands dangle between his knees. He leaned forward and covered his face with his hands. After a moment he straightened and looked directly at Angelina. "Then I think he did a good thing." He paused a moment before continuing. "I wonder if Mrs. Walton knows, or if Hanna knows, or if Aunt Grace knew? I wonder if that is why the Waltons invited us to live with them at Daufuskie."

Angelina moved to and sat on the bed with Eric. "You know Danni Walton's husband was killed, and a man was killed in the Walton residence in Atlanta shortly before they asked you to come and live with them."

Eric slowly glanced over to Angelina, "I didn't know anything about that when we moved to Daufuskie. I sort of pieced it together over the years. I didn't think much of it at the time, that sort of stuff happens all the time from where I grew up."

Angelina wondered how far she could take this line of questioning before Eric would resist. "You were living on Daufuskie when those men broke into Mr. Helton's house. Tell me what happened there."

"It was the night Hanna's husband, Major Madison—he was a Captain then—was supposed to visit. We were expecting him when the knock came to the front door. But it was four men—all with guns—two at the front door and two through the back; they were on us before we could do anything. All night they kept saying that their boss was coming to get his money. I don't think anybody knew what they were talking about. Mr. Helton said he would pay whatever they wanted, just to tell him how much, but they had to wait for their boss.

"About 10 p.m., Major Madison knocked at the front door. The men untied Mamba to answer the knock, and I heard her try to get James to go away, but he wouldn't leave. When he came inside the men put a gun to his head, but—cool as a cucumber—he said to them, 'The man you are waiting for isn't coming. If you leave now, nothing will happen to you.'

"The men didn't believe him and tried to call their boss on their cell phones, but got no answer. The next thing I knew, the two of the men at the back of the house were laying on the floor, somebody shot them through the back windows, and the man with the gun to James head was on the floor with James' knee on his throat.

"James shot the fourth man in the leg when he ran back to find out what happened."

Angelina listened to every word Eric spoke. The description of the night ended too abruptly. "Well, what happened?"

"The men were dressed in black. They came in the back and one of them stopped the bleeding of the two wounded men, and then left. Buford Long called the medics and police, and they came and took the men away. They haven't had any trouble since that night."

The story sounded eerily similar to the description Gerald 'Frenchy' Guidry's gave her of the invasion of the men at the Tyrell Biggs' mansion.

"Did you know two men, drug dealers, were killed that same night on the Savannah River?"

Eric turned to Angelina and looked directly into her eyes, "No, I didn't know."

"Do you have any idea who the men in black were, or who could have killed the men on the river?"

Angelina felt Eric stiffen. He stood and buttoned his shirt. Angelina knew she had reached her limit when Eric's answer was a simple, but final, "No."

~~

Karen and Rachael considered Wednesday the safe day. They knew meetings consumed Ken's mornings and he would usually work through lunch. He would then catch up on paperwork until about 3 p.m. and then slip out to the deli and down a sandwich before returning to work.

It really didn't matter if Ken caught them together, after all, they were sisters, and more than likely he would avoid them like the plague, but these Wednesday meetings served for more than shopping and a delicate lunch—the meetings also served to discuss other things—more private things.

They always reserved the corner table on the second story balcony adjacent to Oglethorpe Square, one of the 21 historic squares in the Savannah Historic District. From the balcony they were above the bother of traffic and the gawking eyes of the tourists, and could look down upon those less fortunate than they. The elegant ladies always tipped well and the restaurant lavished them with fawning service. They formed a beautiful portrait of Southern living with their expensive dresses, jewelry, hats, and the soft tone of their conversations carried just a hint of snobbery that some tourists found enchanting.

Today their conversation was anything but enchanting as Karen explained her concerns to Rachael. "Something is different in Ken."

"What do you mean...different...how?"

"He must have a lot more money than I thought. He hasn't even blinked when he wrote the last four or five checks. He's got something working. I don't know what, but something."

Rachael slowly sipped her coffee before commenting. "Then I suppose we should find out what. Do you have any ideas?"

"Of course I do." With that comment Karen turned to her sister and slowly and gently traced her fingernails along the neckline of her dress and down across her breast. It wasn't simply the touch that aroused her and engorged the nipple, now pushing hard against the fabric; it was also the challenge that lay ahead. "I'm going to make up with Ken."

Karen's audacity amazed Rachael. "Do you think that will work?"

Karen's grin turned into a sneer of contempt before she answered. "It always has."

~~

Ken did indeed have something working; and it was working well.

The most difficult component of investing in the cartel was the liquidation of investments in the American stock markets. After all, you can't just cash in millions of dollars without raising suspicion. Ken kicked himself for not being more aggressive in generating cash. The process of transferring funds to the cartel banks in the islands was slow and tedious, but he kept chipping away. Now he had nearly $6,000,000 at his disposal in off-shore accounts.

And he had put that money to good use. He earned $200,000 on a new resort in Rio. He earned $500,000 on a shipping deal in Liberia. He earned almost a million in black market computer chips. Half his profits went to paying off his bank loans at Coastal, and the remainder he left in the Barclay bank in the Cayman Islands. Millions of dollars earning interest tax free.

This was the world of big finance, and Ken knew he belonged.

Only a few more investments and he would be set, and Jerry Evans was almost giddy with excitement with news of the next deal.

"Ken, it's the mother lode…deep water drilling rights off the coast of Libya! This is going to be big! Get ready to pull out all stops." Jerry didn't have a firm date or location on the bid, but simply wanted to alert Ken of the opportunity.

Ken's day ended with two strange phone calls. The first was from Ed Helton.

"Ken, have you talked with Reverend White about purchasing my Daufuskie stock?"

Ken had put out a gentle feeler, but the good Reverend didn't jump at the offer. "Yes sir, I did. He didn't seem real excited about the offer."

Ken could feel a certain amount of frustration from Helton. "Look, tell him I'll double the buy-back offer. He can make a 20% return in a month. Hell, his charity can buy the stock and make a bundle."

Ken knew exactly why Ed Helton was in a rush to generate some cash. He would have bet his last dollar that Ed Helton was stockpiling cash to bid on the Libyan oil rights. Ken promised he would put the offer to Reverend White.

Ed Helton's phone call was interesting, but he was totally surprised when the screen on his cell phone showed a name that had been absent for a long time; the call was from Karen. He momentarily debated simply ignoring the call—after all Karen had proven to be nothing but bad news. But his curiosity got the better of him. "Hello."

"Ken, please don't hang up. I've made a terrible mistake with you. I've destroyed something that was very special to me. I don't know what came over me. I want to see you, and try and get things between us straightened out."

She wants a meeting…fancy that. The last time he and Karen met the only thing he had to show for it was an incriminating sex video and $40,000 a month in blackmail payments. "What's the matter Karen did your computer crash and you lose the file of the video; do you need to make another?"

Ken heard the subtle change in Karen's tone from one begging for forgiveness to a more sultry and seductive one, "Only if you want to make one. Please Ken, we've got to talk."

Ken knew it was a dumb idea, but she seemed somewhat vulnerable. If what she said was true, then maybe he could work his way out of the monthly extortion payments. "I'll call you when I leave work."

The meeting place Ken selected was one of their favorite seafood restaurants. Before the economic crash Johnny Ray's Shrimp House was a thriving business located on the access road to the county boat ramp and near the shrimper's dock. Now that the restaurant closed, the only business that wasn't totally covered with weeds was a small bait shack that opened only on the weekends. Not only was it secluded, but once you were in the parking lot you had unobstructed view of every car that came across the bridge.

Karen pulled next to Ken's car, driver's window to driver's window. Ken took his time to lower his window.

"Ken, can we talk in your car? This seems so impersonal."

Ken waved her to his vehicle and when she sat in the passenger seat it was as if she was cowering in shame. Ken tried not to stare, but when Karen bent forward in the seat he could almost see her entire breast. She kept her head lowered, not making eye contact with Ken.

280

"I was afraid I couldn't make it on my own. If I could take it back, I would. I hope you can forgive me."

This was just like a woman. So tough when they think they have the upper hand, but always they come cowering back during the tough times.

"Why should I? I trusted you. I thought we had something special between us, and you used our relationship to threaten me. I don't know if I can ever trust you again."

Karen turned to Ken. There were no tears, but Ken could see the distress in her face.

"Ken I need you. You make me feel like a woman. I don't know what I'll do if you don't take me back. You don't have to tell me you love me, just don't leave me."

"What about the money?"

Karen again lowered her head. "It's gone."

"You spent it all?" Ken knew this woman could go through money like crap through a goose.

"I spent most of it. I'll do anything to make it up to you."

Ken knew what she meant. So he had her; first in the car and then in the parking lot between the cars. And when he finished with her and sent her on her way he felt flushed with power. This is the way it would be.

Chapter 37

The pictures of an American officer with Israeli forces attacking into the Gaza Strip caused violent uproar in the Arab states. The uproar in the Arab states resounded loudly in the halls of the United Nations. The speeches in the United Nations reached the grounds of the White House in Washington, D.C. The displeasure of the Administration to the criticisms of world leaders rolled down hill to the Pentagon. The Secretary of Defense's and the Chairman of the Joint Chief's instructions to General McLaughlin were clear. "Get Madison the hell out of the Gaza Strip!"

Colonel Wetzel wasn't treated much better by the Israeli Ministry of Defense for allowing Madison to accompany the lead brigade.

"Major Madison, it would be better if you weren't seen around the headquarters until after the operation. I'm sending you to the Golan Heights and the Lebanon border. You will have a driver and an escort officer to be your guides. I'll see you when you get back."

"The Golan Heights? That's at the other end of the country!"

"That's the idea, Major Madison. You should be safe up there."

Major Madison's inspection of the Lebanon border started at the Mediterranean Sea. By the third day they had made their way to the Golan Heights, the disputed area at the northeast corner of Israel.

The driver was an experienced combat veteran who, at 18 saw his first combat in the 1982 Israeli invasion of Lebanon, and at 42 saw what he hoped was his last combat in the 2006 Invasion of Lebanon. The 1982 invasion drove the Palestine Liberation Organization from the northern border, and the 2006 invasion drove Hezbollah from the same positions. Neither operation brought peace or security to either side of the border.

It happened on the evening of the third day, deep in the Golan Heights, that area still contested by Israel, Lebanon, and Syria. The blast came from the right side of the vehicle. Madison always wondered how fast the brain would process your life before you died. The image of his wife and unborn child flashed through his thoughts the moment of the explosion, replaced by the immediate disintegration of the escort officer's head. The driver was spared when the escort officer's body absorbed most of the blast and James was spared by the luggage piled in the back seat next to him.

The vehicle was blown off the road and tumbled down the embankment into a dried wash. Bleeding through the nose, ears and mouth, Major Madison tried to maintain consciousness during the bone jarring fall to the valley floor. He was alive, and if he was still alive it meant he still had a chance to get back to his family. His delirious thoughts of his wife and child were interrupted by the sounds of machine gun fire, strange men speaking strange languages, and the rough hands of someone pulling him from the now burning wreckage. The smell of burning diesel was the last thing he remembered before the descending blow of a rifle butt crashed into his skull.

~~

The beach where James lay was deserted, or nearly so. Perhaps in the distance, it was difficult to see through the haze that always lingers where the sea and land meet, were children at play. Though the sand plugged his ears, James thought he could hear their young voices when the breeze shifted just right.

There must have been a great storm, James thought, to have washed him ashore like so much driftwood, and to have buried him in the sand just above waves. Only the left side of his face and left foot were exposed; the remainder of his body buried deep within the sand. Only the largest waves reached his face, but each time the water washed over him sand would cover his face making it even more difficult to breathe. Some obnoxious crab or maybe a seagull picked at his exposed left foot, he couldn't turn his head to see, and it was beginning to irritate him. James tried to call out but was unable to purge the sand filling his mouth.

Each wave that passed over him carried more sand and soon he would be completely covered. He wondered who would discover his body; he hoped it would not be a child. Major James Madison came to the realization that he was dying. He was helpless to clear the sand filling his nose and nothing would stop the rising tide. His thoughts turned to his wife and child. Hanna was young, strong and beautiful and she would mourn his passing, but she could find another. His true regret was that he would never hold his child.

"You will hold your wife and child James Madison."

Who said that? James held what breath he had as the next wave washed over him. There, on the beach, walking toward him a tall slender man in white linen. James could not see his face. The sun seemed to follow behind him, and James could not look into the bright light. As the wave receded James felt the sand being washed from his face. When the wave retreated back to the sea the man in white linen sat in the sand and placed James' head on his thigh.

As the man gently brushed the sand from his face James felt no fear and knew this man was his salvation. He knew he shouldn't be so bold as to speak, but he did. "Will you take me?"

The man in linen spoke, his voice pleasing to James' ear, "No, James Madison, it is not your time. It is here where you can serve me best. You have many battles yet to fight."

James was dejected beyond belief. Here was his salvation yet he was being rejected. "But you must take me for I cannot breathe and I am dying. Please do not leave me here as food for the vultures and rats."

The man placed one hand on James' face and the other on his heart. As if from above, James saw the water and sand pour from his mouth and nose; the flow of water was substantial. James knew he had been saved and even the tugging at his foot was nothing more than a minor bother.

"Major Madison, wake up!"

Who spoke those words? The man in white linen was gone and there was no one else on the beach. With the sand removed from his lungs and nose James felt the need to sleep and he closed his eyes.

"Major Madison, wake up!"

As James came back from the brink, he felt the throbbing in his head and it took a moment to realize he was not on the beach. He looked at the man kicking him in the foot. The man was sitting next to a wall and James could see that his clothes were in tatters and charred as if burned.

"Who are you?"

"I'm Ari Sharone, I was your driver. You don't remember?"

James tried to sit up, but when he did a bolt of pain shot up his back. He vaguely remembered something about a driver. "What happened?"

"We ran into an ambush. I think we ran over a mine. I'm not sure."

James remembered another figure. "Wasn't there another man with us? Where is he?"

"He didn't make it."

James looked up from his position on the floor at Ari. Ari's body was blistered and bloody. "You don't look so good."

Ari seemed to shrug off his injuries, "I'll be fine. It looks worse than it is." After a moment he added, "I thought you were dying. You were drowning on your own blood. I couldn't get over to help you, but whatever was blocking your air must have worked lose."

That would explain his dream. It was then that James noticed the chains that bound Ari's arms behind him. The manacles ran from Ari's arms through a steel ring embedded into the wall and then to a metal band around his neck. James lowered his chin and felt the same collar around his neck. When he tried to pull his arms apart to see if he was handcuffed another burning pain shot up his arm. A groan escaped from his lips.

Ari explained, "Your right arm is broken. I can see the bone every time you move."

That would explain the pain. The dim light cast by the single light bulb was barely enough to reach the corners of the small room. It provided only enough illumination to see that they were in a room maybe 10'or 12' square with a wooden stairs at the far end. James could turn his head to see the ceiling was concrete and his immediate conclusion was that this room was probably used as a bomb shelter. The floor may be concrete, it was certainly hard enough, but it was now covered with layers of dust that had long ago packed into a hardened dirt floor. When he counted the steel rings protruding from the walls and noticed the darkened stains that could not be mistaken for anything but dried blood, his conclusion that the room was a bomb shelter was a little premature— a more accurate description was a dungeon. James tried to focus on Ari. It might have sounded a little too nonchalant, but it is what came to mind. "Not exactly the Ritz is it."

Ari chuckled, "No Sir, it is not the Ritz."

James tried to blink to clear his vision. "I can't seem to see anything out of my right eye."

Ari didn't see the need to tell James he no longer had a right eye, or a right ear for that matter, or that most of the skin and hair on the right side of his skull were gone, leaving the bone of the skull to slowly ooze blood. "You took most of the blast on your right side. Your face is pretty messed up. It must just be swollen shut."

James was beginning to piece together the attack, "What happened to the colonel that was with us?"

"He was killed in the explosion...he may have been the lucky one."

It was a strange thing to say about a dead soldier. "What time do you think it is?"

"I don't know exactly, but they couldn't have taken us too far. It was dusk when they hit us, and since none of these minor wounds have crusted over, I think maybe three or four in the morning, maybe even sunrise. I don't really know, but that would be my guess."

Other than the throbbing in his head and the shooting pains up his arm, the thing James longed for the most was a long drink of water. "I don't suppose there is any water?"

Ari tried to make light of their situation. "None that I can see, I'm sure they will bring some with our breakfast."

That only made the need for water more intense. James forced himself to think of other things. "Do you think the Israeli Army will try to find us?"

Ari leaned his head back against the wall and let his head rest on the steel ring. "If they know where we are they might. In the old days they would have already launched an attack, if for nothing more than recovering our bodies, but my government pays too much attention to world opinion and has become a negotiator like yours. My only hope is they are embarrassed about losing an American. They may come for you, but I doubt it. They are already fighting on the Gaza, and will not want to give the Syrians an excuse to launch an attack from the north."

James knew everything he said was true. The grim reality of their situation became clear. Why would the man in white linen tell him that he had many battles yet to fight, why would he give him hope when the circumstances leading to his probable death were so apparent? It was a cruel twist and James now understood why Ari said the colonel was probably the lucky one. He would no longer know pain and suffering.

James heard the creaking of metal hinges from above, and then the creaking of the stairs. In spite of the pain he turned his head to see the feet of their captors coming down the stairs. James closed his eye and prayed for strength.

Two men dressed in the olive tan of the soldiers of the Hezbollah fighters grabbed James under his arms and pulled him to a sitting position. The pain from his arm was immediate and intense and it forced a guttural cry from James. Once they had him in a sitting position, they placed a folded newspaper on his chest.

"American, look up. We want to take a picture to send to your wife."

In a panic James tried to move his butt to see if his wallet was still in his back pocket. To his horror, he felt nothing but the hard floor of his cell.

They took a dozen pictures of him and did the same with Ari, and then they left. It was a bad sign that their captors did not attempt to conceal their faces. If they had any plans to release them, they would not want their identities known. It was obvious to James they had no intention of releasing them. They would be kept alive only so long as they proved useful, and then they would be executed. James wondered how long that would be.

Chapter 38

Sitting at her desk, Angelina absently sketched a reasonable facsimile of the photograph of the eight soldiers onto a yellow legal pad. The faces, of course, were blank, but she didn't need the faces to assign names to the penciled images. Why was she suddenly so conflicted with what she had learned? There should be no moral dilemmas between her duty and her emotions, but there were. Was her growing affection for Eric clouding her sense of right and wrong?

She had to admit, she wasn't so enthusiastic about her conspiracy theories when they seemed to engulf so many good people; people that were near and dear to Eric. It would be so easy to close the files and simply move on with life, but would that compromise be the first in a spiral of ever increasing judgments where she would enforce justice according to her personal values, rather than those dictated by society? Crossing the line was still crossing the line, even if crossing the line seemed the right thing to do.

Her conspiracy theories, she almost scoffed at her own thoughts – murder and drugs – they seemed so far-fetched and unbelievable when you stood in the same room with the people you suspected. Were the crimes they committed so long ago still worth the effort to bring to prosecution? She found some emotional relief when she quickly reminded herself that she had yet to actually prove crimes had been committed; and suddenly found it hard to even accurately describe the crimes she suspected.

Conspiracy to murder, that was it. That was the first issue she must address. She now knew that Eric's father, Sergeant John Brown Jackson, killed Hanna's rapist in prison, but even that wasn't crystal clear. The death of Bomani Thomas could be considered self defense, the prison yard video clearly showed Jackson was the victim of the attack. Then there remained the deaths of the other three rapists; in her mind they were more closely associated with the drug conspiracy than the rape. In fact, if she stepped back from her emotions, all the killings seemed linked to the drugs, even the death of Bomani Thomas, rather than the rape.

It was depressing, almost unbelievable in some respects, to think that the people she met in Cairo could be involved in one of the largest shipments of heroin in the history of Georgia. When you considered the entire scope of the associated violence, the home invasions in Atlanta and Daufuskie, the deaths of so many known as part of Tyrell Biggs drug operations, and the death of Steve Thunder and Peter Walton, all could be clearly linked to the drugs. What two significant events linked Eric's family and friends to the drugs?

First, who had the foresight to send Aunt Grace and young Eric on the all-expense cruise—a luxury they could never afford—during the exact time the drug deal occurred? Second, what in the world would precipitate Danni Walton's visit to Eric's home and convince Aunt Grace to leave her home—a home she would return to only in death—and move to Daufuskie; a move that was sudden and suspiciously close in time to the drug deal? Aunt Grace would know, but she was dead. Steve Thunder might know, but he was also dead. The only other person who would know was Mrs. Danni Walton.

Motive wasn't an element of the law that needed to be established to prove a conspiracy, but what in the world would be the motive of people like Danni Walton or even Doc Broderson, Steve Thunder and John Brown Jackson, to get involved with heroin. Even with the death of her husband, Danni Walton was still set for life through the wealth of her father. Jackson certainly had nothing to gain; he was in prison on life without parole; he would never enjoy the fruits of the deal. Steve Thunder and Doc Broderson served with distinction after the drug money disappeared and gave no indication of an extravagant lifestyle. Or, was it Peter Walton who was involved in the drugs, and was his death, and the home invasions, and even the kidnapping of Hanna from their home in Atlanta, nothing more than the reckless actions of a drug kingpin trying to get his money back? It had happened many times before.

Why had no report ever been made of the kidnapping of Hanna Walton, and who rescued her? Angelina reviewed the report filed by Buford Long on the home invasion in Atlanta. Not a whisper of the kidnapping. Why would something as flagrant as the kidnapping of a young woman not be filed with the police department? Was it to keep the police out of any investigation simply to cover their involvement in the drugs?

If she assumed the Walton's, Thunder, and Broderson were involved; how would their plan be conveyed to Jackson, and why would they even need to go through Jackson? Why not go directly to Tyrell

Biggs. Surely, if they were sophisticated enough to plan the import and sale of the heroin they were capable of finding a way to directly approach Tyrell Biggs. Or, did they include Jackson simply to ensure they included Bomani Thomas in the deal?

There was no valid reason to include either of the men in prison unless – unless – they used Thomas to smoke out the other members of the gang that raped Hanna, and then brutally kill them under the obscuring cover of the drug deal. Who would know the answer? Doc Broderson might know, but Broderson was already wary of her investigation and she would get nothing from him. Peter Walton, Steve Thunder, John Brown Jackson, Bomani Thomas or Aunt Grace might know, but again, they were all dead. But Aunt Grace had done something none of the others had; Aunt Grace left a written record of her visits to her nephew. Maybe Angelina had missed something.

She pulled from the prison boxes the last four letters from Aunt Grace to Jackson, and the last article she sent him, the one with Eric pictured at the military museum; and then scanned them into her computer. It took her a while, but after a few phone calls to Washington, she got the number of the man she wanted. She and Jose Morales, Joe for short, were the only Mexican-Americans in the basic FBI training class and they had become close. Angelina knew Joe had a crush on her, but felt nothing more than friendship towards him, but she needed his expertise now. Joe was a code buster, one of the best, and now worked for the CIA deciphering coded messages from all over the world.

"Joe, I was wondering if you could take a look at a few things for me—off the record?"

"Not a chance in hell. We're really busy right now. I'm sorry."

"It's not very much; only a few letters and one article. It shouldn't take you but a few minutes."

"Angelina, every computer up here is running full blast on a special project. I can't tell you when there will be any time available."

"I don't mean to be a pest, but could you do it at home? I'll owe you."

"If I could get home, I'd do it, but I haven't been home in four days. I'm sleeping on a cot in the office." Joe must have felt her disappointment because he added, "Look, send them up. If I get a chance, I'll run them through our training programs. There's a chance they can pick something up, but I can't promise anything."

~~

290

If she expected her investigation to move forward then there was no avoiding the decision. She would have to visit Daufuskie and interview Danni Walton. Angelina wondered if she should tell Eric.

The last few hours of their trip was somewhat strained. Eric didn't say anything, but Angelina felt the tension. She had gone too far with her questions. She debated calling Eric's home phone knowing he was at CNN preparing for the evening newscast and simply leaving a message, but that would be a cowardly path.

Eric saw Angelina's name on his cell phone and for a moment considered hitting the silence button, but the sting of her questions and unspoken accusations had softened since he dropped her at the office. She had been so persistent with her questions. Each one peeled away a layer of things he had long suspected, but never felt the need to investigate. His friends were all good men and that is what he chose to believe. Good had triumphed over evil and that is the way the world should be. He didn't really know what happened on the river, at the house, in Atlanta, those many years ago; he simply accepted the justice of the outcomes. He wondered why Angelina couldn't accept the past for what it was; history. He hoped maybe she would, so he answered her call.

"Hello."

"Eric, this is Angelina." She paused before continuing, unsure of how to proceed. "I hope you understand why I asked those questions during our trip. It's my job…I hope you can understand."

Eric understood all right; he just didn't like it. "Angelina, maybe I was a little too sensitive. It bothers me that you suspect men that I hold in the highest esteem. But, I understand it is your job. I'm sorry I acted the way I did. I'm sure you will find the truth, and then we can put this entire thing behind us."

It was a reasonable reply, but she did feel some tension from Eric. "Eric, I called to tell you I am going to Daufuskie to talk with Mrs. Walton. I was wondering if you would like to go with me."

Why would Angelina want him to go to Daufuskie, unless it would make her more comfortable when she questioned his friends? It was a moot point. "I can't take off; if you are still there on the weekend, I will come down, but I can't leave until after the Friday news."

It was Wednesday, if Angelina left soon she could be in Savannah this evening and be on the island Thursday morning. She didn't expect the interview with Mrs. Walton to take more than a few hours. She could catch one of the evening ferries back to Savannah and drive back to Atlanta that night. "I don't think I will be there that long. I'll see you when I get back."

"Okay, but the island has a way of slowing things down. If you are still on Daufuskie, I will see you Saturday morning. Are you leaving today?"

"Yes."

"Then I want you to stay in Thunderbolt. It is a small town just on the other side of Savannah. I will call and make reservations for you at the Oglethorpe Inn, it's a bed and breakfast on the water right next to Mike DeAngelo's marina. Mike will take you to the island tomorrow morning at 8 a.m. I will call Mrs. Walton and tell her you are coming. Does all that sound good to you?"

"That sounds fine, thanks."

"Angelina, next to the Inn is the Thunderbolt Cemetery. Steve Thunder is buried there. Would you mind putting some fresh flowers on his grave for me?"

~~

Angelina's drive out of Atlanta took longer than expected. One accident on the interstate could paralyze the entire city—that, and it was difficult to find a gas station with any gas. Even with her government credit card she was allowed to pump only 10 gallons before the attendant shut off the pump. The attendant didn't care if it was government business, if she wanted more then she would have to get back to the end of the line, or find a government installation to fill up. The irate customers waiting for their turn at the pump hurried her along. If she couldn't get some outside of Atlanta, she would drive to the Robins Air Force base south of Macon and fill up.

The drive from Macon to Savannah along Interstate 16 can be very monotonous. It can be a time of reflection, but Angelina chose to let her mind go almost blank and simply enjoyed the serenity of the drive. She elected to drive through, rather than around, Savannah and the narrow streets and famous squares each begged her to stop and read the plaques. The only stop she made was a florist shop.

The Oglethorpe Inn promised her the best in Southern cuisine at the 7 p.m. serving. The proprietor directed her to the local cemetery. She found Steve Thunder's marker overlooking the river. It was a simple headstone with only his name inscribed in the marble. Set into

292

the earth at the foot of the headstone was a bronzed plaque. Angelina bent low to read the inscription.

> In Memory of Sergeant Major Steve Thunder
>
> Sergeant Major Steve Thunder served the United States of America with distinction and valor in combat operations on five continents. He was the most courageous of men and it was our honor to serve at his side. He was a great patriot.

Angelina bent even lower to read the small names listed on the plague; three names now very familiar to her.

Lucas McLaughlin - Bill Cannon – John Broderson

Her dinner at the Inn was everything they had promised and later that night, from her balcony overlooking the Wilmington River and salt marshes leading to the Atlantic Ocean, she wished Eric was at her side. Her thoughts were interrupted by a soft knock on the door to her room, and at the door was the Inn's hostess.

"Miss Sanchez, I apologize for disturbing you at this late hour. A most dreadful looking man just delivered this and said you would need it for tomorrow."

"A big man—maybe a little over 6'—with big arms, deep chest and beard?"

"Why yes, do you know him?"

It had to be DeAngelo. "I think so. Thank you very much."

Angelina opened the neatly wrapped package, taped to the outside of the box a note, it was from Danni Walton.

> *Dear Miss Sanchez, Welcome to my home and Daufuskie Island. Eric informed me you wish to discuss the events involving my daughter. I must confess it is something I have tried to put in our past, but will help you in any way I can. As you may know, my daughter is living with me while her husband is serving overseas. Perhaps we could discuss the subject matter during a ride around the island. Eric guessed you were a size six. Danni Walton*

Inside the box was a complete riding outfit, nothing too extravagant simply functional.

At 7:45 a.m., she walked to the office of the Saltwater Creek Marina and was met at the door by Mike DeAngelo. He inspected her from head to boots and nodded his approval. "Good morning Agent Sanchez, you look good in that get-up. Eric said you needed a lift to Daufuskie. Are you ready to go?"

DeAngelo didn't look quite as dangerous on this sunny morning as he did with the reporter in Cairo, Georgia. "Yes, I am. Thank you for the ride. How long is the trip?"

"We can take the scenic route and it's about 30 minutes, or we can take the short cut, and it is about 30 minutes. It's your choice."

Angelina smiled at the options and deferred to DeAngelo's experience. From Thunderbolt they traveled north on the Wilmington River and then crossed the Savannah River to Field's Cut. The tall marsh grasses blocked from view all but the tallest buildings, and soon even those disappeared. Not that the web of waterways were terribly confusing, but unless you knew where you were going and were familiar with the few markers and buoys, Angelina believed the novice mariner could easily get lost in the marsh.

As they broke from the marsh grasses, DeAngelo turned and pointed to the tree-lined island. "There's your ride." Angelina followed his arm and spotted the docks slightly off the starboard bow. It was an endearing and very quaint touch to her welcome to the island. On the dock stood an old black man, a ring of white hair circling his bald head, attending a horse-drawn carriage.

Angelina leaned close to DeAngelo's ear. "Is this the way they greet all their visitors?"

"Gas is kind of scarce on the island these days. You'll enjoy the ride."

Enjoy the ride, she did. She was here on official business, but the gentle gait of the horse and the mixed aromas of salt air and pine trees were calming. This was a far cry from the hectic life in Atlanta and she immediately understood Eric's comment; she was already captured by the island.

Mrs. Walton met her at the stables. She was dressed in a riding outfit similar to the one Angelina wore. The carriage pulled to a stop, Mrs. Walton walked to greet her and the smile on her face was warm and genuine.

Mrs. Walton extended her hand to help Angelina from the carriage. "Welcome to Daufuskie Island. I hope your trip wasn't too much of an inconvenience and that Mr. DeAngelo behaved himself."

Angelina laughed, "Mr. DeAngelo was the perfect gentleman and the trip was wonderful. Thank you for seeing me, Mrs. Walton."

"Please call me Danni, Mrs. Walton just seems to formal. I hope it wasn't too presumptuous of me to suggest we take a ride around the island. Eric thought you might enjoy it."

"Not at all, I spent most of my childhood on the back of a horse."

"Good, I thought we would take a ride up the beach. It's always very refreshing in the morning."

The pair walked their mounts down a well beaten path and Angelina could see the Atlantic Ocean through the trees. Their conversations were more appropriate for an afternoon tea party than an investigation, but Angelina let Danni take the lead down the path and in the direction the conversation took. Angelina knew the struggle Mrs. Walton was experiencing. It was the same one she had seen in her discussions with the families of the other victims. She knew Mrs. Walton was building the courage to discuss the event that she had spent years trying to forget. Angelina almost regretted her decision to come to Daufuskie.

Danni was cautious with her initial conversations. Eric told her Angelina was investigating rape cases in Atlanta, and Hanna's case was only one of many, but young Eric didn't know the whole truth. In fact, Danni wasn't sure she knew the whole truth; but she did know there were many people she must protect.

Years ago, when she made the decision to avenge her daughter's rape, she was prepared to sacrifice herself. She knew that possibility always existed, but now there were so many other things to live for: her daughter had married a wonderful man and her first grandchild…Eric and this wonderful girl he had met…and even her love for Bill Cannon needed to be explored. For the first time in many years, she began to regret the decision she made years ago.

Danni didn't realize she had been riding with her head down, looking to the beach, until Angelina broke her thoughts. "Mrs. Walton, there are two people on the beach waving at us."

Danni looked up and broke into a smile. "That's Hanna and Brian Vance. Come on, let's go see them."

Danni urged her horse into a trot and Angelina followed. Even from down the beach she could see that Hanna looked a lot more pregnant in shorts and a tee shirt than she did at the funeral those few days ago; the boy with her struggling to walk in the sand. His right leg seemed to drag behind him and his right arm was carried close to his body.

Hanna greeted her with a beaming smile, like a best friend she hadn't seen in years. "Angelina, Momma told me you were coming to the island. How long are you going to stay?"

"I don't really know. I was just planning to visit for a few hours. How's the baby?"

Hanna ran both hands across her swollen stomach. "Oh, the baby's fine. He's kicking up a storm this morning. Angelina, you've got to stay for a couple of days, at least. We've got plenty of room and why would anyone want to go back to smelly old Atlanta when you can enjoy the island." Hanna turned to the boy walking next to her. "Angelina, meet Brian Vance. He's living with us."

Brian raised his left arm, his right immobile at his side, and extended his hand in greeting. "Very nice to meet you Miss Sanchez, I've heard a lot about you. Welcome."

The group chatted for a few moments before Hanna broke up the gathering. "Enough chit-chat, we've got a couple of miles to go before lunch. We'll see you back at the house."

When they parted, Angelina asked Danni, "Brian lives with you?"

"Yes, he used to work for me. He was the only employee at the resort that spoke against the union. Four union goons jumped him one night and almost killed him. After he got out of the hospital, he didn't have anyone else to look after him, so we took him in. He's a fine young man."

"What happened to the men who did that to him?"

"Nothing. The sheriff said there were no witnesses, so he couldn't prove anything."

"That doesn't seem like justice to me."

Danni turned to Angelina before she spoke. "It's not justice. It's life."

They rode in silence for a while before Angelina mustered the courage to address the purpose of her visit. "Mrs. Walton, you know I am investigating the rape of your daughter?"

"Yes, I know."

"What can you tell me about it?"

Danni started slowly, the pain of the night now vivid in the memory. "I was in New York, on business, when it happened. Mamba called me in the middle of the night and said she had a dream that Hanna was in trouble. I tried all night to get back, but there weren't any flights until 6 a.m. She made a mistake and got involved with a couple of kids from her high school. They went into Atlanta and did some drugs. A gang came into the house and raped her. When I finally got back in town, my husband had taken her to Chattanooga. The police investigated, but never charged anyone. It haunts me to this day that I wasn't there."

"Mrs. Walton, do you think the police did an adequate investigation of your daughter's rape?"

Danni felt the taste of rancor in her mouth. "No, not at all, the investigators told me they had some suspects, but without the DNA they didn't really have much to build a case. It didn't help that Hanna couldn't make a positive identification of any of the suspects they showed her. The police said they had a couple of eye witnesses, but never got anything from either of them. After a while, the police just ran out of leads and put the investigation in the dead file. They could have done more."

They rode in silence for a few minutes. "Mrs. Walton, would it ease your pain if I told you that the five men who raped your daughter are dead?"

Danni snapped her head to look directly at Angelina. "It wouldn't ease the pain one bit. You can't take back what they did to my little girl. How do you know they are all dead?"

"I got a confession from the last one left alive. He died in prison. He confessed to the rape and implicated the other members of the gang."

Danni's face was cold as stone. "God forgive me, but I hope they are burning in hell. Do you know how they died?" It was a little morbid but Danni wanted to know.

"They all died violent deaths except the one I talked with, and he died a slow and painful one; he died of AIDS."

297

As the two women continued their ride Danni said, "They all deserved what they got."

Angelina allowed the pair to approach Bloody Point before she asked her next question. "Mrs. Walton, did you know that Eric's father killed Bomani Thomas, the leader of the gang that raped Hanna?"

There was such a pause after her question that Angelina wondered if Mrs. Walton had heard it. Finally Danni answered. "Yes, I knew that."

"How did you know Bomani Thomas was one of the men who raped Hanna?"

"Hanna saw a picture of him on television when he was arrested for the courthouse shootings."

"You didn't call the police when you found out Bomani Thomas was one of the rapists?"

Danni pulled her horse to a stop and turned to Angelina. "What good would that do? We still didn't have any evidence, he was already in prison on a life sentence without parole, and we didn't want to drag Hanna through a trial we probably couldn't win."

"By 'we', do you mean you and your husband, or you and Hanna?"

"My husband, we never discussed it with Hanna. She had been through so much already."

"How did you know Sergeant Jackson had a son?"

For the first time during the ride it looked to Angelina that Danni Walton was weighing her answer, debating within on what she should reveal. "After my husband was killed, I went to Atlanta to talk to the police. I wanted to find out if they were investigating his death. I talked with Steve Thunder, he did part of the investigation; he told me about Eric."

"Is that when you asked Eric and Aunt Grace to move here, after Sergeant Jackson killed Bomani Thomas? I think you told Aunt Grace that it would be safer here than in Cairo."

"Yes."

"What made you think Eric and Aunt Grace would be in danger if they stayed in Cairo? Did Officer Thunder say they were in danger?"

Danni remembered the letter she received from Bill Cannon, the one that said that the danger wasn't over. If she told Angelina of the letter it would implicate Bill and she didn't want to do that.

"No, it was my assessment, and then I saw how they were living, and I felt it was the right thing to do; to bring them up here."

"Why did you think they may be in danger?"

Danni pulled her horse to a stop, and turned to Angelina. "Miss Sanchez…my husband was murdered, two men were killed in prison, my housekeeper was killed…that isn't enough killing to make a sane person think there may be more to come?"

There was a sarcastic edge to Danni's voice and Angelina had to admit that the security of the present; was a far cry from the violence of years ago.

"Why did you feel it would be safer if Aunt Grace and Eric moved here to the island?"

Again, a longer than normal pause from Danni before she answered, "There had already been so much violence. Thunder said the police hadn't found the men who killed my husband. I didn't want to be responsible for anyone else getting hurt."

Was that a slip of the tongue? Did Mrs. Walton actually say, "I didn't want to be responsible?" Now it was Angelina who took longer than normal to compose her next question. "Mrs. Walton, who was it that rescued your daughter from her kidnappers?"

Why was it that every answer now was constructed with such care?

"I don't know, maybe the police. I was just relieved to get her back. I never even questioned it."

"Mrs. Walton, do you know Buford Long?"

"Of course I do. He's a retired sheriff and sometimes he does security work for my father."

This seemed to be an important connection to the scattered and elusive components of Angelina's case.

"Mrs. Walton, Buford Long lives in Savannah. Why would he be in Atlanta the day your husband was killed, and for that matter, can you explain why it was that he happened to be at your house to walk in and shoot one of the kidnappers? His report never mentioned anything about Hanna's kidnapping, only that the man he killed was robbing your house."

Danni didn't hesitate when she answered, "I never asked him. I never asked my father why he had Buford watching us. After Hanna was raped, we never visited here. Maybe he thought something was wrong between me and my husband. Had Buford been a little earlier, maybe my housekeeper would still be alive."

"Do you have any idea why your husband was killed?"

Danni answered without any reservation. "The police report said my husband was probably trying to conduct his own investigation, trying to find out who was involved. Maybe he discovered some of the other men involved."

Angelina couldn't let the statement go. The one Danni made…I didn't want to be responsible for anyone else getting hurt. The connection hit Angelina like a slap in the face, no more like the kick of a mule in the stomach. How far would a mother go to avenge the rape of her daughter? Was the woman riding next to her capable of murder? Did Mrs. Walton know it was her husband and the hooker Jasmine who were witness to her daughter's rape? Both Crack Daddy and Frenchy told her that the 'Preacher' was in the house when Hanna was raped. Did Mrs. Walton know it was probably her husband who witnessed the rape? Did Mrs. Walton know it was the prostitute Jasmine that was found murdered with her husband? The same Jasmine who was listed as an uncooperative eye witness? Would a mother arrange for the murder of her husband and his consort to avenge the rape of her daughter? The implications of such a scenario were almost too outrageous to consider.

"Mrs. Walton, this may seem very callous, but I have to ask. What kind of a man was your husband when he was away from church? Do you think your husband was involved with drugs? Not necessarily using drugs, but in the sale of drugs?"

It was clear the question stunned Danni. Her response was emotional, "That's ridiculous! My husband was a man of God, a well respected preacher. I can't believe you would make such an accusation! Why would you ever think such a thing?"

"Because, your husband's murder had nothing to do with Hanna's rape; your husband was murdered by a man called 'Snowman' because of a drug deal gone bad." Angelina wanted to add, "Or you set him up to be killed," but held her tongue.

Danni pulled her horse to a stop once again. "You know who killed my husband?"

"Yes, I do. Snowman worked for a man named Tyrell Biggs. Biggs, in his day, was the largest drug dealer in the southeast. Snowman killed your husband trying to recover a large sum of money the organization lost on a heroin buy. After your husband was killed, those same men kidnapped your daughter. Was that another attempt to collect the missing money, and didn't the men who invaded your house here on Daufuskie also want money?"

Danni turned to Angelina with a controlled rage. "If you know who killed my husband, why haven't you arrested them? All you have done is to slander him."

Angelina noted that Danni only addressed the murder of her husband. Was the omission of the other charges intentional or simply of little or no consequence to Danni compared to the murder of her husband?

"I have done nothing but state the facts. The facts are that your husband was killed in the presence of a known hooker by a known drug dealer. The facts are that your husband was well known in the seedier parts of town, so much so that he was known as Preacher by the hookers and the druggies. He spent enough time there that it raises questions as to his involvement in shipping heroin into the United States. As to your question of arresting his killer, I haven't arrested anyone because the men involved with the drugs are also dead.

"My intention, Mrs. Walton, is not to slander the dead, but to establish the facts surrounding not only the rape of your daughter and the deaths of her rapists, but the death of your husband and at least another dozen other killings."

"What other killings?"

Before Angelina could list the other murders, Danni's cell phone rang. Angelina waited for Danni to complete the call. "We have to get back to the house right away."

The horses were well lathered when they reached the house. Angelina recognized Eric's voice broadcasting the news. "Tensions in the Middle East are at the breaking point with the Israeli invasion of the Gaza strip. The Israeli Ambassador to the United Nations announced the military action was in response to what they cited as confirmed intelligence reports that Hamas now possessed chemical weapons, specifically a non-persistent binary nerve agent. The US Secretary of

301

State is calling for an immediate halt to the attack and will attempt to bring all parties to Geneva to discuss their differences.

"In other news from Israel, two military personnel, one an American military attaché, were captured in an attack across the international border between Israel and Lebanon. The organization known as Hezbollah has claimed responsibility for the raid."

Chapter 39

When the telephone rang, the nightmares Mamba forced deep into the recesses of her mind came screaming back with a vengeance. The second ring muffled all other sounds in the room, even the voice of Eric reporting the Gaza Strip casualty figures. At the third ring, Mamba looked at the others in the room, their eyes riveted on the phone, frozen in place as if time stopped. On the fourth ring, Mamba broke the spell and moved towards the phone. "I'll get it."

"No, it's for me. I'll get it." Hanna rose from her chair and, crossing in front of Mamba, removed the phone from the cradle. "This is Hanna Madison."

The others in the room saw the color drain from her face. "General, would you mind if I put you on the speaker? My family is here with me and I would like them to hear this."

Hanna pushed the speaker button on the phone. "General McLaughlin, you are on the speaker, please go ahead." Hanna sat on the couch and Danni moved to stand behind her.

"Hanna, your husband and two Israeli soldiers, while inspecting the northern border with Lebanon, were ambushed. One of the Israelis was killed in the attack. Your husband and the driver have not been found. We assume they have been taken hostage."

The group in the room listened in stunned silence.

"Hezbollah has claimed responsibility for the attack. The Lebanese Army is conducting a search of the area to find your husband. The Secretary of State will address the United Nations General Assembly and request a resolution condemning the attack.

"We are doing everything we can to get your husband back. We ask that you direct any inquires to the Public Affairs office at Hunter Army Airfield, and refrain from making any comments to the press. Any comments you make will surely be monitored by the people who have James, and they may use that against him."

Lucas waited for questions, and when there were none, he added, "And Hanna, just some personal advice, from a friend, it won't do you any good to listen to or even watch the news. The news agencies really don't know what is going on, and they always sensationalize everything, even if they have nothing of substance to report. I will personally keep you informed of all the latest details."

Hanna listened with her chin resting on her chest and her hands clutching her swollen womb. "General McLaughlin, I want you to be completely honest with me. What are the chances we can get James back?"

There was an obvious pause before McLaughlin answered. "Hanna, we are doing everything we can. Right now, I think the best thing to do is to stay calm and pray for his return."

Her face flushed with anger.

"General McLaughlin, this is my husband and the father of my child we are talking about! Please don't patronize me and stop treating me as a child! I want some answers; I am entitled to the truth!"

General McLaughlin sensed the growing anger in the room. "I will tell you what I can."

"Has this type of thing ever happened before? I mean to an American?"

General McLaughlin debated whether Hanna's question was relevant to her husband's situation. The time he took to decide the issue was interrupted by Hanna repeating the question. "General McLaughlin, has this happened before to an American officer?"

"Yes, Hanna, it has happened before, but that has nothing to do with the situation we have today."

Hanna almost whispered her next question. "Did they release him?"

"Hanna, please realize your husband is valuable to them as a hostage. That will work in our favor."

That may be true, but it didn't solve her problem. She wanted her husband rescued and did not want him to become a pawn in the insane game of international politics.

Finally Hanna asked, "Will Israel try to rescue him? There is an Israeli soldier with him. Won't they try and rescue him?"

"Hanna, I don't know what Israel will do."

"So the Israelis would sacrifice my husband."

General McLaughlin felt sick that his answers would only add to Hanna's grief. Lucas knew Israel would not intentionally sacrifice Major Madison, but their priority would be to eliminate the chemical weapons in the Gaza strip.

"Hanna, I know Israel is concerned about your husband. They will do everything they can."

"Will the United States try and rescue him?"

"Hanna, I know the President has been briefed on the situation. His objective is to stabilize the situation in the Middle East. If we launched an attack it would only create more tension in the area. Our best hope is that we can negotiate Major Madison's release."

Her husband had suddenly become Major Madison, and General McLaughlin was discussing him as an object of a military response, not as her husband. Her emotions could not be totally controlled. "So, all that talk about never leaving a soldier behind is nothing but a bunch of crap!"

General Lucas McLaughlin was stung by the criticism, and if it were up to him or many others in the military, a rescue force would be assembling as they spoke. "Hanna, all I can tell you is we will do everything possible to get James back."

~~

The trauma of the phone call was such that nobody said a thing. Danni sat on the couch next to her daughter and gently put her arm around her shoulders. It was difficult for anyone to start a conversation. They all feared the emotional flood from Hanna if anyone spoke.

Hanna made it easier for them. "I'm going to my room."

General McLaughlin was holding something back and Hanna wanted to know the whole truth. It wasn't hard to find on the Internet. Yes, another American military officer had been held hostage by Hezbollah in Lebanon. In 1988, Hezbollah kidnapped an American serving on the International Peacekeeping Force. They held him for over a year, tortured him, and eventually hung him.

Hanna turned off the computer and walked out of her room to the front door. Her mother asked, "Where are you going?"

Hanna paused, "General McLaughlin was right. The best thing we can do is pray. I'm going to the church and pray."

Danni got up and said, "I'll go with you."

"No, I want to be alone for a while. I'll be okay. I just want a little time to myself, please."

In the aftermath of the terrible phone conversation with General McLaughlin, Angelina wanted nothing more of the investigation. "Mrs. Walton, in light of everything that has happened today, maybe I should just go back to Atlanta and come back another time."

"If it's not too much trouble, I would really appreciate that. I would like to go and sit with Hanna." Danni looked at her watch. "You've missed the last ferry back to Savannah. Let's call DeAngelo and see if he can pick you up."

The phone at DeAngelo's marina went to voice mail five times before Danni gave up trying to call. "Mike must be out fishing. We'll call him later."

With nothing else to accomplish, Danni and Angelina with Mamba and Brian, all walked to the small church to pray with Hanna.

Later in the evening, when they tried once again to reach DeAngelo, there was still no answer at the marina.

~~

Angelina felt out of place in the pervasive somber attitude that now inundated the Walton residence. When Danni was unable to reach Mike DeAngelo she extended Angelina an invitation to spend the night in one of the guest bedrooms. Angelina slept soundly enough, maybe there was something to island living, but decided the investigation could wait and would make arrangements for her return to Atlanta. At breakfast all she felt safe to ask was if Hanna was alright. Hanna's weak smile and red eyes belied her answer that she was fine.

"Mrs. Walton, I think I should get back to Atlanta. Did Mr. DeAngelo ever return your call?"

Danni looked up from scrambling eggs, "No, he never did. I called again this morning. A young man answered the phone. He told me that Mike called him yesterday and told him to run the marina until he got back. He didn't say where he was going, or when he would return.

"If you must go, you can catch one of the ferries that run to Savannah. You will have to catch a cab to your car, but it is the only way off the island. Are you sure you wouldn't like to stay with us until DeAngelo gets back?"

"No, thank you. I better get back. When do the ferries run?"

Danni looked at the wall clock. "The next one leaves in a little over an hour. Eat some breakfast and I will take you."

Angelina collected her belongings and bid Hanna a goodbye. "Hanna, I have a few contacts in Washington, if I can help you in any way, please don't hesitate to call me. I will pray that everything works out for you and your husband."

Hanna got up and hugged her, "Thank you Angelina. Are you sure you don't want to stay for the weekend?"

"No, I must really get back, but I'll keep in touch."

Part of Angelina wanted to stay with these wonderful people and help them weather this latest storm, but she still had responsibilities in Atlanta. She did what she could to make a gracious exit, and then waited for Mrs. Walton to meet her on the front drive. Angelina took a moment to listen to the quiet of the island and breathed deeply of the salt air. The small sounds, the birds, and the wind, and maybe a fox squirrel or two running through the trees was interrupted by the offensive ring of her cell phone. Damn modern technology. Angelina looked at the screen. It was Jose Morales, her code breaker from the CIA.

"Hello Joe."

"Angelina, I've only got a minute. I've been trying to call you for a day. I had to call your boss for your cell phone number."

Oh, great. Now she had to worry about Mr. Jefferson running her through the wringer again. "I'm sorry, Joe. I should have given you my number. What did Jefferson say?"

"He said you were probably picking flowers with you new boyfriend."

"Jefferson's full of hot air. What did you find?"

"I don't have a lot of time to explain the details, but the letters you sent me were all clean. The newspaper article was full of code. See if any of this makes any sense to you. 'Target B. Thomas X...heroin bait three large dealer outside...six has your boy...thunder.' Does any of that make any sense to you?"

"Is there anything you can tell me about the code?"

"Yeah, it's a simple code used by special ops types in the military; it's easy to crack. I ran it through the training program computers to get it. It's not secure, but useful if you want to pass something quickly. Some of the code is probably code itself, the X is probably a kill sign, and six is normally the number assigned to the commander of a unit. I don't know what, 'has your boy,' would mean. It could be anything."

Angelina knew exactly what, 'has your boy,' meant. "Thanks Joe, I owe you."

The picture began to fill in for Angelina. The only question left was, why?

Angelina was lost in her thoughts when Danni drove up in a one-horse buggy. "I guess Mr. DeAngelo wasn't lying when he said gas was scarce on the island."

Danni smiled. "That and I wanted to talk with you before you left. Climb on up."

With a flick of the reins the buggy eased into motion. Angelina saw that Danni was an expert managing the buggy. "Is there any news from General McLaughlin?"

Danni glanced her way, "No. Not yet. I watched the news this morning and there wasn't anything about James. I doubt anybody really cares about what is happening in Israel, much less what will happen to James; out of sight, out of mind." Danni paused. "Angelina, yesterday you said some things about my husband. His death has always been a mystery to me. What exactly do you know?"

Angelina felt awful about the way in which she addressed the issue of Danni's husband. If she had to do it again, she would not have lost control of her emotions in the manner in which she did.

"Mrs. Walton, I feel terrible about some of the things I said yesterday. I apologize for my insensitivity."

"If I didn't want to know the truth, I wouldn't ask. You mentioned something about my husband involved with drugs?"

"I said he was killed because of drugs. A man named Tyrell Biggs got cheated out of $3,000,000 on a drug deal. He thought your husband knew where the money was."

"And that is why they killed him?"

"Yes."

"You also said my husband was well-known in that part of town."

Angelina was firm in her facts. Too many people had implicated her husband and that he frequented the hookers, but was it necessary to reveal more about his conduct than she had already done, and hurt this woman in the process?

"Mrs. Walton, are you sure you want to hear this?

"My husband's death, the kidnapping of Hanna, the visions of the terrible men who broke into our home here, they have haunted me for years. I never understood why all that happened. Most of the time, I just keep the memories buried deep, but every once in a while I have nightmares about the whole thing. If I knew the truth, maybe the nightmares would end."

What was the point of doing this? Angelina knew the truth would be harder to bear than the nightmares. "Mrs. Walton, let's not talk about this anymore."

Danni pulled the buggy to a stop.

"Eric tells me you are investigating the rape of my daughter. Obviously you have discovered additional evidence, or you wouldn't be here asking about my husband. This happened years ago. Why are you digging it all up again? You tell me that all the men who raped my daughter are now dead. It would have been better if they would have been brought to trial and executed, but they have all paid the price for their deeds. I hope they are burning in hell. I would think that would close that case, but obviously it hasn't. What exactly are you investigating? You won't tell me what you have found about my husband, but will I hear about it in some federal court? I have already suffered the rape and kidnapping of my daughter, the murder of my husband, and now my son-in-law is held captive by some terrorist group that will execute him for some fanatical political gain that has nothing to do with my family, and you are afraid to tell me the truth? Don't you think I finally deserve to know the truth, Ms. Sanchez?"

Angelina was stung by the comments. She took a few deep breaths to clear her head and create time to think. If the tables were turned, and Mrs. Walton was the investigator, would she want to know the truth? As painful as the answer was, Angelina knew she would want to know.

"Alright, Mrs. Walton, you won't like it, but I'll tell you the truth. Your husband's behavior was deplorable. When the police found his body, there was a dead prostitute in his car—the same prostitute that was an eye witness to the rape of your daughter." Angelina didn't rush with the details, she wanted to be accurate.

309

"There was one other material witness to the rape, listed as a John Doe. The police never found him. That man, that John Doe, was your husband. He was having sex with that prostitute in the same house and at the same time that your daughter was raped and beaten."

Angelina saw the shock on Danni's face and hesitated to continue. Danni almost couldn't catch enough breath to ask, "My husband left my daughter there?"

"There is no evidence your husband knew the girl in trouble was Hanna, but he could identify Bomani Thomas. He got a good look at him."

Angelina waited for another question from Danni, but Danni was struggling with an overwhelming sense of nausea. It was painful for Angelina to continue, but now was the chance to get all the facts out in the open.

"When your husband did so much to erase the DNA evidence of the rape, and when he failed to notify the police, or provide information, or identify Bomani Thomas the only conclusion I could come to was that his actions were of a man involved in something more."

Danni sat with her head down and Angelina saw the tears in the corner of her eyes; she appeared to be a totally beaten woman. Angelina could only guess at the torment she was suffering.

"For the longest time I suspected a police cover-up, maybe even a vigilante killing by the police when they couldn't get anything to trial. When I started looking into that, I discovered too many ties to the busted drug deal. The more I looked into it, the more the drugs seemed responsible for all the violence."

To Angelina, Danni looked ill. She wondered if she should continue. "Mrs. Walton, do you want me to continue?"

Danni, one hand on her stomach and one loosely covering her mouth, struggled to answer and only nodded.

"Mrs. Walton, Steve Thunder, the Atlanta Police Officer who investigated your husband's murder was the same officer who broke up the drug deal. Today I learned he sent a coded message to Eric's father setting up the drug deal. In that same message he also passed instructions to kill Bomani Thomas."

Angelina watched Danni closely. There was much to be learned from the reaction of a suspect.

"Mrs. Walton, it is hard for me to believe all this is coincidence. Maybe it's time you started telling me the truth."

Danni dropped the reins and jumped from the buggy. She ran to the side of the dusty road and bent forward at the waist. Angelina didn't move from her seat and only heard the convulsions coming from Danni's direction. When the retching stopped, Angelina looked to Danni and found her kneeling on one knee with one hand braced against a pine tree for support.

Angelina felt terrible. She never expected her questions to have such an effect on Danni. She walked to Danni. "Mrs. Walton, I'm so sorry. I shouldn't have told you any of that."

With her free hand Danni wiped some spittle from her mouth. "Take the buggy. The ferry is straight down the road. I'll pick it up later."

"Mrs. Walton, I…"

Danni stopped her before she could continue. "I don't want to hear any more. Please take the buggy and go."

Angelina wondered how Eric would respond when he learned what she knew.

~~

Danni watched the carriage until it was obscured by the pines. She felt weak and would have preferred to rest and let the world stop spinning before she tried to stand. Could all the things Angelina Sanchez said be true?

Every time she thought of her husband…the prostitutes meant little or nothing to her now…but to leave their daughter behind…the retching noises once again filled the pine woods. Tears streaked her face. All the years of pain…the nightmares…even her terrible act of revenge…could have been averted if her husband would have found the courage to stand like a man and defend his own daughter. But that would have taken a man, and that he was not.

The years of guilt she carried, that her act of revenge to kill Bomani Thomas had somehow caused the death of her husband, now carried with it a hint of justification that a man who would leave his daughter to the ravages of a gang rape deserved to meet such a fate.

Danni struggled with her emotions concerning her husband, but once she began to gain control over those, another emotion began to overwhelm her. She had been used, and again betrayed by a man she

311

believed she loved, and that he loved her. The image of Bill Cannon's letter was clear in her mind. She had read it many times and knew it by heart. Bill Cannon's words, "I regret many things in my life, but none more than the pain and sorrow I brought your family. The loss of your husband will weigh heavy on my soul…please know my intentions were always to help you, not hurt you…" His words were all lies. He had used her lust for revenge to fill his own pockets with drug money. He was no better than the human scum who had raped her daughter and at this moment she felt nothing but contempt.

When Danni finally made her way home, it was Mamba, who noticed the change in her. And Mamba spoke a strange warning.

"My child, the worst death is a slow death where you allow half-truths to poison your mind and your heart. Be careful."

Chapter 40

Bill Cannon walked with Prince Al-Sabah through the rubble that only a few hours ago was the bustling Bank of America lobby in Kuwait City. Bill assumed the bloody mass in the front seat of the smoldering vehicle was all that remained of the suicide bomber. The rear of the vehicle was gone, blown off in the blast. It was the third attack against American businesses in the last month.

Bill turned to Prince Al-Sabah. "Who did this thing?"

The broken glass of the teller cages crunched underfoot as the pair made their way deeper into the smoking ruins of the bank. "I don't know. There are so many groups hiding behind the cloak of jihad that it could have been one of a dozen. But let us not become distracted from our true objective."

Bill looked around the smoking building. "What is our objective?"

"To preserve Kuwait; to preserve the peace."

"This is peace?"

"No my friend, this is not peace, but these attacks are only the arms of the beast that seeks our destruction. If we cut off this arm it will have reason to grow more, and it can grow new arms like the lizard can grow new tails. If we cut off all the arms, then we may never find the path to the heart, and we must strike to the heart if we ever wish to live in peace and prosperity. I am afraid we must suffer through these attacks until we have the power to kill the beast. It is something that will take great leadership."

Bill found his friend's answer almost idiotic. "I guess the $30,000,000 you paid to Abdul Nardiff doesn't feel like such a good investment now, does it?"

"It depends on your perspective. These are American companies, not Kuwaiti. That may seem to be very callous, but I must first protect my people. I wonder what the American government will do to protect theirs."

Another rather odd answer from his friend. "Ahmad, you act as if you don't want American businesses here, why?"

Prince Al-Sabah stopped and turned to his friend, "Bill, it is not a question if I want American business in my country; it is a question if America will choose to remain an economic influence throughout the world. They have already withdrawn their armies and left us to find our own way in a very dangerous time; it is not hard for my people to believe they are only here now to bleed Kuwait dry of resources, and leave when it is no longer profitable for them to stay."

"Is that what you believe?"

"I believe only the American people can turn the tide."

What in the hell was Prince Al-Sabah talking about? Bill was prepared to ask just that when General Al-Wadi rushed into the building. He bowed slightly before he addressed Al-Sabah, "Excuse me great Prince, but something has happened in Israel, an American Army officer has been taken."

Bill Cannon felt a chill run through his body. It was not his place to interrupt, but he asked, "Do you know the name of the American?"

General Al-Wadi turned to Bill, "Yes I do. The name of the American is James Madison, Major James Madison."

~~

James Madison and Ari Sharone were confined in the dimly lit room for now what seemed to be a full day. Except for the visit to take photos, their suffering had been a lonely ordeal. In spite of the searing pain from his right arm and the throbbing in his head, James had finally worked himself into a sitting position. If he pressed his broken arm against the cold concrete just right the pain was bearable. James didn't mention it, because it would only make the lack of it worse, but he would kill for a simple drink of water.

Their solitude was finally broken by the hinges on their prison door and the creak of the stairs. A young man about 30 years old led a group of four down the stairs. He crouched before James, the others moved to Ari.

The man in front of James pulled a wallet from the pocket of his fatigues. Though his one good eye was blurry, the wallet looked like the one James carried. There was no doubt when the man pulled the identification card from it. "Major James Madison, United States Army, is that you?"

314

James assumed it was a rhetorical question and found no good reason to answer. The man reviewed his driver's license. "Major Madison, your driver's license will expire next year. I wonder if you will be back in America in time to renew it?" James noted a familiarity in the man's voice, as if he was discussing events in a coffee house back home.

It was painful to speak, but James asked, "You've been to America?"

The man broke into a big grin. "Oh yes, many times. I lived in America for six years. I received my degree in political science from Michigan State, class of 1994. Go Spartans." He looked closely at the card. "I assume we can find your wife at this address?" He dug deeper into the wallet and pulled Hanna's picture from the plastic holder. "This is your wife? She is a very pretty woman. I wonder if she has thought to cancel these credit cards? Maybe we should call and remind her. What do you think? Or maybe we should bring her here, so she can pleasure our fighters. Would she do that to save you?"

A shiver of fear ran through James. Thank God Hanna was with her mother. It would make it slightly more difficult for these animals to find her there.

"Major Madison, I would like to ask a favor of you. We would like you to make a video message for us."

James knew this demand was coming. Just about every hostage taken by Hezbollah or Hamas ended up on television. The terrorists knew the videos would be seen on newscasts around the world, and it was a means to spread their political message. They used the videos to demonstrate their power, and it was an effective recruitment tool for the terrorists. The military and politicians ignored the videos, and they had no effect on policy or operations, but the influence on the civilian population was often dramatic. James always thought the videos simply served as justification for the barbaric acts inflicted by psychotic terrorists.

Most military men would advise you to avoid the torture and make the video, but James had his own reason to refuse. He didn't want Hanna to think he was a beaten man.

James turned his head away from the man and closed his eyes. He felt more than heard the blow delivered to his head. The blow knocked him to the floor and the bone in his right arm once again ripped through the skin. James felt the blood begin to flow from his nose and face.

The man to his front was incensed. "Don't turn away from me. Your life is mine to do with as I wish. You will make the video."

James ignored the burning pain in his arm and turned his head back to his captor. "Fuck you."

The man stood and kicked James in the groin. The pain was so intense it caused convulsions. The man kicked him again and again until panting from the exertion withdrew to admire his work. James could barely make out his image through the blood streaming from his head wound.

"You will make the video now?"

James could barely talk, but he forced out a weak, "No."

"So the American wants to be like Rambo. Maybe we should ask this Zionist pig if you should make the video."

James watched in horror as the men near Ari produced a steel rod and with all the force possible smashed Ari's left knee cap. James heard the bone break and Ari's scream. The second blow missed the knee and caught Ari on the shin. They enjoyed their work and would kill Ari unless he stopped them.

~~

When Eric didn't return her message, Angelina was sure Mrs. Walton had called and told him everything. It was probably the end of their relationship. She wondered if Mrs. Walton told Eric that Steve Thunder ordered his father to kill Bomani Thomas. Did she tell him that Steve Thunder and his father were involved in the biggest drug deal in Georgia history and that his father was nothing more than an assassin? Maybe assassin was too strong of a description, but there was no doubt Thunder targeted Bomani Thomas and asked Eric's father to kill him.

If their relationship was over, Angelina wanted to explain her side of the story. She called the CNN newsroom and asked for Eric.

Eric was in a production meeting, but if Angelina would hold, she would sneak in a note that she wanted to see him. In a moment she returned to the phone. "Eric can't talk with you right now, but if you want to come to the newsroom, he will break free."

It was all that Angelina needed. She picked up her files and drove to the CNN Center. She waited for 10 minutes before the guard buzzed her through. "Miss Sanchez, you can go in. Eric will meet you inside."

Angelina dreaded the walk down the corridor, the same one where Eric first discovered she was a federal agent. The low buzz of activity from the newsroom was louder than she remembered, and when Eric emerged from one of the offices the big smile on his face told her that Mrs. Walton had not called.

"Angelina, my favorite cop, you look great!" Eric walked up to her and kissed her on the cheek. "How was your trip to Daufuskie?"

"That's what I wanted to talk to you about. You didn't get my message?"

"I slept on my couch in the office last night. This Israeli thing has really got us hopping. The Egyptians have demanded the Israelis withdraw from the Gaza Strip, and are moving some armored divisions into the Sinai. The Iranians are trying to get the Middle East OPEC members to shut off all oil shipments to the West until Israel pulls back, not only from Gaza, but the West Bank as well. The price of crude has almost doubled in the last few hours and the stock market is dropping like a rock. We think the President is going to announce he is going to open the strategic oil reserves and try to strike a deal with the Iranians to keep the oil flowing to us. I haven't had time to check my messages. Now that you're here, I don't need to check my messages."

The greeting put Angelina somewhat at ease. "Is there somewhere we can talk?"

"Come on, we'll use my desk. I only have a few minutes. I'm supposed to anchor a special on the conflict, and have a meeting in a few minutes." Eric held her arm close to his side until they were seated at his desk.

"Eric, about my trip to Daufuskie, that's what I wanted to talk to you about. I've found out some things that I think you will want to know…"

Angelina was interrupted by a man shouting to Eric from across the room. "Eric, we have some video coming in that we want you to use. Check out the big screen."

Eric swiveled in his chair and directed his attention to a huge screen suspended above 30 other sets. Angelina followed his gaze. The blue screen flickered to life with the snow of the satellite feed, and eventually the solid lines of a test pattern. The picture flickered to life with the image of a masked gunman standing over Major James Madison. The sound faded between static and the garbled voice of the

317

masked gunman. The camera panned down to the bloody face of James Madison.

Angelina could not make out the words Madison spoke. Maybe the others in the room could ignore the bloody mass that was once his face, but Angelina could not. The still photo she had seen yesterday was just a picture, but the blood oozing from his head wound and eye socket brought home the true horror of the scene. James left eye was swollen almost shut. His lips were cracked and bleeding and the scrapes on his face were fresh. Somebody from off camera held the paper from which he read. The horrible picture froze on the screen.

Somebody from within the CNN newsroom cursed, "Damn, we've lost our sync, we're going to have to send it again. Somebody fix that sound! We can't put this on the news without sound. Now get to it!"

Angelina was stunned by what she saw. After only a brief pause the bustle in the newsroom returned to normal, and most returned to their work without a second glance at the horrible picture frozen on the huge screen. All returned to their work except Eric. Eric's eyes were riveted on the picture of his friend. Angelina saw tears streaming down Eric's face. The muscles in his jaw twitched with pent up rage.

Angelina stood and moved to his side and held his head to her breast. She could feel his emotion. Through clenched teeth he told Angelina, "They're going to kill him."

The buzz of the newsroom faded to the background. She didn't know how long she stood there holding Eric, but only when Eric pulled back did she release him. It took only a moment for him to regain composure. He wiped the tears from his face and turned back to Angelina.

"I shouldn't let that happen—I'm a newsman—I'm not supposed to let this stuff bother me."

Eric held his head in his two hands and rubbed his face. After a moment he looked up and asked, "I'm sorry, Angelina, what did you want to talk about?"

The folders containing her report didn't mean much anymore. "Nothing Eric, I just wanted to see you. When you get done here, give me a call and I'll cook you some dinner, okay?"

~~

Eric alerted Danni Walton that the Middle East bureau had information and pictures of James. They would air it on the 6:00 o'clock news. In spite of the warning from General McLaughlin to avoid the television, Hanna, Danni and Mamba would not leave their seats for fear of missing the broadcast.

Ed Helton watched the report in his office at Coastal Bank.

General McLaughlin and Terri Toth watched the broadcast in the Emergency Operation Center deep within the Pentagon.

Senator Reynolds watched from his office in the Senate building.

Angelina watched the report from the comfort of the couch in her apartment.

When the horror of the video filled the television screen the words James spoke were mumbled and slurred, "...withdraw all forces...or America...will burn...fires of...death..."

The words meant little or nothing to the reporters. The demands of Hezbollah never registered with the civilians, but they did with Senator Reynolds, General McLaughlin and Terri Toth. They all knew Israel would ignore the demands to withdraw from the Gaza and the West Bank, and that the current administration would study and debate their response until the kidnapping moved off the front page, and then probably do nothing.

Hanna tried to maintain her composure, but the last video broke her resolve. The words meant nothing to her. The bloody mass that was once her husband's face, the buzzing of the flies around his wounds, it was a picture of a man near death.

Her husband was dying a horrible death and she was powerless to help. James was being denied the dignity of an honorable death by the news anchors discussing his fate as if he was nothing more than a pawn on the larger stage of international politics.

The debates speculated and postulated what would occur if the United States conceded to Hezbollah's demands, or whether the prudent thing for Israel to do would be to withdraw from the Gaza and re-enter negotiations with the surrounding Arab countries, or continue the attack and simply hope for the best. They wondered if the coalition of Iran and Egypt would actually attack Israel and what impact that would have on the stalled Middle East peace process. How would the price of oil be affected by the continued fighting? Were Israel's claims that chemical weapons were being smuggled into the Gaza even true? The administration pushed for a United Nations resolution to investigate the claim, but held steadfast to their position that it was a regional problem.

All this was discussed and her husband was only a catalyst to ignite the discussions. Only Eric Brown pushed his reporters to focus their questions on the release of Major Madison, but after so many evasive answers from the White House and Pentagon they moved to other subjects. And now even General McLaughlin avoided her phone calls. His office only responded that McLaughlin was unavailable.

Hanna cried and Danni and Mamba tried to comfort her. Ed Helton held his head in his hands and prayed, and then turned back to his work. Angelina Sanchez repeatedly tried, unsuccessfully, to call Doc Broderson to find out how serious were James Madison's wounds and how long could he survive without medical treatment.

~~

The horrible image of Major Madison only moments removed from the newscast, Prince Al-Sabah's memory was taken back to a scene all too similar to the one just witnessed on television. Almost 20 years had passed since the Iraq invasion of Kuwait, but the images of the torture chamber where Prince Al-Sabah found his dying wife were still vivid. The same dark chamber, the same dirty floor, the same weak lighting, the terrible smell of death, and the beautiful body of his wife mutilated almost beyond recognition. His son and daughter would have surely suffered the same fate if not for the brave man at his side. If not for Bill Cannon and the American force that led the rescue mission into occupied Kuwait, and then deep into Iraq, it could be his own son chained to that wall, or his daughter with half her face blown away. The precious lives of his son and daughter was a debt owed to Bill Cannon that the Price of Kuwait could never repay.

"Prince Al-Sabah, do you know where he is being held?"

There was only one reason Bill Cannon would ask such a direct question. "My friend, you do not have the American Army backing you up. It would be suicide to try and rescue Major Madison."

There would be danger involved in helping his friend, but it was the honorable path. Bill Cannon, unlike his government, would not sit idly by and let his friend die a slow death.

"Maybe, but that is not what I asked you. Do you know where he is being held?"

"You already know where he is being held."

Bill thought back to DeAngelo's marina and the pictures sent to him by Prince Al-Sabah, "The house in Lebanon near the border?"

"Yes. That building is the headquarters of Hezbollah in Lebanon."

"Those pictures you gave me, you knew what was going on, didn't you? You knew about the chemical weapons being smuggled into the Sinai from Syria."

Prince Al-Sabah nodded. "It was my hope that they would have been put to better use, but your government now only panders to the forces that will destroy what peace we have. We are on the brink of war and America will wait to respond to a crisis rather than take risks to prevent crisis."

"What is in the Syrian desert?"

Al-Sabah stood and began pacing as he talked. "After the first gulf war Saddam moved all his chemical weapons and the nuclear weapons he was trying to build to Syria. It is those same chemical weapons that are now being shipped into the Gaza."

"Ahmad, why didn't you get this intelligence to the US?"

"Bill, I walk blindfolded above a pit of jackals and vipers. One false step and I will be devoured. I have done what I can to warn your country, but since they have done nothing I must now eat in the tents of my enemies, or be swept away."

Bill knew everything his friend said was true. "Ahmad, I hate to put you in harm's way, but I need your help." Bill moved to a desk and scribbled out a list of equipment he would need. When he finished he handed the list to Al-Sabah. "Can you supply me with this equipment? I will need it delivered to a safe location in Lebanon. Can you arrange that?"

Al-Sabah looked over the list. It was quite impressive, but was easily filled. His intelligence staff had many covert locations throughout the Middle East from which they operated; making one available to Bill Cannon would not be a problem. The problem that lingered with Al-Sabah was losing his friend on what he considered a suicidal attempt to rescue someone that was as good as dead.

"I can provide you with this equipment, and with a location in Lebanon from which you can operate, and all the money you will need, but you will not be able to save him. Madison will die from his wounds and your efforts will be in vain."

Bill knew his chances of success were not good. Bill knew James Madison would die from infection within a week. It left no time for error. "If I am not in time to save him, then I will have all the time I need to avenge him."

~~

Their farewell was somber. These two men had been through the worst of times, and now each of them had their own battle to fight. Prince Al-Sabah's duty was to his small country in the face of the belligerent giant across the Persian Gulf, and Bill's was to his friend in the chamber in southern Lebanon.

Prince Al-Sabah's farewell would stay with Bill forever. He put one hand on Bill's shoulder and looked him directly in the eyes. "Bill, I love you like no other man not of my own blood, and I am indebted to you. I am indebted to you for my life. I am indebted to you for the lives of my children. In a large sense I am indebted to you for the life of my country. For those things I will eternally be in your debt. I will pray for Allah to watch over you. It is my greatest honor to be considered your friend."

There was only one part of Al-Sabah's farewell that Bill didn't understand. When Bill turned to leave his friend said, "Bill, I want you to know that I have always loved your country. I have always considered America the guiding light of freedom in the world. When I am gone, please remember that what I must do, will be to preserve her, not to destroy her."

It was a strange comment that deserved discussion, but Prince Al-Sabah turned and walked away without looking back.

~~

After Bill Cannon left the palace, Rayhan Al-Sabah, the heir to Prince Al-Sabah's Kingdom, and General Al-Wadi joined the Prince. Prince Al-Sabah greeted his son as any father would. They briefly embraced and then the Prince held his son at arm's length.

"Soon you will be leaving for America. Are you prepared?"

"Yes father I am."

"Good, I am proud of you."

Prince Al-Sabah handed Bill's equipment list to General Al-Wadi, "Colonel Cannon will need this equipment. Please see to it."

General Al-Wadi hesitated. "My Prince, I do not understand. First you ordered an American to be taken, and now you help Colonel Cannon to rescue him. Why are you doing this?"

"I did not know the American would be a friend of my friend. It is right that I give him a chance to rescue him."

"My Prince, I understand your debt to Colonel Cannon, but you are surely sending him to his death…"

"If it be Allah's will."

"…or helping him to kill our Arab brothers."

"General Al-Wadi, the Americans will do nothing to free the officer. Everything we have done has failed. Nothing will move the Americans to action. It is now a matter of honor that I help Colonel Cannon."

"Your Highness, everything we have done I have understood, but now this does not make sense."

"You do not agree with my decision?"

General Al-Wadi did not answer immediately.

"My Prince, I am in your service. I do not envy the weight of the decisions you must make. We face many dangers. There are many ways to die but there is only one way to live and that is in service to Allah. We cannot beat the Iranian army without the help of the Americans, but I think Allah frowns upon us that we allow the infidel to kill our brothers. There is more honor dying under your neighbor's sword than dying from the corruption brought to our country by the Americans. I often wonder which way to point my gun."

Prince Al-Sabah's voice grew stern. "You must place Kuwait above all other concerns. That is what we must do or we will be swallowed by the Persian Army. Our only hope to survive as a country is to force America to action."

"Then your actions…everything we have done…was not to turn the Americans away, but to bring them back. Your deceit brings shame upon you and will not be tolerated by our Arab brothers."

"Our brothers do not understand that we cannot continue to live in the past."

General Al-Wadi stepped back. "Our brothers will not let your treachery go unpunished."

"They have no reason to know. I am sworn to protect Kuwait. I will do what I think is best for my county."

Al-Wadi's posture was a challenge to the authority of the Prince of Kuwait. "And I am sworn to Allah and I will do what I think is best."

Prince Al-Sabah reached beneath the folds of his robe and withdrew a pistol. His hand was steady and aim true. The bullet entered Al-Wadi's heart and he slumped to the floor.

Rayhan jumped with the sound of the gun. It happened so fast that he was stunned. "Father, what have you done?"

"He did not believe. He was more Arab than Kuwaiti. He would sacrifice our country rather than ask the Americans for help. He had become dangerous to our cause. I will miss him, but it had to be done.

Chapter 41

It was another day with no news of James. Hanna spent her time in front of the television and next to the phone; desperate for anything that would give her hope. Her mother and Mamba were in the kitchen, trying to make the day seem like any other, but she knew they alternated passing by the door and glancing in her direction; as unobtrusively as possible and still keeping an eye on her.

Hanna knew another night-long vigil, waiting for the call that never came, would be in vain. The stress on the baby couldn't be good, so she forced herself to relax. Although she told her mother she still had hope and that she was holding up well, the dark bags under her eyes and the nervous tremors of her hands said otherwise.

The ring of the phone startled her. It had never seemed so loud. She snatched it up before the first ring was complete. It was her grandfather, Ed Helton. "Hello Papa."

"Hello sweetheart. How are you?"

"Pretty good…I just wish General McLaughlin would call, but he has been out of his office for two days and nobody else will tell me a thing."

"I know, I called Senator Reynolds, and he was no help. Don't give up."

"I won't. Are you coming to the island tonight?"

"If I do, it will be late. By the way, has anybody seen DeAngelo? I will have to get him to bring me."

"Papa, we can't find Mr. DeAngelo. Nobody's seen him for two days."

Ed didn't want to spend another night in Savannah, but unless they could find DeAngelo it would be another microwave dinner. "Hanna, is your mother available?"

"Just a minute." Hanna carried the phone to her mother in the kitchen. "It's Papa. He wants to talk with you."

When Hanna handed the phone to her mother she left the kitchen and reassumed her position on the couch.

"Daddy?"

"Hello Danni, how are you doing?"

"I'm fine."

"Danni, Reverend White just purchased my stock, you can start buying the hotel stock."

"Okay, but I'm not sure the union will approve the plan."

"They are greedy men. They already own almost half the stock. Once you start buying the stock, the price will go up, and their holdings will increase. They will do it because they know Daufuskie is about the only resort still standing, and that they have the influence to get the big government conference business. You can make it happen."

Danni couldn't believe her father was so callous to discuss business when there were so many events that required their concern. "Daddy, do we have to talk about this now?"

"Danni, I understand what you're feeling, but we can't do a thing about James and our timing is critical."

~~

It's hard to say how Hanna would react, would she be more nervous or less, if she knew that half a world away a man not suited for debate or compromise, a man of honor and action, would not allow her husband, his friend, to take his last breath as a captive of cowardly terrorists.

Bill Cannon slowly inched his way up the drainage ditch that led to his target. His crawl started at midnight and he would easily be in position by 3 a.m. His approach was made more difficult by the added weight of the assault rocket launcher and M32 grenade launcher strapped to his back.

It took Bill three days to pick and assemble his team; an American, one Israeli, a Russian, a Brit, a South African, Doc Broderson for medical support and Mike DeAngelo for seaborne evacuation. It wasn't a hard thing to do if you had an unlimited bank account, and knew where to go. Bill knew exactly where to go and who to see for a list of men willing to risk their lives for money; he knew of this list because his name was on it.

To Bill's advantage, the target was built on a small knoll, and although surrounded by dozens of other houses, it commanded a complete view of all the surrounding terrain; which made it easy to identify and therefore easy to engage. The only significant defensive advantage it possessed was that it was surrounded by civilian structures; a characteristic that in other conflicts protected it from attack by Israeli aircraft or long range artillery.

The house was built in the fashion of boxes randomly stacked upon each other; one formed a tower three stories high, the rest only two. The compound was surrounded by a mortar and brick wall roughly 10 feet high. The wall provided protection from small arms fire but would not stand long even against something as simple as a .50 caliber round.

At 3 a.m. Bill would initiate the attack by launching six thermobaric grenades into the upper windows, and then his rocket at the front gate. The blast would either clear the gate or weaken it to the point where Doc Broderson and the Israeli, in the truck that would serve as a battering ram and evacuation vehicle, could smash through the gate. Bill's partner in the ditch, Snake Patterson, trailed him by 20 yards. Snake would attack the house to the southwest that served as a defensive outpost and then follow him into the house.

The South African and the Russian would serve as flank security and would attack the two houses to the east and then establish a strong point at the primary intersection leading to the target. They would prevent any reinforcements from using the roads. They would be picked up when Bill and his assault team withdrew.

Mike DeAngelo and the Brit were located on a rocky outcropping overlooking the house and their escape route, the Litani River road. They would attack the house to the northwest and provide suppressive fire for the entire operation and then launch the three Katyusha rockets into Israel as a signal for artillery support to cover the withdrawal.

The Katyusha rockets were Colonel Wetzel's idea. Wetzel could justify an artillery barrage into Lebanon, in response to a rocket attack into Israel, more easily than gaining the Minister of Defense approval to support a rescue.

Earlier in the night, Colonel Wetzel and Major General Lucas McLaughlin walked into the command post of the Israel Defense Force Northern Command. The conversation with the Commanding General took no more than 30 minutes. When the trio entered the operations center the commander presented a detailed fire support overlay to the operations officer. It didn't take long for the IDF to call forward their artillery and plot the fire missions.

The IDF Commander, Colonel Wetzel, and General McLaughlin huddled around the portable tactical computer that displayed a satellite image of southern Lebanon. They watched as Broderson's truck pulled into position. The IDF commander stared in wonder at the screen. You could count the number of men moving in each of the targeted houses, but there was no sign of Bill Cannon or his team creeping up the ditches. "I don't see your men, general. Maybe they have cancelled the mission?"

This was a logical question, but Lucas McLaughlin knew you never saw Bill Cannon when he was on the attack. "He is there. Take my word."

Lucas McLaughlin and Colonel Wetzel walked to the highest observation point on the Israeli side of the border. They looked north into the darkness of the night.

Colonel Wetzel had to ask, "Do you think he will do it?"

Lucas McLaughlin turned toward Wetzel, his silhouette barely visible in the starlight. Wetzel asked the question because it would be asked by any sane man who didn't know Bill Cannon. Lucas could only say the truth. "He'll do it."

"You have fought with Colonel Cannon?"

"Many times."

"It is suicide, this rescue. Tomorrow morning we will see his dead body and the bodies of the others on Al Jazeera TV, and you will have much to explain."

"It's not suicide. Tomorrow they will say it was murder."

There was nothing left to do but wait.

~~

Bill did not rush his preparations. His first round would be in the tallest part of the structure. That was probably an observation point and was the most likely part of the structure to be manned. His next shot would be the room directly below the OP. That room would probably be barracks or the command post. The bottom floors were protected by the wall so he would launch his remaining four rounds into the other windows. If the terrorists were using those rooms as barracks, he would kill them in their sleep.

As the seconds ticked by Bill reviewed his plan. Breach the wall within a minute, clear the bottom floors within three more, find and evacuate Madison, and be clear of the building in five. Any more time than that and Hezbollah fighters may be able to regroup and stop their escape.

With 10 seconds to go, Bill raised the M32 to his shoulder. He launched his first grenade. There was no smoke or muzzle flash to mark his position, only the soft thunk of the round leaving the launch tube.

He lowered his sights to the window below the OP and launched his second round even before the first crashed through the window and detonated. He ignored the fireball and moved his sights to the third window. He vaguely heard the explosions from grenades launched on the other houses.

At the first explosions, Doc Broderson started the engine of the truck. He was parked in the bottom of the ravine not more than a quarter a mile from the house. His night vision goggles provided all the light he needed to keep the truck on the road. Doc hoped Bill's calculations, that the rocket would destroy the gate, were correct.

After Bill's last round, he slung the M32 on his back and raised the rocket launcher. The warhead on the rocket was four times the size of the grenades and if Bill hit center mass on the gate, he was sure it would destroy any locking device. The fire from the rocket motor lit up the night. Bill followed the flight to impact—the ground shook even where Bill crouched.

Bill turned his head to see Snake Patterson approaching his position in a low run. He slid into position at Bill's side. "So far, so good, let's go."

Bill and Snake left the cover of their position at a full run; Bill on the right side of the road and Snake on the left. Something peppered Bill's legs as he ran, ricochets from his rear—someone was behind him. Bill felt his body lifted from the ground, something like a sledge hammer hit him in the back. He was spun to the right and thrown from his feet into the ditch. The depression of the ditch saved his life. As Bill gasped for breath and tried to regain his senses, the ground at the lip of the ditch erupted with bullet fragments.

Doc Broderson saw the bullets tear up the road behind Bill Cannon. The trail of tracers from a machine gun slowly gained on Bill. Doc saw the rounds impact the walls of the houses on the far side of the road and then suddenly Bill Cannon was down. There was no other option than to continue the attack. The loss of Bill Cannon would be a costly price to pay for failure.

The bullet that hit Bill first caught the M32 and then the armored vest he wore before grazing his right shoulder. It took him a moment to realize he wasn't seriously hurt. It was impossible to see where the shots were coming form, but he knew Doc Broderson would drive into the same field of fire if he wasn't stopped.

Over the radio, "Doc...Stop now! Hold your position!"

Doc slammed on the brakes and peered through the dust and smoke. There in the ditch ahead was Bill Cannon, lying on his back with his fist in the air, bullets skimming the top of the ditch. Doc grinned. "You lucky son-of-a-bitch!"

Doc heard Bill's call to Mike DeAngelo. "Mike...Mike! We're taking fire from a building on the east side of the road. Doc can't get through. You're going to have to take it out."

From his position high in the rocks, Mike focused his attention on the houses that could bring fire on Bill's position. There it was...the third house from the end, the muzzle flash of weapons. It would be a long shot, but then again the rockets didn't need absolute accuracy to be effective. He answered on the radio, "I've got 'em. Stand by."

The rocket flew true and the explosion crumbled the face of the building. Bill regained his feet and made towards the wall. To Bill's left, Snake was up and keeping pace.

At 50 yards he began to feel the heat of the fires the grenades and rockets started. He and Snake reached the wall and pressed their backs against it. As Doc's truck approached, they lobbed grenades over the wall. The explosions ended slightly before Doc's truck smashed into the gate.

Bill called to Doc, "Hit the lights!"

Snake was the demo man, and placed a charge at the base of the door leading into the house. The explosion caused the third floor, the box that served as an OP, to collapse; fine with Bill, one less threat to contend.

They fanned out in the house to search for Madison. They cleared the room with grenades and shot anything that moved. Snake found the door leading to the cell. "They're down here."

Doc was first at the stairs. Even from the top of the stairs Doc recoiled at the horrible stench of gangrene. He ignored the bile building in his stomach as he tried to find a pulse in Madison…there it was, but just barely. His bolt cutters made short work of the locks binding his hands and the collar around his throat.

As he moved to the Israeli he heard footsteps coming down the stairs. It was Bill Cannon. "Are they still alive?"

"Barely. You take Madison and I'll get this one."

Bill lifted Madison; his broken right arm dangled lifeless down Bill's back. They made their way through the smoke filled rooms to the truck. Bill dumped Madison in the bed and then helped Doc with the Israeli. Doc pulled the wounded men as far forward as possible while Bill backed the truck from the gate. Bill looked at his watch—seven minutes, two minutes too long.

Bill could see the tracers from the machine guns at the intersection guarded by the South African and the Russian. He slowed enough for the two to swing aboard. Bullets pinged through the metal cab of the truck and splintered the wooden sides of the bed. Doc looked up when he heard the distinctive sound of a bullet hitting flesh. A single round ripped through the shoulder of the Russian and then buried itself deep in the side of Snake Patterson; two men down from one round—not good. It didn't stop the others from continuing to cover their escape with a barrage of automatic fire.

~~

General McLaughlin and Colonel Wetzel watched the raid unfold on the screen. The grenades and rockets exploded as white plums of heat; the explosions were virtually simultaneous. They watched Bill and Snake leave their concealed positions and charge the house, and saw the heat signature of the machinegun that knocked Bill into the ditch. The fiery stream of the rocket Mike DeAngelo launched, pinpointed his position on the rocky crag. Colonel Wetzel described the attack with a single word. "Damn."

The fires started by the grenades and rockets did not burn as brightly as the explosions, but McLaughlin could tell they were spreading. It seemed an eternity before the small white figures of six men emerged from the burning house. McLaughlin turned to Wetzel, "They've got 'em. Put the artillery on alert."

They watched as the truck began to pull away from the building. Once the truck slowed to pick up the men at the intersection and finally made itself clear of the area they could see people begin to emerge from the surrounding houses. Bill's truck made its way to the Latani River basin before the Hezbollah fighters organized a pursuit.

The Israeli counter-battery radars picked up the launch of the Katyusha rockets and the siren familiar to all Israelis screamed a shrill warning into the night. Wetzel turned to McLaughlin, "I hope those things don't kill anybody." General McLaughlin only nodded his agreement.

They heard the order for counter-battery fire go out from the command bunker. The Latani Road was plotted by the Israeli gunners. The first salvo of eight 155mm rounds caught the pursuing force strung out on the road and eliminated a third. The second and third salvo, although not quite as effective, completely disrupted the pursuing force. Bill Cannon was clear of the target. He would be without any external support until they reached the coast.

~~

Bill turned and yelled to Doc through what remained of the rear window. "Doc, what's going on back there?"

"We've got two wounded. Neither critical at this point. I've got IVs in Madison and the Israeli. They're still touch and go."

In 20 minutes they were below the Latani dam where DeAngelo hid the inflatable Zodiac. DeAngelo pointed the bow to the open sea. He knew the ride wouldn't be pleasant for the wounded, but he didn't want to get caught on open water in the daylight so he pushed the throttle wide open. He ignored Doc's plea to slow down.

The bottom of the boat was awash with blood. At first glance there wasn't a man aboard that wasn't bleeding from some minor wound. Snake Patterson and the Russian looked pale from loss of blood. The two men in the bottom of the boat, the two prisoners, were unaware of the pounding of the waves on the hull.

Bill leaned close and sniffed of the infection in Madison's arm. "Is that gangrene I smell?"

"I'm afraid so."

"You know that arm will have to come off."

"Yes, I know."

There was nothing more they could do except wait for rescue.

Chapter 42

Hanna didn't fall asleep until well past midnight, and the ringing phone was an annoyance. She looked at the clock; not even 4 a.m. With the phone halfway to her ear she paused; whoever it was at this hour it couldn't be anything but bad news.

"Hello?"

"Hanna, this is Eric, turn on the news; there's something going on in Lebanon and Israel. I'm on my way to the studio. If I find out anything, I'll give you a call."

It wasn't the news Hanna hoped to get, but at least it wasn't the bad news she dreaded; Hanna felt a glimmer of hope. "What happened?"

"This morning, well…morning in Israel, there was an attack on the Hezbollah headquarters in Lebanon. Hezbollah, Syria, and the Lebanese government are accusing Israel of an attack across the international border. Israel denies the whole thing. It doesn't make much sense. All of Israel's forces are on their side of the border. We have reporters all over the region and they would know if Israel made an attack. Maybe the U.S. did it, but I doubt it. The fact is that somebody attacked that headquarters and the entire region is about to explode. Look, I'm in the parking lot, I'll call you once I get inside and find out more information."

Hanna and the other women rushed to the den. There was no doubt that an attack of significant magnitude had taken place. The camera accurately captured the scope of the destruction. Smoldering buildings and dead bodies littered the landscape. The obligatory film footage of children's bodies wrapped in bloody sheets being rushed to hospitals received the majority of coverage. Film coverage that looked vaguely familiar to Eric; it was the same video footage used to incite public opinion in the past, only shot from different angles. A fact Eric mentioned to the producer, which the producer promptly ignored.

The west-coast anchor announced with an appropriate amount of gravity, "A Hezbollah spokesman called this attack on a residential neighborhood as a terrorist act of aggression and the murder of innocent residents. The damage here is quite extensive, and removal of the dead and wounded is a slow and painful process.

"The Israeli Prime Minister released a statement to the press that, and I will read the statement, 'This morning at 3:10 a.m., Israeli Defense Forces deployed along the northern border of our nation responded to an unprovoked rocket attack from Hezbollah forces in Lebanon. Our response was limited in scope and appropriate.' The Israeli government released this video of the rocket attack and their response."

The video showed three faint streams of fire that were the Katyusha rockets, and then the impact of the warheads, followed shortly by the Israeli artillery response.

When the phone rang, Mamba was there to answer. It was Eric calling from the CNN headquarters in Atlanta.

Mamba put the call on speaker for all to hear. "Hanna, we're trying to confirm this before we put it on the news, but that house was where James and the Israeli soldier were being held. We think whoever attacked that house rescued them. We don't know where James is. I'll keep you posted on everything we find."

~~

Two days later, the reception for General Lucas McLaughlin's return to the Pentagon was less than cordial. The Secretary of Defense was in a foul mood, one more appropriate for the death of an American soldier, rather than a successful rescue.

"What the hell were you doing in Israel?"

The Secretary's delicate facial features, more fitting for the political circles in Washington than the hardened soldiers of the institution he now led, always brought out the worst in Lucas McLaughlin. He didn't trust the Secretary any more than he would any politician who would sacrifice his moral position to further a political goal. McLaughlin wasn't about to give the Secretary any more rope to hang him than was absolutely necessary.

"I was on vacation. I went to see the holy sites in Jerusalem."

"Yeah, right! What did you have to do with that fiasco in Lebanon?"

"I didn't know we had any operations going on in Lebanon."

"Don't play cute with me General. I'll have you in a court-martial so fast it will make your head spin."

"That should be a real big hit on the news—Secretary of Defense court-martials Army General Officer for rescuing a kidnapped American soldier."

"What happens to you may not be up to me. Both the President and the Secretary of State are mad as hell. What am I supposed to tell them?"

"Why don't you tell them that somebody did what we should have done a week ago. Tell them they should thank whoever rescued Major Madison."

The Secretary of Defense wasn't impressed with McLaughlin's appreciation for a job well done. His reply was filled with rancor.

"Whoever rescued Major Madison may have started World War III. The Syrians are mobilizing and Iran and Egypt have crossed the Suez, OPEC is threatening to shut off our oil! There's a lot more to international negotiations than running around blowing up buildings. The Secretary of State told me she was near an agreement with the Palestinian Authority to negotiate Madison's release."

McLaughlin was pretty sure the Secretary understood the difference between the Palestinian Authority in Jerusalem and Hezbollah in Lebanon, but even if the Secretary of State was nearing any sort of deal for Madison's release, she was taking the horse the long way around the barn to get to the stall.

"Mr. Secretary, Major Madison was being held by Hezbollah, not the Palestinian Authority. All the Secretary of State would have negotiated was the return of his dead body."

"General McLaughlin, I'm not sure you understand the delicate nature of our policies in the Middle East. The President is walking on egg shells since that incident in the Persian Gulf. He is trying to improve relations in the area—not destroy them. This raid makes it look like his promise of new relationships with the Arab Nations was nothing but the same old policies of his predecessors. The President wants to know who conducted this operation."

"Mr. Secretary, with all due respect, the President is getting pushed all over the map in the Middle East. As far as who did this, I already told you I wasn't on the raid. It could have been anybody."

The little sneer on the Secretary's face reminded Lucas of the Cheshire cat in Alice in Wonderland. He almost purred his question. "You served with Colonel Bill Cannon, didn't you?"

Where was the Secretary going with this question? "Yes I did. A fine officer."

"Our attaché in Kuwait said that Colonel Cannon disappeared from his office in the Prince's palace right after Madison was kidnapped. Do you know anything about that?"

"Colonel Cannon retired some years ago. His whereabouts mean nothing to me."

Lucas McLaughlin felt like knocking the sneer off the Secretary's face when he said, "We're going to find out who made that rescue."

"Mr. Secretary, you said it yourself; the entire Middle East is on the brink of war. Why waste any time or effort trying to find out who rescued Major Madison?" Lucas paused for effect, "Or does the President plan to give Hezbollah another hostage since the one they had got away?"

~~

Since her return from Daufuskie Island, Angelina had been filled with a sense of despair. Her investigation was going to destroy the future she hoped to share with Eric Brown. She declined Eric's invitation to dinner, telling him she wasn't feeling well, and no, there was nothing he needed to do. She just needed rest.

She was relieved Eric didn't mention her interview with Mrs. Walton. She knew it would only be a matter of time before Mrs. Walton would tell Eric of the things she had learned about his father and friends. How would Eric respond when he learned his father killed Bomani Thomas on orders from Steve Thunder? How would he react when he learned his father was directly involved in the drug deal? There was little wonder why Angelina wanted to avoid the confrontation with Eric.

There still remained the questions of the people involved. Obviously, she had not uncovered the complete cast of characters. Somebody other than Steve Thunder and John Brown Jackson killed Tyrell Biggs, the drug lord in Atlanta, his assistant Brownie, and the men that broke into the Helton house on Daufuskie. They were killed after the deaths of Thunder and Jackson.

Angelina forced herself to go back to the basics of the investigation. She remembered her first day in the academy. Her instructor wrote on the blackboard, "Who, what, when, where, why?" He said over and over again through the years, "Answer these questions and you can solve any case."

336

Angelina had a pretty good idea how to answer what, when, and where, but the motive, the why, she hadn't ever given much thought. Why would anybody get involved in drugs? The obvious answer is money. Okay, if money was the motive behind the drugs then it should be pretty easy to check the financials of everyone involved. The e-mail to Director Jefferson requesting a Federal Warrant to review the tax returns and bank accounts of Ed Helton, the Waltons, and Steve Thunder was simple to write. She then added Buford Long and John Roger "Doc" Broderson as an afterthought. Getting her boss to approve such a request was probably a pipe dream.

Angelina received two nice surprises that afternoon. The first was the e-mail reply from her boss, "I'll get you the warrants, but you are wasting your time—you won't find anything." The second was a phone call from Eric.

"We're going out to celebrate. Where do you want to go for dinner?"

Eric was obviously excited and happy about something. "What are we going to celebrate?"

"You haven't been watching the news? Jimmy Madison, Hanna's husband was rescued! Nobody here at the station give's a rat's ass, but I want to celebrate. How about it? You up for dinner and a few drinks?"

Eric's attitude was infectious and Angelina accepted the invitation. She had to face him eventually. Maybe she could explain things on her terms before Danni Walton found the time to call him. Maybe there was still time to salvage their relationship. Eventually she knew Eric would have to choose between her and the future they may have, and his friends. How many times had that challenge been laid before a prospective mate? Angelina grinned; probably in every relationship throughout history.

Over dinner, Eric told her everything he knew of the rescue. How, at 3 a.m. the five houses were attacked simultaneously. How the people who rescued James and the Israeli soldier pulled them from a building that was burning to the ground, and how the Israeli artillery barrage covered their retreat. The genuine excitement of Eric began to soften Angelina's worry about her discussion with Danni Walton.

After Eric completed his narration and while he ordered another round of drinks, Angelina asked, "If the United States or Israel didn't do it, who did?"

337

"Our Pentagon reporter said the Secretary of Defense dropped Bill Cannon's name."

Angelina vaguely recalled the name. "Is that the same Bill Cannon that worked with your father? Why would the Secretary of Defense put out a rumor like that?"

"Colonel Cannon isn't exactly liked up in Washington."

"Eric, how come I've never met Colonel Cannon?"

"He's been working in Kuwait. He's a special advisor to the Prince of Kuwait—they're good friends. He has been in Kuwait since we met."

"Eric, even if he could do something like that, why would he?"

Eric gave a little grin as if he was about to reveal a juicy piece of gossip. "I think he and Mrs. Walton are an item. He would do it for Danni Walton."

Colonel Bill Cannon would do something this dangerous for Danni Walton? The thought flashed through Angelina's mind like an electric spark. If he would do this, then what else was he capable of doing? Was Bill Cannon the missing piece of her puzzle? It took restraint for Angelina to focus on the discussion with Eric.

She planned to use this night to discuss with Eric the things she found out about his father, but now there was another lead to follow. She could allow herself a reprieve from the confrontation with Eric and enjoy the night.

Once she allowed herself to distance herself from the investigation the conversations became more pleasing and soothing. Angelina came to realize Eric was her only release from the lonely life of an investigator. The biggest surprise of the night was when Eric started to casually discuss the future, and the questions gave her the strong sense that he was talking about a future with her. Why now? This just added more confusion to the decisions she knew she must make.

~~

William Jefferson was called to the Attorney General's office the following morning. The purpose was not relayed to him. After pleasant greetings and polite but meaningless banter, the Attorney General asked about the ongoing investigations in Georgia. It was a strange request since Jefferson provided the Attorney General a weekly report on the very subject. The real purpose of the meeting was revealed in his next question.

"The investigator we have in Georgia, she is relatively young." It was a statement not a question.

"Is she competent?"

"Yes sir, very much so. She's doing a great job."

"I have a project that will require some discretion. If she is interested is going straight to the top, then this should do it for her."

What exactly was the Attorney General insinuating? "Well, sir, from what I know of Ms. Sanchez, she should be able to handle just about anything you send her way. What's the project?"

The Attorney General sat behind his desk. "The President is mad as hell about that thing in Lebanon. He's trying to improve relations with the Arab world and we have some loose cannon running around shooting up innocent civilians. The President sets foreign policy, not some out-of-control nut. Everything the President has worked for is on the brink of collapse, and all because of this unnecessary act of violence.

"The Secretary of Defense thinks that a man named Bill Cannon had a hand in it. Cannon was working in Kuwait on security issues, but disappeared right after Major Madison was kidnapped. Cannon lives in Georgia, somewhere on the coast. So does Major Madison. I want Sanchez to find out everything she can about this Cannon character."

William Jefferson wondered why the United States Attorney General would want to investigate Bill Cannon on such a vague accusation by the Secretary of Defense. For that matter, why would the Secretary of Defense even suggest Bill Cannon had anything to do with the rescue?

"Sir, why are we going to investigate this thing?"

"Mr. Jefferson, the President said we are, 'determined to act boldly and collectively on behalf of justice at home and abroad.' If Colonel Cannon was foolish enough to make an armed attack on foreign soil, in a nation we have an extradition treaty with, then he should be prepared to face the consequences. The President is trying to establish an international framework to combat extremism within the rule of law. We will lead by example in this area. If we allow Americans to go around shooting up peaceful neighborhoods only two things can happen. First, we can only expect more attacks on our institutions and our citizens, and second, the President will lose credibility with those that mistrust us the most."

This line of reasoning was incredulous to Jefferson. "Sir, assuming Colonel Cannon had anything to do with that rescue is pure

339

speculation at this point; we have no grounds to conduct an investigation."

"Mr. Jefferson, look at this situation from a global perspective. If a foreign terrorist group made such an attack in the United States, and we requested information from their government, would we not expect their full cooperation and assistance? I see no reason why we shouldn't be prepared to do the same."

It seemed to Jefferson the Attorney General was jumping the gun. "Have we received any such request?"

The Attorney General sat down at his desk as if he no longer had time for the discussion. "Not yet."

Not yet. Just the way the Attorney General spoke led Jefferson to believe the request would be forthcoming. Would that request be the result of an investigation by the Lebanon government, or would it be the result of some State Department back-channel message naming Cannon as a suspect? Would the President go that far to avenge an insult many years ago?

"Sir, that raid was not against the government of Lebanon, but against a known terrorist organization that has become so powerful that the government can't throw them out of the country. Lebanon should be apologizing to us for their failure to protect American citizens from a terrorist organization they allow to operate in their country. What did Lebanon do to free Madison? I'll tell you what they did; they did nothing."

"Mr. Jefferson, the State Department was in the process of drafting a request to Lebanon to assist in the release of Madison. Colonel Cannon's actions have damaged the credibility of the United States."

Jefferson couldn't believe it; the Attorney General was prepared to extradite an America citizen as a token to the new global view of the administration. "Sir, I'm not sure Americans would go for turning over someone that most would consider a hero. I don't think Congress would go for it either."

The Attorney General was no longer in a mood to debate. "Jefferson, the world must stand together to demonstrate that international law is not an empty promise, and that treaties will be enforced. We will do our part. You don't worry about the Congress. The President can handle them. As for the American people, they are for the President; they believe what he tells them to believe."

340

The Attorney General apparently had a weak understanding of the phrase innocent until proven guilty. What in the hell was happening?

Chapter 43

The Georgia State Capital was directly across the street from Angelina's office, and the barricades were up when she arrived. The purpose of the protest didn't cross her mind; there were so many of late that one more carried little significance. Yesterday it was the cost of living and the high prices caused by creeping inflation; and what was the government going to do about it? The day before it was late unemployment checks; today it was probably going to be the lack of gas; and what was the government going to do about it?

The crowds usually gathered just before noon. The chants of the protesters rarely reached her window. Today they were louder than usual, but she didn't really notice, engaged as she was in the bank statements in front of her.

Jefferson was right; she hadn't found a thing. Helton, Walton, Doc Broderson, Steve Thunder, even Buford Long were all clean as a whistle. She found what she expected. Ed Helton was rich, not obscenely so, but he was a smart businessman and very conservative and had amassed a small fortune over the years.

Danni Walton was comfortable and the life insurance check she received on her husband's death wasn't nearly as much as Angelina would have expected. Everybody else lived a normal existence with normal bank accounts and well within their means. Another dead end and it caused her to go to the window overlooking the street to clear her mind and contemplate her next move.

She saw the whole thing unfold. How she picked out the shooter in the seething crowd was a mystery to her, but she saw it all. Maybe it was the Haitian tee-shirt and dreadlocks protruding from the rainbow colored knit stocking that drew her attention, but it was like she was 5 feet not 100 feet away.

The police and metal barricades were holding their own against the growing crowd. As quietly and unobtrusively as they could the police were reinforcing their lines with reserve officers, but any more protesters and the police would start pushing back. Angelina saw 'rainbow hat' pull the pistol from his pants and hold it down to his side.

He moved next to the wall of protesters and had maybe two bodies between him and the police line. Angelina saw the gun snake between the bodies of protesters. Angelina yelled and beat on the glass window to warn the officers, but no one looked. She frantically searched for a handle to open the window, but these windows were bullet proof and bomb resistant, and she was trapped inside.

She couldn't hear the shot, but she did see the officer's legs crumble and he fell to the ground. The crowd didn't flee in panic. The sound of the gun only served as a trigger for their anger to be released upon the symbol of all their troubles, and they overwhelmed the barricades and swarmed over the police.

She saw 'rainbow hat' move south on Washington Street, forcing his way through the crowd, against the flow of people. She didn't hesitate. She didn't wait for the elevator and ran down the stairs. If she used the loading dock entrance maybe she could catch him before he crossed under the interstate into the area of Atlanta where small businesses once thrived, but were now only run down shells of a once proud heritage.

She was breathing hard when she finally made it to the underpass. Sixteen lanes of traffic above her echoed off the steel and concrete, but there was no sign of the man with the hat. Maybe he had discarded it. Angelina ran to the east side of the underpass…nothing. She watched the people closely hoping that they could hold a clue to where a man trying to hide may have passed, but they revealed nothing. Maybe the shooter didn't come this way, maybe he continued south along Washington.

Angelina ran the three blocks up the hills leading back to the capital and turned southwest on Washington Street. The teargas used at the capital drifted down the street and stung her eyes and made her nose run. This was hopeless. Washington Street ran southwest and under the complicated interchange of three converging interstates, I-20, I-75, and I-85. Angelina never ventured here on foot. She passed by in her car many times, and marveled at the number of cardboard structures and piles of dirty blankets that staked out squatters rights to the dry spots for Atlanta's homeless. It was alien territory.

She made her way over the guardrail and through the empty liquor bottles, needles, and filth into the darker recess of the overpasses. There, up ahead, a glimpse of color. The Glock was out of the holster and at her side as she worked from piling to piling to get closer to the group of men sharing a bottle. Stepping from behind a concrete piling,

Angelina raised the Glock and walked boldly into the group. The rainbow hat was the first to take notice.

"You sir, are under arrest." Her voice didn't waiver, neither did the Glock. "Get your hands up and get on your knees. The rest of you move away."

Rainbow's hand moved close to his belly, where Angelina saw him hide his weapon. "One more inch and I shoot. Get your hands up and get down on your knees, or I will shoot you right here like you just did that police officer."

Rainbow moved his hands away from his shirt, but made no move to get down. "This ain't no place for a girl. You're in way over your head. You can't be taking me out of here without no help."

She caught the movement in the corner of her eye, but was not ready for the brick that was thrown from almost behind her. White light flashed in her eyes and she staggered and fell to her knees. She could feel the blood from the cut above her ear. Her vision was blurred and she could barely make out the figures to her front, but what she saw was enough. Rainbow had his gun pointing directly at her. He was going to shoot her.

They fired almost simultaneously. Angelina felt the bullet rip into her ribs. As she fell to the pavement, she hoped someone would call her mother.

~~

When the medic arrived, Sanchez was lying in a growing pool of blood. He ripped open her shirt...no vest and no back-up, brave but foolish decisions. The bullet hit the ribs below the heart, was deflected along the rib cage and entered her arm just above the elbow. He hoped the blood was from the ulnar collateral artery and not the main artery of the arm. He could pinch off the ulnar artery and stem the flow.

"Sanchez...wake up. Sanchez...wake up." The wound to her head concerned him now. The brick could have caused a brain hemorrhage.

Angelina opened her eyes and focused on the man above her. "Doc, is that you?"

Doc leaned over his patient and watched as her eyes focused on his face. "Angelina, you've been shot. I stopped the bleeding, but I am concerned about the wound to your head."

Doc pulled a small light from his kit. "Follow this light with your eyes."

Angelina did as requested. The danger was over. She would have a hell of a headache in the morning, but the blow to the head was probably nothing more than a concussion.

Angelina remembered what happened. "Doc, there was a man…in a rainbow hat…he shot the officer at the capital. Did he get away?"

Doc looked over to the man in the rainbow hat, lying still in his own blood. "No, he didn't get away. We got him."

It was hard to explain, but Angelina felt completely safe with Doc hovering over her. She wanted to thank him and when she started to do so it was then that Angelina noticed the burned and scabbed face above her. "Doc, what happened to your face?"

Only a woman would notice and only a woman would be so blunt as to ask. The burns from the fires in Lebanon, and the cuts from the chips of rocks from the bullets fired at him had not completely healed. "I'll tell you later. Now I think we should get you to the hospital and get you stitched up properly."

Doc held her hand the entire way to the ambulance.

~~

Waking from a deep sleep, one so deep you never dream, is slow and can be confusing. It was the bright lights Angelina first noticed - even before she opened her eyes. The comforting soft beep of something to her right was the first sound she recognized. Through blurred vision she saw a splash of color and a sense of panic enveloped her. The beep grew louder and faster. The colors she saw were the colors of the rainbow hat! She felt a warm gentle hand on her arm, "Miss Sanchez, are you awake?"

Angelina struggled to shake off the fog that clouded her vision. She blinked and squinted and finally the person standing over her came into focus. It was a nurse in the surgical green gown of the operating room. "How do you feel Miss Sanchez?"

The drugs from surgery still numbing her pain, Angelina answered truthfully. "I feel fine. What did you do to me?"

The nurse was busy monitoring the equipment and making notes in the chart she carried, but took time to answer.

"Three broken ribs and a broken arm, and we removed a bullet from your arm, topped you off with about five units of blood and then stitched you up. You'll be out of action for a while, but there is no permanent damage. You were lucky."

Angelina looked left and her arm was bundled in white bandages over a hard cast from her hand to her armpit. With her good arm, she raised the sheets and noticed the neat wrappings around her ribs. "When can I get out?"

The nurse laughed. "Not for a couple of days at least…we need to keep a close eye on the arm and make sure you don't get an infection."

Thirty minutes out of surgery and already Angelina didn't like the confining walls of her room. She looked to the foot of her bed and noticed the flowers that only moments ago caused her some panic.

"Who sent those?"

The nurse walked over to the multiple arrangements. "Atlanta PD sent the big one…" she narrated as she walked down the row, "these are from Ed Helton and Danni Walton, these are from Mike DeAngelo and Doc Broderson…Doc's the one who probably saved your life, and these red roses are from Eric Brown." The nurse paused before continuing, "He's better looking in person." The nurse turned to Angelina and smiled, "Lucky girl."

Angelina was happy that Eric sent her flowers, but wished he was here. "Has Eric been here?" She hoped she meant more to him than a simple arrangement of flowers, even though he did send roses.

"He's been in the waiting room all day. All the nurses are just giddy about it. He must have signed a hundred surgical gowns. He had to get back to work, but said he'll be back as soon as possible. You do have another visitor, a Mr. Jefferson. He flew down from Washington. Once we get you cleaned up, I'll let him come in for a visit. Do you feel up to it?"

What was Jefferson doing here? The beeping of the monitor showed her concern. Was she in trouble? "I guess so. I might as well finish it."

The nurse left when Jefferson entered the room and warned her boss not to upset the patient. Jefferson carried a folder at least an inch thick. A folder he attempted to straighten and close as he walked up to her bedside.

"Sanchez, I've read the police report. I thought we trained you better than trying to arrest dangerous suspects on your own. I'm proud

346

of you, what you did was very brave, but next time I wish you would call for backup."

Angelina saw the smile on Jefferson's face. It was a gentle side of her boss that she always knew he possessed, but rarely showed. "I know. Next time I will. Is that the police report?"

Jefferson pulled a chair next to the bed. He placed the closed report on the bed near her feet.

"No, this is a report on some banking irregularities; nothing to do with you. What is the status of your investigations?"

"Which one?"

"The bank files."

Angelina sighed. "I found nothing, you were right. There's nothing in any of the records that looks out of the ordinary. I can't put it all together. There's a missing piece out there, I just haven't found it."

"Sanchez, that Eric Brown; is he the one who sent you the water lilies?"

Angelina knew she blushed when her boss mentioned the water lilies. That seemed so long ago. "Yes it is."

"I mentioned to him that you get 45 days convalescent leave, and that you would either have to go home or come to Washington for care. He offered to let you stay with his family on Daufuskie."

Angelina almost laughed. Moving to Daufuskie was probably the last thing Danni Walton would allow. "I don't know if I would be welcome on Daufuskie." She then relayed the conversation she had with Danni Walton about her husband. William Jefferson listened in silence.

"Well, it's your choice, but it would help."

That statement puzzled Angelina. "Help with what?"

Jefferson pulled his chair closer, "Do you know who Colonel Bill Cannon is?"

"I know of him, but have never met him. I know he's friends with Eric."

"The attorney general suspects he was involved in the rescue of Major Madison. He wants us to start an investigation on him. If you're on the case, I wouldn't have to send anyone else down here."

What was going on in the Justice Department? "Why would the attorney general investigate Bill Cannon?"

"I think he wants to build a case and extradite him to Lebanon."

"Good Lord, why would he do that?"

Jefferson shrugged his shoulders. "To get closer to the Arab states, trade him for oil - so to speak."

Angelina felt more than heard the concern, or was it frustration, in Jefferson's voice. Jefferson picked up his report and turned back to her at the door.

"You can take a couple of days to think it over. Don't discuss this with anyone else...not with anybody in the Justice Department, the FBI, or DOD. This is just between you and me. If anybody asks you about it, tell them to discuss it with me. Oh, and Sanchez, no written records on this one. I'll be in touch. Heal up fast and stay safe. If you need anything, don't hesitate to call me."

~~

The Israeli doctor, blood still showing on his surgical gown sat down next to Bill Cannon.

"I think he'll live. We had to take his arm. We can't do anything about his eye or the right side of his face. We grafted skin from his leg to cover the bone. Our biggest concern is the infections. We've pumping him full of antibiotics."

"When can I see him?"

"He's in recovery now. They will come and get you when they clean him up."

"When can he be moved?"

"The Minister of Defense wants him out of Israel as soon as possible. As soon as we get his infection under control, you are going to have to get him out of the country."

The doctor stood to leave. "The family of the Israeli soldier you rescued asked me to thank you. We're going to have hell to pay, but you did the right thing. God bless you and good luck."

Madison looked more like a mummy than a human being. Bill leaned close to his ear. "James, can you hear me, it's Bill Cannon."

Bill saw the left eye flutter and open. James couldn't turn his head. "Yes, I can hear you. Where am I?"

"You're in an Israeli hospital."

It took a moment for James to arrange his thoughts. "Has anybody called Hanna?"

"No, we can't do that. The Israeli government doesn't want anybody to know you're here. We can't call her until you are out of the country. As soon as you're able to be moved, I'm going to find a way to get out of the country without being seen. Once we're out, we can call."

"Bill, what happened to the soldier who was with me? Did he make it out?"

"Yes he did."

"Bill, did you do it?"

"Do what?"

"Get me out."

"Jimmy, you're out. How you got out shouldn't matter. Let's just leave it at that."

"I understand."

James struggled to remember that dark room of his prison, and the words spoken by his captor. "Bill, one of the men who held us, he said America would burn in the fires of hell. He laughed when he said my wife would burn with the rest..."

~~

During General Lucas McLaughlin's military career he had received many midnight phone calls, but none as ominous as the one that came at 3 a.m.

"Lucas, this is Bill Cannon. Listen carefully; I don't know how good this connection is and my battery is running low." Lucas could hear the wind and the rumble of a moving vehicle in the background. "They have a nuke in the States. The target is Washington. I don't know when it got there, or where it is now, but the information is solid."

"Christ Bill, this isn't a secure line! This isn't the kind of information we can discuss in the clear."

"Lucas, I don't have a secure line. I got the information from Madison."

"Bill, where are you?"

"Israel. Can you arrange a transport?"

"Go charge your phone and wait for instructions."

349

Lucas called the emergency operations center at the Pentagon. A simple code word started the notification of the highest officials in the government. Within an hour he was at the podium deep beneath the Pentagon.

The White House Chief of Staff chaired the briefing. The information was greeted with stoic silence until the Secretary of Defense raised the question. "How reliable is the source."

Lucas answered, "Colonel Bill Cannon reported it. He got it directly from Major James Madison."

~~

Doc Broderson scolded Angelina as he pushed the wheelchair from the hospital. "I know all you Feds think you can't be killed, but if you ever do something like that again you may bleed out before anybody can get to you."

Angelina accepted the reprimand; she knew her lone pursuit of the rainbow man was against all her training. "I know. It won't happen again. Thank you for saving me."

Doc expertly maneuvered the wheelchair down the hall, taking care not to bump her protruding arm into the chairs, beds, or carts that blocked their path. Her ribs hurt more than her arm, but the two were connected and she winced at every near miss. Doc's face was almost completely healed, but not enough for Angelina not to ask. "You never told me what happened to your face."

Doc directed his attention to avoiding the obstacles and didn't look at her when he answered. "Hunting accident, well, not a hunting accident, but when I was hunting I didn't clear enough brush from around my fire, and the fire got out of the pit. It was a mother to extinguish."

"Is that what you were doing for the last couple of weeks, hunting?"

Doc slowed the pace, "Yep, I didn't get anything, though. I'm not much of a hunter."

"Are you taking me to Daufuskie?"

"I'm taking you to Savannah. DeAngelo will take you to Daufuskie. Mrs. Walton will meet you on the pier. They're all set up for you. Eric said he will be down this weekend."

Angelina didn't know what she should be feeling. The invitation to let her convalesce at the Helton residence was genuine, but her

350

conscience told her that she was going to Daufuskie under false pretenses. It wasn't a good feeling at all. Doc must have read the concern on her face.

"Miss Sanchez, Danni Walton would not have extended the invitation if she didn't want you there. Don't worry, you'll do just fine." What did Doc know?

As they made their way to the loading dock Doc asked, "Would you rather ride up front or in the back?"

"I think I would like to ride up front with you if you don't mind."

Doc grinned, "No, I don't mind. That's better for me, I won't have to move any stuff around."

Doc helped her into the cab. She could prop her arm against the back of the driver's seat. As she was finding the most comfortable position she glanced to the back of the ambulance. Loaded to the rafters, so to speak, boxes and boxes of food; canned vegetable of all sorts, canned meats, juices, and medical supplies. "Good Lord Doc, what are you doing with all this?"

"Ed Helton asked me to bring a load of stuff down. You can't get anything in Savannah, so I went to the military commissary and loaded up. I don't think you'll go hungry."

Angelina laughed, "I hope they don't think I eat that much."

The drive out of Atlanta was under police escort, compliments of the Chief of Police. Their drive to Savannah was pleasant and unhurried. They talked about the shooting…the police officer was recovering nicely, and the constant protests, now a daily event at the capital. They talked about Eric, and Doc wanted to know if her intentions were honorable. Angelina laughed and expertly avoided the questions of which Doc seemed to have an endless supply. They talked about the economy and the rising unemployment and the oil embargo and the price of gas. And they talked about the fighting in Israel and the Middle East. As casually as she could Angelina asked, "Bill Cannon is over there, isn't he?"

Doc didn't slow the ambulance, but something had changed in the truck. "Yes…yes he is."

"Do you worry about him?"

Doc thought about the question before he answered. "There aren't many of us left. I would hate to lose him. He's a good man...the best."

"When was the last time you talked with him?"

"Oh, a while back; before he went to Kuwait."

"Why didn't he come back with you?"

Doc turned his head and gave her a mystified look. "What?"

"Why didn't he come back with you?"

"What in the hell are you talking about?"

Doc hadn't taken the bait. She didn't really expect that he would. "Nothing, what I meant to say was Eric told me he thinks Bill Cannon is in love with Mrs. Walton, why doesn't he come back home?"

Doc turned his head back to the road and gave a knowing little laugh. "Everybody knows those two are in love...except for those two. I guess they're both afraid to be the one to say it first. Who knows, love is a goofy thing." Doc turned and looked at Angelina. "Just look at your relationship with Eric."

Before long they were at the pier in Savannah. Angelina supervised the loading of the boat from a comfortable bench. The two men seemed to enjoy the effort of tossing the cases, first from the back of the ambulance to a stack on the pier, and then from the pier to the boat. When Doc bid them farewell, Mike DeAngelo helped her to a comfortable seat in the cabin next to the helm.

"You don't worry about a thing, Miss Sanchez. Eric told me to take good care of you. We've got calm seas and I'll take it slow, if you need anything, just yell."

DeAngelo loosened the bow line and let the bow of the ship turn with the river current before he eased into the river. Angelina had never seen River Street from the water and DeAngelo kept up a running commentary of the historic sites.

When Savannah was to their stern Angelina asked, "The last time you took me to Daufuskie I couldn't get in touch with you for the return trip. Where did you go?"

"Fishing."

That's it? Fishing? That was Mike DeAngelo's only answer for his disappearance for two weeks? She didn't expect anything more.

When they finally docked at the pier on Daufuskie, Mrs. Walton, Hanna, Mamba, and the young man from the hotel met her on the dock. Angelina couldn't really explain why she felt the way she did, but it felt like she was coming home.

Chapter 44

Ken Carson had never been airsick his entire life, but here he was puking his guts out in the small lavatory of the Lear Jet, and his briefcase only made the process of cleaning up more difficult. It couldn't be anything he ate because he hadn't eaten more than a few bites since yesterday afternoon. It had to be nerves.

He wondered if the nerves were caused by the anticipation of the Vegas trip or the money he would make, or were they nerves that he was risking his entire fortune on a single roll of the dice; or was he more worried that Rachael would check their safe deposit box and discover her diamonds were missing?

He told himself that this would be his last syndicate play. After this, he would take his profits and retire to an Island in the Caribbean; which island he wasn't sure, but this investment would end it. Still he wondered why he was no nervous.

Maybe it was the menacing guard at the forward end of the cabin. The way he kept looking at Ken and the others; as if the barrel-chested man expected one of them to attack the cockpit or try to grab one of the other three briefcases all stuffed with money. The guard could barely speak English for God's sake; Ken thought he was either German or Swiss. The compact machine gun, obvious under his coat, and the armored vest under his shirt only added to Ken's discomfort. You would think the Cartel would at least hire an English speaking guard.

Ken, Hans Dieter, and Jerry Evans boarded the jet this morning at 7 a.m. at Macon, Georgia and the only stop was in Dallas to pick up the Texas oil man, Henry Dobson. Ken remembered Dobson from the first meeting on the yacht. Maybe it was the cowboy hat, or the silver belt buckle, or the snake skin boots, but unlike the meeting on the yacht where the big Texan seemed inviting, now Ken sensed Dobson could be trouble.

Dieter, Jerry, and Dobson huddled around one of the executive tables. Their conversations tended to exclude Ken. That was fine with Ken because he was more concerned with the queasy feeling in his stomach than making pointless conversation.

They would land at Henderson Executive Airport south of Las Vegas. The Cartel never used the large commercial airports; the security was never sufficient to protect the huge amounts of cash the cartel members brought to the bids. The arrivals of the syndicates were staggered and each syndicate was placed in different hotels to protect the identities of the members. Ken's syndicate was placed on the floor just below the penthouse of a golf resort 30 miles into the desert. Two guards patrolled the hall to keep any nosy guests away.

Ken would need a market price on his diamonds. Once he was settled in his room the Cartel sent an appraiser to price the stones. For the first time the entire syndicate would meet to discuss the cartel's investment proposals and their strategy.

At 10 p.m. they would be transported to the bid site, location undisclosed, and arrivals staggered for security purposes. Bidding would conclude at 1 a.m. and the members could enjoy the Vegas night life or return to the hotels. Their departure flight was scheduled for 7 a.m.

The syndicate meeting was a strange affair. Each member had his own agenda, but understood there was strength in their collective bids. It was like eight chefs baking the same cake with each controlling key ingredients. Sometimes it worked out; other times it did not. One member holding back could cause the cake to fall and tonight it was the oil man from Texas, Henry Dobson.

Of the four investments up for bid: the production of the latest flu vaccine—the project Hans Dieter led Ken to believe was a sure thing, drilling for oil in Venezuela, a new casino in Rio de Janeiro, and a diamond processing plant for the UNITA (National Union for the Total Independence of Angola) rebels in Angola, and Henry Dobson had the most money to invest and favored the flu vaccine the least.

Hans Dieter took the lead in trying to change Dobson's mind.

"God damn it Hank, I thought we were in agreement we would try and tap out on the French deal. You can't pull your support on us now."

"That was until Chavez decided he was going to put down more wells. I don't know shit about flu vaccines. I know a lot about oil and I've made a killing on Chavez."

"Hank, the flu vaccine is the quickest turn-around for our money. If the French firm owns the complete rights every nation in the world will be beating down their door. You put your money in Venezuela you won't recover it for years. We should double our investment within a week of the first flu outbreak anywhere in the world, and everything after that will be pure profit. Just think, on a $100 million dollar investment we will earn $500 million within a year. A lot of places can drill for oil, but only the French will own the rights to the flu vaccine."

All Henry Dobson said was, "I'll think about it."

Ken contributed little to the discussions when the syndicate started to put together the collective bid. Ken was almost embarrassed to add his $12 million to the pool. Henry Dobson put $250 million in Venezuela Oil and $50 million each in the diamonds and casino and would consider $10 million in the flu vaccine depending on how the other biddings went, and when the flu was offered. He made no promises and indicated his priority was oil.

Others in the group followed Dobson. The Canadian member put $100 million with Dobson's bid and even Hans Dieter followed suit. By the time the syndicate completed their planning they had $750 million in Chavez Oil, $350 million earmarked for the diamond project, $300 million for the casino, and only $70 million earmarked for the flu vaccine, but Ken's $12 million was the high bid in their group.

When they were done and waiting for transport to the bid site Ken leaned over to Jerry. "I'm almost embarrassed that my contribution is so little. Where do these guys get all their money?"

Jerry looked to Ken and said, "I wouldn't worry about it. A lot of these guys started out small just like you; they've been at it a lot longer than you have. You stick with it and you'll get there."

"How solid are these bid projections?"

"They're pretty solid. That doesn't mean someone won't change his mind at the last minute, but usually they won't change much unless another group slams a bid and closes everybody else out. It can be interesting."

The trip to the bid location was executed with precision. More black suits, more concealed machine guns, and everything done quickly. The guards took them as a group down the service elevator. Two stretch limos carried the syndicate with an armed driver and a shotgun man in each vehicle. Two midnight-black armored SUVs flanked the limos and they made good time on almost deserted highways around the bright lights of the Vegas Strip.

Ken turned to Hans. "Where do you think we are headed?"

Hans looked out the front window of the limo. "It looks like we are headed to one of the smaller casinos in the older part of town. We

356

have used the casinos before. It's perfect. It's in a quite part of the town and totally secure, and limos pulling up to the back entrance never get much attention."

Ken watched as their convoy pulled to a stop on a subtle rise overlooking the back entrance to a small casino. In the early 50's and through the 60's, the casino was a hot spot on the old Vegas Strip, but now it was dwarfed by the modern giants near the airport. Only one small light above the rear entrance pierced the darkness. Ken could see the taillights of a convoy similar to theirs unloading passengers. They were too far away to identify any of the people. The passengers didn't hesitate once the vehicle doors opened. When the convoy pulled away, Ken wondered why their vehicles didn't move.

His silent question was answered when a green light flashed in their directions and only then did the vehicles start to move. He heard the driver of his vehicle report over his radio, "This is car 2, all clear here." The driver turned to address the passengers.

"Everything is ready for you. When we pull up to the door wait for the guard to open the door. Proceed directly into the building. Keep your head down and don't look around. Do not leave anything in the vehicle. You will be picked up in this same manner at the conclusion of the meeting."

They pulled up to the single door and when the guard opened the car door the group quickly entered the building. Once inside, they were in a well-lit hall that appeared to be built into the shape of a gently curving semi-circle. The guard directed Ken and the group to the left. Another guard, about thirty yards down the hall stood at the open door that led into a well appointed room with a heavy curtain at the far end. In the rear of the room was a well stocked standing bar and leather chairs gathered around a coffee table full of all sorts of delightful appetizers. The front of the room, the part closer to the heavy curtain, was more business-like. Eight chairs were evenly spaced on the near side of a long conference table.

Ken turned to Hans, "What kind of place is this?"

"At one time this was the ballroom for the casino upstairs. When the big casinos moved near the airport they converted it to a strip club, more accurately a sex club. When they open the curtains you will see the stage where the girls danced. These rooms were used to entertain the high rollers. When the city council made the hookers move out of town, it fell into disuse. This is the second time the Cartel has used it for a bid."

When all eight members of the syndicate entered the room the guard at the door also entered and pulled the door shut behind him. Ken heard the loud click of a deadbolt lock secure the door from the outside.

"Gentlemen, welcome to Las Vegas. The bidding will start in about 30 minutes. You are the sixth group of eight that will be bidding tonight. Everything you should need has been provided. You will not be allowed to leave until the bidding is complete. Your restroom facilities are located in the room behind the bar. For security purposes, there is a yellow line painted on the floor at the front table. Do not cross the yellow line. The bidding order will be the oil project in Venezuela, the French flu manufacturing process, the Angola diamond operation, and then the casino in Rio. May I remind you that you must cover your bids before you leave this room and only cash, transfers from approved accounts in one of the Cartels approved banks, or collateral approved by one of the Cartel's appraisers are authorized for bid. Enjoy your stay and good luck to you all."

Ken, having no monetary interest in the oil bid, took a seat near the bar to watch and learn. When the curtains opened, lights flooded the stage. From the stage, the lights would be blinding and the people in the eight rooms were completely obscured.

A distinguished gentleman with silver hair and dressed in a finely tailored suit, walked to center stage. His Swiss-German accent easily reached the rooms.

"Ladies and gentlemen," he said bowing slightly to the assembled bidding teams, "welcome to Las Vegas. I hope the accommodations have met with your approval. You have all been provided the prospectus on the four investment opportunities we will offer tonight. The order of the bids will be the Venezuela Oil project, the French flu vaccine production, the Angola diamond project, and finally the casino in Rio. Through a random draw the bidding will begin with Team 2. Team 2 please offer your opening bid on the oil project."

Ken watched as a beautiful woman walked on stage and stood next to the charts marked with individual team numbers. Behind the auctioneer another woman stood next to another chart where the sum of the collective bids would be posted. Ken also noticed at least four guards spread to the rear of the stage.

Ken understood the bidding process instantly. Team 2 opened with a bid of $20 million. The bid was listed on their chart and a cumulative total was listed on the center board. When Henry Dobson called out his bid of $30 million, the total was already at $150 million.

There was no rush between bids. It was obvious each team was calculating their standing with each successive bid. With each bid Henry and the others at the table would scribble notes on where they stood and given the amount they knew they would invest, which teams remained a threat to secure the largest bid and earn bonus returns. It was like bidding on a bridge hand you didn't get to open, against teams who couldn't look at their cards and they wondered how much interest you had in the investment and how much you had to invest. It was the most exciting thing Ken Carson had ever witnessed.

By the end of the second round Henry Dobson had $250 million on the board and the total was at $900 million. The third round would be critical. Ken sat and watched in wonder. These men threw millions around like it was play money and other teams were as well financed as his own.

Henry Dobson slammed his hand on the table and abruptly stood, sending his chair skittering towards the bar when the team bidding immediately before Dobson closed out the oil deal. Ken could hear the celebration in the next room.

Dobson was livid, "Shit! I knew I should have gone heavy on my second bid. Crap!"

Henry went to the bar and poured a stiff drink and threw it back in a single gulp. The auctioneer waited a few moments before asking, "Team 6, do you have a bid?"

"Yeah, raise our bid to $500 million." Henry had to settle for second high bid. Still in place for a substantial part of the bonus money, but not where he really wanted to be.

The investment bids were copied and the charts cleared for the second bid. As Ken took his seat at the table his only worry was that Dobson would shake off his disappointment and get involved in the flu bid, but when he overheard him say, "We're going to get the top spot on the diamond bid!" Ken knew he was safe for at least a little while.

The random selection for opening bid went to Team 7. Ken couldn't quite figure out if that was good or bad and anxiously waited for the bid to get to him. The first bids averaged $5 million and the bidding around the room twice before coming back to Ken's syndicate. The table was set and Ken knew he had a lock on the top spot and bid the remaining $70 million.

Ken would let the other teams fight over the scraps. It was time for celebration. Within three rounds he ensured their syndicate would secure the top investor spot, something that the more experienced Henry Dobson was unable to do. Only Hans and Jerry offered congratulations. The others were plotting to refine their diamond bid.

The first drink was good the second even better, and the third simply wonderful. Ken sat in the deep leather chair and mentally counted his money. He paid no attention to the bidding until deep into the diamond bidding when he distinctly heard a familiar voice calling out a bid for Team 4. He stood and moved to the conference table and asked no one in particular.

"Wasn't that Ed Helton's voice? I swear that was Ed Helton's voice."

Jerry, probably Ken's closest friend in the syndicate voiced cautioned. "Ken, sit down and shut up."

Ken didn't think a single peek around the wall would be noticed by anyone, but the moment his foot touched the yellow line he felt the barrel of a gun trying to poke a hole in his temple.

The words of the guard were not so pleasant as when he first talked to the group. "Please sir, step back from the line."

Jerry jumped up from his seat at the table and grabbed Ken by the collar. "Damn Ken, what in the hell are you trying to do? You want us to get thrown out of here? Nobody crosses the yellow line."

Maybe it was the alcohol talking, but his attitude didn't endear him to the group. "Shit, what's he going to do? Shoot me?"

Ken decided he had maybe gone too far when the guard placed his thumb on the hammer and cocked his weapon. "I hope I don't have to. Please step back from the line."

Ken was ashamed of his conduct and sulked near the bar for the remainder of the bidding. He repeatedly apologized to the members of the syndicate and promised nothing like that would ever happen again. Ken was perceptive enough to know the syndicate members were patronizing him when they said they accepted his apology. When the rest of the team enjoyed the Las Vegas nightlife it was only Ken who returned to the hotel. Ken couldn't wait for the flight back to Georgia.

~~

When Ken returned to his office Monday morning he was informed that Mr. Helton wouldn't return from a business trip until later in the week, but could be reached by cell phone if necessary. Ken had no reason to call the president of the Coastal Bank. He would bet his last dollar Ed Helton was still enjoying the casinos in Las Vegas.

Chapter 45

Angelina cursed herself for removing the bandages from around her ribs. The blood had seeped through during the night and stained the sheets. It wasn't a terrible amount of blood, but enough to be embarrassing, and she didn't want to be a bother to anyone in the house. Now, every movement was like an electric shock of pain. The stitches didn't look torn, but her entire side was an awful shade of purple, red, and blue, and the cast on her broken arm was useless. Every time she tried to clamp the bandage beneath it, it slipped. Maybe if she wedged the end of the elastic wrap in the bathroom door she could stretch the bandage to full length and then roll herself into it. Working with one arm the progress was slow and she had to rest often to let the pain subside. A soft knock on her door interrupted her efforts.

"Yes?"

"Miss Sanchez?" It was Mamba from the deep musical tone of her voice. "Hanna wants to know if you would like to take a morning walk with her. If you allow me to help with your dressings, I think you would enjoy the fresh air and the exercise should do you some good."

The statement caught Angelina by surprise. Her door was closed and she didn't think her moans could pass beyond the walls. "Excuse me?"

Mamba cracked the door a few inches, enough to stick her head through. "Let me help you with your bandages and I will wash your sheets. Hanna takes a walk every morning before breakfast. She would enjoy the company."

Mamba's hands seemed to have a magical quality to them. Every time they moved over Angelina's bruised skin the pain seemed to recede. Mamba cleaned the blood from her ribs, and much to Angelina's surprise the antiseptic she applied didn't sting. As Mamba taped another gauze pad over her ribs, and in the most casual of tones, she said, "It must be hard on you."

Angelina thought Mamba was asking about her cast, but she asked, "What?"

"Having so much knowledge, but yet you do not know the truth."

Angelina thought it was an odd thing to say, but didn't think a debate was in order. Mamba ended the session with, "I have great confidence that you will," and she smiled before she left the room.

Her ribs once again tightly wrapped Angelina was anxious to stretch her legs on the packed sand.

The two women were quite a sight. Angelina's cast arm sticking out for any seagull to perch upon, and Hanna suspending her swollen belly with her hands and waddling like a duck; both women focusing on their breathing to ease their pain.

They didn't talk during their walk south until they reached the exposed end of the island nearest to the Atlantic Ocean. Only when they paused to take in the expanse of the ocean did the tension begin to build between them. "Angelina, why didn't you ask me?"

"Ask you about what?"

"About the rape. That's what you're investigating, aren't you?"

"Yes, that...among other things."

Angelina didn't really invite Hanna's narration of the rape. Hanna simply stared to the horizon and started. "It was horrible. I thought they would never stop. I thought I would die, and then another would take me, and then again, and again, and again, and again. It haunted me forever. When Bomani Thomas was killed I thought it would be over, but it never was. It wasn't over until my mother told me they were all dead. I always thought they would be back. They were in my soul, they had me every night. I couldn't make them go away. I know I should forgive them; if I said I did it would be nothing but a lie."

Angelina had nothing to add to the story, but waited before responding, just to make sure Hanna was finished. "I'm sorry Hanna, I wish it hadn't happened."

Hanna turned back to Angelina, "And now you investigate my family because somebody killed those awful men. What you should investigate is not that they are dead, but how they escaped the law for so long, and how they became what they were. You should investigate why the law fails to protect the citizens and only arrives to determine how the crimes were committed. You should investigate why the law applies only to those who choose to obey it; and overlooks those who fail to abide by it and carry it in such disdain."

Hanna's statement was deeper than she expected, but it was an argument that she would expect from the victim of a terrible crime that was avenged outside the parameters of the law. "Hanna, we can't have citizens taking the law into their own hands, we can't have them killing people, and don't take this literally, just because they deserve it."

Hanna turned to Angelina, "You did. You saw a crime, an unprovoked attack on that policeman, and you tracked down and killed the man who did it."

"Yes, but I am an officer of the law and I only shot him in self-defense; without the law we would have anarchy."

"If it was purely self-defense, then you wouldn't have gone after him and we're close to anarchy now. The law didn't protect that police officer when that man shot him for no reason. The law showed up after the fact, again, and if you hadn't killed him and he killed you, he probably would have gotten away with shooting the policeman."

"But he didn't and he paid the ultimate price for his crime."

"And the men who raped me have paid for their crimes. My mother told me the men who killed my father have paid for their crimes. Justice has been served and I am glad those men are dead."

Angelina never had the intention of questioning Hanna, but there were two incidents where she was a direct witness, and since she broached the subject Angelina didn't think it impolite to ask. "Hanna, when you were kidnapped and taken to Tyrell Biggs estate, who was it that rescued you?"

Hanna didn't hesitate. "I don't know."

"Who do you think it was?"

Hanna gave a little chuckle, something between a sneer and a laugh. "Is that the kind of question you would ask in court? Who do I think it was? I think it was the Lone Ranger and Tonto."

"And the men who broke into your house, who killed them?"

"I don't know...Robin Hood and his band of merry men?"

It was clear that she would not get help from Hanna. She began to wonder why this family was so gracious to allow her to convalesce in their home when they knew she was investigating them. "Hanna, why did your family let me come here?"

Hanna smiled a genuine smile, "Because Eric's in love with you. He's been talking crazy about you ever since you met. Whether you know it or not, you're part of the family, you just haven't made the choice yet, but you will."

It was probably the nicest thing Hanna ever said to her, but it only served to confuse Angelina's emotions even more.

Hanna saw the perplexed look on Angelina's face. "Look, you've got a job to do and there isn't anybody in my family that will try and keep you from it. In fact, they will respect you more if you give it your best effort, but you're wasting your time."

"Why is that?"

"You will never catch them, they are like shadows."

Like shadows; it was a strange description provided by Hanna. "Hanna, do you know Colonel Bill Cannon?"

Hanna's face brightened. "Of course I know him. I love him to death. He's my hero. He rescued me from a shark attack right over there." Angelina followed Hanna's arm to part of the beach north of where they stood. Hanna hooked her arm around Angelina's and gently pulled her to start their walk back up the beach. "Come on. I'll tell you about it on the way back."

There was a strange quality to their discussion. They were at odds over many things, but they walked back up the beach like sisters without a care in the world.

~~

Ed called him shortly after lunch. "Ken, call Reverend White and tell him I'm ready to buy back the hotel stock."

Ed sold the stock to Reverend White at $10 per share when the selling price was actually at $11. The stock was now valued at just over $13. Reverend White would realize a 30% return, and it would cost Ed $2,600,000 to get his stock back. The stock was increasing in value almost every day and Ed couldn't delay the buy-back any longer.

Ken didn't relish calling Ed Helton with Reverend White's decision. "Mr. Helton, I have just talked with Reverend White and he stated he wants to retain ownership of the stock you sold him."

Ken could feel the anger building on the other end of the phone. "He can't do that. We had an agreement. I told him I would guarantee him 20% or the current price. He's going to make 30% for God's sake. Is he an idiot?"

"He feels the stock will continue to increase in value. He does not want to sell at this time."

"Well, there is no way I can buy it back if it goes up any more. He has to take the deal now."

"He doesn't want to sell. He said there is nothing in your agreement that requires him to sell."

"What!? Are you telling me that he can keep my stock? Why didn't you warn me about that possibility? You're supposed to be the expert."

"Mr. Helton, if I may remind you, I only brokered the deal; I didn't review it in detail. I assumed you did your own due-diligence." Ken felt the frustration from Ed Helton, but he really could have cared less. Helton had been pushing him around and holding him down for years. It was about time Helton got cut down a couple of pegs.

"Well, you can call the Reverend back and tell him I will see him in court.

"Mr. Helton, that may be a problem, Reverend White's lawyers have already reviewed the deal, and I am afraid I agree, your transaction provided the options of buying back the stock, but there was nothing requiring Reverend White to sell the stock back to you. His lawyers have prepared a formal rejection of your offer and a release of any further claim on the stock you sold him. I am afraid you have no options."

Ed slammed the phone down and the sharp noise caught Ken by surprise; the sneer on Ken's face was most unbecoming of an officer of the bank.

Ed Helton waited in his office until his secretary announced the arrival of the documents from Reverend White. Reverend White's lawyers were very thorough. They covered every aspect of the agreement and ensured Ed Helton would never have claim on the stock again.

Ed neatly folded the documents and placed them in his personal safe. He calmly picked up the phone and dialed.

"Danni, we're free and clear."

~~

Danni took the call from her father and then placed one to the stock broker managing the stock buys for the resort. "Buy all you can with the money that is left."

It was a simple instruction that Danni knew would be executed with the utmost urgency. Danni turned off the desk lamp and tidied up her desk. She looked around the office to make one last check if there was anything of a personal nature she would want to take with her. There was only the double frame with pictures of Hanna and James at their wedding. She closed the frame and placed it in her purse. She glanced out the window that overlooked Calibogue Sound where only a few guests lounged on the beach, and then she walked to the door and turned off the lights.

When she walked through the reception area the secretary, as she always did, asked her, "Where can I reach you?"

Danni took a moment before she answered. "I'm going home, but don't bother trying to call. You may call all the department heads and tell them I am resigning my position with the resort. I won't be returning. Tell them all good luck."

The word of her resignation traveled faster than Danni could exit the hotel. A few of the employees that had been with Danni since her arrival at the hotel, asked her of the rumor about her resignation. To those few she confided that it was no rumor, she would not be returning to the hotel.

The majority of the employees, those brought in by the new union, only watched her departure and showed nothing but indifference. She was management and it was they who toiled to make the hotel run.

Once off the grounds she didn't look back. She had loved the Daufuskie Resort since her childhood and wanted to remember it as the grand resort that it once was, not the uncaring and sterile building it had become.

All these things Danni left behind. The more distant the hotel became, the more the pressures she had endured left her. Her walk home started to feel like a walk from bondage to freedom. The weight of responsibility had been lifted from her shoulders and her step quickened. She wanted to run, but her heels and skirt prevented that demonstration of freedom. She was refreshed and strong and wondered if Hanna would like to go on a picnic tomorrow.

~~

The Negev Desert at night was a beautiful place. Bill Cannon found it difficult to pick the most endearing feature; was it the glitter of stars against the black sky, or simply the solitude of the desert. If not for the distant rumble of artillery exchanges between the Israelis and Egyptians it would be the solitude.

Bill checked the I-V drip for Madison and then cocked his ear to the Israeli command post to see if he could glean any information on the American C-130 that would evacuate them to Germany. The Israelis wanted both Bill and Major Madison out of the country, and quick; and without the international press finding out they had been harboring the man responsible for the destruction of Hezbollah headquarters in southern Lebanon; hence the nighttime extraction in the remotest part of Israel.

"Jimmy, you're kind of quiet tonight. You okay?'

With his injuries and bandages it was difficult to form the words he wished to speak, and often difficult to understand them. "What do you think Hanna will say?"

Bill knew what Madison was thinking. Marrying a man in uniform was one thing; helping a soldier convalesce from horrific wounds was another. If Hanna left, she wouldn't be the first military wife to do so. For some, the revelation that the effort required was more than they could shoulder came quickly; for others it could take years; in either case the results were the same.

"She is going to say she loves you, because she does. Your wife is a good woman, a strong woman. She married you because she loves you. She'll be there." Bill paused before he added, "Besides, you were never that pretty in the first place. If she wanted a pretty boy she never would have married you."

Madison appreciated the rather crude attempt at humor, and a chuckle that sounded more like a rasping cough drifted across the abandoned desert. "You know what I really worry about? How my kid will handle it. What is he going to do when they say he has a freak for a father?"

"You mean before he kicks their ass, or after?"

"Seriously Bill, you know how cruel kids can be."

Bill turned to Madison. His face not visible in the dark, but James could hear the emotion in his voice. "Jim, I don't know what to tell you. It's going to be tough on everybody, but it's going to be part of your life. If you're a good husband and father, and Hanna a good wife and mother, then your kids will be proud of you."

"Yeah, you're right. I don't know why I even brought it up."

The night didn't seem so dark. Only the distant rumble of exploding artillery broke the silence.

"Bill, what are you going to do when you get back to the states?"

Bill absently tossed a pebble into the darkness. "I don't know. I'll keep on teaching until something else comes up."

"I didn't mean that. What are you going to do about Mrs. Walton? Hanna thinks her mother is in love with you."

For the briefest moment Bill allowed himself to believe what James had said was true, but he was only fooling himself. "That will never happen."

"Why not?"

"Because, I killed her husband; she doesn't know."

"You didn't kill her husband those thugs working for Tyrell Biggs did."

Bill nodded in the darkness. "Maybe they pulled the trigger, but I was the one responsible. Danni's husband was a real jerk, but he would be alive today if I'd done a better job planning."

"Damn Bill, how do you figure that?"

"When I retired, I went to work for Home Depot in Atlanta. Danni started to work the same day; we were in the same orientation class. I think I fell in love with her the first time I saw her; but she was a married woman, and I respected that.

"We worked together for over a year, and then one day she was gone. She just disappeared without as much as a goodbye. I found out later she left because she needed to take care of Hanna." Bill didn't think it was necessary to talk about Hanna's rape.

"I didn't see or hear from her for almost two years. She was a nervous wreck. She asked me if I knew anybody who could get to Bomani Thomas and kill him."

"She asked you that, straight out?"

"No, she wouldn't tell me exactly what she wanted. She knew I worked with special ops. She wanted to get in touch with somebody who would take the job. I set up a snatch with Doc and Thunder. They found out she wanted Thomas killed. They didn't like the idea, too risky."

Bill looked deep into the night before he continued.

369

"I would have done it alone if I had to, but I came up with a plan to use JB Jackson and Bomani Thomas as the connection between us and Tyrell Biggs for a drug deal. We planned to grab the money and Thunder would make sure the drugs stayed off the streets. We hoped Biggs would be so pissed with Thomas that he would have him killed. JB would do it as a last resort. We arranged for the money to be given to Eric as payment on his father's life insurance.

"We had great cover for the whole thing. It would have worked except Danni went to JB's funeral. That's where Tyrell Biggs got the lead on them. The rest is history."

James Madison had suspected the same, or something similar, for years. "Does Eric know the origin of the money?"

"No, and he doesn't need to know. He doesn't know any of this. The military abandoned him after JB got arrested, but I wasn't going to let him live the rest of his life in poverty."

Bill took a few moments before he continued. "I don't think Danni Walton knows the whole story. I think she suspects I was involved, but she doesn't know for sure. That's why it will never work between us. I don't think she could ever really love me if she found out my planning got her husband killed. I don't want to risk losing her to the truth, so I keep my mouth shut. Being near her drives me crazy, but I can still be near her."

"Bill...who were the men with me that night on Daufuskie?"

"Mike DeAngelo and Doc Broderson."

"Were they on the raid to free me?"

"Yes...and some others."

"Bill, why did you do it? Why did you rescue me? It could have been suicide."

"A lot of reasons: You are my friend. You are part of Danni's family. Hanna has seen enough tragedy in her life already, and I was responsible for you being in Israel in the first place.

"There is a Federal investigator in Atlanta looking into Hanna's case. I asked Lucas McLaughlin to send you here so you wouldn't get involved in the investigation. So I was responsible for you. I'm sorry; I didn't think it was going to turn out this way."

Bill heard the distance hum of turbo-props. "Our ride is near."

"Bill, why did you tell me about the drugs and what JB did?"

"Because I owe you; I've messed up the rest of your life. My life is now in your hands; you can do with it what you will."

Bill got up from his seated position on the desert floor and started securing the tubes running into Madison's body to the stretcher. As the engines on the C-130 reversed to bring the aircraft to a halt, Bill took the head of the stretcher and an Israeli soldier the foot and they carried James Madison to the rear of the aircraft.

With his remaining eye James looked up at Bill Cannon.

"Bill…" Bill Cannon had to lean close to hear James, "…thank you for what you did for Hanna.

Chapter 46

James Madison slept between clean sheets. As he shook off the effects of anesthesia from yet another surgery, the voices he heard comforted him; they were American and the sheets were in Walter Reed Army Medical Center in Washington, D.C. He recognized the recovery room nurse; he did not recognize the three men standing a discrete distance away. They stood close enough to the gurney to shoulder their way to the bedside once the nurse left.

"Major Madison, I'm so sorry, these men said they must talk with you just as soon as you woke." The nurse placed a buzzer in James left hand. "If you need me just push this button."

When the nurse retreated, she pulled the door closed and the three men approached the bed.

"Major Madison, I am Martin Trenton. I am a Deputy Director in the Department of Homeland Security." Trenton turned to introduce the other men in the room. "This is Ron Yarbrough from the Central Intelligence Agency, and this is Gerald Hanson, from the Department of Justice. I apologize for the inconvenience of doing this now, but your message has created quite a stir in Washington."

Madison didn't know these men from Adam. "Do you have any credentials?"

"Certainly." The three men produced identifications and presented them for review. The credentials could be library cards for all that James could see, but he needed a little more time to clear his head.

"Where is General McLaughlin?"

"He is in the waiting room. When we are finished, he will be allowed to visit you. Major Madison, I must tell you your report that there is a nuclear weapon being targeted against Washington is very disturbing. We have every asset at our disposal on full alert, but we haven't found a thing. Can you please tell us why you think such a weapon is here?"

"They basically told me so."

"They…being your captors?"

372

"Yes."

"What exactly did they say?"

"The leader, he had my wallet and a picture of my wife, and he knew my address was in Washington—he took great joy in describing her death. He said if she didn't burn in the fires of hell, then she would die a slower death from the radiation."

It wasn't the only thing his captor said. He took some evil pleasure in describing how the bomb would burn away her skin, how it would burn out her eyes, and how her blood would burn and turn brown, how she would be helpless, and anyone passing by could take her, and James could do nothing. They would keep James alive and show him the videos, and maybe he could pick her burned body from the dead. Or they would show him how the radiation would eat away at her body. They would keep him alive until that day. James simple description was enough for these men, the rest of the threats he would keep within.

"Did they say how big the bomb would be?"

"No."

"Did they say how they would transport the bomb into the United States?"

"No."

"Major Madison, that isn't much information for us to build a plan around. Why do you think they told you these things? Do you think they were giving you false information to simply cause us to react to a nuclear threat, to study our response?"

James felt like pushing the red button to ask the nurse to get these idiots out of his recovery room. "Mr. Trenton…that's it, isn't it…Mr. Trenton? I don't think they expected me to get out of that room. I see no reason to think it wasn't the truth. If I were you, I would plan accordingly."

The man from the CIA stepped forward. "Major Madison, do you think you could recognize the man if I showed you photos of known terrorists?"

"I think so. I won't forget his face for a long time."

Mr. Yarbrough took his time with the pictures. There were numerous shots of each man, some as if taken during booking at a jail, others maybe from yearbooks, and still others taken from great distances with telephoto lens, or even computer enhanced photos from satellites.

Mr. Yarbrough was a third into the album when the face that had haunted James Madison once again fixed him with his evil stare.

"That's him. He was in charge of the house. Who is he?"

Yarbrough turned the book to read the text under the picture. "Khalid Al-Hazmi, born in Syria, member of Al-Qaeda, and a player in a splinter group run by a man named Achmad Nardiff. I hate to tell you this, but we had this man in custody in Guantanamo; but there is some good news...he didn't make it out of the house. He's dead...burned to a crisp."

"We had him in custody? How did he escape?"

Yarbrough let a look of disgust cross his face, but only for a moment. "He didn't escape. We let him go. The Attorney General didn't think we had enough evidence to convict him, so we sent him back to his own country."

If the man from the Attorney General's office felt any remorse about the decision to release Al-Hazmi, he didn't let it show. "Major Madison, do you know who rescued you from the house in Lebanon?"

"I'm sorry, what was your name again?"

"I am Gerald Hanson. I work directly for the Attorney General. Do you know who it was that rescued you?"

"Mr. Hanson, I don't remember a thing after making the video. I don't know how I got out of that house, or who came to rescue me. I don't remember anything until I woke up in the hospital in Israel. I always assumed it was Israeli Commandos, or Delta Force, but nobody will tell me. I'm sorry I can't help you with more."

"Major Madison, do you know a retired Army officer named Bill Cannon?"

"Yes sir, I do; about every Ranger in the Army knows who Bill Cannon is."

"Colonel Cannon was with you in Israel—we know that—did he have anything to do with your rescue?"

"Not that I'm aware. I already told you I don't remember anything about it. Unless you have any additional questions, I need to get out of this hospital and get home to see my wife."

~~

Bill Cannon and Lucas McLaughlin waited for the investigators to finish with James. The waiting room of the hospital was not suitable

374

for discussions of the events recently passed, so their attention wandered to Eric Brown reporting the news. Eric's report raised the eyebrows of both men.

"This is Eric Brown reporting from CNN headquarters in Atlanta. The south Texas community of Laredo is on edge today after the brutal murder of three U.S. Border Patrol agents 20 miles west of the town. The killings occurred sometime this morining between the hours of midnight and 4 a.m. The three agents were bound and gagged and then executed by a gunshot to the back of the head.

"The Commander of the Laredo Sector suspects the agents discovered a major drug transaction and Mexican drug-runners killed the agents. The commander has vowed to bring the people responsible for these atrocities to justice. The Border Patrol, with all local law enforcement agencies as well as elements of the FBI have blanketed all roads as far away as Dallas, New Orleans, and points west."

Bill Cannon turned to Lucas McLaughlin. "Laredo is a dumb place to cross; the road network out of south Texas is pretty limited."

Lucas nodded. "Exactly what I was thinking. That must be some big load to kill three border agents. Agents get shot at all the time, but to execute them, it makes you wonder. It's not good business. What could be so important about a load of dope to kill three agents?"

Bill Cannon agreed with his friend. If anything, the drug runners into the US from Mexico tried to avoid conflict, and the massacre on the border would now only heighten everyone to the drug trade.

"The news said they missed a commo check at midnight, but I think you have to assume whoever shot those boys, may have two more hours of a head start. They probably make a check, what…every two hours? So for planning purposes, let's assume the thing went down at 10 p.m., maybe earlier, those drugs could be in Atlanta by now."

"It's still hard to get past the fact that any amount of drugs would be worth killing those agents."

"I know."

~~

Mamba found Danni Walton standing alone, silhouetted by the rising moon, on the southern most end of the island. Mamba expected a vastly different reaction from Danni when they received the news that Bill Cannon would be escorting Major Madison home from Walter Reed Hospital. After the initial burst of excitement for her daughter, the complexity of Bill Cannon's return began to weigh on her. Only Mamba could see the change.

Danni heard her approach and turned, but did not exchange a greeting.

Mamba stood next to the woman she had raised from a baby. Even in the 90 degree heat, the gloom surrounding Danni was chilling. "Danni, this is not like you. What is it that worries you? Why has the return of Major Madison and Colonel Cannon brought you such discomfort?"

Mamba knew Danni heard her question and could wait as long as Danni took to answer.

Danni took in a deep breath and exhaled before she answered. Her answer was not what Mamba expected.

"Has my father told you he plans to close the bank? He has purchased a small island in the Caribbean and plans to move the family there."

"No, your father has not mentioned anything of that nature to me. Why would he do such a thing?"

A strained smile crossed Danni's face. "He said he's tired of fighting the government and all the new taxes and regulations. He said we've got enough money; we're going to camp out beneath a palm tree and watch what happens. He said if we don't get out now, then we will be pulled down with all the other private businesses."

"That's interesting, but I don't think that is what is bothering you."

Danni signed and smiled. "No, that's not what's really bothering me." Danni took most of a minute to compose her thoughts. "My life is not what I expected it to be. So much has happened. First Hanna and then Peter, ...James will never fully recover...so much pain and suffering...what ever happened to love and joy and happiness?"

Danni looked to Mamba and there was no compassion in her eyes, only a look of disappointment. "I didn't think you would understand."

Danni regretted her comment the moment she spoke it. If anyone in the world would understand the tragedies of life it would be Mamba. "I'm sorry, Mamba, that was terrible of me to say."

It wasn't the comment; it was the self pity Danni allowed to overwhelm her life that bothered Mamba. "Danni, there is much to celebrate. Hanna will bring you a grandson soon. That alone is enough…"

A small smile crossed Danni lips. The thought of being a grandmother was enough to brighten her outlook.

"…and the man who can make you whole is coming home tomorrow. I see it when you are together…your eyes smile like those of a child. Yet you always push him away. Why is that?"

"Bill Cannon?"

"Yes, Colonel Cannon! If you still mourn for your husband, then it is you who are choosing a life of misery. Your husband was never worthy of your love."

Danni turned back to the rising moon. "There was a time when I thought I loved Bill, but I am not so sure now. I thought he was a man I could trust, but I have found out he is like all the others; he used me – he tricked me."

Mamba and Danni never directly discussed those terrible times of years ago. To Mamba, there was no need to discuss events that to her were already clear.

"Who is this woman who cries out for pity? Revenge is a dangerous game. When you needed someone with the courage to exact your revenge, you choose Bill Cannon. Look within your own soul. Did Bill Cannon use you, or did you use Bill Cannon's love for you to send him down a dark path, and now you will turn your back to him?"

Danni was taken aback by the force of Mamba's comments. "It's more complicated than that."

"My dear child, true love is never complicated, either you give yourself totally, or it should not be considered love. Bill Cannon knows who you are, and what you did, and he would lay down his life for you. And now you withhold your love based on things you only suspect, but do not know. You can stand here all night, but it will do you no good until you open your mind and heart to the truth. If you do that, I believe you will find happiness."

Mamba turned and walked alone back to the house. Danni stood on the beach for another hour before she turned away from the ocean. Tomorrow would be soon enough to talk with Bill Cannon.

~~

It didn't take Hanna more than 30 minutes to conclude the cheap plastic chair in the small terminal at Hunter Army Airfield was the most uncomfortable piece of furniture she had ever encountered. Sitting on it was like sitting on a tree stump. There was no comfortable position and the baby wasn't helping.

With one foot, the baby was trying to kick out her ribs, with the other he was trying to push the contents in her stomach back up her throat, and one little fist was punching her bladder while the other beat a calypso tune on her spine. Maybe he knew daddy was coming home and wanted out to greet him.

Hanna couldn't take the pain any longer; she paced the polished floor of the hall leading to the flight operations office. The sergeant behind the wooden counter looked up and smiled. He knew what it meant to wait for a returning soldier. The last hours were always the hardest. He shook his head slowly, "They are still on the ground in Charleston. They have a couple of patients to pick up for transfer to the burn center in San Antonio. I'll let you know when they are in the air."

Hanna smiled and thanked him. The hard floor hurt her feet as she waddled back to the visitor lounge. The smell of jet fuel and strong coffee permeated the building. It was a comforting smell. A pilot brought her a pillow from the ready-room; it might help with the chair, he said. Hanna tried sitting on the pillow, and it did help some; but not much. Maybe if she took a walk she would feel better.

She walked back to flight operations, but didn't bother the nice sergeant. She walked to the doors leading to the tarmac and stepped outside. The Savannah heat and humidity was oppressive. Without the sea breeze of the island, Savannah's summers were almost unbearable. The heat didn't seem to bother Doc Broderson or Mike DeAngelo as they strolled on the tarmac in deep conversation, the waves of heat distorting their bodies.

General McLaughlin is the one who called her. He told her that James would be on the medical transport flight landing at Hunter Army Airfield today. Hanna was thankful that James was on a medical flight, and not one of the cargo aircraft they used to transport coffins.

Broderson and DeAngelo insisted on greeting her husband, as did everyone else, including her mother, Angelina Sanchez and Brian Vance. The chairs didn't seem to bother them. Only her grandfather could not attend the homecoming; he had important business at the bank he could not defer, and Eric Brown would come down for the weekend after the news.

Hanna sat on a cement bench just outside the operations office. It couldn't be any more uncomfortable than the torture devices in the waiting room. A gentle knock on the glass and Hanna turned her head. The operations sergeant smiled and pointed to a flash in the sky to the north.

Hanna yelled to her friends on the tarmac. "Doc...Doc...look!"

Hanna was pointing to the faint shape of a white jet aircraft with a huge red cross painted on the fuselage.

~~

It wasn't the kind of welcome home ceremony you see on television, where the bands are playing and the politicians are making the rounds. It was like most arrivals, the wife and family standing alone on the tarmac for their loved ones to return from battle. But still, it was exciting and joyous for the few who gathered, until they were reminded of the purpose of this flight.

The first off were the litter patients still confined to the transport gurneys. They were lowered from the back of the aircraft, bottles and tubes still connected, and immediately loaded into waiting ambulances. Next were the wounded in wheel chairs, maybe missing a foot or leg, or having a cast that prevented safe passage down the steep stairs. Finally those that could walk started to exit from the front of the plane.

Hanna wasn't quite sure the tall man in the khaki pants and white knit shirt was her husband. The bandage that covered his head hid his features, but he had the build she remembered. General McLaughlin had warned her of his wounds - he had lost his arm, and that he had been wounded in the head. Now she watched the man with one arm struggle down the stairs, as if he was unsure of his ability to make each step without falling. Was that her husband?

The man was now on the ground and walking with a cane. Where was the man who ran with her on the beach on their honeymoon, or walked with her in the moonlight? Tears streamed down her face, she couldn't breathe, and she wanted to run and hide from the sight of all the pain and suffering. Not just of this man walking towards her, but from all those who had been carried away. This was worse than a nightmare, this was reality.

Hanna felt a strong hand on her arm and turned to look into the eyes of Doc Broderson, and she remembered what he had told her. "He will look to you for strength."

It was then that Hanna realized she married James Madison not for the way he looked, but for the man he was. This was not the way to welcome the man she loved. She dried her eyes and stepped forward.

379

The man with one arm and only half his face stopped before her. His greeting was simple. "I'm so sorry."

It was the release she needed. "Oh, James..." She circled his neck with her arms and smothered the side of his mouth that wasn't scabbed and torn with kisses. The commitment was total. The man she loved had returned. His cane clattered to the pavement as he circled her waist with his left arm. When he pressed his lips against hers, and her breast against his chest, there was nothing else. When he pulled her close he could feel his son moving in her. This is the woman that kept him alive—this was the woman he owed his life to—this was the woman he loved. The return was complete; his wounds were now just part of life.

The others waited. The passion of the embrace was a beautiful sunrise. They all stood to honor it. There was no rush. The tears of the bystanders were real, and they felt no shame. Of all the things that people pay homage to, they all pale in comparison. This reunion was an honor few are privileged to witness.

"Let's go home."

Chapter 47

Angelina watched the medical flight taxi to a stop near the small terminal. The reflecting heat made the bodies of Hanna and Mrs. Walton and the others, shimmer within the refracted light. She hung back and took advantage of what little shade the awning provided. Beads of sweat trickled into her cast and the wandering drops began to bother her. She considered herself the only outsider—it would have been better if Eric was with her; Eric would have made her feel more like a part of the family.

She watched as the patients confined to stretchers were transported to the ambulances, and the walking wounded struggle down the steep stairs. The inconvenience of the sweat running into her cast became less of a bother.

Angelina saw Hanna recoil from the shattered image of her husband; and then she watched as they embraced. Their meeting was in public view, but private in every respect.

Angelina's eyes followed Doc Broderson and Mike DeAngelo as they left the immediate family and made their way to the rear of the aircraft. There, a tall man assisted other patients from the aircraft. Broderson and DeAngelo called to the tall man and he turned and greeted the pair. There was an obvious bond between these men. From the distance Angelina could not see any tears, but the men embraced as brothers, and their meeting was genuine and emotional. The tall man must be Colonel Bill Cannon.

Angelina saw Hanna give control of her husband to Mrs. Walton and Mamba, and almost ran to the rear of the aircraft where Bill Cannon and the others were standing. She could see the tears on Hanna's face as she wrapped her arms around the neck of the tall man. Colonel Cannon had to bend at the waist to accept the smothering hug, and it appeared he was embarrassed at the emotion of her welcome. It took him a moment to gently separate her arms from around his neck, but even then Hanna would not release his arm.

Angelina's study of Bill Cannon was interrupted by Danni Walton. "Angelina, let me introduce you to Hanna's husband...Major

James Madison, this is Ms. Angelina Sanchez. Angelina is staying with us for a while."

Angelina turned to the voice. She hoped her surprised expression was not offensive to Hanna's husband, but his injuries were vividly gruesome and almost overwhelming when viewed from three feet and not from across the tarmac. James saw the surprise on her face and smiled with what was left of his mouth. He leaned his cane against his leg and extended his left hand.

"Nice to meet you Ms. Sanchez, I hope your recovery is going well."

It was the last time Angelina would ever feel sorry for herself because of her injuries. Here this man, obviously once a good looking man and now a gnarled mass of scars, burned skin and bandages, greeted her with genuine warmth and without even a hint of self pity about his own situation. Angelina took his hand in her right hand, the left still perched away from her body, and she smiled as she replied, "Better than I could have ever hoped. I hope your own goes as well."

"Looks like I'll be spending a lot of time here, we can heal up together. I understand you are keeping Eric Brown on the straight and narrow."

"I'm trying. Welcome home."

Their small talk was interrupted by a call from Hanna. Hanna was dragging Bill Cannon across the pavement. "Momma, look who I found!"

Hanna finally released her grasp of Bill when they neared Danni Walton. Angelina found it odd that Bill Cannon hesitated—almost unsure if he should close the distance between him and Danni. All on the pavement watched and waited without movement. It was as if they were holding their breath for the next step.

Had they lost the ability to move? Angelina wondered what kept these two apart. But then they embraced—Bills arms around Danni's body and hers around his neck. Their kiss was long and with passion and Angelina could see tears streak Danni's face. It was a reunion not to be interrupted and she noticed the others step back, but they did not look away. When Angelina looked into the faces of those watching, the tears and smiles could only have been those of happiness.

Bill stepped back from Danni, realizing after the outburst of passion, exactly where he was and who was watching. Danni must have realized the same for her hand nervously tried to fix a wayward strand of hair that had become unruly during the embrace. The flush on their faces was an embarrassment to them both and it took a moment for them to untangle. They may have been embarrassed at their emotional embrace, but all those who politely allowed them their privacy turned away with smiles on their faces; even Mike DeAngelo smiled.

~~

The procession to DeAngelo's boat was an odd looking parade. Angelina and Brian Vance set the gentle pace, followed by Hanna waddling along and Major Madison keeping pace with his cane making little sucking sounds on the sidewalk bricks. DeAngelo and Broderson politely but forcefully bumped away onlookers whose gawking at the group went beyond a simple double-take and crossed the line of being impolite. Mamba majestically followed and ignored the din of the street, and Bill and Danni brought up the rear.

Danni slid her arm around Bill's as they walked to the county pier. Her soft touch convinced Bill that if his life was to be complete he must confess the truth to this woman. If she rejected him, then his love for her was not meant to be. It was a risk he had to take. His guilt was that which kept them apart. He would tell her tonight if he could find a way to find a private moment.

Danni could feel the tension leave her body and enjoyed the musical sounds of River Street. Nothing was said during the walk and the solitude of the procession gave her the time to come to a decision. She knew Mamba understood her fear, the secret she had kept within for so many years; and now with Bill walking next to her, Danni understood what Mamba said about true love being an uncomplicated thing.

For years she harbored the fear that Bill would consider her act of revenge as a critical flaw in her character. Fear of his rejection was real, but since his return, it was clear that life was rewarding with him and so empty without him. She would tell him tonight. She would arrange a quiet walk along the beach perhaps.

As they walked along the riverfront the world seemed to be a peaceful and secure place until Bill's cell phone broke the spell. Danni noticed his body tense at the ring, but he resisted the urge to take the call. After a moment the phone fell silent, only to erupt again.

She turned to Bill, "Go ahead and answer it. I know it's driving you crazy."

Bill grinned at Danni, this woman knew him like no other. He reached for his phone.

"Hello."

"Bill, this is Lucas. I thought you should know. Nawaf Al-Mihdhar got into the country yesterday under a false passport in Miami. The FBI is on the hunt, but they haven't had any luck yet."

Danni couldn't hear any of the conversation, but felt the muscles in Bill's arm tense.

"And there's something else. Since yesterday, Immigration has picked up three other known terrorists attempting to enter the country; all under false passports. The documents were excellent and even Homeland Security admits they were lucky to get the men they did. No telling how many got through."

"Any idea what the target is?"

"None at all. Watch your ass, old buddy."

Danni felt a new tension from Bill. He didn't look any different, but he was no longer simply enjoying the walk, he was now scanning the buildings and alleyways, and he removed Danni's arm from his.

"Bill, what's the matter?"

Bill didn't turn to answer, his reply was calm but short and to the point. "Nothing, but I want you to walk with Mamba, and see if you can get the others to walk a little faster."

Danni saw the hand signals Bill flashed to Doc Broderson, and then Broderson whisper something to DeAngelo. DeAngelo announced to the group. "I'm getting thirsty and I need a drink; why don't you people get it in gear, this ain't no picnic."

Danni saw James slow and turn his attention to Bill, and again the hand signals. The pace of the sucking noises of James cane on the sidewalk dramatically increased, and Danni knew something was not right. Bill, DeAngelo and Doc now flanked the group by placing themselves between the group and the few tourists on the street, and it seemed an eternity before they boarded DeAngelo's boat.

Bill was the last aboard. "Mike, are you packing anything?"

DeAngelo looked up from preparing to launch. "Yeah, two pieces, one here..." tapping a locker beneath the cockpit, "...and the other in the rear fish locker."

"Good enough. Let's go."

~~

384

About the time they got to mid-river, DeAngelo slowed to allow the *Crescent Moon* to gain the navigation channel. Danni recognized the yacht and moved next to Mike DeAngelo. "Isn't that the yacht that was berthed at your marina?"

DeAngelo glanced up. "Yep."

"Where are they going?" It was the same vessel where she and her father enjoyed the dinner cruise.

"I don't know. They're paid up for berthing space through the end of the year."

Danni looked closely at the flag flying from the staff at the most aft portion of the yacht. It was three strips of green, white and red, and a black shape at the base of the flag. "What flag is that?"

DeAngelo squinted and focused on the flag. "That is the flag of the Kingdom of Kuwait."

~~

The Daufuskie Hotel and Resort Board of Directors meeting turned ugly and Reverend White removed himself from the long table. He tried to ignore the shouting and finger pointing and directed his attention to the huge yacht navigating Calibogue Sound to the north. It was the people on that yacht—those people that had the money to buy something so grand—that used to come to the resort.

And those people weren't coming to the resort. In fact, not many people of any monetary means were coming to the resort. Their connections paid handsomely with government conventions, but the government demanded huge concessions and only with low pricing were they able to secure the business—often at a loss to the resort. Government purchasing agents told the hotel they would make up for the room discounts with purchases made by those attending the conferences. But the Government employees didn't spend money.

Federal stimulus programs of tax rebates for families taking vacations at Government sponsored resorts didn't produce the expected results. The rebates were pro-rated based on income, and it didn't take long for those of moderate means to feel as if they were paying for the vacations of their less fortunate vacationers and they stopped coming; and those of lesser means didn't have any money to spend once they got to the resort.

Dewade Henstep, the senior union member, blamed the economy and bad advertising. The advertising agency blamed poor customer service evidence by almost no repeat reservations. Whatever the reasons, and there were many, the resort was no longer meeting their loan obligations; bankruptcy was near and Reverend White's stock was in a freefall.

Reverend White's call to Ken Carson solicited only laughs. Ed Helton wouldn't touch the stock. Reverend White could roll up his stock and stick 'em you know where. Carson laughed, "You got suckered."

As the yacht passed the Hilton Head lighthouse, Reverend White turned back to the group. "We're ruined."

Henstep growled, "Quit whining! We can still get out from under this."

"Jesus himself couldn't save this place."

Henstep got up from the table and started to the door. "Just keep your mouth shut and leave everything to me."

~~

Ken Carson was sitting in his office as DeAngelo's boat passed the bank. He was finding it more and more difficult to concentrate on the spread sheets arrayed on his desk. Every time he tried to focus on the mundane numbers his attention would wander, and he began to replay his fantasies on how he was going to spend the profits from the Las Vegas investments.

His secretary's call on the intercom destroyed the mental image of his estate overlooking the blue waters of the Gulf Stream. "Mr. Carson, you wife just called. She asked me to tell you to meet her at the River Street law offices of Taylor, Bean, and Smith. She said it's urgent."

"Is she still on the phone?"

"No sir, she just gave me the message, and asked me to tell you to please hurry."

The request had him puzzled. What happened to require a meeting at a law office? He didn't think she had any rich relatives that may have left her something in a will; but she said it was urgent and he was needed right away.

It took longer than expected to find a parking spot, and when he finally did, he had an additional walk of a quarter mile. Ken ignored the tourists and cursed his misfortune; the humidity was already causing beads of sweat to soak his collar. When he arrived at the law offices and entered the double doors that opened directly onto the famous street the frigid blast of air-conditioned air chilled him.

The receptionist, in that special condescending way that puts visitors on the defensive—asked if she could help. It took his eyes a moment to adjust to the subdued lighting and appreciate the luxury of the furnishings and the delicate and sculptured beauty of the receptionist; this was an expensive law firm if they could afford both the furnishings and the receptionist.

"Yes, I am Ken Carson; my wife called from this address and said I was urgently needed."

"Of course, will you please follow me?"

Ken enjoyed following the receptionist up the winding staircase, not only was the view intriguing, but the aroma of perfume she left in her wake was alluring, almost enchanting. He would find out the name of the product and give some to Karen.

The receptionist led him to dark double doors finished in the style of judge's paneling. When Ken stepped into the conference, Rachael was sitting at the end of the long conference table and Karen was sitting next to her. Karen appeared to be quietly sobbing and Rachael had her arm around her sister trying to comfort her. Ken ignored the two men in the room and asked of Rachael.

"Rachael, I came as quick as I could. What's wrong?"

Rachael did not respond to his question, and Karen's sobbing increased. "Mr. Carson," it was one of the suited men in the room, "I am David Taylor. I am a lawyer at this firm, and I am representing your wife in these proceedings."

The color drained from his face. "What proceedings? What is going on here?"

"Mr. Carson, your wife has filed a petition of divorce citing your adulterous behavior." The lawyer pointed to the other gentleman in the room. "This is a deputy with the Chatham County Sheriff's Department; he will be serving you with the original petition of divorce, and a restraining order prohibiting you from any contact with your wife or her sister." The lawyer paused and turned to the deputy. "Deputy please serve Mr. Carson with the petition and restraining order now."

The deputy informed Ken that he had 30 days to respond to the divorce petition. Any violation of the restraining order would lead to his arrest. After the deputy served the papers he left the office.

Ken, now holding the documents said to no one in particular, "I can't believe this is happening."

For the first time Rachael spoke. "What did you think would happen? I can't believe you forced my sister into an affair! What kind of a man are you?"

"That's a lie. She came on to me. She's the one that started it. You know how she is. I can't believe you would believe her." Ken held the two documents before him. "There was no need for this. Why couldn't you come to me, and talk with me before all this?"

The lawyer interrupted the conversation. "Then, Mr. Carson, you admit to having an affair with your wife's sister?"

Ken turned abruptly back to the lawyer. "I didn't admit to anything, I misspoke. You can't trap me that easily, counselor."

"I am not trying to trap you, Mr. Carson. You did that yourself."

The lawyer reached down and slid a computer to Ken's side of the table. There on the screen, playing in all its sordid detail, the recording Karen made of their night in the hotel at the banking meeting in Atlanta.

The lawyer continued. "There is one additional issue we need to discuss. Your wife's sister is considering filing an extortion charge against you. She states you have been using this video to blackmail her."

"Blackmail? That's ridiculous. You people will be hearing from my lawyer. This is an outrage!" Ken turned to leave.

Rachael yelled after him. "You can't go to my house. Karen and I will be there. You will have to find somewhere else to stay."

Ken turned back, "You're going home with her, after what she's done?"

"She is my sister and she needs me now more than ever. You can go find a whore to stay with for all I care, but you can't go to the house."

Rachael was right. The restraining order in his hand prevented him from even getting his clothes out of the house. The fact that his wife seemed to hold all the cards tempered his anger. "Rachael, what is it you want?"

Rachael didn't blink when she answered. "I want it all, you son of a bitch."

~~

Bill debated if Nawaf Al-Mihdhar's entry into the U.S. was cause for alarm; enough to mention it to Danni's family. What were the

388

chances that two of the three men he captured in Iraq would surface so close together? First it was Khalid Al-Hazmi in Lebanon, and now Al-Mihdhar in Miami; and it would be foolish to ignore the three terrorists nabbed by Immigration. Were they all part of a larger plot or could it be possible that Bill was a target, if not by the group, but by Al-Mihdhar?

It was during dinner, a small feast prepared to honor the return of James, where Mamba forced the issue. "Colonel Cannon, you are troubled. Will you not tell us what weighs so heavy upon your mind?"

In the absence of Ed Helton, Bill was seated at the end of the long table. Danni to his left and Hanna and James to his immediate right, DeAngelo and Doc sat on the left side with Danni and Angelina Sanchez next to James, and Mamba in the seat of the household matron facing Bill. When she asked the question the conversations at the table stopped and all eyes turned to Bill.

It wasn't a difficult decision to make. If these people were in danger, then Bill owed them an explanation.

"Years ago, in Iraq, we captured some terrorists. They were held in Guantanamo. Earlier this year the Attorney General released them"

Angelina felt her face flush with embarrassment. She had nothing to do with the release of the men, but she was working for the Department of Justice and these people all knew it; it was guilt by association.

"One of those men, Khalid Al-Hazmi, was part of the group that captured and tortured James. Another, Nawaf Al-Mihdhar, entered the United States under a false passport yesterday in Miami. Immigration picked up three other known terrorists trying to enter the country; no telling how many they missed.

"That is a lot of activity in a short amount of time. I don't know the purpose, but I don't think it's prudent to dismiss the possibility that I, or even James, may be a target."

Mamba was not afraid to continue the conversation. "Is there danger to this family?"

"There may be. It's hard to say right now. If either of us is a target, then yes, we are all in danger. If they have other plans, then we are in no more danger than anybody else. I'm sure the government is doing everything they can to find and arrest these men. The only reason I tell you this is to make you aware of the possible situation and I would like everyone to keep their eyes and ears open, and wits about you."

Angelina sat silently at the end of the table. Would the men detained at Guantanamo go to such extent to seek revenge against their captor for something that occurred years ago, or was there a more recent occasion that would serve as catalyst for their actions? Was this the reason William Jefferson asked her to stay on Daufuskie with this family, to build a case against Bill Cannon? Was she betraying the trust of this family if she dared ask the question?

"Why would you be a target, Colonel Cannon?"

The breathing at the table came to a perceptible stop. "Because..."

Mamba completed the answer. "Because Colonel Bill Cannon is a man of courage and integrity and is not afraid. He is the type of man that has and will continue to stand against them. That is why he may always be a target of those who hate this country, and that is all that will be discussed at this table."

It was an awkward moment. Angelina looked down and studied her lap. Hanna came to her rescue. "Angelina, do you think Eric will come down this weekend?"

The question broke the silence and the conversation began once again. By the time Mamba got up to remove the dinnerware; the question had been largely forgotten.

Danni leaned closer to Bill and slid her hand close to his. "Is it safe enough to take a walk on the beach?"

Bill glanced around the table. No one was paying particular attention to them. "I think we can still manage a walk on the beach; let's go."

Chapter 48

The night air was warm and the sea calm. They walked together for many minutes before Danni turned to Bill. "Do you know Angelina is investigating Hanna's rape?"

Bill looked straight ahead into the darkness. "Yes. I know."

"She said that all the men who raped Hanna are dead."

Bill glanced at Danni. "That's good to know."

Danni wondered, why didn't Bill ask how they died; or was it that he already knew? It would have been a question most others would have asked. "The last one died in prison earlier this year."

Bill didn't answer, what did Danni expect him to say…gee, that's too bad? This was a strange conversation.

"Bill, did you know that Eric's father killed one of the rapists?"

In all the years since the rape, Danni had never once mentioned Bomani Thomas as one of the rapists. If Bill acknowledged that he knew JB Jackson killed Thomas, and that Thomas was one of Hanna's rapists, then all the care he had taken to conceal his part in the revenge killing would be revealed.

How many times had he been on the verge of telling Danni everything; only to retreat to the safety and security of his intricate plan of deception?

"Are you talking about the fight in prison? I saw it on the news."

"She also told me my husband was killed because of a drug deal. Tyrell Biggs had him killed because he thought he was involved. Do you know anything about that?"

This was it. Danni wanted to know the truth. Bill could continue to live with the lies, or reveal the truth to Danni.

"Danni, I know about it all, but there are others I must protect; men who expect me to take these secrets to the grave." Bill turned to Danni, "I will give my life to you and you may do with it as you wish, but there are many men who trust me to keep their involvement secret. Those men I will not betray and you will have to decide if you can accept the man who stands before you for what he is today, and what he will be tomorrow, or reject me because of what you think my past may have been."

Danni released Bill's arm. "Why would you ever expect that I would betray anyone?"

"Danni, you have listened to Agent Sanchez and now you question me like a suspect in something I thought you would rather forget. I will tell you whatever you want to know about what I have done, but I will not go beyond that. I hope you understand. Let me ask you a question first. Does agent Sanchez suspect you?"

It was an instinctive reaction. "Me? Why would she suspect me of anything?"

They were now standing apart in the darkness. "You see, Danni, we all have our secrets, don't we."

Danni felt panic. "I can't believe you would say such a thing!"

The charade was over. It was a dangerous way to start the rest of your life with the woman you loved.

"Why does this bother you now?"

"I thought you loved me, but you only used me to fill your pockets with drug money, and got my husband killed doing it."

The seconds ticked by. The gentle lapping of the waves on the shore were the only sounds. Bill's emotions were concealed by the darkness.

"That is the kind of man you think I am?"

"Is it true? Did you use me to do the drug deal?"

"Danni, the drug deal was intended to generate money for Eric. As for your husband, he killed himself when he started running the hookers. I feel responsible for that...but I will tell you that when I found out what he was doing, I wanted to kill him myself; for what he was doing to you and your family. If you think..."

Bill stopped in mid-sentence. Danni began to regret her decision to ask Bill about the drugs. "Bill, I'm so..."

Bill grabbed her arm and pulled her into a crouching position. "Quiet!"

Bill cocked his head, "Can you smell that?" Bill raised his nose to what little breeze there was. "That's smoke! There's a fire somewhere."

Once Bill mentioned it, she could also smell the smoke. It was drifting from the northern part of the island.

Bill pointed to waters of Calibogue Sound, "Look, isn't that a boat?"

The boat was maybe four or five hundred yards to the north. At full throttle, a small skiff bounced through the swells coming in from the Atlantic. The skiff had pulled away from beach and was now heading north.

"Wait here."

Bill disappeared into the night. The smell of smoke was heavier now. Danni heard her name being called. She could see the vague outline of Bill with his hands cupped around his mouth. He was trying to tell her something.

"The hotel is on fire! Go back home and call the fire department!"

Danni rushed back down the beach. There was a small trail that would cut five minutes off her trip if she could find it. There it was! Twice she tripped on protruding roots, and she felt her face being slashed by low hanging branches. She rushed into the kitchen.

"The hotel is on fire! Call the fire department!"

Danni turned and started to make her way back to the hotel, but was quickly overtaken by Doc and DeAngelo in one of the golf carts the Helton's kept for quick trips around their property. Danni sat in the rumble seat with Angelina and watched Mamba, Hanna and James trail in the dust cloud their cart kicked up as they hurried to the hotel.

The glow of the fire reflected off the smoke and was visible over the trees. When they turned onto the drive leading to the resort, Danni noticed hotel employees capturing the flames in their video cameras. Doc and DeAngelo ignored the people, but Danni didn't.

"Put those cameras away and help the people get out of the hotel!"

"Screw you lady, this is going national, and I'm going to sell this to the news."

393

Danni took a step in their direction, but Doc put his hand on her arm. "Don't waste your time. We've got people to help."

Smoke billowed from both the north and south wings of the resort. Hotel guests in their night clothes streamed from the main entrance. Parents shouted for their children and once found huddled in tight groups on the front lawn. The first guests out were fortunate. The ones that followed were not so lucky, but once clear they all turned and watched with some sort of fixation at the flames that began to blow out windows and lick at the roof.

Danni Walton did not hesitate when she arrived at the hotel. She turned to Angelina. "Angelina, move the guests to the other side of the road and keep them off the front lawn. The front lawn is the only spot where you can land a helicopter, and that will be our medical evacuation point. When the fire department arrives, have them fight the fires in the main lobby. It is the only way out and we have to keep it clear."

Danni turned to Doc. "Doc, set an aid station up at that pool house, there," she pointed at the resort pool. "There should be a first aid kit in the office. Break down the door if you have to. Mamba, you and Hanna help Doc, and James you help Angelina..." she turned to DeAngelo, "DeAngelo, you're with me. There are fire hoses in the lobby. We need to get them going."

Danni and DeAngelo fought their way against the outflow of guests. Those now making their way to the lobby showed signs of burned or singed clothing. Those still inside were nearing a panic level. Danni was not surprised to see Bill Cannon directing the evacuation of hotel guests from the south wing. It was comforting so see Bill kneel down to calm the fears of a child, and assign an adult escort to ensure the child was evacuated.

Danni yelled to Bill, "How many left in that wing?"

The noise in the hotel was almost overwhelming with the roar of the increasing fires and chatter of people making their way from the burning wings. Bill's clothes already dark with soot replied, "I don't know. I banged on all the doors on the bottom floor and I think they are all out. I'll check the top floor in a minute."

Danni nodded and turned her attention to getting the fire hoses operating. Once they had one hose out Danni stopped some of the male guests. None of the employees manned the hoses or stood their ground in the face of the fire to assist the guests. "Man this hose until all that can have escaped." They stood their posts until the fire overwhelmed them, but they saved many lives.

The island's volunteer fire department did all they could, but they had no chance against a fully engaged fire. Doc triaged the injured and help prioritize the injured for aerial evacuation and did what he could for the others.

The grand hotel shuddered and began to collapse from the wings. By morning there was nothing more they could do. Covered in soot, Danni Walton stood with her family and watched the hotel she loved burn to the ground.

"What a tragedy..." Danni turned to identify the man who spoke. It was Dewad Henstep, the union's principal at the hotel. Compared to Danni, Henstep as pristine as the sunrise. Not a wrinkle to his suit as if he had just arrived at the scene, "… it's a good thing we were insured."

Danni felt nothing but revulsion for the man. Pain and suffering all around and his concern was only the insurance. She didn't make any comment. She was too tired to argue with this idiot.

Danni turned back to the smoldering ruin. "Has anyone seen Bill?"

~~

The *Crescent Moon* moved ahead at dead slow. Her slow speed in this area of tight turns would not attract undue attention, especially at night, and it would allow for the boarding of passengers from the small skiff off their port side. Rayhan Al-Sabah supervised the boarding of the passengers from the bridge. Once the passengers were aboard he left the bridge and met his new guests in the stateroom.

Rayhan bowed slightly at the waist, "Allah Be Praised. I hope your journey has not been unpleasant."

Achmad Nardiff returned the bow, "Your highness…through the grace of Allah, our journey was without incident. We have everything we need to complete our jihad."

"How much time will you require to complete the assembly of the weapon? We expect to be near the outer banks within two days."

Achmad Nardiff straightened and his tone changed to one more commanding than accommodating. "Your highness, we have considered the plan offered by your father, and we believe our cause will be better served if we place the weapon in Washington rather than the beaches of the outer banks."

Prince Al-Sabah had warned his son of just such a situation. "May I remind you that our objective is to demonstrate our power, not to start a war with the United States. Attacking Washington would only enflame their wrath and desire for revenge and many of our brothers would be killed by their retaliation. Our objective is to demonstrate our power. Through that power we can bend them to our will."

Most of what Rayhan said was true, all except Prince Al-Sabah's objective. It was a terrible day in Prince Al-Sabah's life when he understood—after all other efforts had failed—that only something as terrifying as a nuclear explosion on the shores of America, would rekindle the spirit of the only country that could save the world. His objective was to awaken the spirit of America.

Nardiff was condescending and hateful in his reply. "You are the son of your father. Your mind has been poisoned by the West. We must strike at the infidel wherever he is. Our brothers here and throughout this land are prepared to sacrifice their lives to gain the Kingdom of Heaven. You and your father are as non-believers. You will be consumed by the earth beast and be defecated into Haawiya, and there you will be tortured by the serpents and scorpions. Your only salvation is to join us!"

It was a terrible curse to place on anyone, much less the first born of the Crown Prince of Kuwait. Rayhan pulled from his garment a pistol and pointed it directly at the head of Achmad Nardiff. "You will do as you have been told, and exactly what you have been paid to do. Anything less than your solemn oath that you will do these things, or before Allah, you will no longer be of the earth; the choice is yours to make."

Rayhan didn't hear the shot until well after the bullet entered his back, pierced his lung and exited from his abdomen. His own gun slipped from his hand as he grabbed for something to help him regain his balance. He staggered past the man who shot him in the back. He had to escape.

His legs would not support him when he tried to climb the ladder leading to the bridge. He did not yell or cry out as he slipped and fell from the yacht into the murky waters below. If he could swim to the shore, he could find help and he would warn his father. They had been betrayed.

~~

Ken Carson formed his plan just after dark and before the drinks muddled his mind. It would be easy to start his retirement a few years earlier than originally planned. His money was secure in accounts

396

offshore in places where his wife and that bitch Karen could never touch it, and the bartender seemed to be the only person interested in his story.

"That bitch don't know who she's messing with." Ken's words had become slurred, and even the bartender was becoming bored. "They're both bitches! I knew they were trash. You try to do your best, and what do you get…you get betrayed…that's what. If they think they gonna get any of my money, they can both kiss my ass."

Ken Carson could smell the smoke as he staggered to his car and when he woke it was with a splitting headache and with a kink in his neck that felt like a knife entering his neck. Sleeping in your car will do that.

Ken knew he would have to check into a hotel and clean up before work, and his watch told him he would be late. He would call work and make an excuse for his tardiness. His secretary surprised him when she answered his call.

"Mr. Carson, is everything okay? Mr. Helton and a deputy sheriff have already been in your office looking for you."

"What did they want?" A deputy sheriff; the implications could only mean one of two things. Either the deputy was there serving more papers for the divorce, or Ed Helton had wised up.

"I don't know exactly. They took a lot of records from your desk. Do you want me to put you through to Mr. Helton's office?"

"Hell no! Don't do that. I won't be in, I'm not feeling well."

~~

Ed Helton, Buford Long, and a police detective from the Savannah Police Department surrounded the coffee table in Ed Helton's office. Each of the men thumbed through the report prepared by Buford Long on Ken Carson's fraudulent accounts.

The detective spoke first. "I think any judge would sign an arrest warrant with this information. How long did this guy work for you?"

Ed closed his report. "Long enough. I'll call my lawyer and have him file the appropriate paperwork."

The phone on Ed's desk rang. It was Ken Carson's secretary. "Mr. Helton, Mr. Carson just called. He is not feeling well and won't be in this morning."

Ed nodded, it was what he expected. "Carson said he is sick and won't be in today. I want us to move ahead with the charges."

~~

Bill Cannon had *Old Ironbelly* at a comfortable cruise moving south on the Intercoastal; the smoke of the fire now well to his stern. There was nothing more he could do at the hotel and there would be nothing to gain from continuing the conversation with Danni. He was bound for a small fish camp at Shellman Bluff, a place of solitude where he could sort out the strange happenings of the night.

The burns from the fire stung, but not more than the words of Danni Walton. She thought of him as a selfish man, a devious man, capable of nothing more than using her misfortune for his personal gain. Not even the clear ocean air or the soothing tones of the twin outboards could expunge the terrible sense of loss that he felt. So this is how it felt to be rejected by the woman you loved. It was an empty feeling, a feeling of helpless frustration. He couldn't change the past, and now his future looked bleak and lonely.

He welcomed the sting of the shower on the raw burns on his hands and arms; it relieved his mind from thoughts of Danni. The shower complete, he turned on the news and lent some attention to the reporter as he dressed his burns with ointment and gauze bandages.

The hotel fire was featured. Bill marveled at how quick the news could respond to tragedy; four known dead and another dozen or so still missing. He hoped Danni would report the small skiff they saw leaving the hotel to the police.

It must have been a busy day for fire departments. After the Daufuskie fire, the reporter transitioned into another, this one at a chemical plant in Arkansas. No injuries or deaths reported, but for the safety of the local population the police evacuated residential areas within one mile downwind of the plant. Neither the plant manager nor the local fire chief could explain the cause of the explosion and fire, and both explained that the chemicals produced at the plant, chemicals used in the production of weed killers, by themselves, were non-toxic to humans. The evacuation was a precautionary measure.

Exhausted from the long night, Bill stretched out on the Army surplus cot. His dreams were filled with visions of black smoke and fire, and of the woman he feared he had lost.

Chapter 49

The drive to the small bank in Richmond, on the outskirts of Savannah, even in the rush-hour traffic was less than an hour. Ken Carson withdrew all the cash from his account, a sum of less than $10,000, and his passport from the safety deposit box. Ken always expected that one day he would need an escape route, and his was well planned. The cash was enough to get him to Miami and then to the Cayman Islands. The millions he had in the Cayman account were enough to help him forget the treachery of both Rachael and Karen. He would be out of the country and living a life of leisure before any on those bent on his destruction would be aware he was gone. The grin on his face would be described by most as evil.

~~

Ken Carson was near the Florida State line when Bill Cannon woke from a troubled sleep. A sleep tormented by terrible dreams of billowing smoke and flames. Danni Walton was there, standing in the flames, one moment pleading for help, and the next floating away above the flames. He ran into the smoke and flames and jumped to grab her, but she was out of his reach. He watched her clutch at her throat and then the convulsions began, and she doubled over in pain.

When Bill woke and took a moment to separate the dream from reality, he understood most of it. He understood the smoke and fire. He had just left the burning hotel. He did not understand her death.

But he had seen it before; the runny nose, the constrictions of the chest and then the drooling and all her body fluids being squeezed from her body. How she began to twitch and jerk and muscles so tight she could no longer breathe and she suffocated. It was terrible to watch even in a dream. He had seen the same deaths in the Kurdish mountains of northern Iraq. It was the death caused by nerve gas.

Call it a survival instinct; Bill had learned to trust his. His call to Lucas McLaughlin in the Pentagon was answered immediately. "Lucas, I've got something banging around in my head, I need to bounce it off someone; you got a minute?"

"Sure Bill, but be careful, this isn't a secure line."

"Yeah...not a problem. Lucas the other day we commented on the border crossing that was on the news; do you remember...how we thought it was strange the three border agents were killed? Has anybody got a lead on who did it, or any packages that crossed?"

Lucas didn't think the fact that all the agencies involved in the search turned up a big donut would be classified. "No Bill, they don't have lead one."

"Just what I thought; now, you remember what was being shipped into Ezbet Abu Sagal?"

"Of course."

"Did you see the news about the chemical plant explosion in Arkansas?"

"I saw a brief report on the news, what's the connection?"

"Humor me for a moment. We've got bad guys coming into the United States from multiple points, we've got a border crossing where agents are killed for no apparent reason, and now we've got a chemical plant explosion where one of the things they produce is weed killer.

"If you stole a gallon of gas from your old man's car, what better way to hide the fact you took some than to burn the rest?

"If that chemical plant produced or stored isopropylamine for their weed killer, and any drug store in America will sell isopropyl alcohol, and what was smuggled across the border wasn't drugs, but methylphosphonic difluoride; then we may be the target of a chemical attack."

Lucas hoped his line wasn't being monitored. "Damn Bill, I told you this line wasn't secure!"

Bill understood the concern his friend had about security. "I know Lucas, but I wanted to tell someone. If I'm wrong so what; if I'm right, then everybody in America will know soon enough."

Lucas had fought with Bill Cannon in many battles and had learned to respect his ability to "see the battlefield," but this scenario was beyond the pale and caught him by surprise. "Bill, how did you ever come up with this?"

Bill took a moment to debate if he should tell his friend the truth; he would. "Lucas, it came to me in a dream."

~~

It took Lucas McLaughlin more than an hour to research the chemical plant explosion and type up a memorandum of the conversation with Bill Cannon. Bill was correct; the plant in Arkansas produced isopropylamine. If their records were correct, four drums of the chemical were missing.

He spent another hour trying to convince the Under Secretary of Defense for Intelligence to get the issue briefed in the daily briefing to the President. The Under Secretary was not impressed, but General McLaughlin was persistent and demanded the Secretary of Defense be informed of the scenario developed by Bill Cannon.

The Secretary of Defense allowed five minutes before he had to leave the Pentagon for a meeting of the national Security Council. The Secretary of Defense, like the undersecretary for intelligence, was not impressed. "General McLaughlin, your Colonel Cannon already has us running all over creation looking for a phantom nuke. Now he wants us to drop everything and go running around looking for chemical weapons...without a single piece of concrete evidence."

"Mr. Secretary, I've known Bill Cannon for more than 20 years...he doesn't make up this kind of stuff. The more I think about it, it makes perfect sense. In fact, a nerve gas attack is more probable than a nuclear one. Somebody is smuggling nerve gas into the Gaza strip...we know that, and it would be easy to smuggle in the components of nerve gas into the United States. We picked up three known terrorists within the last week on both coasts...how many others got through? We should at least raise the alert system and let the local authorities know."

The Secretary of Defense stopped in his tracks. "General McLaughlin, let me make myself perfectly clear. You will not...I repeat...will not, notify anybody outside this building of the possibility of an attack by chemical weapons. I'll mention your theory to the President's Chief of Staff...if he thinks this is important enough to get into the daily brief I'll give you a call. Other than that, you will keep your mouth shut. Now, why don't you go back to your office and make yourself useful and find that nuke ...if there even is one."

Lucas stood his ground. "Mr. Secretary, why don't we send an interrogation team and question one of the terrorists we caught trying to get in the country."

"We can't do that. The Attorney General wouldn't allow it."

"I guess the Attorney General wouldn't let us put out a bulletin that the police look for middle-eastern men leaving Arkansas, or would that be considered profiling."

The Secretary hurried away. "General, you already know the answer to that."

~~

The White House Chief of Staff chaired the meeting of the NSC; apparently the President and Vice President had tired of negative reports and lack of any substantial evidence that the threat of a nuclear attack was imminent. Reports from the various departments were all the same; nothing to report.

The Secretary of Defense debated keeping the information from Lucas McLaughlin to himself. But, if something did happen now, and it became known that he withheld the information, well, then he could be the one blamed. If he could have expected the Chief of Staff's response, then he would have kept the report to himself.

"Chief, General Lucas McLaughlin is filing a report that the border crossing in Laredo may have not been drugs at all, but the components to produce nerve gas."

The Chief of Staff could at times be brutal, and this was one that would help nurture that image. He threw his briefing folder onto the polished table. "You people at the Pentagon are always coming up with a terrorist under every bed." The look on the Chief's face was one of contempt. "First this nuclear bomb and now a chemical attack. What in the hell makes you think that?"

The Secretary could tuck his tail between his legs and retreat, or stand his ground. He could almost hear the snickers of the others at the table. He hoped he was as convincing with this group as General McLaughlin was with him.

"Nerve gas is being smuggled into the Gaza Strip, we know that. There was an explosion at a chemical plant in Arkansas last night. That plant can't account for 200 gallons of isopropylamine, a critical component of binary nerve agent. We've got terrorists entering the country on both coasts. It's not too much of a stretch to think the border crossing at Laredo wasn't drugs but a component to binary nerve gas. I think there are enough questions here to at least warn the local authorities."

The Chief of Staff shook his head. "Who came up with the bullshit idea?"

"General McLaughlin submitted the report."

"General McLaughlin was the officer in Israel when that thing went down in Lebanon, and isn't he chummy with Colonel Bill Cannon?"

"Yes sir, he is."

The Chief of Staff turned to the Attorney General. "I thought we had someone looking into this guy Cannon and his involvement in Lebanon."

"We do. I've got an investigator down in Georgia right now building a case."

If the Chief of Staff was concerned with the possibility of a chemical attack he certainly hid it. To the Attorney General, "The President expects results. When can I tell him to expect the investigation to be done?"

"Soon."

~~

Eric could have simply returned to his apartment and left in the morning, but the videos of the fire caused concern and he wanted to make sure Angelina wasn't hurt. That and he had come to a decision and the anticipation he felt from that far outweighed his concern for Angelina's safety.

The sun was well set when he turned east on I-16 in Macon. The ride from Macon to Savannah was always a lonely stretch of road, but now it was even more so. The 'No Gas' signs plastered on the exits were stark reminders of the impact of the oil embargo.

Mike DeAngelo would meet him at the marina in Thunderbolt and take him to the island. When Angelina received Eric's call that he would arrive around midnight, she insisted on going with DeAngelo to pick him up. Getting off the island would be a change of pace and maybe the salt air would clear the stench of smoke from her nose.

The night crossing had a surreal quality to it, like they were approaching a huge, dangerous, and slumbering beast that could wake and turn on them if disturbed. The mainland had become alien and dangerous territory. Only on Daufuskie was there security and peace.

The dock at Salt Water Creek Marina seemed forbidding. The street lights cast ominous shadows that hid evil images, figures that darted and slithered between the trees. When Eric appeared on the pier Angelina felt a moment of panic and wanted to scream to Eric to run.

She met Eric on the dock and his embrace was tender and loving and the kiss they shared was too long for DeAngelo. "You two should get a room. The tide is going out and if we don't shove off, we may be marooned here until morning. Let's go."

The escape from the mainland was without incident. Eric and Angelina sat together on the folding seat at the stern of the boat; Angelina's awkward cast resting on the back of the seat and Eric's body providing soothing warmth to her cracked ribs. Eric leaned close to her ear and whispered, "I missed you."

With Eric now seated next to her, the return to Daufuskie served to connect and confirm the union between Eric and Angelina. If Angelina knew what was on Eric's mind and what was in his pocket, the crossing may have been filled with more than the pleasures of a gentle ride on the ocean. It most probably would have been filled with suspense and anticipation.

When they docked at Daufuskie, Eric declined the electric cart and chose instead to walk the beach. It was late, but the hour meant nothing to them, they wanted the solitude of a walk in the moonlight.

Eric walked on Angelina's right. When he circled her waist with his arm he bumped the brace holding her left arm and felt her wince. He made do with simply holding her hand as they walked. "Angelina, how do you like living on the Island?"

"Everybody told me it would grow on me, and it has. Except for that terrible fire it's been great. It's kind of boring without you here," Angelina gave Eric's hand a little squeeze. "Not quite as exciting as swimming naked in a rock pool."

Eric laughed, "We can do something about that you know. We can sneak into the hotel pool if you are up to it."

Now Angelina laughed, "I would, but Doc would get mad at me if I got my cast wet."

Eric's mood seemed to change from one of a man very relaxed in an environment where he was in control to a man unsure of himself. "Angelina, have you given much thought to us...I mean to what kind of future we have...together? After your investigation, are you going back to Washington?"

Of course she had given thought to their future, but she took the easy way out and answered the second question and ignored the first. "I really don't know. I'll go where I'm assigned I guess. I can always request an assignment in Atlanta."

"That's another thing I want to talk to you about. I'm not so sure I want my wife in a job where she can get shot."

Angelina's heart jumped a beat. Did she hear Eric correctly? Was Eric serious? "Would you mind repeating that?"

"I said I'm not so sure I want my wife in a job where she can get shot."

If this was a proposal of marriage it wasn't what she expected. Where were the roses and the romantic setting, and the carriage ride? Eric had a different romantic side to him; it was more of substance than show. Every time she thought of the water lily after the rock climb she always laughed. He had integrity and was courageous. He had shared with her his darkest secrets and she loved him in spite of his past. They had talked around the issue many times and she had to admit that when she was away from him, he was always on her mind. For some reason she always thought him out of reach, that he would always marry a celebrity and in later years she would see him on the red carpet in Hollywood. Yet, now, on this beach in the middle of the night, he had proposed. Or was it a proposal?

"Eric you're pretty good on television, but if that was a proposal, it was the worst one I've ever heard."

Eric shuffled his feet in the sand. "Well, I haven't had any practice. If I did ask you to marry me would you say yes?"

Angelina smiled in the darkness. "Are you serious?"

"If I was, would you say yes?"

Angelina turned to Eric. "Can you cook?"

"Not a lot, but I can learn by watching the food channel."

"Then I would probably say yes, if I was asked."

Eric took from his pocket a small case. The diamond inside shimmered in the moonlight. It was not overly extravagant, she would describe it as solid, the same way she knew Eric would be in their marriage. "Angelina Sanchez, will you marry me?"

It was a strange feeling; committing your life to someone else. Most of her girlfriends always made a grand announcement of their engagements, but to Angelina she only wanted to announce to Eric her love for him. It was enough.

"Yes, Eric Brown, I will marry you."

They both laughed when Eric slipped the ring on the third finger of her left hand. Perched far out on her arm that could not be lowered next to her body the ring brightened their way. It was easy to talk of the future, and they did, but the concerns of the present always have a way of creeping into all dreams.

"Eric, can you afford to keep me in the style the wife of a famous television personality should be kept? You've got your image to think about, you know."

The comment was innocent enough. They were just fooling around with silly comments and dreams of their future like all young lovers do, but the answer shocked Angelina.

"Yeah, I hadn't thought about that. Maybe I can get a part-time job on one of DeAngelo's shrimp boats. I think I can take care of you with what I...oops, excuse me, with what we have in the bank. The reality is that we don't really need to worry about money unless you are more of a shopper than I think you are."

Eric never talked about his money. He wanted a woman to love him for what he was, and not what he had. With Angelina he had no reservation sharing his secret. She had his heart and it was time to be completely open and honest. He stopped and turned to Angelina. "If we don't blow it, then we already have more of a nest egg than most newlyweds."

Angelina was amused at the bravado. "Oh really...all right mister big spender, just how much do we have in the bank?"

"Over $3,000,000."

The number stunned her. "How did you ever get that kind of money?" Angelina knew Eric's life was always on the edge of abject poverty. He had a decent job when working with CNN, but never one that would allow him to amass such a small fortune.

"My father had an insurance policy. I never knew anything about it. I've used some of it to get through college and to care for Aunt Grace, but the rest is drawing interest in a bank in Panama."

Angelina tried to control her emotions. Millions of dollars...in a bank in Panama...after his father died...was there any way Eric didn't understand the connection; or was Eric involved? Angelina was glad it was deep into the night and that the stars were only sufficient to ignite the sparkle of the engagement ring, but was not enough to reveal the concern on her face.

Chapter 50

The Cayman Islands were different, but Ken could make do. The British influence was pervasive, but there was so much of America here; the weather channel and American baseball were on the television, and even the news was in English. It was not like you were banished to the far reaches of some frozen land where the sun never shined. The turquoise waters near the shore slowly blended into the darker waters of the depths, and it was beautiful. But the most alluring things about Grand Cayman were the tanned and shapely bodies of the women lounging near the hotel pool.

The tropical depression forming in mid-Atlantic was no immediate threat to his new paradise—the Weather Channel said as much—and the islanders, and Ken already considered himself as such, could expect only blue skies and full sun. His first days as an islander Ken avoided work and made himself available to the women at the pool. His painfully burned skin forced him to take shelter under the shade of the palm trees. In the shade it was possible to enjoy the breezes off the Caribbean Sea and the scenery at the pool. He found it odd that he spent the nights alone in his room and convinced himself that would be remedied when he settled into a grand residence befitting a man of his means. There was so much he could offer a woman.

Today he would tour the main island for his villa, but first a visit to the bank to get his financial affairs in order. The flowered shirt and shorts grated on his skin, but it was what a rich American would wear.

Ken knew he struck an imposing figure as he approached the Barclay's International receptionist. "I am Ken Carson. I have an account with this bank. I would like to talk with one of your personal bankers."

The British accent of the receptionist was music to his ears. "Certainly Mr. Carson, may I ask the purpose of the meeting?"

"I am moving my permanent residence to the island. I plan to go house hunting this afternoon and I would like to arrange for a local checking account."

The cool air from the air conditioner was a magic salve to his burned skin. While he waited the receptionist served him a tall iced beverage of fruit juices and Ken thought how good it would taste if laced with the dark rum that was preferred by the islanders.

"Mr. Carson, Mr. Hawthorn will see you now. Please follow me."

Hawthorn's office was one of the first doors in the long hallway that led to the double doors of the conference room. This was obviously a junior bank executive to be located so near the entrance. Ken deserved an executive closer to the conference room; after all, six million dollars surely wasn't the largest account maintained by the bank, but it was substantial. The chair in the small office was comfortable.

"Mr. Carson, I am Ian Hawthorn, the receptionist mentioned you would like to open a checking account at the bank."

"That's correct. I am starting to search for a home to purchase here on the island. I think it is wise to deal in the local currency."

"I can handle that for you. How much would you like to deposit in the account?"

"I would like a portion of my account transferred to a checking account."

Mr. Hawthorn cleared his throat. "Mr. Carson, the receptionist mentioned that you stated you have an account with us, but I have checked our records and there is no account at Barclay's International in your name."

It was more than the chill of the cool air that shivered through Ken Carson. "That's ridiculous. I have been making deposits to this bank for more than a year. I wrote a draft on this bank less than a month ago for $12 million, and it was processed. You need to check your records again."

"Mr. Carson, I have already checked our accounts twice. There is no account in your name."

What kind of scam was this? Ken offered, "Perhaps my account is listed under the International Investment Cartel under my name."

Hawthorn dutifully typed into his computer, "No, Mr. Carson, we have no accounts listed under any International Investment Cartel."

Ken Carson's breathing increased and spittle started to collect at the corners of his mouth. When Ken reached for his briefcase, Mr. Hawthorn reached for the panic button under his desk. When Ken opened his briefcase he produced the documents that would put this crooked banker in his place.

"Mr. Hawthorn, these are copies of electronic transfers and deposit receipts I have made to this institution for the last year. I have over $6,000,000 in this bank, and unless you want to find yourself in court, then you better find my money!"

Hawthorn took one of the deposit slips from Ken, "Mr. Carson, these deposit slips were not issued by this bank. This is not our international bank routing number. I don't know what bank issued these, but it was not this bank."

Ken was dangerously close to losing all control of his emotions. "I demand to speak to your supervisor. This is an outrage!"

Ken's voice reached down the hall to the office of one of the vice presidents. He expected the phone call from Mr. Hawthorn. To avoid more commotion in the bank, normally a place of stately efficiency, he hurried to Hawthorn's office to quiet the disruptive visitor. He extended his hand to Ken and felt the clammy sweat of panic on his palm.

"I am Mr. Downing, how may I assist you?"

"Are you this idiot's supervisor?" Ken cast a scowl in the direction of Ian Hawthorn.

"Yes I am. How can I help you?"

Ken flourished the deposits slips under the chin of Downing. "I've been making deposits to this bank for over a year…these are my receipts…and this jerk says I don't even have an account here. Somebody better come up with some answers or there will be hell to pay!"

Downing turned to Hawthorn, "Mr. Hawthorn?"

Hawthorn turned the computer screen so his supervisor could view the screen. "There are no accounts listed under Mr. Carson…I have checked it twice. Those receipts are not from this bank. I don't know what else to say, but we did not issue those vouchers."

Mr. Downing took a moment to review the computer screen and the slips offered by Ken Carson. Mr. Hawthorn was correct. The receipts were not issued by the Barclay's International Bank of the Cayman Islands.

"Mr. Carson, I regret to inform you, but you have no account with this bank. You are being disruptive to our business and I must ask you to leave."

Almost before Mr. Downing could complete his statement, Ken Carson was at his throat. "Liar! Thief!"

Ken's eyes were insane and his strength overwhelmed the object of his rage. As the men crashed over the leather chairs and to the floor, Mr. Hawthorn's finger was on the button calling security. It took two officers to subdue Ken Carson.

Ken's third night in the island paradise of the Grand Cayman was a cell in the local police department's jail; the view through the door was not nearly as nice as from under the palm trees. The night alone gave him time to think.

What had gone wrong? How could the bank have been so careless with his money; how could they deny the existence of his account? It was the same bank used by all members of the syndicate. Jerry Evans, Hans Dieter, and even Ed Helton used Barclay's International. Ken had seen the bank logo on Ed Helton's computer. Ken had transferred money from this very bank to fund investments on many bids. They were all electronic transfers, but why would the bank not honor withdrawals in person?

Ken paced the small cell late into the night; four paces in one direction and four paces to return. The hall was dimly lit and only the police locking up rowdy drunks broke the monotony. With each turn the circumstance of the situation became clear. He never should have invested in the syndicate. He was doing fine at the bank. Nobody would have ever discovered his secret source of income. It would have taken more time, but his money was never at risk.

Looking back he wished he had simply ignored the invitation from Jerry Evans to join the syndicate. But it seemed so easy. Both Evans and Dieter proved how easy it was to make money in the syndicate; they paid millions back to the bank within a week with extra profits to invest. Ken had seen the money, he had seen the checks.

Ken only dozed, never slept, during his night in the jail. Every time he started to slip into sleep, a panic gripped him. A horrible feeling that the entire syndicate and the International Investment Cartel were nothing more than an intricate scam; and the face of the man behind the scam was none other than Ed Helton.

In the morning his only visitor was a junior officer from the American Embassy. "Mr. Carson, you are being deported back to Miami."

"But they have my money! You must help me, they are stealing my money! You can't let them get away with this, I'm an American citizen…you're supposed to help me. You can't let them send me back…you have to help me get my money back."

The young man from the Embassy had seen this before. Maybe it was too much sun or too much rum, but Ken Carson wasn't the first to lose touch with reality on a visit to the island. "Mr. Carson, we have reviewed your case. I suggest you contact a lawyer back in the States, but you are not going to cause any more trouble here." The young man dangled a pair of chrome handcuffs in front of Ken. "We can do this the hard way or the easy way. The choice is yours."

As the young man from the Embassy watched Ken Carson board the flight to Miami he turned to the policeman standing with him. "That is one crazy son-of-a-bitch."

The policeman laughed. "All you Americans are crazy."

~~

Bill Cannon traced a line in the packed sand with his big toe. What exactly had gone wrong? One moment he was one with Danni and the next she had turned on him. From the first time they met her laugh and smile had drawn him to her like a moth to a flame. It was more than that, it was her heart—she was a good woman, but now she had chosen to shun him.

He had always held his love for her far above the raging torrents of life and away from the prying eyes of others because there would always be questions; it was as it should be. There would always be the question if his actions were pure, or would they say he arranged the death of her husband to satisfy his selfish desires?

He believed he knew the answer, but did Danni see something different? Did she see things in him that he had kept hidden even from himself? It is easy to lie to yourself; you only have one person to convince. Was he the man he wished to be, or was he really someone capable of such a devious omission, an omission hidden so deep that even his mind turned away from it? Was he a man capable of allowing the death of her husband to gain the reward of her love?

Why is the nectar of love, so sweet in your dreams, so bitter in the light of day? Is there no valley or mountain peak to find the truth, is there no such place where his love could be shared free of the terrible events of the past? Tell him where such a place may be and he would make the journey on bloody hands and knees to find the truth.

For how many years did the sun rise with her approach and set when she would depart? The cold and dark fog of her absence could only be endured with the hope that she would return.

If this is the way it would be, then why did she ever come into his life? What cruel twist of fate would bring her so close if their love was to always be forbidden?

If there was an answer, it would not be revealed today; it would not be revealed on this deserted beach. The ringing of his cell phone would not allow it. He would not have reached for the phone, but there was a chance it could be Danni. It wasn't.

"Is this Bill Cannon?"

"Yes, who's this?"

"Mr. Cannon, I am Sheriff Horace Gates...from Cherokee County in North Carolina...my friends call me Hat...I've got a little problem up here, you may be able to help me."

Hat seemed to be a nice enough guy. "Okay Hat, but how did you get this number?"

"Our forensic lab got it off a cell phone."

The forensic lab—an odd way to find his cell phone number, "Whose cell phone?"

"That's my problem, I've got a body up here and I can't identify it. Your number was the only number in the phone. I was hoping you could help us identify the body."

~~

The county morgue was in the same building as the coroner's office, in fact, it was in the same office as the sheriff's office, and it was only a short walk to the basement where the body was being kept.

"We found him the other day. He looks kind of rough, he was in the water for a couple of days and the crabs got to him."

Hat threw back the sheet covering the cold body. There on the table was the son of one of his most dear friends. There on the table was the body of the young boy he had rescued from the torture chambers of Saddam Hussein. There on the table was Rayhan Al-Sabah, the son of the Crown Prince of the Kingdom of Kuwait.

412

"Do you know who he is?"

"Yes…yes I do…that is Rayhan Al-Sabah, he is the son of the Prince Al-Sabah of Kuwait." Bill turned away from the decomposing body. How would he tell his friend of the death of his only son?

"How did he die?"

"Somebody shot him in the back. We found him in the water, but the coroner said he didn't drown because there wasn't any water in his lungs."

"Do you know who did it?"

Hat covered the body and slid the slab back into the refrigeration unit. "We don't have a clue yet. He was obviously on the water because there are no roads in the area where he was found. I don't think he was transported there and dumped. If he was dumped then whoever did it would have wanted his body to wash out to sea. My guess is he was shot when on board a vessel in the Intercoastal."

"Hat, you need to look for a large yacht named the *Crescent Moon*. She sailed from Savannah on Friday – she was heading north. That boy was probably on that yacht. Find the *Crescent Moon* and you will find the killer."

Bill paced back and forth on the sidewalk fronting the sheriff's office. Twice the international call to Prince Al-Sabah was dropped before the connection was complete. In one way Bill was glad the calls didn't go through. He would have to tell his friend about the death of his son, but he also wanted to tell him at the same time that his son's killer had been caught or even better yet, that his son's death had already been avenged.

A third call to Kuwait failed. It would be easier to walk away and let the State Department notify Al-Sabah through diplomatic channels, but to do so would dishonor their friendship. What would his friend ask him to do? Would he ask Bill to escort the body back to Kuwait? He would do that if asked. Would his friend ask Bill to avenge his son's death? He would do that also.

Why hadn't Prince Al-Sabah told him about his son's visit to America? Did he mention it to Bill during their last meeting? No, only his friend's strange farewell, the one that confused Bill at the time was, "I want you to know that I have always loved your country. I have always considered America the guiding light of freedom in the world. When I am gone, please remember that what I must do, will be to preserve her, not to destroy her."

413

What was concealed in the message? The shiver that passed through Bill's body was real. Was his friend so bold, or so filled with frustration, that he would dare such an act? Bill dialed once again—this time the call was answered.

Lucas McLaughlin noticed Bill Cannon's name before he answered the call. He dispensed with any pleasantries, "Bill, I hate to tell you this, but your name is mud in Washington."

"Yeah, well screw all those pencil necks. Lucas, we may have a problem. Prince Al-Sabah's son has been murdered. He was on his yacht. They launched from Savannah and were heading north. I think there may be more than his killer aboard that boat."

"Bill, I'm tired. Quit talking around in circles and tell me straight what you mean."

"You want the long version or the short one?"

"Make it short."

"I think the bomb is on that boat."

Good Lord…Lucas McLaughlin respected Bill Cannon, but sometimes it was hard to defend him against the 'pencil necks' in Washington. How did Bill Cannon come to conclusions that the entire staff of the National Security Agency missed?

"Damn Bill, first the nuke and the chemical thing and now this, how do you expect me to present this when nobody in the NSA has come up with a thing on the bomb or the chemical weapons?"

Bill understood the pressures his friend was under, but he also knew that Lucas was his only link to the assets in Washington and the Pentagon.

"You know just as well as I do that most of the intelligence analysts couldn't win a game of Clue, and they don't believe anything unless if comes to them on a computer screen. Look…Lucas…I understand the trouble I'm causing you, but you've got to find that yacht. Make up some kind of military exercise, put some helicopters in the air, get the reconnaissance office to reprogram some satellites, and find that boat. Hell, it's big as a football field, there can't be too many of those."

"Finding it shouldn't be a problem, but how do I justify stopping and searching the royal yacht of one of our allies?"

"Make something up. Tell DEA they are smuggling drugs, or have immigration check their passports, anything, just stop that boat."

"Okay Bill, I'll see what I can do. What are you going to do in the mean time?"

"I'm coming to Washington."

"Bill, when we find the yacht, you aren't planning to do anything stupid, are you?"

Bill knew what his friend was asking. "I can't say that the thought didn't cross my mind."

~~

Senator Steve Reynolds sat with the members of the Senate Intelligence Oversight Committee. The picture the analyst was painting in the Middle East was anything but comforting.

"Gentlemen, the entire Middle East is a powder keg ready to explode. Our satellite images show that Iran has moved an armored division near the Fakka Oil on the border with Iraq.

"Iran and Iraq have been fighting over this particular oil field for a quarter century. The movement of an armored division indicates Iran is prepared to escalate the conflict.

"Iran had also moved four divisions within 50 miles of the southern border with Iraq and Kuwait. The movement of these divisions is offensive in nature and there is nothing to stop them if they decided to attack through southern Iraq and into Kuwait. They could be all the way into Saudi Arabia before they would have to refuel."

The senior Senator interrupted the briefer. "What forces do we have in the area if the Iranians cross the border?"

It was a question that should have been asked years ago, before the decision to pull all US forces out of the area, and before the fleet was moved to Diego Garcia. The briefer had no choice but to lay the bare facts before the committee. "None Senator, we don't have a combat ground force or a Navy combat ship within a thousand miles of the Persian Gulf. If they attack, all we can do is watch."

The briefer waited for additional questions. When there were none he turned to his next point. "We have received information that there has been an attempt to assassinate the Prince of Kuwait. The attempt was unsuccessful, but the Prince has gone into hiding. We believe the assassination attempt was part of a growing insurgency of Shia Muslims in Kuwait that want to overthrow the government of Prince Al-Sabah."

~~

General Lucas McLaughlin sat with Terri Toth in her office in the Office of Strategic Reconnaissance. It didn't' take much for Lucas to convince Terri to help find the missing yacht.

Her fingers flew over the keyboard. "There she is."

Terri pointed to an oblong shape confined in the narrows of the Intercoastal Waterway on Friday night in North Carolina. It was easy to track the progress of the yacht. Saturday she was off the coast of North Carolina, by Sunday afternoon she had cleared the Outer Banks and on Sunday evening she had entered the Chesapeake Bay.

Chapter 51

The hairs bristled on the back of her neck. She was being watched…again. In the reflection of the window, from far across the room, it was finally clear who it was that was causing her discomfort.

Mamba stood transfixed…almost statue like…with her knowing gaze somehow peeling away the secrets and questions that Angelina wished to remain buried. It was as if Mamba had entered her body and could easily move that which Angelina had erected to conceal her thoughts. Mamba found what she knew; and then began to search for what was in her heart. It was a painful and disturbing experience.

Eric said the millions in his accounts were from his father's life insurance, but why had he not questioned the veracity of such an endowment? Life is not a fairy tale and there are no fairy god mothers. How could anyone be so naïve as to believe, after being forced to live in pain and poverty for so many years, that his father would have resources and foresight to care for his son only after his death? It was a paradox, a father who would let his son live in squalor, but would sacrifice his life to care for his son.

The innocence of Eric's answer, and there was no attempt to obscure the amount or where the money came from, led Angelina to believe Eric was not involved in the drug conspiracy. That was a conclusion that even the most novice of investigator would conclude; Eric was no more than 15 or 16 when his father died.

So now she had come to the crossroad. Should she reveal to Eric what she had learned; that his endowment was nothing more than tainted blood money? Would he still love her if she did so? Would she still love him if he didn't respond in the manner she would expect of her husband?

For that matter, even in her own mind, how did she expect him to respond? Did she expect that he would simply take her at her word and that her conclusions were correct; or would he challenge her? Would he force her to prove what she believed to be the truth? What if her argument was not compelling enough to convince him? Would he consider her love to be nothing more than a means to invade the memory of his father and the good names of his friends? Could she still love him if he refused to believe her?

If after he learned the source of his money, would Eric simply consider it to have been earned by his father? How far removed must money be before it is considered clean? Are we responsible for the sins of our fathers? Some would always say yes. Angelina could understand the point if he raised it. The money didn't belong to anyone. It had come from the ill-gotten gains of a bunch of murdering drug dealers. Angelina struggled with the question, to whom should the money be returned? Should it go to the government simply because Eric didn't earn it? It was an option that even Angelina didn't find appealing.

"You have decided to test your new love." The voice came from behind her, and she turned to face Mamba.

"Excuse me?"

Mamba faced the table where Eric, Hanna, and James Madison were exchanging pictures of gowns in bridal magazines. It was where Angelina should have been. "It is difficult to sit in judgment of the ones you love. I have lived many years; I have learned to sit only in judgment of good and evil. Learn to accept love and reject evil; it will make your life easier."

Angelina heard clearly the words Mamba spoke, but the meaning was unclear. "I don't understand."

"You will. Now, if you intend to marry that boy, then I would help them pick out your wedding dress."

Mamba smiled, and Angelina felt as if a weight had been lifted from her; she could not explain why. The wedding dress was an important part of her future and she turned to join her friends at the table. Page after page and the light hearted critiques entertained all in the room until Eric's cell phone broke the mood and brought reality to the table.

There was only the look of disappointment on Eric's face. "I have to go back to work. They're calling everyone in, there's something big going on in Washington."

~~

During the drive from Miami, Ken Carson did everything he could to make contact with his syndicate partners, but his calls to Hans Dieter and Jerry Evans were met with the automated operator's message of, "This line is no longer in use, please check your number and try again."

418

The seething rage within Ken increased with each mile marker on the Interstate. He had been duped. Could it be possible that the entire syndicate and International Investment Cartel was nothing more than an intricate charade? Other than the money in the Cayman Islands, he had sold his entire stock portfolio, converted it to cash to invest in the syndicate, and now there was no paper trail to prove his suspicion that Ed Helton and his friends were nothing but scam artists. Carson tried to calm his fears; the meetings were real, the yacht was real, Miami, New Orleans, and Las Vegas, they were not figments of his imagination, they were real! Now it was as if everyone associated with the syndicate vanished into thin air. How could he have been so foolish!

The person with the answers had to be Ed Helton, but he would probably deny any involvement. The loans Ken made to Helton's friends at the direction of Ed Helton, Evans and Dieter, they were real, Ken had destroyed all the paperwork, but he had made the loans himself. He knew they were real, but what did he have to prove those loans were even made? Nothing!

Ken slammed his fist against the dashboard. Damn! He wished it was Ed Helton's face that he was pounding. The pain brought a moment of sanity back to Ken. He would have to keep his wits about him if he was to recover his fortune. He would challenge Helton directly! No, that would accomplish nothing, but he could send his wife. Rachael would help him if for no other reason than unless he recovered his money, there would be no money for her.

These were the thoughts of a desperate man quickly losing his grip on reality.

~~

The pool deck seemed to be moving as Rachael Carson walked to the patio bar. The four fingers of bourbon she poured almost finished the bottle. She hoped there was another in the house, she wasn't sure. The vodka and gin were long gone. She would drink the scotch that Ken left behind only as a last resort. She was now glad she hadn't poured it down the drain as she intended to do.

The ice in the decanter had long ago turned to water and she didn't want to waste the energy to refill it. She cursed as her robe caught the wrought iron of one of the patio chairs. She heard the garment rip as she pulled away from the chair and cursed again when her shin banged against the lounge chair. She saw her stuffy old bitty-of-a-neighbor hurry her husband inside the house and responded to the disapproving look with an obscene gesture. Screw the old bitch. If her husband had

419

never seen a woman in a nightgown in the middle of the day by now, it was about time that he did. Rachael made little attempt to cover her half naked body.

This was the turn her life had taken. One crisis after another that forced her to the bottle.

First it was her sister. Rachael never should have listened to Karen about Ken. It was true she envied Karen and her freedom, and it all seemed so easy. How they would trap Ken in a web of his own vices, and then share the spoils. It had all worked to perfection, but now that Ken had disappeared, half of nothing is still nothing. Her lawyer was no help, he reminded her that Ken had 30 days to respond to the divorce proceedings, and until that deadline had passed the judge wouldn't do a thing.

But sharing of Ken's wealth with Karen was the farthest thing from Rachael's mind; Ken was nowhere to be found and the mortgage was a more immediate concern—that and how her jewelry disappeared from their safe deposit box. She was sure Ken removed it, but if she found out that Karen was wearing any of her jewels, well, the terrible thought of her sister's death did cross her mind.

Everything she had done for Karen…the ungrateful bitch! She took her into her home when she moved to Savannah. She had allowed her the affair with her husband and promised her half the proceeds from the divorce. And what had Karen done for her? Nothing! And now Karen wouldn't answer her call for money. The empty bottle clattered to the pool deck as Rachael finally gave in to the effects of the liquor.

Rachael didn't know how long she slept, but the sun had severely burned the exposed parts of her tender skin. The incessant ringing of the phone woke her from her drunken slumber. She staggered to the phone. She picked up the receiver. She didn't voice a greeting and only listened.

"Rachael, is that you?" It was her husband.

"You sorry bastard! Where have you been? What did you do with my diamonds?" The barrage of insults poured forth until finally she stopped, almost gasping for breath.

"Rachael, something has happened. There has been a big mistake. Something has happened to my money."

"That's a lie! Karen said you had money! She said you have millions!"

"Rachael, listen to me. I know I've made some mistakes. But what I did, I did for us. I've got money in off-shore accounts, enough for us to get out of the country and live like royalty, if you'll only give me a chance to make things right. Now is our chance to start anew."

Rachael swayed as she tried to analyze what Ken had just said. "Oh yeah, how much do you have?"

"Millions…I've got millions off shore. Rachael, everything I did was for us. But, there is a problem with the accounts. I think Helton locked me out, but I have a plan and I need your help."

As strange as it may seem, and as much as she hated her sister, it was always Karen who knew what to do; what would Karen do if she was in her shoes? Karen would follow the money, and Rachael's choices were limited. Help her husband or take nothing.

"I'm listening."

~~

Eric quickly packed the few belongings he needed for his trip back to Atlanta. Mike DeAngelo offered to take him to Savannah. Angelina asked if she could ride with Eric, and DeAngelo had no problem with another passenger. DeAngelo made a big deal that he would even bring her back to the island.

Angelina looked forward to the time alone with Eric. Even though the trip to Savannah would be less than an hour, time with Eric always seemed to calm the waters of her troubled mind. When they were alone life had clarity and focus, and maybe the questions that seemed to constantly wage war with her heart and mind would drift away with the breeze. She would simply enjoy the crossing.

As they were preparing to leave Danni Walton called from the kitchen, "Hey Mike, I need to catch a ride to Savannah."

It was the last thing Angelina wanted to hear; Mrs. Walton serving as chaperone during the few moments Angelina had with Eric. But other than Danni commenting that they made a beautiful couple she left them alone on the stern seats and sat with DeAngelo at the helm.

Their arrival at the county dock was uneventful and Danni gave Eric a big hug, and Angelina gave him an embarrassing kiss and both watched as Eric turned to walk away.

Out of earshot from even the keen ears of Mike DeAngelo, Danni commented, "Have you decided what you are going to do?"

Great...another bout of sparring; this is exactly what Angelina wanted to avoid. At least the boat ride from the island to Savannah was without incident or pressure, but the minute Eric left it returned, "About what?"

Danni ignored her question. "Mamba told me your brain and heart, are at war...her words not mine." Danni laughed, "She has a strange way of defining things, doesn't she."

Angelina looked into Danni's eyes. She didn't see a challenge, only kindness. Angelina returned the laugh, "Yes, she does. Is that why you wanted to come to Savannah, to see what I was going to do?"

"No, you are going to do what you think is best. That much I know about you. I think you can be happy with Eric regardless of the decision you make. He is a good man...you are a good woman...still even with all that it will be hard to find love. I will not interfere, I have enough regrets to last my own lifetime, getting involved with you and Eric is too much of a risk. I love him like a son, and I think you love him too, but it is you that will choose the road you will take."

Angelina turned to Danni. "What should I do?"

"About what?"

"About Eric's money, he said it was from his father, but I don't believe that."

"You don't?"

"No, I think somebody funneled the money from the drug deal to him, but I don't think he knows where it came from."

Danni smiled a slight but knowing smile. "So you must choose between love and the law. May I offer a caution?" Danni thought of her own careless words with Bill Cannon on the beach before the fire, "Words can cut deep as any knife and the wounds may never heal, be careful with accusations you cannot prove."

Angelina was expecting something more profound. She was disappointed in Danni's advice. "That's it? That's all you can tell me?"

Danni laughed a hearty laugh. "Angelina, I don't know what to tell you. I wish this whole thing would just go away, but I want you to make the decision. Look, I have to meet my father at the bank. Why don't you come with me, and afterwards we will grab lunch and see if we can't solve all the world's problems."

Angelina toyed with the idea for a moment. She smiled when she answered. "Thank you for the invitation, but I have to get back.

Hanna and James will have my wedding dress picked out and ordered if I don't get back."

Danni smiled and leaned forward and hugged Angelina. "Angelina, you do what you think is right. No matter what you decide I am glad you are part of the family. Tell Mamba I should be on one of the late ferries. I'll call before I leave. She can send one of the buggies for me."

Angelina boarded DeAngelo's boat and helped him cast away the mooring lines. Their short talk hadn't solved a thing, but for some reason she felt more at peace.

As they floated into the river current she looked to the bank. Danni stood alone high above the river, and she waved, but she didn't drop her hand, almost as if she was debating if she should call for them to return. It was a gesture that should have been so simple, a wave goodbye, but if Angelina would try to explain the feeling that overwhelmed her, it was that Danni Walton was on the deck of the Titanic and the last lifeboat had left without her. Danni Walton had given her seat to salvation to Angelina; it was a terrible burden to carry.

Chapter 52

Angelina couldn't explain why Danni's farewell was so unsettling. She stood at the stern of the boat and allowed the bow wave and the churning wake to calm her. Over the rumble of the engines and the wind rushing through the superstructure she barely heard her cell phone ring. She hoped the call would be from Eric. She needed someone to say I love you, and that everything would be alright.

To her disappointment, it wasn't Eric, but William Jefferson. She hadn't given Jefferson a second thought since the hospital. The island did that to you. It was easy to become disconnected from the mainland and the responsibilities of you profession. She hadn't done a real lick of work since she arrived. She hesitated to answer the call, but Jefferson would continue calling until she did.

As was his way, Jefferson didn't waste time with platitudes. "Sanchez, be on your toes. The Attorney General is sending two investigators to interview you."

"Do they want a briefing on the letter the President received?"

"What letter?"

"Mr. Jefferson, the letter the President received about the rape killings. I don't think I am prepared to come to any solid conclusions or even make a recommendation in the case. There are a lot of loose ends to tie up."

Angelina couldn't explain why she said what she did about the investigation, but she felt better for doing it. She knew she had enough to make a substantial report; something held her back. Maybe Mamba was right, maybe she was learning to sit in judgment of good and evil, and beyond any doubt, she was beginning to believe that Danni Walton, and those others…even those she could not name with certainty…were good and not evil. She felt no remorse bending the truth.

"I doubt they will ask about that investigation. I think the AG is getting pressure from the White House to build a case against Bill Cannon. Have you uncovered anything of substance?"

"Mr. Jefferson, the man only got home the other day and he was here for only a short time. I haven't seen him since the hotel fire."

"What hotel fire?"

"The resort on the island burned to the ground. I saw him at the fire, but not since then."

The investigator in Jefferson wanted to ask about the fire, but more pressing matters were at hand and he forced himself to focus on the Cannon investigation.

"What have you found?"

"Nothing at all. They will be wasting their time. What should I tell them?"

"Tell them exactly that…that you have nothing. I know they want to interview Major Madison. You might want to brief him on the investigation. If Cannon is on the island you may want to tell him to make himself scarce. I don't know if they would try and arrest him, but I wouldn't put it past them. Give me a call after they leave."

Angelina closed her phone. DeAngelo slowed and turned his head, "What was that all about?"

"Just my boss, he wanted to know how my rehab is going. That's all."

DeAngelo grinned, "Did you tell him you were engaged?"

"No, I didn't even think of it."

DeAngelo knew she was lying. There wasn't a woman alive who would admit to forgetting her engagement unless the discussion was a lot more intense than her recovery.

~~

Danni watched DeAngelo turn the boat into the current and paused to wave goodbye to Angelina. It wasn't long before they were hidden by the bends in the river and she turned to hail a cab. She felt alone on the mainland. She was a stranger to those wandering the streets…an islander. There was safety on the island, but here the buildings hid the predators of the concrete jungle; and the predators could strike without warning.

As she waited for the cab, she could feel the approach of something evil. She whirled…but there was nothing. The people on the street ignored her, but the shadows between the buildings would be where the vermin would hide and she couldn't penetrate the darkness;

and she couldn't shake the feeling. Where was Bill Cannon when she needed him?

The cab was filthy and the driver surly and it was an eternity before they arrived at the bank. She would conclude her business with her father as swiftly as possible, and with luck she could catch the next scheduled commercial ferry back home.

The guard at the front door asked for her identification before he allowed her to enter. The décor of the bank was as it always was, but the mood was much more somber. The tellers sat idle and only those serving the drive-up windows were engaged in productive work.

Danni glanced into the empty office of Ken Carson and found that odd. Her father's receptionist greeted her, "Hello Ms. Walton, your father is in a meeting and asked for you to wait. Can I get you anything?"

"No thank you, I'm fine," and Danni settled into a comfortable chair and picked up a magazine.

~~

Rachael Carson sat across the desk from Ed Helton. Ken had schooled her on exactly how to approach him.

"Mr. Helton, I hope what I discuss with you will remain confidential. It is rather embarrassing, but I am concerned about my husband."

Ed was cautious. "Go ahead."

"We have been having some troubles…in our marriage…I filed for divorce. I haven't seen or heard from him since, and he controlled all of our finances."

Ed nodded, but didn't answer.

"My personal finances are in a mess, bills are starting to come due."

If Rachael expected a response from Ed Helton, she was disappointed. She expected at least an expression of concern, but nothing but stony silence filled the office. She had no choice but to continue.

"I have checked our savings accounts, our checking account, and even our safety deposit box, and they are all empty. Did my husband transfer these funds to another account in the bank?"

Ed thought for a moment. "Mrs. Carson, I am sure you understand that I can check the information on any joint account shared by you and your husband, but would require a court order to reveal any other financial information about your husband."

Rachael nodded; it was as her husband told her it would be. "I was afraid you would say that. My husband, before he left, mentioned that he was involved with you in offshore investments. I think he said you were a member of a group investing in something called the International Investment Cartel. Is there any chance of accessing money in that account?"

Ed Helton leaned back slightly in his chair. "Mrs. Carson, I don't have the foggiest idea what you are talking about; what exactly are you alleging."

Rachael expected that answer; so did Ken. "Mr. Helton, I was hoping that you would be more helpful. You know that all my husband's investments will be made known during the divorce hearing. I recall him saying that these offshore accounts were very private. I hoped you would understand my situation and help me without getting the courts involved."

It was a weak attempt at extortion, but Ed Helton had heard enough. "Mrs. Carson, what your husband was involved with was his business, not mine. I have no idea what you are talking about...offshore accounts...investment cartels, they don't mean a thing to me. What I do know is that your husband has more legal problems than just your divorce. Now, if you will excuse me, I have other business to attend."

To be dismissed so easily was an insult to Rachael. "I am sorry to hear that Mr. Helton. You will regret your decision; that I can promise you."

Rachael left the bank in such a state that she didn't notice Danni Walton sitting patiently in the waiting room.

~~

Danni watched as Rachael Carson almost ran through the waiting room. She would have called to her in greeting if she had not looked ready to explode.

When she was invited into her father's office she asked, "Wasn't that Rachael Carson? What's bothering her?"

Ed Helton smiled as his daughter entered his office. She was the first pleasant surprise in a never ending day of one problem after another. They met and hugged, and Ed gave her a loving kiss on the cheek.

427

"Her husband left her high and dry with some bills. I didn't tell her, but I just finished the paperwork to arrest her husband."

That explained the empty office. "Really, what did he do?"

"He was writing fraudulent loans and banking the money... pretty slick operation. We were lucky to catch him."

"How much did he get?"

Ed Helton, as would any bank president, hesitated to disclose their specific amount of loss; it was in a banker's blood to protect the integrity of the bank. "More than I would care to discuss."

Danni understood why her father would conceal the amount. "How did you catch him?"

Ed smiled. "I was in his office one day and noticed a list of names on his desk. I asked him what he was doing. He said he was checking the status of loans. One of the names on the sheet was Mamba's full name, Miranda Castillo. I knew Mamba didn't have a loan with the bank, she would have come through me; it had to be bogus. I've had Buford Long on his tail since then."

"How did you cover the losses?"

Ed busied himself with some documents on his desk. "I personally covered the losses."

Danni was shocked. She understood that her father was a man of integrity and would put the welfare of his customers before his own, but to cover the bank losses with his personal funds was ludicrous. "Good Lord, Dad, how much did it cost you to cover the loans?"

Ed looked up and grinned. "Danni, let's just say that I have made arrangements to recover all my assets. I'm in good shape. Now let's get to why I called you here today. I want you to sign these documents to allow me to transfer your money to offshore accounts."

"Daddy, I don't want to put my money anywhere but in your bank."

Ed nodded his head. "I understand that, but soon I will be closing the bank. If you leave your money here, it won't be safe."

"Did you tell the employees? They are walking around like zombies."

"Yes, I told them about an hour ago."

Like the Daufuskie Resort, the Coastal Bank was a local institution. Both had weathered many storms, and now the hotel lay in smoldering ruin, and her father was closing the bank. The world was changing and Danni couldn't say she liked the changes.

"Daddy, why are you doing this? Some of your employees have been with the bank for 20 years. What are they going to do when you close the bank? Don't you feel any sympathy for them?"

"Of course I feel for my employees, but the fact is that they are part of the problem, and I'm tired of fighting the battle. I've worked for more than 30 years trying to make this bank work. I think I did a pretty good job, but it's just not worth it anymore."

Danni was shocked that her father would describe his employees as a problem. "You have great employees. If you want to see sorry ones, you should have visited the hotel more often. That still doesn't explain why you are closing the bank."

Ed stood and walked to the window overlooking the Savannah River. "Come here and tell me what you see."

Danni walked to the window. In the distance was the port of Savannah. Where there would normally be 40 to 50 ships in various stages of discharging and taking on cargo, now there were maybe five or six. Closer to the bank were two partially complete hotels in various stages of construction, and now falling into disrepair with pieces of insulation blowing in the breeze, and equipment sitting idle next to mounds of dirt or stacks of rusting steel. Across the river was one of the largest and most prestigious hotels in Savannah with union workers walking in circular protest in front of the hotel. To the south of the river were the tops of the homes of the citizens of Savannah.

"I see Savannah."

"No, what you see is the shell of what was once Savannah. What you see now is a city that has fed upon itself until there is nothing of substance left. And those people in the houses you see allowed it to happen."

"Daddy that's ridiculous. Most of those people are good people."

"I didn't say they weren't good people, but for years they have demanded more from men like me, and even from women like you, but they have ignored the warning signs that a society dependent on the government will eventually collapse. They have used their vote to enslave me to their demands for more. They have taken America for granted; life was good, always had been, and probably always will be. They have become complacent with the bounty provided by this country, but apathetic to the freedoms that allowed the nation to prosper. Our government has done such a good job of bestowing public money to our population that many now believe they are entitled to it. And we are going broke doing it.

"I am not going to stand by and let them take what I have earned over my lifetime and squander it on programs I don't support or give it to people who won't work."

Danni had never seen her father so engaged. It took him a moment to calm down.

"So you're going to close the bank and retire."

"Yes."

~~

Danni could not say that she disagreed with her father, just that she held out more hope than he that America could still recover from the economic mess. She signed the documents allowing the transfer of her money to various accounts around the world and was eager to get back to the security of Daufuskie. She didn't look forward to another cab ride.

Her father tossed her the keys to his car. "Leave it in the ferry parking lot. I'll pick it up later."

The waiting room for the ferry was nearly vacant, only a few islanders returning from work on the mainland, and two men dressed in rather cheap suits. The men sat across from Danni and were obviously impatient for the arrival of the ferry.

"We're going to be really pinched for time." He looked at the ferry schedule fixed to the wall. From his seat his finger traced the arrivals and departures. "If I am reading this thing correctly, there are only two more runs from Daufuskie back here to Savannah. We miss that second trip and we are stuck on the island."

"That shouldn't be a problem; we only have two people to question. At most it should take only a couple of hours."

When the first man leaned back in his chair his coat opened, and the butt of a pistol and gold badge hooked to his belt were quite visible. "Who is it we have to interview again?"

The second man pulled a small black notebook from his pocket. He flipped through the pages. "We have to get a report from…here it is…Angelina Sanchez, and then a Major James Madison."

Danni was instantly alert. She hoped her reaction wasn't noticed by the men.

"What exactly are we supposed to do?"

"The Attorney General wants this Colonel Cannon. We don't have anything on him yet, but Sanchez has been working on the case."

"Who is this Sanchez?"

"She's FBI on assignment to the department. She's been planted with the family."

The first man asked, "Do we have anything to charge against him?"

"Not yet, we'll make something up if necessary. The Attorney General will back us. Don't worry about it."

Danni felt her heart pounding. How could what these men were saying be true? What could be their purpose? Why would his own government want Bill Cannon? It was not something she could understand, but what she did understand was that she must warn him. She quietly left her seat and walked back to the pier and onto the street.

Bill Cannon did not answer her call. Where was he?

Mike DeAngelo didn't answer her call. The boy at the marina said he was on a night fishing charter and wouldn't return until morning. The boy would get him a radio message, call Danni Walton, it was an emergency. How long would that take? The boy didn't know.

Doc Broderson would know how to get in contact with Bill. It took her 20 minutes to get through. First it was the police department. Then it was the fire and rescue department, and they wouldn't release his number, department policy. Danni pleaded with the sergeant, it was an emergency. Please have Doc Broderson call her immediately.

Danni waited an eternity for Doc's call. Finally it came.

"Doc, I need to call Bill. It's an emergency. I have his cell phone, but he is not answering it. Do you have any other numbers?"

"I've got a couple, but what's the emergency?"

Doc, there are two policemen, not policemen, but men from the government. I think they are going to arrest Bill. I have to warn him."

"Hang up and wait for my call. I'll try the other numbers I have. I'll call you right back."

431

Danni watched as the men boarded the ferry and then slowly leave the dock. They didn't pay any attention to the lady making the phone calls from the road.

She answered her phone at the first sound of the ring.

"Danni, he is not answering at his gym or his house. He sometimes stays at a small fish camp in Shellman Bluff. I don't think he has a land line to his trailer. That's the only place he could be."

Danni got the directions from Doc. If she didn't get lost, it shouldn't take more than an hour. There was nothing else to do and she had to warn Bill.

~~

Mamba walked to Angelina's room. "Somebody is coming."

"I know."

Angelina was struggling to get a starched white shirt over the brace. Mamba helped guide the fabric over the cast. Once dressed Angelina went to the top drawer in the dresser and removed her badge and Glock and clipped them both to her belt.

"Mamba, would you mind calling Major Madison and ask him if he would walk with me to the county dock? I'll meet him on the road. Tell him to come alone, I don't want Hanna there. Maybe you could ask her up for coffee or something like that?"

"Certainly my child," Mamba paused slightly before she continued, "What are you going to do?"

Angelina looked her directly in the eyes. "I hope the right thing."

Mamba smiled. "I am sure you will."

~~

Angelina met James on the road leading to the county dock. The walk would take 30 minutes, maybe longer in the soft sand. James struggled to keep pace. It was painful to watch James struggle with the walk, but Angelina needed the time, and the solitude for what she had to say.

She told James why she was sent to Atlanta and the letter received by the President. How her investigation led her to Hanna's rape. How she discovered the sordid details of the death of Hanna's father, and the death of those who raped his wife. She told him of the conspiracy with the drugs, and the money she believed was delivered to

432

Eric. She told him everything she discovered. James Madison listened in silence.

"The only thing I don't know is who put the whole thing together. Now I think I do."

"You do…who?"

"Bill Cannon."

There was no perceptible change in James when he commented. "That may be a difficult thing to prove."

Angelina turned to face James. "I am no longer concerned with proving it, but I am worried about Bill Cannon. Two investigators from the Attorney General's office are coming here to arrest Bill Cannon. I don't think they have anything concrete, but the Attorney General is out to get him. I think the government suspects he was the man who rescued you. I was sent down here to build a case against him."

"And what did you?"

"I found men who have honor. I have found love in a man, and a family that I will not betray."

"That may cause you some trouble."

"It may, but it is a simple choice really; the choice between good and evil. There is no choice really."

"I'm glad to hear it. Welcome to the family."

Angelina smiled, "That doesn't help with the men who are coming to question us. I wanted you to know the whole story."

~~

Angelina and James waited on the pier. They were a strange couple. Angelina's arm still braced away from her body, and James leaning on his cane and bandages covering the wounds to his face and head. Angelina spotted the investigators immediately when they stepped off the gangway. She stepped forward and introduced herself.

"I am Special Agent Angelina Sanchez and this is Major James Madison. I understand you have some questions for us?"

"We do, but we would like to talk with you first. Is there any place where we can have a little privacy?"

"No, you only have a few minutes before the ferry leaves. You can talk to me right here, or you can get back on the ferry."

"Agent Sanchez, we have been sent down here by the Attorney General to discuss things that are highly confidential. I don't think it is appropriate to discuss it on this dock."

Angelina didn't back down. "Look, this is my case, and I don't need any help from you. You can write in your little notebooks that I haven't uncovered anything. When I do, I will report it through my proper channels."

"Sanchez, you don't understand the sensitivity of our investigation. We have an international incident on our hands. The man or men who conducted the raid to rescue this man have violated an International Treaty. Somebody is responsible and we are going to find out who it is."

"You're looking in the wrong place. Get back on the ferry and leave."

The two men turned away and quietly discussed their next action. "So Miss Sanchez, you have nothing to report?"

"I have nothing to report."

The men turned to Madison, "Major Madison, do you have any idea who could have been involved in your rescue?"

James Madison straightened as much as he could. "No sir, I have no idea who rescued me."

The small notebooks went back in their jackets. "This could be the end of your career Sanchez. This will go in our report."

It was a threat that carried no weight with Angelina Sanchez. She had done what was right.

As they watched the men board the ferry Angelina commented, "Mrs. Walton should be on the next ferry. I think I'll wait for her."

Danni Walton wasn't on the next ferry. As the sun went down Mamba and Hanna arrived in a carriage. They patiently waited for the final ferry of the day. Danni Walton wasn't on that ferry either.

Chapter 53

Bill caressed the steel of the .45 in the door side-pocket; it was the only thing that gave him comfort during the drive to Washington. The weight of the loaded weapon helped provide focus. Twice he had stopped and walked in the rest areas debating the merits of his decision. He told Lucas he wouldn't do anything foolish, but if he could find Rayhan's murderer and the situation presented itself, he would kill him, and he would feel better about calling Prince Al-Sabah. Bill knew the probability of finding the man depended on the government finding the *Crescent Moon*.

The decision to kill Rayhan's murderer wasn't the only thing that bothered Bill during the drive. The other and more perplexing problem was Danni Walton. Maybe his decision to go to Washington was made in haste. Too many emotions told him he should be back on Daufuskie finding the words that would convince Danni Walton that he loved her beyond his own life. If given a chance, he could find the words to explain what happened those years ago.

The light on his cell phone illuminated, it was Lucas McLaughlin. "Bill, where are you?"

"I'm just south of Richmond; any news on the boat?"

"Yeah, it's in the southern Chesapeake. I'm taking a helicopter to Yorktown. Homeland security is setting up a command post there. Meet me there."

"What's the plan?"

"Homeland Security has the lead and is planning to have the Coast Guard board the vessel, but the State Department has them in a holding pattern. State says the boat has diplomatic immunity and they don't want an international incident on their hands. Right now they are shadowing the boat. We'll have to wait and see what State decides to do. Bill, you will have to leave your vehicle on the road from Richmond, I'll send a vehicle for you. No weapons, cameras, phones inside the perimeter."

~~

435

The closer Bill got to Yorktown the less his thoughts were on Danni Walton and more on the *Crescent Moon*. The command post was established on the site of the National Park where Lord Cornwallis surrendered his British Army to George Washington, marking the beginning of the end of English rule in America. It was a perfect location; only one road leading in and plenty of space for flight operations.

The command post security was tight. Lucas McLaughlin met Bill at the entry control point and they walked the half mile to the command post.

"Any change in the situation?"

The rancor in McLaughlin's reply was quite obvious. "Bill, you're not going to believe this. The President is at a Broadway play and the White House isn't going to issue any orders until he gets back."

"How long will that take?"

"Another hour or so; nobody up there will make a decision. The Secretary of Defense and Secretary of State almost canceled the entire operation when they learned the lead came from you."

"You know something Lucas? I hope they're right and I'm wrong. They can crow all they want, but for God's sake, you're telling me we can't do an inspection on a boat in American waters without the President's approval?"

"Apparently not," a frown crossed Lucas McLaughlin's face, "Bill, have you been able to contact Al-Sabah?"

Bill shook his head. "No, and I've been trying all day. Every time I've tried, the connection goes dead in Kuwait."

"Then you haven't heard?"

"Haven't heard what?"

"There was an assassination attempt on Al-Sabah. He has gone into hiding. There is a full-blown Shia insurgency rising against him. Kuwait City is in shambles. The State Department has ordered evacuation of all the Embassy personnel and is recommending that all US business interests leave the country."

"So he probably doesn't know about his son."

"Probably not."

Bill thought for a moment before he asked. "Lucas, has there been any movement of Iranian forces in the direction of Kuwait?"

"Iran has moved four divisions within fifty miles of the Shat Al Arab waterway."

"Pretty good diversion wouldn't you say? We're over here worrying about a terrorist nuke and chemical attacks, the entire US combat force in the Middle East is pulling up poppy plants in Afghanistan, and the 5th Fleet is getting suntans in Diego Garcia; and we're waiting for the President to come home from the movies."

As Bill Cannon and Lucas McLaughlin entered the command post, the cell phone in Bill's truck came to life. There on the small screen—the name he was hoping to see all day during the drive to Virginia—the name of Danni Walton, and then Danni again, and then Doc Broderson.

~~

Achmad Nardiff was the first to notice the Coast Guard helicopter loitering a mile off their stern. There could be no doubt, they had been discovered. He cursed his bad luck and his decision to forgo recovering Rayhan Al-Sabah's body. It would have been difficult to reverse the boat in the narrow channel of the waterway, and that in and of itself would have attracted too much attention and they would have lost valuable time. It was bad luck that the body did not float out to sea or that is was not consumed by the alligators the Americans claimed were so dangerous.

The helicopter was soon joined by a Coast Guard Cutter, but it also hung to the stern. Why did the Americans not attack? Every minute they delayed only worked in Nardiff's favor. Every minute the American's delayed brought them another mile closer to the Potomac River. Every mile in the Potomac River brought them another mile closer to Washington, D.C.

Achmad checked the compass heading and knelt for prayers. He prayed for the strength and courage to complete his mission. The bomb was ready and thousands, if it was Allah's will, maybe hundreds of thousands of the infidels would burn in hell after this day. And every minute the Americans delayed brought him closer to paradise. Allah Be Praised.

~~

Danni Walton slowed to read the map. The map light in the mirror was worthless and trying to read the map and manage the winding two lane roads of the Georgia lowlands was almost impossible. She was now sure she had missed the turn. Maybe if she hadn't spent so much

437

time watching the car in her rear view she would have seen the road junction. She scolded herself, the car wasn't following her, for God's sake, there were no side roads to take anyway—she had to get a grip on her emotions.

Was the car behind her the government men from the ferry? Was she leading them to Bill Cannon? Would Bill consider it an act of betrayal is she led the investigators to him? She glanced in the mirror, the car was still there, and even though she had slowed, the car maintained its distance. If she pulled off the road, she had to reverse course anyway, then they would either pass her, or she would know she was being followed. If she was being followed, she would lead them far from Shellman Bluff. She would not lead them to Bill Cannon.

Danni pulled to the side of the road; her tires sinking in the soft shoulder and her car at a precarious tilt almost sliding into the drainage ditch that had been excavated to build the road bed. The dark waters and reeds that filled the ditch had an ominous sense to them, seemingly alive with a force that would pull her into the ditch and consume her. She would be careful not to spin her tires when she pulled away. One false move and she would be in the ditch.

Danni watched the car approach. Had it slowed when she pulled off the road? No, the car was now moving; she could see the blinding headlights in her side mirror. It was 100 yards away, now 50, now 25, and they would pass her.

The explosion of metal and glass was violent. Danni saw the glass shatter and the sparks from the colliding metal briefly light up the night. She felt the car slide from the road into the ditch. The shock of the water pouring in through the broken window was that which kept her from slipping into unconsciousness. The dark water was quickly filling the cab and she frantically fumbled with the seat belt. If she couldn't release the seat belt, she would drown.

The man that stood above her was a black shape silhouetted by the headlights of the car that crashed into her and pushed her into the ditch. She saw him reach down. The knife in his hand was unmistakable and the blade hovered near her throat. The water was to her neck and quickly covered her face, and with her last breath she thought of Hanna and the baby, and of her father and Mamba, and of Bill Cannon.

As the blackness started to overwhelm her, she felt something pull on her hair and her body began to float. Was this the death call? Was this what death felt like? She had passed from panic to accepting her fate, and only the tugging on her hair was unpleasant.

It was the instinct to survive that forced her to take a breath when her head broke the surface of the water. Her eyes fluttered open and when she coughed, the water that had filled her lungs spewed forth. She struggled out of her watery tomb and on her hands and knees on the hood of her car, now inches below the surface, she gasped for life-giving air. With each breath she coughed up more water and she knew she would not die in this ditch.

When she finally looked up, it was the shoe of the man that had saved her that caved in the side of her face and sent her back into the blackness once again.

~~

The President was escorted to the briefing bunker far below the White House. Those familiar with him could tell he was controlling his impatience.

"What's the situation?"

Homeland security took the lead in the briefing. "Mr. President, we have reason to believe the Kuwaiti yacht *Crescent Moon* may be transporting a nuclear weapon into territorial waters in the Chesapeake Bay. We have a Coast Guard cutter shadowing the vessel, and with your permission, we are prepared to board and inspect the vessel."

"Any reason we can't do that?"

The Undersecretary of State cleared his throat. "Sir, that vessel may be considered sovereign territory, like an embassy. Any intervention with the free navigation may be considered a hostile act by the Kuwaiti Government."

"Has anybody talked to the Kuwaiti Government, or the Prince of Kuwait? If they understand our concerns I am sure they will grant total access."

One of the many CIA deputies at the briefing spoke up. "Mr. President, there is a civil war going on in Kuwait. We haven't been able to talk with anyone in the government for over a day."

"If the Kuwaiti government can't answer the phone, then we can't be held responsible. The safety of the American people is our responsibility."

The President fixed the Secretary of Homeland Security with an icy stare. "If this things turns out to be nothing, and that's exactly what I expect to happen, I want the people who led us on this wild goose chase strung up by their balls, you understand?"

439

"Yes sir, do we have your approval to board and inspect the vessel?"

The President squirmed slightly in his chair. Answers and orders in response to direct questions were not something that could be easily explained, and his administration was doing too much explaining of late.

"Yes, board the damn boat."

~~

Bill Cannon and Lucas McLaughlin listened with the others to the radio traffic between the Coast Guard Cutter and the command post.

"Yorktown, this is Chesapeake Cutter, we have ordered the vessel to secure and prepare for boarding, but they have not responded. Request permission to fire a warning shot across their bow."

It was the request the leadership in the command post dreaded more than any other. It meant the *Crescent Moon* would have to be forcibly boarded, a task that was never easy.

"This is Yorktown. You are authorized one warning round across the bow of the vessel *Crescent Moon*."

The Captain of the Coast Guard cutter acknowledged his orders. The entire command post went silent as they waited for the report.

"Yorktown, this is Chesapeake Cutter, round fired, target vessel continues on northern track. Sir, she isn't stopping."

The Coast Guard Admiral commanding the interception cursed. "Shit! Don't these people know we're serious about this? Fire another round, closer this time."

The command post waited an anxious minute before the cutter reported. "Yorktown, target vessel has ignored the warning shots and continues north."

The Admiral turned to his operations officer. "Get the White House on the line. I'm not going to sink this bastard without somebody giving me a direct order to do so."

~~

The night sky flashed bright white, brighter than even the brightest sun. Every head in the command post turned to the windows and all motion stopped. There was no doubt the magnitude of the event on the Chesapeake. It was the unmistakable brilliance of the first nuclear attack on the United States of America. Somebody in the rear voiced the

440

truth that everyone present now knew. "Son of a bitch, they really did it."

The military personnel and some of the other agents in the command post knew what was coming and dove for cover behind anything of substance. Those who stood in ignorant wonder of the fading light took the full force of the blast wave and shattering glass.

Bill brushed away the shattered glass from his clothes. "How far out was the boat?"

"About 20 miles."

"Then we have about a minute to get to higher ground. That thing had to move some water."

Bill exited the command post at a full run. The guards outside, blinded by the flash, were staggering aimlessly trying to find their way in the darkness. Bill and Lucas each grabbed a stunned guard and drug them up the rise leading to a bluff overlooking the Bay; others did the same.

The park lights survived the blast and cast pools of light on the ground, but nothing was directed towards the sea. The group assembled on the bluff could hear the approach of the wave more than they could see it. Some crossed themselves in a last prayer, others knelt, some turned to the man or woman to their side and muttered a soft wish of good luck or good bye, but there was no panic.

Bill turned to the blinded soldier he helped to the bluff. "Can you swim?"

"Like a rock."

"I won't let go of you. Just relax when the wave hits. We're going to make it."

Bill turned to Lucas McLaughlin, "Lucas, if I don't make it, tell Danni I loved her."

The roar of the wave grew louder. "Bill, it has been my honor and privilege to have known you. Please look in on my wife and kids when you can."

"Always. Good luck."

The winds pushed before the waves were hurricane strength. Some on the edges of the group on the bluff were blown from their feet. They didn't have time to recover before the wave hit. The steep bluff took the brunt of the wave, but the waters kept rising and the small group was washed away. One moment they were there, the next moment only water covered the ground where they stood.

The force of the water hit Bill like a train, but he held his breath and held the vest of the blinded soldier. They were carried with the raging water as if they were nothing more than twigs. Bill could feel the branches of trees grab at his legs, and things you would never consider to be a hazard, power lines, chairs, bodies banged into him. His lungs were burning and he would drown, but giving up meant death, and he pulled to the surface of the torrent—the body of the soldier now nothing but dead weight—but he had promised he would not let go.

His head broke the surface and he gulped in life-giving air and just as quick as he was forced to the surface he was pulled under again. The churning motion began to slow and there ahead stood the forest that could be his salvation if he could grab a branch.

They hit the trees with a force that shocked even Bill, but he held on to the branches with all his strength. He pulled with all his might and raised the soldier to the branch and Bill put the branch between them and held his arms. Bill yelled to him, "Wake up!", and Bill was rewarded with a flicker of his eyelids and convulsions that spewed water from the man's lungs. "Breathe! We're going to make it! Breathe!"

Bill watched and waited as the waters slowly receded. When they finally reached the ground Bill surveyed the damage. There was nothing left of the command post. There were very few survivors. The waves had cleared the ground of almost every living thing.

It was an hour before the first helicopters arrived from the Naval Base in Norfolk, and another before they started to evacuate the dead and wounded. There was nothing to be found of the Crescent Moon, the Coast Guard Cutter, or any of the dozens of boats that were within the mouth of the Chesapeake Bay up to Mobjack Bay.

Bill left the wounded guard with the medical personnel, and what would have been no more than a simple hour forced march to return to his truck, took three. The truck was a mile clear of the rushing waters.

He would have returned to search for Lucas McLaughlin, but for the text message on his phone. "Danni Walton is missing."

Chapter 54

Angelina would describe the look on Mamba's face as one of stunned disbelief. When she walked close, Mamba said, "I did not see this."

If the truth be known, and if Mamba would have asked, Angelina would have had to say that she did. From the moment of Danni's strange farewell from the riverbank, Angelina knew something was different, something was wrong. That is why, after dismissing the federal agents, she waited on the Daufuskie pier for Danni's return.

Angelina looked at Hanna and Mamba huddled in conversation. The answer to Hanna's questions, "How did my mother miss the ferry, and where is my mother?" were all too obvious. They didn't know.

"Hanna, call your grandfather and find out if your mother is staying with him. Then call Mike DeAngelo, maybe he is bringing her back, then call everyone you can think of in Savannah she may have gone to visit; I'm going to talk to the crew."

The crew was no help. No, there were no more ferry runs tonight. The next run would be at 7 a.m. Yes, she could inspect the ferry. They would certainly call the departure dock in Savannah. No, there was no one at the departure location. They wished her good luck.

Hanna finally got hold of her grandfather. At near 10 p.m., he was still working at the bank. Danni left the bank just after 5 p.m. Ed had given Danni the use of his car. She said she was going straight to the ferry. Ed Helton would call a cab and check the ferry.

By the time they reached the residence, Ed Helton had checked the ferry parking lot; his vehicle was nowhere to be found.

Angelina called the Savannah Police Department.

"My name is Angelina Sanchez. I am a federal investigator with the US Department of Justice. I want to talk with the senior officer on duty."

The operator was impatient and rude. "Lady, we're kind of busy. What exactly do you want to report?"

"A missing person; she was last seen at the Coastal Bank this afternoon at around 5p.m. She didn't return home and we can't find her car."

"Give me the details; I'll put it in the computer."

Now Angelina became rude and impatient. "That's all you intend to do? Put it in the computer?"

"Look, she'll be in the computer. If she turns up we'll notify you. We don't classify anybody as a missing person until they've been gone for over 24 hours. Maybe she's shopping."

Angelina was well aware of the normal protocol, but Danni Walton would never do such an irresponsible thing. Her patience evaporated in an instant and she yelled into the phone. "I know the protocol! I want to talk with your supervisor right now!"

The operator at the police station didn't budge an inch. "He's kind of busy right now. There's nothing more that I can do. She's in the computer. If we find her, we will let you know."

Angelina fumed, "Get your supervisor out of the donut shop or the cafeteria and get him on the phone, or you will be hearing from the Attorney General of the United States! What in the hell is so important that he can't come to the phone?"

"Jesus Christ lady, don't you watch the news?" Angelina heard the click of the phone line going dead, and simply stared for a moment at the phone.

Hanna was nervously hovering at Angelina's elbow. "What did he say?"

"He put her in the computer."

Before Hanna could begin the barrage of questions Angelina knew were coming, and questions that she knew she couldn't answer; Angelina turned on the news.

~~

The picture was of a darkened street on a waterfront. The only light was that which came from the television camera. It was not unlike the immediate aftermath of any hurricane after the flood waters recede. But the only storms were still well out in the Atlantic and for a moment Angelina wondered if the scene was from Europe or perhaps South America. The reporter was completing his report.

"Eric, the waves were at least 20' high when they crashed into downtown Norfolk." The reporter turned and pointed to a small boat wedged into the third floor of an office complex. "That boat once floated peacefully in the calm waters of a local marina, and demonstrates the fury of the unexpected flood. We have no estimate on the number of dead or wounded and reports from the local authorities say the same type destruction can be found all along the Chesapeake Bay from here to Mount Vernon.

"Almost a third of the Chesapeake Bay Bridge has been destroyed, and both tunnels under the navigation channels have been flooded.

"One survivor reported a bright light far out over the bay minutes before the waves hit. Whether this may have been a natural event like the impact a meteor or an explosion of another nature, we can only speculate.

"The Governor of Virginia has mobilized the National Guard to help with the rescue operations and to restore order, because…" the camera scanned to the street, "in the aftermath of this terrible event the ugly side of human nature has raised its head. Bands of looters are robbing the dead and passing wounded or trapped citizens to pillage local merchants. Eric, Norfolk, Virginia is a scene out of Dante's Inferno. Help better arrive soon before this city is destroyed from within; now to our reporter at the White House."

From their broadcast location on Pennsylvania Avenue the news team had a clear view of the yellow police tape that cordoned off the White House. The guards were not the uniformed police officers that normally secured the residence, but soldiers in full battle dress. The automatic weapons, flak jackets and menacing posture could not be mistaken for anything but the highest level of security.

"Eric, for the first time since the terrorists attacked on September 11, 2001, the White House is being evacuated. The White House Press Secretary just informed us that the President has been flown to a secure location aboard Air Force 1, and the Vice President has been moved to a secure location on Air Force 2. Not 10 minutes ago one of our staff noticed the Speaker of the House being moved under heavy guard to an undisclosed location. If our national leadership continues to abandon the Capital at this rate, soon there will be no political leadership left in Washington.

"The White House Press Secretary said the President will reserve comment on the events in the Chesapeake Bay until a more thorough investigation is conducted. Eric, that's all we have from the White House, back to you in the studio."

The studio backdrop behind Eric was a still photo of the devastation at Norfolk, Virginia. "Thank you all for those reports. Here is what we know right now. At a few minutes after 9 p.m. tonight, something exploded in the Chesapeake Bay. The light of the explosion was seen as far away as Charlotte, North Carolina. The number of fatalities that were caused by the explosion is unknown at this time, but the tsunami wave caused by the explosion has killed tens of thousands. The waves have flooded the entire coastline of the southern Chesapeake Bay.

"The governors of Virginia and Maryland have mobilized the National Guard in their respective states, and we know that the President, Vice President and Speaker of the House have all evacuated Washington.

"We will stay with this breaking story all through the night." Eric Brown was preparing to close the segment and go to commercial break when he held his finger to the earpiece. "We have just received word that the President will address the nation at midnight, Eastern Standard Time. We will carry that report live. We will be back in a moment."

Not a person in the room moved or said a thing, each struggling with the magnitude of the reports.

~~

Ed Helton stood on the bank overlooking the Daufuskie Ferry. The parking lot was vacant. He rushed to those passing by and frantically questioned them. Have you seen my daughter? She was driving a beige Lincoln. The look in his eyes made the people shy away. He knew it was a waste of time, she wasn't here. He returned the call to his granddaughter and then he called the man he trusted and the man that had served him well over the years.

"Buford, I need your help. Danni is missing."

"Where are you?"

"On River Street at the Daufuskie Ferry terminal; I gave her my car, she was going back home, but she never got there."

"The streets may not be safe. Go back to the bank and I will meet you there."

~~

446

It had taken Fast Eddie Bennett almost a month to earn enough money to purchase the surplus Geiger counter from AAA Pawn in Virginia Beach, Virginia. Fast Eddie, the nickname, would give pause to most, was not earned through any scandalous behavior, but at the blackboards in school. Fast Eddie was a wiz, a child prodigy if you will, and his prowess at solving math problems had earned him the name, Fast Eddie. Fast Eddie could make short work of almost any equation.

Fast Eddie got the Geiger counter only this morning and he started making readings right away. The granite foundation of the old bank building barely moved the needle. Eddie stuck the probe into the ground at various spots hoping to detect something of interest but the needle didn't move. He sat in the waiting room of the dentist and watched the needle bump with every x-ray, but it was so small that Eddie began to wonder if the Geiger counter was functioning properly.

But after the strange bright light over the Chesapeake the needle jumped to near 200 on the scale. What the 200 represented Eddie didn't know, but it was interesting enough to show his mother.

"Momma, I think that bright light was a nuclear explosion."

Mrs. Bennett smiled. Fast Eddie was always entertaining her with a 13-year-old perspective on the world. "Now how would you know that?"

Eddie showed her the reading on the Geiger counter, now hovering near the 100 mark. "This was at the 200 a few minutes ago. I'm going to call the Sheriff's Department and see if they know anything."

Mrs. Bennett warned Eddie, "Didn't the Sheriff warn you about calling the station all the time?"

"Yes, but this is important!"

Eddie's call to the Sheriff's Department was met with constant busy signals. If he couldn't get through to the police, then he would go right to the top. He sat at his computer and in the address of the e-mail he typed, 'ericbrown@cnn.com.' He trusted Eric Brown would put his discovery to good use.

~~

Eric Brown was finally relieved at the anchor desk at midnight. He had been on-camera for six hours straight and was scheduled to anchor the special report on the explosion at 8 a.m. He loosened his tie and leaned far back in his chair. The magnitude of the news he had been reporting started to sink into his own world. The disaster was quite enough to upset even the most hardened reporter, but what really bothered Eric was the outbreak of riots and the complete disregard for the sanctity of civilized behavior by those using the event to loot and rob.

Yes it was late, but he needed contact with someone who would allow him to unwind. He hoped Angelina would understand his need and that her cell phone was near her bed. The call was answered on the first ring.

"Angelina, I'm sorry for calling so late, but I need to talk with someone."

Angelina seemed impatient. "Eric, I'm glad you called. I know you've had a tough day. I've seen what's on the news, but we have a problem down here; Danni Walton in missing."

Eric quickly forgot his fatigue. "What?" The statement caught him completely by surprise and his outburst was noticed by others in the newsroom.

"Danni Walton is missing. She went to her father's bank. She left the bank at five. Nobody's seen her since. She hasn't called you, has she?"

Eric's mind raced, "No, she didn't call me. Have you called the police?"

"Of course I've called the police. I can't get a thing out of them. Have you heard of any reports of an accident—or anything—that may give us a clue as to where she is?" It was a long shot, but it couldn't hurt to ask.

The fatigue Eric felt was replaced by a surge of adrenaline. "No, but I'll call the Savannah office and check all the reports. Maybe I can find something. How is Hanna doing?"

Angelina looked to where Hanna was sitting. With one hand on her belly and the other daubing tears from her face, it was obvious the events of the evening were taking a heavy toll on her. "She's doing as well as can be expected."

"Should I come down there?"

"No, you can do more good up there. Keep watching for anything that may come in from your reporters. Maybe you can call some of the newspapers, radio stations and television stations and see if they have anything. I'll call you if something breaks."

Angelina didn't allow time for Eric's "I love you," before she closed her phone. It bothered Eric some, but not enough that he didn't

448

immediately turn to his computer. He would email all his contacts and follow-up with phone calls.

The first message he saw made him forget his immediate task. He printed the e-mail from Fast Eddie and rushed to the production room. The producer was engrossed in preparing for the President's address to the nation and ignored Eric's intrusion until Eric shoved the paper directly in his face.

"It was a nuclear explosion!"

The producer quickly read the e-mail. "Can it Brown. We can't use that. That could be a hoax for all we know. If it was nuclear then we'll let the President tell the country. We're not going to announce something like that unless we have hard proof."

Eric turned to the large screen to watch the President's address. The five minute address wasn't worth the electricity it took to broadcast it. He promised a full investigation and called for calm.

Scripted words from the security of an underground bunker did not inspire Eric Brown.

~~~

Danni Walton was shocked when the cold water hit her directly in the face. She slowly fought through the pain and delirium and slowly opened her eyes. It wasn't so much what she saw that caused her to wretch, but the stench that filled her senses; it was beyond revolting.

"So finally the rich bitch wakes up."

Danni had heard the voice before, but she couldn't place it. The room was dimly lit, only slightly brighter than the glow of a bathroom night light. She felt the hard steel of a column in her back, and her arms pulled behind her, and she realized she was seated on something hard but slimly. With the slightest movement she could feel her butt slide on the floor. Was she handcuffed? Was the floor covered with mud?

The voice answered part of her question. "It's chicken shit you're sitting in." The voice giggled, "Just goes to show you can make chicken salad out of chicken shit, doesn't it," the laugh got louder, almost insane before it calmed.

Danni struggled to speak, "What do you want?"

"I want to find out if your daddy loves you. Do you think he loves you?"

"This is crazy."

Danni felt the steel of the knife that freed her from the flooding car trace a line on her neck. "Is it? Your daddy owes me some money. We're going to see what he loves the most, his money or his daughter. It should be fun, don't you think?"

Danni didn't answer. The man moved to her front and knelt down, the knife slipping under her blouse and cutting the buttons that held her shirt closed. Danni closed her eyes and shuddered with each cut of a button. "You'll never get away with this."

"Oh yes I will."

The knife moved up under her chin. Danni could feel the point cutting into her skin. Danni recognized the voice. She opened her eyes and stared into the leering face of Ken Carson.

"Now what can we send to your father to find out if he loves you?" The knife moved slowly to her ear, "An ear maybe? He should recognize the earring, don't you think?" The knife moved down her arm, "Or maybe a finger. Would he recognize your rings? Maybe he would." The knife moved under her eye. "But maybe we don't have to be quite so crude."

Chapter 55

It was odd—the way in which James Madison took the phone call. The hour was late, near 2 a.m., and perhaps he stepped outside so he wouldn't disturb Hanna, who found a few moments of sleep on the couch. That may have been a rational explanation. But the manner in which he moved and shielded his voice raised the question as to why there were secrets he needed to guard.

Angelina followed him to the front porch. "Who was that at this hour?"

He took his time answering the question. Could this woman be trusted? Only yesterday he would have considered her a subversive charlatan using her association with Eric Brown to spy on his family and friends. Her confession to him earlier in the day could simply have been another subterfuge to hide her true objective.

"That was Doc Broderson. He and DeAngelo are coming to pick me up. We are going to search for Mrs. Walton."

Was Madison hiding something about Danni's disappearance? If he had any idea where she may be, Angelina would have expected him to tell her hours ago. "Do you have any idea where she is?"

"It's only a long-shot. Mrs. Walton called Doc Broderson yesterday afternoon looking for Bill Cannon. She was trying to warn him…" James let his statement trail off, as if to continue would offend Angelina.

"Warn him about what?"

James started to hobble away, "About the investigators who came to see you yesterday."

Angelina felt relief and embarrassment at the same time. Relief that they may finally have a lead, and embarrassed that in some small way she could be held responsible for Danni's disappearance.

"Has anyone tried to contact Bill Cannon?"

"We've tried, but he hasn't answered any of our calls. We're going to drive the roads. Maybe we will get lucky."

451

"Where are you going to look?"

Confession or not, Angelina's questions continued to raise suspicion in James, and he would not allow the location of Bill's trailer in the Shellman Bluff fish camp to become part of her file. "We'll keep you posted."

"I want to go with you."

"No. You might be needed here. If we find anything I'll call you. When Hanna wakes, please tell her what I'm doing."

As she watched James Madison struggle though the soft sand she wondered, what could a man with only one eye, half his face and only one arm do, that she couldn't? When she turned to stomp back into the house her left arm, still braced away from her side, banged into one of the columns on the porch. The jolt was painful, but not debilitating. The brace had to go.

She was quiet as possible as she walked to the kitchen. The television cast a gray light in the living room and Hanna slept peacefully on the couch, and Mamba appeared to be dozing.

Angelina braced her arm against the sill above the sink, and the serrated knife made short work of the plaster cast forming her brace.

"Shouldn't you ask the doctor if that should be removed?"

She was so engrossed in cutting off the cast that she hadn't heard Mamba enter the kitchen. The question startled her.

Angelina didn't stop her work. Small beads of sweat had formed on her forehead. "It will be fine."

"Why are you doing that?"

The brace finally fell from her arm and clattered into the sink. She threw the brace into the trash and slowly lowered her arm. It was a strange sensation, but nothing broke and it felt good to flex the muscles in her arm once again. She walked to her bedroom and returned with the Glock. With effort she could operate the slide of the automatic, and if she fully extended the piece she could even reload the magazine.

"I need to talk with Mr. Helton. When is the first ferry to Savannah?"

Mamba knew it was useless to attempt to get Angelina to change her mind. "The first ferry is at 7 a.m. You better get some sleep; you have a big day ahead of you."

The last thing Angelina did before laying her head on the kitchen table was to call William Jefferson to explain the situation with Danni Walton. She wanted to ask for a contact in the FBI to help with her investigation.   Angelina hoped for more than the sterile voice announcing Jefferson was not available; but that's all she got.

~~

At 4 a.m., Ed Helton unlocked the door to the bank only long enough to allow Buford Long to enter. "What took you so long?"

"Damn city is a mess…gangs are running the streets. I couldn't get anybody at the police department so I stopped there to check the desk sergeant's sheet. I checked the hospital emergency rooms, and even the morgue; she isn't in Savannah."

Ed was tired and appreciated the efforts his friend had already accomplished. "I'm sorry Buford, I'm a little tired."

"Ed, has anybody contacted you? If somebody grabbed her, we can expect contact."

"No, nothing."

"Is there anybody that would have a grudge against your daughter, anybody at all?"

"Buford, I've been sitting here racking my brain. I can't think of anybody that would want to hurt Danni."

Buford Long took a moment before he posed his next question. "What about that stuff with her husband?"

"What do you mean?"

"Come on Ed…Danni was mixed up with some pretty rough people back then.   For God's sake, how many were killed, a dozen…maybe more? Those kind of people don't forget."

Ed got up and paced the room. "Buford, I don't know what to tell you. We never talked about it. The rape of Hanna, the death of Danni's husband, it was all too terrible to talk about. I think we all just wanted it to disappear. I thought it was behind us, but maybe you have a point. I wouldn't know where to tell you to start looking."

"How about I start with Bill Cannon?"

Even the question stunned Ed Helton. "Bill Cannon would never hurt Danni; I think he is in love with her."

Buford slowly nodded, "Love can do strange things to a man. If you ask me, Cannon has always been kind of scary, like he could go off at any time. They didn't have any fights or anything like that lately, did they?"

"Buford, he just got back from the Middle East the other day. Danni couldn't wait to see him."

"Okay, I'll accept that for now, but that leads us to you. Anybody you do business with that may have it in for you? Anybody you've screwed that would hold a grudge and try to use Danni against you?"

Ed hoped his friend would accept his answer and not pry for more details, "Only Ken Carson."

"The guy we just investigated? I would think he would want to lay low. He might face a few years in jail in some low security prison farm for bank fraud, but kidnapping could get him a life sentence. Is he crazy enough to do that?"

"You asked."

Buford Long got up from his seat and moved to the door. "Cannon has a gym here in Savannah doesn't he?"

"Yes he does, it's on Jenkins Drive, right across from Hunter Army Airfield, but you're wasting your time."

"Ed, do you want me to help find your daughter, or not?"

Ed Helton hung his head and replied, "Yes...help me find her." Ed hoped he was correct and Buford wrong about Bill Cannon. "Be careful out there."

Ed Helton was exhausted. There was nothing more that he could do. The couch in his office was the only rest he would get tonight.

~~

Angelina had just closed her eyes when she felt the shaking of her shoulder. "It's 6 a.m. You should eat before you go. Here is some coffee."

Angelina raised her head from the kitchen table where she had laid it only moments before. The comforter Mamba draped over her shoulder slid to the seat cushion. The aroma of the coffee beckoned to her.

"Is there anything new on the Chesapeake Bay explosion?"

"I am afraid not. The death toll continues to rise. The cameras have seen many terrible things. It saddens me to see that only one such event can strip away the façade of civilized behavior for so many."

Angelina looked up from her coffee. "The looting?"

"It has only gotten worse through the night, and it is not just near the explosion, it has spread like a cancer."

Angelina couldn't do anything about that right now, she must focus on Danni Walton. "Did James call?"

"No…no one has called. Shall I call Mr. Helton and make an appointment for you?"

Angelina heard movement from the living room. "Where's James?"

Angelina swiveled in the chair and faced Hanna. "He went with Broderson and DeAngelo last night. He didn't want to wake you."

"Are you going to Savannah to see my grandfather?"

"Yes I am. He was the last person to have contact with your mother. Maybe he missed something."

"I'm going with you."

"Hanna, I don't know how long this will take."

"Miss Sanchez, we're talking about my mother. I'm going with you."

~~

Hanna first noticed the missing brace when they were on the ferry. "Did you cut off your brace?"

Angelina smiled, she really hadn't thought about her arm, it almost felt normal to have her arm once again hanging from her shoulder rather than poking straight out from her body.

"Yes."

"Does it hurt?"

"No, it's weak, but I think everything is in the right place."

It was many minutes before they spoke again. "Angelina, can you find my mother?"

Hanna held her head in her hands and Angelina could tell she was quietly weeping. She felt great compassion for her and moved closer, put her arm around her, and simply held her.

The few passengers on the first ferry walked up the gangway and stopped. Angelina and Hanna had to push their way through the crowd. The entire street was trashed. Trash cans that were always emptied every night were now dumped on the street. The benches that lined the river bank were pulled from their foundations and some thrown over the railing and others were used to break the windows of the merchants overlooking the river. The few cars on the famous street were all sitting on the rims, tires slashed and windows broken. It was not the River Street the workers from Daufuskie left last night.

Angelina walked to the ticket office. "Will you please call a cab for us?"

"I'm sorry the cabs aren't answering our calls."

Angelina turned to Hanna. "We're going to have to walk. Are you sure you don't want to go back to the island?"

Hanna held her stomach. "I'm fine. Let's go."

~~

The doors of the bank were locked when they arrived; a practice that the bank employed for many months; a security measure now even more appropriate. Angelina recognized the man standing with the guard who unlocked the door. It was Buford Long, the man she had interviewed many months ago, the same man who had William Jefferson's telephone number memorized.

Hanna went directly to her grandfather's office and left Angelina and Buford in the lobby of the bank. Buford showed some surprise when he recognized Angelina.

"Agent Sanchez, what are you doing here?"

Angelina still carried some ill-will to the way in which Buford Long deflected her investigation by calling William Jefferson. Now he addressed her as if she was violating his space.

"I'm here to talk with Ed Helton about his daughter."

Long disarmed her aggressive attitude. "Sanchez, I heard about the shooting in Atlanta. You are due congratulations."

Congratulations for killing another human being, albeit in self defense, seemed an inappropriate offering. "Congratulations for what?"

"For not getting killed, that's what. You were brave but foolish—timely but reckless. We're outnumbered...always...we can't trade the life of a lawman for a criminal," Long grinned a sly grin, "We would lose just by sheer numbers. Call for backup next time."

"I will, and thanks."

As they walked to Ed Helton's office Buford asked, "What ever happened with your investigation?"

The investigation of the Walton murders; funny how that classification had a distinctive ring to it...the Walton murders...seemed to have become so insignificant when compared to the current events.

"It's not finished."

"You asked me about a drug conspiracy and the Atlanta Police Department. What did you find?"

Angelina remembered her strong belief that the police department and Buford Long were involved in the drug conspiracy, but now she knew they had nothing to do with the drugs or the money it generated.

"The police department came up clean." Angelina wondered why Buford Long was now interested in an investigation that he effectively killed, when their attention should be focused on Danni Walton. "Look, Mr. Long, I'm not here to discuss that case. I'm here to focus on getting Danni Walton back."

Angelina allowed Hanna and her grandfather the time to regain their composure from the embrace and words of encouragement to each other. Angelina glanced at the television in Mr. Helton's office and noticed Eric signing on with the special report segment on the Chesapeake Bay explosion. The sound was turned to a barely perceptible level and was muffled by any activity in the room.

"Mr. Helton, I will do everything I can to help find your daughter."

"Kidnapping is a federal offense isn't it? You can call the FBI and get them down here, can't you?"

"Mr. Helton, I have already called the Department of Justice asking just that. They haven't called me back." Angelina nodded her head towards the television. "With the Chesapeake Bay thing, I don't know if we will be on the top of their priority list. The first thing we are going to have to establish is that she has been kidnapped. Has anyone contacted you?"

Ed Helton grimaced, "No...not yet. I don't know what to hope for; I don't want to even think she has been kidnapped, but any contact would tell me she is still okay."

Angelina didn't want to dampen Ed Helton's parade, but even if kidnappers did make contact, there was no guarantee that Danni would be returned unharmed.

Angelina turned to Buford Long. "I tried to get anybody at the Savannah police department. I had no luck. Is there anyone you can call?"

"Same thing with me; Savannah PD has every officer on riot patrol. But, even under normal conditions, they wouldn't do anything until 24 hours. I don't think we can wait that long. If Mrs. Walton has been kidnapped, then we are the ones who will have to find her."

Angelina looked between Ed Helton and Buford Long. "Do either of you have any ideas on who would have any motivation to kidnap Mrs. Walton?"

Ed Helton sat behind his desk; he looked exhausted. "I think the only viable lead is Ken Carson. He was the manager of our loan department. I caught him making fraudulent loans and had Buford investigate him. We filed the paperwork to have him arrested about a week ago. He hasn't shown up for work since then. He's the only person I suspect."

The ringtone on Ed Helton's phone almost made him jump. Everyone in the room waited in silence as he answered the phone. "James is coming up. They've found Danni's car."

Chapter 56

Hanna met James at the door to her grandfather's office. James managed a smile and put his hand on her swollen belly. "How's the baby?" It was an unexpected way to begin the report on his search for Danni's car. Maybe it was a way to soften the news they brought.

Hanna and the others were impatient for the news, but it was such a natural concern and it seemed to have a calming effect on the room. "The baby's fine. I think he wants to get out and see his daddy pretty soon."

"We found your mother's car south of Savannah on Highway 17. The left side was all bashed in and it was submerged in the drainage ditch on the side of the road. The driver's side window was missing. Your mother must have gotten out through the window, but her purse was still inside."

There was a palpable sense of hope in James' report. If Danni had escaped from the car then she may be in a hospital or clinic, or even someone's house. James could feel their hope and knew the remainder of what he had to say would not be pleasant.

"There was another car involved. Only one man was in the car. We think he pulled your mother from her car, to his, and put her in his trunk. There were drag marks up the bank and a man's footprints to the rear of the car. There was some blood on the ground; we can only assume it was your mother's blood."

"How do you know it was only one man in the other car?" It was Buford Long that challenged their findings.

"Mr. Long, we've tracked enough men to know. There was only one man."

"Not conclusive proof of a kidnapping, but it sure looks like it was."

"Yes."

Ed Helton looked to Hanna and James. Hanna was ashen and James concerned. Doc and Mike DeAngelo were standing silently in the door to the office; Angelina and Buford Long looked engaged only in their thoughts. Ed hoped they were analyzing what they had learned and were coming up with a plan to find and rescue his daughter.

"Okay, what do we do now?"

~~

"Oh my God!"

The words came from Ed Helton's assistant in the front office. It was loud enough to attract the attention of everyone in the room. Normally a woman of impeccable manners and decorum, this morning she simply yelled to Ed Helton from her desk.

"Mr. Helton, turn on the news!"

Ed turned up the volume using the remote, the bars taking an eternity to climb the scale. Eric was reading from a prepared script.

"...that makes the fourth attack this morning. The death toll in the New York subway station is well over four-hundred. The office of the Mayor of New York released a written statement that the New York Fire Department has not yet determined if a combination of a natural gas leak combined with hazardous material somehow mixed to form the lethal gas that was responsible for the fatalities.

"Police officers at the scene say that the victims had the same symptoms as the fatalities at the elementary school in Orlando, the passengers aboard Delta Flight 28 from Atlanta to Chicago, and the hotel in New Orleans.

"Ladies and Gentlemen, it is the opinion of this reporter that this country is under a well coordinated terrorist chemical attack aimed at our most vulnerable targets...innocent American citizens, and it is time for our government to be truthful with us and let us know exactly the situation."

~~

How was it...why was it...that life could repeatedly lay such calamity in your path with such disregard to the pain and suffering she caused? His entire life had been one battle after another with only brief respite between engagements. The last five years had been such a calm. The last five years had given him hope that maybe...just maybe, there was such a thing as peace in his life.

But now, he had lost another friend, and yet another was in hiding from those who would kill him simply because of his ties to the West. And if Prince Al-Sabah survived the uprising in his own country, would he be able to survive the loss of his son? For that matter, would

460

Bill Cannon be able to survive the loss of Danni Walton? Bill knew his life would be empty without the hope that one day he could make Danni one with him, and it urged him through the growing exhaustion of the night. He vowed he would not lose the woman he loved.

Bill drove until exhaustion finally overtook him and the adrenaline finally left him. At 4 a.m. he pulled to the side of the road. His truck had survived the flood waters with minor exterior damage and the waters soaked the interior; she ran a little rough, but it was enough to get him from the destruction caused by the tsunami waves. He placed the .45 in his lap. The cab had the musky smell of wet carpet, but Bill had slept in worst places, as he drifted off to sleep.

Bill woke with the sun; only four more hours to Savannah. Bill cursed when the cell phone still failed to connect with any of the people with which he needed to talk.

~~

James held his wife close. Ed Helton, Angelina Sanchez, and Buford Long seemed almost paralyzed with the news. Only Doc Broderson and Mike DeAngelo, in quiet conversation by the door, understood the threat for what it was—a terrorist attack using chemicals instead of bullets and explosives to kill their victims.

"Doc, do you have any atropine injectors?" Atropine injectors were the known antidote to nerve gas poisoning.

"I've got a box in the ambulance."

"We may need those."

Hanna was the first to ask. "I can't believe it. Who would do such a thing?"

"The same people who would set off a nuclear bomb in the Chesapeake Bay, that's who." Mike DeAngelo had a blunt way with words.

Angelina Sanchez said, "There's no proof that was a nuclear weapon last night. If it was, don't you think the government would inform the public?"

"Shit lady, if it was a nuke, then the government is the last that would want the public to know."

"What should we do?"

461

James answered, "All we can do is stay away from big crowds and closed-in spaces. If it is nerve agent, then it will only be effective in closed-in spaces or in the immediate area of dispersion."

The discussion broke the terror in the room. Ed Helton brought the discussion back to his daughter.

"I'm sorry for those people killed in those attacks, but can we focus on Danni? We still have to find her, and now we will probably get less help than before. Does anybody have any ideas?"

Angelina did, "We can get a search warrant for Ken Carson's house. Maybe his wife knows something."

Buford Long agreed, but had reservations. "We'll never get a search warrant in time."

"Then we'll have to do it without a search warrant. It may not stand up in court, but I don't think we can wait."

~~

The guard at the front door saw the boy approach. He carried a box wrapped in the morning newspaper. The paper was taped to display the headline, "Explosion Rips Chesapeake Bay," on the top of the box.

The video cameras dutifully recorded the event. The boy knocked on the door and spoke into the speaker. "I have a package for Mr. Helton."

"What is it?"

"I don't know. I was just told to bring it to Mr. Helton. A man gave me fifty bucks to bring it."

"Remove the wrapping and open it." When the paper was removed, "Hold it up to the camera."

The reddish brown mass in the box looked harmless enough. "What is it?"

The boy looked into the box. "It looks like a wig to me."

The guard called Ed Helton's office. "Mr. Helton, there is somebody at the front door with a package for you. Check the video camera. Do you want me to let him in?"

When Ed saw the contents of the box he almost gagged. "Yes, bring him right up."

~~

462

It was a simple note. "Is your daughter's life worth $4,000,000?"

"Why $4,000,000?" Angelina thought it was an odd number to demand for a ransom.

"Because Ken Carson knows that is how much cash we are required to keep at the bank."

"Why no drop location? If he wants his money he is going to have to tell us how and where to meet. That's where most kidnappers make their mistake. It's hard to make a drop where we can't track them."

"Miss Sanchez, that may be true under normal circumstances, but these are not normal circumstances. This is the perfect time for such a crime. The entire country is in turmoil, and we couldn't get a policeman to write a traffic ticket right now."

"What do you want us to do?"

There was no decision Ed had to make. He would pay the ransom to ensure the return of his daughter. "I'm going to pay it, and then we're getting the hell out of here."

Angelina knew the chances of getting Danni back unharmed were not good, but was confident the FBI would eventually find Ken Carson and bring him to justice. "Mr. Helton, I'm sure we will catch this man."

"Miss Sanchez, I appreciate your efforts, but look at what's happening outside. The country is under attack and we can't get any help from the FBI or even the local police department. If I can get Danni back in one piece, then I'm taking my family out of the country."

Ed Helton turned to Mike DeAngelo. "Mike, do you have a boat big enough to get me and my family to the Bahamas?"

"Sure, you would have to top off in Florida before you made the crossing, but I've done that a hundred times. Not a problem."

Hanna almost crept up to the box that all had gazed into except her. The lid was only placed over the container and not pushed or seated on the sides; it was easy to move the lid away. The morning paper was only loosely assembled around the contents. It was brown with a reddish tint. Pieces of bloody flesh still clung to the roots. Inside the box was her mother's hair. She had been scalped.

The horror in the box set off a chain reaction in Hanna. First, the convulsions to catch her breath; she had taken in too much air with the shock of the contents in the box. She was wracked with spasms of coughing and hyperventilation, and then her water broke, and then the blood started to flow, and then the violent contractions, and then the clear amniotic fluids.

Doc and James rushed to her side at the same time.

"She's hemorrhaging. James, go and get as many towels as you can find. Do it quickly."

Doc laid Hanna on the couch. He placed his hand loosely over the mouth and nose and leaned close to her ear and spoke clearly. "Hanna, calm down. Breathe slowly." Doc's hand slowly opened to allow a limited amount of air into and from her lungs. He could see the panic in her eyes.

Doc grinned at Hanna, it was a calming gesture. "Hanna, do you have a name picked out for your baby?"

Hanna frantically searched for her husband. "Where's James?" Hanna winced with the contraction. Her eyes widened, "Was that what I think it was?"

Doc smiled, "If you mean, was that a contraction, yes it was. Hanna you are going into labor."

James returned with almost an armload of paper towels. "Did you say she was going into labor? Shouldn't we get her to the hospital? Why are we waiting? Let's go!"

It was calming the way in which Doc reassured the father to be. "Relax dad, women have been having babies even before there were any hospitals. We'll make it."

Hanna turned to her husband, "James, call my mother and tell her to bring my suitcase, it's already packed; and also ask her to bring the gown for the baby."

In her excitement she had all but forgotten about her mother. When she realized what she had said the excitement in her eyes disappeared. "Oh, I can't believe this is happening now. I always thought my mother would be with me."

Doc turned to Mike DeAngelo, "DeAngelo, make yourself useful and carry this young lady to the wagon."

DeAngelo easily lifted Hanna. As she clung to his neck she called to Angelina. "Please find my mother before I have the baby...please."

Angelina didn't need any more pressure on her than she already felt, but put up a solid smile. "Don't worry Hanna, we'll find your mother."

~~

Buford Long insisted on going with Angelina to question Rachael Carson. "You've only got one good arm, missy. If things get rough you may want some help."

The ride to Tybee Island was in silence until Buford, from out of the blue, offered, "I can tell you who set the whole thing up. It was Bill Cannon."

"The kidnapping?"

"No, that thing in Atlanta."

Bill Cannon, the man Angelina has come to suspect, but could never find a direct link from him to the drugs or the killings. She turned to Buford Long.

"You know that for a fact? You can prove that in a court of law?"

"That ain't my job; it's yours."

Why would Buford Long offer-up Bill Cannon so easily? Months ago he had called William Jefferson to block her investigation; now he fingers the central figure in the entire Walton case, why? It seemed so out of place that anyone associated with Ed Helton or Danni Walton would offer up such a damming accusation. Was he still trying to deflect attention from his part in the deal, was he trying to eliminate someone who could testify against him?

"Why didn't you tell me that months ago?"

"Let's just say that I gave it more thought."

"That's a serious charge. If you don't have any evidence, what makes you suspect Bill Cannon?"

"Danni Walton one day, out of the blue, asked her father for a quarter of a million dollars. She wouldn't say why she needed it. Even for a man as rich as Ed Helton, $250,000 isn't something you give to your daughter without a few questions. Ed asked me to look into it.

"During my investigation I saw a video of Bill Cannon and Danni Walton coming out of a hotel room in Atlanta late one night; back even before her husband was killed, and back before all the killing started. Think about it...Danni Walton married to a famous

465

preacher…she makes a mistake and gets a little too close to Cannon…realizes what she has done and tells Bill Cannon to get lost. Cannon gets pissed off and blackmails her so he won't spill the beans to her husband. He may have loved her, but I wouldn't put it past him to blackmail her."

Angelina listened to Buford Long's explanation. It was a scandalous charge against Bill Cannon and Danni Walton.

"If he was blackmailing her, explain why they have been seeing each other for the past five years."

Buford Long shrugged his shoulders. "Who knows? Maybe the two of them wanted her husband out of the way. Maybe they set it up together. It wouldn't be the first time two lovers capped off a husband to get the insurance money. Once her husband was out of the way, they could do whatever they wanted."

"Did you ever mention this to Mr. Helton? He seems to like Bill Cannon a lot. I don't think he would put up with someone who was blackmailing his daughter."

"Ed Helton loves his daughter, but he never liked her husband. Back when they were married, the good Reverend never brought the family to Savannah or Daufuskie to visit. Helton was a lonely man. Maybe he found out the good Preacher was running the hookers; he wouldn't be the first father to look the other way when a shitty husband is found dead."

Now the charges were getting ridiculous. "Are you telling me that you think Ed Helton may have been involved in the murder of Peter Walton?"

"I didn't say that. What I said was that he may have just looked the other way when Peter Walton turned up dead. There was a lot of shit going on in that family. You know that report about the shooting at the Walton residence in Atlanta? In my report, I said that I shot the guy that broke into the house."

"Yes, I am familiar with the report."

"Danni Walton really killed him. When I went in to check the house the guy shot me in the back. I was able to get a shot off and hit him in the shoulder. He was completely defenseless and Danni Walton came in and shot him through the heart. She executed him."

"Good Lord Buford! You filed the report that said you shot him! Why?"

"Sanchez, I've been in law enforcement for my entire life. You're going to find that a lawman's pension doesn't go very far…I did it because Ed Helton paid me to do it, and the guy deserved to die; nobody cares who killed him. If we would have arrested him there would have been too many questions to answer in court."

The Tybee Island residence of Rachael Carson was just ahead. "Buford, after we get Danni Walton back, you and I have to have a serious discussion."

"If we get her back."

Angelina knew Buford Long's reservations about getting Danni Walton back safe were realistic. "How do you want to handle this?"

"I'll be the bad cop, you be the good cop. Maybe we can get something out of her."

~~

Ed Helton was left alone in his office. DeAngelo and Doc were with James and Hanna at the hospital, and Buford and Agent Sanchez were on their way to Tybee Island. The bloody piece of Danni's scalp stared at him from the bottom of the box. It was a chilling reminder of the lengths to which Ken Carson would go to collect his ransom.

Ed Helton hoped the phone would not ring. He didn't know what he would tell Carson if he called. Yes he did, he would tell him he could have the money—no questions asked—just return his daughter safely to him.

The entire scheme to recover the bank's funds from Ken Carson now seemed a silly game…a deadly game. He wished he had let the money go. It wasn't worth his daughter's life.

There must have been some optimism still left in his soul, there was always the hope that Danni would return safely. He picked up the phone and dialed his residence on Daufuskie.

"Mamba, I want you to start packing for an extended trip to the Bahamas. We'll be leaving as soon as we get Danni back, and after Hanna has her baby."

It was as if Mamba had been expecting the call. "Yes Mister Helton."

Ed held his head and prayed. He prayed for the safe return of his daughter. And he prayed for the safety of his granddaughter and her husband and their new son, and he prayed for the country. The intercom interrupted his final thoughts.

467

"Mr. Helton?"

"Yes?"

"There is a man at the front of the bank who wants to see you."

A chill ran through Ed Helton. Was it the devil outside?

"Who is it?"

"Mr. Bill Cannon wants to see you."`

Chapter 57

Rachael wanted to turn on her side but couldn't. The sheets on the bed seemed rougher than normal, but it wasn't the sheets she minded so much, it was the cold. Oh, how her head hurt. She must have drunk too much after the investigators left. The gall of them both! How dare they try to question her without a search warrant or allowing her to call her lawyer. She knew the law…she didn't have to testify against her husband, everybody knew that. She saw right through the silly game they were trying to play. She had seen the same technique on television a thousand times, good cop—bad cop. There was no compassion in the Mexican whore who said she was from Washington. What a bunch of crap.

The cold started to reach to her core. She tried to turn to wake Ken; she would make him adjust the thermostat. Once again she couldn't turn and remembered that Ken no longer slept in her bed. Damn, it was dark tonight, darker than she could ever remember and she couldn't see a thing. She tried to reach for the light on the night table, but her arm wouldn't move; neither would her legs.

She heard something move in the darkness. Was it a chair sliding across the floor? Someone was in the room! She could hear him breathing! Panic consumed her. Her body strained to rise up and run, but something held her fast. She had to escape! She strained madly against what held her. Her body thrashed about. She screamed, "Help! Somebody help me!" She banged her head against the hard surface that once was her pillow. "Help me! Oh, God, somebody help me." The terror started to eat at her and she started to sob. "Oh, please somebody help me."

She lay exhausted on the hard bed. It had to be a dream. If I relax the dream will go away and I will wake. When the sounds of her screams evaporated into the night, all that was left was the breathing. She could hear the breathing, and he was near. "Please, help me, please!"

But the breathing didn't alter its rhythm nor did it go away, and her fear infected her bladder and her urine slowly leaked out, and she couldn't stop it. Through her sobbing the breathing was always there. It was maddening—the dream had to end.

A strange sound and she gasped and screamed as a weight fell upon her body. She was on fire, no, she was now even colder than before. It was nothing more than water, but the water filled her nose and mouth and she was drowning. What a horrible way to die. But she sputtered and coughed and the water was forced out. The water in her nose burned as her body began to shiver. The water on her skin trickled down her sides and between her legs.

Over and over the water cascaded over her body. Would it ever stop? She began to sob almost uncontrollably. "Please...stop...please." Her sobbing echoed off the walls of her dungeon. She long ago quit struggling against her bonds. It was useless to struggle.

The breathing came closer; it was near her ear, and again the sound of something moving on the floor. She jumped as much as her restraints would allow when gentle hands touched her shoulders. They were large hands, rough hands, the hands of a man.

The hands were so gentle and caressed her skin and slowly rubbed her neck and shoulders and down her arms. The hands were so gentle they could not be the hands of someone who would harm her. "Please, help me, please."

The hands moved from her neck and shoulders and gently moved over her breasts. They were so gentle and even in her fear the sensation was pleasing. The hands moved back up to her throat and then gently massaged her jaw muscles and she began to relax. The fingers moved under her jaw and pressed up and held the pressure. Her body was racked with pain. Electric jolts shot through her body and up to her brain and the paralyzing pain did not stop until the hands released the pressure from the nerves.

She gasped for breath and tried to regain her strength. Never had she felt such pain, and her body convulsed when she felt the hands on her shoulders once again. This time, when the hands massaged her neck and shoulders there was no pleasure in it, only mounting fear. Fear of the pain so intense it burned all through her body. And the hands were now again on her breasts and then moving back up her throat and onto her jaw. When the fingers pressed up on the nerves her body shook and convulsed, and the pain didn't leave until the hands moved away.

She could barely whisper, but she begged for mercy. "Please stop. Don't hurt me again." And she whimpered like a baby.

The breathing moved next to her ear. "It is your choice…pleasure or pain."

Rachael didn't understand the choices, pleasure or pain; her mind still in a panic. "Please don't hurt me again. I beg you. Please stop." Her pleas ended in sobs of pain and panic.

The breathing moved away and Rachael had hope.

The breathing returned and laid a cold hard object on her chest.

The hands massaged her arm and hand and then removed the object covering her breasts. Something bit her on the little finger of her hand. No, it wasn't a bite—it was the constant pressure that told her it wasn't the jaws of an animal, but the jaws of something more sinister and painful.

The voice leaned close to her ear. "Do you trust me, Mrs. Carson?"

Rachael did not understand the question. Did she trust him? When she struggled to form an answer the pressure on her finger increased and the pain started to build.

The voice asked again. "Do you trust me, Mrs. Carson?"

Her mind in a fog of fear she hoarsely whispered, "Yes…yes, I trust you. Let me go and I won't tell anyone. I promise. I swear to God I won't say anything, just let me go."

"First you must tell me what I need to know. Where is your husband, where did he take Danni Walton?"

"I don't know anything!!" She almost screamed it. "Honest, you have to believe me!"

The voice didn't change inflection. "Then you will suffer great pain for nothing. Where is your husband, and where has he taken Mrs. Walton?"

"I don't know…"

Rachael felt and heard the bone in her finger break even before the pain shot up her arm. This pain did not subside. It burned like fire and was so intense she almost collapsed from the pain. Her screams of agony filled the space.

"Mrs. Carson, you must trust me on this. The pain will not stop until you tell me what I want to know." Rachael felt the grip move to another finger. "Where is your husband and where did he take Danni Walton?"

"I…" Rachael felt the pressure increase on her finger and heard the sickening sound of the bone snap. In an instant she knew it was too much to bear. "…no wait…stop…please stop. I don't know anything…please…have mercy."

Pain can be a wonderful thing if applied correctly, and Bill Cannon was expert in its application. It wasn't long before Rachael Carson understood the futility of the situation. Either tell this man exactly what she knew, or the pain would never stop.

When he had the information he needed Bill stood, "Mrs. Carson, pray that what you have told me is the truth and that Mrs. Walton is unharmed," there was a long pause, "or you will die in this place."

It was a farewell that Rachael Carson believed to her core.

~~

Her screams filled the room. James tried to save his remaining hand from the vice grip of hers'.

The doctor stood from his examination. "Mrs. Madison, the baby is crowning, I want you to stop pushing. Try to relax. We're going straight to delivery."

James had trouble keeping up with the gurney as the attendants quickly pushed Hanna to delivery. No one stopped him as they pushed through the double doors to delivery. He didn't offer to stay behind; he wouldn't leave his wife until they forced him to do so.

The doctor entered the operating room and quickly donned his surgical gown and bent to the task of the baby and Hanna. When he glanced up at James all he said was, "Get a gown, mask and gloves on dad."

There were times during his captivity when James Madison questioned why God would allow him to suffer such pain at the hands of his captors. Why had he been forced to endure the torture? It would have been easier to let him die and for the pain to fade away. But now, in this operating room, he knew the answer. As he watched the miracle of childbirth and as his son took his first breath, he knew he had earned the right to be a father.

The doctor laid his son on Hanna's breast. He reached down and placed his hand on his son and he looked to his wife. "We have a son."

"I know."

James and Hanna's hands met on the small body of their baby and the eternal bond of family was formed.

The nurse was rough with the baby, turning him over and over and wiping the blood from him. It seemed much too rough for James. When they took him from Hanna's breast James started to get up and follow, but Hanna held fast to his hand.

"Don't worry my love, they will bring him back."

And James bent to kiss his wife, and their tears flowed freely, and their love was worth the pains they had suffered. When the nurse returned their son swaddled tightly in a blanket they laid him next to his mother. And James smiled as his son's lips moved.

"May I hold him?"

James worked his arm between the baby and Hanna. The nurse moved close to assist, "Do you need help?"

It was strange coming from Hanna, but her voice was not soft. "That's his father. He doesn't need help to lift his own son."

The nurse backed away and James lifted his son close to what remained of his mouth and he whispered to him, "Fear not my son, God loves you, I love you, your mother loves you, and we will always protect you."

Hanna looked to her husband and the baby he cradled so tenderly in his arm. His face and head were covered in bandage, and the gown was loose where his arm once hung, and he had to lean against the bed to maintain balance, but Hanna felt no fear facing the future with the man that had proven to be worthy of being the father of her son.

The nurse approached the bed, "Have you decided on his name?"

Hanna answered. "Yes we have. His name is William Cannon Madison."

Hanna, exhausted from the labors of the birth, relaxed her head on the pillow. James cradled William in his arm. The nurses busied themselves with cleaning the delivery room. It was then that she longed for her mother.

"James, give William to me. Go call papa and find out if there is any news on my mother."

~~

Eric Brown was working through the field reports. More gas attacks across the nation and the death toll continued to rise; more bodies

473

recovered from the tsunamis, and more panic from the population. The governors of twelve states activated their respective National Guard to restore order and to assist the authorities to secure the most vulnerable targets.

The production rooms were overwhelmed with video not only of the death from the gas attacks, but of the senseless murders of shop-owners or any citizen who tried to bring order to the rampaging mobs. Each killing only seemed to feed the mob's blood lust. There were two classes in America now, those on the rampage and those cowering in their homes hoping and praying the surging beast would pass them.

The senior producer sat heavily at Eric's desk. Maybe the level of violence coming into the newsroom had finally sunk into a man who always seemed to enjoy the tragedies they reported as entertainment more than news. But now the bodies of the innocent contorted in death on the streets of America, the senseless violence of the rampaging mobs wrecking destruction on the lives and property of those they considered the oppressors—seemingly for no reason other than they could—caused tremors in his hands and voice that he could not control.

"I was in LA during the Watts and Rodney King riots. I thought that was the worst thing I would ever see, but this…" he waved his hand over the reports, "…this is from another world. This can't be America." His voice trailed almost to a whisper. "Why don't they fight back?"

Eric knew how he felt—he had moments of the same depression. "Who are you talking about, the police? They can't be everywhere and they are outnumbered and outgunned. They will wait until the fury of the mob has been satisfied, and then maybe they will venture out to count the dead; but they will not risk their lives trying to reason with a mob that has lost all reason."

"I'm not talking about the police or the military. I'm talking about the people. Why don't they fight back?"

Eric thought he knew the answer. They, the people, had for too long allowed the moral decay of society, they had allowed the gangs that were now ravaging the streets to go unchecked, because it was easier to look the other way or move to the suburbs and their gated communities rather than confront the growing resentment to civilized standards of society. They, the people, had allowed the rule of law to be compromised by the few, and they believed as they were told; that it was the right thing to do. They, the people, turned a blind eye to the inconvenient truths of moral decay and, in their ignorance, allowed the wound to fester into a cancer that could be the death of their society.

"Because the few that have the courage to stand before the mob will perish when their neighbor's refuse to stand with them. They have become victims of their own complacency. They hide like frightened children from sounds in the night, and their only hope is that the mob will choose someone else to ravage. After this is over, they will crawl from their homes and demand change, but will once again only throw enough money at the mob to keep it placated and sated, rather than demand they contribute to society. We have allowed the evil to live among us and now we are suffering the consequences."

The producer was shocked at the things Eric said. "Maybe you're right, but somebody has to stop them."

"What are we going to do if the mobs try to break in here?"

"We discussed this upstairs. We'll transfer operations to New York. We have vans parked in the underground parking deck and we will be driven to safety."

"Will the guards use their weapons to keep the out the mobs?"

The producer looked stunned. "Oh, heavens no, we'll evacuate the building before we have to resort to violence."

It was the answer Eric expected. "That's what I thought."

Somebody yelled from the floor, "Eric, phone call line three."

Eric turned away from the producer; maybe it was Angelina. "Hello?"

"Eric, this is Steve Reynolds. Do you know where Bill Cannon is?"

Eric had to put his finger in his ear, "Senator, nobody down here has seen him for three days. What's up?"

"We know he was with Lucas McLaughlin in Virginia when the bomb exploeded. We have found McLaughlin's body, but we haven't found Bill's. There's still a lot of area that hasn't been searched, but I hoped you may have heard from him."

Eric noticed the slip of the tongue. "Senator, are you confirming it was a bomb that exploded on the Chesapeake Bay?"

Eric could sense a level of frustration from Senator Reynolds.

"Stop being a newsman for a minute, okay Eric? The President has ordered a full scale cruise missile attack on Kuwait. I can't follow their reasoning, but the Secretary of Defense said that Bill knew about the bomb and the nerve gas being smuggled into the States, and somehow they are linking that to Kuwait. I've got to get hold of Bill; maybe he can talk some sense into the administration."

"Damn Senator, why would we attack Kuwait? They are our only real ally on the Persian Gulf."

"Eric, they need to blame someone…and Eric…the FBI is going to release a report on the bomb and the gas attacks. In that report they are going to name Bill Cannon as a 'person of interest.'"

A person of interest, the newest method used by law enforcement at all levels to convince the public they were making progress in an investigation. It was a cowardly way to deflect attention to someone only suspected, but not proven to be guilty of a crime. It was the most outrageous charge Eric could imagine against a man of Bill Cannon's character.

"That's the biggest bunch of crap I have ever heard!"

~~

"Will you bring me some water, please?" Danni yelled her request. She could hear Ken Carson in the room above her, and if she could hear him then he damn well could hear her.

The blood from the wound to her scalp had long since dried. The pain was only made worse by her insatiable thirst. "Will you bring me some water, please?"

Danni heard Ken's footsteps on the wooden floor above and heard him move to the door leading to the stairs. Her eyes were fixed on the bottle of water he carried. He held the water to her lips and she drank deeply of the cooling liquid.

"Thank you."

Ken talked to her as if they were in the waiting room of the bank.

"This should be over soon. Your father should get my demands, and if he does as he has been told, then you should be home by tomorrow night."

"What happens if he refuses to pay?"

"Then you will die."

Danni didn't think Ken Carson had the guts to kill her until he answered her next question.

"Why are you doing this?"

Ken's eyes had a crazy look to them. "I am nothing without money. You will die, I will die, but I will not go alone. You should pray that you father loves you and will pay for your return."

"Even if he pays, you will not get away with it. He knows it is you that has done this thing."

"Yes I will. A lot of things have happened in the last two days. Nobody will come looking for me for a long time. I will be out of the country before the chaos is over."

Danni found the answer odd. "What chaos?"

Ken rubbed his hands together, "The night I took you, there was an explosion, a huge explosion on the Chesapeake Bay. It killed thousands. Maybe it was a terrorist attack, I don't know for sure, but what I do know is that everybody is going crazy. And then I saw on the news that there have been gas attacks all over America, and your boyfriend is involved."

Danni didn't want to believe what her captor had told her. "My boyfriend?"

"Yeah, that Army guy you had at your party, the big man."

"Bill Cannon?"

"Yeah, that's him. The government is looking for him. He may have been killed in the blast or by the tidal waves it caused—they haven't found his body; he's probably already dead. That's why they won't catch me. Everybody...the police, the Army are trying to control the riots. They won't even look for me." Ken Carson ended his statement with a bizarre little laugh.

Danni was stunned. She leaned back against the post that held her prisoner. It was not that hope was lost; it was that her love may be lost forever. She hung her head and silently wept. Sitting here in the filth of a makeshift dungeon she did not lament her situation, but she did regret the many times she could have told Bill Cannon that she loved him, but did not.

~~

Buford Long listened half-heartedly to Sanchez's plan for the drop. His mind was focused on the money; how to get it, how to keep it, and how to conceal the fact that once he got it, that he had it. He would be damned if he would be left with nothing when the Helton's were living the life of luxury in the Bahamas.

The objective was the money. When would the money be most vulnerable? Not in the bank, but during transport, during the drop, or after. Sanchez offered to make the drop; one more person between Buford Long and the money.

Chapter 58

Danni's head hung to her chest. She had been drifting in and out of sleep. The feeling had long ago left her arms and legs. The noise of someone coming down the stairs stirred her from her exhausted slumber. It was Ken Carson struggling under the weight of two bags.

Ignoring Danni, he placed the bags on the floor and carefully removed the contents. He removed two large gas cans and a car battery from one of the bags, and another three cans from the other. He took his time and was careful when he assembled the bomb. Danni sat calmly among the containers that may cause her death; she felt great contempt for Ken Carson.

"You are such a coward."

Ken looked up from his work. He connected the last wire to the car battery and then walked to Danni. When Danni looked up the flash of his fist was all that she saw. Her head snapped to the side and her body fell to the floor. Carson pulled her up from the floor with what remained of her hair.

"Shut up bitch! You only live if I get what I want. Maybe I should kill you now. Nobody will miss just another snobby rich bitch."

Danni struggled against the blackness that tried to envelope her. Carson placed a newspaper on her chest and took a photo of her.

"You have 12 hours bitch. If anything goes wrong, if anybody tries to stop me, then that pretty skin of yours will burn like paper."

When Ken Carson left the room the only thing Danni Walton was left with was the digital clock ticking off the seconds of her last hours on this earth.

~~

Ed Helton opened the package that was once again delivered by a young man randomly selected off the street. To his relief, there was only a crude map marked with an intersection of two country roads between two small rural towns in the lowlands, and a time to meet. There was no other note or instruction.

479

Buford Long was the first to comment. "That's wide-open terrain. He could be anywhere in the surrounding area; he will be able to see everything approaching that point."

Angelina traced the roads leading to the intersection. "What am I supposed to do, just drop the money and leave?"

"I don't think that's a smart idea for a couple of reasons. First, anybody could drive by and take it. That wouldn't do a thing for us. Second, we need proof of life and a reasonable assurance that we will get Ms. Walton back before we turn over the money."

Ed Helton listened in silence. He trusted the experience and training of both Buford Long and Angelina Sanchez. "Buford, what would you describe as a reasonable assurance?"

"Ed, I don't know exactly what to tell you or Ms. Sanchez. I think it's a gut feeling. Carson holds all the cards. He knows if he gives up your daughter he has no leverage. There's no mutual trust in deals like these. He doesn't trust us, and we can't trust his word. It's a Mexican standoff." Buford turned to Angelina. "I can't stress enough; you can't turn over the money until you have proof of life."

Angelina hoped neither Buford Long nor Ed Helton would notice, but her legs were shaking. Was it her ego that demanded she be the one to make the drop? Now Danni Walton's life may depend on her decisions. Life was simpler when all she had to do was piece together the mysteries of the Walton murders. She turned to Ed Helton.

"I'm ready."

Ed and Buford helped Angelina load the three suitcases into the car. The two men watched as she drove away. Ed turned to enter the bank and when he noticed Buford was no longer at his side he turned to find out why. Buford was leaving the parking area of the bank.

"Buford, you're not coming back inside?"

Buford stopped, "Ed, that little girl may need some help. I'm going to the police department. I know it's a long shot, but maybe I can find us some help."

Ed Helton would be forced to wait alone for news of his daughter.

~~

James Madison paused in the waiting room to watch the news. The banalities of the President's speech and the reports from members of the Cabinet were superfluous and more apropos to political campaign than to the defense of the country. James didn't expect much more, but the scandalous report linking Bill Cannon, in any manner other than the one who brought the threat of the bomb and gas attacks to the attention of the country, was outrageous and defamatory.

James looked to where Doc Broderson had been patiently waiting and noticed his absence. It was probably just as well, if Doc had seen the same report he probably would not have been so controlled as James. Thank God DeAngelo wasn't here or the waiting room probably would have been completely trashed.

On the balcony leading from the hospital, the smell of smoke was pervasive. It was not the city he remembered. James hoped the call to Mr. Helton would bring better news.

~~

The information Rachael Carson provided was accurate. Now Bill hoped he wasn't too late.

His reconnaissance of the abandoned chicken house was almost complete. The trees that lined the plowed fields would provide concealment only up to a point, but any approach would have to be made across open ground.

How many were in the house was unknown. He assumed only Ken Carson, but there could be more. Would the house be secure? What kind of locking device? Would there be any trip wires or explosives devices with which he would have to contend? What measures would be required to free Danni? For that matter, what would be the medical condition of Danni? Would she be ambulatory or would she require assistance? That was the reason he stopped by the hospital and picked up Doc Broderson.

"It will be nice to tell Hanna her mother is safe."

Bill turned to Doc, "Focus on what we're doing. If we get her then we will have all the time we want to call."

Some could have taken offense at Bill's brusque manner, but Doc was not one to object—Bill's focus had saved his life many times over the years.

"What's the plan?" Doc had paid attention during the recon, but it was always Bill who had the eye for the ground.

"We're coming in from the south. We'll put the truck in the trees and should only have a half mile on foot. We'll come up in the tree line...that will leave us only a couple of hundred yards of open field to cross. We'll hold in the trees and try to determine how many are in the house."

Bill backed his truck into the trees and checked his equipment. "You ready?"

Doc took one last deep breath. "Let's go."

~~

"Brown, get up here!" The call was yelled from the upper level of the newsroom.

Eric left his desk and took the stairs two at a time. The call had urgency to it. The network bigwigs were all in attendance.

The executives were working over a stack of still photos of Bill Cannon from his time as a young lieutenant to his testimony before Congress just before his retirement.

"Where did you get those photos?"

"The FBI got them from the Pentagon. We want you to anchor a special we're putting together on Cannon. We want to air it on the 6 p.m. newscast. The White House is going to send down some narrative. Think you can put it together by this afternoon? We'll give you priority of support."

"Why me?"

"You're the best we've got, and our surveys tell us that you are our most trusted anchor."

"What's the objective of the report?"

"The FBI thinks this Cannon character is behind these terrorist attacks. We want to help smoke him out; to help them to build a case against him."

"That may be the most ridiculous thing I have ever heard. Why would the FBI think that?"

"The FBI thinks he went rouge and has been working with terrorists elements from the Middle East."

"That's the dumbest thing I have ever heard. If the FBI had any evidence they would arrest him, not blast his name all over the news."

"They're working on it. We want to be lead network on this. It will make a great report."

The executives were stunned when Eric stepped back from the table. "I won't do it."

"You'll do it or you can find another job."

Eric gave a few moments of thought before he answered.

"Are we a news network, or just hatchet men for the White House? Our society is crumbling and all the White House is concerned with is Bill Cannon? Why don't we ask the White House what our intelligence agencies have been doing for the last year to discover and prevent these attacks? Why don't we do a report on how inept the Pentagon and the FBI and the CIA have been in protecting our country? Those are the questions a real news network would be asking. I won't be a part of it."

"Then you are no longer working for this network. Clean out your desk."

Eric stepped back. Never in his career did he see such a disregard for the truth. He knew his life would be better away from such deceitful men.

He didn't look back when he left the building.

~~

Angelina stopped her car at the intersection marked on the map. Once she shut off the engine the silence was deafening. She got out of the car and scanned the distant tree lines that formed a natural visual barricade surrounding the intersection. She was sure she was in the correct spot, but the map showed the roads leading to the intersection as basically straight, but in reality the roads contained many turns and dips that restricted her ability to see more than a quarter mile in any direction.

The ditches that formed the shoulder of the roads were filled with dark brackish water that smelled of fertilizer and decaying vegetation. Only one field was plowed and allowed any measure of unobstructed observation; the other three contained wheat or grass for livestock feed. Carson could be anywhere. How long was she supposed to wait?

Carson could be in the fields, there was enough vegetation to provide complete concealment, but he wouldn't do that—because he would need a car to transport the money—unless he would simply take her car and leave her stranded…or dead in the field. No, he wouldn't take her car because he would think there would be a tracking device planted somewhere in it. For that matter, there could be a tracking device in the suitcases containing the money. He would probably transfer the money to his own bags; Angelina would if she was in his place.

How long had she been waiting? Damn, she should have checked her watch when she arrived. It felt like an eternity. She pulled the map again and traced her route with her finger. This had to be the spot. She hoped this was the spot—maybe she should go back to the main road and drive the route again just to make sure. No, that would be foolish; she was in the correct spot.

The sound of her cell phone took her breath away until she realized Carson would not have her number. She was on edge when she answered, "Eric, I can't talk with you now."

"Angelina, I only need a minute. You must be busy, but I just quit my job at CNN. I'm coming to Savannah." From Eric's tone of voice Angelina could tell he was not feeling the anxiety that almost overwhelmed her.

Eric expected some sort of reaction, something that would have let him know that she was concerned, or happy, or confused, or something, but Angelina's response was terse and final. "Eric, I can't talk now," and without any explanation abruptly ended the call.

Eric stared for a moment at the phone. That was completely out of sorts for Angelina. Was this a side of her that he had not seen? He almost pushed the redial, but reconsidered. If Angelina said she couldn't talk right now, then obviously she wouldn't appreciate him questioning why. It bothered Eric, but he would see her in a few hours and find out why she was upset.

The phone call made Angelina even more nervous. The call was a world away from the surreal surroundings of the field. Should she have confided in him her fears? No, she must keep her attention focused on saving Danni Walton.

The ringing of the phone bothered her. She had just told Eric she couldn't talk. But, her phone was not lit up. The ringing continued. It was coming from the ditch behind her. Three rings and it stopped. She walked to the ditch. A short pause and the ringing began again. There in the tall grass, the black shape of a cheap cell phone.

"Hello?"

~~

Bill and Doc lay prone in the grass. Bill turned to Doc, "It's clear on the outside. I haven't heard a thing from the inside, have you?"

"Not a thing."

"Dead run to the north end. Stay in the shadows. If anything happens we will evacuate to this spot and then work our way back to the truck. Any question?"

"I'm ready Bill, let's go."

Bill carried the weapons; Doc carried the equipment and medical bag. Although the pace was brisk, there was no heavy breathing and the two men moved silently through the grass until they crouched in the shade at the north end of the building.

Bill leaned his head against the tin of the building. There was nothing moving inside. Could it be that the building was abandoned?

Bill whispered to Doc, "Padlocked from the outside. I don't think we can get inside without waking the dead. This tin will only magnify the sound. I think we need to go full bore and be ready to shoot."

Doc gave him the thumbs up. Bill held the padlock away from the door as Doc cut it away. There was only the softest click as the bolt cutter cut through the shank. Bill signaled he would take the left side of the room, Doc the right.

Doc pushed open the door and Bill dove through it, rolling as he hit the floor and came up with his pistol to his front; and Doc now to his right. There was nothing moving in the long room. Bill pointed to footprints in the dust. They were fresh footprints and they were leading to a hatch set in the floor.

Bill approached the hatch and bent low. There were no trigger devices he could see, but there was no reason to be careless. He attached a line to the ring that served as a handle and both he and Doc moved as far away as the line would allow.

Doc lay prone on the floor, but Bill had to stand erect to gain leverage. There was no explosion. The reflection in the mirror Bill held below the edge made his heart race. Danni sat in the middle of the room. It took considerable restraint to control his urge to abandon all caution and rush down the stairs, but just because the door wasn't rigged didn't mean there was no threat. Too many of Bill's friends had walked into ambush when they thought the danger was over.

Bill whispered to Doc, "Danni's in the middle of the room tied to a pole. The stairs look clear. I'll go first."

Danni heard the shuffle of feet, but couldn't force her vision to focus on the objects that moved silently in the dust. She felt the tension release that held her arms. She was lifted, or was that just a dream, or

485

was she dying? It didn't matter; she was off the filthy floor. The angel who rescued her was strong but gentle.

Bill and Doc carried Danni up the stairs, and paused for only a moment at the door before they covered the open ground between the building and the tree line. They didn't slow down in the trees and continued the pace until they reached the truck. In the back seat, Doc worked on Danni's wounds. The stinging liquid shocked Danni. Her trip back to consciousness was slow and things unclear.

"Bill?" Danni's voice was unsteady and the surroundings confusing.

Bill glanced back, but only for a moment. "Danni, you're safe. We're taking you home."

Danni tried to move. "I don't understand."

Doc placed his hand on her shoulder. "Danni, please sit still for a moment more." Doc finished wrapping her head.

Danni sat in silence for the ride to the hardtop road. The world was spinning and all that had passed intermingled with the present and it was confusing. "How did you find me?"

Bill answered, "We got lucky. Danni, why don't you rest; we're not out of the woods yet. I'll tell you all about it later."

Doc climbed over the front seat to allow Danni to use the back seat as a bed, but the adrenaline of safety surged through her. She leaned forward and placed her hand on Bill Cannon's neck. It was a comforting gesture to them both. She heard Bill make the call.

"We got her. She's safe. Do you want to talk with her?"

Bill handed the phone to Danni. "It's your father."

"Daddy, it was Ken Carson who took me."

"We know. You're safe now. Bill will get you back home." Ed felt relief beyond anything that he could have expected; his daughter safe, and his granddaughter giving birth to his first great-grandchild. It was something that made the kidnapping quickly fade in importance. "Danni...Hanna is in the hospital. She had a baby boy!"

In spite of the pain Danni literally squealed. "NO! I can't believe I missed it! We're going there now!"

"Danni, talk to Bill, it may not be safe downtown."

"If my daughter is there, then it is safe enough for me. We're going. I love you daddy, I'll see you after the hospital."

486

"Bill, Hanna is in the hospital. I want to go there."

Bill wanted to stop and hold her rather than counsel her on the wisdom of going into downtown Savannah. "Danni, a lot of things have happened since you were taken; it may not be safe to go through downtown."

Danni's voice had regained some of the command that Bill remembered and always loved. "Mr. Cannon, if downtown Savannah is not safe enough for us, then it damn sure isn't safe enough for my daughter and grandson. We're either going there for a visit, or we'll go there to get them out, but we're going!"

Bill smiled. The old Danni wasn't lost in her ordeal. Once out of danger she was only thinking of others. "Okay Danni, we'll go see your daughter." Bill handed her his phone. "Call James, tell him we're on our way and then call your father. Tell him where we are going, and then find out where the drop is."

~~

Bill pulled to the emergency room entrance; the scene was chaotic. He addressed both Doc and Danni. "I know it may be difficult, but get the baby, James and Hanna and go to the bank. DeAngelo has a boat ready to get you off the mainland."

Danni looked to Bill. "We can't take the baby and leave!"

Bill understood her concern. "Danni, it's not safe here. Doc will be with you. Hanna and the baby will be fine."

"You're not coming with us?"

"No, not now, I'll meet you later. I have a couple of things I need to do. You go on ahead."

"What are you going to do?"

"Angelina might be in danger. Eric would never forgive me if she got hurt."

"Bill, the money doesn't mean a thing. Let it go. She will deliver the money and then come back."

Bill wasn't smiling when he answered. "Maybe," then Bill turned to Doc. "Take Danni and get moving."

Bill would try and protect Angelina. He would try and recover the money. But the real reason he was going was that he would not allow a man to treat any woman, much less the woman he loved, in such a manner and go unpunished.

487

Chapter 59

Angelina Sanchez looked around the fields. Surely the phone was intended to be answered. She approached it as she would a snake—slowly and carefully. The phone went dead once again after the third ring.

When she finally mustered the courage to retrieve the phone, the screen read only unknown number. How long before it would ring again?

Angelina almost dropped it when it rang again. "Hello?"

"Who are you?"

"My name is Angelina Sanchez."

"I saw you on your cell phone. Take it out and hold it in the air so I can see it, and then throw it in the ditch."

Angelina did as the voice requested. The phone made a plunking sound as it sunk into the dark water. Angelina knew Ken Carson was close enough to see her. She tried to look deep into the trees without being too obvious.

"Do you have the money?"

"Yes."

"Put the money on the ground and leave."

"I can't do that."

The phone went dead. Angelina's hand shook with tremors of doubt. Was that too bold a move? She prayed she had not made a critical—a deadly mistake.

She walked 20 or 30 paces from the car. She shaded her eyes from the sun and tried to discover where Carson could be. Would he be near one of the roads leading to the intersection or was that too obvious?

Again she failed to note the time of the first call. It should be on the phone. It was—it was 10 minutes ago. Why didn't he call back?

She felt the vibration of the phone almost before it rang. "Yes?"

"Are you stupid? Can't you understand? I said put the money on the ground and leave!"

It was clear to Angelina that Carson also felt the pressure of the transfer. Could she use that to her advantage? Don't get ahead of yourself. Stay in the moment.

"I need proof of life."

"You…"

Angelina closed the phone before Carson could complete his statement. She didn't' plan to do it, the idea came only as a flash. If Carson wasn't prepared to provide proof of life, then they had nothing to discuss. She had stepped up to the challenge; she would not be overwhelmed by a man who had proven to be coward.

Ken Carson was a smart man, a methodical man, accustomed to detailed analysis and movement of numbers or dollars on the stock exchange. How could he handle making decisions without the luxury of a pace that he set and in a situation where failure could mean life or death? Angelina would watch closely for any sign of weakness or doubt.

Angelina understood; she held more sway than she first believed. She had the money…Ken Carson wanted it. Ken Carson didn't care about Danni Walton. She was only a tool to gain what he wanted.

It was another 10 minutes before the phone rang again. Carson had calmed considerably.

"Are you armed?"

"Of course."

"Remove your weapons and throw them in the ditch." Ken Carson was preparing to come out.

"I will not."

The calm demeanor evaporated. "You will do what I tell you or you will be the one responsible!"

"Mr. Carson, calm down. You are the one responsible for the safety of Danni Walton. You have Danni Walton and I have the money you want. I am prepared to do the exchange. I am not here to harm you."

"You are wasting time, and time Danni Walton cannot afford." It was a threat that tried to put control back with Ken Carson. The phone went dead once again.

Angelina saw dust rise from a distant corner of the fields. Ken Carson was leaving his concealed position.

She removed the Glock from her belt and held the weapon down to her side. Carson pulled to a stop a few paces from her. He left the car running when he opened the door and stepped out. A chrome plated revolver stuck from his belt.

"Do you work for Helton?"

"Not really. I have lived with his family for the last few months. I volunteered to do this for him."

"Where is the money?"

"It's in the trunk. You won't see a penny of the money unless you have proof of life."

"You make me nervous with that gun. Toss it and I will give you proof of life."

"Mr. Carson, let's not play games. You put that gun back in the car, and I will put my weapon on the road."

Carson pulled the pistol and tossed it into the front seat. Angelina knelt and placed the Glock on the road and then took two steps back. "You have proof of life?"

Carson stepped closer and tossed his cell phone to her. "Open it."

The picture was of poor quality but it was enough. Danni Walton sat in the middle of a group of containers connected by wires, a digital clock in the foreground. The paper on her chest was from today.

"That was taken this morning. About four hours ago. That will go off in eight more hours. There's your proof of life. When I am safe and secure, I will call the cell phone you have, and give you the location. If anything happens to me, you will never find her in time to save her life."

"What guarantee do I have that you will call?"

"Ed Helton will get over losing money; I don't think he would ever rest if he lost his daughter. I don't want her dead, I just want the money. It's a business deal."

It made sense to Angelina, and she believed him. It was the gut reaction Buford Long had talked about.

"Okay Mr. Carson, I believe you. Do you want to count the money?"

"There is no need. If the amount isn't correct, I won't make the call. I don't think Mr. Helton would be so foolish as to try and short sell me on this deal." Carson walked back to his vehicle and pulled four canvas bags from his back seat. "Load the money in these bags."

Angelina loaded the stacks of money into Carson's bags, showing him each block before she placed them in the bag. Carson watched with interest as she transferred the blocks of bills.

Angelina was sweating through her shirt by the time the transfer was complete. "Load the bags into the trunk, and then step back."

Angelina did as she was told. She stepped back and allowed Carson room to close the trunk. She held the cell phone that Carson gave her.

"You will call this number?"

Carson moved toward the door of his car. When he looked up to address Sanchez, it was as if he was leaving for the supermarket. "I will call that number…" and then his eyes widened, and his mouth tried to form the next words, but all that could form was the grunt of all air blown from his lungs.

Angelina heard the explosion of the gunshot, and felt the compression of air as the bullet passed her. Ken Carson grabbed to his chest and his warm blood covered his hand. How could this girl have betrayed him? His legs were weak and he staggered and fell against the car. He slowly slid to the ground and sat in his own blood, and his hand fell to his lap.

Angelina stood frozen in place. There was no explanation. What happened? She was as surprised as Ken Carson. He was dying before her eyes. She stepped back to move closer to the Glock still lying on the pavement.

"Nobody will miss him."

The words came from behind her. Angelina slowly turned and looked into the smoking barrel of a gun trained at her and into the eyes of Buford Long.

"Why? Why did you kill him?"

"Don't be stupid Sanchez…for the money. I couldn't have him complaining to Helton that he didn't get his money. He had to be eliminated. I'm sorry I have to do this, but you understand I can't let you live."

"You won't get away with this."

491

Buford sneered, "I don't need to get away with this. Everybody will think Carson killed you, and he disappeared. You are just in the wrong spot at the wrong time."

Angelina knew he would shoot her, and that she would die. Angelina saw his finger begin to tighten on the trigger. She could see the grasses sway in the gentle breeze, and could hear the insects buzzing in the air. They would be the last things she took from this earth and she closed her eyes.

But the final shot never came and the only thing Angelina heard was the collapse of something to her front.

Buford Long lay sprawled on the road, his arms and legs spread out and the gun he once held now lay next to his hand and not in it. It took a moment for the scene to register; the small entry wound on his forehead, and the blood pumping from the back of his head explained everything.

From across the field Angelina saw a man jogging toward her. His gait was without effort and he covered the distance quickly. The dust he raised and the great distance distorted his image, but she could see the rifle he carried in his right hand.

Bill Cannon slowed to a walk when he neared the cars. He glanced at Angelina but didn't speak. He walked to the still body of Ken Carson and poked him with the barrel of the rifle, and the body slid from the sitting position of a rumpled heap now lying on his side, his eyes staring blankly at the pavement.

Cannon moved to the body of Buford Long, the blood from his head only now slowing to an ooze of red matter mixed with skull and brain rather than a flood of pumping blood. He took the barrel of the rifle and moved the gun away from his reach; out of habit Angelina supposed.

Cannon finally looked at Angelina, "Are you okay?"

Angelina felt numb. The building tension of the exchange, the subtle maneuvering with Ken Carson for dominance, Buford Long's finger tightening on the trigger of the gun, the responsibility for Danni Walton's safety—taken away with the sudden impact of two bullets. She was simply an observer in a world where things were not debated and negotiated, but brutally solved with the finality of death—a world where those who would resort to violence with ruthless disregard to anything but survival always won. But, still, there was the matter of Danni Walton.

"How will we find Mrs. Walton?" It was almost whispered. How would she tell Mr. Helton that she had failed?

Cannon was at the trunk removing the bags from Carson's car. "Danni's safe."

"Safe...how?"

Bill Cannon ignored the question and carried the bags to Angelina's car. He nodded in the direction of the Glock. "Is that your weapon? Pick it up...you may still need it."

Angelina moved in slow motion. It had all happened so fast. "He was going to shoot me."

Bill slammed the trunk. "It looked that way to me."

Bill stuffed Angelina's pistol in her belt and led her to the passenger door. "Get in."

Bill circled the car and picked up Buford Long's weapon and tossed it in the back seat, he placed his rifle between Angelina and himself. As he backed to avoid the bodies littering the road he almost yelled at Angelina. "Sanchez...Sanchez...snap out of it. We're not out of danger yet."

Still dazed, Angelina had trouble forming her question. "How did you know Buford Long was going to steal the money?"

Bill focused on the road. "I didn't. I came to kill Carson for what he did to Danni."

Angelina began to feel her stomach churn. It was a struggle to fight back the urge to vomit away her fear. "Would you really have killed him? I mean...Mrs. Walton was safe...would you have killed him anyway?"

Bill Cannon didn't answer; he simply momentarily turned to Angelina. In that instant, what she saw in his eyes made her shudder. Deep within the eyes that seemed to want to smile; there was steel cold death. She recoiled and shuddered. Sitting next to Bill Cannon was like sitting next to death itself. How many had looked into these eyes before they were sent to hell?

It took a moment to regain composure before she gathered the courage to ask, "Where are we going?"

"To my truck and then I'll escort you to the bank. Ed has arranged a boat to get us out of the city...and Sanchez, Eric is coming down. He's going with us."

Bill thought the mention of Eric might bring Angelina back to the present...it took some time.

A few days ago, Eric Brown filled her thoughts. It was sad that she allowed so many things to come between them. She had dodged death once again and would not make the mistake again. Maybe Eric could bring sanity to her world.

"Eric is coming here?"

"Yes."

"Mr. Cannon," Angelina's voice was still unsteady, "thank you for saving my life."

Cannon smiled as he turned to her, "I had to; Eric would be pissed if I let anything happen to you."

Angelina smiled; it was good to be alive.

~~

Cannon stayed with her until she was in sight of the bank. Before he left her car, he told her, "Tell Ed and DeAngelo to go ahead and launch as soon as everybody is ready. I'll meet them at the Dolly Madison Reef."

"You're not coming with us?"

"I will, but I have something I must do. Be careful."

~~

"I won't leave without Bill!" Danni was adamant.

Ed tried to reason with his daughter. "Danni, think about Hanna and the baby, it's not really safe here."

Mike DeAngelo stood at the glass door that looked down on River Street. As he spoke he pulled a pistol from beneath his shirt. The mob was slowly working its way to the bank, ransacking the windows of the businesses as they progressed. "We need to do something. Either we get moving, or we will have to fight our way to the boat."

Angelina was the last to talk with Bill Cannon. "Mrs. Walton...Danni, Colonel Cannon said for us to go with Mr. DeAngelo and that he would meet us." She glanced over her shoulder through the glass door. "If we stay here, there will be bloodshed."

It was Hanna's plea that finally convinced her. "Momma, Bill will meet us. He always has, he always will. You must trust him."

Doc and DeAngelo were the first out the back door of the bank. The trip to the waterfront was direct and they quickly boarded the 45' fisherman. The accommodation would be tight, but there was safety on the water. As they left the mouth of the river and were on the open ocean, Danni looked back at the city she loved her entire life. There was a pall of smoke hanging over Savannah. It bought a tear to her eye.

Over the Dolly Madison Reef, DeAngelo cut the engines and drifted. Doc and Mamba went below with James, Hanna and little William, and helped tidy up a crib for the baby. Angelina and Eric sat together on the foredeck, their conversations quiet and private. Danni, her father, and Mike DeAngelo scanned the horizon from the bridge.

Ed Helton asked, "How long will we wait?"

"As long as it takes."

"What if he doesn't come?"

DeAngelo could see worry on Danni's face. "He always has."

~~

Bill Cannon parked the truck in the underground garage of his condo. He would need clothes and weapons during the crossing to the Bahamas. He flipped on the TV as he packed; it was his only source for intelligence on the situation. He quickly sorted through his documents. He packed only the most important ones. Bill threw a picture of eight men in battle dress taken in a jungle clearing many years ago in his bag.

One document he did not pack was the certificate he framed when he received his commission as a second lieutenant. What was it that suddenly made Bill feel guilty?

"The latest death toll from the chemical attacks is now well over 10,000…"

Bill's eyes went to Sergeant Tex Graham, killed in the Colombian jungle protecting the United States of America.

"Forty-two school children were found dead in a small town in Colorado…"

Bill put his finger on the image of Sergeant First Class Thomas "Sparks" Edison, killed in the Mogadishu Bakaara market in Somalia; on the Horn of Africa serving the United States of America.

I do solemnly swear that I will support and defend the Constitution of the United States…

495

Bill threw a waterproof jacket, a pair of boots and three boxes of .45 shells in the pack.

"A mob in Chicago killed three fire fighters trying to save the homes of..."

The eyes of First Sergeant William Edwards followed Bill around the room. Edwards died in Iraq serving the United States of America.

...against all enemies, foreign and domestic...

"The water supply for Little Rock, Arkansas, is contaminated..."

Sergeant First Class John Brown Jackson died in a Georgia prison yard, but his spirit was killed while serving in Africa by the actions of an unfaithful wife.

...I will bear true faith and allegiance to the same...

Major General Lucas McLaughlin died in the blast of a nuclear explosion on the Chesapeake—defending America. Command Sergeant Major Steve Thunder survived combat on five continents and died in the jungles of Atlanta protecting humanity from that which was now running amok across the country.

...so help me God...

Of the eight, only he and Doc Broderson remained to watch over the legacy. It was these dead comrades that would not allow Bill Cannon to run before the threat. It was the memory of these brave men that caused Bill Cannon to hang the citation back on the wall and leave the comfort of his home without completing his packing. He hoped Danni would understand.

~~

The wait turned from one hour into two. When the others went below for dinner Danni stood alone in the fish tower high above the deck. There, against the dark line of the distant shore, a splash of white; and then again, but now it was no longer simply a splash of white, it was the distinct shape of a boat, and it was on a direct course to them.

Danni yelled once, and again, "Mike! Somebody is coming!"

DeAngelo appeared on deck and with binoculars announced. "That's Bill."

Danni couldn't explain it, but she felt short of breath. It was a childish sensation.

496

Chapter 60

Danni watched as Bill maneuvered to the port side of the boat. DeAngelo and Doc secured the bumpers and tied the two boats together. They were the first to greet Bill as he swung aboard.

She heard the muffled conversations, but the breeze blew the words to the sea. She saw Bill turn and smile and try to make his way to where she stood, but James intercepted him. The men almost pushed Bill below to introduce him to his namesake. As Bill disappeared below he called up to Danni.

"I'll be right back; I need to talk with you."

Danni smiled, she wished he had come straight to her, but it would have been impolite to try and upstage the new parents. She waited for a moment, but became impatient and made her way to the galley where the others gathered.

The scene below warmed her heart. Bill cradled young William in his arms; dwarfing the infant. Hanna and James were almost giddy explaining that they had named the baby after Bill. There was no fear in this cabin, and the troubles they left in Savannah seemed so far away. Mamba came and stood next to Danni.

"He is a wonderful man."

"Yes he is."

"Will you be wise enough to make the correct choice?"

"What do you mean?"

Mamba smiled and moved away, and Danni felt the strength of a rough hand on her arm.

"Danni, could we go on deck?"

The others in the cabin noticed their departure and DeAngelo dug an elbow into Doc's side. "What do you think she'll say?"

Doc turned to his friend. "I don't know. We'll have to wait and see."

~~

Bill walked Danni to the transom and froze. He had rehearsed his little speech during the cruise out, but now that it was time to speak, he found himself stammering.

"How do you feel?"

Danni hadn't thought about her wounds since Doc had worked his magic on her. "I'm fine. It doesn't hurt much anymore since Doc patched me up." This is what Bill wanted to talk about...her injuries?

"You know that Ken Carson is dead."

"Yes, I know. Angelina told us about the whole thing. I never thought Buford Long would turn bad."

"Yeah, well, money can do that to some people."

Then came the same long silence that Danni had seen in Bill many times in the past. A man of confidence and action reduced to a stammering school boy when they were alone. She decided to help him along.

"Bill, is there something you wanted to talk to me about?"

Bill cleared his throat. "Well, yes, as a matter of fact there is, but I don't really know how to start."

Danni recalled the times in the past when she sensed Bill would try and talk of their future, and she almost laughed because he always arranged for a private walk on the beach, as if he needed to be moving when they talked.

"Bill, I know this may be hard for you, but we're stuck on this boat and don't have the luxury of a long walk on the beach. You might as well man up and get to it."

Danni's blunt comment caught Bill a little by surprise. It didn't leave him much maneuvering space.

"Well, Danni, I...um...was wondering if you are dead set on going to the Bahamas?"

It was not what she expected to hear. Why would he ask that? "My father says we will be safe in the Bahamas. He has worked a long time moving his banking business there."

"I know, but...you see...I can't go...I'm not going...I can't."

Danni felt her heart drop. "For God's sake Bill, why not?"

"Danni, too many of my friends have died protecting America for me to run from the battle to save her."

Danni felt a sense of panic. Was she to lose the man she loved to an ideal that had little or no chance to succeed? "Bill, you can't do it on your own!"

Bill turned to Danni, "I don't want to do it on my own. I want you to come with me...as my wife."

When Danni didn't move, and when she withheld comment, Bill was the one who felt panic. "Danni, I know you may have doubts of me, but I will be a good husband. I have loved you from the first day we met. You will break my heart if you say no."

She had heard the proposal correctly. There was no doubt about that, but why now? Why now when the world was quickly falling apart? Why now when her daughter and grandson would be in the Bahamas? Why now when her father had provided for their safety far away from the surging mobs that were destroying the fabric of society and the heart of the country?

Danni knew she had always loved Bill Cannon, but she never expected that her coy move to have Bill get to the point would produce something so dramatic.

"Bill..."

Why was she stammering? It was not the way a woman in love should respond. Why did Bill tell her he was going back? Should that make any difference if she really loved him? Would her life with Bill just be another tragedy, like her first marriage? No, that was unfair; Bill was a man of integrity and moral convictions. But, would the tragedy be trying to make a life in a society that was crumbling?

She knew Bill told her he was returning to the mainland. He would do just as he said he would, he would continue to fight to save the country. Was that a warning to her, or was it simply a metaphor? No, with Bill it was never a metaphor. He was a man that did not play with words.

If she accepted his proposal, did that mean her life would forever be filled with the danger that she knew Bill Cannon would always face, and from which he would never retreat? Would one day she be kneeling over the body of the man she loved because he would step forward when the need arose or his country called?

Did she love him? Yes, beyond all others. But, did she love him more than her daughter and grandchild? In the instant where your heart and thoughts collide, Danni paused. Since the death of her husband, Hanna was all that she had. But now Hanna was married to a good man and her focus would be on her child. Had she become so callous to her own happiness that she believed it would only come from her daughter and new baby and that no man could make her happy?

But then again, Danni knew that she was only truly happy when Bill Cannon was near. In her heart, she knew there was only one answer.

"Bill, I..." Before Danni could form her thoughts, her father shouted from the cabin.

"Bill...DeAngelo just told us you are not going with us." The faces of all the others could be seen gathered behind him.

Bill, waiting patiently for Danni's answer, turned. "That's right. I'm going back."

"Bill, that's crazy. Why would you do that? It's crazy back there."

Bill thought for only a moment. "Ed, I know you mean well, but unlike you, all I have is my country. I will not stand by and let her die."

Did Ed Helton take Bill's comment as a veiled insult? "That's ridiculous! You can't change the way things are. You saw what was happening back there. You'd be crazy to go back. We can go to the Bahamas and be safe. I've got it all set up!"

Bill felt Danni put her arm through his. "Mr. Helton, I appreciate what you've done, but it won't change my decision. I must go back. I couldn't live with myself, I couldn't live with the memories of the friends I have lost, if I cut and ran when the country needed me the most."

"Bill, this is idiotic! What can one man do? Everything is against you."

"That may be, but one man can get another, and then another. If you want to live your life running from that which provided you the means to become what you are, to have what you have, then you are free to do so, but I will not."

Ed cursed and turned away in disgust. "I can't believe this. You are committing suicide if you ask me, but we're going to the Bahamas. Clear your boat, we need to get under way."

"I'm not going either."

Ed Helton turned back to face his daughter. "What?"

Danni held Bill's arm even tighter. "I'm going back with Bill."

Ed looked as if he had been punched, but Bill ignored his reaction. He turned to Danni.

"Does this mean what I think it means?"

Danni turned to Bill and circled his neck with her arms. "Yes my love, it does. I love you, and I would be proud to be Mrs. Bill Cannon. I hope you won't regret asking me, I can be terrible in the morning."

And Danni stood on her toes and kissed the man she had loved for so many years. The kiss melted away any fears the future may bring, because this is the man that always made her feel safe.

It took a moment for the announcement to be understood by those in the cabin. The first to realize what had just unfolded was Hanna. She shrieked with delight. With baby in arms, she rushed to her mother.

"Oh, momma, I know you will be so happy!" Little William slept blissfully through the hugs. Hanna turned to Bill, "I am so happy for you! I've have always known that you were the man to make my mother happy. What took you so long?"

The celebration consumed the group. The tension of their escape from the mainland and the confrontation between Bill and Ed Helton momentarily forgotten until Mamba approached Bill.

"Colonel Cannon, if you have room in your boat, I would like to go with you. There is no other place for me. America has become my home."

Eric Brown and Angelina Sanchez, arm in arm, approached Bill. Eric asked, "Colonel Cannon, do you have room for us?"

Hanna turned to Ed Helton, "Papa, James and I have talked about this. We are going back with Bill and Momma."

Ed Helton leaned heavily against the fish chest. He hung his head. All the preparations for their escape and safety now discarded. All those that he loved had now chosen to stay and face the challenge of rebuilding America. He could not say that their decisions upset him, no, in fact their decision made him proud.

Ed Helton raised his head and stood. He smiled when he said, "God help us; we're going to need it."

~~

Their celebration went deep into the night. Mike DeAngelo announced, "As Captain of this vessel, on the high seas of the Atlantic Ocean, I now pronounce you man and wife."

It was an unnecessary ceremony and carried no legal weight, but it was enough for those who smiled as Danni and Bill separated *Old Ironsides* from the larger boat.

With the morning sun at their backs, the small procession of two boats made their way back to Daufuskie Island. Danni leaned against her husband. The smoke hanging on the horizon didn't carry the same fear as it did just a day past.

Epilogue

On the fifth day after the Chesapeake attack, the President ordered an attack on Kuwait. An unmanned drone marked the target. The cruise missiles were launched from a nuclear submarine operating in the Indian Ocean. The reconnaissance aircraft from the USS Ronald Reagan flew from south to north over Kuwait City at angles 10, Mach 2. The high speed digital cameras recorded the devastation. Prince Al-Sabah lay dead in what remained of the Royal Palace of the Kingdom of Kuwait.

The pilot put the aircraft in a 90 degree bank for another pass over the city when his eye caught movement on the highway below. What he saw was amazing, and he reported it to the circling AWACS over Riyadh, Saudi Arabia.

"Control, this is Navy Recon over Kuwait City. You're not going to believe this, but there are hundreds of tanks down here. They stretch all the way back to the Iranian border. I think Iran is invading Kuwait! What should I do?"

Before the AWACS could respond, the shrill alarm for missile attack sounded in his headset. He outmaneuvered the first two missiles, but by then his airspeed was down, and the third detonated and blew away his vertical stabilizer and most of his right wing.

His calls of Mayday were monitored by the fleet. The rescue operation escalated into a running battle between aircraft from the fleet and the armored columns from Iran. When all was done, the burning hulks of tanks littered the highway and the Iranian attack was stopped.

The White House called the cruise missile attack a just response to Kuwaiti's involvement in the attack on the United States. The Pentagon called the battle on the road to Kuwait an unfortunate misunderstanding between Iran and the administration. The Iranian Ambassador to the United Nations explained the armed excursion through southern Iraq as a defensive measure to stop the civil unrest in Kuwait.

Bill Cannon turned to Danni. "That's the biggest bunch of crap I've ever heard. That was a full-fledged invasion force. If the Iranians

503

hadn't shot down that recon aircraft, they would have been to Riyadh by now."

"Bill, do you think Prince Al-Sabah did all those things the Government says he did?"

"Danni, Ahmad was a man who loved Kuwait and this country. I think he saw what was coming. I believe he did everything in his power to warn us. If he was involved, it was to warn us and not to harm us. Nobody listened to him and now he is dead, and I will miss him."

~~

On the eighth day after the Chesapeake attack, the Tybee Island Police Department responded to a citizen complaint of 'shots fired.'

The Tybee Island PD, at full strength, was only 14 officers. Eight were detailed to the 24 hour barricade on the only road leading to the island. The other six were on overlapping shifts, with one team in the residential areas, and one team always on the water to prevent looters from getting on the island by sea or through the tidal marshes. The two officers responding to the complaint were the only men available.

The residents were skittish. They had seen the news. They knew what was going on in Savannah and across the country. Their complaints, until this call, were limited to panic reports of strangers roaming the streets; none of which proved to be accurate. But this report, with shots fired, could be different. Both officers knew the possibility of looters slipping past the road block, or the seaborne patrol, were real.

They slowed as they neared the address. They parked in the drive, using the house to provide cover. They removed the shotguns from the vehicle and only one officer approached the door, the other nestled into a position where his back was covered, but he could provide support to the officer at the front door and could also cover the street.

An elderly woman answered on the second ring. The officer was polite, "Good afternoon ma'am, you filed a complaint with the police department, something about gun shots?"

"Yes I did. We both heard them." The officer noted the husband sipping coffee at the kitchen table.

The woman didn't pause to even catch her breath. "Something should have been done about them a long time ago. They're nothing but trash. Always running around half naked and yelling all the time, and that woman is nothing but a drunk."

504

The officer had to slow her down. "Yes ma'am, who are you talking about?"

The woman turned and pointed to her neighbor's house. "Those people over there. He's some kind of a banker. I don't know how they ever let them on the island. We don't need their kind here. It's embarrassing to the rest of us."

"That's where you hear the shots?"

"It started this morning. Two women, one of them lives there, were arguing. We could hear it over here. They were yelling and screaming at each other, and then we heard a gunshot, at least I think it was a gunshot, and then a few minutes later we heard another. Since then…nothing."

The police officer called to his partner and pointed to the residence next door. "Run that address through the computer."

As the officer ran the check, the husband left the kitchen table and approached the door. He wasn't as concerned about the shooting at the neighbor's house. "How are things in Savannah?"

"Not good, but it looks like the worst of the looting is behind us."

The officer from the cruiser called to the door. "That house is owned by a Mr. Ken Carson. The captain told us to investigate."

The officers approached the front door with caution. Repeated rings and knocks only echoed through the house. The officer tried the door and, to his surprise, the knob turned easily and the door opened without resistance. Shotguns at the ready they cleared the front rooms.

They slowly made their way to the back of the house. Nothing seemed out of place until the kitchen. One delicate foot snaked from behind the island. The officer kept his eyes moving as he bent to feel for any pulse. The body was cold. The bullet entered the chest. The blood stained the delicate silk blouse and formed a small pool under the body.

They left the body undisturbed. The neighbors reported two shots, and there was only one hole in this woman. They approached the den overlooking the pool.

There, the body of another woman, the left side of her head missing, the gun still clutched in her right hand. Her blood smeared on the glass door as her body slid to the floor.

As his partner called the station, the officer commented, "These two could have been sisters."

One month after the Chesapeake attacked, Angelina's report reached the desk of William Jefferson.

The box sat squarely on William Jefferson's desk. There, beneath the letter, the glint of gold and cold of gray; the gold was the shield of the Department of Justice, and the gray was the surface of the Glock pistol. Beneath the badge and weapon, in neatly package envelopes, the files of a year's work.

The letter from Sanchez was polite, concise, and to the point; exactly the way William Jefferson liked his correspondence.

"Mr. Jefferson, my report concerning the investigation directed by the President is contained in the files shipped with this letter.

"After exhaustive research, it is my conclusion there is no evidence to support the allegation of police murders in Atlanta. Although four of the five suspects in the case met with violent deaths, all were involved with an extensive drug network and died as a result of attempting to procure and distribute narcotics.

"It is my recommendation the facts be reported to the President and the case closed.

"Concerning the death of Buford Long, I can only surmise that each of us has a breaking point; he crossed the line. It may bring you some level of comfort to know that he did not suffer in death.

"On a personal note, it has been my privilege to serve with you. However, the actions of the Attorney General and his unrestrained legal pursuit of Colonel Bill Cannon is clearly an abuse of his office, and my conscience forces me to submit my resignation rather than support policies I consider contrary to the law."

William Jefferson smiled when he read the last paragraph. It was a scathing indictment of the Department of Justice; but it was all true. It was why he picked Sanchez for the assignment. She was smart enough to understand the truth.

~~

On the 45th day after the Chesapeake attack, the United States Senate convened a hearing to investigate the intelligence and security failures of the government.

Senator Steve Reynolds was allowed two minutes of questions during the hearings. He did not intend to use his time to pontificate his displeasure with the failures of American Intelligence, as the other members of the panel had so eloquently done, but to establish the facts of the failures.

"First Miss Toth, I would like to congratulate you on your promotion to the Director of the Office of Strategic Reconnaissance."

"Thank you Senator."

"Miss Toth, chemical and nuclear weapons do not simply appear out of a vacuum, when and how were you made aware of the possibility that terrorist groups had access to weapons of mass destruction?"

"A year ago, Prince Al-Sabah of Kuwait provided photographs of suspicious activity concerning the shipment of chemical weapons into Egypt for transfer into the Gaza Strip. He provided these photos to Colonel Bill Cannon who in turn gave the photos to me."

"The photos were the first indication American Intelligence had of these weapons?"

"Yes, Senator."

"And this threat was briefed at the highest levels of our government?"

"Yes, Senator. It was considered a regional problem and not a threat to our country."

"Miss Toth, when were you made aware there was a direct nuclear threat against the United States?"

"Major James Madison reported the threat after his rescue from Lebanon."

"Who reported the chemical threat to the United States?"

"To my knowledge, Colonel Bill Cannon came to the conclusion that chemical weapons were being assembled in the states. He reported his suspicions to General McLaughlin who in turn briefed the White House Chief of Staff."

"Miss Toth, am I to conclude that one man, Colonel Bill Cannon, currently under investigation by the United States Department of Justice, was primarily responsible for warning us of the threats that so tragically devastated this country?"

"Yes sir. That is my opinion."

507

~~

On the third month anniversary of the Chesapeake attack, Brian Vance looked up from his desk at WDAU, a small radio station broadcasting from Daufuskie Island. "Good morning, Mrs. Brown."

"Good morning Brian. Can this tin can of a radio station spare a cup of coffee?"

Brian pointed to the coffee in the corner of the office. "Just brewed not more than 20 minutes ago. Help yourself." Brian sorted through the papers on his desk. "Do you have anything we can put in local news?"

Angelina removed the heavy belt holding her sidearm and handcuffs before settling in the only vacant chair in the office.

"DeAngelo said somebody stole one of his crab pots, but I think he just forgot where he put it; other than that, it's quiet."

Angelina enjoyed the aroma of the coffee before she took her first sip. "Eric tells me you are going back to the Citadel next semester."

Brian looked up and grinned. "Yes ma'am. I'm really excited. Mr. Helton set up a scholarship fund for most of it, and gave me a student loan for the balance of the fees. Mr. Brown said I could work here on the weekends."

Angelina smiled. The scholarship fund was a pet project of just about everyone on the island. "Eric told me you have been doing a great job getting the show syndicated. How many stations do you have now?"

Brian beamed with the complement. "Thirty; and we're meeting with a group out of Florida this afternoon! 'Eric Brown – your voice of reason' it has a ring to it, don't you think?"

Angelina smiled. "Yes it does. I never would have dreamed a radio show could be so popular. Is Eric on the air now?"

Brian looked to the clock and then the schedule on his desk. "He should be finishing up the news. You want to listen?"

"Sure."

Brian flipped a switch on a panel to the rear of his desk and Eric's voice filled the room. Angelina never tired of hearing his voice.

"…the final news item is something that was long overdue. The White House today announced the President accepted the resignation of the Attorney General and the Secretary of Defense. Both men had come under fire since the attacks on the United States. The President said the

508

resignations were for personal reasons and not in response to any political pressure. That does it for today. This is Eric Brown, your voice of reason. I'll be back tomorrow."

Angelina got up from the chair to welcome Eric as he exited the booth. He kissed her gently when they met.

"Did you hear the news?"

"Just the last part…why?"

"Major Madison announced his candidacy for Congress. I think he has a good chance of winning."

Angelina beamed. "Oh, that's great. I can't think of a better man for the job. Come on let's go, I don't want to be late for the dedication." Turning to Brian Vance, she asked, "Are you coming?"

Brian finished stacking documents on the desk. "I wouldn't miss it for the world. Let's go."

The trio left the office and walked the short distance to Main Street. Doc Broderson and Mike DeAngelo carried a #4 washtub overflowing with ice, beer and an assortment of liquor bottles.

Eric asked, "You don't think Bill and Danni will have refreshments there?"

DeAngelo answered, "Better to be safe than sorry. I don't want to get stuck at some snobby party with just tea and crumpets."

A few steps behind DeAngelo and Broderson walked James and Hanna Madison, little Bill bundled in a blanket and cradled in his mother's arms.

Eric met with James and Angelina went directly to Hanna and the baby.

Eric extended his hand. "Let me be the first to say, good afternoon congressman."

James laughed, "That is certainly premature, but thanks. I hope I can get the support of the 'voice of reason.'"

"Absolutely."

Eric turned to watch Angelina take the baby from Hanna. "This little guy must be quite a load. I'll carry him the rest of the way."

Little Bill wasn't a strain on Hanna, but the baby only smiled when Angelina took him from his mother. Eric smiled; the baby looked so natural in her arms.

Ed Helton and Mamba caught the group and the greetings were warm and unhurried. They could have chatted in the street the rest of the afternoon if not for Mike DeAngelo, "Alright, everybody knows everybody and if we don't get going this ice is going to melt."

The little group turned up the lane leading to the new Daufuskie Island Bed and Breakfast. There on the porch, the proprietors, Bill and Danni Cannon.

Danni took control and narrated the tour of the house. DeAngelo snuck Bill Cannon a couple of beers to help him get through the details of color pallets, fabrics and accent pieces.

The tour moved slowly through the rooms until finally the little group was led to the veranda overlooking the Atlantic Ocean. Danni led the group down the wide staircase leading to the patio and then to a red shroud covering a rectangular object at the base of the flag pole that already flew the star and stripes. Bill Cannon handed his empty beers to DeAngelo and walked to the front of the group next to his wife.

"Thank you all for coming." Bill paused for a moment. "We have been through a lot together. Not all of it pleasant. I have come to realize that there is still the miracle of happiness for me. Danni and all of you have had a part in that miracle. I will never forget that.

"Many I hold in high regard are not here to share in this day."

Bill spread his arms to encompass the manicured grounds and the building to their backs. "It is only fitting that we dedicate this to those who have made the ultimate sacrifice and made this day possible."

Bill grabbed the red cloth and removed it from the object beneath. Boldly carved into the polished granite were the simple words, LIBERTY, FREEDOM, PEACE. In smaller letters, Dedicated to Those Who Served. MG Lucas McLaughlin's name was carved there. CSM Steve Thunder's name was carved there. A tear ran down Eric Brown's face when he read the name SSG John Brown Jackson also carved into the stone.

Made in the USA
Charleston, SC
12 March 2011